In 1836 when she was nine years old, Cynthia Ann Parker was kidnapped from her family's settlement by Comanche Indians.

She grew up with them, mastered their ways, and married one of their leaders. Except for her brilliant blue eyes and golden mane,
Cynthia Ann Parker
was in every way a Comanche woman. They called her Naduah—
Keeps Warm With Us.
She rode a horse named Wind.

This is her story, the story of a proud and innocent people whose lives pulsed with the very heartbeat of the land. It is the story of a way of life that's
gone forever.

RIDE THE WIND

...will thrill you, absorb you, touch your soul, and make you cry as you celebrate the beauty and mourn the end of the great Comanche nation.

Quanah Parker, circa 1880.
Shown as a child on our cover painting by the artist Tom Hall, Quanah was the son of Cynthia Ann Parker and Wanderer and was the last free war chief of the Comanche.
Photo courtesy of Western History Collections, University of Oklahoma Library.

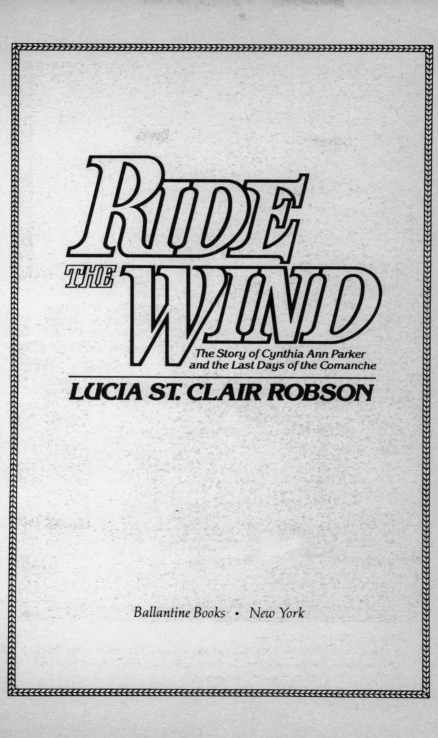

RIDE THE WIND

The Story of Cynthia Ann Parker
and the Last Days of the Comanche

LUCIA ST. CLAIR ROBSON

Ballantine Books • New York

Acknowledgments

I want to thank Darlyne and Bill Morales for giving so generously of their enthusiasm and help, and Joseph Cotton for sharing his collection of materials on the Parker story. Thanks also to the members of the Comanche tribe who graciously agreed to correct translations and pronunciations of names and words in their language.

I also want to acknowledge an enormous debt of gratitude to libraries and librarians. They are among this country's greatest resources.

To Sallie Ratliff Taylor, teacher and friend, who said she'd wait on the other side.

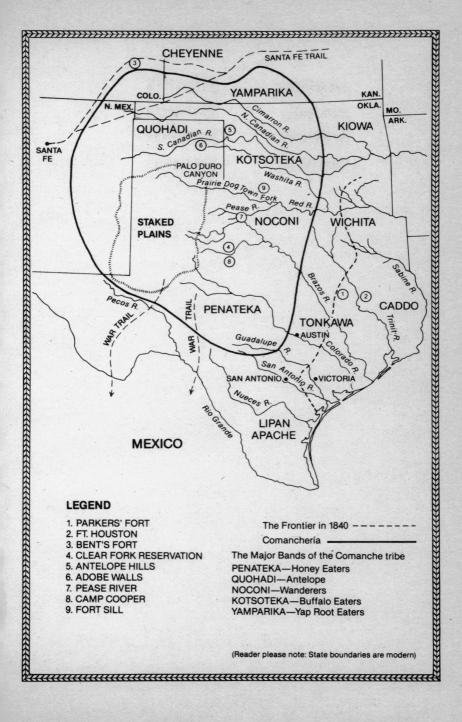

CHEYENNE

SANTA FE TRAIL

YAMPARIKA

COLO.
N. MEX.

KAN.
OKLA.
MO.
ARK.

KIOWA

SANTA FE

QUOHADI

Cimarron R.
N. Canadian R.
S. Canadian R.

KOTSOTEKA

Washita R.

PALO DURO CANYON

Prairie Dog Town Fork

Red R.

Pease R.

STAKED PLAINS

NOCONI

WICHITA

Sabine R.

Brazos R.

CADDO

PENATEKA

Pecos R.

WAR TRAIL

WAR TRAIL

Guadalupe R.

AUSTIN

TONKAWA

Trinity R.

Colorado R.

San Antonio R.

SAN ANTONIO

VICTORIA

Nueces R.

Rio Grande

LIPAN APACHE

MEXICO

LEGEND

1. PARKERS' FORT
2. FT. HOUSTON
3. BENT'S FORT
4. CLEAR FORK RESERVATION
5. ANTELOPE HILLS
6. ADOBE WALLS
7. PEASE RIVER
8. CAMP COOPER
9. FORT SILL

The Frontier in 1840 – – – – – – –

Comanchería ——————

The Major Bands of the Comanche tribe

PENATEKA—Honey Eaters
QUOHADI—Antelope
NOCONI—Wanderers
KOTSOTEKA—Buffalo Eaters
YAMPARIKA—Yap Root Eaters

(Reader please note: State boundaries are modern)

Prologue

Eighteen thirty-six was an uneventful year. In the remote wilds of Texas a slender, mild-eyed twenty-one-year-old named John Coffee Hays joined the newly formed Rangers. In February, the U.S. Patent Office burned to the ground. Among the waterlogged papers rescued from the debris were the sketches and specifications on patent number 138, the clever innovation of another twenty-one-year-old, Samuel Colt.

The first women crossed the plains in a wagon train that year. A self-taught painter and ethnologist named George Catlin rode thousands of miles desperately recording the faces and folkways of a doomed race, the American Indian. God still owned the real estate between the ninety-eighth meridian and the Rocky Mountains. It was a useless piece of property dismissed on maps as "The Great American Desert."

On April 21, 1836, Sam Houston's ragged army cornered Santa Anna's forces at San Jacinto, drove them into a quagmire, and, ever frugal with their ammunition, clubbed them to death. Texas became a nation bordering the United States at the Sabine River. Refugees from the Mexican War began trudging back from Louisiana to their homes and fields, many of which had been burned by Houston's retreating troops the month before.

Among the refugees were members of the Parker clan, their friends and in-laws. Perched on the rim of the frontier, the last settlement before the wasteland west of the Brazos, Parker's Fort had escaped devastation. Its people returned and picked up the threads of their lives.

Not much happened in 1836.

SPRING

I will say of the Lord, He is
my refuge and my fortress:
My God, in Him will I trust. . . .
Thou shalt not be afraid for the
terror by night;
Nor for the arrow that flieth by
day;
Nor for the pestilence that walketh
in darkness;
Nor for the destruction that wasteth
at noonday.

Ninety-first Psalm

"If it is ordained that we should die here,
then the Lord have mercy on our souls."
Elder John Parker

❧ *1* ❧

A rolling sea of deep grass flecked with a foam of primroses washed up on islands of towering oaks and pecans and walnuts. The pale blue sky was fading at the edges as the sun heated up the day. Soon it would be hot enough for the children to sneak down to the nearby Navasota River to splash in the cool, shaded waters. The warm East Texas wind blew through the stockade door, bringing company with it. It was a morning in May; a time of sunshine and peace, an open gate and Indians.

Inside the high wooden box of Parker's Fort, twenty-six people stood frozen as though in a child's game of statues. Outside the gate scores of painted warriors sat sullenly on their ponies. One of them dropped the dirty white flag he had been holding. It fluttered slowly to the ground where his nervous little pinto danced it into the dust.

Give them a cow, Uncle Ben. Please. If that's what they want, give it to them. The cracked corn felt cool around nine-year-old Cynthia Ann Parker's fingers as she held the small gourd of chicken feed. Cold chills prickled her skin under her father's scratchy, tow linen shirt. Patched and frayed and altered down to only three or four sizes too large, the shirt looked as though it had been dyed with the same pale, gray-brown dust that covered her bare toes. She watched the men at the gate like a baby rabbit staring into a snake's eyes.

They were begging, Uncle Ben had said. A cow? What would a hundred Indians do with one cow? Roast it outside the fort? Would all of them leave driving one cow ahead of them? It didn't matter. Uncle Ben wouldn't give it to them. The Parkers didn't hold with begging. He'd tell them to move on, and everyone would go back to their chores. Maybe her grandfather, Elder John, would preach a sermon on sloth at the service Sunday. Foreboding swelled in her stomach and spread to her chest. She heard her heart pounding in her ears.

Her cousin, fifteen-year-old Rachel Plummer, hovered nearby. Her hands were dusted with flour and tangled and rigid in her coarse linen apron. The other women stood in the doors of their cabins, built in two rows against the stockade's north and south walls. The houses were tiny and crowded, but all seven of them fit inside the fort for safety. From the corral opposite the gate Ben Parker's big roan neighed in answer to a sly-eyed war pony's whinny.

In the center of the bare yard Rebecca Frost was poised over the huge, noisome vat of lye and fat boiling into slimy soap. She

1

clenched the long wooden paddle like a club in her right hand. The smell of morning coffee mingled with the smoke of her fire and the warm, heavy odor of the corral. Outside Elder John's cabin, Granny Parker sat on a worn log bench, her knitting lying in her lap. Her Bible story had trailed off into silence as she and the young children stared at the bronzed mass of bodies outside.

Feathers swayed and bobbed on the Indians' slender, upraised lances. The brass cones on their leggings jingled merrily. Sunlight streamed around them and through the gate that faced east to collect it each morning. The tranquil, muted coo of mourning doves mocked the carelessness that had left the heavy wooden door open. The few men who had stayed in from the fields that morning were far from their guns.

"If you're not a good boy, John, we'll trade you to the Indians." The memory of her mother's soft, slow voice, speaking to her little brother, echoed in Cynthia's head. *"We'll trade you to the Indians."*

From the corner of one wide blue eye Cynthia could see Samuel Frost sliding along the front wall of his cabin, the rough wood plucking at his heavy cotton shirt. The big log chimney hid him from the Indians' sight, but in the stillness of the yard his movement seemed to set the very air in motion. Surely the eddies would reach the warriors and warn them. She held her breath until he was safely inside with his new breechloader. It could fire over three times a minute. One hundred Indians, and a gun that could kill three of them a minute.

Please close the gate, Pa. Close it now. Paralyzed by fear, she stood mired in the dust and watched the scene play out. Cynthia's uncle, Ben Parker, shrugged off his brother Silas's hand and moved toward the Indians. Big, beloved Uncle Ben with laughing blue eyes, silky black hair, and hands that dwarfed the toys he was always whittling for the children. Now he looked small and alone framed in the door's wooden jaws. Her father, Silas Parker, stood by to close the heavy gate.

"Oh, Lord," whispered Rachel.

There was a surge of ponies that engulfed Ben. When the wave receded he lay, Comanche, Kiowa, and Caddo lances quivering in his body. Howling like all of hell's condemned souls, the raiders split around him and pounded through the opening. Women and children scattered with the squawking chickens before the battering hooves. Their screams ricocheted against the wooden walls and fell back into the din.

Huddled in the angle of a chimney and wall, Cynthia stared out at the nightmare. Across the yard, young Henry White leaped from a bench and threw his arms over the lip of the low cabin roof. He kicked and heaved, his bare toes seeking purchase on the logs of the wall, his hands scrabbling for a grip on the warped roof boards. He hung there for a century, suspended in time, before he managed to pull his long legs over the rim and start to crawl up the slope. A hundred miles ahead of him lay the abutting stockade wall and safety. Under his baggy, torn corduroy trousers his knees were bloody, the skin scoured by the eaves' ragged edges.

A Comanche galloped the length of the cabins toward him. His horse plowed through the pile of rock-hard hominy corn, toppled Mr. Frost's work bench, and strewed the crude wooden tools behind him. Standing up in full career, the raider grabbed Henry's thin ankles and tugged. The boy clawed at the saplings holding down the shingles. Long splinters drove up under his nails before he was pulled loose like a piece of green fruit. He screamed as he was whirled and thrown into the madness below.

Robert Frost thrashed at the riders with his father's long-handled adz, trying desperately to cover the retreat of his mother and sister. At the top of a swing the weapon was wrenched from his hands, throwing him off balance. He fell under the horses' hooves and curled into a ball in the dust, vainly shielding his head and stomach. The raiders wheeled and spurred their rearing, protesting ponies back and forth over him until there was little left to recognize as human.

Naomi White ran for the gate, her long skirt flapping about her legs. As her stride widened, the hem snapped taut. She pitched forward, her arms flailing for balance. Gathering the faded cloth in her hands, she pulled it up over her knees and fled like a startled deer through the clamor. A squat iron bake oven, dribbling a trail of beans, rolled through a doorway and into her path. She leaped it and one bare foot landed hard in the soft, bloody pulp of her favorite hen. Screaming and sobbing in horror, she stopped to scrape and twist her foot in the dust, mindless of everything but the warm, wet flesh and feathers between her toes.

There was a sharp, stabbing pain in her side and another in her chest. Sighting up the lance shaft, she stared into a painted face flanked by half a dozen others. They herded her, still sobbing, to the center of the yard, where Mrs. Duty and Rebecca Frost stood at bay near the soap vat.

Big, raw-boned Sarah Nixon defended her doorway like a mother bear her lair. Hot grease from the morning's salt pork splattered as her huge iron spider rang against a Kiowa's hard thigh. Men crowded around for the fun. Laughing and clucking, they poked at her, jousting with her frying pan from horseback. Two of them finally dropped nooses over her head, catching the long graying hair

3

that tumbled from the bun at the nape of her neck. She choked and stumbled, running to keep from falling and being dragged, to where the other women were.

Over the screaming and the war whoops there was a steady thunk, ka-chunk. Some of the Indians were pounding on the bulbous iron kettle with the butts of their lances. Others wedged their shafts under its rim and heaved. Slowly it tilted, the viscous gray mass inside flowing toward the far edge. The kettle wavered, then toppled, spewing the boiling lye and fat like lava onto the women's feet. The sight of them slipping in the steaming slime, their legs already turning red and raw, was a grand joke. One by one they were lassoed and dragged off through the mud to serve those who circled them, jostling for a turn. Little Susan Parker's screams sliced through the din as she was roped and towed through the fire, sending sparks and live coals flying.

With the primal reflexes of predators, the Indians chased anything that moved fast. Cynthia didn't move at all. Cowering against the cabin wall, she still clutched the gourd of corn. Through the chaos in the yard she saw only one thing; like an object at the wrong end of a telescope, the image seemed far away yet sharply defined. Her father hung suspended, a dozen arrows driven into his back, pinning him to the heavy gate he had been trying to close. One arm dangled limply in the big wooden bolt slot. His head drooped, and the top of it was flat and bloody.

Cynthia's terrified whimper rose to a shriek as she tried to block the sounds of death. Dust rose in billows, blinding her to the sight of Silas Parker hanging lifeless as a rag doll. She was still screaming when her mother spun her around and shook her, sending the gourd flying. Lucy Parker's nails dug into the child's small round arm, the pain wrenching her back to sanity.

"Find John," Lucy Parker said. Her voice could scarcely be heard, but her lips formed the words clearly. Carrying two-year-old Orlena and holding little Silas by the hand, she nodded toward the rear of the stockade.

Cynthia slid along the line of cabins, stunned by the horror in the yard. She squinted through the dust and smoke and horses' legs, searching for her younger brother. If he was out in the open, he was dead. Some of the Indians had driven the hysterical animals out of the corral, stampeding them with flapping buffalo hides. Now they careened blindly through the compound, neighing shrilly and trampling everything in their path.

She spotted John peering wide-eyed from behind the hogshead used to store water. She sprinted across the open space and pulled him around the corner of the last cabin to the rear of the fort. There in the palisade wall was a small opening cut for those fetching water from the spring down the hill. Lucy Parker had already crawled through it.

Cynthia pushed John after her and crouched to follow him. She heard a familiar voice and swung her head around. A mob of Indians cawed and hooted and shoved Granny Parker as they tore her clothes off. She shouted at them and pushed at their lances as their points caught her skirt and ripped it. The child stared as her grandmother was pushed onto her back. Two men held her arms while two others spread her legs. A fifth stood straddling her. He raised his lance, then drove it with both hands through her shoulder and into the ground. Cynthia could almost hear the scrape of the metal blade on bone, like fingernails across slate. The Indians began loosening their breechclouts. She knew instinctively what they were going to do and that Granny's age wouldn't save her from it.

The image of her grandmother's thin, white body, pinned squirming and screaming, followed her through the opening. The inhuman cries rang out across the silent hills, tearing the air. The jagged edges of the roughly cut hole snagged Cynthia's braids and ripped her smock. Sobbing, she jerked her head, leaving wisps of wheaten hair dancing on the light breeze that sucked in through the door. She raced after her mother, who was headed for the dense thickets along the river bottom to the west. The hillside was covered with burs and sharp stones hidden in the tall grass, but she felt them no more than the dust and dung that coated her feet.

Behind her Rachel Plummer ran ponderously, a fifteen-month-old Jamie bouncing on her hip. Rachel was with child again, and she supported her slightly swollen belly with her other hand. Mounted Indians swooped in and out at her, yapping and whooping as she swerved and stumbled to dodge them. Stirrup to stirrup, two riders bore down on her. Just as they were about to run her over they split apart. With graceful precision they lifted her onto one horse and Jamie onto the other. Then they wheeled and raced back to the fort.

For the Parkers, sanctuary was close. Once they reached the thickets Cynthia could hide them. Their tangled mazes were her refuge from the fort, where she was as much communal property as the hominy mill or the water barrel. Solitude was never officially listed as a sin, but the search for it was. The stolen hours spent listening to the sun go down or watching a line of ants were her biggest iniquity. Now she could see that they were part of God's plan. He wouldn't let anything more happen to them.

The ground under her feet vibrated as a dozen ponies overran and surrounded the family. While the riders circled, herding them like cattle, four men broke from the ring and cantered to the center of it.

They halted in front of Lucy, who tried to hide her children behind her long, faded skirt. She kept her small face passive, but her skin was pale under the light scattering of freckles across her nose and cheeks. Her ice-blue eyes stared up into the painted masks around her. John darted out and stood in front of her, arms akimbo, small mouth set fiercely, a pudgy field mouse standing off a pack of wolves.

The outer ring of riders halted, and a few peeled off in search of other game. The rest sat on their restless ponies. The brightly colored feathers on their shields and horses riffled in the wind, giving them a carnival air.

"Don't you touch my mother, you filthy heathens." John's high voice rang out in the moment of silence.

One of the four warriors walked his round-bellied pony the few steps to where John stood. He was so close and the moment seemed so long that Cynthia felt she would never forget him. His lean legs were encased to the tops of his naked thighs in soft, tan leggings with long fringes and tinkling brass beads. His buttocks and upper body were bare and tightly muscled. His dark blue breechclout fluttered behind him like a flag. Strung across his narrow chest were his bow and quiver. Four long cylinders dangled from his right ear lobe and swayed as he turned to stare at John. Straight black hair framed a face that was young and aristocratic under the gaudy red paint slashing his cheeks and chin.

He sat high above little John. The child never flinched, but glared at him through his mother's wide blue eyes. Cynthia froze, crumpling a handful of her mother's skirt and waiting for the Indian to skewer John on the delicate point of the fourteen-foot lance he held carelessly. Suddenly John drew back, cocked his arm, and hurled the rock hidden in his shirt. The hours spent driving crows from the fields had sharpened the six-year-old's aim and strengthened his arm. The rock thunked on the Comanche's cheek, leaving a dark welt.

The Indian swooped, and Cynthia screamed as all of them fell back. Leaning off his horse until only the loop braided into its mane held him, he reached toward John and tapped the boy's shoulder.

"*A-he*, I claim him!" Like a chorus of coyotes, the warriors laughed at the coup. The white cub was a worthy foe.

Motioning with his lance, the thin, hawk-faced man ordered Lucy to lift John onto his horse. When she paused, there was a tensing of the circle. It drew in a little tighter and the men shifted their weapons. Lucy grabbed John under the armpits and hoisted him up behind the lean rider. The little mustang cantered off toward the fort with John bouncing on his broad rump. Clinging to the rawhide

6

surcingle, he looked back at his mother, his face wrinkling as he fought tears.

A tall, lithe warrior wheeled his coal black pony in a tight circle to face Lucy and the children. The black rings around his eyes gave his face a startled, Satanic leer that couldn't hide the handsome set of his features. His full, sensuous mouth was grim as he pointed first to Cynthia and then to the back of his pony. One raven feather hung from his scalplock, and otter fur was wrapped around his long, thick braids. When he reached out to pull the child up onto his horse, she saw the wide leather band that protected his wrist from the bowstring. Though he was hardly more than sixteen years old, his grip was painfully strong. He lifted her as easily as a doll.

As she settled behind him, she smelled smoke and tallow and leather. She tried not to touch his bare body glistening with sweat and oil, but when he quirted his horse, she lurched and grabbed him around the waist. Together they raced after his companion. The circle of Indians, bored now that the small white warrior was gone, scattered for the shelter of the stockade before the white men discovered them in the open. Lucy and her two younger children were abandoned to the two remaining men, who would kill or enslave them as whim dictated.

From the thickets along the river bottom nearby, David Faulkenberry watched the surrounded Parker family and swore under his breath.

"Damn them. Damn them to hell." Whether he meant the Indians or the Baptists of Parker's Fort he couldn't say himself. Prime raiding weather and the gate left wide open, like as not. He had warned them so often, but they wouldn't listen. They had all the answers in that Bible of theirs. "The Lord will provide and the Lord will decide." Old Elder John's favorite maxim. And look what the Lord has provided this day, John Parker.

The big farmer rested his battered Hall carbine on one strong forearm. Sweat ran down the channels in his tanned cheeks. He had prayed and sworn as Lucy and her children ran toward him. There had been no way to help her alone in the open. Now she was trapped, so close and so impossibly far.

He steeled himself for what he would have to do. He could only get off one shot, so it would have to count. It would be for Lucy. When the Indians tried to rape her, he would charge them and shoot her. There could be no error in his aim. He hoped they killed him quickly after he'd done it, but the chances were they'd kill him very slowly indeed.

David Faulkenberry was a veteran of a dozen battles. He had been at San Jacinto when Santa Anna lost Texas just four weeks earlier, but for the first time in his forty years of trouble he felt not simple fear, but terror. He was terrified of what he would have to see and do. He tensed into a sprinter's position as the thin raider and his tall companion took the older children back to the fort. If only his son Evan or Abram Anglin were here to draw fire, he might stand a chance of rushing them. Swearing at Parker was just a way of cursing his own stupidity in coming to the river alone.

When Lucy was left with only two warriors, David reacted almost reflexively. He charged silently from the bushes, devouring the distance with his long, powerful legs. One of the Indians had pulled Lucy and Orlena up onto his horse. The other one reached for little Silas. They looked up, startled by the white man who had appeared like a ghost from the tall grass and waving flowers on the hill. They stared at the steady, lacquered barrel of the carbine aimed at the chest of the one holding Lucy.

"Now, sir," David said levelly, advancing on them. "You just put the little lady back on the ground or I'll blast you into a puddle of paint."

His meaning was clear. Lucy slid down, then reached up and took Orlena. The raiders backed their ponies, reined them hard around, and galloped for the safety of numbers. David let them go. A shot might bring the rest back. Indians didn't like to leave a dead or wounded comrade. They were like rattlesnakes that way.

"David, they killed Silas. They scalped him. My God, you should have seen him." Lucy swayed, struggling to keep calm.

"Miz Parker, we have to get to cover. It's just a little farther."

"No. They've taken John and Cynthia. I have to go back. Don't you know what they'll do to Cynthia?"

"We can do nothing, Miz Parker. And if we don't get out of sight, little Silas and Orlena will be dead or worse."

Lucy wasn't listening. In shock, she had already turned and started up the hill, still absently carrying Orlena, who clung to her neck. David gently stopped her, his big hand on her shoulder. He picked up Silas in one arm, put the other around Lucy, and guided her toward the trees near the river. On hands and knees he pushed them ahead of him into the tangle of wild plum bushes and grape vines. He forced them to crawl, until they could no longer hear the noise of fighting over the rush of the Navasota River. Thorny twigs tore at their clothes as they burrowed through, hauling themselves along on their elbows and knees.

David rolled to clear a small space with his tough body and pulled the children down next to him. He laid a calloused finger to their lips. Exhausted, they didn't need to be told to keep quiet. They lay with their faces pressed to the humous, breathing its thick, musty odor. Lucy stretched out next to her children. With his carbine in his left hand David threw his heavy, corded right arm across all three of them and settled down to wait. He knew he should try to reach the other men pinned down in the grove of trees below the fort to the north, but for now he would stay here.

Reaching up with his big, scarred hand, he pulled a leaf out of Lucy Parker's tangled, honey-colored hair and pondered his next move.

❧ 2 ❧

With his large, luminous eyes in a heavy fringe of lashes and his cherubic face under the smeared yellow paint, Potsana Quoip, Buffalo Piss, looked like a child playing at war. But he carried a fresh, bloody scalp on his lance. It was the first foray of the season for the Penateka Comanche and his first raid as a war chief. He wasn't ready to end it yet. The few of his men who had guns stood watch on the roofs of the cabins that jutted like lichens from the stockade wall. Those who weren't busy elsewhere sat on their ponies and listened as the raid leaders of the three tribes discussed strategy. Every man there was his own commanding officer, and decisions took time.

The settlers, frustrated by the carefully cleared land around the walls, were sniping from the trees and deadfalls of the grove below the fort. The snap of their gunfire sounded like corn popping in a skillet. The Indians were pinned down. Attacking the entrenched white men across the open space would be suicidal. Still, Buffalo Piss refused to give up.

"Are we turkeys," he snarled, "to roost here helpless? These white eyes don't know how to fight. We can kill them all instead of amusing ourselves with their women."

Ooetah, Big Bow waited a beat to give his words more weight. His features seemed chiseled from walnut and polished to a luster. His deep-set eyes reflected the wisdom and generosity that made men follow him willingly on raids. His braids were long, and wrapped in deerskin. He was solidly built and as graceful on the ground as on horseback. He carried few tokens of his coups, yet everyone knew he had more of them than any man in the party. At twenty-three he was the youngest member of the Kaitsenko, the Society of Ten, the Kiowa's highest honor.

"It is time to go," he said. "We have scalps and horses and captives and goods to take to our women. They will be happy and dance for us and warm our beds. There is no need to make them cry when we don't return. I say we should scatter, pick up the extra horses at the Nav-vo-sata and meet at the ford of Three Rivers. We can divide the goods there and go our separate ways. The day grows old. We can do no more here."

While the raid leaders talked, a few men finished with the women, who were mercifully unconscious. Others packed the stolen loot onto the settlers' horses. Some still ransacked the cabins. Patient ponies stood outside the open doors as the muddled sounds of breaking china and furniture drifted out. Feathers from a torn blue comforter floated dreamily down around the bodies sprawled in the wet, slimy mud.

Sitting tall and loose on his black pony, To-oh-kar-no, Night, with Cynthia still clinging to his back, Wanderer studied the littered yard. Quinna, Eagle reined in beside him, John perched behind him. He grinned at his friend and looked around.

"Nocona, Wanderer, my brother, I wish these white people would come west so we could raid them all the time. They have such wonderful things, and they're soft like newborn pups. I may spend more time here in the east."

Wanderer grunted, but his thoughts were on the small, round mirror he held in his hand. It was backed and bound by a silver frame of intricately intertwined flowers and vines. He rubbed the raised design and ran his finger over the cool, smooth surface of the glass itself. He stared at his reflection, the large black eyes and the planes of his face shown as truly as if he were another person looking at himself. It gave him the curiously detached feeling of not being in his own body. The one who made this had medicine, powerful medicine.

He wrapped the mirror in a piece of torn calico and put it into the fringed bag slung on his surcingle. Something about this raid was nibbling at the corner of his mind like a mouse hidden in the winter's pemmican supply. Something unseen, yet disastrous. He considered the new breechloader slung over Big Bow's shoulder, replacing the old musket the Kiowa had given away already.

No. Quinna, Brother Eagle, was wrong. White people weren't soft. A soft person didn't make weapons like that new rifle. Always they had new and better weapons. The white eyes were like the river, never still, always changing. The people who made these

10

things were not soft or stupid. Untaught in a land that was new to them, but not stupid. And what would they be when they learned to survive here? What would the pups grow into? What new kind of animal was moving toward the land of Nermenuh, the People? Who would be the victim and who the prey?

Aside from the Kiowa, Big Bow, Wanderer was perhaps the only one in the party to ask such questions. Suddenly he felt restless and alone. He wanted to return to the wild, desolate Staked Plains where his people, the Quohadi Comanche, lived. All these trees and bushes made him feel uneasy, penned in. They screened the view and gave the enemy too many places to hide. The wind moaned through the leaves like dead souls denied paradise.

While the two men were absorbed in their thoughts, John leaned over to whisper to Cynthia, who sat almost knee to knee with him. Eagle casually elbowed him in the stomach, knocking the wind out of him. The child gulped for air, gagged, and turned red, then purple. Cynthia feared he would die before he finally caught his breath. He didn't try to speak again. His sister sat with her face buried in the crook of her arm, her head pressed against Wanderer's back. But even in the darkness she could see the picture of her father hanging from the gate.

The raid leaders had reached a decision. It was time to go before the desperate white men found a way to attack them.

"Huh! Oti, Hunting A Wife, Paroni, Skinny And Ugly, leave that woman. Throw her away," Buffalo Piss called to his men. One of them was spread-eagled and humping atop the motionless form under him. With his head buried in his victim's large breast and his birdlike legs stretched along her heavy white thighs, Skinny And Ugly looked like a suckling child. Digging his bony fingers into her soft, doughy shoulders he worked on, oblivious to the horses' hooves passing nearby and the debris scattered around him. While he held Skinny And Ugly's piebald, Hunting A Wife tore a calico skirt into strips to hang from his own pony's war bridle.

"Do you want to be left here like a dog stuck in a bitch?" snarled Buffalo Piss from across the yard. He didn't like having his decisions voted down. All his men had best steer clear of him for a while.

With one last thrust of his pointed, naked buttocks and a grunt of pleasure Skinny And Ugly pulled himself up and tucked himself back into his breechclout. He straightened his leggings and brushed the mud from them. Then he took his patient little piebald's reins from Hunting A Wife and checked the knot holding the battered copper kettle to the broad leather band of his surcingle. Around the yard raiders were vaulting to the backs of their war ponies and

11

moving toward the gate to hear their instructions. There was a clatter and clank of pots, pans, and tools tied to the settlers' horses.

The warriors lined up in splendor. The yard was crowded with them. Strips of gingham and calico, linen and wool waved with the scalps and deer tails on bridles and shields. Sleeves had been ripped from coats to make vests. Sunbonnets bobbed in and out, their ties fluttering in the fitful breeze. Granny's gray shawl was wrapped around a naked waist. A red union suit hung limply from a lance, the legs stirring now and then as though something still lived in them.

Wanderer and Eagle jumped down from their horses and lashed each child's ankles together with ropes passed under the horses' bellies. Tied tightly in place they might survive the flight ahead. Then the men remounted and walked their skittish ponies to the rear of the war party swarming at the gate. Wanderer knew there was no need to be in front. Night, his friend, his brother, his favorite pony, could outrun them all. He and Night would both be glad to leave this place.

Scattered through the grove of pecan trees were the men who had been in the fields when the first faint sounds of death floated over the hills. Their tanned faces and hands and faded, dust-drenched homespuns blended into the cool, thick leaf mold of the grove's floor. Sun dapple and shadows camouflaged them even more. Irridescent blowflies, gleaming in shafts of light, buzzed around the body of a small skunk, the remains of an owl's midnight meal. The carrion smell burned the men's noses.

L.D. Nixon, his wispy, blond hair sweat-plastered to his round, pink head, cried softly. Sweat and tears blurred the spectacles that perched on his small nose. His pale blue eyes were red-rimmed and raw. Stretched next to him behind the huge fallen tree trunk was Luther Plummer. His narrow shoulders shook as he swore with an imagination no one would have expected in him. He fired mechanically at anything that moved above the spiked walls or outside the gate, though the Indians were beyond his range. He continued blaspheming under his breath as he reloaded, ramming the lead balls viciously down the muzzle of his old Common.

Whatever James Parker's thoughts were, he kept them to himself as usual. His hooded dark blue eyes never left the fort above them, sweeping the blank wall from front to rear and back again as he searched for some sign of his family. Seth and Ashbel Bates and George White held quiet council, rifles cradled, backs hunkered against a massive gray limestone boulder. White's deep voice rose and fell, counterpoint to the whine of the flies' song.

"Elder John, Silas, Ben, Samuel, and young Robert Frost are up there. Dead if they're lucky. I saw someone running down the hill toward the river. Indians ran 'em down, though. Looked like they brought 'em around back the other side of the walls. I don't know if anyone made it to the bottomlands or not. Where's Old Man Lunn and the Faulkenberrys and Anglin? Do you think they could hear the noise all the way to your cabins?"

"I reckon so," said Seth. "It ain't much farther than the fields, and the wind's right."

"David went down to the river to fish, first light. He's probably holed up there. If anyone makes it to the river he can help them. He's got his carbine with him," Ashbel said.

"The others were working on Anglin's well. They must have circled around to the river. Looks like we're the only ones anywhere near firing distance," said Seth Bates.

"How many Injuns do you suppose there are?" White asked.

"A passel, seventy-five or a hundred at least. The Caddos are from around here, but the Kiowas and Comanches are a long way from home. There ain't that many Injuns in this whole territory," Seth answered.

"Is your wife and young-uns up there, George?" asked Ashbel.

White nodded and continued to study the fort from around the edge of the rock. "They're all in there. All of them." His self-control almost cracked.

"George, James, we've got to do something," Plummer called.

"What do you suggest, Luther?" James Parker answered, but his eyes never relaxed their vigil.

"What about the opening in the back?"

"We planned well when we built that fort. We left no cover standing around it," said Parker patiently. "You know we'd be porcupines before we could get around to the back. The grass isn't as trampled there, though. If the other men are at the river, maybe they could crawl up the hill to the back door. And then what? These guns are no match for arrows at close range."

There was a piercing howl from the fort. The white men jumped. A mass of riders exploded from the gate and fanned out across the hill, flowing down and outward like water bursting a dam. As it spread out, the pack turned and fled in a wide circle around the grove and north, paralleling the Navasota River.

"Don't shoot," White shouted. "Some of them are riding double. They must have taken captives."

There was little chance of hitting anyone at that range anyway. The Indians rode low on their mounts and moved fast. The flapping cloth and feathers whipping in the wind blurred them as targets.

13

The last one of them cleared the gate and his black pony pulled up on the rear horses, passing them one by one. The rider lashed him on with a long quirt, heedless of the small child clinging to his waist, her blond hair streaming behind.

In silence the men watched Wanderer and Cynthia Ann Parker top the next hill to the northeast. They seemed to pause a moment at the crest, outlined against the sky, hock-deep in waving grass and flowers, before they disappeared over the edge and into legend.

❧ 3 ❧

David Faulkenberry and James Parker returned to the fort late in the afternoon of that same day. They knew that someone had to search for wounded survivors and collect supplies for the refugees hidden in the thickets of the river bottom. From the bushes at the base of the hill they scouted the slope leading to the back of the fort. James laid a hand on David's arm.

"What is it?" David whispered. James pointed.

David raised himself on his elbows to peer through the bushes. Three-quarters of the way down the hill between their hiding place and the back stockade wall, the grass was waving as though a large animal were pushing through it. Whatever it was, it moved slowly and low to the ground.

As they watched its approach, David listened to the cricket's twilight celebration of spring. Black vultures, like angels of death, circled silently over the toothed walls, silhouetted against the pink and gold sky. They had to hurry. There was barely an hour of light left.

"I'm going to take a shot at it," James's jaws were clenched.

"No. Wait a few more minutes. Whatever it is, it will hit that stretch of rock soon."

David readied his carbine, tracking the path of the animal. The minutes inched by. Then a clawlike hand reached through the edge of the thick grass. It was followed by a thin arm caked with dried blood. The dirt-encrusted fingers clutched a gash in the rock and pulled the body forward as though scaling a sheer, vertical cliff. Granny Parker's coarse, gray hair lay spread across the lighter gray of the limestone. The blood-soaked rag tied clumsily around her shoulder clung to the yawning wound there. Her frail form was blotched with purple bruises and crosshatched with red gashes and scratches.

All caution forgotten, the two men raced up the hill. Granny moaned as David picked her up in his arms. He lifted her as easily as if her translucent skin were filled with feathers and not flesh and bone. He carried her back down into the trees. James cleared a spot, and he laid her gently in the bushes, hidden from view. He took off his shirt and draped it across her, almost covering her entirely. James brought her water in his leather hat.

"We'll be back, Mother," James whispered close to her ear. She couldn't see the tears in his eyes and David ignored them. The old woman barely nodded, her eyes closed. Her cracked and swollen lips twitched in something like a smile of recognition. David and James started wearily up the hill, foreboding churning in their stomachs.

David stared down at Elder John's eyeless sockets, crawling with jewel-like flies. The crows had already begun turning the day's dead into useful forage. They delicately picked out the choicest morsels, the eyeballs, first. There wasn't time to dig holes for the bodies, and when help finally arrived from Fort Houston, there would hardly be enough left to bury. But under no circumstances would he allow any of the Parker people back up here for a burial detail. He could at least spare them that last horror.

Shadows crept across the compound floor, yet Faulkenbery continued staring at Elder John, whose thick, steel-gray hair and beard had turned snow white. He was over eighty years old, yet he had been tall and robust. He had always looked the part of the religious patriarch he had played for so long. Now his stripped, mutilated, and drained corpse was shriveled and old. The buzzing of the flies set David's eardrums vibrating. He had seen war and death in quantity, but never anything like this.

Forgive me for cursing you, John. If you erred, you paid a higher price than ought be demanded of any mortal.

David leaned one hand against a log in the stockade wall, lowered his head, and retched helplessly. James was silent, his face rigid as he stared at his father's body.

"It looks like there's no one here alive," said David, knowing there were no words that could comfort James. "Lucy Parker says Rachel and little Jamie were taken, and she thinks Elizabeth was too. We have to be sure, though. You start checking at that end of the cabins, James, and I'll look here."

Puddles of night collected in the hollows and angles of the debris in the yard. They lapped around the men's ankles as they searched and called through the jumbled desolation that had been home for thirty people. David picked his way around the huge, groping talons of a broken grain cradle. Angry at being disturbed, crows cawed from their perches along the cabin roofs and stockade walls.

A patch of snow stood out against the darkening earth, flour that the raiders had scattered in a blizzard of destruction. Shattered hand-hewn furniture lay about. A small china doll, its face crushed by a horse's hoof, sprawled like an elfin corpse. David knew he would find no metal or weapons, nothing the Indians could use to pursue their favorite pastime of war.

He and James filed silently out past Silas Parker, a lonely sentinel hanging against the gate. His brother Benjamin still lay where he had fallen. They had to hurry down the hill before it became too dark to find Granny and the path to the river. David turned one last time to look up at the fort standing starkly against the wide sky, an abandoned ship on a desolate ocean. Each of the logs in it had taken days to cut. The settlers' axes had bounced off the rigid hardwoods. Their lives were bound up in it, committed to it. He wondered if they would come back, bury their dead, clean up the mess, and start over. He felt sure they would. They or others like them.

He shuddered as the cool evening wind blew across his bare shoulders, raising chicken flesh along his back and arms. The cricket chorus was pulsing steadily around them, background noise to his thoughts. He and James would carry Granny Parker to where the others were hidden. She needed care and water badly, but she was amazingly tough. They all were.

Tomorrow he and some of the men could scavenge food, clothing, and horses at his and Lunn's and the Bates's cabins, *if* there were no signs of Indians returning. He'd send one man ahead on the fastest horse, Old Blue probably. The other animals could carry the worst of the wounded. The rest would have to walk the fifty miles to the nearest settlement. He didn't relish the prospect. And by tomorrow two of the wounded women would probably be dead. More death and more suffering for the living. He didn't even want to think about Rachel and Elizabeth and Cynthia Ann. For them it was just beginning.

Oh God, he was weary with the weight of worry and sorrow. But methodically he resumed planning for the next day. The survivors could hide and rest by the river and start out late in the afternoon. The moon would be up shortly after dark. It was at the round, ripe, luminous phase, so bright you could read by it. The Comanches preferred that kind for raiding, or so he'd heard. He'd circle his people away from the fort. The buzzards might upset the women even more. And by evening, who knew how far the innocent breeze would carry the smell.

Rachel Plummer's hands were bound to the rounded pommel of the saddle that was chafing her hour after hour. The skin on her inner thighs was raw and bleeding. Matted blood pulled at the hairs on her legs, but that was minor. A rawhide noose choked her, now loosening, now jerking her up tight as her horse fell behind the one leading it. When the rope tightened it gagged her until her gorge rose, washing her mouth in the sour taste of bile. The pain in her neck then shot down across her breast bone in a spasm that almost paralyzed her arms and left them tingling.

It took all her concentration to keep her balance, even though her feet were cruelly bound by the horsehair lariat passed under the animal's belly. The coarse black rope left a bright red circle around each ankle. Blood ran in rivulets across her bare, swollen feet. Her shoulders cramped and her muscles ached from the tension of fighting the forces pulling on her hands, feet, and neck as her pony raced headlong after the one ahead of it.

When she fell behind, pulling too hard on the leash that held her, the short, stocky Indian at the other end of it wheeled back and lashed her with his quirt or beat her with his bow. Her blouse hung in tatters from her shoulders and her back was ridged with long, purple welts. Her dark brown hair stood out in a tangled thicket around her face, blinding her when it blew into her eyes. Her head drummed with pain and her mouth was parched. The heavy, swollen club that had been her tongue stuck to her lips when she tried to coax moisture from it. The flaring sun burned her raw back, and the constant jolting jarred even her internal organs. Her poor unborn child could never survive this.

The throbbing pain burrowed its way into her pores, spread out under her skin, and wrapped around her bowels until she could no longer imagine being without it. The raid that morning seemed to have happened years before.

The sun had already been hot and high five hours earlier when the twenty Comanche warriors had ridden out of the glare into the cool shade of the pecans and sycamores along the Navasota River to the north of Parker's Fort. They had left their spare pack animals there before the raid. A whinny was the only sign of the two dozen or more horses hidden in the dense growth of bushes. Two boys about fourteen years old appeared soundlessly from among the trees. Without a word they began leading pack horses and fresh riding mounts into the clear area at the edge of the copse.

17

In an eerie silence amid deep shadows, strong, calloused fingers swiftly freed the stolen loot from the sweating war ponies and transferred it to the fresh animals. Pots and tools and other metal objects were wrapped in rags and hides to muffle them. Smaller things disappeared into heavy leather pouches hanging like huge bloated ticks from sweat-stained surcingles.

Tiny, wiry, nineteen-year-old Mo-cho-rook, The Cruelest One Of All, stuffed Elder John's big black Bible into the square deerhide pack he carried at his side. He would have looked like a puckish schoolboy off to classes with it except that one half of his pinched face was painted red and the other black. The paint extended down onto his naked, pigeon-breasted chest. His thin mouth looked like a gash, and his large black eyes held only hatred.

As Wanderer untied his captive's chafed ankles, Night curled his short, sleek neck around. Puckering his velvety lips, he nibbled his friend's shoulder. Wanderer swatted him absentmindedly as he worked at the knots. In pique Night snorted and turned to nuzzle the pinto next to him. Cynthia sat mute, trying to make herself as small as possible, her mind and body numb. She knew instinctively that if she made any trouble at all she would be killed as casually as her mother would pick a louse and crush it between her fingernails.

The thought of her own death shouldered everything else out of her mind. How would it happen? She'd heard that Indians took babies by the ankles and dashed their heads against trees or rocks. Did she weigh too much for that? She saw the gnarled cream-and-brown-mottled trunk of the sycamore spattered with her own brains and blood like the plank floor at hog-killing time. Maybe they ate children. Would they roast her alive? Were the rest of her family dead? Why wasn't anyone trying to save her? Where was her mother?

Wanderer pulled her roughly down from the horse, yanking her back to reality. He signed that she was to take care of any physical necessities right there. She hid herself in the long tail of the shirt she wore and squatted at his feet like a dog. To deflect the shame, she stared fixedly at the bright brass cones hanging from the fringe on his leggings. Then he lifted her onto another horse, a red piebald with wild eyes that seemed to leer at her. The horse pulled his blotchy upper lip back over his long yellow teeth as though smelling something rotten. He laid his pointed ears back, sidestepped and half reared on his bandy legs, but Wanderer held him and retied Cynthia as she'd been before.

One of the boys brought water in a rounded pouch that looked like the stomach of some large animal. Wanderer took a long drink while the boy led Night away to water him lightly with the other war ponies. Cynthia looked longingly at the drops running down Wanderer's chin. Without thinking, she passed her tongue over dry lips.

For the first time since her capture, she found herself staring into the tall warrior's deep, aloof eyes, made even larger by the black paint around them. She tried to keep her face neutral, not knowing what expression might enrage him. He glanced around as though to make sure no one was watching. Then he handed her the water. She had barely wet her lips before he snatched it away and passed it to his friend who had John. Since Eagle had knocked the breath out of John, neither of the children had tried to speak to each other. John must have displeased Eagle somehow though. One of the child's eyes was purple and his mouth was swollen and bleeding.

The Indians divided into small parties, separating the captives.

In less than half an hour they all had mounted and headed east toward night and the Trinity River.

By the time darkness fell, Cynthia was only aware of the pain in her body and the rhythmic movement and incessant pounding of the horses. She still rode behind Wanderer, and both of them were drenched in sweat. Her face was burned and raw from the stinging wind and sun. The men and horses had to be phantoms, demons, despite the smell and feel of them. No mortal beast could run like this, hour after hour across the sweltering prairie. They moved on relentlessly, alternating their pace from a fast walk to a canter and then to the stomach-jolting trot. Cynthia felt like her insides were bruised.

Just after sundown a brilliant full moon rose over the hills ahead, spilling light across the rounded peaks and sending it flowing down into the valleys. The sea of grass shimmered silver as the wind brushed it into rippling patterns. Dappled nighthawks swooped across the moon's bright face like moths at a candle. Far away a wolf howled a cry of despair. Cynthia's flesh crawled, as much from the lonely, wailing sound as from the wind's chill breath on her wet skin. All she saw of the ethereal landscape was the bronzed, smooth back ahead of her. She had memorized its cordillera of vertebrae and the long ridge of a scar that curved around under the left shoulder blade.

The moon was high, marking the hour of midnight, when the group rode into another stand of tall trees. They picked their way single file among the massive columns, dodging the thickets of thorns that reached out to rake their legs. The friendly moon followed, winking through openings in the leafy roof overhead. Through the trees flames flickered as though the forest were ablaze, yet the men continued to thread their way toward the fire. An eerie howling and moaning grew louder as they moved deeper into the woods.

They began to pass the shadowy forms of hundreds of picketed horses cropping leaves, bark, and the sparse grass of the small clearings. The fire was so big that the crack of burning logs could be heard above the whoops and howls. As Cynthia peered around Wanderer's back, she knew that Elder John had been right. And he had been wrong. There was a hell, and it was just as he'd described it. But you didn't have to die to be condemned there.

The vast tree trunks circling the clearing towered eighty feet into the air. Their columns turned the space into a pagan temple. The incandescent frenzy there was intensified by the looming black maw beyond the inner ring of trees. Reality became as tenuous as the flames that leaped and twisted, making even the trees and bushes undulate and dance. Daylight's smudged, painted faces became ghastly, demonic masks. Light flickered across shining mahogany cheekbones and shadows formed gaping black pits where eyes should be. Leaping and whirling and waving bloody scalps, dozens of raiders celebrated.

Wanderer slid down from his pony and flexed gracefully up on his toes. Casually, he sauntered toward the circle of watchers, calling to some of the men swaying and chanting there. Cynthia's stomach and chest felt cold where his warm back had been pressed against her. She bit her lip to keep from crying out after him, begging him to stay. As bad as he was, he was the only security she had.

A few men from the circle came toward her. She jerked futilely at her tether and flailed with her small arms and fists as fingers dug into her ankles and held her while others untied the knots. The memory of her grandmother threw her into a panic. She fought as she was pulled headfirst from the horse and dumped on the ground. Urine stung her chafed legs as terror made her lose control. Struggling like a beached fish, she was flipped on her stomach and her wrists and ankles tied. Choking in the churned-up mold of the forest floor, she was dragged by her hair into the ring of dancers.

They dropped her near the sprawled forms of John and her cousin and aunt. As the men passed, they kicked the cringing bodies or lashed them with their bows. She could only see and feel their moccasins as they thudded into her stomach and ribs, and she wondered bitterly if a pair of them belonged to her captor. The fire was so close that she feared her clothes would flare up from the intense heat. The pounding of the drums never ceased, and the monotonous chanting was punctuated by screeches that hurt her ears.

She could see John and her Aunt Elizabeth from where she lay.

Their backs and legs were bloody and lacerated. From the feel of warm, sticky wetness on her own body she knew she must look the same. Each blow sent a crest of pain breaking over the general ache. She sobbed, her tears turning the black soil to mud under her face.

After what seemed like hours, the dancers tired of the game. Two of them dragged her and John out of the circle and threw them against a tree trunk, as though they were rubbish swept out of the campsite. As her head hit the knotted root of a gnarled old oak, she slid gratefully down a ringing well lined in black velvet.

Someone was slaughtering hogs and doing a sloppy job of it. Their shrill squeals meant the sticker had missed the vein and the animals were bucking and twisting to escape. Cynthia hated hog-killing time, and ran and hid when she could.

Something sharp was digging into her cheek. She tried to brush it away from her face, but found her arms were paralyzed. No, tied. The dream faded, and the nightmare came into focus. Still the animal screams went on. Cousin Rachel and Aunt Elizabeth were near the flames, their bodies painted in yellow light. They had been stripped and were bound spread-eagled to stakes hammered deep into the soft ground. The raw shame of their exposure shocked Cynthia almost more than the killing and tortures she had seen.

A few Indians still jerked and twitched in a trancelike state in front of the fire, but most of them stood or squatted around the women. Ignoring their screams and moans, they laughed and joked with each other as they waited their turns. Men who had finished wandered off to sleep a few hours before the long day coming. The others were in no hurry. There were many of them and only two women, but they had all night. While they waited they recounted the stories of the morning's coups and speculated about how the raid leaders would divide the wealth up among their men. It had been a very good day.

$❧ 4 ❧$

Cynthia smelled coffee. Coffee and love and family and home. A rooster crowed in the chill hour before dawn. She and her brothers John and little Silas curled together under the huge, blue goosedown comfort-

er. The smell of coffee drifted up through the cracks in the floor-
boards of the low loft where they slept. Her father's big arms
wrapped around her while they rocked in front of the morning fire.
She ran her fingers through the thick, black hairs on the back of his
hand as he held a mug of hot coffee. Aromatic wraiths floated over
steaming bowls of cornmeal mush sweetened with wild honey.

But the world had gone awry. Her beloved coffee was mixed with
the stench of fresh dung and stale sweat. With rancid grease and the
biting odor of urine that splashed near her head as she lay huddled
against the tree root where she'd been thrown. She looked up to see
an Indian shake off the last drops and shuffle sleepily back toward
the fire.

It was the hour before dawn. It was chilly. Coffee was in the air,
along with death and terror and cruelty. Her breakfast was dirt, and
there was grit between her teeth.

"John?" No answer. He was gone.

The coffee was being brewed in Mrs. White's new copper kettle,
now coated with fine black ash from the open fire. Drooping red
banners of buffalo steaks hung from long, sharpened sticks planted
around the fire. The flames popped and sizzled as the juice dropped
on them. The rich odor of roasting meat knotted the child's empty
stomach with hunger. Raiders squatted on their haunches around
the fire, tearing at the charred flesh, grease running off their chins
and elbows as they talked in low, guttural tones. Others rounded up
horses for the day's ride.

The Indians coalesced into separate groups. The lean Caddoans,
with turkey feathers behind their ears, skinny legs, hooked noses,
and bobbing crests of hair, looked like a flock of tattered birds. Their
plucked skulls were painted with wavy red lines. Bright tin rings
dangled from their noses. The paint on their faces was cracked and
peeling, giving them a scabrous look in the dim dawn light filtering
through the trees.

Elizabeth Kellogg lay unconscious and almost naked across the
flanks of one of their ponies. Her arms and legs were tied together
by a rope passed under the horse's belly. She seemed dead, her
head lolling from side to side as the group moved off single file
through the woods. Their course would take them north and out of
Cynthia's life.

The Kiowa were a handsome and arrogant lot, much more graceful on the ground than the stockier Comanche. Many of the Comanche didn't braid their hair but wore it pushed behind their ears.

A thin, quavering wail rose over the camp's clamor. Little Jamie
Plummer had been snatched from his cold cradle of leaves and twigs
and tied onto a horse. His mother followed him, her haunted,

red-rimmed eyes sunken in the dark hollows of her gaunt face. Her shredded clothes fluttered about her. She walked stiffly, jerked along by Tsetarkau, Terrible Snows, her owner. Eyes bulging in his round face, he waddled ahead of her, balancing precariously on his strangely thin legs. His paunch hung over the edge of his narrow breechclout cord. His long arms ended in large, bony hands that dangled halfway to his knobby knees. Rachel shuffled after him to the horses. Head bowed, she was pulled through a gauntlet of men who reached out to pinch and slap her.

Near the fire, Big Bow, Buffalo Piss, and the other raid leaders were huddled, dividing up the spoils that lay heaped around them. Runners delivered the goods to the men who were to receive them. Cynthia could see Wanderer's head above all the others as he moved toward her, weaving in and out among the groups. Desperately she told herself that he couldn't have been one of her tormentors the night before. She almost prayed it wasn't so.

Hunkering down, he untied her feet. With the black paint washed off his face, she had a fleeting glimpse of youth and innocence and intelligence before he lifted her head up by the hair and slipped the noose around her neck. Lights exploded in front of her eyes as he yanked her to her feet by the cord around her throat. She swayed and stumbled, needles shooting through her cold, numb legs. Her feet were lumps of clay hanging on her ankles. Every muscle was outlined in pain. Her back, legs, and arms were stiff with dried blood and scabs.

Something in Wanderer's eyes had seemed human, had tricked her into expecting some small kindness from him. She had been lured into thinking she could predict his behavior. She stared at his lithe, tapering back as he stalked ahead of her, trailing her leash loosely. And she felt deeply and brutally betrayed for the first time in her life. With the singlemindedness of a child, she blamed him for all that had happened to her and her loved ones.

All she wanted in the world were freed hands and a long sharp knife. She would plunge it to the hilt between his tawny, smooth shoulder blades and hang on it until it sliced all the way down the length of his spine. She wanted to feel his blood spurting on her arms and watch him topple face down into the dirt. She hated him, and she knew she would always hate him.

Maybe it was the hatred that kept her sane that second night. She concentrated on the revenge she would take when she escaped, and avoided the problem of *how* she would escape. A tight gag cut the corners of her mouth and soaked up what little moisture was left. Staked out on her back, her throat tethered by a thong passed tightly across it and tied to small posts on either side, she couldn't even huddle up against the cold.

She stared up at the stars glittering like slivers of ice in the black sky. The cool night air blew across her sunburned skin until she shook with chills that passed up and down her body. She had had nothing to eat and little to drink in the thirty-six hours since the attack. Her mouth was lined with dirty lint. Her stomach seemed shriveled. The insides of her eyelids were fine sandpaper. She couldn't see John, but she could hear the slapping, slurping noises of the men using Rachel.

They were back at the Navasota River in the small clearing where they'd picked up their horses the day before. Why were they here? Would they attack the fort again? Was she doomed to watch the same grisly scene over and over? It couldn't be. There were only fifteen Indians now, and surely help was coming. Her family and friends must be searching for her. Cynthia pulled quietly and desperately at her ropes. If she could escape, she could follow the river home. This nightmare would fade into stories to frighten her own children. Her father would be alive and her mother would welcome her lost child back. But the rawhide held against her feeble tugging and she had to stop, weeping with frustration, when she saw Cruelest One watching her. He never seemed to take his black, glittering snake's eyes off her, as though waiting for an excuse to kill her.

She had no way of knowing that in the Comanche's vast territory a hundred-mile detour for a rendezvous was nothing. They weren't happy to be back at the Navasota, though. There was no fire and no noise. The few men still awake got up often to stand at the edge of the trees and stare out at the bright, moonlit hills. Scattered around the small clearing were the humped forms of the others, sleeping under warm buffalo robes.

Cynthia could feel tiny legs tickling her as night spiders explored her body. Jibbering thoughts of snakes slithering alongside her for warmth kept her tense and wide-eyed for hours. When she finally fell asleep, she never heard the eerie, bubbling call of the screech owl.

There was an argument going on when she woke up. Without understanding a word she knew that she was its cause and that she might die. Cruelest One was talking softly but savagely. He stabbed the air in her direction with his bony finger. The others squatted or stood and listened attentively, their faces stolid and unreadable in the dim light. Wanderer spoke next, his voice almost too low to hear. When he finished, the rest grunted and went off to saddle their ponies.

Wanderer walked over to her and sat on his heels. He studied her as though she were a kitten to be drowned. She stared up at him dumbly, her blue eyes enormous under the tangled straw of her hair. One tear sneaked from the corner of her eye and fled down her cheek, but she kept the rest of her face under control. He was so young to be a murderer, scarcely older than Robert Frost. Wanderer pulled his scalping knife from the leather sheath strapped to his bare thigh. Cynthia closed her eyes, tensed her muscles, and tried to remember the prayers her mother had taught her centuries ago. But there were no prayers left, only rivers of blood, mangled limbs, naked women, and babies with their heads burst like melons.

She felt a slight tug at her throat. He was using the knife's point to loosen the knots in the rawhide. When he had her neck free, he untied the gag in her mouth. He held the flat of the blade against her lips. Then he drew the tip lightly in a graceful, curving line from the hollow beneath her left ear, around under her chin, and up to her other ear. His meaning was clear. She nodded, assuming that he in turn would know what her nod meant. She could never take life for granted. Wanderer held it quivering in his hands.

"He's not so bad, you know."

"John, how can you say that?"

It was the second day after leaving the Trinity River. The sun had burned off the morning's haze and now blew its hot breath across the low hills. A fairy cloud of gnats danced around the children's faces as they sat tied against an old pecan tree. Its rough, furrowed bark hurt the striped grid of bruises and scabs on their backs. They shook their heads, flailing their hair at the winged motes that tangled in their lashes and crawled over their mouths and nostrils.

In front of them bucked the Brazos River, swollen by invisible spring rains somewhere to the north. The Comanche called it To-hopt Pah-e-hona, Blue Water River. Its sly, sapphire eddies and foamfrosted pools had almost drowned the lot of them as they swam their horses across. The last drops of their soaking were drying up, forming shrinking oases of coolness on their bodies.

"Well, he hasn't beaten me any more, and this morning we sneaked away and he showed me how to get honey. He let me have a little. His horse is faster than anybody's except Wanderer's. His name means Eagle, and he's teaching me sign language. Did you know the word for honey is *pena*?"

Cynthia was no longer nine years old. She had aged a lifetime in three days. Now her little brother was trading it all in for a fingerful of honey from a murderer.

25

"John, listen to me." She dropped her voice to a whisper. "Don't you remember what they did?"

"Eagle didn't kill anybody. It was the others." His small mouth set into the tight line that closed out all argument.

Maybe he hadn't noticed his father's thick, curly brown hair hanging from the war lance nearby. Maybe he didn't understand what was happening to Cousin Rachel. Rachel's sweet, fey voice floated across to them from where she huddled among the roots of a cottonwood, suckling Jamie. Shame hovered around her like the cloud of gnats. She never raised her eyes, never spoke except to croon nonsense to her child. She was as alien as the Indians. And now John was defecting. Cynthia felt old and alone, but she tried again.

"Don't you miss Mother and little Silas and Orlena?"

"Of course. Maybe tonight we can escape or the Rangers will find us. . . ."

Their whispering had alerted Cruelest One. He glared at them from the circle of men studying the notched sticks that guided them through strange territory. His look silenced the children.

As they rode that day and the next through country that became flatter and more barren, Cynthia went frantically over each day's march, searching for some carelessness that would let her and John slip away. Landmarks became fewer and fewer as they moved away from the hills and onto the plains. The sky soared higher over them, and the horizon stretched out into infinity. Hopelessness yawned at her feet, and she was sliding into it. But death in the desert was better than what was happening to Rachel. It was better even than watching it happen to her.

Rachel knew she would never be clean again. An ocean of water and a continent of soap wouldn't do it. Not all the world's scrub brushes could scour the salmon scent of dried semen from her skin. Keening softly, almost silently, like the high-pitched whine of summer's mosquitoes, she drew her finger up her arm. It left a furrow in the film of grease there, rancid beaver oil that their bodies smeared all over her.

Absently she rubbed and kneaded the tattered rags of her skirt. The cloth around her thighs was stiff and black with grease and dirt and sweat salt. When they weren't tied her hands were moving up and down against her legs, wiping and massaging first the palms and then the backs and the palms again.

Maybe Luther, her husband, was alive and looking for her. And if he found her? What then? He would never want to touch her. No one would. She hated to touch herself. She saw herself back among civilized people. She heard the murmur of whispers that parted before her and closed in behind her back as she passed.

Death tantalized her, dancing like a mirage of water in a baking desert. Die and abandon Jamie to the savage who hung him carelessly in a leather sack on his packhorse along with the other loot. Who fed him by throwing a pan of dirty, congealed corn mush in front of him and letting the child live on what he could dig out with his tiny, unlearned fingers.

At least they let her nurse him now and then, not knowing that her milk was drying up, curdling inside her. The few minutes cradling him at her breast were all that kept her living. That and the necessity of killing Cynthia. Rachel didn't know how she would do it, but she knew it would be inevitable eventually. It was only a matter of time before the child's innocent, vulnerable beauty caught their attention. Rachel would try to be ready when it happened.

Constant hunger ate at her insides, keeping her weak and disoriented. On the fourth night out her master tied her hands behind her and propped her against a prickly, stunted juniper tree just outside the warmth of the fire. As the raiders ate they occasionally tossed sizzling pieces of buffalo meat onto her bare thighs. They laughed at the sight of her crying from the pain and struggling to eat the small bits after they fell in the dirt. It gave them endless enjoyment, but not much nourishment for Rachel.

That was the night they invented another new amusement. When those who used her finally finished and allowed her to fall into an exhausted sleep, two of them crept up with a glowing coal held between green sticks. Cruelest One thrust the live ember up her left nostril. He and Terrible Snows giggled when she woke up screaming and writhing, lashing her head from side to side and pulling at her bonds to rid herself of it. When she didn't stop screaming Cruelest One placed his dirty moccasined foot in her mouth and, leaning down, held his knife's point to her throat. Rachel stopped screaming. But whenever Cynthia awoke from her fitful sleep that endless night, she heard her cousin sobbing quietly.

❧ 5 ❦

Ahead of the small party stretched a carpet of blue. The flowers flowed for miles across the gently undulating plain. At the horizon they curved upward and blended into the cornflower-colored sky. Cynthia sat loosely on the tattered old packhorse Wanderer had given her to ride. Her legs barely reached across his back and the leash was still around her neck, but she felt a twinge of pride in having her own mount. The ache in her body was now only what she used to feel after a hard day in the fields back home.

A gentle wind ruffled her honey-colored hair and sent the horse's ragged tail fluttering out behind him. She was grateful for the bit of calm after five days of horror, even if it were the peace in the eye of the hurricane. That morning Cruelest One and three others had ridden off to the northwest. Another group had followed them with Rachel, Jamie, and John. Now she was alone with Wanderer, Eagle, Big Bow, Howea, Deep Water, one of the herder boys, and a warrior of Mexican birth named His-oo-san-ches and called Spaniard. The last one in the group was Buffalo Piss, the raid leader.

She missed John, even though she'd been upset at how quickly he had begun to enjoy the wild, Indian life. He seemed more unhappy at Eagle's betrayal as he had casually traded the boy off for two blankets, a bolt of cloth, and an iron skillet, than by all the atrocities he had seen.

In a way the loss of the captives was a weight lifted from Cynthia. It had been painful to watch Jamie's legs and arms shrink into sticks from malnutrition. She no longer had to see John turning into a savage or hear the nightly moans of Rachel and the obscene noises of the men rutting. Rachel had become a shameful reproach, making Cynthia vaguely guilty for not suffering more. Her presence constantly reminded the child of unspeakable acts and terrifying threats.

There was a tug at her leash. While the other men discussed their route, Wanderer turned his black pony to face her. He pulled a small bag from his belt and poured black powder into the palm of his left hand. He mixed it with water from his pouch and, dipping his fingers into the paste, began smearing thick paint over the exposed area of Cynthia's burned shoulders and face. Expecting blows, she flinched as his hands touched her. Now they were gentle and firm as he tried to protect her from the sun.

When he stroked the sticky black paint onto her cheeks, she was startled by the intense look in his eyes as he stared into hers. Fear from a source too deep to have a name caused her to lower her head and jerk away. Frowning, he pulled her back roughly and held her until he finished. Everyone in her family had the same brilliant azure eyes; she couldn't know the fascination they held for an Indian. The acres of blue brushing the ponies' hocks intensified their color under her long yellow lashes, making her seem like a growing thing that belonged on the prairie.

* * *

28

The acrid smell of burned feathers hung over the campfire. A turkey carcass, charred black and looking like a huge, jagged lump of coal, lay in the embers. Deep Water, the herder, raked it out with a stick and set it aside to cool. Huddled outside the ring of men, Cynthia felt the night wind on her back and the faint warmth of the flames on her face, chest, and shins. The dried black paint on her cheeks and body pulled at her skin. She picked at it with her fingers, peeling it off in flakes. Her stomach churned with hunger.

Deep Water drew the skin back from the neck of the carcass. He slid it down the length of the body as though removing a glove, taking off the burned feathers and exposing juicy, steaming white meat seasoned with spicy smoke. The odor of roast turkey blended with the incense of burning juniper and perfumed the air. Wanderer passed her a wing and a handful of crunchy roots that tasted like chestnuts. She brushed the dirt off them and chewed slowly, never sure when or what she would eat next. She saved the turkey for last, savoring it.

Overhead, a lopsided moon sailed along as the clouds raced past it. Tall pecan trees crowded along the quiet river, lying like black velvet below them. The deep green ribbon of trees along the water was an oasis in the expanse of short grass and stunted oaks and twisted junipers. The plain stretched for miles in all directions before bumping up against low, flat mountains dim in the distance.

The group had passed an invisible line that day. The ninety-eighth meridian was behind them, and now they were in the Comanchería they ruled. When Cruelest One and Terrible Snows, Rachel's owner, left, they seemed to take the tension and rancor with them. Wanderer sat until late that night, smoking, talking, and laughing with the other men around the fire. Cynthia watched him deftly make a cigarette, sprinkling the tobacco on a cottonwood leaf, rolling it neatly, and licking the edges to seal it. He lit it from a burning twig and settled into a quiet, bantering argument with Eagle, Big Bow, and Buffalo Piss.

Cynthia's head drooped, jerked up, then fell against her chest. She woke long enough to brush away last year's crop of rotten pecans. She lay down on her side, hands pressed between her knees for warmth, barely daring to breathe for fear Wanderer would remember that she was only held by the leash around her neck.

When she woke up hours later, the moon and the fire were low. A corner of Wanderer's buffalo robe was draped over her legs where he had thrown it as he stretched out. She cautiously nestled a little farther under it, inching down with agonizing slowness rather than risk waking him. Wanderer did nothing carelessly. He meant the robe to be there and he knew she wasn't tied up, but she had no idea what the limits to his astonishing kindness were or what price she

29

would have to pay for it. In this new game the rules were not only unwritten but unspoken. Learning them could be painful, even fatal.

She lay listening to the lonely night sounds of crickets and a manic mockingbird serenading a sleeping world. The yipping howl of a solitary coyote and Wanderer's small act of humanity brought tears to her eyes. The trickle turned to a flood that burst the dam she had built against all the battering horrors of the past five days. The knowledge that she was totally alone and helpless in a brutal, hostile world washed over her, overwhelmed her, and swept her away. She sobbed silently and convulsively for the loss of everything she loved.

Escape was impossible. The plains stretched away on all sides, vast and dry and featureless. There were wolves out there, and bears and snakes and hunger and thirst and slow death. Even if she managed to hide in a land where there were no hiding places, where would she run? Her father was hanging from the fort's gate. The curly brown hair that she had loved to play with would decorate some savage's shield. Her mother and brother and sister were probably dead. If her mother was a captive somewhere, she was suffering as Rachel suffered. The thought almost forced her to cry out in pain. No. Not that. She bit her lip until blood beaded on it. She squeezed her eyes shut and concentrated on exorcising that picture. It took her hours to do it, and it happened only when she had finally cried herself dry.

The howl sounded near her head, followed by a stench thick enough to stir—like a vat of fresh cow dung. Cynthia reared up, heart pounding. Across the fire Deep Water was leaping and shaking his right arm and yelping in pain and surprise. It looked like he was celebrating the scalp dance all over. Then she saw the skunk, its sharp little teeth buried in the fleshy base of the boy's thumb and still stubbornly chewing as it was whipped back and forth. Blood flew in a spray, spattering everyone around. Buffalo Piss grabbed it by the tail and, jerking it free, swung it against the nearest tree trunk, splitting its skull.

Dawn was still an hour away, but Big Bow built up the fire while Deep Water nursed his lacerated hand. Buffalo Piss carefully removed the skunk's anal glands, handling them as gingerly as though they were made of spider webs. He hacked off the animal's legs and head, gutted it, and held it over the flames to singe off the hair. Then he cut a long green stick, sharpened the ends, and skewered the body on it. He stuck the branch in the ground and slanted it out over the fire. While the meat roasted, the men made ready to move out.

Buffalo Piss's hand and forearm were stained green by the fumes, but no one seemed bothered by the smell that clung to him and Deep Water. It was so strong it burned the linings of Cynthia's nose, and she kept as much distance between herself and the men as possible. She could do that because she was no longer burdened with the humiliating leash. It had been part of her for so long that there was a white ring circling her sunburned neck when Wanderer finally took it off.

Her stomach revolted when she realized what breakfast would be. She fought down nausea when Wanderer gave her a small share of it. Was this another of their cruel jokes? She watched the others bolt theirs down, then sniffed her own suspiciously. She nibbled a piece, knowing she would get nothing else to eat until nightfall. It tasted like roast suckling pig, and she wished he had given her more.

The gently rolling plain was washed in the pastels of sunrise when the party left the cover of the trees and headed into the dry, ever-present wind. The short, curly buffalo grass swept in front of them like a lawn thousands of square miles in size. Buffalo grass made the very best grazing, and it was too much temptation for a pony. The ponies slyly slowed the pace to a walk and began snatching mouthfuls as they went. Night finally feigned a limp, and everything came to a halt as the animals started grazing with singleminded fervor. The men had been expecting rebellion, and let them eat until they had had enough. A contest of wills developed over the definition of enough, but the horses lost it. Cynthia had almost smiled at Night's limp. He was a wonderful horse, she had to admit. She resolved to slip him some of the grass he so obviously loved.

As the day wore on the plain flattened out. Prickly pear grew into deadly thickets as tall as a man. Agave stabbed skeletal fingers up through the sward. A jackass rabbit, all legs and ears, leaped almost from under the horses' hooves and bounced crazily away.

To the south the occasional black dots of buffalo expanded and blended into a wooly mat that stretched to the horizon, where the heat set it to dancing and shimmering. The cat-hammed, spindle-legged little ponies began to prance under the soaring blue canopy of sky. Even Cynthia's lumpy old packhorse lumbered into a spastic cavort and looked sheepish about it. Unable to hold himself in any longer, Wanderer whirled his black pony around and gobbled like a turkey.

Whatever he shouted after that was an insult and a challenge. Buffalo Piss yelled to Deep Water as they raced off. The boy looked murderous as he rounded up the spare horses to drive them after the men. He lashed about him with his quirt and beat the slower horses with his bow.

"*Ob-be-mah-e-vah,*" he snarled at Cynthia, although there was no

31

need to tell her to get out of the way. She had been keeping up wind as far away from him as possible since his run-in with the skunk that morning. At least he had no chance of sneaking up on her to do her harm when Wanderer's back was turned.

Wanderer pulled out in front of the others. Throwing one leg over the black pony's back, he flung himself around to sit backwards, facing the others. He finished that way, making hideous faces and taunting them. When Deep Water and Cynthia caught up with them, they were amusing themselves by inventing new and impossible ways to ride. Eagle was standing on one foot atop his pony's bare back and steering a careening course between mesquite bushes. Hooting like a mad ape Spaniard hung upside down under his galloping horse's belly. The others competed to see who could pick up the heaviest boulder while riding at full speed.

Bewildered, Cynthia watched them. Where were the murderers and rapists of a week ago? When would their boyish play turn into death and torture? Their erratic behavior left her more confused and warier than ever. She would never forget what they did to her father and grandmother and cousins. Cruelest One lurked in all of them, no matter how harmless they seemed. In play they were just as crazy and senseless as they were at war.

She had seen no liquor, yet they all seemed totally intoxicated. They were. They were home.

The rumbling could be heard for miles out on the plains. The Comanche called the Colorado Talking Water River for good reason. The racing, leaping rapids tumbling over its rock-strewn bed drowned out conversation. The group rode for ten miles along the north bluff overlooking the rich, narrow bottomlands. Late in the afternoon they stopped at a massive pile of boulders. Buffalo Piss resumed command and sent Spaniard grumbling off toward the west along the river. The rest dismounted and began riffling through their packs.

Cynthia watched in rising panic as they pulled out their war gear. Was there a settlement in this howling desolation? Her grandfather's fort had sheltered the last group of whites west of the Trinity River as far as she knew. Hope and fear played tug-of-war with her. Maybe there were enough of her own kind to rescue her. No. The Indians surely wouldn't attack if they knew they were outnumbered. It must be a lone cabin of defenseless people. They were probably going about their business, cooking dinner, milking the cows, playing with the dog. Or perhaps it was a rickety, dust-covered wagon, dwarfed by the distances it was crossing, and led by weary pilgrims looking for their own Eden. Whichever; as soon as the raiders got within hearing distance she would start screaming to warn them. And she would scream until her captor killed her.

Big Bow shouted and pointed to the northeast. Cynthia could see nothing at first. Then a small cloud of dust rose against the empty horizon. Whoever it was moved fast. The cloud seemed to grow as she watched it. The men went on dressing, pulling up their fancy leggings, smoothing the wrinkles out of them and tying them to their breechclouts. They painted themselves and greased and rebraided their hair. War shields were slid carefully from their soft leather cases and shaken to straighten the feathers rimming them. Wanderer tied Night's tail up as though for war, and braided feathers and bells into his mane.

While he was busy, Cynthia searched for some sign of settlers. If she only knew where they were, she could race to warn them. The memory of Wanderer riding backwards ahead of all the others taunted her, but she felt she had to try. As though reading her mind, he came over and slipped the noose around her neck again, leaving the other end tied to his wrist.

Then she recognized the leader of the approaching four riders, and her legs went weak. She clung to the girth on her old horse for support, burying her face in the strong damp odor of his bristly hide.

Please, God. No. Please. No more killing.

Cruelest One was painted for death and riding up fast, beating his lathered, crazy-eyed piebald and raking him with spurs until blood mixed with the foam on his sides. Hunting A Wife, Skinny And Ugly, and the loud one called Esa-yo-oh-hobt, Yellow Wolf, followed. All of them rode with streamers flapping and lances held at the ready. Their bows and quivers were strapped on their backs, their shields hung from their left arms. Wanderer lifted her onto her horse as the rest of his group mounted and rode to meet the newcomers. They conferred briefly, then turned and headed along the river bluff into the setting sun.

The light below them showed a settlement, but not a white one. Hundreds of squat conical tents were scattered among the tall cottonwoods by the river. Only the ones near the center of the village could be seen clearly. There was a roaring fire there that sent shadows leaping on the ghostly pale yellow curves of the nearest lodges. The other tents faded into the darkness, marching off through the trees like a spectral army.

Buffalo Piss gave a long, ululating cry, echoed by his men. It was taken up and multiplied by hundreds of throats below until the wide, low canyon reverberated with it. Spaniard had alerted the

People that they were coming. The ponies raced over the edge of the cliff and plunged headlong down the steep, black slope. They almost outpaced the small avalanche of stones and boulders ricocheting in front of them. Cynthia clung desperately to her horse's neck, ready to leap clear when he stumbled and pitched forward. For once she was glad he was so slow. Wanderer had let go of her leash and there were few horses behind to trample her if she fell. She remembered the dense clumps of prickly pear and cringed at the thought of rolling into one.

The horses smelled home. They all reached level ground with a jolt and headed toward the village. The raiders reined them in at the outlying tents and paraded slowly and solemnly through the narrow streets. Their kin and friends surrounded them, chanting and yelling. A troop of small boys fell in behind them, whooping and waving their small bows and lances. A few women called and held out their arms, promising their own form of reward. The celebration built in pitch and intensity and lasted long into the night.

For Cynthia it was a blur of blankets and robes and leather fringes. Abandoned to the mob, she saw only a living forest of hands and arms, reaching, clutching, touching and pinching her. The waving limbs seemed to grow directly from round, malevolent faces. Young and old, male and female, they all looked alike and they all looked evil. She cowered, trying to protect her face.

Then someone grabbed a piece of her smock and ripped it. The others began laughing and hooting and tearing at the tattered remnants of her clothes. Everyone wanted a souvenir of the yellow hair. When they started pulling her hair, she flailed at the hands and shrieked in anger and terror and shame. She grabbed a handful of the nearest coarse wiry mane and hung on. She was still pulling and kicking and screaming when everyone scattered. A monument of a man towered over her.

Looking up, she saw a stomach. Folds and cliffs and escarpments of earth-colored flesh plunged into and over the rift of his breechclout, then surged out from under it and flowed down to make two vast, smooth columns of legs. She couldn't see his face atop the mountain of his body, but he was so enormous she wouldn't have been surprised to find his shoulders wrapped in clouds.

Bending down, he lifted her easily and tucked her under one arm like a sack of flour. The crowd parted in front of them as he thudded through the village. Most of the lodges were dark and vacant, their inhabitants silhouetted against the fire. The emptiness of the streets and tents was almost as terrifying as the clamor. Suddenly Cynthia was seized by the wild fear that this giant was going to eat her. She started kicking and squealing and squirming again. But she bothered him only a little more than the horseflies that swarm in summer.

A dim light showed through the side of a lodge in a quiet section. Cynthia's captor pushed aside the hide flap covering the door and called to the woman inside.

"Tsatua, Takes Down The Lodge, Wanderer has brought a yellow hair. I had to save the People from her. She was starting her own scalp collection." His broad, flat face wrinkled in a smile.

Silently Tabbenoca, Sunrise, a solemn-faced man with short-cropped hair appeared next to Cynthia. She was passed over to him and he carried her inside. She still clutched long black hairs in her fist.

"Thank you, Pahayuca," Sunrise said quietly as he brushed by. "Takes Down The Lodge needs her."

"Thank you, Pahayuca," the woman's low voice called from inside. Pahayuca, He Who Has Relations With His Aunt, crouched to look in the doorway. He filled the opening and overflowed along the sides of the tent.

"I did nothing." His deep, guttural voice rumbled up from his throat like tremors reaching the earth's surface. "Thank Wanderer when you see him, Ara, my nephew. The trip was a long one. You might give him an extra present for his trouble."

"Of course," said Sunrise. "I will tomorrow when I pay him for her. We feared he wouldn't find one."

"This one looks suitable enough. She's strong. She'll be a good worker," said Pahayuca.

The garble of words passed back and forth over Cynthia's head as she stood swaying on the hard-packed dirt where Sunrise had set her. The close heavy air and the wild medley of odors in the tent made her dizzy. As she wove in and out of consciousness, she wondered vaguely what life as a slave would be like. Then exhaustion took over, and she pitched forward.

Her mind seemed to hover at the top of the tent as she felt hands lifting her and laying her down. Something heavy closed out the dim light and noise from the dance. She was asleep too soon to feel the six-legged creatures that shared her bed. She woke up late the next morning to the shrieks and screams of children's laughter.

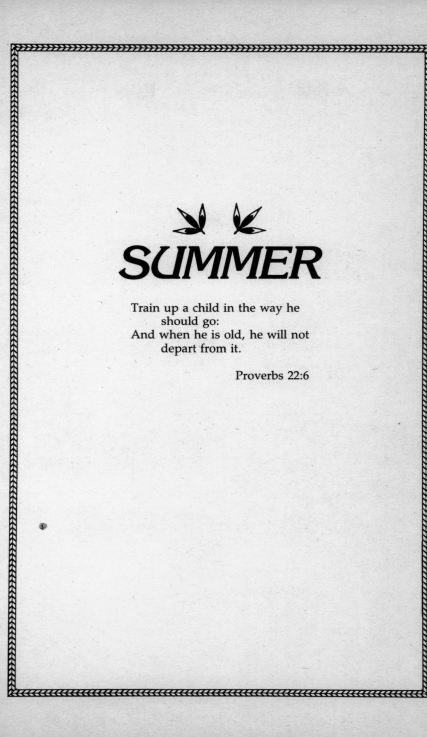

SUMMER

Train up a child in the way he
should go:
And when he is old, he will not
depart from it.

Proverbs 22:6

Cynthia lay under the heavy, scratchy robe, listening to the sounds outside the lodge. For a brief moment she thought she was under the old blue comforter and had been allowed to sleep far past the usual time. Her cousins were already up and playing in the compound outside. She could hear dogs barking and horses thudding by. Men and women laughed as they went about their morning chores. Above the everyday morning sounds the shrieks of children at play rose again. There were only two things wrong. There were no chickens clucking, and she couldn't understand any of the words that filtered, muffled, through the hide wall next to her head.

What waited for her out there in the light? In the morning? In a camp of savages? She cowered under the robe, too frightened to move or peek out. She knew she couldn't hide there all day, but she intended to try. The sun was already warming up the side of the tent. She could feel that part of the bed getting hotter, and she was beginning to sweat. Maybe they'd forget she was there and she could sneak away. But she could hear someone moving around inside the lodge, and she would have to get up soon. She had the same pressing need she had every morning, no matter what else might be happening. Her very life was in danger, and all she could think about was that she had to relieve herself. Where did Indians do that sort of thing?

She would have to face whoever was out there. And she would have to make them understand her need. What would they do to her? What did they want with her? She had a horror of peering out from the covers into the stony eyes of Cruelest One. She'd heard that Indians roasted babies, and tortured captives or made them slaves. Would she have to work from dawn till dusk hauling and chopping and toiling for them? She prayed her family would rescue her soon.

Low voices sounded nearby. There was a clatter of wood and kindling dropping, then silence. She tensed in the suffocating blackness, trying to guess everything—personalities, intentions, motives, attitudes—from the small, anonymous noises that reached her. Then she felt something warm and alive snaking up under the covers. It brushed against her side. She screamed, threw off the robe, and scooted across the narrow bed until she was backed up against the taut wall like a cat cornered by a dog pack. A small brown hand and arm lay on the robe that covered the pole and rawhide bedstead. It belonged to a doll with an impish face and shiny, shoe-button eyes. A tiny, perfectly-curved mouth lined with even white teeth grinned from behind a curtain of wavy, black hair.

39

"*Hi, tai*, hello, friend," she said. "*Asa Nanica*, Star Name." And she pointed to her own small, naked chest. The imp laughed and, stretching all the way across the bed, tickled the yellow hair. Cynthia squealed and hit out, pushing harder against the hot tent wall that pressed like a drumhead at her back. She heard a noise like hens settling in for the night, a rustling and clucking of feathers being shaken out and roosts disputed. The tent was filling with people.

They all looked alike and they all smelled alike. The odor of smoke and sweat, leather and bear grease made the air almost too thick to breathe. Outside she could hear the thud of running feet as more women and children ran to join the crowd already at the door. An audience had come to see a show, and the main attraction was naked. Cynthia grabbed the stuffed deerskin pillow and held it in front of her. There were boys in that mob. It was easy to tell since they had nothing on either.

"Go away. Leave me alone. Leave me alone, will you!" she yelled at them. But they only laughed, the women tittering behind their hands. The group bobbed forward, pushed by those crowding in behind them. The air thickened like barley soup boiling down. Children crawled between the legs of the adults and squatted down in front, staring up at her with big, black eyes under their tousled hair. One of them inched forward to touch her and she looked wildly around for a weapon, a missile, anything.

Then the woman who lived in the lodge gave a quiet command. The crowd began to melt away, backing out through the opening like a scene played in reverse. One last urchin peered in, his hair standing out in spikes around his head, even white teeth flashing in his brown grin. Takes Down The Lodge shooed him with the buffalo rib she used as a stir stick. It was such a familiar gesture, so like her own mother waving her big wooden ladle at little John, that Cynthia was for an instant home again. Then the instant was gone.

It was quiet in the tent. The air thinned out. Only Takes Down the Lodge, her husband's mother, Pohawe, Medicine Woman, and the child, Star Name, remained. They stood staring at their guest, who had found a heavy stick by the bed and now brandished it at them. Cynthia's hair stood out in tangled tendrils around her face, and the sunlight filtering through the leather wall ignited the tips of it. Tears had left salty tracks in the dust on her cheeks. Her sturdy body was tense, and one muscle in her shoulder twitched. Her wide blue eyes had a deranged look in them.

As though approaching a cornered and dangerous animal, Star Name crooned in a low, soothing voice while Takes Down The Lodge and Medicine Woman watched. Star Name reached out a tiny hand and touched Cynthia lightly on the wrist. The gentle touch released the tension. Cynthia dropped the L-shaped club, Takes Down's shinny-ball stick, and collapsed onto the bed. She sobbed into the pillow and burrowed back under the covers like a desperate horned toad digging into the sand.

The Indian child crawled up next to her and pulled the robe back. She wrapped her arms around her and rocked her gently, smoothing the snarled, dirty yellow hair and wiping the tears away with the side of her palm. Star Name was dressed in a breechclout and was as brown as saddle leather, polished smooth.

"*Ka taikay, ka taikay, Tohobt Nabituh*, don't cry, blue eyes. *Toquet*. It's all right."

It was the first warm, human contact Cynthia had had since the attack on the fort. She huddled in the lean brown arms, inhaling the sweet, smoked smell of Star Name. She clung to her like a baby squirrel to a tree limb a hundred feet in the air.

"*Mi-pe mahtaoyo*, poor little one," said Medicine Woman. Backing slowly off the bed on her knees and one hand, Star Name pulled the yellow hair, still clutching the pillow, onto the bare hard-packed dirt floor, studded with worn-down tufts of stubborn grass. Cynthia allowed herself to be tugged to the small fire in the center of the lodge. The smoke spiraled lazily up from it and was sucked through the hole fifteen hazy feet above. She stared around her. The tent was as big as the cabin she had lived in at the fort, once she got used to its cone shape.

Motes of dust danced in the shaft of morning sunlight that sliced, straight-edged and solid looking, through the open door. Around the curved wall was a jumble of furs and buffalo robes on the three raised bedsteads. The light that came through the translucent leather washed the heaps of bags and bulging rawhide boxes in a warm, golden haze.

On one of the beds lay a half-finished shirt of smooth, soft doeskin. The bone awl, worn to polished ivory with use, was stuck into a seam. The rib stir stick, a turtle-shell bowl, and a large butcher knife lay on a piece of hide next to the fire. Hanging from a peg driven into one of the tent poles was a plain, square shaving mirror with holes punched through the wooden frame and feathers dangling from it. Clothes and weapons hung from pegs or were draped over a line stretched between the poles. Permeating everything was the smell of roasting meat.

Cynthia glanced nervously toward the door, cowering behind her pillow. Through the oval opening she could see camp life going on as usual. No one even glanced her way, and it didn't seem necessary to be embarrassed in front of the three who were with her. Takes Down The Lodge was short and plump, with a plain, round face and a shy smile. Medicine Woman was older, tall, and slender, with kind eyes. Star Name squatted on the floor with her arms wrapped around her knees, as though trying to contain her excitement over the yellow hair. The glint in her eyes made her seem like a jack-in-the-box about to explode.

The lodge looked as though a high wind had passed through it and the survivors were still living in the wreckage. But Cynthia knew better. In spite of the curved walls that tapered up to the smoke hole, the lodge poles crowding through the opening, it didn't seem very different from the cabin she had left. The tools and clothes were simple, but made with skill and care and cherished by those who used them. Everything was where it could be reached easily when needed. She was in someone's home. Someone without pretense. She was in the kind of home she had always lived in.

Takes Down The Lodge handed her a pointed stick with a piece of blackened meat dangling from it, drops of grease falling and leaving dark stains in the dirt. Cynthia bit through the crisp, charred crust into the pink, juicy flesh underneath. Wiping the grease and cinders off with her fingers, she transferred them to her thigh and ate the meat off the stick. She squatted to dip her fingers into the glob of corn mush that lay like a lump of gray clay in a bark dish. The main seasonings were grit and bark chips, but it eased the hollow hunger ache in her stomach. If the place only had a privy, she'd be almost content.

Takes Down The Lodge worried a hot stone from the coals, balanced it on the broad end of her stir stick, and dropped it into a paunch full of water. When the hissing stopped, she dipped a piece of rag into the warmed water and began scrubbing off the layers of dirt and grease, black paint and dried blood that had accumulated on her new daughter. Medicine Woman opened a small, elaborately beaded bag lined with fresh leaves. She scooped out some of the spicy smelling salve and smeared it onto the cuts and scratches that hadn't healed yet.

Star Name had slipped out while Cynthia was eating. She popped back in, pulling her mother along with one hand and trailing a long strip of cloth with the other. It was one of her breechclouts, a present for the yellow hair. Her mother, Tuhani Huhtsu, Black Bird, murmured a greeting and stood by the door. She stayed out of the stream of light, as the others worked and chattered around the new child. She was a heavier, even shyer version of her younger sister, Takes Down The Lodge, and she seemed to prefer being part of the furnishings.

While Star Name and Takes Down showed Cynthia how to put on the breechclout, Medicine Woman flitted about like a hummingbird. She softly chanted a high-pitched song that seemed to vibrate in her sinuses. She darted in and out with a long leather thong, laying it down Cynthia's back and around her chest, then knotting it in various places. The child stood with her arms held out from her sides and watched the flimsy breechclout cord being tied around her hips.

She wondered what the old woman was doing. Medicine Woman reminded her of her grandmother in a way. She wasn't fat like the other women, and she had narrow, sharp features. Her eyes were dark pools with sunlight glinting in them. There were lines in the skin around them, where the laughter had spilled over and run down her cheeks. Cynthia reached out timidly and touched her hand, to see if the brown skin felt like her own. It had the same velvety feel of her own grandmother's, of denim worn smooth with time. And like Granny Parker's, Medicine Woman's fingers were long and deft, and her palms were paved with callouses. Medicine Woman had the strong, gentle hands of a healer. She smiled at Cynthia, laid three spidery fingers lightly on the child's cheek, and went back to her thong.

Next, Takes Down attacked Cynthia's hair, pulling at the snarls with a brush made of a porcupine tail stretched over a block of wood. Still kneeling, her breath soughing on Cynthia's cheek, she braced one hand on the child's head and raked the tangles from the long, thick golden mane. Star Name picked up a lock of it, stroked it, and held it up to the light to show her mother its color.

On the other side of her, Medicine Woman laid her thong, now lumpy with knots, along Cynthia's foot. She giggled and did a little dance to escape the tickling. In her need to relieve herself she danced anyway, from one foot to the other. The pressure in her bladder was almost painful. How much longer could she hold out? How could she tell them of this most basic need?

Takes Down The Lodge tapped her on the shoulder with the brush to make her stand still, and began braiding. Cynthia stared straight ahead, unable to focus on the woman's face so close up. It was a face she couldn't help liking. Takes Down had large, sad doe's eyes with an oriental tilt. Her narrow mouth seemed to stretch across her face and dive into the round cheeks on either side. A straight, aquiline nose gave her a look of quiet dignity and intelligence in spite of the moon-shaped face around it. Her hair was cropped short and tucked behind her small ears.

Star Name plaited a crow's feather into the thin braid on the crown of Cynthia's head, and she and Takes Down tied the two side braids with blue ribbons. Cynthia wondered where they had come from. Had they been taken from some settler child as she lay dying? Cynthia hoped they'd been bartered from a trader.

Finally done with the ritual of the thong, Medicine Woman

43

painted a red line down the center of the yellow hair's part, using a blunt stick dipped in the thick paste of paint. Then they sat back on their heels to admire her. Cynthia ducked her head shyly under the weight of their attention.

Takes Down The Lodge heaved to her feet with a grunt and went to get the mirror. She walked as though wading through deep mud, swaying from side to side and barely lifting her feet. She held the thick, square glass out, the bright metal cones tinkling and the feathers revolving slowly on their thongs. Cynthia jerked her hand to her part, startled by the red line there. For an instant she feared she was bleeding, that they had numbed her with their sly kindness while they treacherously cut her. Then she remembered the paint, and she smiled sheepishly. As she looked around at their beaming faces, she felt a little guilty for thinking ill of them.

"Tsa-tua, Takes Down The Lodge," Takes Down poked her own breast, her fingers sinking into the soft flesh that billowed out like twin sails. "Tsa-tua."

"Chatua?" Cynthia rolled the strange syllables around in her mouth and tried to spit them out as the woman did.

"Tsa-tua." Takes Down patted her own chest with both hands.

"Tsa-tua." Cynthia was a fast learner. "Asa Nanica," she added, reaching out and giving a light tug on Star Name's shiny black hair. Still standing by the door, even Black Bird laughed, hiding behind the deerskin she was chewing. The tall, delicate woman stepped forward.

"Pohawe, Medicine Woman," she said.

Cynthia reached solemnly to shake Medicine Woman's hand. Not understanding the gesture, Medicine Woman took her hand and pressed it to her heart. Cynthia could feel it fluttering under her fingers like a bird caught in the bony cage of Medicine Woman's chest. Then Star Name pulled her over to introduce her to her mother, Tuhani Huhtsu, Black Bird. Black Bird bobbed her head and smiled shyly around the hide she was chewing as part of the tanning process. She kept it in her mouth as much for cover as for the need to be chewing it.

Now Cynthia knew them all by name, but they didn't know her.

"Cynthia," she said, pointing to her pale chest. "My name is Cynthia."

"Tsini-tia?" They burst out laughing and chattering.

"What's so funny?" She stamped her feet and hugged her elbows, shut out by their laughter, unable to understand her own joke. Were they laughing at what she said, or what she was? She wanted to cry again from the loneliness and frustration.

"Tsini-tia." Takes Down The Lodge grabbed her in strong, plump brown arms and hugged her, jerking her off her feet and immobilizing her. As she was crushed against the rough deerskin her arms were pressed into her stomach and she could smell smoke and horses, dust and wild onions. *Please, God, don't let me wet myself and this woman. She might kill me for it.* She closed her eyes and gritted her teeth, tensing until her muscles ached. As Takes Down set her down, she heard her name being passed from mouth to mouth. If only she knew what it meant. Tsini-tia, Little Stay Awhile. It was a wonderful omen for her new family.

Star Name took Cynthia by the hand and started gaily for the door, chattering as though her new friend understood every word. Cynthia planted her feet so firmly and suddenly that Star Name almost fell over backwards.

"Oh no you don't. I'm not going out there." She knew they couldn't understand her, but she didn't care. After all, they didn't care that she couldn't understand them. Her mouth set in the stubborn Parker line, the line that had brought her family through thousands of miles of howling wilderness. The whole tribe of savages was outside, waiting to grab her and taunt her and throw things at her as they had the night before. She was staying right here, even if she had to wet herself where she stood. It wouldn't be the first time since she had been kidnapped by these people.

Anyway, she didn't have any clothes on. In her nakedness she felt vulnerable and exposed. What would her mother say? Or her father? She blinked and gave a small shake of her head, trying to rid herself of the image of her father as she had last seen him. What would Grandpa say? She could hear Elder John at the evening worship, preaching about modesty. His deep, booming voice had always sounded like a cannon to her, blasting at the forces of Satan. She used to bow her head more to get out of the line of fire than from reverence. "I was afraid because I was naked: and I hid myself. Genesis three, ten."

Not only was the breechclout shameful, but it was embarrassing. She was wearing a diaper. Little John would laugh at her if he could see her. The rough wool felt itchy and tight along the crease at the top of her thighs. She was so aware of her bare legs and chest and buttocks that she could feel them tingling with shame. Besides, she could never run away from anybody in this thing. It tickled her legs. It would probably fall off. What if the cord broke, or she caught it on a thorn and pulled the cloth loose? And the sun would burn unladylike freckles on her shoulders and face.

She tried to back up, pushing against the rock-steady hands of Takes Down The Lodge as they pressed into her shoulder blades. Her feet plowed furrows in the dirt as she was shoved and hauled toward the door, while Black Bird and Medicine Woman called encouragement. She teetered in the opening, a fledgling about to be pushed off the edge of the nest. The noises of camp, the barking and neighing, the shouting and pounding and scraping and laughing, seemed to crescendo.

"*Mea-dro*, Tsini-tia. Let's go!" Star Name grinned at her as she tugged her hand. Cynthia stepped over the threshold and took a few tiny steps into the sunlight. She looked around, ready to jerk away and flee back to the safety of the cool, dark hole in the lodge wall. She shivered in the heat and waited for God to part the sky, lean down, and scold her for her shamelessness.

As she moved farther out into the day, she had the vague feeling that she was being washed helplessly along, adrift in a fast, deep stream. When she looked back at the lodge it seemed as alien and forbidding as the rest. They all looked identical, the lodges. They squatted like fat cones, scattered among the oak and mesquite brush and the masses of prickly pear on a high plateau. But the lodge she had just left had a big, yellow sun painted on one side, and she noted it carefully.

She memorized the shape of the tall pecan that stood behind it and the meat rack alongside it. The rack had three poles to hang the drying strips on while most of the others only had two. She had learned long ago to be always aware of her surroundings and to take her bearings on whatever was available. It would be easy to stumble into the wrong tent. She had a horror of that.

Takes Down The Lodge, Black Bird, and Medicine Woman followed them out, watching. They lined up in front of the tent with Medicine Woman in the middle, and the two sisters on either side, like bookends. The sight of them, solid and smiling, reassured Cynthia a bit. She wasn't completely alone.

Life went on in camp. No one jeered. No crowd formed. There was no pause in the steady, rasping rhythm of the bone scrapers as the women bent over the hides pegged out on the ground. Children raced among them, chased by the puppies and young dogs who thought they were all part of the same pack. Now and then one of the longlegged, unkempt animals would jump onto a child's chest and send him sprawling. Then they would roll, growling and laughing, in the dust. The older dogs had no time for play. They were constantly policing the camp for offal and defending their territories. There were few men in camp, mostly older ones, bundled in buffalo robes and sitting together in the hot sun.

The other children don't have any clothes on either. A quick look around showed her that she was better dressed than most of those her own age or younger. And naked or not, there was at least one piece of information Cynthia needed quickly. In the hand talk and pantomine of children she began talking to Star Name. Together they headed for the latrine, several thousand square miles of countryside.

Cynthia timed her dodge badly and shrieked as the grizzly ate her. Mo-pe, Owl was built like a bear cub, and Cynthia screamed as the strong brown fingers dug into her sides, gouging and tickling her until she squirmed and writhed on the ground. She rolled in the dust, limp from laughter. The other children darted in, trying to steal handfuls of sand, the "sugar" that Owl was defending. Those who had been tickled were out of the game and sat on the sidelines watching the others. When they had all been eaten, the children sprawled in heaps, panting with laughter and the midmorning heat. Some of them emptied their breechclouts of sand that had either sifted in during the game or had been stuffed inside. All of them were covered with red dust that was striped with channels of sweat. Their hair was powdered with it and plastered to their flushed faces and necks.

Cynthia let the fine grains run through her fingers and looked over at Star Name. She'd known her less than a week, but she was sure her friend wouldn't sit quietly for long. She was right. Star Name leaped to her feet and sprinted in the direction of the river.

"Mea-dro, let's go!" The tangle of bare limbs writhed and kicked as the children scrambled to unsnarl themselves and catch her. They fled through the village, howling like a pack of mad wolves, flashing bare, red bottoms and calloused soles. They used gear and cooking fires as hurdles, scattering belongings and breaking up dog fights. The dogs would have stopped fighting anyway to dash for the overturned meat racks. The women dropped their hide scrapers and their sewing and ran to beat them off the food supply. Owl's mother, Tah-hah-net, She Laughs, grabbed a slab of buffalo steak as it snaked by her and held on. Brought up short, the dog on the other end worried and shook it, trying to dislodge her, but he was no match for her. She detached him with a feint and a solid kick to his bony ribs. He slunk off with his ragged tail between his spindly legs, and she hung the meat up to finish drying.

As the red dust cloud blew off, dissipating like smoke in the wind, the women shook out their work and settled back down, laughing and gossiping as though nothing had happened. The old men relit their pipes and picked up the threads of their stories. Those who were gambling, woven into tight knots around their dice games, had never even looked up.

Cynthia raced with the others toward the edge of their new camp and the cool river that slid silkily along between high limestone banks. She stretched her legs as far as they could go and pumped harder to catch up with Star Name. She leaped rocks and bushes, dodging the thorns of the deceptively delicate-looking, pale green mesquites. She could feel her muscles stretching, flexing, flowing under her skin. She was an antelope, a racehorse, a startled hare bounding free across the plain. She threw back her head and howled like a wolf from the sheer joy of it. Freckles, shame, unladylike behavior, they didn't matter. The old rules didn't apply here, and the new rules seemed few and simple.

The last of the tents were cleared as they approached the edge of the bluff. At the bottom of it was the river, hidden by the tops of trees. She was so high up she almost expected clouds to roll by. Far below, rolling hills covered with bushy live oaks swept to the horizon. The undulating layers of them went from deep green to dark blue, each row fading until the last one almost blended with the sky. She felt like a bird soaring above it all and able to see a hundred miles in all directions.

The children flung themselves over the edge of the cliff and ran down the steep path that wound through the grove of cedars. Cynthia grabbed a handful of the cedars' small, hard, gunmetal-blue berries to pelt Owl and Star Name. Some tiny, unseen flowers perfumed the air with the smell of roses. Cynthia ran with her toes pointed in as Star Name had taught her. Takes Down had made her a pair of moccasins and they had hurt her feet until she learned the trick of walking pigeon-toed in them.

They raced along the narrow, sandy red beach at the base of the cliff and clambered over boulders until they came to a deep pool. Rocks rimming it let the water flow in one side and cascade down a smooth gray limestone face before joining the main stream again. A dense, deep green canopy of towering pecan trees hung over the pools, allowing sunlight to warm only a few patches on the cool rocks.

The first naked bodies dove off the boulders and into the largest pool like a hail of arrows. Cynthia stood, caught in the trap of her upbringing again. The breechclout wasn't much, but at least it was something. Star Name and Owl surfaced, puffing and blowing and splashing each other. Owl climbed out and leaped in again, tucking her short, powerful legs up and aiming for Star Name. The backwash drove out a thick, black water moccasin that slithered up the opposite side of the pool and disappeared among the rocks.

Spray from Owl's cannonball splashed on Cynthia's chest and cheeks, cooling her and making the decision for her. She kicked off her moccasins, dropped the breechclout where she stood, and, holding her nose, jumped in after her friends. It didn't occur to her that she couldn't swim. As she went under, her mouth and eyes filling with water, she churned desperately for solid ground. She fought her way to the surface with a push against the firm, gravelly bottom, but gasped and went under again. A strong hand grabbed her and hauled her to the surface. Owl grinned and held her while she spluttered and dog-paddled frantically. Star Name rolled over on her back and spouted water, her hair slicked to her head.

The children slid like otters down the sleek rock ramp into the other pool. They swam to the edge, clambered out, and raced to dive in and do it all again. Star Name found a thick grapevine hanging from a tree limb over the water, and for an hour they swung on it. They sailed out to the top of the vine's arc and dropped, kicking and squealing until they hit the water.

Finally, Star Name and Owl and Cynthia pulled themselves onto a flat, cool boulder at the pool's rim. Hanging over the edge of it like slick brown sea slugs, Cynthia's friends scooped sand from the beach below and began rubbing it into their hair. They grabbed Cynthia and rubbed her down. Ignoring her wriggling, they pulled the ribbons and bedraggled feather from her hair and worked the sand into her scalp with hard little fingers. It left her feeling tingly and clean and shiny, like the pots she and her mother used to scour the same way.

They dove in to rinse off, then climbed out and lay in a patch of sunlight. They ate the handfuls of dried grapes and hunks of pemmican that Star Name and Owl had snatched as they ran through camp. Cynthia found her breechclout, but didn't put it on. Lying naked in the sunlight was the headiest freedom she had ever known, and she wanted to savor it as long as possible. She napped like a cat in the warm grass by the beach while the others played the afternoon away.

When the breeze began to blow cold across them, they came out of the water, shaking like soaked dogs, their fingers wrinkled from being wet so long. Cynthia looked away as the boys strolled by, their small, wizened penises nestling like brown mice between their legs. Some dried themselves with handfuls of grass and slowly put on their clothes. Others set out for camp with their breechclouts in their hands and trailing in the dust behind them. Cynthia shivered in the cool shade of the cedars as they toiled back up the slope.

They left Owl at her lodge near the outskirts of the village, and hand in hand, Cynthia and Star Name wandered through the sprawling camp toward home. The three hundred lodges of Pahayuca's Wasp band meandered for a mile along the bluff, with some families or groups of families choosing to set their tents up apart. Without Star Name as a guide, Cynthia would have been lost.

"*Yo-oh-hobt pa-pi!* Yellow hair!" Star Name dropped Cynthia's hand and whirled to face her seven-year-old brother, Pahgatsu, Upstream, and his gang of friends. Cynthia realized that she hadn't seen many boys in camp older than Upstream. They must wander far afield.

Star Name glared at him and spoke from the corner of her mouth. *"Tah-mah,* Brother." It was one of the words Cynthia had learned. Star Name had pointed him out one morning, or rather his back as he raced off with his friends. But this was the first time their paths had crossed. Upstream was collecting a crowd of shouting children like iron filings to a lodestone. He had his sister's impishness, with a dollop of meanness added. Cynthia braced herself for trouble. Upstream was Star Name's own family. And these children were probably her friends. Why should she suffer for an outsider, a freak? Cynthia looked around her for clues as to the direction of Takes Down's lodge. She was tall for her age and she was long-legged. She'd give them a good run.

Star Name bent down and selected a large piece of chocolate-colored chert from the gravel at her feet. She rubbed the polished surface with her thumb as she hefted it skillfully, almost absent-mindedly, to test its weight. With a graceful, fluid motion she swung her arm back and bounced the rock hard off Upstream's head with a satisfying thunk. He yelped. The other children lost interest, skittering into tents or scuttling around behind them.

"Tahmah Kuyanai, brother turkey!" Star Name added an insult to the injury and picked up another rock. Upstream retreated, looking back at his sister, as though hurt that she would humiliate him so. A stone whirred past Star Name's ear and clipped Upstream on the heel, spurring him on after his retreating army. She spun around to find Tsini-tia grimly tossing a spare rock into her throwing hand and raring back to let fly. Star Name laughed and clapped her hands with delight.

"Toquet," she said. "It is well."

Cynthia grinned back at her. *"Keemah,* come."

Linking arms, they swaggered through the village. As they rounded one of the lodges and entered the bare open space in the center of the camp. Cynthia braked suddenly, yanking Star Name backwards. Sitting in front of Pahayuca's big tent were Eagle and Wanderer, Pahayuca, Buffalo Piss, and Cruelest One. And Star Name was heading right for them. Cynthia only allowed herself to be dragged toward them because to fight it would have created even more of a scene.

Cruelest One's eyes were hooded and hostile as usual. His thin, tense body seemed about to explode with the violence packed into it. How could Star Name stand there casually chatting with them?

They all were fiends and assassins. They murdered women and children. Cynthia watched in astonishment as Star Name acted out the fight with Upstream and his friends, mimicking the yellow hair perfectly, down to the accent of her few Comanche words. Eagle, Pahayuca, Buffalo Piss, and even Cruelest One laughed.

Wanderer didn't laugh. He didn't even seem to hear Star Name. He lay against a pack saddle with his long legs crossed in front of him, and looked at Cynthia with his solemn, steady stare. His gaze moved down her body and up again, catching her eyes and holding them. He seemed to be searching around in her mind to see what she was thinking. She dropped her head, studying the ground intently, feeling his eyes on her bare legs and chest. She glowed a deeper pink under her sunburn. She wanted to roll up like an armadillo, disappear in a dust devil, die. Anything but stand here helplessly with him laughing at her behind his solemn face.

She began edging away, dragging Star Name reluctantly behind her. She tried not to limp, though the moccasins were hurting her feet. She had forgotten to walk toes-in at times during the day. And every time she looked back he was still following her with his gaze. As she stalked along, she clenched her fists. She hated him. She hated him even more than she hated the small vicious man, Cruelest One. At least she knew what Cruelest One was thinking. He might want to kill her, but he didn't humiliate her. Star Name's chatter annoyed her suddenly. It annoyed her because the only word she could clearly understand was Nocona, Wanderer. She could tell Star Name about Wanderer, if only she could speak her friend's language.

In the pale evening light the war shields stood tall on the spindly tripods that held them, like spectres against the darkening sky. She remembered those shields with their feathers flapping on the arms of the painted raiders. They had followed her across the plains like a flock of monstrous, vicious birds. The sight of them made her stomach churn with fear.

She almost broke into a run when she saw the lodge with the bright yellow sun on it. Star Name waved and turned off toward her own tent nearby. Takes Down The Lodge sat outside, mending a pair of stubby moccasins by the fading light. Takes Down patted a spot next to her on the thick buffalo hide. The child sat obediently, wrapping her arms around her knees to keep warm. She shivered in the freshening night wind, and Takes Down grunted as she pushed herself to her feet and went inside. When she came out, she carried a brown and white robe of beautifully pieced rabbit skins, with white ermine tails sewn at the edges as a fringe. She draped it around Cynthia's shoulders, fur side in.

It was made for a child. But certainly Takes Down The Lodge hadn't sewn this in one day. Was it Star Name's? Cynthia looked down at it, stroking the silken hair and nuzzling a corner of it with her cheek. The cool fur took on her body's heat almost immediately and seemed to glow with warmth against her skin. She had never owned anything so elegant and warm.

"Thank you, Tsatua," she said in English. Did Comanches have words for thank you? She looked up from the robe and saw tears in Takes Down The Lodge's huge dark eyes. And she knew suddenly to whom the robe had belonged, and why Takes Down had wanted her. Her own eyes stung with sympathy, and Takes Down's round, kind face blurred. She groped for the square, work-hardened hand and held it tightly.

"It's good, Tsatua. *Toquet.*" She sorted through her few words of Comanche language for the one she needed. She had learned it while playing grizzly and sugar, when Star Name took the part of the mother protecting her children from the bear. "*Toquet, Pia,* it's good, Mother." She knew why Takes Down was so quiet and sad. Surrounded by her own people, her friends and her relatives, Tsatua was lonely, mourning a lost child of her own. It was something Cynthia could understand. It happened often on the frontier.

What had she been like, that other daughter? What did Takes Down expect of Cynthia? Of a white child who couldn't even talk to her? Perhaps when she learned enough of the language she could explain that her own mother grieved for her, and needed her. Perhaps Takes Down would understand and let her go. In the meantime, until she was rescued or could escape, Cynthia would try to make her happy.

❧ 7 ❧

Why was Takes Down The Lodge cooking so much food? The big dented copper kettle hanging on the tripod over the fire was full of hunks of meat. The stew bubbled and steamed under a thick, brown-flecked foam. She asked Cynthia to brush the dirt off the wild onions piled in a heap in front of her, then cut the dried tops off them and threw them into the pot. The aroma curling up toward the black hole above made Cynthia's mouth water, and the smell of the coffee heating at the edge of the fire made her homesick.

"*Kaka*, onion. *Too-pa*, coffee." As she worked, Takes Down told her the names of everything in the lodge, repeating each word over and over until Cynthia could say it. Now and then she would hold an object up. "*Hakai*, what?" And Cynthia would name it. It was a start. But what were the words for lonely and homesick and afraid? When would she learn those so she could tell Takes Down The Lodge how much she wanted to go home?

It had been hours since she had had the sparse lunch of stolen dried grapes and pemmican at the river with Owl and Star Name. Her stomach was growling, and the smell from the pot was more than she could stand. There was no telling when they would eat. It must be close to nine o'clock at night. She fished out a piece of meat with the flat stir stick and blew on it to cool it before picking it up in her fingers and eating it. She looked guiltily around her, but Takes Down only smiled.

Cynthia missed Star Name, but she didn't dare leave the lodge to go looking for her in the dark. She didn't know how to ask permission to leave, or even if she had to ask permission at all. Star Name never did. She took what she needed and gave just as freely. Cynthia was wearing one of her simple dresses over her breechclout. And she had brought an extra pair of moccasins for her friend. Cynthia wriggled her feet in them. She couldn't understand how the women could be so kind and the men so cruel. Most of the men anyway. Takes Down's husband, Sunrise, wasn't and neither was Pahayuca, the big fat one.

Sunrise sat on his low bed across from the doorway, stretching wet rawhide over the bent wooden stirrup frames. Sewn on damp, the leather shrank as it dried, molding to the wood like bark to a tree. In the dim light from the fire he hunched over to see his work, his black hair swinging forward to curtain his face. Takes Down kept up a flowing conversation with him, like a narrow mountain stream burbling over rocks. He punctuated her talk with an occasional grunt, and Cynthia wondered if he was even listening to her.

The front of the lodge shuddered as though a heavy wind had blown against it, and Pahayuca forced his way through the small opening. The side pulled inward along his shoulders and rebounded with a snap, sending tremors up the hide in ripples. As he lumbered across the dirt floor he waved his arms and grumbled loudly. He obviously thought lodge doors should be bigger. His swaying gait made the muscles on his back and shoulders undulate like huge boulders rolling around in a leather sack. He patted Takes Down The Lodge on her plump arm as he went by and growled something that set her to giggling into her hand.

As he lowered himself onto the bed next to Sunrise, the rawhide straps creaked loudly and the poles bowed slightly in the middle. Pahayuca shifted to the end, where there was more support, and leaned against the back rest at the foot of the bed. He raked his fingernails across his chest, and with his other hand reached up under his long leather shirt to jiggle himself into a more comfortable position in his breechclout. He gave a long, rolling belch and began pointing out the right way to sew stirrups.

He created such a furor in the quiet tent that Cynthia almost didn't notice the fifteen-year-old girl who followed him in. She entered as silently and as gracefully as a leaf blown through the doorway. Only the low, musical tinkling of bells caught Cynthia's attention, and she stared open-mouthed. Tsa-wa-ke, Looking For Something Good, was too beautiful to have been produced by chance. Her features looked as though they had been carved in cedar by a master, then rubbed smooth and oiled until they glowed, and flowed in graceful curves from her rounded chin to her vaulting black eyebrows.

Her two-piece dress was of muted yellow chamois. The skirt clung to her narrow hips, sliding across them as she walked. It hung down her long legs at the sides and scalloped up over her knees in front and back. The heavy fringe at the side seams swayed as she moved. At her slender waist a half-moon of red-gold skin showed through the fringe of her beaded poncho. The slit that formed the neckline was deep, angling down across small firm breasts. Cupped around them were loose, heavy curls of hair. Something Good had a mane as ebony and as irridescent as a raven's wing.

"*Hi, tai.* Tsa-wa-ke," the girl murmured, naming herself and turning to look full at Cynthia. Her nostrils were slightly flared, giving her the untamed look of a wild mare.

"*Hi, tai.* Tsinitia." Hello, friend? Was it possible to be friends with someone as beautiful as this? Something Good glided across the lodge floor, crossed her thoroughbred's legs and sat in one flowing motion, like water running down a stick. Cynthia tried to sit the same way. She crossed her arms around her knees and pulled her rabbit robe tighter around her so her plain dress wouldn't be as visible. She felt like an urchin next to Something Good. Was the girl Pahayuca's daughter? She'd ask Star Name when she saw her. There was so much to ask Star Name, and she understood so little of the answers.

Just then Star Name and Black Bird came through the doorway in a fog of steam that rose from the heavy kettle they carried between them. Star Name strained with both hands to hold up her end, grasping the leather wrapped around the hot metal handle until her knuckles were white. Upstream herded them in, trying to crowd around them in his efforts not to miss anything. He sat near Pahayuca and grinned and waved at Cynthia as though he had never teased her and she had never thrown rocks at him. When he smiled he looked just like Star Name. Maybe she wouldn't tell the Rangers to kill him when they rescued her.

Star Name only nodded to her after she set the kettle down by the fire, and Cynthia wondered if she had offended her somehow. It was hard to tell what was the right thing to do. Did they have any rules of courtesy like white people's? At any rate, her friend hardly smiled and sat solemnly next to her mother. The people in the lodge shifted subtly so that the men now sat around the fire and the women and children ranged behind them along the edge of the tent. Cynthia found herself separated from them all, as though there were some invisible screen around her. But there was no way she could find out what would happen next except by waiting patiently and quietly until it did. Even Medicine Woman sat apart from her when she entered.

Owl entered next, leading her grandfather, Kavoyo, Name Giver, by the hand. Name Giver was square and solid and powerful like Owl, but his muscles were beginning to slacken under his skin, as though it were a size too big. He too was dressed in his best clothes, but they were worn and frayed and the leggings had been patched. He was ramrod straight and walked with the dignified air of faded gentility. As Owl guided him to a place of honor next to Pahayuca, he turned to look in Cynthia's direction with cloudy, opalescent eyes.

Everyone seemed to be waiting for something, and the talk was low. Then there was a rhythmic jingling of bells from outside, and Big Bow and Eagle and Wanderer stooped to enter the lodge. The thick clusters of metal cones sewn to the long fringes on their leggings kept time with their footsteps. Somehow the delicate noise was intensely strong and masculine and martial, and it stirred something inside Cynthia. The two men turned left as they came in the door and paced all the way around the circle to the right before they sat in a shower of bells, their legs crossed in front of them.

Cynthia crouched down even further among the piles of bundles and furs and hides, trying to make herself as small as possible. Wanderer looked magnificent, even to a nine-year-old who disliked him. He was taller than all of them, even Pahayuca. His hunting shirt was a pale cream color and hung almost to his knees over his dark blue leggings. The front of the shirt was decorated with tassels of wavy black scalp hair and white ermine tails. His braids reached to the middle of his back and had otter fur wrapped around them. Two eagle feathers hung from a hole in the center of a beaten silver disk at his scalplock. His high moccasins were bright with intricate beadwork, and there were long fringes at the calves.

He too turned to look at Cynthia, and she wanted to melt through the lodge wall like hot wax through cloth, to find herself outside, curled up with the dogs for the night. It wasn't his clothes that awed her. They were beautiful, but no more splendid than Pahayuca's or Eagle's. It was his face that held her spellbound. With only three small stripes of red paint on his chin, he wasn't the grim, masked warrior she had known on the raid trail. And he wasn't the exuberant boy racing Night toward the far horizon. Nor was he the arrogant young man who had stared at her as she was coming home with Star Name earlier that same evening.

She stared at his classic profile, outlined in fire, the flames burnishing his copper skin with golden highlights. He was only sixteen, but he had the calm face of a man totally at ease with himself and with leading other men. And although she didn't realize it, that was what made Cynthia so uncomfortable around him. Anyone that sure of himself must often question the ability of others. And judge them. And find them wanting, as Grandpa Parker used to say.

Wanderer had obviously come to spend the evening, and already he was making her miserable by just being there. She started inching back, pushing with her feet and sliding the hide she was sitting on toward the lodge wall. They were all so busy talking among themselves she doubted if they'd miss her if she sneaked out under the tent's edge. She was so intent on making her escape she didn't notice the sudden hush that fell over everyone.

Name Giver had held up his hand. He waited until he was sure they were all watching. Then he drew his medicine pipe from the narrow, beaded bag Owl gave him. She used two green sticks to pull a live coal from the fire and carefully lit the pipe with it. It was a task that a young man always did, but no one questioned Owl's right. She was Name Giver's eyes, and he was important to all of them. If it was his wish that his granddaughter be his pipe lighter, then so be it.

Name Giver sucked in a deep breath and blew smoke toward the top of the lodge. He blew another puff toward the earth, and one in each of the four directions. Then he chanted a long invocation in a loud voice. When he finished, everyone turned to stare at Cynthia, who froze in horror. All of this apparently had something to do with her. Had their kindness been a sham, a ruse? Were they planning to torture her after all? Is that what they'd gathered here for?

Sunrise stood and walked over to her. Taking her by the arm, he pulled her to her feet and led her to the center of the circle around the fire. She felt like a calf being led to slaughter as she stood in front of the old man. Name Giver groped for her, and she tensed as he grasped her around the waist. She stiffened when he lifted her off her feet, chanting as he did it. She was big for her age, but it seemed to cost him no effort to raise her three more times, each time a little higher than the last. It was his way of asking the Father in the sun to make her grow big and strong. As he held her up the fourth time he threw his head back and, with his eyes closed, began a droning chant. The word *"nanica"* gave Cynthia the first clue. *Nanica.* Asa Nanica, Star Name. She was being named. Surely they wouldn't name someone they were planning to kill. Would they?

"Naduah." The old man said it four times. That must be her name. She wondered what it meant. One more thing to ask Star Name. The girl was a wonderful mimic, and she was teaching Cynthia, Tsini-tia, Naduah sign language. Star Name would know what the name meant. Cynthia was weak with relief. They weren't going to hurt her.

Sunrise stood next. He was a listener. He drank people's words with his eyes. Words fell into them like pebbles into deep pools and left no ripples on the smooth, calm surface of his face. In the six days Cynthia had lived in his lodge, she had rarely heard him speak. She was surprised now at his clear, strong voice. She couldn't understand the words, but she almost knew what he was saying from his face, suddenly alive and eloquent, from his tone and his gestures.

He was thanking Wanderer for bringing them a new daughter. Wanderer nodded slightly in response. He was asking the Father in the sun to make her strong and wise, and to help them teach her the ways of the People. He spoke for half an hour before he let her sit in the center of the ring of men. Each of them then took turns speaking while the others listened attentively. It was almost eleven o'clock before the meal was finally served, and they all ate as though it were the first food they'd had in weeks.

There was going to be trouble again. Wanderer sighed as he watched Eagle watch Something Good watch Pahayuca, her husband. If he'd known that the girl had left her father's band to marry Pahayuca, he would have had doubts about suggesting this trip to the Penateka territory. Even when Wanderer had seen her, leggy as a filly, four years ago, he could tell what she would become. Just as he could see that Naduah, Keeps Warm With Us, would someday be a woman worth many horses to have. Already there was the look about her, the sleek, rounded, barely contained look of a bud about to burst into flower. And she would be a rare flower among the People, unusual and exotic. Someday she would be worth all the trouble it had been to bring her here.

In the meantime, there was Eagle to deal with. And Something Good. Something Good was Eagle's type of woman—female. And beautiful. And married. A dangerous combination for his friend. Still, Wanderer had to smile, turning it inward where no one could see it, as he remembered the deceived husbands and forlorn wives littering Eagle's trail. He was eighteen years old and should know better, but he never seemed to learn. At the rate he was going, he wouldn't live long enough to steal the horses he needed to buy a wife of his own.

Not that stealing a woman was a killing offense. It wasn't like taking a man's favorite pony. But someday he would push someone too far, someone who wasn't willing to accept payment for the insult, slit his wife's nose, and forget about it. Wanderer suspected that Eagle preferred to pilfer his women. It was a game with him, just as raiding for ponies was. He was always giving his ponies away or losing them in dice games so he could go after new ones.

But this was different. Something Good belonged to Pahayuca, bought and paid for with fifty horses. An unheard of price. Her father, Tsocupe Mo-pe, Old Owl, was proud of her, and so was Pahayuca. That was evident. No one dishonored Pahayuca. Wanderer had been a herder on a raid four years ago when Pahayuca had ridden into a crowd of armed Osages. He had throttled two of them with his bare hands, shaking each like a dog with a rag before dropping them to the ground. In the face of that kind of medicine, the band had fled.

He was a master at spooking the enemy into panicking. The Osages could face arrows and lances, but not a madman who cut off their route to paradise by strangling them. Their souls couldn't escape through their mouths when they died. They would be imprisoned in the rotting, stinking corpses, mauled by wolves and vultures, then tethered to the bones as they bleached and dried in the sun's kiln. Even in the hot tent full of laughter and chatter, Wanderer shivered at the thought. Who but Pahayuca would have thought to use his crazy courage and bear's strength to stampede a herd of Osages? The coup would be told around campfires for years to come.

He was good-natured, Pahayuca was. Anyone who weighed a third as much as a young buffalo could afford to be. But even the northern bands respected him. That was part of the reason for Wanderer's trip south. Pahayuca was his great-uncle, the younger brother of his father's mother. He hoped to use family influence to persuade Pahayuca to join them on the staked plains, or at least to stop trading with the whites. No good could ever come of it. It weakened the soul.

The Penateka, the Honey Eaters, had once been great warriors. Now they were called Sugar Eaters by the young men of the Quohadi and Yamparika, the Tenawa and Kotsoteka bands of the north. The Penateka were selling their manhood for the sweet white sand, and the cloth and metal and old, misfiring guns the traders brought. Soon they'd be drinking stupid water, and he'd seen what that did to a man, making him as helpless and as foolish as a newborn child.

As Something Good helped Takes Down The Lodge serve the coffee, Wanderer saw Eagle touch her hand. She looked up, startled, and he held her eyes captive for only a second. Too late. It had started. Wanderer glared at Eagle, but his friend wasn't noticing him. Something Good dropped her eyes and passed on to Sunrise.

Wanderer felt a hand rocking his knee. He looked down to find Star Name grinning up at him. She crawled into his lap as he sat crosslegged. Only Star Name would have dared such familiarity, and most warriors would have dumped her back onto the ground. But Wanderer encircled her, resting his forearms on her legs and propping his chin on the top of her shiny head.

She snuggled down to listen to Pahayuca weave one of his funny stories. And then Name Giver was sure to tell one. Wanderer was even quieter than usual, worried about Something Good and Eagle. By now the looks were flickering back and forth between them like summer lightning. They could only be seen if one were looking in the right direction at the exact time they occurred. He'd be glad when the women left the lodge so the men could smoke in peace. Until then, it was going to be a long evening.

Cynthia lay cupped against Star Name's back, sharing her narrow bed. Black Bird's lodge was smaller than her sister's, and less cluttered. It had no tools or weapons that a man would use. When her husband's body had been carried home after that disastrous raid five years ago, she had given away or burned everything that had belonged to him. Whenever the band passed near his grave she rode to the crevice where his bones lay and put fruit and flowers next to it. Now she was Sunrise's second wife, and Star Name was Cynthia's foster stepsister as well as her foster cousin.

Cynthia and Takes Down had abandoned their own lodge when Sunrise had pulled out his plain pipe of green soapstone. The men's voices rumbled from next door, their talk and laughter rising and falling into the cool dark hours of predawn. Cynthia lay listening for Wanderer's laugh. She refused to admit to herself that the sound of it pleased her. It reminded her of the only pleasant time she had had on the long trail from the fort, when Cruelest One and Terrible Snows left with Rachel and the men sat smoking and talking around the fire.

Just outside the tent a dog whimpered in his sleep, his nails scratching the hide as he chased a rabbit in and out of his dreams. Miles away, in the rolling emptiness of hills and bluffs and canyons, coyotes began interlacing their eerie, intricate fugue.

Cynthia was exhausted, but she couldn't sleep. There were too many frightening images and strange words and customs spinning in her head. Obviously the Comanche didn't hold with the belief that early to bed and early to rise would make them better. The night before everyone had still been celebrating the return of Buffalo Piss with his raiding party. They had chanted and drummed and danced, screeching and whooping around the scalp poles all night long, while Cynthia huddled in the lodge, afraid they would come for her to torture her again. And afraid she would see her father's scalp among those on the pole. Cruelest One had taken it. At least he was the one carrying the lance that it decorated. Had Wanderer killed anyone? Uncle Ben or her grandfather? Had he been the one to pull Henry White from the roof? Or smash Robert Frost's skull? It had all been so confusing, she couldn't remember. And now, suddenly, it was important to know.

She had been working and playing since the sun rose, and it was almost dawn again, and still people were awake and talking. Nothing they did made any sense to her. She couldn't find any routine in their lives. True, she had to gather wood and bring water every morning, but after that the day was hers. It had been fun, she had to admit, but she was an outsider. Alone. And at moments, when she realized the enormity of her situation, it frightened her so much she would begin to shake.

Tonight had been the worst, standing there waiting for them to do something horrible to her. Even Star Name had deserted her, hanging onto Wanderer. Wait until she could tell Star Name how he had treated her. Then she wouldn't snuggle up to him or hold his hand or chatter to him. She probably had no idea what a monster he was away from camp.

What did it matter? She'd be leaving soon. There must be search parties scouring the countryside for her even now. She lay listening to the night sounds of camp. The last drummers had stopped and there weren't many noises, besides the dogs' growling and whimpering as they slept in heaps. Not even the babies cried at night. She strained to hear the furtive snap or clank of a Ranger company coming for her, perhaps the very one her father had belonged to. A small jingle jerked her eyes wide open, as she listened for their horses. Then she closed them again, her heart pounding when she realized it was the metal cones of a shield cover blowing in the wind.

She listened to Star Name's even breathing and envied her serenity. She breathed the leather smell of the wall so close to her face. It reminded her of the corner of the cabin where her father had stored his bridle and saddle and harnesses. Tears stung her eyes when she thought of it. She longed to hear his voice and feel his arms holding her safely again. She reached out from under the light robe and stroked the smooth, freshly peeled pole that was one of the lodge's main supports. It was new and hadn't had a chance to soak up the dust that made most things smell alike. Its rich cedar odor was comforting, like the shavings in the trunk of clothes back home.

She had to get home. They had to find her. What had happened to them? Where were those who had been away when the Indians struck? Were they all dead? Was her mother dead?

> *Oh, that I had wings like a dove:*
> *For then would I fly away and be at rest.*

Silently she recited the Bible verse. Then she repeated to herself, over and over, *Please come soon. Please come soon,* until she finally fell asleep.

James Parker leaped into the river after the skunk. He grabbed it as it swam frantically, its wet body almost slipping through his fingers. He squeezed it tightly and held it under water, even after it had gone limp, to make sure it was dead. Dripping, he waded ashore and clambered up the bank, dangling the sodden corpse by the tail. It hadn't had a chance to spray him, but the heavy odor of musk was still there. The ones who would eat it waited for him, their eyes following the body as it swung back and forth. Eighteen people and one small skunk. It was the only food they'd had to eat in the two days since they'd left their hiding places downstream from the fort. To James Parker it seemed like a lifetime ago that he had covered his father's mutilated corpse and lowered his brother's body from the gate.

The ten children old enough to walk sat resting in the grass, their eyes empty of everything but hunger and pain. Becky Frost was still holding little Sam White, and Mrs. White carried her baby. Only the two men and Mrs. James Parker and Mrs. Frost had shoes. The others' bare feet were red with blood. It would be easy to track them by that alone. Everyone's clothes hung in shreds, clawed by the riverbottom brambles. It would be much less painful if they could leave the dense thickets along the rivers, but there were too many Indian signs to risk it. They didn't know that they were trailing the outriders of the raiding party back to the Trinity. They thought they were being hunted, and they would have been if they had been discovered.

Traveling only at night, they forced their way through the tightly woven, head-high growth, tearing at it with their hands. Tall trees blocked most of the moonlight, and they knew they were passing through patches of waist-high blackberry thickets only when they were torn by them. They found the huge bull-nettle bushes when their fingers closed around the hairy stems, burning and stinging their hands until it was agony to touch anything.

Parker and White took turns using their bodies to clear a path, often shielding their eyes with an arm and falling onto the green wall to batter it down with their weight. The other man carried whichever child was the most exhausted. Mrs. Frost had been crying for her dead husband and son for two days, and there was nothing anyone could say to calm her. The children were quiet, too worn out and terrified to whimper. They seemed to know it wouldn't help.

The water at least soothed James's hands a little. He would have everyone bathe their hands and arms and feet. His nose twitched as he looked at the dead creature swinging in front of him. They would have to make a fire. He offered a small prayer of thanksgiving for the flint in his pocket. Indians or no Indians, the children had to eat. He wondered briefly if he would be able to cut the throats of the women and children if they were caught. He had abandoned his gun, hiding it when it ran out of ammunition at the fort. But it wouldn't have been fast enough to dispatch everyone in time anyway.

Faulkenberry and Anglin must be having a hard go of it too. They had taken another route, carrying the wounded on makeshift litters of torn blankets and poles. At least they didn't have to see the children suffer, since only Lucy and her two were with them. The eighteen survivors stood around the naked, half-cooked skunk. Stripped of its black and white pelt, it didn't look as bad. More like a squirrel or a rabbit or opossum.

"Oh, Lord, for what we are about to receive, we thank you." He cut the carcass up, neglecting to serve himself a piece. There was hardly a mouthful for each as it was. Then they lay down to sleep, generally keeping their family groups together and huddling for warmth. James Parker's eyes filled as he watched his children try futilely to pull their tattered clothes around them in the wind. The Lord was testing them. James prayed that He would also give them the strength to endure.

John Carter and Jeremiah Courtney were repairing a hole in the side of the ferry when James Parker limped and staggered into the clearing at Timmin's Crossing on the Trinity. He had eaten nothing for six days and had still walked the last thirty-five miles in eight hours. Carter and Courtney saddled their five horses while James told them the story. He was with them when they rode out after the others, who had been too weak and footsore to walk any further.

Around midnight of May 25, the same time that Pahayuca was carrying Cynthia Ann Parker toward Sunrise's lodge, her uncle and cousins and friends shuffled into the bare dirt yard of Carter's cabin. The soft dust felt like velvet under their feet, and the candle shining through the open doorway seemed to dance and beckon.

Soon the yard was littered with bodies as the women and children slumped where they stood. They lay or sat, too exhausted even to walk to the house. Anna Carter bustled among them, giving out blankets and what little food she had. The men carried the weakest and most badly hurt into the tiny cabin. The others spent the night on the ground, sleeping as soundly as if they were in featherbeds.

James Parker was up at dawn. Borrowing one of Carter's horses, he set out for Fort Houston to recruit volunteers for a rescue party. But there were none to be had. Rumors were flying that Santa Anna was gathering a force to invade Texas, and once again the men marched off to stop him. The women grimly piled their pitifully few belongings beside their doors and prepared to flee again. No one could even spare horses to go looking for the captives.

In despair, Parker made his family as comfortable as he could in a crumbling abandoned cabin, one they would share with the Whites. He built a box to hold the bones of his father and brothers and friends, and went back to bury them. It was July before he could travel to San Augustine to beg General Houston for soldiers to help him in his search for the captives.

Martha Parker was emaciated and her eyes had black smudges under them from the weeks she had spent with the measles. The settlement's doctor had given her and her child up for dead, but James had begged medicine from him, and nursed and swore and prayed them back to life. He had only left to ask for troops when he was sure they would live. Now Martha could tell the news wasn't good as soon as he came in the door.

"What did he say, James?" She sat halfway up in bed, supporting herself on one elbow on the hard frame.

"He says he'll send someone to talk to them." James sat wearily on the bed next to her. It was the only piece of furniture in the room besides the splintered puncheon table and a log bench.

"Talk to them! How can you talk to savages?"

"Force won't do, he says. We have to make treaties with them."

"But doesn't he realize what must be happening to Rachel and Elizabeth and little Cynthia Ann?"

"I suppose he does. But he won't send troops. I told him there was no use talking to them until they'd been whipped, and soundly at that. But he won't listen. Said he was sorry. Sorry!" Parker stood and began pacing, his hands jammed into his pockets. Above his

long, unkempt beard his eyes were glittering with fury. "Talk to
them. I wish he had been with me when I gathered up my father's
bones. The buzzards and coyotes had scattered them all over kingdom come. I wish he had seen my mother when David carried her to
the river. Seventy-nine years old and you know what they did to
her. It's a miracle she lived. Talk to them. 'Let death seize upon
them and let them go down quick into hell: for wickedness is in their
dwellings and among them.' "

"What will we do?"

"Trust to God and keep trying."

James Parker and others who had lost loved ones to the Indians
would never understand Houston's policy of treating with them.
But he was right in a way. If a force had attacked the band that held
the captives, the Comanche would have slaughtered them rather
than let them be retaken. It was a tragic lesson the people of the
frontier would learn over and over again.

❧ 8 ❧

When Something Good had asked if Naduah and Star Name could come
with her on the honey hunt, Cynthia had begged Takes Down The
Lodge to let her go. She would have three days with Something
Good almost to herself. Three days to be in her company and not
have to watch her talking to dozens of people, always working,
always busy. Cynthia was so excited that Takes Down couldn't say
no. As the girls rode away, Cynthia turned and waved to her and
Black Bird. She didn't notice the worry on her foster mother's gentle
face. Takes Down spoke without taking her eyes off her daughter's
diminishing back.

"Maybe I should go with them."

"Something Good knows what to do. She's a better shot than
some men her own age. But I'll deny it if you tell anyone."

"Yes. And an old woman like me would spoil their fun."

"I wonder why Something Good didn't take her own friends
along, though. It's strange that only the three of them are going."
Black Bird was even quieter than Takes Down, but she had a keener
eye for brewing gossip. Nothing escaped her, especially breaks in
the pattern of camp life. And Something Good was no longer spending as much time with the other women.

"The child has been with us less than fourteen days. She is so new. What if she tries to escape?"

"On that mule? I know you're fond of her, Sister, but you have to admit she's not much of a rider."

"She'll learn. She learns everything fast." With her hand shading her eyes, Takes Down The Lodge stood stolid and unmoving in front of the doorway until the small group was out of sight, lost in the bustle of camp. Short and square in her buff-colored dress, Takes Down The Lodge looked like a block of limestone that the ground had eroded away from, leaving her standing solid and firmly planted.

Naduah learned fast, but would she learn fast enough? The People's world had little patience for learners. Only survivors. And if she did try to escape, she wouldn't survive long. If the bears and snakes didn't find her, Piam-em-pits, Cannibal Owl, might. Or nenepi, the malevolent little people. And there was the tribe to the south, the Nermateka, People Eaters. The sun had been up almost an hour, and it shone in Takes Down's face. She blinked her big, dark eyes to dismiss the thought of her new daughter alone and hurt somewhere, and squeezed out a tear in the process. From the sun perhaps. She turned back to the hide she was scraping. It was only for three days. And Naduah would be all right.

"We have to kill a deer before we can collect the honey." Cynthia was sure that was what Star Name was telling her, acting it out as they rode double on the old, swaybacked mule. Cynthia slid sideways on his scabby, broad back so she could look over her shoulder at Star Name, and shift her weight off the cutting edge of his backbone at the same time. They were riding on a pad saddle, a leather bag stuffed with grass and held on by a strap. After a long day it had flattened out until it was little use in separating Cynthia from the mule's bony spine. She clutched his short mane for balance as they jounced along.

They had to kill a deer? What could killing a deer have to do with honey? Was it for some crazy religious reason? They had plenty of those. Would they eat the meat for strength? At any rate, Something Good was carrying a bow and a quiver of arrows as she rode next to them on her skittish, clay-colored pony. Surely she wasn't going to shoot the bees with it, and women usually only carried knives. Takes Down had given Cynthia one, and it rode strapped to her waist, over her dress. She rested her hand on the polished antler hilt, feeling grown up and brave.

Although she had been with Pahayuca's band less than two weeks, her vocabulary was growing rapidly. She could only pick out isolated words and phrases in the constant flow of conversation around her, but it wasn't for lack of teachers or ability. She just needed time. Everyone taught her, pointing out objects and repeating their names.

Even the children sometimes stopped in the middle of a game to quiz her. But though she could usually see what people were doing, she couldn't ask why they were doing it. And she always wanted to know the how and why. Like this business with the honey, and the deer. They had come out here to hunt honey, not game. She could ask Star Name why, but she'd learned that why was much harder to explain. She'd have to wait patiently. Perhaps the doing of it would explain the why.

Why, for instance, did Tse-ak, Lance, drone and chant every morning when he woke up? And why did everyone enter a lodge and turn left, then pace around to the right? Why did the women paint red lines down the parts of their hair? And why were even fierce warriors terrified of thunder and lightning? Why did Takes Down insist that she lay one end of the stick in the fire, rather than just dropping it across?

Maybe Something Good could answer some of her questions. From the corner of her eye Cynthia studied the girl's delicate profile as they rode along, and watched how she handled her pony. Her long, bare legs gripped the mare's sides, lifting her body slightly in time with the stride. Her thin suede dress was hiked up past her knees, and the fringe at the hem had fallen away to show her strong, smooth thighs. She sat lightly and swayed from side to side, as gracefully as tall grass rippling in the wind.

Long curtains of fringe swung from the high curved pommel and cantle on her saddle, and from the V-shaped yoke on her dress. The reins lay loosely in her right hand as it rested on her thigh. Her left arm was bent, her hand riding at the crease where her leg met her body. She sat straight and supple, moving in perfect time with her pony. Her hair was tied into two thick braids wrapped with thongs, but wisps of it blew around her face in the wind. The bells and dew claws dangling from the side boards of the saddle made a lilting castanet clatter.

Something Good was the wife of Pahayuca, who was Medicine Woman's brother and Sunrise's uncle. That made fifteen-year-old Something Good Cynthia's foster great-aunt. Around camp Cynthia watched her, finding excuses to stay near Pahayuca's group of lodges. Once she had even ventured into Something Good's own tent, and stood in the doorway while Star Name delivered the message they had been given. Star Name walked in casually, calling out only to make sure Something Good was inside. Cynthia followed her timidly and stood mute, as usual.

Something Good had handed them each a piece of the bread she had just baked on a flat stone propped in front of the fire. The bread was thin and brittle, and made of a meal of ground pecans, sweet mesquite beans, and honey. It had a delicious, nutty flavor, and Cynthia nibbled hers to make it last longer and to give her an excuse to be silent. While Star Name and Something Good talked, Cynthia looked around, missing very little.

Old Owl, Something Good's father, was a civil leader, and his daughter's possessions were beautiful. The poles were hung with necklaces of shells and beaten silver and brass disks and bone cylinders. There were dozens of fringed leather bags, most of them beaded or painted. Hanging between two of the lodge's support poles was a painted buffalo robe such as only a chief or a chief's wife would wear. The dresses and leggings hanging from a rack along one side were dyed in pale yellows and greens and decorated with bells and fur, shells and tassels. Against a pole leaned Something Good's four-foot-long, L-shaped shinny stick, the shaft smooth and polished from the oil of her hands. The floor was covered with buffalo robes, and a saddle sat on top of her folded red saddle blanket. Her bridle, braided of rawhide and red flannel, hung nearby. On the bed, pulled up like a quilt, was a robe made of ermine fur.

The only war gear had been the bow and quiver that Something Good now carried, its strap loosened so that it rested on her pony's back. But what caught Cynthia's attention that day in Something Good's lodge was a stuffed doll sewn of soft doeskin. It was dressed in a perfectly detailed woman's outfit. Its painted face was almost rubbed blank, and it was worn from years of being carried around. It had been patched, but a bit of white cottonwood fluff was leaking from a seam. Next to it stood a miniature beaded and tasseled cradle board. Over everything, even the smell of the baking bread, was the faint perfume of sage. Something Good burned it often in her fire.

Something Good had noticed the yellow-hair watching her, and she had been amused. And touched. She knew what it was like to be a stranger. She missed her own family and friends, and asked for news of Old Owl's band whenever there were visitors in camp. Sometimes in the middle of the everyday chaos Naduah's face would take on a lost, lonely, frightened look, and Something Good wanted to hug her and tickle her out of the mood. She looked so out of place with her indigo eyes and corn yellow hair, like a golden kingbird in a raven's nest. So she had invited the girls to come with her. She couldn't go out alone, and she didn't want anyone older along. There was another reason for the trip, and she was sure the girls would keep her secret.

They chattered beside her now as she rode, staring intently at the ground, searching the rough caliche limestone soil for deer signs. They were traveling through a deep ravine, the preferred route of the People. Whites usually chose the easier, level, exposed ridges, often to their sorrow: they made excellent targets there. The sides of the narrow game trail were tightly woven with underbrush, small plum trees, roses, currant bushes, and gooseberries. And meshed with them were huge masses of prickly pear and wild flowers. A fat yellow rattlesnake, six feet long, lay basking on top of the wild green mat. The few tall pecans were festooned with grapevines, the undersides of their leaves shimmering silver in the breeze.

Tiny brown canyon wrens darted nervously among the trees, their clear, liquid "tee tee tee tee, tew tew tew tew" cascading down the scale. The girls' passing disturbed the yellow kingbirds too and they flew overhead like flashes of sunlight, chattering their rapid "queer-a-chi-queer, queer-a-chi-queer." Rose-colored tanagers watched from the limbs overhead, and the dapper woodpeckers ignored them, rapping out their tatoos on the tree trunks.

For an instant Cynthia found herself face to face with a tiny, jewel-like hummingbird, its head and neck gleaming irridescent green in the sun. It hovered at eye level as though inspecting her before vanishing, its vibrating wings forming a halo around it. She turned to see if Star Name had seen it, and they grinned at each other. The smell of the warm earth and dense foliage and spring flowers was intoxicating. Old One Hundred began ringing in her head, and she hummed it to herself, hearing her grandfather's rumbling bass and her mother's delicate soprano.

> *Praise God from whom all blessings flow,*
> *Praise him all creatures here below.* . . .

Her song ended in a gobble from the line of six turkeys that strutted single file along the top of the ravine opposite the stream. They took flight in an explosion of flapping wings.

Something Good ignored the noise and concentrated on the ground. They were following a cold, spring-fed creek that bumped noisily into the rocks in its path as it rushed to get to the river several miles to the east. Crickets hushed under their horses' hooves and started up again after they had passed. It was late afternoon, and the insects thrummed and pulsed until the blood in Cynthia's temples seemed to beat in time with them. Something Good held up her hand, signaling the other two to halt, and put a finger on her lips.

She crooked a leg and swung it over her saddle, jumping off lightly. Her knees bent as she landed, and she crouched in one smooth motion. *Something Good never flails around*, Cynthia thought grimly as she struggled to get down from the mule's bony back. She hung with her stomach across the sharp ridge of his backbone and kicked, stretching her legs and feeling for solid ground. When she was riding him it seemed as though his two ends were going to fold up and pinch her in the middle, but swaybacked as he was, it was still a long way down.

Star Name had pushed back on his rump and slid off that way, using his tattered tail to steady herself. *If I did that he'd kick me sure, or break wind on me.* He had fired off one loud, popping explosion after another, all along the trail. They'd been giggling about it for hours, pounding his sunken sides with their heels to hurry him out of his own stench.

The three girls squatted around the prim, curved, twin indentations in the wet sand by the creek.

"*Adeca,* deer." Something Good breathed the word almost silently. They remounted, Star Name cupping her hands to give Cynthia a boost. Then she took a short running start and leaped on herself, Cynthia hauling her up by the back of her dress. They retraced their steps a little way, then climbed a steep trail to the top of the ravine. They kept downwind of the deer tracks and avoided the faint deer path that lay like a part in the bushes. Cynthia would never have noticed it if Something Good hadn't pointed it out. The deer would be coming to drink soon, drifting like twilight shadows down the trail.

Something Good led them a mile through the bush-covered hills to a large bowl-shaped depression, the remains of a limestone cave that had collapsed. At the bottom of the sinkhole bubbled a clear spring, forming a pool rimmed with a green velvet carpet of moss. The pool was shallow except at the center, where the water was the color of pale blue silk. It was so clear that the bottom was plainly visible, and it looked only a few inches deep all the way across. But it wasn't. The spring went down fifty feet before joining the vast underground lake that flowed through the dissolved limestone bedrock.

The sides of the depression were covered with tall plumes of ferns, solidly massed. The air was ten degrees cooler there. At the top of the bowl was a grove of pecan trees and scrub cedar, and Something Good motioned for them to tether the mules among the trees. She didn't dismount, but turned and disappeared in the direction of the deer trail.

There were only two hours of daylight left, and Star Name wasted no time. She led the two mules down to the spring and watched while they drank, pushing aside the flocks of black water bugs that skated over the surface. Water oozed into their hoofprints in the moss, making tiny green ponds. Then she brought the animals back and slipped the twisted rawhide hobbles around their front legs, chopping with the edge of her hand behind their knees to make them lift their feet. She fastened the hobbles with a wooden toggle that fit through a slit in the leather. Then she pulled a pair of long, sharpened stakes from the pack and pounded them into the hard ground with a heavy rock. She tethered each animal to them by fifteen-foot lines of braided buffalo hair, tied at the ends with thongs to keep them from unraveling. She yanked at the knots and the stakes to test them. The mules weren't much, but without them they'd be in serious trouble.

Cynthia stood watching Something Good ride off, a hollow feeling growing in her stomach. What if something happened to her? Would Star Name know the way home? The beauty around her grew ominous and threatening.

"Naduah. *Kee-mah*, come." Star Name beckoned, and Cynthia walked over to untie the load from the pack mule. He bit at her in thanks, and she socked him hard on the tender muzzle as Sunrise did. Her foster father's meaning had been clear. Never let a mule or horse get the upper hand. And never let an animal sense that you are afraid of it. She stood now, glaring up at the mule, her hands on her hips. He towered over her, but the bluff worked. He lowered his head docilely, looking at her innocently from the corner of his eye, and began ripping up mouthfuls of the thick grama grass.

Star Name dug a fire pit and began bringing in loads of wood while Cynthia carried the bundles to the campsite. She rummaged around in them until she found the parfleche of jerky, but Star Name shook her head and motioned her to put it back. Cynthia sighed, her stomach rumbling in protest. No wonder Indians ate so much. They ate so rarely. At least they wouldn't have to worry about being attacked by Comanche. As they chopped brush for a shelter, a smile chased the thought across her face.

"*Hakai*, what?" Star Name caught the look, but Cynthia wouldn't have explained it if she could. She shrugged and grinned and went back to tying up the poles for the lean-to frame.

Star Name was teaching Cynthia to light a fire when Something Good returned. They were huddled close to block the wind and taking turns pulling the small bow of the fire drill back and forth. The rawhide thong was looped once around the drill stick, which twirled as the bow was pulled from side to side. It was a long, tedious process. While one child twirled the stick, pressing down on the flat rock on top of it with her other palm, the second girl steadied the hearth, the piece of wood with the hole into which the drill stick

70

fit. She also fed small handfuls of tinder into the smoking hole and blew it gently. Star Name was using the stringy, frayed inner bark of the cedar trees, and it smelled good as it smoldered.

They were both so intent on what they were doing, hypnotized by the teasing little curls of smoke and the tiny sparks, that they didn't hear Something Good sneak up behind them. They had just coaxed a real flame when she screamed an unearthly, blood-congealing, ululating war cry that echoed eerily among the ragged hills and bounced off the bluffs that loomed against the darkening sky. It sent spasms of terror down Cynthia's spine and stood her hair on end. Her heart was pounding so hard she could hear it as she whirled around, her knife drawn. Something Good sank down onto one of the beds of cedar boughs that the girls had cut and covered with a buffalo robe. She was laughing too hard to stand up.

"You should never let anyone surprise you like that. I wish you could see your faces." Star Name and Cynthia stood stunned for a few seconds, then, without even looking at each other or saying a word, they attacked. They dived onto Something Good, tickling her until they were all crying with laughter and too weak to wrestle anymore. They rolled in the dirt together in a wild tangle of flailing arms and legs, and finally sat up, brushing the sand and bits of gravel off each other.

"Some scouts you two are. I could have taken both your scalps."

"Some wife you are. Where's the live coal to start the fire? Why should we wear ourselves out with this drill? At least you could have left the flint." Star Name kicked the drill with her foot. Her pride had been damaged.

"You know you need the practice, bright eyes. And you may be caught somewhere without a flint or coal, but you can always make a bow and drill. *Namasi-kohtoo*, quick, quick. Make the fire, and I'll skin the deer. Unless you would rather butcher it and I'll start the fire."

"I'll start it." Star Name grumbled a little as she gathered the scattered tools. It wasn't often that she was on the receiving end of a joke, and she didn't like it. She sawed at the bow almost viciously and the flame caught faster. Cynthia fed it dried moss, then twigs, until it was burning brightly.

Something Good tied a line around the neck of the doe she had shot, leaving it in place on the back of her pony. She threw the other end of the line over a low limb. Swinging her whole weight on the rope to hoist the carcass up, she fastened the end of the line around the tree trunk. The body revolved slowly as she cut the skin around the neck, just above the shoulders. The girls helped her peel it down toward the heels, tugging on it as, with her skinning knife, she cut it away from the tissue underneath. They ended up with the entire hide in one piece and inside out.

She tied the arrow hole and the four legs shut with buckskin thongs, twisting tiny pegs into them to keep the thongs tight and in place. They all took turns blowing up the skin, until it was distended like a bladder, then Something Good tied the neck closed. She held it up.

"Our honey container."

"Oh." The why was answered. "That's what the deerskin is for."

"Of course. Were you planning to carry the honey home in your hands?" Star Name held her hands out, bloody from the skinning. Cynthia was glad Something Good had shot a small deer. She was filthy and exhausted, and there was still the carcass to butcher. She washed off with some of the water from the gourd canteen.

By the light of the fire Star Name put together a small drying rack, a tripod of five-foot poles with three more sticks lashed across them horizontally for hanging the meat strips. Cynthia cut long green sticks and whittled points to toast the fresh steaks for their evening meal. The thin strips that Something Good was cutting to take as travel rations would smoke and dry next to the fire. What they couldn't eat or dry, she stuffed into a buffalo stomach liner and tied tightly shut. She went off into the night, carrying it and a burning brand to light her way.

"Hah-ich-ka po-mea, where is she going?" It was very dark now, and it made Cynthia nervous to see Something Good disappear again.

"She will put the meat into the water to keep it cool." Star Name had become so used to clarifying her explanations with elaborate gestures that she did it automatically now. When the wood had burned down to coals, Star Name laid the liver across them, and the smells almost made Cynthia dizzy with hunger.

Something Good appeared again, like a wraith materializing from the darkness, and brought a treat for them. They each dipped into the small leather bag and scooped out fingerfuls of mush made from buffalo marrow and crushed mesquite beans. It was sweet and took the edge off their hunger. Then she threw some water-lily roots from the pond into the ashes.

When they had eaten, the three of them leaned against a broad trunk of the nearest pecan and watched the fire dance. Something Good had built it up so that the light from it played high in the limbs above them. She had tied one end of a thirty-foot rawhide line to an arrow and shot it over one of the limbs. Then she had bundled what food was left and the swollen deerskin and hoisted them far up

among the leaves, safe from bears. She dragged the remains of the
deer carcass off behind her pony and dumped it into a crevice.

"If any bears come looking for food tonight, all they'll find is us."
She settled back between Star Name and Cynthia. She seemed
relaxed, at ease there, yet restless, her eyes searching the dark
around them, looking not for danger but for something else.

The sounds of night insects were all around them. The wind
soughed through the canopy of leaves. Otherwise it was quiet.
Above them the stars were so thick and brilliant the pebbles on the
ground around them threw tiny shadows. Something Good tried to
teach them a lullaby, her voice low and soothing.

> *The wind is singing.*
> *The wind is singing in the leaves.*
> *The wind is singing me to sleep.*

Cynthia tried to learn it, repeating the words and imitating the
simple tune. But it was too hypnotic for her, and the day had been
too long. Her voice trailed off and she fell asleep with her head on
Something Good's shoulder. On the other side, Star Name soon
followed. Neither of them heard Something Good's second song.
She sang it even lower, each word wrapped in spider webs of
melancholy.

> *Nei-na-su-tama-habi.*
> *I lie down and dream of you.*
> *I rise up and think of you.*
> *When the wind blows through my hair,*
> *I know you are moving in my heart.*

Neither of the girls remembered her helping them into their beds of
fragrant cedar boughs. And not once during the long day had it
occurred to Cynthia to try to escape.

They were up early the next morning, and Something Good gave
them their orders as she divided the small amount of honey she had
brought along as bait.

"Find a flat rock in an open place over there, on the other side of
the sinkhole. If you can't find a clearing, make one. Use your knives
to cut down the bushes. Save the ax.

"It's going to be a hot day, which is good. The deer hide and the
meat will dry more quickly. The sun will evaporate the honey, and
the smell will attract the bees faster.

"Don't follow the first bee. Let her go back to the hive and bring

the others. When they have their supply line set up you can see
which direction they're traveling and go that way. If you lose one,
there'll be more to follow. I'll do the same here. Where we meet, the
hive will be. We'll cut down the tree and wait until they've settled
down some. Then we'll come back for the honey. The hide should
be ready to hold it by then.

"The bees will be all stirred up, of course, but don't swat them.
Ignore them. You'll get stung, but not as often. And when one does
sting you, don't pull the stinger out. Scrape it out with your knife
blade. If you squeeze it to get it out you'll release the venom in it. Do
you have any questions?"

Cynthia didn't understand enough of the instructions to ask any,
and Star Name said no. It wasn't her first hunt for the white man's
flies, the imported gift that the People accepted as they accepted
horses and metal.

The sky was the color of bleached denim and the day was already
hot. Star Name and Cynthia wore only their moccasins and breechclouts as they walked around the huge bowl left by the collapsed
cave. They peered over the ragged limestone boulders fringed with
ferns at the edge. Sweat was collecting under their arms and the
pool looked inviting below, like a pale sapphire in an emerald
setting. It was the color of the sky, complete with reflections of small
clouds floating in it. Later they would enjoy it. There was work to do
now.

Star Name carried the bait honey carefully in a few broad, triangular cottonwood leaves. Cynthia carried an ax very much like the one
her father had owned. Star Name poured the honey onto a flat rock,
and they cleared a comfortable place in the shade of a pecan. Star
Name repeated Something Good's instructions again in the hand-
talk/pidgin/pantomime language they had worked out between
themselves. She gathered a handful of the pale pink flowers that
grew around them and held them out for her friend to sniff. She
patted her stomach and smiled. It would be delicious, fragrant
honey.

The first bee landed and inspected the bait. She seemed to be
taking its measurements and testing it, stroking it with her an-
tennas. Star Name and Cynthia froze, watching her. When she took
off it was tempting to chase her, but they resisted, waiting in sus-
pense to see if more would return. It seemed to take forever before
another one lighted, then a third. Cynthia held her fists tightly
clenched, urging them to hurry and fly. Bees had never seemed like
such slow, methodical creatures before.

Finally one rose, circled twice to gain altitude, and took off. The
girls raced after her, caught up in the excitement of the chase. They

shouted and laughed and hooted as they tore across the hills. It wasn't easy to keep a tiny insect in sight in rough country, but they were determined to make as straight a beeline as their prey. They crashed through stands of scrub oak and the occasional roly-poly cedar, swerving to avoid only the thickets of plum and grape and prickly pear that were too tall to leap. They plowed through meadows of wild flowers, leaving a swath behind them. They toiled up hills and raced down the other side, sometimes sliding to the bottom in a hail of gravel.

As they neared another grove of pecan trees near a stream they saw Something Good running toward them through an open stretch of grass. Then a second figure broke from the brush. Eagle had found her. They trotted up, almost as scratched and dirty as the girls. Eagle grinned as he held out his hand for the ax, but Cynthia scowled when she surrendered it.

What was he doing here? They didn't need him, and they didn't want him. Now he would take charge and spoil everything. Not only were men arrogant, but women went all mushy and helpless when they were around. Something Good would forget how to do anything. And they wouldn't have her to themselves anymore. And what if Wanderer had come with him? They went everywhere together. She searched the bushes suspiciously, waiting for Wanderer to appear, and was relieved when he didn't. One of them was bad enough. If Wanderer came she'd get on the mule and head back to camp by herself.

There was no problem finding the bee tree. They heard the faint, ominous buzzing, like a storm about to break. The opening for the nest was thirty feet up in a dead tree. The trunk shivered as Something Good and Eagle began chopping at it. They laughed as the cloud of bees came boiling out of the hole and swarmed around their heads. As they landed on Cynthia's arms and shoulders and face she panicked and slapped at them, trying not to cry as they stung her. Something Good and Eagle chopped methodically in the middle of the cloud of angry bees, until the huge tree creaked and toppled slowly, bouncing a little as it landed. Then all hell did indeed break loose, and the four of them retreated in wild disorder.

They ran for two miles and collapsed, exhausted and laughing, on the beds in the brush shelter. They were filthy and covered with scratches, their bodies glistening with sweat. Their hair was tangled with twigs and wood chips and dead bees. Something Good had a large bruise on her arm where she had fallen. Cynthia's eye was fast swelling shut, and Star Name's upper lip was puffy. Eagle pulled the big butcher knife from the sheath on his belt and beckoned Cynthia to him. She came reluctantly and knelt in front of him. He scraped at the bumps on her face and shoulders, cleaning off the dirt and sweat as well as digging out the stingers. Something Good did the same for Star Name. Then Eagle sat cross-legged in front of Something Good and took her small chin in his left hand. She flinched ever so slightly and looked fixedly at the ground while he removed the stings from her face and neck.

"*Mea-dro*, let's go." Star Name jumped up and raced for the edge of the sinkhole. She ran down the side, through the ferns, and scrambled up onto a large boulder, that had rolled partially into the pool. She dropped her breechclout and cannonballed off it, holding her nose. Cynthia followed her, gasping as the icy water hit her.

"You didn't tell me the water would be this cold."

"You didn't ask me." Star Name scudded the heel of her hand across the surface, sending a broad spray into Cynthia's face. They battled back and forth across the shallow part of the pond, then dove and swam under water, racing to see who could go farthest and stay under the longest. Star Name won, but Cynthia was pressing her.

They swam to the far edge, skirting the crystal spring in the center. As they passed it they could feel the turbulence from it. But they knew better than to dive in and explore it. There were stories of children, and adults too, being sucked into springs like that and never being seen again. Sometimes entire trees washed out of them, carried by the underground stream.

They headed for the small waterfall that cascaded down from the steepest side of the hole, about eight feet up. It sprayed down over the rocks and ferns like a fountain in a garden. They lay under it, leaning their heads back like chicks to drink from it. Then they rested on their elbows in the shallows, letting the cold water wash the last of the dirt and sweat from them.

"What's the matter?" Cynthia could tell something was wrong. Star Name was more than just irritated that Eagle had come. She was worried. It wasn't a look Cynthia had seen on her face before, but she recognized it.

"Eagle shouldn't be here."

"Why not?"

There was a moment of silence. The why again. Star Name sat in the water and held up her right forefinger. "Something Good." Then she raised her left forefinger. "Eagle." She placed them far apart. "*Toquet*, all right." She brought them together until they were touching. With her right finger she made a sudden slicing motion across her nostril. "Something Good."

It took a few seconds for the connection to close in Cynthia's mind. Then she remembered the woman with the horribly disfigured nose. The one none of the other women spoke to much.

Adultery. It was a word she knew. It was part of the Ten Commandments. And the woman in the village had had her nostrils sliced four or five times. Even the tip of her nose was missing. Had it been done for only one transgression, or once for each? She shook her head in amazement. An eye for an eye. But how could anyone do that to Something Good? Surely kindly Pahayuca wouldn't. Would he? She was a chief's wife. Surely she wouldn't do anything wrong.

Cynthia almost cried with relief when she saw Something Good appear over the rim of the bowl and run down through the ferns. She pulled her dress over her head as she ran, and dove off the rock like a sleek brown otter, swimming toward them with powerful strokes. She lay her head back in the water to slick the tangles of her blue-black hair, and they made room for her between them. They began talking about the bee chase.

Eagle could sense the hostility. It wasn't hard to do. It radiated from the two girls like the heat from the fire between them. And it was difficult to be hostile during a dinner like the one they were eating. When their venison had roasted, each of them had loosened a peg holding the cord tight around a leg of the bulging deerskin hanging nearby. They let a stream of honey flow slowly over the meat, before retwisting the peg and shutting it off. With the meat they ate more of Something Good's delicious nut bread, spread with a paste of pounded plums.

It didn't matter to Eagle that the girls were angry with him. But he was naturally charming, and he turned it on them now. They were, after all, Something Good's friends, and whether they knew it or not, they were going to be his friends too. Cynthia refused to look at him or talk to him. She picked some bits of powdered bark and a few deer hairs out of the honey. Then she fished out a dead bee with her thumb and forefinger, holding it up and letting the honey drip off it before flicking it behind her. She concentrated on her food with a ferocious intensity. Next to her Star Name did the same.

They're like two soft, fierce panther kittens. Eagle tried not to let his amusement show. He would win them over because it made Something Good unhappy to have tension among them. And he knew he could win them over. They would know he was doing it, but they wouldn't be able to help themselves. Not any more than the panther kitten he had once raised could stop herself from batting at a wriggling thong, even when she saw Eagle's hand at the end of it. Women were the same at any age. Helpless against a sincerely charming man.

When they had finished eating and had wiped their hands on the thick piles of cedar needles around them, he reached into the pouch he carried at his waist. He pulled out a small bone disk, polished smooth by years of handling. He held his two fists out, palms down, in a gesture that triggered an immediate response in the girls. It was the old pea-under-the-shell trick. Button, button, who's got the button? Maybe it was the racial instinct of a predatory species. Into which hole did the rabbit run? In which pool are the fish biting? Without thinking, Cynthia reached out and pointed to Eagle's left hand. He grinned at her and turned the hand up, uncurling long thin fingers slowly to show her his empty palm.

"Let me do it. I can guess." Star Name hunched forward and watched closely, her forehead wrinkled into a scowl, while he waved his hands and passed them back and forth over each other to confuse her. He held them out again and let them both guess before he opened them. Cynthia guessed right, leaving Star Name with the empty palm.

"Give me another chance." Star Name knew she had it figured out.

"No. Not unless you make it worthwhile. What will you bet?" He was teasing, and Star Name rose to it.

"I'll bet you my part of the honey." She forgot that he couldn't very well ride into camp with honey. He wasn't supposed to be here. Cynthia was shocked though. Was Star Name really going to give away so easily what she had worked and suffered to get? Her small, full mouth was so swollen she could hardly talk, and she was covered with welts. "What will you bet?" Star Name was all business.

Eagle got up and walked over to his saddlebags. He brought back a large, thin disk cut from an oyster shell. He had traded with Big Bow for it, and the Kowa had in turn liberated it from a dead Nermateka, a People Eater from the coast. It had a hole drilled near one edge so it could be worn as a necklace. He held it up by its thong and twirled it slowly. The fire shone through its translucent surface in muted yellows and oranges, but in the sunlight it would glow with opalescent color, pale pinks, delicate greens and blues and purples. Something Good rummaged through her bundles and pulled out a pair of brass trader's tweezers. She passed them over for Star Name to inspect. There weren't many around, and they were a prize to have.

In her mind Cynthia searched through her scanty possessions for something to bet. Everything she had Star Name or Takes Down or Medicine Woman had given her, and she didn't want to bet someone's gift. She could bet her part of the honey, but that would deprive Takes Down and Sunrise. She had been counting on giving it to them in return for all they had done for her.

"Naduah is new. She doesn't have much. Let her play without betting," said Star Name.

"No one plays without betting. She can take care of the winner's horses for a month," replied Eagle.

"But I don't have any horses. What if she loses to me?" asked Star Name.

"She won't. Something Good and I will be on one team and you two can be on the other." Eagle pulled a log over and laid a stick across it. Then he picked up several twigs and began breaking them into smaller pieces. When he had twenty-one of them, he laid them out between the two teams. He passed Something Good the bone disk and began the gambling song in his clear tenor, beating out the rhythm on the log. Star Name and Cynthia kept time by pounding the ground in front of them. Something Good waved her hands, twining them to the beat. When the song ended she held them out to Cynthia. She guessed right, and a stick was slid over to her side of the fire. Then it was her turn.

She had picked up a little of the chant, but she didn't sing. She was concentrating too much on hiding the bone. She couldn't fool Eagle, though, and his team received a stick and the bone. Hours went by as the two piles of stick counters grew and dwindled. By midnight they were all yelling at each other and screaming with laughter. Fortunes had been won and lost again. And Cynthia and Star Name were to take care of Something Good's and Eagle's ponies.

Star Name was allowed to keep her honey. The victors would have returned it to her anyway as a gift. They both knew that her family needed it. Sunrise provided for Black Bird and Star Name and Upstream, but one man was hard put to feed six mouths. Something Good and Eagle sang the victory song while Cynthia and Star Name beat on the log.

Finally they all went to bed, Something Good lying between Cynthia and Star Name under the brush lean-to. From the other side of the fire, near the horses, Eagle could be heard singing his medicine song to himself before he went to sleep. His voice was hypnotic as it rose and fell for an hour. Cynthia fell asleep long before that, but Something Good lay awake staring up at the stars beyond the shelter's frayed eaves. When she had left on the hunt she had made it clear where she would be, and she had thought Eagle would follow her. He had been hanging around for days with that intensely wistful look on his face. Now he was here, after heading out in the opposite direction, then doubling back to meet her. And she didn't know what to do with him.

She resented the girls for being there, for the accusation in their silent concern. For their presence that formed a barrier between her and Eagle. But at least they wouldn't tell on her. They knew the consequences. That was evident. Her hand went to her nose, unconsciously feeling to make sure it was whole and unblemished. And another part of her was glad they were there. They kept her from having to make the decision to betray Pahayuca.

As she listened to their soft breathing, she forced herself to lie still, knowing that Eagle was so close and awake too. Fear and frustration and longing and guilt tugged at her. She wanted to get up and go to him. To kneel over him and run her hands down his hard, slender chest and into the curve of his waist, then down along his thighs. She wanted to see his face looking up at her, lit by the lantern of the stars. She wanted to stretch out against him and feel his arms around her. She wanted so desperately to touch him that she closed her fingers into tight fists, the nails digging into her palms.

Tears ran down her cheeks and into her ears. She rolled over and buried her face in the small robe she had folded to use as a pillow. Softly, she cried herself to sleep.

❧ *9* ❧

The breeze off the river cooled the glistening bodies of Wanderer and Eagle as they sat in the thick grass. Their lathered ponies grazed nearby. Wanderer had won the race, of course, but Eagle expected that. He was only trying to shorten his friend's lead.

"Someday I'm going to steal a pony as good as Night."

"There aren't any ponies as good as that."

"There must be one somewhere, and I'm going to find him. It'll be worth a lot of trouble to beat you and take that smirk from your face."

"I don't smirk."

"Only after a race."

"Is that why you're always raiding for horses? You want to beat Night? If you really want him, I'll give him to you."

Eagle gave a small start and was silent. It was an offer such as no one ever made. Nor was one like it likely to be made again. A man cheerfully loaned his wife or risked his life for a brother or a friend. That was natural. He could always expect the favor in return. He shared his sacred pipe and on rare occasions might bestow one of his coups on a friend or son or nephew. He even gave away horses, but never his war pony. Not while he lived. Not a horse like Night.

"Night is yours, *Tah-mah*, Brother. To take him from you would be very bad medicine. But I'm honored. Anyway, he bites me. Even worse than that, he bites me in embarrassing places. I think he does it deliberately. I still have a scar on my buttocks from the last time."

"I'd tell him not to. He bites everyone. It's his way of keeping people from taking liberties with him."

"He doesn't bite you."

"Of course not. I'm his brother."

"Exactly." Eagle pitched a small clod of dry dirt at Wanderer. It crumbled as it hit him on the shoulder. Then Eagle stretched out in the cool grass, crushing it under his weight until the smell of its juices washed over him. He pulled a wide blade of it and made a small slit with his thumbnail. Cupping it between his thumbs, he blew. Night threw up his head and snorted at the high, piercing wail it made.

It was almost three weeks since Sunrise's feast celebrating the arrival of the yellow hair and her naming. There had been feasts and dances and nightly talks with the men of Pahayuca's band. They had moved camp every few days, and this was the first chance they'd had to be alone. Wanderer prepared himself for the talk he knew he had to have with Eagle. It was his real reason for coming out here. The race was an excuse. He only raced horses to win more horses, and Night's reputation was such that few people would bet against him anymore.

"Brother."

"Yes." Eagle rolled over on his stomach and propped his chin on his sinewy arms, pretending to study a parade of ants dismember a grasshopper. From the corner of his eye he watched his beloved friend, the man he called brother, sitting straight against the deep blue sky. Here it was. A lecture from Wanderer. He should never have been so wise so young. It wasn't natural. There was time enough for wisdom when they were codgers, permeated with pipe smoke and chuckling about their misspent youth. If Wanderer wasn't careful he'd spend his youth so carefully he'd have no scandalous memories to amuse himself and his friends with when he was old.

"You know that Pahayuca is a relative of mine." Wanderer knew it would be best to translate the problem into one of honor, not courage. Eagle wasn't afraid of anyone. He'd take on Pahayuca with a grizzly thrown in for interest and fight until he was torn apart. But family honor, favors to a friend, those were something else again.

A flicker of pain passed over Eagle's proud face. It was gone before even Wanderer, who had been with him since childhood, could see it. Eagle sensed what he was about to be asked.

"Yes. I know that," he said.

"He seems to prize Something Good." Why was this so difficult? She was only a woman, after all.

"Of course he does. Pahayuca isn't stupid."

"No. He isn't. And to dishonor him would be to dishonor me."

"I know that also."

"Will you smoke with me, Brother?" The tension tautened between them like a rawhide thong. They were bound to each other, yet wanted to be free of this conversation. Eagle sat up, hunched over, and fingered the gold, Mexican eagle coin hanging on a delicate chain against his thin chest. It was the only way he ever showed strain.

Wanderer remembered how he had gotten the coin. It had been on their first raid for horses, three years ago. They'd ridden south for days through the brittle hills and ridges, bristling with cacti and clumps of agave that fanned like clusters of swords. As hot as it had been they'd had to wear their leggings to protect themselves from the thorny mesquite that grew barrel high to their ponies and carpeted the stony ground as thickly as buffalo fur. Even the sky had glowed a hot, shimmering white.

They'd penetrated far into Mexico and ridden through small fields of withered corn, strangling in the baked soil. The white-plastered adobes, looking like frosted loaves of bread, glowed and pulsed in the sun's glare. The dirt grubbers rarely fought, but they did that time. They were a people born to be victims. To see them fighting with their shovels and hoes and sticks was like seeing rabbits challenging a pack of wolves.

Eagle had spotted the coin glinting on the rumpled white shirt of the first man he ever killed. Drunk with the ultimate power of life and death, he became careless. He jumped down from his horse to get it. Blind to the three men who ran toward him, he bent to pull the chain over the man's head as it flopped loosely on the neck. He was tugging it from around the ears when Wanderer rode into the fight. He shot two of the peasants, pinning them together with one arrow. Eagle killed the third with his knife. He took the two scalps skillfully, even though they were his first. He was a born warrior, Eagle was. Making a deft, circular cut around the hairline, he braced his foot on the man's shoulder and gave a quick jerk. With a loud sucking pop the hair came away in one piece, almost as neatly as if the victim had been alive.

It was satisfying to kill. Wanderer thought no more of the right and wrong of it than a hawk or a coyote does. It was part of the cycle of life. And a better death than wasting away of age and disease, like the old buffalo bull that stumbles after the herd, his hide lacerated by the horns of the younger males. Wanderer wished to die quickly of an enemy's arrow or lance. He hated the thought of spending his last years like Name Giver, being led around by the hand.

He wasn't sure which he liked better, to ride screaming into battle or to sneak into an enemy's camp and steal whatever he wanted. Once he and Eagle had crawled into an Osage camp and touched each sleeping warrior before stealing their horses. He smiled to think of it. They'd been little more than boys, and his father still boasted of it.

He glanced back at Eagle. The coin was one of the newly minted ones, with an eagle on it. It was Eagle's most sacred medicine. But he was too vain to hide it away with his other holy items in the small pouch that hung inside his breechclout. Still Eagle stroked the coin, and Wanderer waited patiently for his reply. He waited so long Wanderer was trying to imagine life without him as a friend.

"Yes, *Tah-mah*. I will smoke with you." The words fell into the hot air like pieces of metal into a brass kettle. They were quietly spoken, yet seemed to ring in the shimmering air. Wanderer gave a small sigh of relief. It was settled. Eagle would forget this folly and leave Something Good alone. The smoke sealed every important agreement between men. And the seal was broken only at risk of great shame and dishonor, a burden too heavy for a man to bear. He stood and walked to where his pipe and fire-making tools lay in their slender, painted bag. Now he could relax and enjoy the summer here. Whatever the Penateka's reputation as warriors might be, their hospitality was the best anywhere. And he wanted to see how the yellow hair, Naduah, adjusted to her new life.

Cynthia knelt over the fresh hide, paring off the worst of the fat and muscle with the heavy elk-horn and flint adz. Star Name and Owl were working on their own hides nearby, and the hum of the women's conversations droned around her. After three weeks she was catching many of the words she heard, but she couldn't follow the gossip.

Pahayuca's four-year-old daughter, Eta-si Kawa, Dusty, was tussling with a clumsy puppy, all ears and feet. They rolled in the dust, growling good-naturedly at each other and worrying a frayed piece of rawhide between them. Under a brush arbor fifty feet away Name Giver and his friends were practicing their stories in front of Owl's lodge. Narabe, Gets To Be An Old Man was telling one that involved hopping around and cackling like a chicken with a hot foot. His friends were laughing and choking and slapping each other on the back. Cynthia wished she could hear and understand what he was saying.

Star Name and Owl were arguing happily about something, and Black Bird was chewing on a skin, a faraway look on her face, like a cow with a particularly juicy cud. Takes Down The Lodge was going through the last series of steps in the tanning process. After the antelope hide dried in the sun she'd be ready to smoke it to keep it supple. It would retain its shape even after getting soaked by rain and river crossings.

It had taken two weeks of watching Takes Down scrape and flay and bury and trample and beat the hide, but at last another of Cynthia's whys was answered. Why did the People's buckskins always look so much neater than those the men wore back home? The settlers' leather pants turned black and greasy and stiff and misshapen with use. Getting caught in the rain with them was an embarrassment and a disaster. Cynthia remembered the wedding for that schoolteacher in Fort Houston. She giggled a little, bending to hide her face so no one would think she was laughing at them. She started working out the description in the language of the People. They'd appreciate the story. She would rehearse it and spring it on them one of these days. Right now it was still too hard for her to explain.

The schoolteacher's name was gone. But she'd never forget him. He was the homeliest man she had ever seen, all knees and elbows and adam's apple. He was six foot six inches tall, and gentle. His wide, myopic eyes gave him the look of a startled ostrich. He was a good, kind, peaceful man. About as suited to the frontier as an ice flow in hell. But he jumped into the life with innocent enthusiasm. He had a suit of buckskins made for his wedding, then got caught in a rain, one of those Texas down-spouts, the day before the ceremony.

The trousers did what they always did when they got wet. They turned to slimy mush and flowed down his ankles, collecting in a puddle around his moccasins. So he took a knife and trimmed off the excess. Then he sat next to a hot fire to dry them out. As they dried, the hems retreated back up his long, lanky legs, taking a stand somewhere near midcalf. The knees remained sitting, projecting out in rounded bulges. And that's the way they preceded him down the aisle.

People had laughed quietly about it for months. They were probably still laughing about it. The thought disturbed her. Were they still laughing? Were they joking, gossiping, teasing as they always had? Were the men still cursing the Mexicans and boasting about their escapades in the war, as though nothing had happened at

Parker's Fort? Did they gather outside their doors in the evening to talk about the flight from Santa Anna, the Runaway Scrape? Did no one miss her? Not even her mother? Was her mother even alive? It was impossible that life could go on back home as before. That horrible morning, the dead and dying, the wounded and violated, the terror were always in the back of her mind like a scream that rang endlessly. It was a cry that could be muted by other noises, but never stilled completely. If she let herself think about it, the day came back to her, but with an unreal quality, like a recurring nightmare.

The world had ended that day, and would never be the same again. Surely they couldn't forget. But if they hadn't forgotten, where were they? Almost a month had gone by. The moon would be full again soon. She remembered what it had been like, riding under that moon, clinging to the silent, stony figure ahead of her. Wanderer had been part of the nightmare. The memory of it brought tears to her eyes, and one dropped onto the hide.

"Naduah." Takes Down grunted as she lowered herself to kneel next to her daughter. Her voice was as close to reproachful as it ever got as she pointed out the lumps and ridges Cynthia had left while her mind roamed. The child ducked her head to wipe her eyes surreptitiously on her arm, pretending to brush the sweat from her face. The hide was staked down with small pegs pounded through holes punched around the edge of it, and her knees hurt from kneeling over it.

In the midmorning heat the smell of curdled blood made her gorge rise. The slime and grease were all over her in flecks that prickled her skin as they dried and hardened there. Sweat trickled down her forehead and into her eyes again. Her elbows and armpits and the backs of her knees itched. She wanted to walk away from it all and go swimming. The river was low and tepid, the color of weak tea, but at least she and Owl and Star Name could lie in it and feel it surge sluggishly around them.

She knew they would go to the river later, but no one suggested quitting now. She set grimly to work, trimming off what she had missed. It was more painstaking than it looked. The hide had to be shaved down a little with each stroke. Takes Down had told her again and again how important it was to make the surface even and smooth. Not that this particular piece of leather was going to be used for anything good anyway. It wasn't the right time of year for prime hides. The buffalo were shedding their winter coats, and the hair was matted with mud and dung, dust and dead insects. It flaked off in wads of filthy felt.

Getting all the hair off was going to be even worse than scouring the flesh. It was harder to pull out, scraping against the grain. It stuck to her wet skin, blew in her nose, and made her sneeze. The wood ashes and water that Takes Down worked into it loosened the hair a little, but not much. Maybe Takes Down would make soles for everyday moccasins out of it, or a rug or a pemmican box. So much work for a piece of roughly finished rawhide.

Cynthia's arms ached as she dragged the flesher back and forth. It was hard to scrape just the right amount of flesh off. Sometimes she dug too deeply and then had to scrape the rest down to the level of the pit she'd made. The flesher had been made for an adult, and it was heavy, and getting heavier every minute. Fatigue was making it harder for her to stroke evenly with it. The rawhide lashing that held the flint blade at a right angle to the horn handle was rough, and her hands were raw. Callouses, in the form of blisters, were starting, but they were slow to form. She rested a moment, head down, while thousands of tiny, pinpoint lights exploded in front of her eyes and the world reeled around her. The talk seemed to be coming from far away, from deep in a cave. She closed her eyes and thought about flax. It was just as miserable to prepare. She had always hated scutching, beating the stinking, rotted flax stems to separate the fibers. And no one else here seemed as tired as she was. She had to finish what she had started. She couldn't disappoint Takes Down The Lodge.

Takes Down wiped her hands on a scrap of leather to clean off the worst of the tanning compound that she was rubbing into her antelope hide for the fifth and last time. It was pernicious stuff, the tanning mixture. The first time Cynthia had seen it she had almost been sick to her stomach. Takes Down had opened the rawhide sack of it and scooped handfuls out onto the center of the hide they were working on. Cynthia's nose had wrinkled when Takes Down began spreading it around, rubbing it vigorously into the leather. She had poked at it gingerly with one finger, dreading to get it on her hands. Finally, she had taken a deep breath and dug in. The compound was made of basswood bark pounded fine and mixed with grease and liver and buffalo brains. It was a revolting, smelly, slimy gray mess that didn't improve with age. It took an hour of scrubbing with sand to get it all off her body. Even then, the smell lingered, though perhaps only in her imagination.

Takes Down knelt beside Cynthia again and reached for the flesher. Cynthia held onto it stubbornly and shook her head. She went doggedly back to work while Takes Down smiled at her. She got up, went into Black Bird's lodge, and came out with another scraper. Together they finished the job. Later Takes Down would finish her own piece of buckskin, pulling and stretching it into shape around a sapling, then rubbing it with a smooth stone, pulling it back and forth through a rawhide loop to make it supple. Finally she would stake it out to dry and bleach in the sun one more time. After all that it would be ready for smoking, which was another process altogether.

"Enough." Takes Down stood and carefully returned the flesher to her sister's lodge while Cynthia wiped hers off and put it in its special case. Then Takes Down waddled toward the river with the three girls like ducklings in a row behind her. As they passed through the village, other women and girls put away their tools and joined them. Something Good brought along a gourd, and Cynthia knew they would have a lively game of water keep-away. They passed through the open area near Pahayuca's lodges in the center of the camp, and Owl and Star Name stopped at the guest tent.

Eagle and Wanderer were sitting under the brush arbor, talking while Eagle repaired his hunting bow. Star Name chattered to Eagle, and Wanderer seemed to be ignoring them as usual. Star Name had developed a fondness for Eagle since the honey hunt. He had sworn them both to secrecy there, pantomiming passing the pipe with them. Star Name had been shocked at his joking about anything as serious as that, but she had enjoyed it. And under the laughter, the girls knew that their silence was important. Cynthia liked knowing something about Eagle that Wanderer didn't. He always looked so cocksure of himself, that Wanderer, so smug. He looked that way now, acting as if they didn't exist.

She watched him from the corner of her eye and thought she caught just a glimpse of a smile, like the flutter of a leaf when there's no wind. But when she looked again to make sure, it was gone and he was studying the six-foot thong loop stretched between his fingers. He wound it around and around, sliding a middle finger under a loop on the opposite side and pulling it taut, then reversing the process and repeating it, until it looked like a hopeless tangle. By now he had both the girls' attention and several young women had stopped to watch too.

Not that the women needed much excuse. Addlepated, was what Uncle Ben would have called them. Addlepated and cow-eyed. Always parading around in front of Wanderer. They were so obvious, giggling and cooing and batting their lashes at him. It was disgusting. They could have him. She wanted no part of someone who could treat an innocent child the way he had treated her.

He casually flipped the last loop over his fingers and pulled his palms apart, holding up an intricate lattice pattern. He looked straight at Cynthia then, and grinned, almost shyly. He beckoned her slightly with his head, and mesmerized by his piercing eyes, she came forward to where he was sitting. He carefully slipped the string figure from his own long, strong fingers onto her smaller ones. She flinched when they came in contact. It was the first time he had touched her since the trip from the fort.

"My heart is glad." She stumbled on the words and blushed.

"Come back later. I'll teach you how to make it." He smiled at her again. As she walked to the river with Star Name, she wondered how she could keep the latticework intact. She'd rather figure it out herself and show him she wasn't stupid, than have him teach her anything. If he thought he could win her over and make her giggle and moo like those other women, he was mistaken.

❧ *10* ❧

There had been dew the night before, and ground fog that rose like thick steam from the warm earth. It still lay in the valleys between the rows of low, dark hills below Cynthia, like icing on a cake of many layers. The quilted mass of clouds overhead was a deep rose color, a vast satin comforter thrown over the world. The sun had just come up and would burn it all away soon. But for now she sat on the edge of the cliff with her long, tanned legs dangling, savoring the view and the solitude.

On the plateau behind her three hundred horses and mules grazed, making a steady, loud tearing and crunching sound as they ripped up the sweet grass. She was alone for the first time in her month with the People. She had gotten up before the sun on purpose, to have the dawn to herself. There had been a dance most of the night before, and she knew the village would sleep longer than usual. Below she could hear the first quavering notes of Lance's good-morning song.

Star Name had translated the song as best she could, but basically it had no particular meaning. It had become as familiar to Cynthia as the songs of the birds. And like the birds, Lance sang every morning just for the joy of it, celebrating the beginning of the new day for himself and for anyone else who happened to be awake. She lay in bed each morning listening for it, and it gave her goose bumps and peace of mind all at the same time. She would have felt cheated in some way if she didn't hear it. It reminded her of what Sunrise had told her when she woke up out of sorts one morning.

"You should be happy to greet each day. And if you're not happy, look inside yourself for the reason."

Smoke began to rise from the lodges as the women built up the morning fires. She could picture them moving softly around their tents, trying not to wake their sleeping families as they raked back the ashes and blew on the tiny embers that nestled under the warm cover all night. Pahayuca's camp spread out below her on the other side of the shallow river where the bottom lands were a quarter of a mile wide. The bluff where she sat rose steeply from the riverbank on her side.

She watched the tiny camp dogs separate from the piles they slept in and stretch, their hind ends in the air and their front paws reaching in front of them. Then they began their daily rounds, sniffing out offal and marking everything with their odor, setting up their territories. Soon the boys would come out, yawning and tightening their breechclout belts and pulling on their moccasins. They would splash in the river, taking their morning baths, then pad sleepily up the trail toward the horse pasture. Lance had ridden through the village at twilight yesterday to announce that they would be moving today.

Cynthia had moved six times in the month she had been there, and she knew the trips were leisurely affairs. There was no need for her to hurry. But the boys would begin moving the horses down onto the flat area outside camp. The herd was up here because there was a spring and better grass, but it was unusual for them to be this far from camp. It wasn't a wise practice because it left the People vulnerable to attack. But they were rarely disturbed here, deep in their own territory and in such large numbers. Pahayuca's band had seventy or eighty lodges and could gather sixty warriors in seconds.

She decided to leave before the boys arrived. The horse herd was their responsibility, and they didn't like to see a girl doing their job. She wasn't afraid of them. She had learned to glare them down the way Star Name did. But they were noisy and rude and it was too beautiful a morning for that. She looked for Night, hoping to give him the thistles she had brought for him. She knew it was unlikely he would be with the rest of the herd, but she looked anyway. He hadn't been outside of Pahayuca's guest lodge when she had passed it earlier, so Wanderer and Eagle must be off somewhere. Hunting probably.

She found patient little Tabukina Naki, Rabbit Ears, Takes Down's pony. Rabbit Ears was shy too, and seemed to know she was knobby and ugly. She took the thistle delicately in her mouth, her lips rolled back, and pulled the spiny stem in with her discolored teeth. She swallowed it with a blissful expression.

Cynthia gathered up Sunrise's mule, three pack ponies, one riding horse, and Rabbit Ears, holding all of their lines loosely in her right hand. The mule led better if she was casual about it, as though he were just politely accompanying her. Sunrise's buffalo pony was already in the village, tethered near his lodge as usual. One of her jobs was to gather armfuls of grass each day for him, but this was the first time Sunrise had asked her to bring in the rest of his small herd. Star Name's brother, Upstream, always brought them in with his own mother's animals.

Her foster father had asked Cynthia casually, after Lance had ridden through with his message about moving the camp. But she knew it was a test. There was nothing to stop her from getting on one of the horses and riding off into the rising sun to find her family. Nothing except the fact that she wasn't much of a rider, nor did she have any provisions. She could handle the docile pack animals or Takes Down's favorite mare, but a horse fast enough to get away would be too much for her. And Spaniard could track her down in no time.

Besides, what would she find if she escaped? Even if she managed to find her way home? She had a horror of riding into Fort Houston or Parker's Fort and having everyone stare at her as though she were a ghost come back to haunt them. To accuse them silently of abandoning her. Maybe they had forgotten her. Or maybe her whole family was dead and she would be an orphan. At least here she had people who cared about her.

Worse yet, she might be put into the charge of her Uncle Daniel. And she couldn't remember ever, in her nine years, having seen him smile. He must have sometime. But she couldn't remember it. She knew what his idea of proper conduct for young ladies was. She would be confined to the cabin and yard, unless accompanied. She would never be allowed to ride or explore miles of wild countryside. The thought of it was like a pillow over her face, smothering her.

Anyway, she would be a freak to them, a wild Indian. As she led the six animals down the path that zigzagged across the face of the bluff she felt her braids, still greased from the night before when Takes Down had fixed them for the dance. Would the children back home taunt her and throw stones at her the way they did at Puss Weber's mulatto offspring? She tried to remember her mother's face, and her brother's and sister's, but they kept fading out of focus.

A strong, familiar smell and a patch of feathery, gray-green bushes caught her eye. They waved flat clusters of tiny pink flowers at her, bouncing and beckoning in the breeze. Milfoil. Yarrow. What was it doing here? It grew by the acre back in Illinois. Her mother and grandmother had brought it with them to east Texas so they would have it when they needed it. They planted it and gathered it carefully, but it spread like gossip around the fort, its roots creeping everywhere and sending up new plants.

The flowers' spicy fragrance reminded her of the bundles of it hanging from the fireplace to dry, and filling the small cabin with the aroma. *Achillea Millefolium,* named in honor of Achilles, who used it in the Trojan War. Or so her grandmother always said. Granny Parker claimed it would cure anything, influenza, gout, liver and kidney ailments, wounds.

Thoughts of home were forgotten. Here was something she could give Medicine Woman. She had never seen her use it. Perhaps the plant was rare here. She could show her how to steep it in boiling water and treat wounds with it. She was so excited that she wanted to gather it right then, but she had her hands full with five ponies and a stubborn mule. And besides, she had no bits of food to put in the hole as an offering as Medicine Woman had taught her to do.

She noted the location of the yarrow so she could find it again as soon as she delivered the ponies. She would come back alone for it because she wanted it to be her secret, her gift. She did a little jig step as she imagined the smile on Medicine Woman's face. She skipped as she hurried the animals along, splashing through the shallows of the river and heading for camp. As she walked along she rehearsed the speech she would make to Medicine Woman, rummaging through her store of Comanche words for the ones that would express what she wanted to say.

Eagle and Wanderer were a few miles from camp, scouting for second-growth saplings to make arrow shafts, when they heard the rumble. It sounded like distant thunder in a cloudless sky, but they knew better. Without a word they kicked their ponies into a head-long gallop, the lash of their quirts counterpoint to the drumming of their heels against their horses' sides. Mile after mile the ground whipped by under them, long after a grain-fed horse would have collapsed.

When they hit the outskirts of camp they hardly slowed down. Wanderer went one way and Eagle another, both shouting as they rode. They tore among the lodges, scattering kettles, drying racks, dogs, and children. As though they had kicked an ants' nest, the village exploded into action, a chaos that spread outward from the riders. Women screamed for their children, dogs barked, ponies whinnied and plunged at their tethers.

Cynthia was threading her way through the maze of lodges, her precious yarrow plants clutched in her hands. Each time the camp was moved it was set up in a slightly different pattern. Pahayuca's lodges were always at the center, and Sunrise's were nearby, but the neighbors usually shifted, and the lodges still looked alike to her. She was following the route she had carefully memorized, and as the hysteria engulfed her she started running toward home. A wrong turn brought her up short. She fled down another alley between tents and knew she was lost. In panic she began running aimlessly.

"Takes Down The Lodge. Star Name. *Ha-itska ein*, where are you?" All around her people worked quickly and grimly, dismantling the lodges and packing them away. With the precision of years of practice, the camp fell apart. Tents collapsed around her. The coverings weighed 125 pounds each and took two or more women to fold. The towering skeletons of the lodges toppled slowly after the hide slid off them. Cynthia dodged the heavy poles as they swayed and fell. She leaped aside to avoid being trampled by a herd of wild-eyed ponies driven in from the outskirts of camp by a dozen yelling boys. Others thundered by on all sides of her.

Sobbing, she ran on, knowing that something terrible had happened. Maybe it was an attack. Maybe her family had come after her. If so she had to find them. To tell them not to kill Takes Down or Sunrise or Star Name or Medicine Woman or even bratty Upstream. Or Owl or Name Giver. And Pahayuca had been kind to her, and Something Good. She had to save them.

She veered instinctively when she heard more hooves pounding behind her. A pair of strong hands gripped her under the arms and swung her onto the back of the coal-black pony. Wanderer held her in front of him as he galloped through the village. The lodge with the bright yellow sun on it was gone. In its place were the four main poles with the beds and possessions still lying about, strangely naked and exposed. Wanderer leaped down before Night had stopped and ran to help Black Bird and Star Name pull down their lodge.

Night was heaving and retching, his eyes rolling and his legs trembling with fatigue when Cynthia climbed down from his back. She threw her arms around his wet neck and hugged him before running to help Takes Down. Without thinking, she began folding the heavy hides from the beds, bouncing up and down on them to crease them. Sunrise was already loading everything onto the pack-horses and mule that Cynthia had brought in earlier. Caught up in their frenzy, she forgot about the soldiers and being rescued. She had moved with Takes Down and Sunrise five times, but this time was different. There was no order of packing. She just picked up armloads of things and stuffed them into whichever saddle bag or pouch had room.

The People had already begun to pack when Eagle and Wanderer arrived. And they could dismantle a village of a thousand souls in less than fifteen minutes. It wasn't fast enough. Over the shouts and banging of the poles and gear, Cynthia heard a dull rumbling. It grew, ugly and ominous. The pace increased as people began driving their ponies full speed toward the low bluff. A long, creamy wave, beaten to a foam and a mixture of almost equal parts sand and water, crept along the wide bottom lands to the canyon walls on either side. It hissed like a million snakes as it slithered along.

Already it was lapping at the heels of the laggards in the western edge of camp. About sixty feet behind it came a mass of water four feet high. Heavy rains in the uplands far to the west had sent it coursing through the narrow channels and gorges of the high plains. It spewed into the broader river bottoms downstream with the pressure of a colossal fire hose. More and more horses and mules labored up the slope toward the safety of higher ground. Poorly tied loads fell, scattering household gear with a clatter on the rocks. The lodge poles, tied into travois behind the horses, bounced crazily along. Tiny, wide-eyed children clung to the edges to keep from falling off.

Leaving what hadn't been packed yet, the People raced across the bottom lands. Cynthia rode double, bouncing in front of Takes Down on Rabbit Ears. She could see the load slipping on the mule in front of them, but there was nothing she could do about it. The hastily tied lines were loosening, and the pile of her family's robes was falling off to one side. She knew now the effort that went into making them, and she watched them fall with despair. A corner of the hide Cynthia had labored over dragged in the thick wet sand that flowed under them like thin cornmeal mush. She clenched her fists, willing the lines to hold until they reached safety.

Sunrise galloped ahead of them, herding the other packhorses. Suddenly he swooped down, sliding off his pony until he held on only by one foot hooked over the horse's backbone. He grabbed at something under a scrub oak bush and came up with a wailing child, a baby who must have fallen off one of the travois in the confusion.

All around them the villagers fled through the trees and up the slope, floundering as the sand crumbled under them and slid down the side of the bluff in sheets. Kettles and pots, racks of meat, toy bows and arrows, dresses and robes lay strewn about. Eagle was helping Something Good calm a mule that had panicked and bucked everything off, sending it flying through the air. As Cynthia and Takes Down passed, Cynthia saw a doll floating almost under Rabbit Ears' hoofs.

"Stop, *Pia*." Rabbit Ears braked and Cynthia jumped off. She grabbed the doll and Takes Down pulled her back up. It was Something Good's doll. She held it to her chest as they raced up the sandy bluff, the pony pawing desperately for footholds.

As they reached the top of the bluff, Takes Down turned the horse around to look back. The four-foot wall of water rose gradually to the rear until it was fifteen feet high and studded with logs and debris, entire trees rolling and plunging like twigs in the flood. The noise was deafening, like being under the biggest waterfall Cynthia could imagine. At the top of the crest the body of a mule whirled slowly, his four legs sticking out of the foam. A few lodges were still erect where their owners had abandoned them. One stood alone, like a lighthouse in a stormy sea. The hide covering was still in place, and it seemed deserted.

Cynthia watched Wanderer head for it with the water swirling around Night's hocks. As he slid down and disappeared inside, Night gave a shrill cry that rose over the oncoming wave. He poked his head through the door, as though urging his friend to hurry. Wanderer ran out with a few bags and looped them over his saddle horn. Then he ducked back in and came out with a large bundle of robes and blankets in his arms. He balanced it in front of the saddle and leaped on from the rear. Holding it with one hand, he headed Night toward the bluff.

The water was belly high now and the huge wave loomed over the campsite. The exhausted horse struggled desperately with his double load, and the scene seemed almost frozen, acted out in slow motion. Night lost his footing and was swept thirty feet before he regained it. He surged a few feet closer to higher ground, then began swimming, his eyes bulging with the strain while the wave hung poised over them.

"Come on, Night." Cynthia's hands were clenched, her knuckles white. Tears were rolling unheeded down her cheeks and everything was blurry. "You can do it, Night. Swim. Please swim."

The wall of water hit and washed over them. They came to the surface and whirled downstream, dwindling until finally lost among the debris. A pecan tree glided sedately after them, its tangled roots jutting up like an enormous, tattered sail.

"He's not so bad, you know." John had meant Eagle when he said that, but Cynthia thought of Wanderer's handsome, mocking face. He hadn't fooled her with his charming ways. She'd been right about him all along. He was a thief. Their hero had turned back to do the unthinkable, to steal from one of the People. All of them in danger of their lives, and he was looting. He deserved to die. She was glad. But did he have to take Night with him?

The pony had been her only friend and solace on the nightmare journey from the fort. She remembered his velvety muzzle tickling her palm as he ate the sweet grass she held out to him. He would lower his head so she could scratch his ears, and he flicked them when she whispered to him, as though answering her. If she stopped scratching before he was ready, he would butt her between the shoulderblades as she walked away.

They both felt guilty about it. Cynthia was afraid Wanderer would be enraged if he caught her making friends with his horse. He was so possessive of Night. And Night seemed to feel he was betraying a trust. When they were together he always looked around him with something akin to furtiveness in his soft brown eyes. Now he was gone because of Wanderer's greed. Cynthia lowered her face onto the pony's neck and cried into the coarse hair. Vengeance was hers, and its taste was bitter.

Takes Down patted her shoulder to comfort her. She flicked the single rein looped around her pony's underlip and kicked her lumpy sides to catch up with the others. The band fanned out across the hills, following Pahayuca and mountainous Hahki, Blocks The Sun, his number-one wife. Cynthia leaned back, sinking into her foster mother's warm, plump body. She felt the short arms curl protectively around her as Takes Down guided Rabbit Ears into the dust of the fleeing villagers.

By the time they found another campsite, it was too dark to set up the lodges. It didn't take much time, normally, to erect the tent and have a paunch of buffalo stew boiling. But now everything was thrown into the packs in a jumble or scattered over miles of wild country. And many people didn't even have what they needed to put up their lodges. There would be a great deal of swapping and loaning and sharing and helping until everything was replaced.

The land had leveled out and bristled with agave, prickly pear and an occasional mesquite. Against the horizon, their tops sheared off, a ring of bluffs encircled them. They hulked there, brooding and black against the graying sky. At first glance it looked like a grim, inhospitable place, but at the edge of their camp was a ravine. It was choked with wild grape and plum bushes, and a cold stream ran through it. There was buffalo sign all around, and some of the men were getting ready to start a hunt in the morning. Pahayuca always said that with so much territory to choose from they'd be fools to camp in any but the best places. Staying along the flooded river was out of the question. The water was too foul and muddy to drink, and it rampaged between its new banks like a wild animal rattling the sides of its cage.

Fires flickered against the black sky as each family gathered for a quick meal of whatever they could find in the jumble of their possessions. Cynthia shivered in the night breeze as she sorted through the saddle bags, searching for her rabbit fur robe. She looked over at Upstream, his face outlined by the fire. He usually buzzed around like a cicada on a string, but now he sat with his lower lip pushed out and his eyes bunched. A few tears made furrows in the dirt on his face. Sunrise simply stared into the flames while Takes Down and Black Bird talked quietly together. They would be talking about Wanderer's death, and she didn't want to hear it. To hear them mourn Wanderer as though he were special. Pieces of the day whirled in her head, a kaleidoscope with Wanderer's elegant, arrogant face at the center. Was he going to haunt her because she had wished him dead?

Star Name caused a ripple in the gloom as she appeared silently from the dark and sat down. She had been touring the bedraggled camp, checking up on her many friends, and two were missing.

"*Ha-itska* Nocona, where is Wanderer?" she asked.

"Medicine Woman was sick. He was trying to save her. We do not know if they are alive or not." Takes Down lowered her head and studied the fire, tears streaming down her cheeks. Cynthia froze, her hand in the saddle bag. She had understood most of what Takes Down said.

"Was Medicine Woman in her lodge when Wanderer went in?"

"Yes." Takes Down could hardly talk and her soft voice quavered. "She had the shaking sickness. Wanderer told Pahayuca he would get her. Now they're both gone."

A sudden chill shook Cynthia, and it was more than the night air. Wanderer and Medicine Woman were both dead. And he wasn't a thief. "No," she whispered in English. "I'm sorry, Wanderer. I didn't know." Remorse made the tears sting even more. She remembered the shy smile he had given her when he handed her the string figure. *He's not so bad, you know.* And she remembered Medicine Woman the afternoon she had gone gathering herbs with her. They had wandered the hills and ravines around camp, lost in their quest. Medicine Woman seemed oblivious to time. It stopped around her. The world narrowed to just the two of them, and finding herbs was the only important thing in it.

She remembered squatting over a tiny, delicate plant, feeling its leaves while Medicine Woman tried to explain to her how to prepare it and what it would do. They sat for a long time watching a black beetle, shimmering with irridescent fireworks as he patiently rolled his ball of dung ahead of him, lost in some mission of his own.

"The dung beetle can show you where the buffalo herd is."

"How, *Kaku*, Grandmother?"

Medicine Woman tapped the beetle's horns lightly with her fingernail.

"His horns point toward them."

"Why?"

"Some say it's because they have strong medicine. But I think, perhaps, being so close to the ground they can feel the vibrations of the buffalos before we can. What do you think?" She smiled at Cynthia in that mischievous way she had, all her wrinkles moving and deepening on her face.

Cynthia never went anywhere now without studying everything around her.

"Watch the animals, see what they eat," Medicine Woman had told her. "They know what cures." It was as though she had never really seen the world before. And the more Medicine Woman and Takes Down taught her, the more wonderful it all became. Now there was an emptiness in her life. She shivered as she pulled the rabbit fur robe from the bag and wrapped it around her. She found Something Good's doll and clutched it with her free hand, the other holding the robe closed at her chest.

"Come on, Star Name. Let's go find Something Good." She had to move, to do something besides sit and mourn and think of the injustice she had done Wanderer.

The two of them threaded their way through the groups gathered around fires, stumbling now and then over piles of loose gear and ropes. There was rarely litter in Pahayuca's camp, but tonight everyone was too despondent to care. They were mourning Medicine Woman and Wanderer, but quietly, not officially yet. They knew that if anyone could survive the wave, Night could. They would wait before they grieved in earnest.

"Something Good, I found your doll." Cynthia held the sodden toy out to her.

"It makes my heart glad to see it, little one. Put it over there with my saddle." She sat with Blocks The Sun and Tosa Amah, Silver Rain, Pahayuca's other wives. Something Good was roasting a paste of pounded hackberries mixed with fat for Pahayuca's three youngest children. She pointed the stick at Dusty, who scraped the paste off with her fingers and took a small bite out of it. She smiled bashfully at them, the only smile in the group. Pahayuca's chunky seven-year-old son, Haista Amawau, Little Apple, and his daughter, Kesua, Hard To Get Along With, had already eaten theirs. Their mouths were rimmed with a shiny ring of grease. The roasted hackberry paste was as good as candy, and the girls watched hungrily while Something Good molded more of it around the stick.

"The next batch will be for you, sisters."

"Something Good, will Medicine Woman and Wanderer come back?" Cynthia almost believed that if she asked enough people the question one of them would answer yes, and it would be so.

"I don't know, little one. Wanderer and Medicine Woman have strong spirits watching over them. And Night is the best horse I have ever seen. We have to trust their medicine." The grief in their eyes pained her and she patted the robe next to her. "Sit here and I'll tell you how Ahtamu, the grasshopper, got his beautifully painted robes. He used to be gray, you know." Everyone except Cynthia did know, but it didn't matter. They all moved in closer to hear the story, even Blocks The Sun and Silver Rain.

Around them the camp with its flickering fires was eerily still. There was rarely a night when the drums weren't pounding and voices chanting a song for dancers, or the men weren't boasting about their coups or shouting around a handful of dice. Sometimes a young man would be serenading his love with his flute, and the dogs would howl mournfully in accompaniment.

But tonight there was only Gets To Be An Old Man, lying on his back out on the prairie, alternately quavering and yodeling his medicine chants. From one of the sawed-off bluffs ringing the horizon a coyote took up the song, as though in response. The full moon had risen over the same bluff, silhouetting the coyote in stark relief.

Later that night the two girls lay rolled together in a single robe, their heads drawn in like twin turtles to escape the singing mosquitoes. The insects and the ringing in her ears blended with her memory of the water's thunder and Night's desperate shriek. The coyote began howling again, and she silently asked it what had happened to her friends. Coyote would know. Coyotes could tell the future, Sunrise said. If only she could understand what he was saying.

Finally she threw back the robe, grateful that a rising wind had blown away the mosquitoes. She rolled over, reached out, and put an arm around her friend's slim, smooth waist. Laying her cheek against Star Name's shoulder blade, she let the steady rise and fall of the child's breathing put her to sleep.

She was still asleep when Eagle woke up at dawn. He saddled his pinto, gathered extra supplies and two packhorses, and rode off toward the rising sun. He went grimly in search of his friend, determined to find him alive or to bring back his bones in the empty buckskin sack he carried with him.

❧ *11* ❧

Cynthia coughed and choked on the dust blowing in her face in billows. It settled everywhere, the cloud following them as they rode. And they were near the front of the procession. She wondered what it must be like for those following behind. The column stretched for more than a mile, winding through the hills. The dry, hot wind had seared her sinuses and tear ducts until her eyes and nose burned. Her lips felt like sawdust, and the skin on her hands and legs was cracked like alligator hide, with dry flakes peeling off. An umbrella. What she wouldn't have given for an umbrella between her and the sun. She was riding the old mule as usual, and her bare thighs were sore from his mangy back.

At first it had been exciting to move. Like a parade or a gypsy camp or a circus. Upstream and his friends galloped, yelling, from the sides of the column. They beat game from the bushes—birds and rabbits and mice—and shot at it with their toy bows and arrows. The older boys raced their ponies, charging and whooping as they pretended to swoop down on sleeping enemies. The travois poles, heavy with piles of robes and bundles and with round willow-withe cages of tiny children, clattered over the stony ground. The dogs fought constantly, and the betting was always heavy on the outcome of their brawls.

As they rode, three or four abreast, the women gossiped. Their babies swung in the long, fringed cradle boards that hung from their saddle horns. The two planks that formed the V-shaped back of each cradle board extended above the baby's head and were sharpened into points. Even if the board fell the points would bury themselves in the ground and the baby's head would be protected.

Cynthia envied the four- and five-year-olds as they sat effortlessly atop their fat, tranquil ponies. Their short, chubby legs stuck straight out from their horses' sides. At the head of the women rode Blocks The Sun, Pahayuca's first wife. She always occupied the coveted lead position, out of most of the dust and able to pick the best camping place when they arrived.

No one would have disputed the position with her, even if she hadn't been Pahayuca's favorite wife. She weighed three hundred pounds and had been known to crack a man's ribs in an affectionate hug. No horse could hold her, so she traveled on a specially made travois. She rode backwards on it now, waving her arms and leading the gossip. She was solemn today, but usually her eyes were merry, when they could be spotted among the folds of her face.

Pahayuca liked to complain that he had to ask Takes Down, the band's best lodge-cover maker, to sew Blocks The Sun's dresses. But she was the one who waited on his guests and carried his shield and lance when they moved camp. And she always set up a lodge next to her own for visitors.

The warriors rode apart, some behind, some to the sides, and some ahead, their bows and lances ready to defend their families. A man never carried anything that would interfere with his weapons. There was a constant jingle and clatter of bells and kettles and metal bridle ornaments. Feathers and streamers fluttered in the wind, and the long fringe on the clothes and tack bounced to the rhythm of the ponies' gait. The People were happiest when they were mounted and moving, and they designed their clothes and gear to look best when in motion. Some of the war ponies had brightly painted buffalo robes draped across their withers, in barbaric imitation of the early Spanish conquistadors. It gave the procession a courtly dignity. But it had become so familiar to Cynthia that now she thought more about the discomfort than the romance of it all.

"Why do the People move so often?"

Bemused, Takes Down looked at her. "We have to move."

"But *tosi-tivo*, white people, don't move every few days the way we do." Cynthia blurted it out before she thought, but Takes Down didn't seem to make the connection between her blue-eyed daughter and white people.

"White people don't know how to live. Sunrise tells me they stab Mother Earth with sharp metal sticks and destroy her. They cut down all the trees, not just the ones they need for their lodges. And they let their horses eat all the grass, then grow different grass for them and feed them only the seeds. And the horses can't run as well. The People could never live like that."

"But the People wouldn't have to dig in Mother Earth's breast. Why can't we stay in one place and hunt?"

"There's no reason to stay in one place."

"I liked the last place we camped. I wanted to stay there longer. It was a pretty place."

"But, Naduah, the next place will be pretty too. Pahayuca picks pretty places. There are many of them. We can enjoy them all. And then come back later and enjoy them again. And the animals don't stay in one place, especially when they're being hunted. We have to move on when they leave.

"Besides, if you could smell the big winter camp after the spring thaw, you wouldn't ask why we move. So many people and animals leave piles of dung. Also, if we stay in one place it is easy for our enemies to find us."

And that was the other, unspoken reason that Cynthia wanted to stay longer where they were. She still had a faint hope that her family would find her and rescue her or ransom her. But by now it was probably more from a sense of duty than from a desire to leave her foster people. She thought of her brother, John, and wondered where he was.

"Will we see other bands of the People sometime?" Did she dare mention John? "I would like to see my brother."

"Your brother is with Old Owl's band. We will see them. We will spend the winter with them."

The winter? It was only June. She wondered how John and Upstream would get along. They were alike in many ways. Maybe the two of them and she and Star Name could run away together. She tried to imagine the reception they'd get at Parker's Fort. Then she gave it up and nodded on the mule, drifting off into a nap. Behind the caravan, at the very end of the line, rode Buffalo Piss, setting up stone markers pointing out their direction of travel.

Cynthia sat under the cottonwood and whittled at the L-shaped shinny stick, very much like the one she had brandished at Takes Down and Star Name and Medicine Woman the first morning in their lodge. Now she knew what it was, and was making one of her own. She shaved off long, curling slivers and smoothed it, sighting down it to see where it needed trimming. Star Name sat beside her, sulking because she hadn't been allowed to play shinny with the older girls and women. But it wasn't in her nature to sulk long.

"Look out, Something Good!" She jumped up screaming and waving her arms. But Something Good had already sidestepped the blow that would have crippled her if it had connected with her knees. Most of the people in camp were lined up along the hundred-yard field. They cheered for their favorite team and made bets heavily. The noise was deafening as the twenty players screamed at each other, their sticks flailing in the sun.

They were each trying to knock the flattened deerskin ball toward the other team's goal post. The ball was about the size of a small cannon shot. It was stuffed with hair, and dust colored. Cynthia couldn't sit still either and stood shouting next to Star Name.

"Look at Takes Down. Run, *Pia*, run! Hit the ball." She threw her hands over her eyes. "I can't look, Star Name. Someone's going to be killed."

"No one from this band has ever been killed playing shinny." Star Name spoke matter-of-factly, her eyes never leaving the action. "But a woman was killed last year. Our team was playing against Old Owl's band when it happened. I saw it."

"Look at Takes Down run, Star Name. I never would have believed she could move so fast."

"She's good, but she's not as good as my mother." Actually, the two were about equal, but Black Bird did shed her shy manner as soon as she walked out onto the playing field. She raced and screamed and looked like she would kill anyone who came between her and that lump of buckskin. Behind them sat Cynthia's mangy new friend, scratching her teeming flea colony and panting in the scanty shade. The dog had spotted a soft touch and gradually insinuated herself into the child's life. Now she followed her everywhere.

"What shall we name her?" Cynthia knew that names were important, although she wasn't sure if they were important for dogs.

"I don't know. Why don't you call her Dog?" Star Name didn't seem to think it was a vital decision.

"Dog?"

"Sure. That way everyone will know her name without even being introduced. And if we think of a better name we can call her that." So Dog it was.

Takes Down had been right. Pahayuca had found another wonderful place to camp. The seventy lodges of the Wasp band stood scattered among an open grove of cottonwoods along a clear, deep stream. It ran through a valley about a mile and a half wide, with high, ragged hills on each side. The grass that hadn't been trampled stood waist high, and the horses were grazing contentedly, picking out the most succulent blades. The playing field took up a large part of the level valley bottom that wasn't included in the camp and its pasture.

She allowed her attention to stray for a moment and saw movement at the far end of the valley. Rangers? Her heart skipped. They were really coming for her this time. Should she yell? Should she sneak toward them so they wouldn't attack her friends? She sidled away from Star Name and stared into the shimmering air, trying to sort out the images. Four horses picked their way down the twisting trail and started slowly across the valley floor. As they approached she recognized the proud, ebony pony, his long plume of a tail flowing out behind him.

"Star Name. *Nabone*, look!" Cynthia's voice rang out over the noise of the game. The game ended instantly and became a foot race as the players dropped their sticks and ran toward the riders.

Sitting straight and loose and solemn, Eagle rode first. Behind him came his packhorses, one with an improvised travois and litter. On it rode Medicine Woman. She was hollow-eyed and looked as though her face had been rubbed with ashes from the morning fire.

Wanderer brought up the rear. Pahayuca galloped from camp on the big bay that had once been a Mexican rancher's pride, and rode alongside Wanderer. Wrapping his bear's arms around him, he embraced Wanderer from atop his horse. Wanderer laughed as he gasped for breath.

"Ara, my uncle, spare me your gratitude. It'll kill me."

"Wanderer, my son, we feared that you and my sister were dead."

"I said I would get her for you. You had no need to worry."

Medicine Woman began shivering with the chill that meant another attack of high fever. The malaria had weakened her, leaving her helpless with delirium when the flood hit. Wanderer had managed to save only her most precious things. Hanging from his saddle was the medicine bag that brought people from all over the Comanchería to see her. Silver Rain and Something Good led her pony toward the village. They took her not to Pahayuca's noisy, crowded set of lodges, but to her son's. So it was that Medicine Woman came to live with Sunrise and Takes Down, and Cynthia became a granddaughter again.

Cynthia's temples throbbed in time to the drum that had been beating for hours, along with her headache. The heat and odor and fumes in the tent were stifling. But worst of all was what's-his-name's voice. What was his name? She'd always tried to avoid him. He was an irascible old geezer, seduced only by Star Name's honeyed way. She could make him grin a toothless grimace until he looked like a living death's head. His cheeks collapsed into his empty mouth and the skin around his eyes gathered into tiny pleats.

Now he was naked as usual, except for the greasy, filthy breechclout that always seemed about to fall off his thin shanks. It bagged around his flat buttocks and gaped at his stringy thighs, exposing the worn medicine pouch that rode nestled in his hairless groin. There wasn't much more than willpower holding the breechclout up, and it made Cynthia nervous to see him jumping around so. If his breechclout fell down she would laugh, in spite of everything. And she knew that would make everyone angry with her.

His voice sounded like sandpaper and had gotten worse as he became hoarser with each passing hour. His chanting was marvelous only for its monotony, rather like a machine badly in need of oil. Poor Medicine Woman. This couldn't be helping her.

Gets To Be An Old Man. That's who he was. She remembered Star Name's imitation of him as she acted out his name, sucking her cheeks in and scolding like a jay. Gets To Be An Old Man must be the camp quack, and now he was tormenting poor Medicine

Woman. Why didn't she heal herself if she was the powerful medicine woman everyone claimed her to be? Maybe her medicine only worked for others, or when she was strong and well. The tension and anxiety in the camp added to her own fears for Medicine Woman. She bowed her head and whispered a prayer, asking the God she knew to spare a good woman.

Takes Down came in with another armload of green cedar branches and threw them on the fire. The needles sent up a shower of sparks that crackled like thousands of tiny firecrackers. Fresh billows of pungent smoke spewed toward the top of the lodge. Gets To Be An Old Man blew on Medicine Woman, and fanned her with five eagle feathers. His assistant, a sour-looking boy, drummed on until it seemed as though his beating and the drone of the old man would never cease. She could have left the lodge, but she was afraid something terrible might happen while she was gone.

After six hours the fever broke and the patient's gentle, lined face glistened with sweat. Old Man gathered up his paraphernalia, beckoned to his drummer and trooped out of the lodge, waving his arms triumphantly to those outside, like a circus act making a grand exit. Sunrise went with him to arrange payment and get a prescription. Some aspects of medicine were the same everywhere.

Takes Down busied herself with the evening meal, and a blessed peace settled over the lodge. Cynthia crept over to Medicine Woman's pallet, knelt, and looked down at the still face. When the old woman opened her eyes, there were golden flecks in them, like tiny chips of iron pyrite, fool's gold. The child wiped the perspiration from the soft skin, stretched like parchment over high cheekbones. She brushed wet wisps of hair from her grandmother's high forehead. Medicine Woman smiled and reached out a thin hand that still trembled. Cynthia took it and stroked the back of it, feeling the pulse pounding far too fast in the slender wrist.

"Hi, *Kaku, nei mataoyo?* How are you, Granddaughter, my little one?" They were the first words Medicine Woman had spoken since that morning when she'd been laid, shaking like treetops in the wind, on the bed.

"*Nei chat, Kaku,* I am well, Grandmother." Cynthia, now Naduah, fell into the rhythm of the People's words. And, as the days passed, into the rhythm of their lives.

❧ *12* ❧

It was an afternoon the color of a tarnished gun barrel, and unusually chill for early July. Naduah sat under her rabbit robe with Star Name. Together they watched the small fire. The flames flickered hypnotically, a work of art that changed and danced in patterns of delicate beauty. The few stray raindrops that fell through the smoke hole hissed and turned to steam as they landed.

Outside, the tent was besieged. Rain drummed the sides in random surges, until it sounded like a thousand fists and the air inside seemed to reverberate. Lumps of hail as big as robin's eggs beat an erratic tattoo on the taut hide while thunder boomed like cannons and grumbled off through the distant hills. Wind whipped the rain into a frenzy as it fell, driving walls of it diagonally into the ground with such force that it rose again in a misty spray. The mat of thick grass on the valley floor kept the ground from absorbing it all. It ran in rivers around the lodges until they seemed to float in a broad, shallow sea.

The narrow trench dug around the tent had long since overflowed. Beds and belongings were pulled away from the sides to escape the wet, probing fingers that poked under the dew cloth. This leather curtain hung draped all the way around the walls, tied to the lodge poles about six feet up. It overlapped onto the floor, channeling to the outside the water that ran into the smoke hole. In the center of the floor the children were dry. They sat on carpets of buffalo hides with the hair left on, cushioned by the thick, woolly nap.

As the billowing gray clouds had gathered, herded by a rising wind, Naduah had gone outside with Owl to close in the smoke hole. A howling, gale-force gust snapped the ends of her breechclout around her as the first huge, icy drops splashed on her bare head and shoulders. Naduah struggled with one of the two eighteen-foot poles attached to the winglike flaps at the top of the lodge. She and Owl closed them, like an old man pulling his coat's lapels around his chin to keep out the wind. The pole flexed and pitched, bucking in her small hands, until she wedged it in place. She shook it to make sure it was solidly planted. Owl had finished first, but knew better than to offer help. For someone who had wasted nine years of her life with white people, Naduah was closing fast on the rest of the field. Owl admired her for it.

They pulled back the heavy hide door and stepped over the low threshold into the warm lodge. The weights in the bottom of the door hide kept it closed even in the wind. It was dim and dry inside. Owl's mother, She Laughs, passed Naduah a strip of roasted squash, ballast brought back with the corn and tobacco, the real cargo of the last trading trip to the Tuhkanay, the Wichita, three hundred miles to the northeast. The hot squash was sweet and tender. Naduah scraped the last bits of it off the skin with her teeth, threw the rind into the fire, and wiped her hands on her breechclout. Then she gave Name Giver her full attention. Name Giver took up the story of how the Nermenuh, the People, separated from their brothers, the Shoshone, long ago. As he spoke he worked on a war arrow for Wanderer.

The light was dim, but it made no difference to Owl's grandfather. Cataracts had slowly eclipsed his sight, shrouding his eyes more each year until they were glazed with a thick, milky film, like clouds over the moon. He said they gave him the feeling of already being in the spirit world, surrounded by shadowy forms and disembodied voices. His calm, thoughtful face sometimes did seem to be off somewhere communing with souls unseen.

He was the children's favorite choice for Guess Who because they didn't have to bother blindfolding him. They would sit in a row with their legs stretched out in front of them while Name Giver felt along the line. He would choose a child, pick her up, and sling her over his broad back with her head hanging down. Then he would pace in a circle while the others asked his captive questions.

"Do you have a saddle?" "Do you have a pony?" "Do you have a doll?" When Name Giver guessed who his victim was by the sound of her voice the others rushed him, crying they were going to eat him. They tickled him unmercifully until they were all rolling on the ground with laughter. Naduah had introduced the variation of Blind Man's Bluff, but it wasn't as popular. Probably because no one was tickled.

Now Name Giver was creating long, slender death that sang as it searched out its victims. With Owl's help he still made the best arrows in the band, working by the feel of them in his huge, powerful hands. Sometimes Naduah helped Owl pull the cord that twirled the bowlike lathe used to true the shafts. But only Owl was allowed to buff off the rough spots on them with an ancient piece of pumice, treasured in the family for years, and almost worn away.

Bundles of green dogwood shoots, in various stages of seasoning, lay piled around the lodge or hung from the tops of the lodge poles. As it passed by them the smoke seasoned them and killed any insects in them.

Name Giver was finishing a shaft by greasing the few almost imperceptible crooked places. Then he drew it through two grooved sandstone slabs fitted together to form a cylindrical mold. When the shaft was as round as he could make it and tapered just right, he lined it up with the tips of his fingers and pulled it through a round hole cut in a disk of bone. A sharp spur projecting from the edge of the hole gouged a groove along the arrow.

Name Giver made four such grooves in each shaft. Two were straight and the other two he curved by rotating his wrist as he pulled the shaft through. Owl would later paint the grooves, the straight ones black and the spiral ones red. The grooves kept the arrows from warping and represented the path it would follow with the speed of lightning. They also formed channels for the blood to run out in, weakening the prey faster.

Then the shaft was rubbed until it gleamed, and still it was far from finished. It had to have the feathers added and the point made. The arrowheads were painstakingly cut from the iron barrel hoops and other metal stolen from the white men. They were sharpened with files traded from the Comancheros, and then hardened by heating them in the fire and dropping them in cold water. They took longer to make than the old flint arrowheads, but they were stronger and sharper. And if one was lucky, one could buy packets of ready-made ones from the traders. A dozen points that cost the trader six cents brought him a buffalo hide from the Indians.

For Wanderer's arrow Name Giver would paint three red lines around the base of the shaft. They were his crest, the identifying mark that separated his arrows from others. Each man had a different one. The war arrows had their points set at right angles to the bowstring so they would penetrate between human ribs. Hunting arrows were set parallel to the bow so they would pass between buffalo ribs. Name Giver was making war arrows with the points loosely attached and barbed. When the point entered the body it pulled off the shaft and rotated crosswise in the wound, making it difficult to extract without tearing the flesh.

A warrior usually carried a hundred such arrows with him, and could shoot them from a running horse fast enough to keep one in the air all the time. A good hunting arrow, loosed by an expert bowman, could drive completely through a buffalo's body from a distance of ten to fifteen yards.

Name Giver's arrows were known for the care he took, and for the slender grooves painted red and black. His arrows always struck with the feathered end tilted upward, which meant they were perfectly balanced. Name Giver would have a purpose until his strength failed and his hands trembled, gnarled by arthritis like an ancient mesquite tree. Until Owl married and left and there was no one to gather dogwood or turn the lathe.

The young men didn't want to learn such things now. All they thought about were the clumsy, ugly *ella cona*, the fire rods of the white men. They couldn't shoot as far or as accurately or as fast as arrows. One shot and the game for miles around scattered. They were always jamming and exploding and turning on their masters. Skinny And Ugly was missing the ends of two fingers thanks to his ancient musket. The guns didn't fire at all if their powder got wet. And no matter how many the warriors stole, they could never keep up with the white men.

Besides, they couldn't steal enough powder and shot to practice with, so they weren't nearly as accurate with their precious guns as they were with reliable bows and arrows. Just getting their powder across streams was a major preoccupation. With arrows all a man had to do was shoot them over to the other side and retrieve them when he crossed. Someday the young men would see the folly of lusting after weapons that were of no use to them. Name Giver knew there would always be a need for his craft, when the white men were destroyed and their bad influence washed away like rain washes dust from the lodges.

Naduah sat as contented as a kitten in front of the fire, listening to the fury outside and basking in the cozy warmth inside. Somewhere in her month and a half of work and play and rambles with Star Name she had shed her other name. She thought of herself as Naduah now, She Keeps Warm With Us. She was Star Name's friend and sister, Medicine Woman's granddaughter, and Takes Down The Lodge's daughter. She concentrated on Name Giver's long, meandering tale.

"Rainbows are the breath of the Great Lizard," he said, painting a rainbow across the air of the tent with a sweep of his arm. "The Great Lizard soothes the angry Thunderbird." And his face twisted into a hideous mask as he loomed over the children, a terrible Thunderbird with outstretched wings, spanning the world to the horizon.

"The Thunderbird's shadow is the vast cloud overhead, and lightning flashes from his eyes. The thunder is the sound of his huge wings flapping, and the rain spills from the lake on his back." Name Giver lowered his voice to a hoarse whisper when he spoke of it, glancing up toward the top of the tent from time to time.

Naduah held her breath, straining forward to hear and understand, her blue eyes wide with fear. She looked up when Name Giver did, expecting to see the Thunderbird's baleful, red-veined eye peering through the smoke hole at her. Chills chased each other up and down her spine. No wonder the People rarely went out in the rain, unless it was absolutely necessary.

* * *

"Blocks The Sun sent me to straighten up here. She says men make such a mess everywhere they go. We thought you were both out visiting." Something Good stood just inside the door, looking like a frightened deer about to take flight. The dripping hide she had draped over her head lay in a puddle of water behind her. Her two-piece dress of thin suede was wet and clung to her body even more than usual. The dress was plain except for the heavy fringe at the hem and shoulders, but Something Good had no need of ornaments. Her thick black hair was plaited into braids wrapped with thongs. The rain had blown so hard that they had gotten wet under the hide umbrella.

"Wanderer is with Buffalo Piss and Big Bow," said Eagle. "He probably won't be back tonight. I didn't want to spend the day telling foolish stories when there are things in my heart I can't speak of at all." Eagle stirred the fire with a stick, sparks and flames leaping higher as the air reached them.

"I'll leave you to your thoughts then. You seem to prefer their company these days." Another burst of thunder detonated nearby. Something Good flinched, but turned to pick up her rain covering.

"Don't go back out there. Blocks The Sun shouldn't have sent you here in this storm." He knew why she had been sent. Wives usually got along very well, but one as young and as beautiful as Something Good would suffer from another's envy and jealousy. Maybe Blocks The Sun herself didn't realize that she was treating the girl unfairly, but there was no other reason to make her go outside in this.

As to how Pahayuca must treat her, Eagle couldn't think of it without jealousy and anger putting a hard hand around his heart and squeezing it. Huge, fat, simple Pahayuca and slender Something Good. She was a chief's daughter and the wife of a chief and her life was theirs to command. How often did she feel the tug of the cord that passed from her husband's bed, out under his lodge wall, and into that of her own? What did she feel as she folded a blanket around her naked body and walked, barefoot, hair loose and flowing, to him? A flush of anger and shame warmed Eagle's face, and he bent to hide it. She stooped down, collected the hide, and shook drops from it.

"I would rather go outside than stay here with someone who hates me."

"I don't hate you." But he sounded surly and kept his eyes down, not wanting to look into hers. He knew if he did his soul would fall into their depths and never be his own again. And his promise to his brother, Wanderer, would be the ashes that sift through one's fingers and blow away in the wind.

Some things happen only once in a man's life. Only once does he feel the thrill of killing a buffalo for the first time, of seeing the arrow slant at just the right angle to pass into the tiny spot behind the short rib, then forward and down into the heart, bringing a ton of flesh crashing to the ground. Only once does he sink his knife into another for the first time and see his enemy go limp and powerless, eyes glazed over in the orgasm of death.

There is only one first time to enter a woman's moist, soft passage. He couldn't remember his first woman's name, but he could remember the volcano of pleasure that trembled and erupted, leaving him spent and astonished and delighted with the prospect of doing it for years to come.

He knew there would only be one Something Good in his life, and that he couldn't have her. He folded his arms across his knees and clenched his fists to keep from reaching toward her. And so they remained, silent, while the cold rain drummed outside. Something Good shivered from the damp.

"Come here and dry off," Eagle finally said. "No one will expect you back until this is over. I've wanted to talk to you for a long time." He felt like he was treading a narrow mountain path, with sheer drop-offs on either side and a strong wind blowing. One toyed with one's life, but not with a promise to a brother. He should leave, but his legs refused to obey him.

Staring into the fire, he felt, rather than heard, Something Good silently cross the lodge and sit near him. The smell of her, of smoke and wet leather and a trace of wild sage, made him drunk. Still he watched the flames, his muscles tense and a slow, hot ache building in his groin. For an instant he was angry with her for doing this to him. Then he thought of her gentle face, with no trace of arrogance or guile, and the anger melted.

"I don't hate you. You know that."

"Yes. I know it." She too stared into the fire.

"I promised Wanderer that I wouldn't betray Pahayuca. That's why I've been avoiding you. Seeing you and not being able to have you is like a painful wound that won't heal." He placed another stick on the fire, careful to put only one end in. To lay a stick across a fire was bad luck. "I should leave here and go back to the Staked Plains and the Quohadi."

"No!" She gave a small start and masked it by reaching up to untie her braids. She ran her fingers through them to untangle them and shook out her hair. The plaiting and the dampness made it stand out, a thick, wispy nimbus of ebony and gold firelight around her small, beautiful face. "Please don't go."

When Eagle looked at her at last, all he saw were her huge, dark eyes, gleaming with tears. He reached over and laid his hand along her cheek, his thumb wiping the drop away from the corner of her eye.

"If you leave, I'll still love you," she said. "And if I can't have you, I'll still love you. And if you marry another, I'll always be yours. Even when the fire has been smothered and ashes raked over it, it lives underneath, smoldering there until it's uncovered and someone blows on it."

He slid his hand slowly down her face and rested it in the curve of her neck and shoulder. He paused, then caressed further, stroking her chest and ribs. When he reached her waist, he put his hand under the edge of her cape and moved back up her warm, satiny body. As he cupped his fingers around her small breast, brushing the taut nipple lightly with his thumb, he could feel the pounding of her heart and the shudder that passed over her. His last sober thought before he laid her gently back on the robe was a rueful one. A man had no more formidable enemy than a woman. Against her there was no defense and no victory and no honor.

❧ *13* ❦

Rachel Plummer had reached the end of her tether. She no longer cared what they did to her. She figured if she was lucky they'd kill her and put her out of her misery. She grabbed a thick piece of kindling from the pile she had just hauled in on her back, and swung with all her strength. It caught Awoominot, A Little Less, completely off guard, landing on her chunky shoulder and dropping her like a sack of sand. The quirt with which she had been beating Rachel flew from her hand and spun a few times in the air before it landed. She lay there gaping in the litter around the frayed, patched lodge.

Rachel beat at her as the old woman scrabbled away on her back, pushing with her arms and legs like an overturned turtle doing the backstroke. The stick bounced off the woman's head and shoulders, splitting her forehead. Blood rained into her eyes. *Might as well be hung for a sheep as a lamb*, Rachel thought bitterly. As she struck she waited for a lance to bury itself in her back, or a hatchet to split her skull. She wondered with detachment what it would be like to have one's skull split by a hatchet. Would she feel anything? At least it would be quick.

A crowd of neighbors had gathered, laughing and shouting as though betting on a dogfight. Among them a stony-faced, tow-headed boy stood with his friends. *Give it to her, Rachel.* John Parker's fists were clenched, and he was torn between wanting to help his cousin and wanting to disown her. He felt a flush coloring his face and he turned away, beckoning angrily to his friends.

"*Mea-dro*, come on. Who wants to watch two women fight?" The five small boys stalked through the crowd like bantam cocks. Their miniature bows and arrow quivers hung rakishly across their backs, and ropes and lunch sacks swung from their breechclout belts. John didn't look back, nor to the right or left. He glared ahead to hide his pain and his guilt, and refused to admit that he had ever known Terrible Snows' white slave.

There was a low laugh behind Rachel, and Terrible Snows wrenched the club from her hands, spraining her wrist. She spun on him and went for his bulging toad's eyes, her thin fingers spread and curved like talons. Her eyes were wild, and she was hissing. Flecks of foam gathered in the corners of her bruised mouth. Terrible Snows dropped the stick and grabbed her wrists in a relentless grip. He held her while she writhed, pain shooting up her arms, then he shoved her backwards. She tripped over a broken saddle and fell sprawling. When A Little Less saw that she wasn't going to be clubbed to death, she set up a steady howl, and Rachel screamed back, propped on her elbows in the dirt.

"You filthy savages. You lousy, stupid, stinking savages. May you rot in hell!"

A Little Less was built like a nail keg on legs, and she now lay flailing on her back, unable to get up. Terrible Snows pulled his mother to her feet and kicked Rachel hard in the side to help her up. When A Little Less picked up a stick to resume her beating, he took it from her and pushed her into the lodge. She could be heard still grumbling and threatening as she slammed her kettle and stir stick and knives around, holding a dirty rag to her bleeding head. The show was over, and the neighbors went back to their evening meals.

Terrible Snows pulled off his damp, smelly moccasins and threw them in Rachel's face. But mending moccasins was recreation compared to tanning hides for hours each day or chasing barefoot through the brambles after the ponies. She gathered up the shoes and went to find her sewing materials in the chaos of the tent. She skirted the perimeter of it to avoid A Little Less, staying well out of arm's reach.

It looked like she was going to survive another day. She hadn't been killed or even punished. Yet. And Terrible Snows had laughed, ugly sound though it had been. She held her wrist as she reached up

112

involuntarily to touch the raw, painful spot on her nose where it had been burned again. It throbbed constantly from the torture of A Little Less and her outcast daughter, Toyahbi, Mountain. That would stop. Rachel had had enough. She would be a slave. She would eat scraps, the offal from the family's skimpy meals. She would suffer the horror of Terrible Snows' stinking breath and jutting belly at night, his thick, ugly, blotchy penis battering into her, tearing the dry, tender flesh. But there would be no more beatings or cuttings or burnings.

Rachel had always been thin. Now she was gaunt. There were purple bruises around her sunken eyes, from the beatings, but also from exhaustion and malnutrition. She looked like a scarecrow dressed in the scraps and patches she gleaned from the family's rags and leftover pieces of buckskin. They were sewn crazy-quilt fashion and flapped around her thin legs. The children chased her and threw clods of dirt and dung at her. There were always bruises and sores and open cuts on her arms and legs, and her hands were filthy and calloused. Rachel had just turned sixteen years old, and she looked a hundred. And her belly was swelling with her second child.

The thick chestnut hair that had always been her pride was an owl's nest. It was greasy and snarled beyond the power of a comb to correct, even if she had had one. She'd gotten out of the habit of bathing, but the bottom had come when she found herself popping a louse into her mouth the way A Little Less did. She cultivated her personal disorder, making herself as ugly as possible. She still hoped, after two months of abuse, that Terrible Snows would find her too repulsive to rape. But it seemed impossible to do.

At least she might discourage some of his friends. Terrible Snows was a very generous man when it came to his slave. She didn't wear out from that kind of use, and he found many men eager to try her. At night she lay with her head to one side, her body rigid and her eyes squeezed tightly shut. She tried to breathe as shallowly as possible until Terrible Snows had finished. And she thought of Luther, her husband. Luther with his bony body and the pale spot at the back of his head where the hair was thinning out.

She had done her duty by him. She had borne him a male child, and she was carrying another. And he had abandoned her. As the weeks passed and no one tried to ransom her, she became more and more bitter, dividing the blame for her misery between those who tormented her and those who let them do it. She'd show them all. She'd survive until someone happened onto the band, a trader maybe, or a trapper.

They were out here somewhere, those men. She'd seen them

113

milling around Independence when her family had passed through. There'd been hundreds of them, all outfitting for the wilderness. More people than she'd ever seen in one place. They left in long wagon trains, or in groups or in pairs. Now and then a man with a strange, feral look in his eyes would head out alone, leading a string of pack mules loaded high. The plains had swallowed them up, and the vast emptiness silenced them. At first they had seemed to grow as they rode out onto the prairie, their images distorted by the shimmering waves of heat that pulsed from the ground. Then they had vanished, like drops of water on a hot griddle. But they were out here somewhere. She could see their presence in the ribbons and beads and the new cotton jacket of Old Owl. They were out here. And she would wait for them to find her.

Terrible Snows and his family were plagued with bad luck. His horses were always the ones who died mysteriously of black lung, or were stolen by the Osage. His lodge was the one that had caught fire two years ago and burned to the ground, leaving them struggling to replace what little they had. They lived with cast-offs and gifts from others. Terrible Snows was always borrowing horses so he could hunt, and they were inferior animals. He never brought home as much meat as other men. He could never gather enough ponies to buy a wife, and his sister's infidelity to her husband was a constant reproach to him. He cursed his luck, swore some evil medicine man had put a spell on him. But inwardly he knew he was being blamed for his misfortune. He was treated like everyone else, but he knew there was shame around him, a barely perceptible shame, like meat just before it goes bad.

Terrible Snows and his mother and sister and white slave lived at the edge of the village, away from the more prosperous warriors clustered around the lodges of Old Owl, the civil leader, and Santa Ana, the war leader of the band. Terrible Snows swaggered and he boasted and he took his rage out on Rachel. It was the only life she knew with the People. That and the cruelty of the children, who could spot a weak member of the herd and run it to ground like wolves after a sick elk. Even John pretended he didn't know her. So much for loyalty of her own kind.

Later that night, after her fight with A Little Less, Rachel slipped silently through camp on her way to check the ponies. She ran furtively to avoid being tormented by anyone. She knew she would always be an outsider here, cold while others sat at their fires. Lonely while others talked and laughed in the evening shadows. Abused while others cared for each other. It never occurred to her to ask anyone for sanctuary. They were all alike. No one would help her here. She passed through the center of the village and headed for the pasture on the other side, her path lit by the fires shining through the lodge walls. The pasture would be dark, but there would be some light from the moon, and she would be away from Terrible Snows. Maybe he would be asleep when she returned.

She stubbed her bare toe on a rock and hopped a few steps, massaging it. At least it was warm now. What would it be like when winter came? Best not to think of that. Best to believe she would be long gone and safe in her husband's house. As she passed Old Owl's smoking lodge she heard the men inside, and she cursed them silently before moving off into the darkness.

Like a flock of geese settling in for the night, the cackling of laughter and talk drifted from the softly glowing lodge. Of the eight old men sitting around the fire inside, Old Owl was the runt of the litter. He looked like someone who had fallen on hard times. His shoulder-length gray hair was ragged, thin, and disheveled. A few stray bristles sprouted from his weasel's chin like stubble missed by the plow. He was small, even for a Comanche. The parentheses of his bandy lags, embracing an invisible horse, gave him a rolling gait.

A lone eagle feather dangled from the thin rope of his scalplock like a tattered flag that had been left out in too many storms. His crafty, myopic eyes peered owlishly over a monolith of a nose. Fortunately, his daughter, Something Good, hadn't inherited his looks, although she did have the same intelligent glint in her eyes.

Old Owl's breechclout was torn and dirty, and the stiff, rumpled white cotton jacket was far too big for him. It seemed as though he had shrunk in the wash rather than his clothes. The jacket was already grimy, although it was so new that creases still sectioned it off where it had lain folded among the trade goods.

He had bought it from the traders who had left only a week before. Old Owl thought how fortunate it was that Nabisoa, He Sticks Himself, had ridden ahead to warn the band so they could pack the new white captives off on a fast hunting trip. The boy was eager to go on any expedition, and probably would have hidden from the traders anyway, but the woman would have been troublesome. She wasn't the only one. Old Owl had had to talk long and hard to convince Terrible Snows to miss the traders. Old Owl always avoided trouble when possible, and he didn't want white people coming after the boy. The woman would be sure to tell the traders he was here, and his family would come looking for him.

The nightly meeting in the lodge looked like a convention of grandfathers, which, in fact, it was. And Old Owl seemed the most grandfatherly of all. A kindly man. A deacon perhaps, or a tailor, or a senior bookkeeper. He was a chief and a diplomat and a killer, but a kind man nonetheless. He had never killed anyone unnecessarily, at least not as he reckoned necessity. And he rarely killed at all anymore. Not humans, anyway. He was fifty-four years old and not in shape for it. His arthritis was too painful for the long forced marches and nights on the cold, wet ground. About all he was good for these days was giving advice. And he was very good at that.

As he sat in the place of honor, opposite the door, he saw in the gloom outside a pale, impish face under a thatch of hair like curly golden pine shavings. He frowned and waved his hand slightly at the boy. He wasn't in the mood to have a horse backed into the lodge this night. It would break the silence and he would have to start the opening ceremony all over again. John, or Weelah, Bear Cub, as he was called, had done that once before, and like all boys, he didn't realize that once is enough for any joke.

But Cub vanished into the night and Old Owl watched his cronies file silently into the smoking lodge. They sat without a word and remained silent while Old Owl held up his scarred, greenish-gray soapstone pipe and chanted his prayer to the sun. He laid a pinch of real tobacco, uncut with sumac leaves, on the ground as an offering. He stroked the smooth, soapy-slick bowl, feeling the curve of it in his hand. It wasn't his sacred pipe, the one he used for important councils, but he was very fond of it nevertheless.

His medicine pipe, his special one, had traveled a long road from the red pipestone quarry on the dividing ridge between the Saint Peter's River and the Missouri, nine hundred miles to the north. Once it had been a place of peace where the Father Who Lived Behind The Sun called all the Indian nations together. They had dug for the red stone without fear. Then the white men came, and desecrated the quarry, carrying away the sacred stone to make into bowls and foolish things. They told the Dahcotah Sioux to guard the place and forbid others to use it so they could sell the pipes. Now the People must make war to get the pipes to smoke for peace. And all because of the white men.

Old Owl took a long drag on the green pipe. His cheeks sucked in and the hot smoke burned the back of his throat, making him pleasantly light and dizzy. As he exhaled, he felt the day's small tensions and annoyances floating up with the smoke. He blew the first puff toward the top of the tent for the Father. The next he directed downward, into the ground for his Mother, the earth. Throughout the invocation there was absolute silence, except for the faint wheezing of So Nabehkakuh, Many Battles, which his friends stolidly ignored.

Forty-five years ago an arrow had passed through Many Battles' neck and pierced his windpipe. Sanaco had only been a herder then, but he had pulled the arrow from Many Battles' throat as he lay writhing and suffocating in the grass, trying to yank it out himself. Putting a steadying hand on the older man's shoulder, Sanaco had pushed away the ragged flesh from the edge of the wound. Poking his index finger into the bubbling hole, he hooked it under the punctured pinkish-gray tube that whistled with escaping air.

He pinned the hole shut with a cactus spine while Many Battles, now as calm as though he were being checked for lice, studied the clouds over his head. Around them the retreating horses pounded by, showering them with clods of dirt and torn grass while war screams filled the air. Many Battles hadn't forgotten that day, and he made sure that Sanaco had every advantage his prestige could give in the silent struggle for leadership.

For forty-five years Many Battles' voice had been like a file rasping a metal arrowhead. He preferred to converse in handtalk, although the People didn't use it as much as the other tribes. They didn't have to. Next to Spanish their own tongue was the lingua franca of the southern plains. Now, made equal by time and trials, Sanaco and Many Battles sat side by side at the fire.

Old Owl watched each friend in turn as the pipe passed from hand to hand, always to the right. War and raiding and loving women were the best ways to spend one's youth. Old Owl couldn't conceive of doing things any other way. As long as one had the misfortune to grow old, though, this was the way to spend one's time. Among friends. Without striving or boasting or having to prove one's manhood constantly. It was enough to watch the cycles, the patterns of life. To see the young make the mistakes that their elders made, and to see them discover the joys. To know that spring would follow the worst winter and the sun would never fail to rise. To know that the buffalo would always come back to the People each year and that Mother Earth would send up fruits to feed her children.

The pipe passed to Kwasinabo, Snake. He must have had a bad day. His brows were puckered and his wide, thin mouth turned down at the ends like an old, sprung bow. That meant he was either angry or thinking. And Snake didn't think much.

"How is your woman, White Horse?" Snake would never forgive Tosa Pookuh, White Horse, for stealing her from him thirty years ago. When he was in a bad mood he'd bring it up, even though the cuckolder had given the cuckoldee ten fine horses to soothe him. And he and his new woman had left the band for five years until the scandal died down. Snake was sixty-two years old. The three wives he had were more than enough for him, but the offense still rankled.

"Snake, Brother, I rue the day I let her talk me into marrying her. She gabbles like a flock of jays and fills my lodges with relatives. Her family eats more than a pack of starved wolves, and their snarling and howling and complaining follows me to bed at night."

White Horse rarely smiled. He had an impassive face with a profile that would look good on coins. It took newcomers a while to realize they were the victims of a master flimflammer.

"Would you like her back?" He stared at Snake with an earnest, sincere face. "For twelve horses I'll throw in her sisters, her mother, and three of her aunts. I'll keep my daughter, Deerskin, though. She makes pemmican with plenty of meat and not so much fruit. Think what a comfort all those women will be in your old age. You'll have the strongest pizzle in the band with all the exercise it'll get."

Snake was never sure if he was being made fun of or not. He suspected he was, and his voice had a jagged edge of belligerence. "No. She's just right for you. She's too lazy to tan hides right and they stink. Her shirts feel like bark and her moccasins fall apart after one wearing. I never wanted her anyway. She was always trouble."

"There was trouble at Terrible Snows' lodge today." Sanaco was a plain, matter-of-fact man with a knack for turning aside an argument's point before it could draw blood. Many Battles said he could be on friendly terms with Cannibal Owl. He would drop in on Sanaco some night to steal his soul, and Sanaco would distract him with a game of dice or a long, rambling discussion of horses. He'd stuff his guest so full of stew he wouldn't be able to fly. Cannibal Owl would have to walk home, belching, souls and death forgotten in the warm glow of hospitality.

"The white-eyes woman knocked A Little Less down this evening. It sounded like half the dogs in the village were fighting." There was a general chuckle. Everyone had wanted to knock A Little Less down at one time or another. Santa Ana spoke up.

"They deserve each other, those two. The white-eyes slave is like an animal. My nephew's friend said she clawed him when he accepted Terrible Snow's offer of her. It's like bedding a bundle of thorny mesquite sticks, he says." Santa Ana was hulking, with a bland affable face and a heap of corpses in his past.

"White-eyes women are no good for bedding." Old Owl finally spoke up. "They're only useful as slaves. It's the difference between horses and mules. If you beat a mule enough you can get work out of him, but not companionship. They're too stubborn and set in their ways."

"They can't be worth much, the white-eyes women. Look at the way their men leave them unprotected. They're almost worse that way than the Mexicans." Sibepapapi, Shaved Head, spoke for the first time. The long scar that stretched from behind his ear to the back of his head was hidden by his hair, except where it crossed the part between his braids, like a major intersection. His wife had shaved that side of his head when he had been wounded years before, and the name had been with him ever since.

"At least the Mexicans know how to ride. The white eyes look like sacks of meal in the saddle."

"But they have such fine, big horses."

"They're slow, those horses. And they maneuver like boulders. By the time you get one turned around the buffalo are grazing in the Ute's territory."

"The whites must be almost as intelligent as the People. Their children make good warriors and wives if they're stolen early enough." Old Owl had become very fond of Bear Cub the white captive boy. He had been adopted by Old Owl's nephew and had thrashed an average of two children a day for the first two weeks he had been in camp. Even the older boys left him alone now. And already he was riding almost as well as one of the People. Old Owl had given him a bow and quiver of arrows and a spotted pony of his own.

"Remember Tehan, with Satank's Kiowa? There's a warrior for you." Many Battles' voice sawed into the conversation.

"Is he the one with hair the color of live coals and orange spots all over his skin like a salamander?"

"Yes. And a good man to have next to you in a fight."

"Then it must be that the white eyes have no training when they're young. Otherwise why would they set up their lodges each by itself, with no one to help defend it? They must be crazy."

"And they tear up Mother Earth and rip out her hair, the grass. When they die she won't take their bones to her heart the way she does ours."

"They are so careless with their horses that soon there won't be any left. We will have stolen them all."

"Then we'll have to make those long trips to Mexico again."

"White people are ignorant. They'll never survive here. We should take all we can from them before they give up and go back where they came from."

"Where do they come from?"

"Where the sun rises. They have big villages there, and all manner of strange things, I hear. But I think most of what I hear must be lies."

"I don't want them to leave before I steal one of their new guns. Have you seen the one Big Bow has?"

And so the talk went until the stars seen through the smoke hole showed that it was halfway between midnight and dawn. Old Owl didn't relight the pipe when it went out, and his friends rose to go, their knees cracking as they stood.

"Wait." Old Owl took a burning brand from the fire and a stick. Cub had been up to something. He knew that look. He'd have to teach the boy to rub berry juice on his face until he turned darker brown from the sun, or give him black paint to use as camouflage. He was too light to get away with tricks at night.

Old Owl held the brand up so he could see, and poked around with the stick outside the lodge door. Just as he thought. Hidden under a thin layer of dust was a pile of fresh dog dung. He pointed it out to the other men and they all chuckled. Cub was a fistful all right. And a fast learner.

Old Owl pushed the smelly mess out of the way so his friends could file out. They left, yawning and stretching in the cool black morning. They padded back to their darkened lodges in groups of two or three. Their paths were lit by a soaring sky full of stars, glittering and twinkling like embers flung across the blackness.

❧ *14* ❧

The image of Something Good with the tip of her nose deformed and lumpy with livid red scar tissue and her delicate, flaring nostrils slit haunted Wanderer. He could remember the crone who had scavenged on the edge of camp when he was a child. She had lived on what families gave her to eat, and she had paid for it with their scorn. For a woman the price of infidelity could be high.

He didn't want to consider the possibility that Eagle had gone back on his word, but he had been acting strangely lately. If Wanderer had been a woman there would have been no doubt in his mind. Women can smell love and its intrigue as rain can be smelled before the storm ever breaks. He only knew that the patterns of his friend's behavior, which were as familiar to him as his own, had changed.

Eagle laughed less. Maybe he was finally maturing and taking life more seriously. Eagle went off by himself more often. Perhaps he was getting ready to go on another vision quest to ask for new medicine. That was something strictly between each warrior and his spirits. He didn't even discuss it with his friend and brother. Most disturbing of all was that Eagle had been so lost in his private thoughts yesterday he didn't notice little four-year-old Dusty walk behind him while he ate. Two captured eagles would eat with their backs to each other so that nothing could pass behind them. A man with eagle medicine kept the same taboo.

Wanderer had seen Eagle, in a mindless rage, almost strike a man who broke that taboo once. And he had never seen a grown man fight with his fists like a child. He remembered how upset easygoing Eagle had been after the desecration. He'd packed up and made the two-hundred-mile trek to Medicine Mounds to straighten things out with his eagle spirits. The wrongdoer had moved to another band rather than stay around Eagle.

Now Eagle was off somewhere again. Outside the scruffy brush arbor where Wanderer sat, the sun was sweltering. It baked the ground into hard clay, like the thin, brittle Mexican bread when it had been too long on the flat stones set beside their fires. He'd seen it there often, cracked and turning black, when the Mexican women were chased from their cooking and raped and slain or taken captive. He wondered idly if the sun was hot enough to cook such *toth-tee-ahs* now. Probably so.

Was Eagle avoiding him? His heart had always been a lodge where his friend was welcome to come and go at will. Now the door was not only down, but laced firmly shut. Whatever the problem was, it was time to get away for a while. Maybe on a hunting trip he could find out what was bothering his brother.

"Spaniard, will you come on a hunt with Eagle and me? Life here is too noisy and too quiet."

Spaniard looked up and grinned. "Maybe so." He went back to futilely digging with a small pair of clamshells at the splinter in his palm. Cruelest One loosened his breechclout and pulled out his medicine pouch. He fished around inside it until he found his pair of metal trade tweezers and tossed them to Spaniard, who grunted his appreciation. No one ever referred to Cruelest One as a Spaniard. Or a Mexican. Not unless one were making a collection of dangerous, implacable enemies and wanted to add a prime specimen.

Cruelest One wasn't born one of the People, and if the People had forgotten that, Cruelest One never did. Mo-cho-rook, The Cruelest One Of All. Kwasinabo Nabituh, Eagle called him, Snake Eyes. And sometimes his eyes didn't seem quite human. He was all right on a raid, but Wanderer would rather not choose him for a casual hunting trip. Cruelest One probably wouldn't have gone anyway. He rarely stayed in one place. He had just come back from a visit and would be off soon for another band. He was a wanderer in a tribe of wanderers. He was searching for something he couldn't find in his own soul.

Pahayuca had told Wanderer about finding Cruelest One many years ago in the raid on the Mexican Village.

The men had been gone, grubbing in their fields as expected. But the women had fought.

As the party had approached the quiet village, they flushed a woman from the bushes. Laughing, a warrior chased her as she ran, screaming a warning. When he drew up with her, he leaped from his horse. His weight bore her to the ground as he fell on her, ripping her white cotton blouse open at the same time. But she managed to reach up under her skirt and pull out the thin-bladed knife strapped to her thigh. She sank it to the bone handle in the man's chest. They had both stared at each other in astonishment until he crumpled across her body. She pushed him off, the knife's handle catching in the torn tangles of her blouse as she scrambled to her feet.

She was a young woman and a beautiful one, but the dead warrior's friend, raised his small hatchet and brought it whistling down. The blade, shaped like a miniature Spanish broadax, split her skull to the shoulders, the halves falling apart, and blood spraying. The friend regretted his rashness when he tried to take her scalp. He resolved to be careful to leave the head intact the next time. But to honor her, many of the men leaned down to touch her body as they passed, counting coup on a brave fighter.

The other women fought too. They fought with everything they could lay their hands on as the warriors swarmed down on them, like a school of sharks maddened by the smell of blood. In mindless hysteria one of them threw her baby at a raider just before he speared her. They screeched like wildcats and clawed and spit and hammered with their small fists until the last one of them lay hacked and broken in the pool of her own blood that soaked into the thirsty ground. Their children lay scattered around them too, like rotten fruit in the autumn. No one from the village was left alive, and the only sounds were the occasional whoof of a pony or the jingle of a bridle or the heavy breathing of the men as they looked around them.

Then there came a wail, very faint, from one of the white clay lodges, built up by hand like the home of a mud dauber wasp. Wedged up into the rough mesquite-log rafter poles, along with the strings of red and green chilis drying and maroon corn and crude metal graters, was a bundle of blankets and rags. The baby's face inside was as wrinkled and red as wadded trade cloth. He squalled and kicked, his tiny features gathered in the center of his face like a rosebud and his stiff black hair sticking out in all directions from his head.

Cradling him in one massive arm, Pahayuca pulled the blanket away from his face. The infant grabbed his finger in a firm grip and his face opened up like a flower. He stared at the painted mountain looming over him with huge, fearless eyes, his cheeks glistening with tears.

Pahayuca had brought him home, and Blocks The Sun had raised him. But Cruelest One was no one's son.

Maybe if he had been bigger, Wanderer thought. Or if no one had told him he was Mexican. But he was barely five feet tall, and he knew he was different. His whole life was spent relentlessly trying to be better and worse than all the others. Cruelest One never took captives. He killed anyone he could on raids. He never smiled, except when he was in the midst of battle and blood ran down the groove in his lance's shaft and onto his wiry arm. Maybe he was brother to nenepi, the little men, the demons who stood only a foot high but who always killed the unwary with their tiny bows and arrows.

There were tearing and crackling sounds as Cruelest One steadily ripped pages from the big, black book. He crumpled them and added them to the pile of paper wads that lay next to him. When he had torn all the leaves from Elder John's Bible, he began stuffing them into the opening left in the lacing of the two disks of tough buffalo hide. Paper made good insulation for shields. It was lighter than buffalo hair and it absorbed blows better than dried Spanish moss. Raiders were always on the lookout for books. From the way the white eyes studied them they must also be good medicine, which made them even more valuable.

Cruelest One's arsenal was the most complete in the band, even more so than Buffalo Piss's. Not many took the time to make their own double shields, even though the shield was their most sacred possession next to their medicine pouch. Cruelest One wouldn't allow anyone to do even the preliminary fleshing and scraping. He patiently heated the tough hide from an old buffalo's shoulder and steamed it several extra times to contract and thicken it as much as possible.

Then he cut two circles from it, and rubbed and pounded them with a smooth stone to make them flat and pliable. He stretched them over each side of a wooden hoop and sewed them together with rawhide thongs passed through punched eyelets. After he finished stuffing the shield and sewing up the remaining opening, he would paint his sacred animal on the front and decorate it with eagle feathers. Holes were already punched in the back circle for the wide strap to hold it on his arm. After all that was done, he would make the round case to store it in.

Cruelest One's whole life was tooled for war, even more than the average Nermenuh brave, Wanderer mused as he watched him. What kind of old man would he be? Probably as cantankerous and ferocious as Satank, the Kiowa leader. Satank would die fighting if he had to get up off his deathbed and go looking for someone to kill. Looking at Cruelest One's stony face, he wondered if he would ever be capable of loving a woman. He felt sorry for the one who finally married him.

Maybe that was Eagle's problem. Perhaps he was involved in another of his flings with a married woman, consoling himself for not being able to have Something Good.

Privacy in a camp of the People was rarer than white buffalo and not nearly as prized. There was little need of it, except for forbidden trysts. But Eagle and Something Good had found a tiny, secluded valley not far from camp. Dozens of bubbling springs flowed down the valley's limestone sides. It was cool here among the rocks and bushes, the air chilled by the misting waterfalls nearby and the trees overhead. If the village had been set on the open plain the task of finding such a place would have been much harder. Even so, the meetings were tinged with the danger of discovery.

Eagle nuzzled Something Good's slim neck and began blowing on her throat and up into her hair, ending with a loud whiffle in her ear. She giggled and rolled on top of him, throwing a brown leg over his own. They lay a moment, drunk with the feel of each other's bare skin. Their legs were almost the same length, and she tickled his foot with her toes as, propped up on her elbows, she glared down at him. Her hair flowed around his face, closing them off with a thick curtain.

"What are you doing?"

He stared up at her in wide-eyed innocence, blowing a tendril of her mane out of his mouth.

"You once said that your love was like a fire that lay buried under the ashes, waiting to be fanned back into flames. I'm just blowing on the coals."

She collapsed laughing onto him, and he lay feeling the warm, lovely weight of her. It was good to take a woman. It was paradise to have one you loved. He ran his hands down the slope of her sleek spine and up the smooth curve of her rounded buttocks. Wrapping his arms around her slender back, he hugged her, dizzy with joy. She spoke against the hollow of his shoulder, and he could feel her lips moving on his skin.

"My dove, my swallow, my soaring eagle, what will happen to us?" From laughter she went quietly to tears. He could feel the wetness of them.

"Something Good, only death will separate us, I promise you that. I'll find a way for us to be together." He stroked her hair again and again to comfort her. "Don't cry. Everything will be good with us, I swear. Do you believe me?"

"Yes, Eagle. I believe you."

Naduah stood with her hands clasped between her knees, trying to peer over Medicine Woman's shoulder and contain her own excitement. Medicine Woman had been working on something for weeks, but she always mysteriously put it away when Naduah came into the lodge. Now she was smiling her secret smile and rooting around in one of the boxes of rawhide stretched over a willow frame. From under one of Takes Down's dresses she pulled something cream-colored. She shook it out with a lilting jingle of tiny bells and held it up. The dress was one piece, an entire deerskin with the legs dangling at the hem. Medicine Woman held it against Naduah while Takes Down looked on fondly. Sunrise put down his equipment repairs to smile at her.

"*Kaku*, Grandmother, it's beautiful!"

"Try it on."

Naduah slipped it over her head. The thick fringe hung from the neckline and shoulders and brushed against her legs at the hem, which fell just below her knees. Dozens of small, metal cones were fastened in clusters at the side seams and yoke. They tinkled delicately when she moved. The doeskin had been tanned and chewed for hours, then smoked until it was as dainty as linen, as soft as velvet, and the palest of yellows, like rich, frothy cream. Even if it got wet, the smoking process would keep it supple. It fit Naduah perfectly.

But Medicine Woman wasn't finished. She brought out a small pair of thigh-high leggings, painted a deep sky blue and also fringed and belled and beaded. The garters that held them up just below the knee were solid red, white, and blue beadwork. Next she handed Naduah a small pair of soft, high-topped moccasins with fringe at the calves and running down the single back seam. When she put them all on, tying the tops of the leggings to her breechclout, they seemed to hug her legs and feet, as though embracing her. She stroked the front of her dress, smoothing imaginary wrinkles.

She knew how much time had been spent making the new clothes. But there was more. Medicine Woman took the rabbit's foot from her neck and put it over her granddaughter's head. It had an intricate design of tiny beads at its base. Medicine Woman knotted

125

the thong so that it hung, warm and furry, in the hollow of Naduah's throat.

"Grandmother, not your medicine. You need this." She groped for the words, frustrated that after two months she was still unable to express so many things.

"No Granddaughter. I'm old. I have lots of medicine. You keep it and it will protect you as you grow."

Naduah stood on tiptoe, threw her arms around Medicine Woman's neck, pulled her head down, and kissed her on the cheek.

"What are you doing, little one? Are you trying to eat me? Do you think like the Nermateka that you can devour my medicine along with my flesh?"

"It's called a kiss, *Kaku*. It's something white people do when they love someone."

"Kiss? Kiss means wait."

"In the People's language, yes, but not in . . ." Naduah almost said "my own," but stopped. In spite of her blond hair and blue eyes, in spite of the fact that she had been with them only two months, she knew they loved her as their own. She changed the subject.

"How did you make everything fit so well, Grandmother? You never tried anything on me."

Medicine Woman took her medicine pouch down from its peg. The bag was bigger than most and made from the entire skin of the rabbit whose foot hung around Naduah's neck. Streamers of red flannel were sewn to it, and a drawstring pulled it shut at the throat. Naduah had never seen what was inside it, and she was afraid to peek. Everyone held the medicine in too much awe.

Medicine Woman held the bag a moment, communing silently with it. When she opened the drawstring, the odor of wild herbs escaped like a djin that had been trapped inside. She laid it along her palm with the opening pointed toward the light of the fire, and peered up inside it. She fished around with her free hand and pulled out a grimy, lumpy cord. It dangled and danced from her fingers like a live snake. Naduah recognized the thong that her grandmother had measured her with that first morning. All her dimensions were recorded on it. At least for another month or two. She was growing fast.

Sunrise finally stirred from his usual place, sitting cross-legged on the thick buffalo robes of his bed. He searched through a pile of boxes and bags and held out a square of folded navy blue wool. It was a brand new trade blanket that he had been saving for a special occasion. Then he gave her a small bow and a dozen arrows.

"Daughter, these are for you. I almost forgot them."

"A bow and arrows?"

"Yes. I'll teach you how to shoot them. I'm making a quiver for the arrows. Soon you'll be shooting better than the boys." He saw the puzzled look on her face. "You must learn everything you can. And you should excel at whatever you attempt. We'll be proud to have you for our daughter, and you'll be proud of yourself, which is more important. There's no reason why you shouldn't learn to hunt your own food and defend yourself. And do it well." It was a long speech for Sunrise. Naduah sometimes wondered if he even noticed her. She was only a girl-child, after all. Now she knew he did. Takes Down spoke next in her low, shy voice.

"I have a small present for you too, Daughter." Takes Down thought she was plain, which she wasn't. Not to those who knew her. She had a way of talking with her hand held to her mouth, as though she didn't want to be noticed. She offered her gift as if expecting it to be rejected. Naduah took it and hugged her hard, her arms going only a little way around her mother's plump body.

Takes Down's gift was a beautifully beaded envelope of deerskin with a shoulder strap. The long, tapering tongue was held firmly closed by a flat brass toggle attached to a cord. The cord ran down the inside of the bag and out through the bottom, where it was knotted to hold it tight.

She untied the knot, pulled the toggle loose, and peeped inside. There were smaller bags of paint powders, two or three brushes in hollow reed cases, a hairbrush made of a porcupine tail, thongs and ribbons and otter fur for her braids, and a pair of clamshell tweezers. There was even her own mirror. Takes Down handed her something else, a doll sewn of buckskin like Something Good's, but with a dress exactly like Naduah's new one and hair cut from Takes Down's head.

Naduah hugged her presents to her and swiveled her body to make the fringe on her dress swirl. Medicine Woman had taken time to add extra layers of fringe and it chased around her like a playful puppy. Naduah loved the feel of it tickling her arms and legs, and the tinkling sound of the bells.

"I'm going to show Star Name and Black Bird and Something Good and Owl."

"When you get back there's a case for you to store your new clothes in." It was Takes Down's gentle way of reminding her that the dress and leggings were for special occasions. She would never forbid Naduah to wear them for everyday use. She only told her what was proper and common sense and left it to Naduah's judgment.

Naduah stood a moment outside the door, listening to the sounds of drums and laughter from the other end of the village. As she walked toward Star Name's lodge, she looked around at the tents with firelight flickering softly through their creamy sides. She looked at the familiar tanning frames with hides stretched between them, and at the heaps of dogs twitching and moaning in their sleep. Her own dog followed closely behind her. She saw the shields standing guard, assuring her that she and her loved ones were safe from attack.

She felt an overwhelming rush of affection for it all. How could she have ever been afraid and lonely here? The camp seemed almost like one big house, with each lodge a room. Standing in the quiet, dusty street, she felt as though she were in a familiar corridor and surrounded by family. She stopped to let Sunrise's war pony nuzzle her. He whiffled her outstretched palm with his velvet lips, searching for the tender grass she usually brought him. She stroked his neck and murmured to him. With her fingers she untangled and separated the thick strands of his mane, picking out the burs. Then she walked in front of him, stood on tiptoe, and reached up, scratching hard behind both his ears, while he stood with a blissful expression on his bony face.

"Do you like my dress and leggings and moccasins?" She stood back and gave him a better view in the pale starlight. The pony snorted. "You're right, old war-horse. They are beautiful."

She whirled and skipped toward Star Name's lodge, dancing in time to the bells on her dress and practicing the heel-toe step of the dances she was learning. She had a sudden desire to show her finery to Wanderer. To show him that she was not a child, that she was as good as those young women who were always staring after him with their big, stupid, cow's eyes. And someday, when she was very brave, she'd tell him that she had thought he was a thief and would apologize for it. Someday. When she was much braver.

❧ *15* ❦

This hunting trip was a mistake. It had seemed like a good idea when Wanderer had proposed it, a chance to get away from camp and disperse the suspicions that were gathering like storm clouds over Pahayuca's lodges. Now Eagle regretted coming. He looked over at his friend, who sat near the fire in the waning light, splitting the stems of turkey feathers, dipping the ends in glue and binding them with sinew to the shafts of his hunting arrows. The silence between them was like Cannibal Owl devouring their friendship, but there was no way Eagle could break it. He dared not let his guard down lest Wanderer verify what he only suspected. Of the two people he loved most, Eagle must betray one.

He pretended to concentrate on the water lily roots and wild onions cooking in the ashes at the edge of the flames. He poked at them, turning them so they would roast evenly. The onions' strong aroma rose with the smoke. Then he stood and went to see how Spaniard was doing with the day's kill, a young buffalo. He was usually full before he ever finished dressing out an animal. He feasted on the heart and liver and entrails unless reminded to share. His favorite delicacy was to cut the udders of a freshly killed doe and suck the warm mixture of blood and milk as it spurted out. At least he volunteered for the messy job of butchering. And he did share, as long as someone reminded him.

If Spaniard had been indolent, he would have been fat. But he was as solid as a piece of mahogany furniture, with arms and legs that looked like they'd been turned on a lathe. His bushy black hair seemed to dance with electricity. Wisps of it always escaped his thick braids, no matter how much buffalo dung he rubbed into them. With his smooth, plucked brows, black eyes, hooked nose that curved into swooping nostrils, and full, sensuous mouth, Spaniard looked, except for his hair, very much like one of the People. His Aztec ancestors had bred true.

Spaniard handed Eagle the remains of the brains and leg marrow he had stirred together on a piece of hide and eaten with a rib bone. Bits of gray matter clung to the corners of his wide mouth, and more spewed out as he greeted Eagle. Eagle took the hide plate and the pieces of flesh that the Mexican had draped over platters of dried buffalo chips to absorb the blood. He went back to the fire and offered Wanderer some of the warm brains and marrow. Wanderer took it in silence, and Eagle bustled about, collecting and sharpening sticks to roast the meat. They would each eat about five pounds of it before the evening was over.

Eagle lay under the robe that night, long after Wanderer had begun to breathe heavily and Spaniard had started his nightly moaning and twitching and tooth-grinding. The misshapen moon shone through translucent clouds as though seen behind a sheet of mica. Eagle searched idly for the old shieldmaker who was supposed to live there. Eagle was uneasy here in the Penateka territory. They were far to the south and east of the Staked Plains, the huge plateau where the Quohadi ranged undisturbed by white men and their destruction. The hills here were too close together and there was too much brush. The countryside seemed to be choking on it. He missed the limitless sweep of home, he missed being always able to see the horizon.

The thoughts that had been buzzing around his head like a swarm of horseflies came back to plague him. It had definitely been a mistake to come along. He was too vulnerable to Wanderer's probing. He had thought he could use the time to think and plan. He had been uneasy in the village, constantly having to see and talk to Pahayuca. He wasn't afraid for himself. All Pahayuca could do was kill him. And he wouldn't do that without a fight. Eagle was used to fighting. But he worried for Something Good. She was the one who would suffer if they were discovered. She would be mutilated, shamed for the rest of her life. If that happened, he knew he would have to kill Pahayuca and suffer exile as long as he lived, if he wasn't killed himself by a relative. Perhaps Wanderer himself.

Could he live without Something Good? Just keep riding north and west and never turn back? No. After only three days away from her the ache had spread from his groin into his chest. It was like hunger in February, when the snow flows in drifts on the currents of the wind, when the pemmican supply runs out and the babies cry for food. He could relieve himself, with his own hands or with other women, but it would be no better than eating bark to fill an empty stomach. He had had many women, but never one like her.

They could run away together. It happened all the time. But this was different. Pahayuca was known and respected all over the land of the People, even in the north. His wife and her lover would be welcome nowhere. They could go to the Kiowa, live with Big Bow. If anyone understood eloping and wife stealing, he did. He'd done enough of it himself. But it would be exile for life, and a hard test for their love. He had promised her that everything would be good for them. And she said she believed him. He wished he could believe it himself.

It had been a hard day's hunt for the three of them, and the sun beat down on them without mercy. As Wanderer lay lapping at the edge of the cold spring that gushed from the bottom of the shallow ravine, he felt chills prickle his arms and back. He leaped to his feet and whirled around. On the embankment about them stood a dozen Tonkawa, arrows nocked and bows drawn. Two of the Tonkawa were already sliding down the slope to grab the three ponies with all the hunting and war gear.

"Nermateka, People Eaters," breathed Eagle. "What are they doing this far north, away from the swamps and their stinking fish?"

The Tonkawa rode clumsily and owned few horses. But they'd managed to catch the three of them by surprise.

"We will go with them now," Wanderer muttered, "They're stupid, these people, and we can get away from them easily." The leader, a tall gaunt man with the deceptive name of Placido, made an arrogant sweep of his arm. Wanderer started up the slope toward him, followed by Eagle and Spaniard.

In the heat of the midsummer day several of the Tonkawa wore sleeveless, painted hide jackets with a curved extension covering their groins. The *cuera*, the conquistadors' leather armor, lived on. Most of the men had vertical stripes painted or tattooed on their foreheads and chins. It may have been the clink of one of their shell necklaces that had alerted Wanderer too late.

As they rode, their wrists tied behind them and their feet lashed under their horses' bellies, Wanderer signalled with his hands to the two who followed him. He knew that the People Eaters weren't horsemen, certainly not the experts that he and his friends were. If the People Eaters had known horses they would have put the captives on their own plodding pack ponies. The three Comanche war ponies were almost like having three invisible warriors along.

Wanderer gave a low cluck to Night, along with pressure from his right knee against the pony's side. Night leaped from the line of march and raced away. Reflexively the Tonkawa whirled to catch him, and from the corner of his eye, Wanderer saw Eagle and the Spaniard bolt in opposite directions. Even with their hands tied they were better riders than their captors. He knew they'd be able to escape easily.

"People Eaters, you stink of yamma roots and fish shit! You're the spawn of toads and soft like mosquito larvae in foul ponds." Eagle's voice rose over the shouts and hoofbeats. Wanderer could picture him sitting proud on his pony.

He hadn't followed instructions, of course. Instead of fleeing, he was trying to distract the Tonkawa away from his blood brother. Wanderer leaned forward and tightened the grip of his knees. As his body moved in rhythm with Night's long stride and mesquite whipped by his legs, he braced himself against his pony's neck and stuck like a bur to his mane.

He could hear the sounds of pursuit getting fainter, and laughed softly with Night. Then there was a wrench at his shoulder, as though a giant hand had shoved him forward. As arrow tore through him and buried itself in the fleshy part of Night's neck. The pony stumbled, gathered his feet back under him, and surged forward. Wanderer tugged backward, but the arrow stayed glued to the shaft pinning him to his pony. He cursed the People Eaters for shooting him with a hunting point, like a deer. His blood mingled with Night's and was blown into his face, almost blinding him. He could feel the numbness spreading through his shoulder and arm, and he could hear the hoofbeats crescendoing behind him. In a fury he pulled at the thong that bound his wrists. He tore the skin, but the cord held.

The Tonkawa chief, Placido, caught up with Wanderer first, but soon he and Night were surrounded. Even with him wounded and his hands tied, it took four men to unseat Wanderer from his pony's back.

Night bucked and reared and lashed out with his hooves as one of the warriors tried to mount him. He whirled on the man and sank his teeth deep into his shoulder just at the base of the neck. Three others had to beat him about the head and mouth to make him let go. In spite of the blood running from his own face, Night drew his lips back over his reddened teeth in something like a laugh.

His victim fell back, the rows of purple punctures spurting blood, and looked wildly for a weapon. Several men dropped lariats over the horse's head and rear legs and pulled on them, keeping him spraddled and off balance. The man he had bitten beat Night's face and tender muzzle with a bow. Night's ears were already laid all the way back. Now he arched his neck and rolled his eyes up into his head. His chest heaved as he screamed with rage. Wanderer was struggling to get loose and help him when something hard and heavy hit him from behind, landing just above his neck. He collapsed, bright lights fracturing and shooting off like comets behind his closed eyelids.

When he woke up, he was tied like a sack of meal across the back of a mule. The blood pooling in his head wasn't helping the stabbing pain there. Every jolt sent fresh spasms through his eyes. The numbness was wearing off in his shoulder and was being replaced by a throbbing ache. Someone had stuffed grass into the wound in a halfhearted effort to slow the bleeding, and it scratched at the raw edges of the torn flesh. Blood still ran down his arm in rivulets and was slung off the tips of his fingers as his body swayed with the mule's gait. The cords had cut off his circulation and his toes curled in the grip of knotting cramps.

Worst of all, Eagle wouldn't shut up. What was the matter with him? Was he trying to get them killed quickly to avoid the ordeal that was sure to come? He smeared the Tonkawa with his contempt as though he were rubbing their faces in fresh dung. There was no mistaking his meaning, and they regularly lashed him with their bows and musket butts. They seemed to take a perverse pleasure in exchanging insults with him in broken Spanish and Comanche. Tied to another swaybacked, hip-slung mule, he rode ramrod straight, and taunted them all the way back to their small hunting camp. At least Spaniard had gotten away. There was little chance of his bringing a rescue party in time to save them, but there would be revenge and a decent burial for their bones.

The shabby brush shelters blended in with the stunted cedars that grew thickly in all directions. But the camp would have been easy enough to find just by following one's nose. The sky was spattered with wheeling crows and buzzards, the usual retinue of a hunting camp. The stench from the carcasses could be smelled a hundred yards away. Several mounds of dead buffalo, like brown boulders rising from the grass, lay rotting in the sun. Their tongues alone had been cut out for the evening meals. The flies were thick enough to slice, and they swarmed around the fresh blood on Wanderer and Night.

These people were stupider than Wanderer had thought. They had stayed far too long at this site, in the territory of their enemies. It was possible that their luck would run out and a party of the People would happen across them. If Eagle didn't get them both killed before sundown, which was a more likely possibility.

With arms and legs tied, they were propped against two mesquite bushes near the fire. The mesquites were chosen on purpose so the prisoners would have the added discomfort of wicked thorns stabbing their backs and shoulders. The Tonkawas began their victory dance slowly, slapping their feet down deliberately to make as loud a thud as possible. Their chants started low and built as the night wore on. As they leaped and whirled, they stabbed at the air with their knives. One of them sliced so near Wanderer's head that he carved a piece from the tip of his ear. The blood tickled as it ran down Wanderer's neck. Eagle was knocked over by a blow with a musket, and someone righted him again. Through the dance and the beating he never stopped taunting them. Wanderer was afraid he had gone mad.

A stocky warrior, his long arms dangling and his eyes close-set, stepped from the circle of dancing men. Another laid the long blade of his lance into the flames. The first man squatted in front of Eagle and said something in his own tongue. Eagle spat at him, the saliva running down his tormentor's cheek. The Tonkawa slapped Eagle hard, bringing a red flow from his left nostril. He hit him again with a fist and broke the fine hawk's nose, pushing it askew on Eagle's face. Still he laughed and jeered.

The man pulled his long knife from his belt. It glittered in the fire's light. He jabbed at Eagle's eyes, but it didn't stop the taunting. He lowered the knife and began sawing a strip of flesh from Eagle's thigh. Wanderer knew then that what he had always heard about the People Eaters was true.

"May it tie your stomach in knots," Eagle told his enemy conversationally. "And may it make your dung run like water from you for the rest of your short life."

A second man cauterized the wound with the glowing lance blade, but Eagle seemed to be so far removed from his pain there was nothing they could do to reach him.

"Is it true that you eat your own babies? And that you breed your women like cattle, to bear tender veal? If I come to your village will you treat me with baby stew?"

"*Tah-mah*, Brother, do you need her so badly? Will you die thus rather than live without her?" Wanderer had finally figured it out.

"Brother, one of us has to die tonight. We both know that. I prefer it to be me." He kicked out at the man as he walked toward the fire, swinging the filet on the point of his knife. As Eagle's feet swung back, the Tonkawa didn't notice the jagged rock that he had sent skittering across the dark ground to land near his friend. Wanderer shifted slightly to cover it with his leg. He could feel it there, pressing into his flesh. He spoke to Eagle.

"I envy you, Brother. You won't have to ride to paradise after this night. You can soar with your brothers, the eagles."

"I hope so." Eagle smiled at Wanderer with the lower half of his old grin. The upper part, his eyes, were already overcast with pain, and remote. But the two friends spoke as though they were discussing a horse race.

The Tonkawa had stopped their dancing and now sat or squatted expectantly around the fire. Like a pack of wolves, their yellow eyes glowed in the light. The real evening's entertainment had begun.

❧ *16* ❦

When Spaniard leaped from his horse in front of Pahayuca's lodge, the pony dropped, his front legs folding under him first. His head hit the ground with a thud and slid forward as his chest and hindquarters followed. He rolled over on his side, and his heart gave a few spasmodic heaves. A shudder rippled through his body. His legs twitched even in death, as though he were running as he had for the past thirty-six hours. He lay there unmoving finally, his eyes staring and lather still foaming off his steaming sides. A trickle of blood ran from the corner of his mouth.

Naduah stared down at him in horror as warriors shouldered past her into the lodge. There was no need for Lance to ride through camp announcing that Spaniard had returned alone. The news spread like pollen in the wind. People came running to hear what had happened to the other two hunters. They stood in small groups, talking in low voices or calling questions back and forth. Naduah wished they would all be quiet so she could hear what was being said inside. Star Name began to cry softly. Naduah, holding her sister's hand tightly, felt tears well up in her own eyes.

"Maybe they're all right, Star Name."

"No. Spaniard would never have just ridden into camp that way. That's not how things are done. A messenger always stays on the outskirts of camp and signals. Something terrible has happened."

The talk hushed when Buffalo Piss appeared in the doorway. He seemed hardly older than the boys he beckoned to, but they jumped to attention. They jostled their way through the crowd to hear their whispered instructions. Then the boys raced for the meadow along the river where the ponies were pastured. Somewhere a baby wailed and was quieted before he could even catch his breath for a second cry. The lodge emptied of warriors, each trotting off to collect his gear. As curious as everyone was, no one tried to stop them to ask questions.

Pahayuca stooped through the opening and blinked in the bright sunlight. As though heralding him, a drum began to throb in some distant part of the village. Others joined it, calling back and forth like coyotes from separate peaks. Pahayuca shaded his eyes with his hand and looked out over the crowd, as though scanning the horizon for the young men they all loved. When he spoke there was no trace of the clown or the storyteller in his booming voice.

"The People Eaters have surprised our men and may have captured Wanderer and Eagle. There were twelve of them, and Spaniard didn't go back to see if his two brothers escaped." There was a murmur that rose slightly, like a low swell on a calm sea. Pahayuca put his hand out and stilled it.

"If they were captured he could not have helped them. If they escaped, there was no need for him to help. He will lead us to them. Spaniard can follow the tracks of a butterfly in a field of flowers. We will find them."

Spaniard came out of the lodge and stood partly hidden by Pahayuca's bulk. As he moved off silently the People parted in front of him. No word was spoken to him, and he seemed to be studying the ground a few inches in front of him as he walked, as though looking for his friends' tracks already.

* * *

It took a long time for Eagle to die. He and the Tonkawa made sure of that. The sky was the deep black that comes a few hours before dawn when Eagle began chanting his death song in a low, clear, steady voice.

> I am a spirit.
> You are making me a spirit.
> Where I am now
> You are making me a spirit.
> Even the eagle dies.

He timed either the song or his death perfectly, and his soul flew as he finished the last line. Wanderer thought he could almost see it, a vapor that escaped Eagle's gray lips and spiraled upward like an eagle soaring on a current of air.

The Tonkawa got up, creaking and stretching after so many hours of sitting, and filed off toward their robes and blankets. The tall, thin one, Placido, lifted his lance in front of Eagle's still, mutilated form. From the concentration in his eyes it was obvious that he was offering up a prayer for the brave warrior too. Then he turned and followed the others, leaving Wanderer to the cold air that crept in around the dying fire.

There was little time to lose, but Wanderer forced himself to stay motionless until he felt sure that everyone was asleep. He hunched down until the jagged stone was within reach of his numb hands. It slipped from his deadened fingers time and again, and the effort sent spasms of pain shooting through his wounded shoulder and back down his arm. Doggedly he kept trying until he had a firm grip and could saw at the thong holding his wrists. It took an hour before the leather snapped when he jerked it. Leaning over, he untied his ankles and drew his legs up to rub the blood back into them.

Stealthily he crawled to where Eagle sat still tied in a sitting position. His legs and arms were flayed to the bone, with the tendons hanging from them like the strings on a broken puppet. With the tips of his fingers, Wanderer gently closed his friend's eyes and lifted the gold chain and coin from around his neck. He rested his hand, palm down, on the cold, narrow chest.

Rest when you get to paradise, my brother. Perhaps someone like Something Good will be there for you. Don't worry about your bones. I'll be back for them. You will be avenged. I need no pipe to swear it to you.

As silently as the bats that flit at twilight, he ran, crouching, to where the horses were tethered. Night pricked his ears forward and flicked them once in greeting, but made no sound. He caressed

Wanderer's cheek with his warm muzzle while his friend cut the
tether line with the same sharp rock. Together they stole off through
the cedars and mesquite, each picking his feet up and laying them
down carefully in the dark.

Naduah sat bolt upright in bed. A piercing, keening wail rose in
the night, carrying Something Good's soul upward on the voice of
her grief. More women's voices joined hers in harmony and dis-
sonance, but none could match the pain of a heart emptied of all
reason for living. Naduah didn't know who was mourning. The
eerie, ululating cry could scarcely be recognized as human, much
less Something Good's. It sent shivers up and down Naduah's spine
as she fumbled in the dark for the breechclout she had dropped in a
heap by the bed six hours before.

Dark figures ran through the night to converge at Pahayuca's
lodges. The fires there had been fanned to life. Women hurried to
help mourn, crying as they ran. The top half of Something Good's
left index finger lay in a pool of blood in the dust, and three women
held her arms to keep her from slitting her own throat. The flames of
the lodge fire shining through the translucent walls silhouetted the
shadowy forms struggling inside. Naduah darted among those at
the tent's door and threw herself at Something Good.

"No, Sister. Don't." She screamed to be heard over her friend's
grief. But Something Good wasn't hearing anyone. Blocks The Sun,
sobbing and moaning herself, pinioned the girl's arms and forced
her down onto the pile of bedding. Four women held her arms and
legs as she thrashed there, screaming "Eagle!" over and over. The
other women wailed and slashed their arms, ripping their dresses
open to cut their breasts. The lodge floor was littered with heaps of
hair that they had cut off. And one or two other finger joints joined
Something Good's. Naduah backed out of the lodge in horror. The
screams and the flickering firelight, in her half-awake state, made it
all seem like a hallucination.

Eagle was dead. And Wanderer? Where was Wanderer? Was he
dead too? She whirled to look for him and almost bumped into a
dusty, blood-caked pony, so filthy and gaunt he could scarcely be
recognized. Naduah threw her arms around Night's neck. And the
air around her suddenly filled with the People's cry of alarm, "T-t-t-
t-t-t-t-t!" like crickets starting up suddenly at twilight. Everyone
knew of Night's viciousness and they feared the child would be
hurt. Night only flinched a little as her hand hit the wound on his
neck. He swung his head around and bumped her gently to bring it
to her attention.

"Poor Night. What happened? Don't worry," she crooned. "I'll take care of it for you. Medicine Woman can heal you." She buried her face in the gritty wetness of his heaving side and whispered so no one could hear. "Where is Wanderer, Night?"

"Naduah, will you care for Night for me?" She looked up startled, almost frightened by the hollow-eyed specter standing behind her. His left braid had been cut off in mourning, leaving the hair ragged. Around his neck Eagle's gold coin glinted in the light that poured through the open doorway. Unable to speak to this ghost, this parody of the handsome Wanderer, she nodded dumbly, her arm flung around his war pony's neck.

"Good. You're the only one he's ever allowed to touch him. If you're not sure what to do, ask Sunrise. I'll come see him tomorrow. Tonight I have to talk with Pahayuca and Buffalo Piss and the council." He half-turned to leave, but stopped long enough to say, "My brother is dead." His voice was almost too low to hear over the din from the lodges, and she was astonished to see that the ruthless warrior, the idol of boys and the ideal of women, was crying.

Men didn't cry. At least not the white ones she had known. Yet there was Name Giver huddled outside his doorway. He had his ragged buffalo robe pulled up over his head and face, and underneath it his body was shaking with sobs. The hysteria spread as the news of Eagle's death was carried through the village on the still night air. And over it all rang the keening cries of Something Good's grief.

Crazy, reckless Eagle. Everyone loved him. Naduah remembered his even white teeth flashing in his wicked grin as he beat her and Star Name at the guessing game. She remembered that night of the honey hunt when the four of them had laughed and played and sung for hours under the stars.

Poor Something Good. Poor Wanderer. They weren't really brothers, he and Eagle. But they were closer than brothers. They were the dark and the light side of the same person. What would Wanderer do now that part of him was gone? In a daze, Naduah gathered a handful of Night's mane in her fist and led him away, ignoring the rein draped over his back. Tonight she had to touch something of Wanderer's to assure herself that he had returned. She and Night walked slowly through the clamor of grief surging and swelling around them. Fires glowed through most of the lodge walls, and the faces of those who passed were distorted with crying. Caught up in their anguish, she cried too, wiping her nose on her arm.

But at least Wanderer was back safely. She had missed him. She had missed his low, resonant voice calling as he entered the lodge to talk to Sunrise. Even though he still made her uncomfortable, she had gotten into the habit of watching him when he wasn't aware of it. Often she stood back, squirming with embarrassment while Star

Name laughed and teased with him until a smile played across his fine face like sunlight on deep water. Now he had left her in charge of his beloved pony and friend. And he had spoken to her as an adult. She held her head a little higher as she led Night home.

Medicine Woman almost hummed the chant around the mouthful of *pouip* root she was chewing. It was the same high, quavery voice that so often sang Naduah to sleep at night, but with a different inflection. She seemed to be listening too. It was like half a conversation between two adults making an important deal. As she chewed and chanted she picked pieces of dried grass out of the wound in Wanderer's shoulder. He lay serenely through it, with his eyes closed. Naduah winced as bits of grass stuck in the dried lymph and blood had to be pulled free. Medicine Woman gently scraped away the scab that had half-formed and motioned Naduah to bring her the rag soaked in warm water.

After she had sponged the remaining dirt away from the ugly hole, rimmed with purple flesh, she spit the *pouip* juice into it and added some of the boiled yarrow that Naduah had brought. She split an oval section of prickly pear leaf, the *nopal*, and placed it, raw side down, against the wound. She bound it with strips of soft leather and rocked back on her heels to admire her handiwork.

"You know you should rest a few days, my son. But of course you won't."

"You know me well, Grandmother." He opened his eyes and turned to look at her, his face pale under the rich chestnut color of his skin.

"When will you leave?"

"As soon as I can gather enough men. Many have left in search of my dead brother and me, but they should be back soon. Spaniard knows Night's tracks and can tell I escaped."

Naduah sat in despair. It would do no good to protest. He would listen to her as one listens to a child. And he would go off to be killed anyway. Perhaps the next war party would return with Wanderer's bones.

Gets To Be An Old Man, who had eagle medicine, made Wanderer and his war party rise before dawn and bathe in the river. Now they all sat in a circle in Old Man's medicine lodge. They wore only breechclouts, and their hair was loose and flowing. Each had put eagle feathers in his scalplock and rubbed his hair with sage. As the pipe passed around the ring Old Man chanted his eagle song, breaking off now and then to instruct them in the proper ceremony.

As he listened to the high-pitched drone, Wanderer's mind turned off onto a little-traveled track. He wondered if Big Bow could be right. The Kiowa laughed at medicine men. A man must get his own power, he said, not beg it from another—besides, they were all self-serving frauds. Wanderer knew that some were. There was the one who was caught hammering the hooves of a fine horse he had put a curse on. Until then the pony's owner had believed the curse was working and causing the inflamed feet.

But there could be no harm in using every source of power available. Who knew what would work and what wouldn't until it had been tried? And it was good for morale. The ceremony separated the warriors from the rest of the band and made them special. It gave them the confidence and strength to do whatever necessary to protect their families.

Wanderer considered the need to have a captive girl take part in the ceremony. The yellow hair would do. He would tell Deep Water to ask Medicine Woman to explain it to her so she wouldn't be frightened. Deep Water, Owl's brother, followed Wanderer everywhere. He now waited outside the lodge, like a young wolf at the mouth of his den, wanting to be of some use to his elders. And at seventeen, the leader of his first war party, Wanderer was now an elder in Deep Water's eyes.

Wanderer looked around at the men in the circle, each sunk in his own thoughts. They were all powerfully built and tightly muscled. He had chosen carefully. He wished his brother could be with him, but he knew the men he had picked could be trusted to fight well. If they ever got out of here and on the raid trail.

He felt bound and helpless here in this hot lodge. He wanted to be riding across the plain with his men behind, racing to avenge his brother. He was impatient to feel the wind blowing his hair and pushing against his shield, to feel the sun hot on his skin and the straps of his quiver and bow across his bare chest. To feel Night surging under him. To find the enemy and charge, screaming over the thunder of the horses' hooves. To be drunk with excitement and the release from tension.

But most of all, he wanted vengeance. He wanted to find his brother's bones and to extract a terrible payment for them. It took great effort to force himself to sit quietly and listen to Old Man, to keep from drumming his fingers on his knees in frustration.

Facing east in her new dress of cream-colored suede, her long, golden hair unbound, Naduah sat next to Wanderer. She was tall for her age, but still he made her seem small. The drums beat steadily and the six singers chanted hypnotically. The men in the war party circled, shaking their gourd rattles in time with the beat and stamping their heels hard in the dust. Little puffs of it rose and drifted off on the west wind.

Each dancer carried a fan made of the wing of an eagle, and the men dipped and rose as they pretended to be young eagles leaving the nest. They cried like eagles and whirled slowly, soaring on imaginary air currents. After an hour they dropped to their knees to rest, and the drums hushed. The midmorning sun was beginning to reach its full heat, and Naduah could feel the sweat running down her back. The dress felt heavy on her small shoulders.

She'd been frightened earlier, even though Medicine Woman had told her it was only pretend. Wanderer and his men were painted for war and looked fierce and dangerous as they surrounded Sunrise's lodge, demanding her as a captive. Even knowing it was part of the ceremony, the sight of them triggered terrifying memories that had begun to sink into the sunless depths of her mind.

Sunrise had pretended to defend her with his lance, but they had brushed past him and carried her off to the center of the village. She had struggled a little. She had been frightened and embarrassed and worried that she might shame Wanderer in front of everyone. Now, except for the heat and the dust, she was enjoying the attention. At least she had been enjoying it until Yellow Wolf stood to tell a story while the dancers rested.

She didn't like Yellow Wolf anyway. She didn't like the way he peered around the thick nose that jutted from bulging brows. His eyes always seemed to her like an animal's glaring from a dark cave. And the story he chose to tell made the sweat on her back turn to ice water. He was acting out Eagle's coup on little John the day he and Naduah had been captured. Yellow Wolf must have been in the ring of men who had surrounded them. When he finished, there was laughter and yelling and a wild applause of drums and rattles and stamping feet.

Naduah didn't look up until he had knelt back with the other dancers and the noise died. Then there was a rustling and stir at the rear of the crowd, and Sunrise and Takes Down The Lodge and Medicine Woman pushed their way through. They shouted and waved knives, threatening to snatch their child away and save her. Instead they laid presents in front of her—a small bag of tinkling metal cones, a yard of blue cloth, a pair of moccasins for everyday wear, a shinny ball. Then Pahayuca came forward, holding a bridle rein in his left hand. On the other end of it balked a long-legged, blood-bay filly. In her high black stockings she danced, alarmed by the noise and confusion. Pahayuca held the rein out toward Naduah to show that the horse was a gift, then led her out of the circle.

Medicine Woman hadn't told her about the presents, and Naduah sat stunned by it all. The dance started up again and went through the afternoon, until the men dropped, one by one, panting and drenched with sweat. Through it all Wanderer sat, impassive as a statue, straight and silent. His eyes had the black rings painted around them, making them look like those of his brother, the wolf. Now he rose slowly and walked to the center of the ring.

Like a scepter he held his fan. It was made of the entire body of an eagle, the curved head and beak forming the handle. The body was wrapped in painted rawhide and the tailfeathers splayed out into the fan itself. Standing tall and alone, his face turned heavenward, Wanderer began his prayer for aid, chanting in a loud, clear voice.

> *Eagle Spirit, you see me here.*
> *Help me.*
> *I go to war to avenge my brother.*
> *Help me.*
> *Send good weather.*
> *Send my brothers, the eagle and the wolf, to guide me.*
> *I have smoked.*
> *My heart is sad.*
> *Give me the horses and the weapons of my enemies.*
> *Give me their lives and the lives of their families.*
> *I wish revenge.*
> *Help me.*
> *I will remember.*
> *Help me.*
> *Eagle Spirit, hear me.*

Although he stood rigid and still, his arms upraised and only his mouth moving, Wanderer appeared to grow, to stretch upward, pleading and reaching for the power he would need to make his raid successful. Naduah told herself it must be dizziness from the heat that made him seem to shimmer and vibrate with energy, that made his voice boom like thunder, the words echoing and rolling off across the hills beyond the village.

When he finished, there was a long silence. He turned and handed Naduah his fan, then strode away without looking back. Each dancer in turn gave her his fan and rattle, then filed off toward the river to bathe. Takes Down brought a large bag to keep the men's sacred objects in. As the People scattered to prepare for the evening's feast, Takes Down and Medicine Woman and Star Name helped Naduah to her feet. Her legs were numb from sitting so long in the same position, but she was proud to have been chosen. Still, she could think of only two things. That Wanderer might not come back alive, and that now she had a pony of her own.

❧ 17 ❧

"What shall we name her?" Naduah was chasing a horned toad to race with Star Name's, but she was talking about her new filly grazing nearby. Naduah crept up on the tubby little lizard as it frantically flung sand over itself in its efforts to hide. It looked like a tiny armored dinosaur that had fallen under a rolling pin. She pounced on it, and two tiny drops of blood formed at the corners of its eyes.

"Look!" She showed them to Star Name.

"Yes. I've heard they can do that, but I've never seen it. We'll ask Medicine Woman what it means."

"Do you think it means something bad has happened to Wanderer?"

"I don't know, Sister."

Naduah held the horned toad until it stopped struggling and settled into the warmth of her hand. She pricked her finger as she lightly poked the spiked frill at the back of the lizard's head. She repeated her first question.

"What should I name the filly?"

"The name will come to you. Be patient."

"But she has to have one. How can I train her without one?"

"Then give her one for now and change it when the real name comes."

"That would be confusing."

"We do it all the time. You were Tsinitia, and now you're Naduah, Keeps Warm With Us. Men change their names often."

"Why do they do that?"

"Because they're always looking for better medicine, or they hear a new spirit, or they do something special, or they just want to change. Sometimes people give them one they don't even want, but they can't get rid of it. Like Pahayuca. Do you think he wants to be called He Who Has Relations With His Aunt?"

"Why is he called that?"

"I don't know. And I'm not going to ask him, either."

"Where did Buffalo Piss get his name?"

Star Name laughed, a bubbling sound of pure joy that Naduah had come to love above all other sounds.

"On his first buffalo hunt his horse fell and a bull buffalo wet him as he ran by. And a bull buffalo pisses like a waterfall. It made Buffalo Piss so mad he mounted his horse and killed that buffalo and another one with the same arrow. Drove it right through them both. Everyone knew then that the buffalo piss was strong medicine, and he's been called that ever since."

"Then what about Pahayuca's daughter, Kesua? That means Hard
To Get Along With."

"Kesua is so good-natured we named her that to tease her."

"And why is this band called the Wasps?"

"Can't you guess?" Naduah shook her head, and Star Name told
her, "Our warriors sting hard and are gone before the enemy knows
what hit them."

"Why don't the women change their names often the way the men
do?"

Star Name had become used to Naduah's constant questions about
things everyone knew, and she answered them patiently. But she
thought of Naduah as one of the People, and the gaps in her educa-
tion sometimes took her by surprise. Of course women didn't change
their names as often as men. But why? She thought about it, sitting
cross-legged in the thick grass, holding her own lizard in both her
small brown hands.

"Because men need medicine to do the things they have to do. To
be powerful in war, to find animals, and to be able to catch and kill
them. Their names are part of their medicine. It doesn't take much
power to tan hides and set up lodges." Star Name stood and struck a
dignified pose. Holding her lizard toward the sun like an offering, she
began chanting through her nose like Gets To Be An Old Man. "O
Great Sewing Spirit, make my sinew strong and my fingers nimble
and my stitches neat so that I may sew the shirts of my husband well."
They both giggled.

"But Sunrise is teaching me to use the bow and arrow. He says I
should know how to do everything."

"He's right. He's promised to teach me too. But it's not what's
expected of you. The women keep the camp running, but the men
keep it alive. They must be always ready to defend us. That's why
they never carry any baggage when we travel."

Kneeling on the edge of the ring Star Name had drawn with the side
of her moccasin, they leaned over and put their lizards in the center of
it.

"If mine wins, Sister, you have to bring in a load of wood for me.
And if yours wins, I'll bring one for you," Naduah said.

"*Toquet*, all right." Still kneeling and holding her hands cupped
over her entry, Star Name looked up slyly at Naduah.

"And if mine wins the next one, I get to be the first to greet
Wanderer when he comes back."

Naduah looked her friend in the eyes, hers contrasting with Star
Name's, sapphire and obsidian. She wasn't going to be tricked into
any confessions about Wanderer. She shared everything else with
Star Name, but not her feelings about him. She changed the subject
slightly.

"Do you think they'll come back all right? Owl's brother, Deep Water, went too, and the whole family will suffer if anything happens to him. They've been gone a long time."

"Not so long. Less than two moons. Sometimes war parties are gone for years." Years. It couldn't be. "They may have to track the People Eaters all the way to the big water. Wanderer will bring his men back safely. Don't worry."

"Do you think so?"

"Of course. He'll be a famous chief someday."

"How do you know?" It pleased her to hear him praised. Perhaps because he had captured her she felt proprietary toward him.

"It's easy to see. He's better than all the others his age, and better than many who are older than he is. Did he ever tell you about the time he counted coup on an entire Cheyenne war council?"

"No," said Naduah. "When did he tell you?"

"He didn't. I heard it from Pahayuca. He was telling the story the night of your naming feast. But you couldn't understand it then, I suppose."

"He counted coup on a war council? You mean they weren't even in battle?"

"No, they were in camp. Getting ready to fight. It was two years ago. Wanderer's brother dared him to do it."

"Did his brother go with him?" Naduah knew she dared not use Eagle's name. It would have been disrespectful to his memory.

"No. It was hard enough for one man to get away with it. It would have been suicide for two."

"It sounds like suicide anyway. Alone! He was crazy!" Naduah chilled at the thought.

"Not crazy. Brave. Listen. He went to each man in his own party and borrowed Cheyenne clothes. The warriors often take enemy clothes with them, you know, especially those captured from a brave man. They wear them to call on the enemy's spirits to help them too. And they use the captured moccasins to make confusing tracks."

Naduah nodded sagely, although it was new to her.

"It was dark, and he rode right through their camp. He held his robe over his head and shielded his face. It was a temporary camp, and the council fire was not in a lodge. He stood with the men gathered around the Cheyenne war leaders, and he touched each leader with his quirt before slipping away. Then he mounted Night and rode out again. *Suvate*, that is all. You never heard that story?" Naduah shook her head. "It was one of Wanderer's brother's favorites."

"I miss Wanderer's brother. He always had funny stories to tell. But I never heard that one."

"I think all of us together don't miss him as much as Wanderer and

Something Good do." They were silent a moment, remembering the honey hunt. Then the lizards became restless, tickling the girls' hands as they explored their sweaty cells.

"*Sem-ah, Wa-hah-duh, Bhi-hee-duh*, one, two, three!" The girls let them go, jumping and yelling as they urged them toward the finish line. The race ended quickly and the field scattered while their owners chased them again. Star Name panted as she picked up the dropped thread of the conversation.

"You can ask Owl's grandfather to name the filly for you."

"The arrow maker?"

"Yes. His name means Name Giver, you know."

"You mean he really gives names?"

"Of course. He gave you yours, remember?" Even Star Name's patience was becoming a little worn with heavy use. "You have to give him a present, but he would be happy with anything you've made. It doesn't have to be anything big. He likes you. We'll talk to him when we get back." Star Name looked wistfully at the bay filly. "I wish I had a pony." She almost never looked unhappy, and it hurt Naduah to see her that way now.

"You can ride mine whenever you want. She'll be old enough soon, Sunrise says. Just be patient. He says when you need something it will come."

A dust cloud formed along the line of trees near the river and billowed toward them.

"*Posa bihia*, mischievous boys." The People didn't swear, but Star Name made the words sound like a curse. Upstream's gang fanned out behind him, all of them riding at full gallop. "There's the pony I should have had." Star Name would always resent the fact that Upstream was younger yet had been given a pony. Of course, if he didn't have one he would "borrow" one. And he did have to start his training. But Star Name still resented it.

"Look, Sister. Look! I killed it." Upstream started yelling before he was even close enough to be understood. But he kept repeating it as he came closer.

"*I* killed it." Sarai Na-pe, Dog Foot, had a different opinion.

"I counted coup first."

"But I killed it."

When they pulled up in a huge cloud of dust and shower of pebbles, it was evident that several had killed it. The female pronghorn was stretched over the rump of Upstream's small red pinto. The young horse had only been recently trained to carry dead game, and he was nervous. Upstream ignored his jumping and thrashing and pointed behind him. The pronghorn looked like a huge porcupine, with a hundred small arrows bobbing to the motion of the horse.

"I see it, Brother. I didn't know you owned that many arrows!"

"The others shot it, but mine killed it."

"Mine did." Dog Foot was sticking to his story. The rest joined in, claiming their own coups or taking sides, and they all rode off in a pack, still arguing.

Star Name turned to Naduah. "There won't be a bit of that meat that doesn't taste like metal. And they probably ran it so much its flesh will be bitter anyway."

Leaving their vanished racing lizards behind, they gathered up the filly's reins, untied her tether, and walked off after the boys.

The stiff frayed buffalo hide lay forgotten, along with Naduah's job of collecting dried buffalo chips to pile on it and drag back to Takes Down The Lodge. As she squatted, looking down at the pitiful little creature in the grass in front of her, Naduah remembered the swollen udders on the pronghorn Upstream and his friends had killed the day before. Why hadn't the boys noticed them? Some hunters. They must have been too excited about their first big kill.

Too weak to run, the fawn looked up at her. The arrow in its leg must have been a stray that hit the animal as it hid in the tall grass. But the groove in its shaft had done the job it was designed for, and the blood had flowed freely from the wound. Now the fawn was too drained to walk, much less run.

"You're a late one, aren't you? You can't be more than a month old." Naduah spoke to it soothingly, resting on her heels and parting the grass with her hands. "Where's your brother? Are you alone?" Single births were rare with pronghorns, unless the mother had bred for the first time. Naduah walked cautiously around the area, looking for a twin. She poked into the grass with the stick she always carried on her fuel-gathering trips. She had learned never to put her hand into grass or bushes where she couldn't see, or to turn over logs or deadfalls with anything but a stick. Too many stinging, biting creatures lived in such places.

While she searched, she wondered what to do. There weren't any pets in camp, except for the young eagles, stolen as fledglings. But they were kept tethered to supply feathers for their captor. Now and then a child would make friends with a dog, but the friendship usually lasted until the dog took on more adult responsibilities. Naduah's favorite, Dog, sat next to her now, head to one side and looking quizzically first at her, then at the fawn.

"No, we aren't going to chase it, Dog."

The dogs in camp had their uses. They pulled small travois and warned of enemy attack. They kept the camp clear of carrion, and their fights were a major source of entertainment. Besides, they were brothers to the coyotes and wolves, who were, in turn, brothers to the People. And dogs were never used as food. Pronghorns were.

She went back to where the fawn lay on her side, panting. Gently Naduah began to stroke her, carressing the silky smoothness of her long, cinnamon-colored coat. She continued murmuring to her even though the baby was too weak to struggle anyway. She stared at Naduah with huge, sad brown eyes under long black lashes. She shook her large, delicately veined ears and solved the question of what to do. The fawn had taken the child's heart captive.

Naduah grunted as she stooped and lifted the animal, being careful not to disturb the small arrow. Pulling it out might start the bleeding again. The fawn weighed about ten pounds, and it was a long way back to camp. She abandoned the hide half full of chips and started off. She considered using the hide as a drag to carry the fawn, but was afraid the bumpy ground would hurt her even more than being carried. So she struggled toward home with the baby's slender, black-tipped legs dangling below her arms and her head resting trustingly against Naduah's shoulder.

When she staggered up to the group of women sewing under the arbor in front of Takes Down's lodge, the laughter and gossip stopped abruptly. The child's blond hair was plastered to her forehead with sweat and the muscles of her small arms were taut with strain. She stood leaning a little backwards to balance the fawn's weight, and she could barely see over its head. Takes Down looked at her fondly a moment before she spoke.

"*Peta*, my child, put it there on that scrap of hide. How far have you carried it? And where is the hide you took to gather fuel?"

"I found her near the bend in the river, next to the gully where the ground owls live. I left the hide there, but I'll go back for it and bring in two loads of chips."

"That will make a tender stew, Naduah." She Laughs was Owl's mother and Name Giver's daughter. She was a widow with no brothers-in-law to marry her, and no one else had been willing to take up the support of her kin. Her fifteen-year-old son, Deep Water, was the only hunter in the family, although Owl brought in small game. They were without meat more than the others, and what meat they had was often from charity, part of a buffalo whose killer couldn't be identified in the chaos of a hunt.

Naduah hugged the fawn's neck tighter as she held the animal's head in her lap. Her mouth set in the stubborn Parker line and her blue eyes flashed.

"No one will eat her. I'm keeping her for a friend." She couldn't think of a word for pet, and suspected there was none.

"Soon Naduah will have more animals running after her in camp than there are outside of it." It was time for She Laughs to change her name, thought Naduah. She didn't laugh enough these days. But she knew She Laughs was lonely, and she understood why she sometimes was biting in her talk. She ignored her.

"Where is Grandmother? I want her to help me cure the fawn."

"Nayiya, Slope, is giving birth. Your grandmother went to help her. She'll be back soon." Takes Down smiled her shy smile. It was good to have a child again. They did such unexpected things. Especially this one.

"Speaking of giving birth . . ." Ekarero, She Blushes, took up the gossip where it had left off. Name Giver's sister had a delicate tracery of laugh lines around her eyes and mouth, although she often looked tired. There was a great deal of work in a family with a blind brother, two children, and only two women.

Naduah paid them no mind. She had wondered for a long time what the women talked about as they worked, day after day. Now she knew, and it didn't interest her much. She didn't have to worry about men sneaking into her bed at night, or labor pains. When they spoke of ·useful things, like the best way to cut a lodge cover, or where to find the juiciest berries, or how to gentle a horse, she listened. Now she just crooned to the fawn and stroked her head while she waited for Medicine Woman.

"Something Good . . ." Naduah's head gave a little jerk at the mention of her friend's name.

"The one who just died . . ." The women's voices dropped and they drew close, their heads together like hens going after the same defenseless beetle. Naduah had to strain to hear them.

"Silver Rain is sure they were lovers. She told me so herself. And now Something Good is with child. Whose do you suppose it is?" Adeca, Deer, looked more like a buffalo cow than her namesake. She was considered the best source of gossip in the village. Naduah avoided her, not because she didn't like her, but because the woman didn't know her own strength. She would playfully clap the child on the back and almost send her sprawling in the dust.

"It's probably not Pahayuca's. She still goes out each night to mourn the one who died. She's cut her hair off and speaks to almost no one." She Blushes managed to contribute to the gossip, yet maintain the air of one who was above such things.

"What do you think Pahayuca will do?" Takes Down broke in quietly.

"He loves her so much he can hardly see anything. He trips over his own feet when he walks." Deer rooted around in the foothills of her vast lap for her lost needle. That was the trouble with the slender steel trade needles. They disappeared so easily.

"Pahayuca hasn't been able to see his feet over that stomach of his for years." She Laughs mumbled around the wad of sinew thread that she was softening in her mouth. With her fingertips she twisted one end of a piece of sinew into a fine point and allowed it to dry stiff. Now she was using her mouth as a spool and pulling the thread out as she needed it to lace the sole to the upper leather of a moccasin. The rest of the yellowish thread lay next to her in a loose, thick braid, just like the one Lucy Parker had had to keep her embroidery floss free of tangles.

"I feel sorry for her." But then Black Bird felt sorry for anyone with troubles.

"I don't." And Deer felt sorry for no one. "She has a chief for a husband and anything she wants. She should be grateful, and not run after other men like a shameless Tuhkanay, a Wichita woman." No man had invited Deer to run after him in a long time.

"Is it true the Wichita women don't wear anything above their waists?"

"So I've heard."

"No wonder the men are always going off to trade for tobacco with them. Sacred rituals. A likely excuse." She Laughs almost choked on her sinew, and the rest of the women joined her. They howled with glee, rocking back and forth in the storm of it. They were still giggling when they took up their sewing again. And so it went.

Naduah sat silent, her face burning and anger seething inside her. Spiteful women. What did they know of Something Good and Eagle and love? She remembered the night of the honey hunt, when the four of them had sat around the campfire under the stars and talked and laughed at Eagle's preposterous stories. Eagle had mimicked many of the people they knew, and they rolled on the ground, aching with laughter. He had Deer down perfectly, even imitating the slower drawl of the Penateka.

Something Good had been radiant that night. Her face glowed with happiness. Now the light in her eyes had been snuffed out, and Naduah despaired of its ever being lit again. It pained Naduah to see her friend moving woodenly around, working silently, never smiling. Maybe Takes Down would have an idea for a present she could make Something Good. And she decided to ask her friend to practice shinny with her. That ought to cheer her up. And she was going to have a new baby. Naduah could help her care for it.

After Medicine Woman helped her with the fawn, she would go check on her new filly. And she had to find Star Name and show her the pronghorn. And talk to Name Giver about a name for her pony. And make a present for him. She'd have to ask Sunrise about that. Then there were the two loads of chips to bring in, and grapes to gather and pound. They would be moving soon, with all the bustle that entailed. The baby pronghorn had to be strong enough to travel before that happened, and she had to think of a way to carry her.

Then there was the bag she was making for Sunrise and the doll she was sewing as a surprise for Star Name. There were herb-hunting trips with Medicine Woman, and Takes Down had promised to let her help with the next lodge cover she was asked to make. Sunrise wanted to teach her to shoot her bow and arrow and help her train her filly. There was the ongoing game of kick ball with Owl and her other friends. And the horses to take care of. Her days were full of responsibilities and an ever more tangled skein of relationships. She had begun to think in the language of the People, and there was little time to dwell on the past.

Over the noise of the camp, the conversations and the children playing, the barking and neighing and the drone of Gets To Be An Old Man's medicine song, like a flock of turkeys with the croup, came Lance's chant. The crier rode slowly through the streets, holding up the buffalo robe that Naduah had abandoned. Lance always looked as though he were about to fall asleep. He had a droopy face with long features, and his expression was undiluted simplicity. But he had a perfect memory. For that he had been chosen by the band's council as the youngest camp crier anyone could remember.

Naduah went bashfully to collect the robe, handing him the piece of hackberry candy Takes Down had given her. He looked down at her in that solemn way of his.

"The boys found this near the gully. Upstream said it looked like Takes Down's."

"Yes, Lance. I had to leave it. I was going back for it." Nodding, he rode off, deep in his own thoughts as usual, and nibbling absent-mindedly on the candy.

She had rescued the fawn just in time. If the boys had found her first she would have been someone's evening meal. She held the baby's head while Medicine Woman worked the hunting arrow out. The back edges of its point had been rounded so that it could be pulled out easily.

As Naduah looked into the fawn's large, trusting eyes, she felt the bond that ties one to a helpless animal. No matter how many pronghorn steaks she would eat in her life, this doe would always be special, an individual and a friend.

↘ *18* ↙

The hills around the camp shimmered and danced in the waves of heat that pulsed upward from them. The sun had seared the grass until it was brown and shriveled, showing patches of dry, light brown gravel underneath. The horses grazed listlessly or gathered in the shade of the few cottonwoods. Dust covered everything, and there seemed to be no color anywhere, just shades of brown rolling to the horizon. The sky was white and cloudless and glared down at them. It was impossible to look outside without squinting and shedding tears. Naduah broke into a sweat at the thought of activity.

The sides of the lodges had been rolled up two or three feet to catch any breeze that might stray through camp. The heavy rolls were held up by stout forked sticks wedged into the ground along the tents' perimeters. Through the open bottoms of the lodges Naduah could see her neighbors lying on their robes or moving slowly about their necessary chores. Most people were sitting outside under their brush arbors as she and Sunrise and Takes Down were.

The village was quiet, and Naduah realized it was the children's laughter she missed. They were all at the river, sitting chest high in its tepid waters. She would have been with them, except that she had promised Sunrise she would help him work on a saddle for her. Parts of it lay spread around him.

Her pronghorn, Pah-mo, Smoke, and Dog lay curled up together next to her. They had tried to include her in the heap as part of the pack, but she pushed them away. Dog was faithful and loyal, but she was also hot and smelly and crawling with fleas. Now the two animals lay sleeping peacefully, exhausted from a hard morning at play. They had formed a strange friendship. Smoke would leap and paw the air while Dog grabbed her slender leg gently and shook it, snarling as though she would tear it from its socket. Then they would chase madly through camp.

At first the other dogs tried to interfere. Two of the biggest ones advanced arrogantly, determined to have pronghorn for dinner. Dog stalked to meet them on her short legs, the hair bristling along the ridge of her back.

"Go get them, Dog," Naduah hissed behind her. That was all Dog needed. She went after the two, running so fast her belly skimmed the ground. Surprised, the other dogs turned tail and fled, and Dog chased them into a huge pile of gear that scattered with a clatter. Finally she and Smoke were left alone, ignored as though Smoke were just another big dog.

Smoke's name had come to Naduah just as Star Name said it would. As she watched the fawn drift silently and lightly among the lodges, dogging her every footstep, Naduah thought of the wisps of smoke rising from the blackened smokeholes and floating gracefully on the wind. With Takes Down's help she had made a tiny collar of red trade cloth backed with buckskin. She sewed on the metal cones she'd been given at the eagle ceremony to make tinkling music wherever Smoke went. Now she could find her if she strayed. Also, the fawn had a bad habit of wandering up behind Naduah and playfully butting her as she tended the fire. Or she would put her cold, wet muzzle against the back of her friend's neck and give a loud whiffle of air. At least now Naduah had fair warning.

Next to her, Takes Down was patiently twisting strands of coarse black horsehair, rolling them rapidly on her round thigh with one hand and feeding more in a little at a time with the other. Some of the long rope she was making would be woven into a heavy, prickly four-inch-wide cinch for Naduah's new saddle. Takes Down was waiting for Sunrise to finish the frame so she could stretch the wet rawhide cover over it and sew it in place.

"*Pia*, Mother, why do most of the women wear red paint in the parts of their hair?" Naduah knelt, holding the twenty-inch-long curved wooden bar for Sunrise. It would be the seat frame when it was joined to the other bar by a pair of carved wooden arches. She held the light cottonwood as firmly as she could because Sunrise was drilling holes in it with a glowing metal awl. The afternoon was so hot already she hardly noticed the small fire he had near him to heat the awl and soften the glue he painted into the joints.

"Sunrise, tell our daughter why we wear red in our hair." Takes Down knew the answer. She had an astonishing amount of information stored up in her, if one asked her the right questions to get to it. But she never discoursed on important matters when Sunrise was around to do it. That was his responsibility. He thought a moment before answering.

"The red line in a woman's part ties her to Mother Earth, from whom everything comes and increases. It signifies the long trail a woman travels in her life, and it asks the spirits to make her fruitful like her mother, the Earth."

"Father, will you teach me to ride?"

"Yes. But why don't you ask Wanderer to help you when he comes back?"

"I wouldn't dare. He wouldn't want to waste his time with a child. And a girl child at that." She was holding the arch in place, lining up the drilled holes in its base and the saddle bar while the glue dried. She didn't notice the look that passed over her head between Takes Down and Sunrise.

153

"Hold this tighter, Daughter. Don't let it slip." Sunrise laced the parts securely together with green deer sinew that would shrink and harden as it dried. Then he repeated the process three more times and set the frame aside until the glue dried. The long, curved bars would parallel the pony's sides, and the arches would fit over her back. While he waited he picked up the graceful, saucer-shaped saddle horn and carved and smoothed it further.

Although Sunrise was quiet, he was rarely still. His hands were always busy at something, carving or sewing or repairing. And he wasn't home much. With two families to feed he hunted often, although he rarely raided far afield, even when he was looking for horses. He had no brother, and he worried about what would happen to his women and children if he were killed. At times he must have felt burdened by it all, fettered when the younger men rode off on their horse raids hundreds of miles south, deep into Mexico. But Naduah never once heard Sunrise complain. About anything.

Naduah and Star Name were working with her filly away from the distractions of camp. Star Name held the new bridle that Takes Down had made. It was a simple one that looped around Wind's lower lip and again around her neck. Naduah climbed onto a boulder and leaned her weight across the pony's back, talking to her in a low voice and moving very slowly. It had taken her a while to learn to mount from the right, instead of the left as her real father and uncles had always done. The People mounted from the right because they held their weapons in their right hands and it saved them the trouble of lifting them across the pony's back.

"When we finish here, let's practice with our bows," said Star Name. "I brought Upstream's target hoop." The hoop was a willow rim four inches across with thong spokes coming from a one-inch ring in the center. The object of the boys' game was to pass an arrow through the center ring while the wheel was rolling.

"He'll be angry with you for taking it."

"No, he won't. He has four or five of them, and this one is too small for him to hit anyway. I think he'd like to lose it. Sunrise made it for him, and Upstream is embarrassed to admit he's not good enough for it yet." She never passed up a chance to take a poke at her brother, and he always returned the favor. "Anyway, they've all gone off on a hunting trip. After grasshoppers or hummingbirds, or some such big game. They took enough food with them to go all the way to Mexico. Which is a good thing. They'll go hungry if they have to depend on what they kill."

"I hit the target three times in a row when Sunrise and I were practicing the other day."

"Good. Soon we can go on hunts together."

"We can't go on hunts. We're girls."

"Yes we can. Women hunt. You haven't met Santa Ana yet. He's with Old Owl's band. But his wife hunts and raids too. We just have to work harder and prove we can keep up. Sunrise can use the help. He'll let us come along. He's not like a lot of men."

Just then the pony stamped restlessly.

"Easy, Wind." Name Giver had thought of a good name for her, just as Star Name said he would. And he had been pleased with the herbs she had brought him as a present. He listened solemnly as she told him how to prepare them and what they would do. He hung the bag she had made for them on a peg driven into one of the lodge poles. It gave her a good feeling to see them there when she visited.

He had explained to her that the wind was the messenger of the spirits. It carried their words to their people. When souls were released it carried them to heaven. The wind went everywhere and saw everything. Nuepi, Wind, would carry Naduah wherever she wanted to go with the speed of a prairie wind.

The girls were interrupted by Smoke, who saw the riders first. She went bounding over the rolling plain in a wide circle, the white patch on her rump reflecting the sunlight and giving off a pungent odor of danger. Her collar of thickly sewn metal cones jangled madly.

"Smoke. Come here." Naduah put her index fingers in her mouth and gave the shrill whistle that Smoke and Wind had been taught to answer. The filly's head snapped up, yanking the bridle from Star Name's hand. Wind looked back over her shoulder at Naduah, who slid down from her pony. She tied a rope loosely around Smoke's neck when she calmed enough to be caught. As usual, they saw the cloud of dust first. Then the riders. One separated from the rest while the others stopped, waiting.

"It's Deep Water, Owl's brother. They're back!" Star Name was running as she shouted. Leaping rocks and gullies almost as gracefully as Smoke. Her braids flopped in the wind as she ran to be the first to spread the word. Deep Water was coming to prepare for the war party's return. Wanderer was back. Or he was dead.

Without thinking, Naduah vaulted from the rock onto Wind's back, catching the pony so off guard she forgot to protest, although she'd never been ridden before. She jumped a little, bringing both forefeet down as though stamping on a snake, then obeyed the knee pressure and firm hand on the rein.

Suddenly the world looked totally different to Naduah. She had ridden before, but always old, broken-down horses, and always surrounded by women as they moved the camp. Now she was alone on the plain with the wind ruffling her half-wild pony's black mane and blowing her own hair. She could feel Wind's muscles rippling between her thighs and knees, and she felt herself swaying with the rhythm of her horse's gait. She felt beautiful and wise and powerful and swift.

She wanted to kick Wind's sides and tear off across the plain as fast and as far as she could go. To feel the wind whipping past her and to see the ground flowing away under her as though she were flying. To know that she was one with a beautiful, powerful animal. Instead, swept up in the drama that pervaded the People's lives, she advanced slowly to meet her friend or mourn him.

Wanderer watched her approach, her body loose and relaxed, her left hand resting on her thigh and holding the rope attached to Smoke's neck. Smoke balked and skittered on the end of it, afraid of the mass of men and horses, the flapping streamers and fluttering feathers. Naduah's right hand held the reins as though she'd been born to ride.

Under the grim mask of black war paint he almost smiled, remembering the dirty, cringing urchin he had carried behind him four months ago. No, she had never been cringing. Not even then. There had always been a spark in her. He recalled her face when she thought he was going to slit her throat as she lay staked out. He hoped he would meet death as bravely.

Her body was tanned a rich, honeyed brown that set off her hair. Hours under the flaming sun had bleached it flaxen, almost white, and it blew like cornsilk around her face. As she drew closer he could see her brilliant blue eyes, fringed with long, creamy lashes. Her eyebrows stood out like downy white feathers against her dark skin. He could tell she had grown, and she carried her new height with dignity.

He would have to talk to Sunrise about her as soon as he could. In spite of decorum and the grim cargo he was carrying, a smile twitched across his face when he thought of the woman she would become. The smile looked grotesque because his face was painted totally black, signifying that he had taken his revenge and the debt was paid. Setting his mask back into its scowl, he raised his lance in greeting, the feathers and streamers waving from it, and waited for her.

"Hi, haitsi." She spoke in a loud, firm voice, unaffected by the fierceness of his look. "Hello, friend. My heart dances like the colt in spring to see my brother back safely."

Solemn as a little brave, she was. The future looked better all the time. And an antelope. What was she doing with an antelope? Did she know he was from the Quohadi, the Antelope Comanche? It was a very good omen. With an effort she made Wind understand

how to turn and came alongside Wanderer. Together they rode
toward camp, followed by the band of warriors, many of whom
carried long black scalps on their shields.

Deep Water, who had left as a herder, rode back with the warriors, a scalp blowing from his lance. Two of the men were bandaged, but Wanderer had brought them all back alive, as well as
horses and pack animals loaded with goods. As she rode with him,
his men ranged wild and fierce behind them, Naduah felt as though
her heart would burst with pride.

And from the large, soft leather bag tied to Night's surcingle came
a muffled, rattling sound. The bones were on their way home.
Wanderer would carry them with him until he could deliver them to
his dead brother's father far away on the Staked Plains.

As they approached the village a throng ran out to greet them.
Medicine Woman led the parade of singing women and girls. She
carried a slender sapling, the scalp pole. Later the new scalps would
be hung there for the dance, but for now most of them decorated the
men's lances and shields. Wanderer's dangled from Night's lower
lip to show his disdain for the enemy. The whole village formed a
huge procession filing through camp with singing and drumming,
the dogs barking and boys whooping from the sidelines. Unsure
what to do, Naduah followed along, feeling self-conscious, and
looking for her family and friends in the mob.

When they reached the other side of camp the warriors wheeled
and headed back the way they had come, each turning off at his own
lodge and handing his pony and weapons to his wife or sister or
mother. Wanderer dismounted outside Pahayuca's guest lodge. He
gave Naduah Night's reins. Then he handed her his lance and bow,
quiver and shield. She sat dazed, cradling them all precariously in
her small arms. She started to protest, but he smiled ever so slightly
and nodded in the direction of her lodge. Then he disappeared into
his tent.

She was still sitting there, trying to balance the fourteen-foot
lance, when Star Name ran up.

"Naduah, he let you take care of his war gear!" Star Name yelled
and ducked as Naduah swung around to face her, the lance curving
in a lethal arc. "Watch out! Naduah, be careful with that."

"What am I supposed to do with it? Help me. Hold the shield for
me."

Star Name shrank back in horror. "I can't do that. He asked you to
hold them."

"Why me?"

"He has no mother or sister or wife here, silly."

"He only has about thirty women who would like to be his wife. Probably more than that if you counted the ones who aren't eligible but would like to be anyway." Naduah tilted the quiver while struggling to keep from poking someone's eye out with the lance, and almost lost the arrows. Star Name put her hand up to catch them as they were sliding out.

"What do I do with all this?" Naduah asked in despair.

"I'll lead Wind while you hold everything. Medicine Woman or Takes Down or Sunrise can tell you what to do." They went slowly, weaving in and out, the lance wedged upright where it couldn't do any damage.

Star Name put the gear in Sunrise's lodge. Then, with a wave, she skipped off to put on her good clothes. Naduah tethered Wind and Night, watering them and rubbing them with handfuls of sweet grass. Then she went looking for her family.

She found Sunrise first, but she didn't dare disturb him. Sunrise was helping Name Giver instruct Deep Water in the proper preparation of his first scalp. The three of them were smoking and offering up a prayer when she passed the lodge. Then they would carefully shave the flesh off the skin and stretch the circle of scalp over a willow hoop, sewing it from east to south to west to north and back to east, the same way they entered a lodge. The hair would be oiled and combed and attached to a pole and allowed to dry all day before being hung with the others on the scalp pole planted in the center of the dance area.

Later it would be backed with red trade cloth and used to decorate a hunting shirt or lance. No one asked if the scalp had been taken from a man or a woman. It didn't matter.

Everyone in camp seemed delirious with delight. The old men were reminiscing about their own youth. The younger ones rehearsed the stories of their coups, acting them out with ear-splitting sound effects. Naduah finally found her grandmother at the dance area set up in front of Wanderer's lodge. Medicine Woman was directing the others as they tied deer hooves to the tall scalp pole so they would rattle when the pole was shaken.

Wanderer was in front of his lodge, but she couldn't get near him. He was surrounded by people congratulating him and receiving presents in return. Naduah gave up her search for Takes Down and went back to her own lodge.

She found Takes Down there, busily sewing more elk's teeth onto her own and her daughter's dresses. Wanderer's shield was set on a tripod outside, facing the afternoon sun. His lance leaned against the tripod and the quiver hung from it, all of them gathering power from the sun's rays. Takes Down held up Naduah's newest dress, shaking it so the dozens of teeth clattered.

"You'll sound like a hundred rattles, Daughter."

Naduah smiled wanly. And the dress would weigh like them too. Now that the thrill of riding in with Wanderer and receiving his weapons had worn off, she felt let down and left out. At least the dress was beautiful. The rows and rows of sparkling white elk's teeth stood out bright on the honey-brown suede.

"Will I have to dance too?"

"Only if you want to." Takes Down had found her best brass bracelets and divided them, giving half to her daughter. Naduah had to hold her hands up to keep them from sliding off, or she would grip them as they dangled against her palms. She sat patiently while Takes Down painted her small face and chin with vermillion, ending with the red line down her part. She giggled as her mother painted the insides of her ears red too. It tickled. Finally Takes Down unbraided Naduah's hair and carefully greased it.

"Pay attention to how the painting is done so you can do it yourself next time."

"Yes, Mother." Outside, it was becoming dark, and the drumming and singing and shouting were intensifying. Naduah squirmed, afraid she would miss something. When Takes Down was finally finished, the child raced from the tent.

"Slow down. You'll ruin your dress if you fall." Takes Down's voice followed her as she ran. She slowed to a fast walk, clacking and jingling among the others hurrying toward the dance area.

Pahayuca, Buffalo Piss, Sunrise, and the others of the council sat in a semicircle around the fire, their robes over their shoulders in spite of the heat. The pole with its grim foliage of scalps was planted in front of them. Lines of dancers, one of men and one of women, danced forward and back, facing each other. Then they formed a circle and moved around the scalp pole. The drums beat steadily and the flames leaped high, silhouetting the dancers.

Suddenly there was a yell, and the dancers stopped. Deep Water rode up on his pony and drove his spear into the buffalo hide laid out at the opening of the semicircle. There was silence while Deep Water told of his coup, and the taking of his first scalp. Then he dismounted and joined his comrades, sitting outside the circle. A second man rode in and did likewise.

"What are they doing?" Naduah leaned over and whispered into Takes Down's red-lined ear.

"They're sorting out the coups. The men of the council will listen and decide who really earned each one. Only two coups can be counted on the same enemy."

"Can't they tell by who has the scalp?"

"No. It's much braver to strike a live enemy with your coup stick than to take a scalp from a dead man. And even if a man kills an enemy, another can count coup on the same body. Battles are very confusing, and this is the only way to really know who earned what."

Naduah waited impatiently for Wanderer's turn, sure he would be last. She was right. She jumped as there was a screech like fingernails across slate. Night careened into the firelight like a piece of the darkness gone berserk. The pony raced toward the circle as though he would trample those inside it. Naduah shrank back, half hiding behind Takes Down's comforting bulk. Takes Down never flinched, but sat placidly as Night stopped just in time, almost in mid-stride, and Wanderer drove his lance into the lacerated hide. He sat on his war pony, both of them burnished by the flickering flames, and he told his story.

As she listened, Naduah felt sick, yet curiously elated, the same feeling she had when she saw boys torturing hummingbirds. After the noise of the rattles and drums and applause for the others' stories, his voice boomed in the stillness.

"We found the Nermateka, the People Eaters. The ones who killed and desecrated our brother's body. We swooped down on them as they slept, like a hawk on a helpless mouse. We captured them. We cut off their arms and legs. We cut out their tongues. We scalped them. But we didn't kill them. We built up their own fires until they were high. We threw them onto it alive and danced around them laughing while they gabbled and moaned with their tongueless mouths. While the grease from their bodies crackled and melted and their skin split and the blood boiled in the heat, even as it ran from them. And so we avenged our brother.

"We chased their women and children like prairie chickens through the brush. We speared them and mutilated them and left them for the ants. There was no one left to cry over their bones. We burned their village. We took everything they had. They will trouble us no more. Hear me, Brother Wolf and Brother Eagle and my brother who is dead. I am avenged. *Suvate*, it is finished."

But it wasn't quite finished. The Tonkawa chief, Placido, and his small hunting party had returned while his village still smoldered. He rode silently through the ruins, stopping only to pick up a Comanche war arrow with three red lines painted around its shaft. He recognized it. He had taken some just like it from Wanderer. Weeping silently, Placido carefully put the arrow into his saddle bag. He rode out the other side of camp in search of the remains of his wife and children, so that he might bury them.

160

❧ *19* ❧

Naduah shifted from one foot to the other. She scratched the welts on her arms and legs and flailed at the mosquitoes and horseflies that swarmed around her. The air she breathed was a stew of insects, thickened with dust, spiced with the heavy odor of horse dung, and heated to just below simmering. Not a leaf stirred. In fact, there were hardly any leaves to stir. Only cactus and a few stunted mesquites and cedars and some spindly post oaks. She wanted to sit down, but there wasn't a rock big enough, and if there had been one it would have been too hot to touch. The ground was gravelly and thickly sown with thorny plants of one type or another. She remembered something her father had said: everything in Texas sticks, stings, or stinks. Worst of all, vanity had made her wear this sweaty dress rather than her loincloth.

She began to regret bringing Wanderer out here to look at her filly. But he had asked to see her, and she couldn't have said no. She had been so excited when he had mentioned it that she'd run home to tell Sunrise and Takes Down. Sunrise had looked up from his awl and sinew and glue stick and smiled at her.

"That's an honor, Daughter. Listen very carefully to what he says. He's trained the best war pony I have ever known. He can tell you much." Then he went back to work.

But Wanderer wasn't saying anything for her to listen to. And he wasn't doing any training either. He was staring at Wind from all angles and running his hands over every part of her body. And he was ignoring Naduah even more than he ignored the mosquitoes. It was bad enough being ignored, but she couldn't even be comfortable while he did it. She looked longingly at the tiny spot of shade under the small cedar bush, wishing she could crouch in it. But that would be undignified and probably disrespectful. She sighed and sucked on a peeled piece of prickly pear, coaxing moisture from it into her cottony mouth. He was inspecting the filly's hindquarters now, having worked his way around from her eyes. Surely he would finish soon.

No wonder he wasn't married yet. He would probably ignore the most beautiful woman in the band the same way. *Serve them right,* she thought with more than a little malice. Any one of them would give her best outfit to be here alone with Wanderer. Much good it would do them. All they talked about was Wanderer. They practically fell over themselves, those women, and the girls too, trying to be chosen to dance with him. She thought of him dancing, his head

161

above all the others, his hands on his partner's waist, moving hypnotically in time to the beat of the drums.

He danced gracefully, abstractedly, as though serenely unaware that the rest of the women were standing around and fretting, speculating as to whom he would court and marry. She thought he regarded women as all right to flirt with. She had seen him do it. But he forgot about them as soon as something important came up. Like a horse.

"Women live to please men," Takes Down once said, laughing. "And men live to please themselves."

His examination of her pony began to make Naduah irritable and nervous. Would he sneer at Wind's flaws? She loved that horse. She didn't know what she'd do if he belittled her. No horse could pass an inspection like that, anyway. Not even Night. What if he disapproved of the care Naduah had given her? What if he said the filly wasn't worth his time? She was starting to feel belligerent, anticipating his criticism. She didn't care what he thought. She loved that filly and she'd train her herself. She'd make her the best around.

"She's a fine pony." Naduah almost choked on the angry retort she had been rehearsing. Instead she blurted the first thing that came to mind.

"How do you know?" It was the right thing to say.

"Come here." He beckoned to her and she trotted over, waving the cloud of insects away with one hand. Wind was becoming impatient and snorted at him, dancing and shaking her head.

"Just a little longer, Wind." He stroked her muzzle. "See the bulge in her forehead?" Naduah nodded. "That means she has a larger brain than the average horse. She's intelligent."

I could have told you that, thought Naduah, but she held her tongue.

"Her eyes are set far apart and are clear. Beware of a horse with puffy or inflamed lids, or eyes that have a bluish tint or a film over them. I'll show you how to check a horse's eyes for other defects later. Right now we'll make this quick. I'll just tell you the main things. Stand here in front of her and look at her chest. Her legs are straight and not too far apart. Her withers are narrow." They walked around to the side.

"If there's too much of an angle where the head sits on the neck, the pony will have breathing problems. Now run your hand over her backbone. Feel the muscles on each side of it? Beware of a horse that has a backbone that stands up too far above those muscles." Naduah thought ruefully of Sunrise's old pack mule. Wanderer continued stroking Wind and feeling her contours, as gently and lovingly as if she were his woman.

"Her back is short. That's good. She has one less vertebra than the white man's horses. That means she's from old Spanish stock. It also means she has a strong back. And her neck arches all the way from her head to her withers. Look out for a horse with a reverse curve in his neck. He'll likely have bad wind.

"But most important are her feet and legs. You have to check every part of them. Be sure her forelegs come straight down from her body and not out to the front or back. Stand in front of her and behind her to see that she's not knock-kneed or bowlegged. Her legs can't be too thin or too fat. And her hooves should be in a straight line from this first joint here to the toe." He crouched to point it out, and she looked over his shoulder, her hands on her thighs. She had never realized how much there was to looking at a pony.

"These are just a few things to look for. There's much more. We'll go over it a little each time. Get on her."

He stood back to let her mount and offered no help. She looked furtively around for a stone, a log, anything to stand on. There was nothing. Was he laughing at her again? She looked up at him, but his handsome face was solemn, still obviously interested only in the horse. She took a few steps back, ran, and leaped desperately, putting every muscle she could to work. She almost made it, and had to scramble only a little to find her seat.

"You'll have to learn to mount from both sides, the rear, or from an angle if necessary. In an emergency you can't be choosy. Walk her around in a circle." Naduah did as she was told, kicking Wind lightly with her heels to get her moving. "When I'm through with you," said Wanderer, "she'll obey signals no one else will even see." He turned with them as they circled him slowly. "Keep your hands low, and don't pull on the reins. Wind plants her feet solidly when she walks and her cadence is regular. Now trot her if you can. Ease her into it and keep your thighs tight against her sides. Sit forward a little and pump with your feet. Don't steady yourself with your hands. Use your legs. Use your legs as much as possible. You may need your hands for other things someday.

"Good. She still has an even beat, and she throws her feet out in front of her. Feel her gait with your calves and knees and thighs. With your seat and your hands and your heart. Feel every twitch and slide of her muscles. You should know what she's going to do and what condition she's in with your eyes closed. Look at her ears. They'll tell you things. When she's trained she can warn you of danger with them and tell you if the danger is man or beast. She will be your best friend. You will know her as you know yourself, and you will care for her as well as you care for yourself. Maybe better."

Wanderer spoke in a calm, firm, almost mesmerizing voice. He never raised it, though Naduah knew she was jouncing around like popcorn in the fire.

"I want you to run her around the village and come back here. Can you stay on her?"

"Of course." Naduah sounded offended, but she wished she was certain she could do it. She kicked and clucked to Wind and they raced off, Naduah clinging for her life and her honor. She pulled up five or six minutes later drenched in sweat and slid off, her legs shaky from the strain of gripping. The two of them listened to Wind's breath. It was even and quiet, not rasping or coughing.

"Watch her flanks just below the hipbone. If the flanks move once when she inhales and twice when she exhales, that's a bad sign. A horse that does that will have trouble breathing. But she's fine. Walk her a little to cool her off. And that will be enough for today."

"I brought some food with me," she said shyly. "Takes Down packed extra. Would you like to share it? We can eat by the river under the cottonwoods." Naduah knew she had no right to take up more of his time. He had important things to do, and he had already spent hours longer with her than she expected of him. But then, she was only beginning to realize how thoroughly he attacked everything he undertook. Why was he doing this, anyway? The thought nagged her some. She was only a girl. She would never be a warrior. His quiet answer startled her.

"All right. I know a good place to eat." He owl-hooted softly to Night, who grazed nearby. It was an inconspicuous signal, and she kept it in mind as she whistled for Smoke and Dog. As they rode toward the river Naduah told him about her new saddle, her eyes glowing. Smoke's collar jingled in time with their hoofbeats as she teased Naduah to race with her. And Dog scrambled off through the underbrush after rustles only she could hear.

"Takes Down is letting me put my own fringe on it. It's going to be the most beautiful saddle you ever saw." She had learned that modesty wasn't admired among the People. Wanderer watched her as she rode barebacked next to him. Her long, strong legs gripped Wind's sides, and she rode with loose-hipped grace. She was a natural, unlike most white people. Of course he could detect Something Good's style in the way she sat. She had picked a good model, but she had a style of her own, too.

She would be an excellent rider, even without his help. Did he want to spend the time necessary to see that she learned the basics and the extras too? But then to Wanderer everything was basic when it came to weapons and horses. The plains didn't forgive carelessness or incompetence or ignorance. It would take a long time to see that she learned right. There was so much to teach her. Why was he doing this? He looked at her again, at her smooth, solid body and her long, cornsilk braids, greased to keep her hair from tangling hopelessly in the constant wind. She stared back at him with her brilliant blue eyes, like bits of the sky trapped there under the white clouds of her brows. She smiled shyly, showing a glint of even white teeth in her tanned face. Then she flushed under the tan and dropped her eyes. She pretended to concentrate on her pony.

He was doing this because he could see her place in his future. That was why. He would teach her as much as he could while he was here. When he had to go back to the Quohadi, the Antelope band on the Staked Plains, he would leave instructions for Sunrise as to what he had taught her and what she still needed to learn. Takes Down and Medicine Woman were already teaching her many things, and he would ask Something Good to help. It would be good for her too, perhaps give her something to occupy her mind.

Naduah walked back through camp after her morning with Wanderer. Sunrise had told her to use all her senses, rather than depend on her sight alone, and she was smelling her way home. She could almost close her eyes and tell what people were doing. There was pecan and mesquite bread baking, and corn and meat roasting. No, the corn was roasting and the meat was boiling. There was steaming horse dung and tanning compound, and one of the dogs had caught a skunk. Someone was preparing to go gathering mesquite beans or grapes. She could smell the faint, fetid odor of rosita, a plant the women rubbed on themselves to keep the bugs off when they went crashing around in the bushes. And Gray Hand had let her meat sit too long again before drying it. It was beginning to spoil.

There was the odor of cut grass for the tethered war ponies, and crushed oak leaves and cedar on the brush arbors. There was sweat of humans and animals. Horse blankets, fresh leather from the hides stacked nearby, and smoke. There were so many different kinds of smoke. She sniffed deeply, closing her eyes to help herself sort them out. Tobacco, with sumac. So the pipe was being smoked just for gossip, and not a council. Buffalo chip smoke and several different kinds of wood. Deer must be using rotten mulberry bark to smoke her new antelope hide. It would make the hide a darker yellow-brown.

Silver Rain was boiling up a pot of dried plums. The sweet tang floated all over camp. And someone was making yellow paint. She could smell the huckleberry roots boiling with decayed oak bark. As she walked among the groups of women working and children and dogs playing, she tried not to look to left or right, depending on her nose to give her information. It was a game she enjoyed, a treasure hunt and a test. She was always trying to add new smells, and to hone her ability to distinguish them.

One of the men must be repairing his bow and filling the air around his lodge with the sharp odor of hot glue made from boiled hoofs and hide scrapings. From the amount of glue he was using, it must be one of those compound bows made of several layers of wood or bone. And there would be a new kick ball soon, judging from the smell of charred wood. Name Giver had promised to make the girls one. The usual method was to hold an oak bole over a fire to char the lumpy areas and make them soft. Then he would scrape the bole smooth and round. Naduah could feel her sore insteps and toes and wished that Name Giver would take the time to cover the ball with mesquite gum so it would be a little softer.

She caught the faint aroma of roasting hackberry candy and veered in its direction, knowing she would be offered some if she dropped by to pay her respects. In one hand Naduah held Wind's empty bridle, and in the other she clutched the thick, furry piece of bearskin that Wanderer had given her as a saddle pad. She hadn't even been able to tell him how happy his present made her before they were interrupted by Buffalo Piss and Pahayuca, and she had left him deep in a cloud of smoke and conversation.

But he had told her the story of the bearskin as they sat by the river, dangling their legs in the tepid water and eating the jerky and honey she had brought. She wondered how she could ever have thought him arrogant. She shuddered now to think of the story he had told her, and tried to imagine what it must be like to face a grizzly bear alone. Wanderer had been inside the bear's grasp, held in the crushing vice of the shaggy forelegs, when he reached up and slit the animal's throat with his knife. He had been drenched in a waterfall of warm blood. One of the thick, sharp claws had left the long, curved, satiny welt under his left shoulder blade.

Wanderer had spoken of it as calmly as though he were telling her about a rabbit hunt. And he showed her the knife, letting her hold it. It was a plain, broad trader's butcher knife about a foot long, with a flat wooden handle. It looked just like the one her real mother had used. This one was only a few years old, but it had been sharpened so many times it was much thinner than her mother's. She could barely make out "Green River" on the flat of the blade. Wanderer had done what most of the People did with their skinning knives. He had ground down the original edge and then beveled it on only one side. And he kept it razor sharp and oiled. Takes Down had one that had been worn to a sliver, and she had made a special, narrow case to hold it.

Wanderer had only been fifteen years old when the bear attacked him. What if he hadn't had the presence of mind to have his knife in his hand and to keep his arm free when the grizzly grabbed him? What if he had died there alone, somewhere in a wild ravine on the Staked Plains, and the wolves and coyotes and ravens and vultures had picked his bones clean and dragged them off and scattered them?

There by the warm, muddy river, in the speckled shade of the cottonwoods, with the sun hot and high over the bristly hills and the crickets singing, she had held the knife, warm from riding in its sheath at his waist. She tried to picture her handsome Wanderer dead, with ants crawling over him. What if he hadn't lived to pull her onto Night's rump and ride away with her? Would she still be at Parker's Fort with her family? No. Someone would have stolen her, probably. The People needed children. And they loved them. Perhaps it would have been Cruelest One. Except that he never took captives. But it might be someone just as bad.

She and Wanderer had talked about the raid on Parker's Fort as they rode double back from the horse pasture. It had been painful, but he seemed to want to be sure she understood what had happened that day. She could still hear his voice, low and matter-of-fact, in her mind. He had turned to look back at her as he spoke, his large, black eyes searching her face in that way he had, like a wolf inspecting something he's unsure of.

"Buffalo Piss had formed a raiding party to go where the white men make their lodges. They are very careless, and it is so easy to steal horses from them that there are often none left worth taking. We met a band of Caddo. In the past we fought them, but several years ago we made treaty talk and gave them presents. When we met them we planned to trade for corn with them. But they invited us to join their war party. They aren't the warriors we are, and they could use us. They were on a revenge raid, to pay back the white eyes for an attack on one of their villages by the white police society."

"You mean the Ranger companies?" Naduah translated it as "roving warrior band," which was as close as she could come.

"Yes. They attacked a village at dawn while everyone was sleeping. They killed many people and drove off the pony herd."

"Why?" Naduah had heard the story from her father, who was one of the first Rangers. But she had heard that the attack was to recover horses that the Caddo had stolen from the settlers, and to punish the thieves.

"Other Caddo had stolen horses to replace the ones white people had taken from them as they passed through." And so it went, with one group stealing, then another, involving people who had had nothing to do with it in the first place. "The fort was a good place to take revenge."

"But the people there hadn't stolen from the Caddo or attacked them." They both avoided mentioning Naduah's relationship with the victims, or the fact that she was white.

"It didn't matter. Those of the Caddo village weren't the ones who had stolen the whites' horses either. The fort was far from other white lodges. The soldiers who had been there had left. And the people who lived there were careless. The Caddo had been watching them and knew their routine. Big Bow and his Kiowa and those of us of Buffalo Piss's party went for loot and horses. We weren't on a revenge raid, but the Caddo were. And when blood is shed, a man forgets why he is there. Blood is like the white man's stupid water."

"You mean whiskey?"

"Yes. *Wih-skee*. It makes him brave and foolish, and he does things he can't even remember afterward. And so it happened. *Suvate*, that is all."

And so it happened. And here she was. And it had been almost four months and no one had come for her. By now she wasn't sure she cared. Deep in her own thoughts now, she walked along, staring at the buff-colored puffs of dust that rose when she put her feet down. She dodged to avoid the stringy vine that sent tendrils running through the dust and gravel. By this time next year the whole area would be covered with them. She kicked at it to uproot it. The vines grew in masses, their thorns clutching at anything that moved through them. But their red flowers, like furry little balls, filled the air with the scent of roses. She could smell it strongly from just one plant.

"Naduah."

"*Hi, tai*, hello, women friends. How are you?" She had tracked the hackberry candy to its lair, a brush arbor in front of Owl's lodge. She Laughs had finished roasting it, and it lay in a small turtle shell. She smiled one of her rare smiles, and it lit up her face. She Laughs was homely, with coarse features, but her smile was beautiful as though to make up for it. Like the ugly little vine with its delicious aroma.

"Is Owl here?" Naduah peered toward the dark lodge opening behind them. Name Giver sat next to it working on the kick ball.

"No. She went to gather saplings for her grandfather."

"We heard that Wanderer was helping you with your pony."

"Yes." Eka Na-pe, Red Foot, was pretty, but Naduah was wary of her. She was vain, and she didn't seem to think about much except finding a husband. Wanderer, preferably. Perhaps Naduah disliked her because she was the one who followed him around the most, always intruding when Naduah managed to get a word in with him. Now she'd had three or four hours with him and apparently the news was all over camp already. She wasn't surprised at how fast it had spread, just that they would bother to talk about a nine-year-old girl. But then, everything Wanderer did was gossip for this crew.

"What did you two talk about?" She Laughs sounded wistful. Could she be interested in Wanderer too? She was old. Almost thirty winters.

"We talked about horses."

"You were gone all morning and you only talked about horses?" The envy in Red Foot's voice gave Naduah a twinge of pleasure.

"Yes. We talked about horses. And how he got this piece of bearskin here." She held it up. "I'll tell you about it when I have the time." *And when I've rehearsed it enough,* she thought as she reached out to tickle the face of Slope's new baby with the crow feather that dangled from his cradle board. Strapped into his V-shaped frame, the baby hung from a pole in the roof of the arbor and swung gently. She tweeked his small penis that stuck out through the swaddling cloth, and he spouted like a tiny spring.

"The candy was good, She Laughs. Tell Owl I'll come by to see her later." And she left before she could be asked any more questions. Smoke and Dog trotted around her, tangling with her legs and almost tripping her. She shooed them with her arms.

She decided to ask Wanderer if Owl and Star Name could come to the training sessions. And she would swear the girls to secrecy about what happened there. That ought to keep Red Foot in a state of agitation. She grinned at the thought. And did a little heel-toe step, and the sideways slide of the love dance.

❧ 20 ❧

The pale reddish soil and short, patchy brown grass looked like a rumpled, mangy buffalo robe thrown across the hills. The rolling plain marched off to meet the horizon with nothing blocking its way. The sky seemed to hang lower to the earth than usual, and it was the color of ashes. From the distance came the steady roar of thousands of buffalo. It was a dull rumbling, as pervasive as the cold wind and the gray sky.

Wanderer sat loosely on Night, and tucked the reins into his belt, leaving his hands free. The reins were twenty feet long, and they would come loose from his belt if he fell while chasing the buffalo. If he was lucky he could grab them in time for Night to pull him free of the herd.

In the cold air of the late October dawn he wore only a breech-clout, moccasins, his skinning knife, and his quiver and bow case. He rode barebacked, unwilling to burden Night with even the weight of a surcingle. He shivered a little as he made one last check of his equipment. He took the coiled sinew bowstring from under his armpit, where he kept it to protect it from the morning damp-ness, and strung it onto his bow. If the sinew became too wet, it stretched, and it shrank and snapped when it was too dry. He had two spare strings tucked into a small pocket on the quiver, in case this one broke.

He slipped the bow under his thigh to hold it and shifted the quiver so that it was at his left side, where he could reach it more quickly than by groping over his shoulder. The wind chilled his back where it had been warmed by the thick fur of the quiver. He shook the quiver so all the arrows were lying in the bottom, the wider part of its tear-drop shape. With the bow gone its case drooped at the ends, out of the way of the quiver that was attached parallel to it. Both cylinders were made from the entire dense winter pelt of a huge white wolf, with the tail turned into a case for the bow. The four paws hung down at both ends of the quiver and were decorated with beadwork and tassels. White wolves were very rare among the red wolves of the plains, and their medicine was powerful.

Wanderer pulled out seven arrows, all of them banded with the three stripes of red paint near the base of the turkey fletching. He put two of the shafts in his teeth and held five in his bow hand. All together, the quiver with its twenty hunting arrows weighed less than two pounds.

The great semicircle of fifty men advanced slowly toward the buffalo herd grazing out of sight on the other side of the long, low ridge. The hunters had no metal, no horseshoes, no saddles, noth-ing to creak or jingle, and the wind was blowing toward them. In the gray light of the overcast dawn they drifted silently through the ground fog that eddied around their ponies' hooves. They seemed like phantom hunters, their heads and shoulders wreathed in writh-ing swirls of steam from their own breath and that of their ponies.

Out of the corner of his eye Wanderer watched Pahayuca sitting like a statue on his big red bay. The People had no need of police societies for hunts, like those of other tribes. Each man was his own master, yet he cooperated fully with the others on a hunt. It wouldn't have occurred to them to do otherwise. The tension vi-brated among the men as they waited for Pahayuca's signal. They were flesh and blood springs wound tightly and held by a hair trigger. Wanderer forced himself to relax, but he still shivered slightly. Night flicked his ears once.

As he waited, Wanderer thought of a hunt three years before and of his cousin's crushed and mutilated body. Wanderer had stared down at it after the wounded bull had finally died and been dragged off with lines tied to several horses. A buffalo hunt could be deadlier than a raid against men. It was harder to predict what buffalo would do.

Wanderer remembered his first hunt and the huge bull he had only wounded. He had been thirteen years old and frightened for the first time in his life. Since then he had felt that expanding bubble of fear in his bowels many times, but the first time had been the worst. He would never forget the smell of the beast's breath, and the hissing noise of blood and steam venting from his mouth and nostrils. He could still see the huge bulk of the animal looming from the cloud of dust. He could see the veins in the encrusted, bloodshot eyes that seemed about to pop from the animal's head.

His broad back, matted with burs and caked with dust, seemed yards across, and his shaggy, tangled mane brushed the ground as he bellowed and pawed. His shoulder muscles bunched and tautened and his head went down, the wicked, curving horns thrust forward. He was preparing to charge. He stood seven feet tall at the shoulder and weighed over two thousand pounds. Of course Wanderer had picked the biggest bull he could find for his first kill. Now it was debatable who was going to be killed. Wanderer knew that even if the bull died, his momentum and will to live and nervous system would keep him going several yards.

The bull charged, and Wanderer froze on his pony. He watched, fascinated, as death thundered toward him. Luckily, his horse had better sense. Wanderer's father, Pohebits Kwasu, Iron Shirt, had loaned him his prize buffalo pony, and the horse was brilliant. He dodged and circled the plunging animal while the buffalo pivoted on his front feet. Hitting the ground with his rear legs and using them to push off in a new direction, he could turn his two thousand pounds as if on a swivel.

For two of the longest minutes in Wanderer's life the pony ducked and dodged, jockeying for the right position on the bull's left side. He had to get Wanderer a bow's length away for the shot to be most effective. The second arrow entered behind the rib, drove all the way through the heart and into the ground on the other side. The buffalo crashed to his knees and paused there, as though paying homage to his slayer, before rolling over dead.

Wanderer had been too elated to retrieve his first, misfired arrow.

He had burned with shame when his sister and her friends presented it to him, taunting him in front of the whole band at the celebration afterward. He had learned two things that day. He vowed never to leave a misfired arrow in his prey, no matter what risks he had to take to get it back. And he knew he would always have the best horse possible under him.

His daydreaming was interrupted by a movement at the edge of his vision, and he tensed, the movement translating into a signal to Night.

Pahayuca's hand rose and fell with a quick chopping motion. Every man leaned forward, and the ponies leaped ahead. The line of naked riders swept over the ridge and circled on the other side, trapping the herd in the magic surround. As the ring of riders tightened, cinching the buffalo ever more closely, the cows and calves milled bawling in the center. The bulls raced around them, using their bodies as a barrier. They ran with their tongues out and their heads down, the air puffing in and out of their mouths.

Wanderer didn't even have to use his knees to guide Night as they rode in among the stampeding bulls. Running full speed through the thick cloud of dust, Night dodged old prairie dog holes that would have snapped his leg like a twig and thrown his rider and friend under the driving hoofs around them. He knew to swerve as soon as an animal was shot, to avoid being gored if it turned on them. And he had the speed to run their quarry down quickly. The meat of an overheated buffalo spoiled fast.

Wanderer and Night were like one animal, like the centaur the Indians had believed the mounted Spaniards to be hundreds of years before. But Wanderer rode better than any Spaniard. He and Night raced through the melee, dodging horns and hoofs and the arrows of other hunters. There was no time for fear or thought or plans. They acted reflexively, unconsciously, weaving in and out in the dust and the stench and the noise.

The herd scattered as individuals found openings and headed across the hills. They seemed clumsy and bumbling at first, until they found their stride. Then they raced off with astonishing speed, veering first to the right, then to the left. They made a zigzag trail to keep their heads turned to one side or the other, one eye looking forward and the other back. Pahayuca said a buffalo herd could eat breakfast in Texas, dinner in the country of the Ute, and supper with the Wichita.

The ground was littered with fallen buffalo, arrows sticking from their sides as uniformly as if they had been measured with calipers. Finally only the yellow and red calves were left, deserted or orphaned. They bleated and lunged in all directions. While the boys, yelling and whooping, rode in to finish them off, Pahayuca signaled to the waiting women and girls, who ran down the slope, racing to count coup on the bodies.

Star Name straddled the calf as it lay on its back, its legs in the air. With a deft stroke, she opened the belly. She made another cut and dug around inside the calf's first stomach. She scooped out a handful of curdled milk that looked like farmer's cheese, picked out a few chunks, popped them into her mouth, and offered the rest to Naduah. Naduah shook her head feebly and almost lost what little breakfast she had eaten.

It was the first hunt of this size she had been on, and the dining arrangements were difficult to adjust to. It wasn't the butchering that bothered her. She had seen plenty of that, although she didn't like it. It was that the People ate everything. And with relish. With the plains for a table and a warm hide as a platter, they feasted.

Some of the animals were still kicking, their nerves still sending impulses to their brains after their hearts had stopped beating. One cow lay panting with life and moaning while the hide was flayed off her. Blood still flowed, and the dust hadn't even settled from the crashing fall of the last bull. The raw livers, sprinkled with green bile from the broken gall bladders, were delicacies reserved for the hunters. Sunrise shared a small piece of his with Naduah, and she was surprised at how good it was. She began to help herself to the entrails. They were all she was going to get, after all, and she found she was craving them. She was unaware of the trace elements and minerals the organs provided. She only knew they appealed to her.

Takes Down bit into a hunk of the soft, yellowish tallow from the bull's loins, letting it melt in her mouth. Her eyes were half closed and she chewed with the same blissful expression Rabbit Ears had when eating a particularly tender thistle.

The dogs were racing to and fro in packs, snapping and barking and howling in a frenzy. Now and then they leaped together, trying to catch a choice piece of offal tossed over someone's shoulder. Tail between his legs, the winner of the toss streaked across the plain, the losers baying at his heels.

The hearts were cut out and set aside, to honor the buffalo and to encourage them to multiply. And as soon as the soft entrails and other organs had been eaten, the men, women, and children set quickly to work, finishing the butchering. Meat that wasn't cut into strips and hung on the drying racks by the following morning would spoil, even in the cool weather. And there was a lot of meat. It took four or five women, working along with their men, to process the animals killed by each hunter.

Takes Down and Black Bird butchered the cows Sunrise had killed for his family. Laying the animal on its side, Takes Down ripped it down the belly and took off the top half of the hide, cutting away the meat from the bones. Then she and Black Bird tied ropes to the feet and turned the carcass over with their ponies to repeat the process on the other side.

Naduah and Star Name and Owl loaded packhorses and rode back and forth together all day between the kill site and the drying racks at the hunt camp. By afternoon Naduah's arms and legs ached with the strain of carrying heavy loads of meat and standing on tiptoe to hang the strips. She was covered with grease and blood that was drying and itching.

While the women worked, Sunrise and Wanderer heaved the heavier bulls onto their bellies with their legs spread. They slashed the hide across the chest and neck, then folded it back so they could cut out the forequarters. They sliced down the center of the back, being careful to leave the sinews intact along the spine. The hindquarters were disjointed, leaving the rump with the back. Next the flank was cut up toward the stomach and removed in one piece with the brisket. The thin slab was rolled, put into a piece of hide, and loaded onto a packhorse.

Sunrise cut up through the stomach to remove the guts, separating the ribs and the sternum. Slicing between the middle ribs, he took their free ends in both hands and pulled sharply upward and outward, breaking rib steaks from the spine. When he had finished, all that was left was the bare spine with the head left on. He cracked the skull and scooped the brains out into a stomach liner. The brains would be saved for tanning.

While Black Bird carefully removed the sinews from the spinal column, Takes Down prepared them before they had a chance to dry and stiffen with their own natural glue. She cleaned the moist tendons by scraping them with a piece of bone, then softened them more until fibers could be stripped off. The process looked easy. It wasn't. The longest sinew was the three-foot tendon along the backbone. The one lying under the shoulder blade of a buffalo cow was only a foot long, but especially thick. Many of them twisted together made a tough bowstring.

As the carcasses shrank, vanishing under the hands of the People, Naduah realized how much their lives depended on the buffalo. Each part had a function. The bladders were saved for medicine pouches. The bones would turn up as shovels, splints, saddle trees, scrapers, ornaments, awls, and even dice for the gambling games. The scrotums were cut off to be turned into rattles for dancing. The stomach paunch liners would replace worn-out water containers, and the hooves and feet were saved for glue and more rattles. The horns would make cups and spoons and ladles, and fireproof, waterproof holders for powder and coals when the camp was moved.

The hair would be used to stuff pillows and saddle pads and shields. It would be twisted into ropes and halters and used for headdresses. The tails were handy flyswatters and quirts and decorations. Even the stomach contents were emptied and sorted for future use. The small pellets of partially digested grass were saved for Medicine Woman to use in treating frostbite and skin diseases. Star Name held up a big hairball, very valuable medicine that Medicine Woman would be pleased to have.

The hides were saved, but they weren't prime yet. Later, toward the end of November or the beginning of December, there would be another hunt to get them when they were thickest. The hides of the four-year-old cows were at their best for lodge covers then. Robe hunters looked for small buffalo with trim, compact bodies. Their hair was as silky as fur, and it made the best bedding.

As the sun hovered over the horizon, it looked as though it too had been dipped in the blood that drenched Naduah and her family. The wind blew colder, and Naduah shivered in her sweat-soaked dress. In a long, tired line the hunters and their families followed the buffalo herd's wide, sunken road back toward the river and the hunting camp. The scouts who had left a few days earlier to pick a spot had done well. The low hide lean-tos were set among an open stand of willows and cottonwoods near a clear stream. On the other side of the stream a bluff protected them from the north wind. The small shelters could hardly be seen behind the hundreds of scaffolds hung with meat. One had to pick one's way through a maze of them.

"Naduah," Star Name shouted between cupped hands, "we're going to the river to bathe. Come with us."

"You're crazy. It's too cold."

"It's not cold," Owl assured her. Not to Owl, maybe. Melted snow probably wouldn't be cold to Owl. She had skin like an old buffalo. But Naduah couldn't resist the unspoken dare.

"I'm coming."

She and Star Name stood at the edge of the stream and splashed water over themselves, shivering and chattering with the cold, a blue tinge under the goose bumps that covered them. Only Owl seemed oblivious to the weather. She had waded in and sat now with only her head showing.

"Cowards," she called. "It's not bad when you get used to it."

"This'll do, Owl."

"Don't complain to me when no one asks you to dance tonight because you smell like a buffalo," Owl shouted. She stood up and walked toward them. They bundled up in their robes and headed toward camp, still talking.

"Pahayuca promised the buffalo tongue ceremony when we get back to the main village," Star Name said.

"And the women are in an uproar about it," added Owl. "I can't wait to see who's chosen to serve the meal."

"I suppose they all want to be chosen," said Naduah. Owl laughed with delight.

"Not exactly. Before she can serve the tongue any man who's lain with her has to shout 'No!' She has to be a virgin, you see."

"A very rare animal," said Star Name wickedly.

"And of course the woman gets teased, no matter what."

"Remember when Red Foot did it last year and Buffalo Piss said she slept with all the dogs in the village?"

"Yes. Then Sunrise said she'd slept with everything with a pizzle."

"Sunrise said that?" Naduah couldn't believe it.

"Yes, he did," said Star Name. "I heard him."

"That's the trouble. Everyone hears it. If no one speaks up, the women all applaud and go 'li-li-li-li.' " Owl demonstrated, vibrating her tongue against the roof of her mouth.

"I can't do that."

"Yes, you can, Naduah. It goes like this." Owl skipped around in front of Naduah and tilted her head so the girl would have a clear view of her tongue and palate. "Practice."

And the three of them practiced loudly all the way back to their shelters.

❧ 21 ❦

Biting her lip, Naduah watched the horses walk toward the line of bluffs to the north. Turning, she stuffed the reins of the painted pony Wanderer had just given her into Star Name's hand.

"Take him. Now we each have one." She choked on the last word, then whirled and ran off among the lodges. She darted through the boys' wheel game. The wheel target and the small arrows flew in all directions, but she never slowed down. Ignoring the threats that followed her, she raced on toward her own lodge. She jumped over the threshold into the dim warmth and threw herself, sobbing, across her low bed.

Medicine Woman came in as quietly as a shadow and waited until the storm subsided. Then she sat next to Naduah, gathering her into her slender, fragile arms.

"He'll be back, little one. Don't cry."

"Not for two or three years. Maybe more. He said so. That's forever." Naduah gulped and hiccupped and blew her nose on a leaf that Medicine Woman handed her. "Why did he have to leave? I thought he was my friend. He was helping me train Wind."

"Do you know what Nocona means, Granddaughter?"

"Wanderer."

"Names are very personal. Each should be different, like snow-flakes, because each person is different. Your name tells others about you, like Keeps Warm With Us. It tells how you act, and what you've done in your life. Nocona is a wanderer. He's special. He belongs to no one and he belongs to everyone. We have to share him."

"I don't want to share him. I have to share him right here in the Wasp band."

"Sometimes there are things in life you have no choice about. Wanderer is one of them. He's special, and he has many responsibilities already for one so young. He must go back to his own band and to the Staked Plains for a while."

"Why is he special?"

"Some just are. All our men strive to be great warriors. All of them are brave. But the coyote can never be a wolf, nor the hawk an eagle. Wanderer is a wolf among coyotes and an eagle among hawks. He won't forget you, little one. And you have to be worthy of his friendship."

"I'll try." Naduah snuffled back a large, wet sob.

"Smile for me." Medicine Woman tilted her granddaughter's chin up and smiled down at her. "That's good. We'll be camping with Old Owl's band soon. We'll spend the winter with them. You'll see your brother." Naduah's smile widened.

"When?"

"Soon."

John Parker, Bear Cub, sat huddled under his buffalo robe in front of his grandfather's lodge, watching Old Owl work on a new bow for him. He was growing so fast that after six months with the People, Cub's bow was too short. It was late afternoon, and the autumn light was failing. The two of them were sitting outside the lodge to take advantage of what rays the sun could send through the thick, swollen gray clouds. Old Owl's eyes had once been like a hawk's, but they were failing him now.

Old Owl had measured the length of the bow that morning before Cub had left on his daily excursion. He had made the boy stand still while he laid the Osage orange sapling along his leg and marked it at his waist. He had been shaping it all day, patiently whittling it into the desired taper. Now Cub was back, and as he worked, Old Owl talked. It was a monologue that went on whenever he and Cub were alone. And often when they weren't. Cub listened carefully.

"Always look for winter wood, Cub. It doesn't split when it dries. Orangewood is best, like this here. But it comes from far to the north, and it's not as easy to get. A young ash that's been killed by a prairie fire makes a fine bow. But elm, cedar, willow, dogwood, mulberry, they'll all do. Trim the bark off the staves when you collect them, and rub them with fat. Tie them in bundles and hang them at the top of the lodge, over the fire. The smoke seasons them. And kills the insects in them."

"How many sticks in each bundle?"

"Oh, ten or twelve. Shape it like this, carving outward from the center, the grip. Then smooth it and polish it with sandstone when you finish." He rubbed more fat onto the stave and held one end of the tapered wood over the fire until it was very hot. He grunted as he braced the end under his moccasin and forced it into a curve. He went on talking as he held it there.

"When this cools the curve will be permanent. The hard part is getting the two sides to curve exactly the same. Sometimes you have to reheat it and start over. The important thing is to be patient, and not stop until it's exactly the way you want it. Never settle for less than the best, unless you're desperate and in a hurry. Your life depends on your weapons. And more important, your family's lives depend on them.

"Be sure the grip is thick enough or the bow will kick when you shoot it. And the cord will burn your wrist." Cub held up his wrist to show his grandfather the wide leather band he had made in case that happened. Old Owl reached out and turned Cub's wrist to see the band from all sides. "Good. But if you burnish the edges with a hot rock, they won't rub you. Where was I?"

"You were talking about making the grip thick enough."

"Yes. And the ends of the bow. They should be the width of your little finger. Hold one out here so I can measure." Cub obliged, then reached under his robe and pulled out a small bag from among those dangling at his waist. He poured some round, dark pellets into the palm of his hand.

178

"I found these today, Grandfather."

"What are they?"

"Deer scats, of course. You said to bring things like this to you."

"That's right. I did." He peered owlishly over at them, squinting to focus. "Where did you pick them up?"

"In a meadow a mile from the river."

"When did you pick them up?"

"In the middle of the afternoon."

"Then we know they're at least two or three hours old. How old do you think they were when you found them?"

Cub picked one apart with his fingernail. It crumbled easily.

"There was no dew this morning to wet them so they would have dried out faster. But I'd say they were left there yesterday."

"And how big an animal dropped them?"

Cub studied the pellets intently, as though deciphering a secret code. "Medium sized."

"Was it a healthy animal?"

"Yes."

"Good. You're right. What kind of grass was it eating?"

Cub separated the bits of the broken scat. "It looks like the short thick grass that grows by the river."

"Were there any other deer droppings nearby?"

"Yes, smaller ones. That means it was probably a mother with a fawn, doesn't it?"

"Probably. Yes. Were the scats piled up or scattered?"

"They were piled up."

"And what does that tell you?"

"That the deer were grazing quietly and not being chased."

"Were there any other tracks nearby?" And so the questioning went. It was almost dark when Old Owl made the bowstring, working by the feel of it between his gnarled fingers and by the light from the fire between him and Cub. He picked up a piece of buffalo sinew about eighteen inches long and split off two strands with his teeth. He soaked them in his mouth, then with his palm he rolled them rapidly on his thigh, pulling back his buffalo robe to bare it. He placed a third piece between the first two, rolled it quickly, then added another and another. When he finished he had a string of even diameter, three times the length of the bow. He folded it into thirds and twisted it into a three-ply cord. He knotted the ends to prevent raveling and tied it between two stakes to keep it stretched as it dried.

Then he rose, creaking at his joints, and began kicking dust over the fire. Cub helped him, scattering the burning logs. A soft glow and low voices came from the lodge, along with the smell of stewing meat.

"Grandfather, may I wear your wolf robe? The one you used when you were a wolf scout."

"It's old, Cub. I don't even remember where it is." Old Owl found it hard to say no to his grandson.

"It's in a case way back under your bed, against the wall of the lodge. I saw Prairie Dog put it there."

Perhaps small children should be taken on raids, mused Old Owl wryly. When motivated they had an uncanny ability to find what they wanted to find.

"You're too young."

"No, I'm not. I'll be careful with it. I want to practice being a wolf scout."

"Can you sit still for hours without twitching a muscle?"

"I'm practicing that."

"How many days have you spent watching wolves?"

Cub should have expected that question, but it caught him off guard. "None. But I've seen lots of them."

"Can you tell a male wolf from a female by their pelts, and by the small differences in their bodies? And can you do it while they're far away and running? Can you tell if a wolf is tired or fresh, hungry or full by looking at his ears? Do you know if he's on a serious trail or just traveling, or if he's going to kill the elk or play with it?

"Do you know about wolves and ravens? Did you know, for instance, that wolves and ravens play together, tease each other? I've seen them play tag like children, wolves and ravens. You'll often find ravens near a pack, perhaps looking for prey for them, perhaps waiting for them to make a kill so they can eat when the wolves are through. Do you know how wolves hunt? Do you know their strategies for hunting different kinds of game? Do you, Cub?" Old Owl peered sternly at Cub in the gloom.

"No, Grandfather."

"Then how do you expect to imitate a wolf? When you can answer any questions about wolves that I ask you, you may borrow the skin. It brought me through many dangers. I am invisible in it. It is very powerful. I can't lend it casually."

"I understand, Grandfather." He looked crestfallen.

"Tomorrow we'll go on a hunt, just you and I. And test your new bow. We'll shoot a grizzly bear and bring it home to throw in your mother's pot." Old Owl hated to deny Cub anything. He put his hand on the child's shoulder as the two of them moved toward the lodge door, a bright yellow sun in the general glow of the tent. They did many things together, and they were a strange pair, the small, stocky, towheaded boy and the shriveled old man, browned and wrinkled like weathered leather.

"Pahayuca's Wasps will winter with us. You'll see your sister, Naduah."

"I'll be glad to see her." It was the first time anyone had spoken to him of her. And he had never asked.

A wolf's howl followed them inside, perhaps mocking Cub. Perhaps inviting him to come learn about his ways.

"Don't call me John. They named me Weelah, Bear Cub, because I thrashed a hundred when I got here."

"All at once?" Naduah squatted in the dust so she could look her brother in the eye. Smoke peered around her and Dog studied the ground for fleas.

"No, of course not. But some of them were bigger than I and one time I took on two of them at once. They kept bothering me, you know." The children spoke in the language of the People, already comfortable in it. Cub was stretched on his belly across the laps of his foster mother, Tasura, That's It, his foster great-aunt, Tahdeko, Prairie Dog, Old Owl's wife, and Wild Sage, Santa Ana's wife. Each of them had a pair of tweezers and they were going over Cub's bare hindquarters, picking out prickly pear spines. As they worked they gossiped among themselves.

Cub was as brown as a hickory nut all over his tough, scratched, stocky little body, except from his ankles down, where his moccasins protected his feet. His hair was as pale as Naduah's, but curlier, and his mother's freckles spattered like paint across his snub nose and cheeks. He wore a leather band around his head in a futile attempt to control the curls that tumbled into his eyes, many of them too short to be caught into his stubby braids.

"Ouch!" Cub twisted around to glare at Wild Sage. She had flicked him hard on a haunch with her fingers.

"Then stop wriggling like a tadpole, or we'll never finish here. I have to start the evening meal soon. There are guests to feed."

In spite of the fact that it was November, the women wore dresses of light deerskin. The whites called weather like this "Indian summer" because the Comanches took advantage of the warmth and the full harvest moon to raid before cold weather locked them in. Naduah could hear Buffalo Piss now, riding through the huge winter encampment with his hand drum. He was beating out an invitation to the young men to join him in one last dash to the Texas settlements before winter closed in.

"What happened to your rear end, *Tahmah*, Brother?" Cub looked a little sheepish, which didn't happen often.

"I was relieving myself and didn't notice the cactus."

"That's what you get for running around with no clothes on like a

Tuhkanay, a Wichita. What if it had been a rattlesnake? Where would they have put the tourniquet?" They both giggled, and Sage flicked him again.

"You look like a Tuhkanay yourself, Sister. Hey, I have my own pony. Wait'll you see him."

"I have one too. And she can cover yours with dust."

"We'll race then, but you won't have a chance. Old Owl gave me mine and helped me train him."

"Pahayuca gave me Wind, and Wanderer helped me train her." Wanderer's name jolted them into the past, to the journey they had made together.

"I was sorry to hear about Wanderer's friend. He was nice to me. I suppose he had to sell me. He had no wife to raise me."

"John. Cub. Do you ever want to go back?" Without thinking, Naduah changed to English for privacy.

"I did for a while."

Wild Sage poked him in the ribs. "Speak as one of the People, Cub. You have no secrets."

"Not until he starts looking for women to poke his lance into." That's It rarely laughed. But when she was around, others did. Wild Sage and Prairie Dog were laughing as they set Cub on his feet. Wild Sage regarded him with a practiced eye.

"He has a long time to wait before that thorn grows into a lance."

Cub rubbed his itchy buttocks and grinned at the women, arching his back to flaunt the item under discussion.

"When I find the right target my lance will be ready."

Still laughing and chatting, the women waddled off toward Prairie Dog's lodge to start cooking for the friends and relatives of Pahayuca's band, the plague of locusts as That's It called them. Cub ducked into That's It's tent and came out carrying leggings, breechclout, and a small, fringed shirt of soft deerskin. He dressed as he talked, steadying himself on Naduah's shoulder and hopping while he pulled his moccasins on. He tugged his shirt down over his head as they started toward the pasture where the ponies were kept. They spoke English for the first time in many months.

"I felt low for a while. Especially when the boys tried to bully me. And I missed mother and father a lot. But now I don't have time to think about them much. No one bothers me. They all think I'm wonderful. Something new, you know. I can do whatever I want. Hunting is more fun than farming, I know that for sure. I have lots of friends and we play all the time. I like it here."

"I know. I have friends too, and my family loves me. Do you think our real family will come after us?"

"Seems like if they were going to, they would have by now."

"What would you do if they did?"

Cub studied the ground and kicked at clumps of grass as they walked.

"I don't know. I might hide. I'd probably hide. The fort was so dull compared to this." With a sweep of his arm Cub took in the lodges, the plains, the horizon, the sky, the herd of grazing ponies, the freedom. "I don't think I want to be a white man again."

"Do you see Cousin Rachel very often?"

"No. Her family left a month ago and went to live with a band further north. I'm glad they went. I think she was crazy, Cindy, and they treated her badly. It was embarrassing to be related to her, although no one here knows I am."

The silence was painful as they thought of the trip from the ravaged fort on the Navasota. Naduah finally spoke.

"I'll race you to the pasture. First one to reach the clump of three cottonwoods wins."

Rachel huddled under the shabby buffalo robe, trying to protect herself and her new baby from the howling wind that blasted gusts of snow around the corner of the tent. Above her, the black tree limbs clawed at the slate-gray December sky, and a flock of crows blew across the clouds. The baby was crying so hard he refused to nurse. His pitiful, weak wails could scarcely be heard over the moan of the wind.

Inside the lodge it was warm, even if it did stink. At least she could have crept close to the fire. Maybe the heat would have eased the pain in the baby's bowels. But Terrible Snows was too poor to have two lodges. When his cronies came by to smoke and brag and laugh like a herd of braying mules, he threw Rachel out as though she were one of the curs that slunk through camp.

A Little Less, Terrible Snow's mother, could go visiting other women. Even her daughter, Mountain, with her hideous, mutilated nose, had a friend she could shelter with. But Rachel knew she would be there outside the door of the lodge, trying to warm her baby, long into the night. She had tried to leave once before, to find a niche somewhere out of the wind. The beating Terrible Snows gave her when he found her was still painful and the bruises had not yet faded.

The cold began to soak through the robe, as though it were being saturated with icy water. She could feel it on her shoulders and flowing down her back. Snow was piling in small drifts around her thin moccasins stuffed with itchy, dry grass. Her toes were numb, like aching clubs at the ends of her feet. She wished she could go snuggle down into the pile of sleeping dogs, heaped like discarded hides against the side of the tent.

She thought of the old woman who had helped her when her time came to give birth. Her hands had been gentle, and she had given the baby a small rabbit-fur robe to be wrapped in. Rachel had fought A Little Less for that robe like a mother badger defending her young, her teeth bared in a snarl.

But the robe and the old buffalo hide weren't enough. Rachel tried not to think of what the temperature must be, and how low it would go before the night was over. She had to find shelter, no matter what Terrible Snows did to her. She stood, and almost fell with the cramps in her legs. With one thin hand she pulled the tattered robe closer as the wind tried to tear it from her. Cradling the baby in her other arm and pushing against the wind, she started toward the lodge of Tasiwu Wanauhu, Buffalo Robe, the old midwife. Ice crunched under her feet, cutting through her moccasin soles like shards of glass.

She wavered at the door of the lodge with its softly glowing fire shining through the walls and the sound of low conversation drifting out. Then, knowing she had no choice, and with a gust of wind pushing her from behind, she shouldered aside the hide flap and stepped through the opening. Crumpling at Buffalo Robe's feet, she clutched the hem of her dress and looked up at her with pleading eyes.

The family moved to make room for her at the fire, and the old woman, clucking like a worried hen, gently placed a warm blanket around her. Her daughter handed Rachel a horn cup of steaming broth, made with a pinch of powdered cornmeal and pemmican for flavoring. The children clustered around their mother, looking around her skirts at Terrible Snows' slave with the shiny, button eyes of a litter of field mice.

Taking the screaming baby, his tiny hands feebly flailing and his face crumpled like a crepe myrtle bud, Buffalo Robe rocked him and sang to him. She used her free hand to mix powdered star grass and blazing root into a bitter tonic for colic. With firm hands that had doctored scores of children, she poured the medicine down the baby's throat before he knew what was happening. Taking a deep breath, he made a fresh assault on their ears. But as the terrible pain in his intestines eased, he fell into an exhausted sleep.

Rachel's teeth finally stopped chattering and her body ceased its shivering. She rolled up in the blanket and lay next to the fire, lulled by the conversation that picked up again, although she was now the subject of it.

Loud, angry voices woke her the next morning. Terrible Snows had run her to ground, and Buffalo Robe was giving her opinion of the case. But the People almost never interfered with another family's affairs. The old woman watched helplessly as Rachel stood and collected her crying baby again. She followed Terrible Snows out into the glittering day, the ice-frosted lodges shining like fat icicles in the pale light of the winter sun.

She looked down at her child. The ache in her chest made her short of breath as she studied his thin, pinched face, his spindly arms and legs, and his tiny, bulging stomach, swollen with malnutrition. His cries were getting weaker, and he stopped from time to time to pant with the effort. She clutched him to her, planning to sneak back to Buffalo Robe's lodge and leave him there, hoping she would defend him against Terrible Snows. For now, Rachel would lay him on the dirty, lice-ridden robe where she slept at the foot of her master's bed. Then she would take her beating and warm herself with her drudgery.

Terrible Snows had other plans. If she had tried to learn more of the People's language in the eight months she had been with them, she might have picked up what he was muttering as he stalked ahead of her. But there would have been little she could have done anyway. As they approached the lodge, Rachel's heart jumped and her throat tightened. Bundled in a robe and squatting by the door, like a rattlesnake coiled to strike, was Cruelest One. When he saw them coming, he rose and stretched like a cat, throwing the robe loosely around his thin shoulders. Rachel moved to one side and tried to scuttle past him through the lodge door, but he grabbed her arm, and his bony fingers dug in like talons.

She tried to pull away from him, too hysterical with fear to notice Terrible Snows coming at her from the left. He snatched the baby, wrenching him from her while Cruelest One held her. Terrible Snows waddled away, casually swinging the screaming child by one foot, like a saddle bag. As usual, his lodge was on the outskirts of camp, and he headed out onto the plain. Only a few people stopped to watch him. A Little Less and Mountain cheered him on.

Cruelest One gave Rachel a shove that sent her sliding across the slippery ground. She fell, ice scouring patches of skin from her knees and elbows. Kneeling there, her bloody knees and palms freezing to the ground, she threw back her head and wailed as Terrible Snows raised the baby over his head and threw him down. The tiny body bounced and slid. Cruelest One picked him up and tossed him ahead of him, then kicked him, as though playing a game of kickball.

Rachel covered her head with her robe and doubled over. She rocked back and forth, shutting out with her own screams the sounds of laughter and the dull thud of the infant hitting the earth again and again. The child that had clung to life so ferociously in the face of overwhelming odds, refused to die easily. When Terrible

Snows finally turned to give the broken body back to its mother, he felt a faint flutter in its breast. He held it out for his friend's inspection.

Cruelest One pulled a coil of rope from his belt and tied it under the child's arms. As though casting bait he tossed him into the middle of a dense clump of prickly pear, a huge thicket seven feet high and twice that around. They dragged the body back toward them and threw it again. When they tired of that, Cruelest One tied the end of the rope to his saddle and rode gleefully through camp, whooping, with the bloody mass bumping along on the frozen ground behind him. When they finished, there was little left that Rachel could recognize as her child.

The men dropped it in front of her and, tired of the fun, went off to brag about it with their friends. As she held it in her lap, she began to laugh. Her face lit up with joy, and she smiled at those around her, trying to share her happiness with them.

"He's dead now, see?" She held him up, babbling in English, tears streaming down her face. "He's really dead now. He won't cry anymore or be cold. He's with Jesus. I'm so happy." Then she fainted and pitched forward to lie face down on the ice.

She awoke when Buffalo Robe gently shook her. The mangled body was gone, and she never asked about it. She followed Buffalo Robe to her lodge and sank into delirium and a restless sleep, crawling with nightmares. The struggle now was not to be alive when traders or soldiers found her, but to be sane.

❧ 22 ❧

The combined winter encampment of Old Owl, Pahayuca, Tosa Wanauhu, White Robe, and old Mookwarruh, Spirit Talker, was huge. Four hundred lodges were strung out for eight miles along the river's edge. And each band was bigger than in the summertime, because the individual families that had gone off on their own hunting trips had rejoined their civil leaders.

The riffles and low water falls of the river had frozen into ice sculptures—candalabras, lace doilies, fragile crystal flowers, and geometric forms. The lodges themselves sat in glowing pools of pale golden light, reflections of the flames inside falling onto the snow around them. The spidery, bare black trunks and limbs of the tall pecan trees seemed to weave and sway in the flickering light before soaring up into the black void of the sky.

Name Giver's lodge was crowded with people. They sat in terraces, on the bedsteads, on the piles of thick furs on the floor, and finally, the smallest children clustered in the center of the ring, near the fire. They filled the big, pale yellow cone with warmth. Shadows from the flames leaped high on the darker walls of the lodge, like playful kittens chasing moths. A radiance from the fire flickered across the red-gold faces, painting them with brightness and shade. Young and old, mothers and fathers, grandparents and children were entranced by Name Giver's story.

Outside, the fairy landscape was lit by a brilliant lantern moon swinging high overhead. The old shieldmaker who lived there must have been smiling down on the scene below him. The path of the moon's light twined through filigrees of frost patterns on the stiff clumps of grass that poked up through the white snow quilt blanketing the rolling hills. Far off, coyotes sang of their hunger, an insane goblin choir that made goosebumps rise on Naduah's shoulders and arms.

A dry snow sifted down, its needlelike crystals forming clusters like the petals of tiny flowers. Naduah hoped it would stay for a while. She and Star Name and Cub and their friends could spend the next day sliding down the hills on old, slick hides.

It was February, the Month The Babies Cry For Food. But no one in the vast camp was crying. It had been a good fall, and there were still stiff rawhide boxes of tangy pemmican piled around the sides of everyone's lodges. There was even honey mixed with melted tallow to drip on it. And there were dishes of boiled dried plums and piles of steaming squashes.

Naduah licked the last of the sweetness off her fingers and snuggled between Star Name and Owl. The two girls had come early to visit Owl, so they had grabbed the best rug to sit on. It was the reddish-brown winter pelt of a wolf, with a double layer of fur, the outer guard hairs five inches long. Warming her lap was Smoke, curled into a ball, but with her big eyes following everything. Dog crowded close too, casually pushing against the nearest warm body that would tolerate her.

Across the fire sat Bear Cub, with his new friend, Upstream, Star Name's younger brother. The deviltry had doubled since they teamed up, but at least they kept things interesting. Old Owl went around shaking his head and grumbling that Cannibal Owl would eat them if they weren't careful. And Sunrise was giving them stillness lessons, the hardest part of their schooling.

"It's boring," Cub told Naduah. "But we have to do it."

"What do you do?" she asked him.

"Nothing. Absolutely nothing. Except breathe. And I think Sunrise would rather we didn't do that if we could manage it. We stretch out on our stomachs behind a log or something and burrow in. We have to stay there until the field mice dance around us and the rabbits run over us. Did you know that mice dance?"

"Of course. I used to spend hours that way whenever I could get away from the fort. I'm probably better at it than you are."

"I don't care. I don't like it. I'd rather be learning to shoot with Arrow Point."

"He may be your father, but he doesn't spend much time with you, Cub."

Cub became defensive. "He's Old Owl's nephew, his adopted son, and he's very important. He doesn't have much time."

Naduah sniffed. "Still, he doesn't seem like much of a father to me." Then she turned away before Cub could retort.

They had spent a lot of time with each other, considering they were boy and girl. Cub seemed older than his seven years and closer to her than he had ever been before they were captured. It was as though what they had suffered together had formed a bond between them. In spite of their friends and their adopted families, only the two of them knew what it was like to be both white and red.

Naduah looked fondly at him as he sat across the lodge from her. He and Upstream had just returned from one of Sunrise's stillness lessons, and they were both huddled under buffalo robes, thawing out. Their teeth were still chattering, and spots of rose painted their cheeks and noses. She would be sorry to see Cub leave with Old Owl's band in the spring.

The People said that winter was the time when love ruled the camp. When everyone relaxed, free from the need to hunt or raid or work very much outside. They were secure in the knowledge that their enemies wouldn't be raiding either. They were free to sneak into the lodge of a beloved and lie entwined under silky robes, listening to the wind complain of the cold outside. Winter was the time to learn new dances and give feasts. To play games until the sun rose, to sing of old battles and new loves. It was a time to visit, when many bands camped together, caught under the net of twisting branches of the tall pecans spread overhead. The People saw friends and relatives who had been distant all year, and there was a great deal of gossip to catch up on.

It was the time when story tellers reigned. Each night, scattered among the four or five hundred lodges that glowed like candles in the dark, older men and women of the tribe held their audiences spellbound. Naduah had been sampling many of them, and she had decided that, of them all, Name Giver was the best.

He knew how to repeat the familiar lines worn soft and pliable with use, like old moccasins that fit better than new ones. He knew when to lower his voice so everyone had to lean forward to hear, drawing them even deeper into the web of his story. He knew how to add a new little twist to keep his listeners alert, and he could mix mystery in his tone, to give it a subtle flavor, like using dried grapes in the pemmican instead of plums or persimmons. He could make the most familiar tale seem as fresh and exciting as the first time it had been told, leaving Naduah quivering with anticipation of the lines to come.

Tonight Old Man Coyote, the Trickster, was among them. Naduah could see him clearly as Name Giver painted him. He was tall and lanky and gangling, with his thin, coarse, black braids hanging like frayed horsehair ropes on his bony shoulders. He spoke to the wind in its own voice, sometimes high, sometimes low. He spoke to all the beasts and trees, to every living thing, in its own language. Everyone liked him, but everyone was very careful around him, because he was the Trickster.

"You know, my children," Name Giver was saying, "that you must never ask for or tell stories of the Trickster in the daytime. And he prefers that you tell about him in the winter. Because he knows that's when his people need cheering the most.

"That's when Piam-em-pits, old Cannibal Owl, spreads his monstrous wings and blocks the moon with his shadow, gliding silently in search of souls, like helpless little mice that he wants to devour." Name Giver rose, spreading his arms and bending over the small children in the front rows. His face contorted into a horrible mask, and he gave the shrill cry of an owl diving for its prey. With squeals and shrieks, the children scattered, hiding behind whatever they could find. Everyone else laughed. But the look on Name Giver's face, distorted even more by the fire's light, gave Naduah chills.

"Nightime is when we can gather here in the light and the warmth and leave the darkness for the spirits of the dead. Listen, can you hear them?" The crowd hushed. Outside, the wind moaned around the lodge. "Those are the spirits, riding on the cold wind, searching for paradise. And Trickster can understand what they're saying. He can understand what everything says. Even you." He pointed a finger at one of the braver children, who had crawled back close to the fire. Who knew how he could tell the child was there. Perhaps by the rustling. Perhaps just by the feel of the air. "Even you, when you whisper with your friends. Trickster may be listening."

"Long ago, it is said, Old Man Coyote was coming along. He strode over the plains on his long legs, and stepped over mountains. He watched all the creatures, and sometimes he stopped to talk to them, and sometimes he tricked them.

"Finally he became hungry from his travels, and he saw just what he needed. There was an entire village of beautifully colored prairie dogs, all plump and juicy. The sight of them made Old Man Coyote's mouth water, and he began thinking of a way to trick those prairie dogs so he could make a meal of them. They called out a greeting to the Trickster as they sat at the mouths of their burrows. 'Tdek-o! Tdek-o! Tdek-o!'." Name Giver, with his milky porcelain eyes, turned into a prairie dog, his hands clutched to his chest and his nose wrinkling and sniffing. "Tdek-o! Tdek-o! Tdek-o!" From somewhere among the audience a child's voice piped up in perfect imitation of Name Giver's. Everyone laughed and applauded. There was another storyteller on the way up.

Name Giver began the hypnotic chant of Old Man Coyote's song, luring the prairie dogs to dance with their eyes closed so he could club them and toss them into his pot.

"In those days," Name Giver said, "the prairie dogs were very beautiful. They were all colors—red and green and yellow and blue. But Trickster didn't care. He killed and ate them all. All except two, who peeked and saw what he was up to. Those two happened to be brown. So now all prairie dogs are brown. They still sit on their mounds and call 'Tdek-o! Tdek-o! Tdek-o!' back and forth and they wag their little tails as fast as they used to. But they never listen to strangers anymore. *Suvate*, it is finished."

The hide flap was pulled back just as Name Giver was ending his story and everyone was sitting still, savoring it. Lance poked his long, solemn face inside.

"Medicine Woman, Something Good's time has come. Pahayuca asks that you help her."

Medicine Woman stood looking down at the girl's face, wet with perspiration. Her thick black hair, still cut just below her ears, was damp. Blocks The Sun and Silver Rain had prepared well, but the birth would be a difficult one. She was young, and her hips were narrow, like a boy's. As the spasms of pain passed through Something Good she bit her lip and flinched, but never cried out. Naduah squatted down beside her and held her hand while Medicine Woman inspected the birth lodge. She often brought Naduah with her. She had found that the child had a natural ability to soothe and heal.

If the baby arrived with no trouble, the lodge would do very well.

The shallow hole in the center of the floor was lined with several layers of thick, soft furs. A stake was driven close to one edge. In another hole water was being heated in a hide by dropping hot stones into it. The steam mingled with the aroma of burning sage. Yes, it would do very well. If there was no trouble. But there would most likely be trouble. She went to the door of the lodge and murmured to Lance, who sat outside, waiting for possible messages to deliver. He rose and raced off, his moccasin soles flashing lighter than the darkness around him. There was nothing to do now but wait for Gets To Be An Old Man.

He arrived in a very short time, and Naduah gritted her teeth through his medicine song. All those rehearsals, when he lay flat on his back for hours, shaking his rattle at the indifferent sky and chanting through his sinuses, hadn't improved it at all. The same gangly youth played the drum, and the medicine man fanned Something Good with the same moth-eaten eagle feather. This time, though, he pulled an otter skin through the gaps between his teeth and passed it over her body as she lay writhing in pain.

He pretended to vomit, bringing up his power, and breathed it into Something Good's mouth. Then he spit into Medicine Woman's hands, to share the power with her. He walked around the fire, skipping a little, like a jolly skeleton. He struck a dignified pose, with his breechclout hung so low in back it revealed wrinkled cleavage, and droned one last verse of his song. If one long syllable could be called a verse. He leaped over the doorsill like an aged grasshopper, thus encouraging the baby to enter the world as easily, and disappeared into the night.

Medicine Woman spread the saliva around in her hands, then rubbed her palms over Something Good's abdomen. As she did it she crooned her own medicine song. The other women helped Something Good to her feet, and she stood with a bare foot on each side of the hole. She grasped the stake with both hands and strained, biting her lips and pushing in an effort to squeeze the baby out. Naduah dared to speak.

"Sister, relax a little. Let the baby come when it will. When the pain comes flow with it, work with it. Don't fight it." She remembered the advice her real grandmother, Granny Parker, had always given. And Granny had seen many babies born.

"It hurts, little one."

"I know. But be calm and talk to your baby. Tell it it's welcome here. Tell it how beautiful it will be and how much you'll love it."

"That's true, little one. I'll love it very much."

"Tell it that we're all waiting for it. Tell it, Something Good." Something Good's drawn, beautiful face softened, the angles melting back into curves. Her eyes closed and peace settled in, the first she'd known in the six months since Eagle's death. Medicine Woman, Blocks The Sun, and Silver Rain were silent as Something Good communed with her unborn child. A contraction seized her, then another. They were coming close together now, but she seemed oblivious to the pain.

Finally the tiny, furry head pushed through the narrow opening, ripping the tender edge of its tunnel. The head was covered with wet, downy, black hair, almost like a fledgling bird. As more of the baby pushed into the light, Medicine Woman reached out and tugged gently, helping it into the dim, quiet world of the lodge. She lowered it onto the soft bed of furs and bit the umbilical. She tied the ends off and massaged the baby until it gave a small cry. She held the child up so Something Good could see it was a girl.

While the mother lay back panting, Medicine Woman wrapped the infant in a rabbit-fur robe and took her down to the nearby stream. Breaking the thin crust of ice at the edge of it, she scooped water up and washed the child as she squalled and kicked in protest. Half an hour later, she threw the afterbirth into the running water in the middle of the stream and watched it whirl away on the current. She sent her prayers after it, and turned and climbed back up the bank.

Silver Rain wrapped the umbilical cord in a piece of soft doeskin and hung it on the hackberry tree outside the lodge. The tent had been set up there on purpose. If the cord hung undisturbed in a hackberry tree, the child would have a long life. Naduah resolved to guard it to make sure nothing happened to it. That a child's fate should depend on the whimsical appetite of crows seemed no stranger to her than what she'd heard the women of Parker's Fort talk about: a knife under the pillow will cut the pain, an ax under the bed will stop bleeding, mother's milk spurted on a hot rock will dry up a breast.

Since it was the grandfather's job to ask the sex of the child, Old Owl hovered near the doorway. If he had had a hat he would have been holding it in front of him, fidgeting and twirling it with nervous fingers.

"*E samopma*, it's a girl." Blocks The Sun pushed her massive shoulders through the small opening, making the lodge itself appear to be giving birth. Old Owl's face fell a little. He shrugged philosophically, hitched up his leggings, which always sagged on his thin, bowed legs, and went off to discuss the newest arrival with friends around a pipe. He knew the rumor that was flying around camp like a shinny ball in a fast game. He knew that the whole tribe would be curious about whom this baby resembled.

Gossip was the main pastime at any season of the year, but in winter it practically took precedence over eating and sleeping. As crowded as the camp was, and as freely as everyone entered each other's lodges, secrets were harder to keep than fresh meat in the summertime. Already women were streaming toward the birth lodge, to pay their respects, to offer suggestions for names and care, and to gawk. Mainly to gawk. Under his bland expression, Old Owl was worried.

❧ *23* ❦

The buds on the trees were taut and shiny. The hills were covered with a fur of green from the recent rains. The world looked washed, and the ponies were cavorting in the pasture, neighing and kicking their heels like colts. They were beginning to lose the lumpy look they had when they grazed all winter on bark and twigs. The air was cool but not chilly, and the birds were out of their minds with joy. They kept up a constant cacophony in the cottonwoods overhead.

The huge winter camp was beginning to stir. White Robe's band had left a week earlier for the north, and Spirit Talker's people had gone the day before, dwindling into their own cloud of dust as though swallowed up by it. Old Owl and Pahayuca's bands had stayed together a while longer, reluctant to say good-bye for another season. They might run across each other, but it wasn't likely. The People's land was vast. There was enough room in it for everyone to hunt.

Spring seemed to be bursting out of everything. Especially Bear Cub and Upstream. They led the gang of small boys that came galloping on their ponies down the narrow path between the lodges. They were whooping and whistling and flapping buffalo hides. They sent dogs and women and children tumbling in all directions. They scattered the cooking fires, sending up great gouts of choking smoke with their flapping hides. The war ponies reared and neighed at their tethers.

The boys' object was the large meat rack outside Old Owl's tent. As they raced by, each boy leaned out and grabbed a handful, stripping the rack as bare as a bleached buffalo carcass. Cub hung by one foot from the loop braided into his pony's mane, his yellow curls cascading around his head. He scooped up the gray fire horn that his grandfather always kept by his door, in case friends dropped by for a smoke. He bounced back on his pony and, to add injury to insult, swatted his sister on the shoulder as he rode by, counting coup.

"*A-he*, I claim her!" They all laughed as they disappeared to enjoy their stolen feast, somewhere on a sunny ledge by the water, or high on a ridge overlooking the countryside. They left Naduah and Star Name and the women to clear up the wreckage.

"I didn't think it was possible," Star Name shook her head, "but your brother is worse than mine."

"You're right. Old Owl indulges him too much. He should never have been given a pony so young."

"It wouldn't have mattered." Star Name stooped, picking up the litter of thongs and awls. "He would just have stolen one. Most of those boys borrowed their ponies."

"Neither his father or his grandfather punishes him for anything. He can do whatever he likes." Naduah felt aggrieved, but she had never been punished either. In fact, she couldn't remember seeing anyone punished. Adults told erring children that the People didn't behave that way. And that sufficed.

As Takes Down rearranged the huge mosaic of hides they were piecing into a lodge cover, she interrupted.

"They're learning to be warriors. What they do today will be good practice for what they must do on raids."

"I pity the Osage," said Owl.

"Or the Cheyenne," added Something Good.

"Or anyone else who gets in the way," Deer grumbled.

"They'll be fine warriors as long as they don't have to depend on stealth," said She Laughs.

"He's a nuisance, that's what he is." Naduah was jealous. Just because he was cute and brash and brave to the brink of insanity, he charmed everyone. Sometimes Naduah hated being a girl.

Takes Down went quietly back to her work, directing the women who were making a lodge cover for Deep Water, Owl's brother. She knew why Cub was so audacious, but she said nothing. Captive children almost always tried harder to prove themselves. She would rather be captured by one of another tribe than by a white who had adopted the red man's ways. Such men were more ferocious, much more inclined to torture their prisoners. Cub would be a terror, although not as bad as Cruelest One. Under his swagger and bluster, Cub was an affectionate child.

As Naduah shaved and sharpened skewers from the pile of sticks next to her, she watched the women work on the huge patchwork of hides. Takes Down was trimming it into a semicircle, cutting along the line she had made by pressing a pointed willow stick into the leather. The lodge was a large investment for Owl's family. It had taken them a long time to accumulate the ten hides for this small one. The hides Deep Water had been given by Wanderer as his share of the raid on the Tonkawa village, plus those from the fall hunt and the ones his grandfather had taken in payment for his arrow-making, had finally amounted to enough.

"Why does Deep Water get his own lodge? He's only fifteen, even if he did bring in a scalp." Naduah's sense of equity was injured.

She Laughs looked up from the hides she was sewing. Her legs were stretched out in front of her and the cover drawn up over them. Her voice was strangely musical, coming from her rough face.

"I wish we could have made him one sooner. Deep Water has to have his own lodge so he won't have to sleep near Owl."

"Why shouldn't he sleep near Owl?" Naduah and her whys.

"It's taboo for him to sit near me. Or for me to touch him. He could kill me if I did."

"Why?"

Takes Down spoke again. "Deep Water is a warrior. He has to have a place to make the medicine he needs to protect his family. He can't be close to his sister. He might adopt some of her womanish ways and fail in battle or on the hunt."

"Besides," added Medicine Woman, "cooking grease is contaminating, and so is menstrual blood. He has to sleep where there is none."

"Are you bleeding already, Owl?" It was something all the girls looked for. Their rite of passage to adulthood.

"No. But I might someday soon."

Naduah finished the last skewer she was whittling. The pointed sticks would be woven through lines of holes punched into the front of the lodge to hold it together. She Blushes was measuring and punching the holes for them. Medicine Woman, She Laughs, Black Bird, Deer, and Something Good sat back on their heels while Takes Down checked their work and did some last-minute trimming. The whole cover should fit together perfectly when it was raised. Takes Down didn't want to have to lower it to make adjustments.

The huge semicircle was twelve feet at its widest and twenty-four feet across its straight edge, with two flaps at the center of that edge to close the smoke hole. There were two smaller half-circles cut from the lower part of the same edge. When the edge was brought together the half-circles would meet to form the door opening.

It was a small lodge cover, but there were still many seams to pull to test for weak places. The lodge would have to withstand the stress of howling gales and hard travel, sun and rain and snow and hail that stripped trees and knocked down flocks of birds. Also, it was a point of honor with Takes Down never to have to take down a lodge to refit it. That was why everyone came to her when they needed a new one.

"*Toquet*, all right," she grunted. "On your feet." The women got up, rubbing their knees and groaning about the pain of it all, and about how hard Takes Down The Lodge made them work. Takes Down ignored them and bustled around putting everyone in position for the lodge raising. It never occurred to them to ask a man for help. No one needed their interference.

The four main cedar poles, fifteen feet long, lay nearby. They had been freshly peeled and they smelled wonderful. Their large ends had been sharpened to stick into the ground. She Laughs tied them near the top, and four of the women set them upright. They pulled the butt ends out until they seemed evenly spaced then planted them firmly. Takes Down paced across inside, starting at the east and walking from one pole to the other, measuring the distance with her feet. She made Deer pull her pole out a little, then had the women stack the other eighteen poles around the four main ones.

Something Good, the tallest and slenderest one there, stood on Deer's soft, meaty shoulders, her feet sinking into the flesh as she lashed the poles in place. Deer supported Something Good's slender ankles with her hands, and kept up a steady stream of harrassment.

"Something Good, just because you're a chief's wife doesn't mean you never have to wash you feet. Whew! When did those moccasins die? Did you forget to tan them before you sewed them? Are you carrying a dead skunk inside them as medicine? If so, it's powerful." Something Good laughed and almost fell, clinging to the poles for support.

"Be careful, Deer." Naduah circled Deer, craning her head upward and ready to break her friend's fall if she slipped.

"Child, we've been doing this since long before you were born." Deer beamed down at her, her eyes disappearing into the folds of her smile like currants into whole-wheat dough. "You're putting on meat, Something Good," she called up, squeezing the girl's calves. "Soon there'll be enough of you to make a whole woman. And you'll be able to wear Blocks The Sun's dresses."

"She could wear them now. She and three or four others together," put in She Laughs. "Did you hear that Pahayuca is saving all his old lodge covers now. He says if Takes Down will let them out a little they'll be fine for Blocks The Sun to wear."

And so it went. And no one seemed to mind. In fact, Naduah was grateful to Deer. There was often a strain when Something Good was around. The girl's nose was perfect. Pahayuca hadn't slit it, although whether it was from his love of her, his friendship with her father, or his own good nature, no one could say. And there was a great deal of speculation on the subject.

Something Good still carried her head high, but she didn't talk freely to many. Nor was she included as often in the things the women did. Takes Down and Black Bird had asked for her help, and Deer had accepted her, which made it difficult for the others in the special circle of friends not to. She had joined them at first because she was fond of Naduah and Star Name, but now she felt comfortable with all of them. Takes Down understood her pain and would have gone out of her way to befriend her anyway, but Wanderer had also spoken to her of it, as a favor to him and to his dead blood brother.

The women picked up the edges of the cover and carried it around the frame. Takes Down and She Laughs went inside with two long poles. Reaching out with them, they snagged the center of the cover between the two smoke-hole flaps and dragged it, flesh side out, up the outside of the frame. They held its eighty-five pounds, their arms straining, while the others climbed on each other's shoulders, and fastened it at the top. Then they pinned it in place along the front seam, down to the door opening, and pegged its hem down. They all stood back to admire it while Takes Down walked slowly around it. None of the seams puckered or buckled or was pulling apart with the strain. Other women gathered until there was a crowd, clucking and cooing and running their hands along the seams to check the workmanship.

Raising a lodge was routine, but there was a knack to fitting one perfectly, especially this one, since it was smaller than those Takes Down usually made. She had had no old cover to use as a pattern, and had drawn this one freehand on the ground. Then she had to fit the assortment of hides to the correct shape. She had approached the problem as she did most things. She thought about it quietly as she went about her chores. Then, the day the cover was to be pieced, she was up early and had the hides laid out by the time the other women arrived. She worked swiftly and efficiently from some plan in her head, and as usual, it was work well done.

"All it needs now is a dew cloth to hang around the sides," said Medicine Woman.

"And a woman to sneak under the wall's edge at night." Deer laughed, making obscene motions with her hands.

"We're working on the dew cloth now," said She Laughs. "He'll have to take care of the other himself." Owl grimaced. She spent all winter scraping hides so her brother could have his own lodge to get away from women so he could smuggle one in anyway.

"He's too ugly for any woman," grumbled Owl.

"No, he's not," Star Name jumped to defend him.

"Were you planning to sneak into his lodge, bright eyes?" It was good to see Something Good laughing and teasing again, even if it was rare.

"Did you hear that Old Owl's band is moving soon?"

"All of us will be moving soon. I pity those who live on the outskirts of camp. The dung is getting deep there. You have to watch where you walk."

"There was plenty to eat this winter. It all had to go somewhere."

"But not outside my lodge."

"Speaking of eating, what's for dinner, She Laughs?" Deer always came to the point. She Laughs was expected to feed the workers and give Takes Down a present.

"There's antelope."

"Good. I like antelope." Deer chuckled and began sidling toward She Laughs' lodge nearby.

"You like everything, Deer."

"That's true. But I especially like antelope. Young antelope." She eyed Smoke speculatively, dressing her out in her mind. Naduah ignored her teasing, and Something Good changed the subject.

"Pahayuca sent a bedding robe as a present to Deep Water. I left it near Weasel's cradle board. Naduah, would you bring it for me?"

Naduah trotted off and Smoke leaped ahead of her. They ran to where Something Good's baby, Kianceta, Weasel, was laced into her cradle board. The board stood braced against a grape bush and the robe, in a large folded square, lay next to it. On top of the robe, like a pretty, brightly colored bracelet, was a coral snake. It was slithering slowly toward the cradle board, as though to inspect what was there. Little Weasel watched, fascinated.

Naduah froze and looked frantically for a weapon. She kept absolutely still, afraid a cry would startle the snake. What if it crawled up the wrapping and bit Weasel's lip or nose? Coral snake bites were usually fatal, certainly to a two-month-old child. But while Naduah stood, Smoke acted, so swiftly that she could hardly be seen.

Rearing, she came down with her sharp hoofs on the snake's head. She reared and pounded again and again, throwing the snake off the robe and into the dirt, where she continued to attack it. It wasn't until Naduah saw the snake smashed and lifeless that she screamed. She ran to Weasel, kicking the snake's body as far as she could when she passed it. Dog assumed she was playing fetch and went after it. She arrived with it in her mouth just as the women were running up.

Something Good took Weasel and crooned to calm her, but she

was the calmest one there. Naduah knelt in front of Smoke and hugged her, then rubbed her muzzle with her own nose. Smoke licked her cheek.

"I'm going to tell Cub about this. He says I shouldn't make friends with the food supply. Says it's hard to eat your friends. As if I'd ever eat you, Smoke."

Naduah and Cub had been having a footrace with Smoke and Dog. Since Smoke could run sixty miles an hour, it wasn't much of a contest. But she loved to run with them anyway, bounding around and around them. Now the two children hung by their legs from a low branch in a live oak tree, with Naduah flailing her arms to keep Smoke and Dog from licking her face. It was fun to view the world from upside down.

"Everyone's packing up in Grandfather's band. Why don't you come with us, Sister?"

Naduah thought a moment, then swung up and straddled the limb.

"I couldn't leave my family, and they wouldn't leave Pahayuca. And all my friends are with the Wasps. I wouldn't see you much anyway. You're always with that pack of prairie dogs, yapping and running around causing trouble. You act like you don't know me half the time."

"I have to or the boys will tease me. You know that."

"I know. But I'm better off where I am."

"What if someone comes for one of us during the year? Soldiers, maybe." John had climbed into a crotch of the tree and was pitching twigs at leaves, trying to spear them.

"I'll hide." Naduah had given it some thought.

"But what if they find you?"

"Then I'll escape and come back. I can do it. I've been learning how to trail and ride and hunt. What about you?"

"I'll fight them. I'll kill them." Cub jumped up so that he was standing in the crotch and stabbing at the tough bark with his knife. "I'll scalp them. I'll eat their livers. Nobody's going to take me away from Grandfather."

"And what if Old Owl sells you back to them?"

"He wouldn't do that."

"You might make him mad enough at you one of these days."

"That's an act. He's never really mad at me. If the Rangers come, they'll have a fight. *Suvate*, that's all."

"How will we know?"

"What?"

"If one of us has been taken back?"

Cub sat down, one brown leg dangling from each side of the tree's fork. He was obviously thinking.

"We could leave signs to show that we're still with the People."

"What kind?"

"Some signal that we could work out. And leave it after we move from each campsite. You know we come across each other's camping places from time to time."

"What kind of sign should we leave? What kind of sign would be standing maybe months later?"

Cub looked a little exasperated with her. "I don't know. We could carve something in a tree."

"If there are any trees. Or if there aren't hundreds."

"Then we'll make a pact. If anything happens to me, I'll make Old Owl or my father swear to get word to you. I know they would. And if anything happens to you, you can ask Pahayuca or Sunrise to send word to me. Do you think they'd do it for you?"

"Of course. The People always seem to know what's happening in the other bands anyway."

From the direction of the distant camp came the incongruous sound of a turkey gobble.

"That's Grandfather calling me." Cub dropped from the tree and answered, a fair imitation. "I have to go. They must be ready to move."

The children untied their ponies and rode toward the site of Old Owl's winter camp.

"I'll miss you, Cub."

"I'll miss you too."

"As bad as you are, at least you're not dull."

"Wait'll you see me next winter. I'll be much worse."

"Promise?"

"Promise." He leered at her evilly. Then he braced his hands on his pony's neck and, gathering his feet under him, stood for a better view. "They're starting without me!" He opened his legs and dropped back into place, spurring his horse into a gallop before he was even firmly seated. Ahead of them, the camp was in the usual turmoil as everyone beat their pack animals and yelled and dashed for the head of the line of march. Cub tucked his reins into his belt and jumped up to stand on his pony's back again. He shouted and waved his arms to get his friends' attention.

"Wait for me, you offal from an Apache dung heap!"

Upstream separated from the group and rode toward him.

"Where've you been? I wanted to say good-bye to you." The two of them rode back toward the gang of boys. Feeling left out, Naduah watched them go. Because he was a boy, Upstream would be able to ride along with the other boys until he tired and turned back. She stopped at the top of the first big ridge and waved at Cub when he turned to look once at her before setting off at a run, whooping. Below her, the long procession wound off through the pale green hills. She sat there for an hour or more until they were all out of sight beyond a far rise. Then she wheeled Wind and headed home to help with her own family's packing.

꙰ 24 ꙰

Naduah had looked over her shoulder at the old campsite as she rode away, remembering the good times she had had there. But Takes Down was right, as usual. It was time to leave. The camp looked devastated and forlorn. The grass was trampled and cropped by the three thousand horses and mules of the four bands that had wintered there. The cottonwoods along the river had been stripped of their lower branches so the ponies could eat the bark.

There were piles of unrepairable equipment and heaps of bones and decaying carcasses from the latest hunt. Naduah thought she saw a slight movement at the outskirts of the site, a coyote come to see what was left. And the vultures overhead were beginning to circle, like the beginning vortex of a storm. She could picture the ants moving in to scour everything that the crows and mice left. And the grass would grow over it all, and it would be even greener here next year. Or the year after.

They had been traveling for two days now, and were farther north than Pahayuca and the council usually chose to come. But there had been reports of large buffalo herds this way. And as though to verify them, a raven had circled over the old camp four times, dipping his head and cawing. Then he had flown off in this direction. So they were following the same trail that White Robe's band had taken when they left the winter encampment almost a month before. It was a major north/south route for the People, and easy to follow. The undulating plain was indented in a broad line that snaked across the hills to the horizon, a shallow trough dug by thousands of ponies and travois passing this way year after year.

Once spring arrived in Texas, it wasted no time. It was only early April and already there was heat in the air and a riot of flowers dancing on the hills. The hundreds of miles of rolling green swells were too much temptation for Naduah and Star Name. They had casually steered their ponies off to one side of the procession and ducked down into a ravine. They worked their way forward until they were beyond hailing range. Then they staged a race to take them even farther ahead.

Now they were where they weren't supposed to be, in front of the scouts who always rode in the vanguard. They were practicing their riding. Star Name had braided a loop into Paint's mane and hung with her foot hooked through it. She skimmed her fingers through the grass, snatching at pebbles as her pony ran.

Naduah was crouched, gathering her feet and her courage under her. "Feel your pony with your knees, your legs, every part of you." She remembered Wanderer's voice as he had taught her for hours under the hot sun. She cleared her mind of everything but the feel of Wind's powerful muscles rippling under her feet. She swayed, letting the rhythm of her pony's stride course up through her body until she was moving in perfect time with it. Without thinking, she rose and stood.

"Star Name! *Na-bo-ne*, look!" And she fell. Star Name rode back laughing as Naduah stood, testing her joints and rubbing her rear end.

"Did you see me stand?"

"Yes. A little more practice and you'll have it!"

It was then that they noticed a camp far in the distance, and the vultures over it. The sky was black with them, like a roiling thundercloud that looked strangely out of place in the clear blue afternoon sky. Something was wrong. Naduah felt the uneasiness grow in the pit of her stomach. There were usually vultures around the People's camps, but never this many. Whose camp was it? Not Old Owl's. Please, not Old Owl's. Or Wanderer's.

Wind snorted as the first faint whiffs of death, mingled with the scent of spring flowers, reached her sensitive nostrils. Smoke was already bounding around in her wide danger circle, her white tail flashing. Dog had caught up with them and sat, whining, under Wind's feet. Naduah and Star Name stared ahead, neither wanting to guess what the cloud meant. Quietly, they waited for Buffalo Piss and his scouts.

Buffalo Piss glowered at them when he and his men rode up. Even with his smooth, plucked brows, his shaggy, tousled hair, and his big, dark eyes he looked ferocious. The girls moved silently behind the men. Buffalo Piss and Sunrise rode ahead as they approached the village that lay under the swirling black cloud.

"It must be White Robe's band," Buffalo Piss muttered to Sunrise. Sunrise shaded his eyes to see better.

"Yes." Sunrise knew the plains as all of the People did. He knew if a stone had been disturbed and he knew if it had happened accidentally, or with a purpose. He knew the patterns of the birds, and the calls of the animals, at different times of the day and in different seasons. He could find trails where a white man would say none existed. And he knew, without a doubt, that there was something terribly wrong in White Robe's camp.

Pahayuca and Medicine Woman and more of the men caught up with them. Their faces were expressionless, but their muscles were tensed as they all advanced toward the lodges. The smell reached them when they were still over half a mile away. The men drew together in a quick council to decide what to do.

"Stay here, little one." Medicine Woman searched through the saddle bags for her medicine pouch. Slinging it over her shoulder, she tied a piece of cloth around her mouth and nose.

"I want to go with you. I can help."

"No. It could be a trap. There must have been an attack, but maybe some of the wounded are still alive."

With her arm across her face to keep out as much of the foul air as possible, Naduah rode back to the waiting women and children. Many of the young ones stood on their ponies to see better, but the women threw their robes over their heads and keened, as much in horror as in sorrow. Dogs howled in answer. The hair at the base of Dog's tail stood up in a ridge, and she milled stiff-legged among Wind's legs.

The steady, hollow thud of Gets To Be An Old Man's small hand drum and the unearthly wailing of the women joined in a dirge that followed Pahayuca, Buffalo Piss, and their warriors as they rode slowly, weapons ready, toward the camp. When they entered the outskirts, there was a roar as hundreds of turkey vultures rose, a living pall lifted by an unseen hand. Those that refused to leave their feeding hissed and grunted and flapped their enormous wings, snatching mouthfuls as they sidled away from the riders. Their red skulls looked like bloody death's heads, and their curved yellow beaks gaped in threat. Crows wheeled and darted, cawing angrily. The men coughed and gagged as the dense stench burned its way into their noses and mouths, coating the backs of their throats.

Decaying corpses lay sprawled among the silent lodges. There were war ponies, dead at their tethers outside their master's tents. And there were humans. Hundreds of them. Aside from a bundle of arrows that fanned out where they had fallen from a dropped quiver, there were no signs of war. There had been no looting, no burning, no fighting, and no scalping. Just death. Riding at the end of the procession that wound among the lodges, Medicine Woman felt the hairs on the back of her neck tingle, as though ants were crawling there.

A tiny baby, covered with wriggling white worms, lay at his dead mother's breast. Tears streamed down Medicine Woman's cheeks, and she silently sang for them. She was unaware of the whimpering that came from her own throat. Warriors, old people, children, a young couple entwined as though making love, all dead. Their faces were unrecognizable, obliterated by time, scavengers, and the elements.

Howling and snarling, a pack of dogs, crazed by fear, careened from behind the biggest lodge, that of White Robe. The leader, a huge yellow cur with his skin laddered over his ribs and saliva flying from his mouth, leaped at Pahayuca. The others attacked, trying to rip the men's legs or disembowel their horses. The men beat at them with their lances and bows and quirts, or fired into their open mouths.

Choking, the dogs stumbled off, pawing at the shafts as they tried to pull them out. Some were pinned to the ground, the arrows driven all the way through them. When the leader went down crying, the others tucked tail and ran, scattering out onto the plain. They fled toward the falling sun as though trying to throw themselves off the edge of the dying world.

At the head of the line, Pahayuca began to chant in his deep, resonant voice. It was picked up by those behind him and swelled over the cawing and flapping of the birds. A requiem for the dead. Desperately, Medicine Woman searched for an explanation. The spirits were never this vindictive. They might take vengeance on an individual or a family, but not on an entire band. The universe didn't work that way. Could they all have died from tainted meat? Not likely. Her mind was numbing with the horror of it when she heard something. It was the first human sound in that graveyard of the unburied dead.

Shouting, she turned and headed toward it, threading her way among the bodies, the overturned drying racks, and the tumbled equipment. The men followed her. An old woman was raving, crawling among the corpses, poking them and rolling them over. Medicine Woman rode slowly toward her.

"Mother, what has happened here?"

The woman gave a small cry and turned towards Medicine Woman. Her sightless eyes crawled with maggots and she babbled on, wound tightly in a cocoon of madness. Her face was rotten, covered with sores oozing blood and pus. She began to laugh, cackling hysterically and clawing at the cankers, rupturing more of them.

Medicine Woman screamed. And screamed again. She couldn't stop screaming. Nothing in her life had prepared her for this. No nightmare. No ghost story. No battlefield of scalped and mutilated corpses had ever been this terrifying. Medicine Woman's terror spread to the men. They all pounded out of the silent village and scattered onto the plain like the dogs they had driven off. The rest of the band galloped after them, strewing possessions and abandoning horses in their blind flight. They ran for miles until exhaustion forced them to stop. And as they retreated they looked back again and again over their shoulders, as though expecting the spectre of death to be pursuing them.

The People had a new enemy. One they had no weapons or medicine against. One they were totally powerless to combat. Smallpox had settled on the plains.

At twilight of the next day, the band finally camped. And it was an almost silent camp. Even the dogs slept where they had fallen, their legs still quivering with the fatigue of trying to keep up with the horses. From the outskirts of the village, Gets To Be An Old Man's medicine songs went on for hours as he lay on his back, chanting to the darkening sky. Small groups of people gathered around their cooking fires, and whispered about the village of death. Even the mourning was subdued, as though people were afraid to grieve, afraid to call attention to themselves lest they bring down the same plague that had struck White Robe's band.

Many lay in restless sleep, although it was still early. Some whimpered and cried out, haunted in dreams by what they had seen or been told. They had ridden hard all night and day after fleeing the dead village. Naduah had drooped and nodded as Wind paced steadily through the dark, picking her way over the rough ground by instinct and the light of the full moon. Something Good had ridden nearby. Her daughter, little Weasel, slept serenely in the cradle board dangling from the saddle horn. With the morning light the older boys and some of the men went to hunt stray ponies, but many of them were never found.

Naduah sat with her arms around Star Name as she sobbed quietly, asking "Why? Why?" over and over. Naduah knew why. She had seen the graves that littered the trail to Texas. She had marched behind caskets and watched them lowered into graves. She knew it was a white man's disease. And she felt responsible for it. She knew its name and she knew what it did. But she didn't know how it spread or what its cure was.

The People knew more about how it spread than she did. They believed that sickness was caused by the breath of an unknown enemy. And smallpox was transmitted by inhaling an airborne virus from its victims. By fleeing the contaminated village and camping in an isolated spot, they had reduced their chances of contracting the disease. They would have been spared if Deep Water had not picked up his cousin's beaded pouch.

Deep Water would probably have passed his cousin's body if he hadn't recognized him by his painted leggings and the silver disks he always wore in his hair. The disks had belonged to his father before him, and Otter was rarely without them. Deep Water had leaned down and scooped up the pouch with the black horsehair tassel as it lay where it had fallen, a few inches from Otter's fingers. He knew that Otter always carried it with him to hold his awl and glue and extra sinews and rawhide for patching his weapons and clothing.

Deep Water had raised his lance in brief salute. He sent a prayer after Otter, to help him along the sad, twisting path to eternity, the path of men who aren't killed in battle. He put the long strap of the pouch over his shoulder, then turned his pony and rode after the other men. At least he would have something to remember his cousin.

Several days later smallpox entered the lodge of Deep Water, Name Giver, Owl, She Laughs, and She Blushes. Medicine Woman came back from their tent looking drawn.

"They all have fires inside them. Their skin almost burns the hand. Gets To Be An Old Man is with them now."

"Maybe it's the shaking sickness, Mother. The same one you had," said Sunrise.

"Maybe. They have chills and their heads and backs hurt them, just as mine did. But I don't think it's the same one. I'm afraid of this sickness. I think it's one we've never seen before."

"What's Gets To Be An Old Man going to do?" Takes Down spoke up from her sewing.

"He'll try to quench the fires in them. He says they should take a steam bath and then bathe immediately in cold water. They should go to the mountains where the springs are the coldest."

"Then we should get ready to move with them," said Sunrise.

"No!" They all turned to stare at Naduah. From the rapidly dwindling supply of English words in her memory she had found the one she needed. Quarantine.

"No." All she could do was repeat it. There was no way she could explain it to them.

"Why not, Granddaughter?"

"We mustn't. We can't go with them. They have to go alone. We have to leave them. Right away." She stood, fists clenched, her wide, blue eyes pleading desperately. They could see she had power, although they didn't know it was the power of experience. Finally Medicine Woman spoke.

"I will tell my brother, little one. We won't go with them." And she held Naduah all night as the child cried convulsively.

The next day Naduah walked around in a daze, her head throbbing from hours of crying. They would have to abandon her friend, Owl. And Name Giver, and the others. As she packed to leave with the rest of the band, she remembered Owl's strong fingers digging into her ribs that morning when she had first played bear and sugar. And it had been Owl who had pulled her up when she jumped into the river and sank like a stone that day.

Quiet, stolid, good-natured Owl, who spent much of her time leading her grandfather through the village and helping him with his arrow-making. Poor Owl. How many times had she wanted to come with Naduah and Star Name, but couldn't? Because she had no pony or because she had to help at home. "Stupid, stupid, stupid!" Naduah dug her nails into her palms. Why hadn't she loaned Owl her pony more often, or helped her with her chores so she could come play too? "Stupid!" Now it was too late. And she began to cry all over again.

She went to Name Giver's lodge, already standing isolated as those around them took down their tents. She stood in the doorway, afraid to enter. Only Deep Water could sit, and he hunched over the tiny fire, feeding it twigs. His slender frame shook under the buffalo robe wrapped around him.

"Deep Water, is Owl here?"

"Yes. But I think she's asleep." He nodded toward the silent forms under the piles of buffalo robes on the beds. "They all are." He looked up at her with hollow, fever-bright eyes.

"And Name Giver?"

"The sickest one." There was a silence, and Deep Water panted, as though even the conversation were an effort for him.

"We have to go, Deep Water. We have to leave you. It's the only way to save everyone. Please believe me." How could one of the People understand being abandoned by the others, when their custom was to help each other through adversity. She was responsible for *paitai*, forsaking someone. They were leaving Deep Water and Owl and Name Giver and She Laughs and old She Blushes because Naduah had told them to.

"Pahayuca and Medicine Woman explained it to us. We understand."

"Sunrise and Takes Down send pemmican and jerky and fruit and water."

"Tell them they are kind. Leave it there." And Deep Water's head drooped to stare into the fire again. Perhaps he was thinking that he would have to follow Otter down that sad, dark road, as a warrior who didn't die in battle. A large pile of supplies, robes, and food that others had brought lay by the door. She left the food there, along with the paunch of water.

"We will see you when you get better." She prayed it might be so, but she knew from experience that the chances were slight.

"Yes." He didn't look up, and she backed from the doorway and ran.

❧ 25 ❧

Summer passed and fall came, and there was no word of Name Giver or his family. The days were getting cool and everyone was preparing for the winter. Naduah clung like an aphid to the gray, scaly bark of the persimmon tree. It wasn't a very big tree, but it looked like a long way down. Her legs were wrapped around the limb, and she lay along it as she shinnied out toward the foliage at the end of it, a stick clutched in her right hand and both arms holding tightly to the limb. Something Good was doing the same in another part of the tree. Star Name was standing on one limb, holding on to the one above her head. She began jumping up and down, causing the tree to vibrate wildly, and sending a shower of small, black *naseeka*, persimmons, onto Takes Down and Black Bird.

"Star Name, stop it! Do you want to kill Something Good and me?"

"Sorry. I forgot."

"At least warn us so we can have a tight grip when you do that, bright eyes," called Something Good from somewhere among the yellow-tinged, club-shaped leaves. Among the whites, Something Good would have looked like a beautiful, angelic boy with her short, thick hair. She kept it cut just below her ears and would probably never let it grow again, in memory of Eagle. And she would always disappear quietly at twilight each night to mourn him.

"There will be plenty for drying and for pemmican."

"If only there were more pemmican to put it in." Black Bird spoke quietly so that the girls wouldn't hear her. But she expressed a worry that they all felt. The buffalo had been scarce this year, no matter what Pahayuca or Buffalo Piss or Old Man did. Even Naduah could tell the difference. She had asked Sunrise where the buffalo had gone.

"Sometimes they just leave for a year," he had told her. "We don't know where they go, and they always come back. Some years there aren't as many of them. This year will be a lean one." He saw the fear in her eyes, and stroked her head. "Don't worry, little one. We will make it through. We always do."

"Do you think the weather will be clear long enough for these to dry?" Naduah spoke as she hit at the persimmons with her stick, knocking them to the ground.

"Yes. We will have two or three days of clear weather."

"How do you know, Mother?" Since the first early frost that had turned the persimmons from sour to sweet the sky had been uncertain, and she'd been unable to read the clouds.

"The spiders told me."

"The spiders?"

"Their webs are long and thin and they're spinning high off the ground. The weather will be clear and dry."

"What are they like if it's going to rain?"

"Everyone knows that, Naduah," said Star Name. "They spin short, thick webs, low to the ground." And Naduah packed that information away. Her first year with the People had come and gone, and it had been crammed with learning. This bit would be added to her store of weather information. Smoke curling down instead of rising meant rain, as did ants in a line rather than scattered. And insects were supposed to bite more just before a storm, though they bit so much anyway it was hard to tell if they were biting more. And of course, there were the clouds to read. There was no end to it, the things she had to learn. Sometimes she despaired of ever knowing it all.

She climbed down with Star Name and Something Good and they all gathered the fallen fruit, piling it onto buffalo robes and dragging them to the large, flat rock nearby. With wooden clubs they started beating the fruit to a pulp, chattering as they worked, and enjoying the pale warmth of the late October sun. When they finished they would separate out the seeds, form the pulp into cakes, and leave them to dry, with Naduah and Star Name standing guard, waving off the birds with long branches.

The grapes and plums had already been dried and stored in bags, ready to boil later. But the persimmons were special. They were for pemmican. Most of the People in the Wasp band preferred persimmons in their pemmican. No one wondered why. They just did. Other bands might use walnuts, or plums or cherries or pecans. But the Wasps used persimmons if at all possible.

The three older women had gone back to their chores, leaving the two girls sprawled on their backs, watching the cloud sculptures and picking out forms they thought resembled things they knew. They waved the long, plumed branches slowly back and forth, and talked.

"In a few years we can be *naivises.*" Star Name was a year older and that much closer to adolescence.

"You mean when the boys get all dressed up and parade around the village showing off?"

"It's called *taoyovises* when the boys do it. *Naivises* when we do it. The older girls did it after the fall hunt last year, remember?"

Naduah remembered. She also remembered, now that Star Name had brought it up, that it hadn't been done this year. Perhaps the hunt had been too disappointing for anyone to have the heart to show off and celebrate. But it had been fun a year ago.

The older, unmarried boys and girls had spent days getting ready. They polished their ponies' coats until they shone, and oiled their own skins and hair until they gleamed too. They decorated their saddles and bridles, dressed in their finest clothes, and paraded on horseback through the village. They were thronged by the adults and the younger children, all calling out how beautiful and handsome they were, and how proud the People were of them. Naduah had been thrilled at the sight of them, young and strong, the future of the band.

She remembered thinking that her pony, Wind, was more beautiful and better trained than any of the horses there. And she dreamed of the day when she and Wind would prance down the street, and she would show everyone what Wanderer had taught her. And he would be there to see her, tall and graceful and proud.

She had drifted off into her favorite fantasy, when she felt the slight vibration of the earth underneath her. She and Star Name both reared up together. *Good,* she thought. *This time I felt it as soon as she did.* They looked for the source of the tremors. A lone rider appeared from the dense bushes behind them. It took them a few seconds to recognize him.

"Deep Water!" They both shouted it at once and ran toward him.

"Are you alone? Where are the others?" Naduah was almost afraid to ask.

"Dead." He hardly glanced at them, but moved on toward the village at a walk. His pony was tired, and they were both covered with dust. No other horse followed him, not even a pack animal. There was a small bundle tied to the pony's rump, a buffalo robe rolled and lashed on top of that, and his weapons, but that was all he carried with him. As he passed close to them, looking neither to the left nor to the right, they realized why it had taken them a few moments to recognize him. His face was pitted with scars, and looked like a piece of ground that horses had trampled.

The girls dropped their branches and followed him, keening for Owl and Name Giver, She Laughs and She Blushes. When he reached the outskirts of camp, Deep Water pulled his buffalo robe up from around his waist to cover his head and shoulders, signaling his sorrow, but with a subtle touch of anger in the angle of his robe as it framed his face. Grief spread from him like ripples from a stone tossed into a pond. For six months there had been no word of Name Giver and his family. Now they would find out what had happened. Blocks The Sun took Deep Water to the extra lodge to rest and eat while the men of the council gathered in Pahayuca's tent. Deep Water joined them later, and they were there until late at night, surrounded by the wails of the mourners.

Sunrise always told Takes Down what had been discussed in council, unless he had been sworn to secrecy. It had taken Naduah a while to realize it, since she so rarely heard Sunrise speak. And Takes Down was seldom silent in the privacy of her own lodge. But Sunrise did speak, so softly sometimes that she had to strain to hear him. As she had to do now. He had waited until they were all gathered for the evening meal, Black Bird and Star Name and Upstream too, all of them exhausted and with heads aching from a night of grieving. Naduah had four cuts on her arms, two parallel diagonals on the inside of each forearm. As she sobbed and wailed, remorse and guilt mingled with her grief, she had slashed her arms, and kept the cuts open now so that they would scar and remind her always of Owl and of Name Giver. And remind her never again to take a friendship for granted as she had Owl's.

After the evening meal, when the family usually shared their day's experiences, Sunrise told them Deep Water's story.

"Deep Water said he would speak of the thing that happened to his family once in council, and then never again. He has made a vow. Do not ask him questions.

"For three days after the Wasps left, the arrow maker and his family were very sick. Their skins were on fire and there were terrible pains in their heads and backs. Then, they began to feel a little better, and Deep Water thought they would get well. But a rash appeared on their faces, and arms and legs, and on Deep Water's too. When the rash became sores and the sores became filled with pus, he knew they had the sickness that had killed those of the village of death. He did what Gets To Be An Old Man had told him to do.

"Even though every movement felt like it was driving hot lance points into his eyes, he carried stones to the lodge to make steam. When they had all lain in the heat, he helped them, one by one, to the river and made them plunge into its cold, spring waters." Sunrise's quiet voice broke, and there was silence, interrupted only by the sobs of those around him and the wails of those still mourning in other parts of the village.

"The water wasn't as cold as in the mountains, but it was still cold. The blind one, his grandfather, was the first. Deep Water says he was dead when he pulled him out of the river. He laid his grandfather's body on the bank and rested. He took his mother and then his aunt to the river and back to the lodge. His sister was last. She died last, but they all died. Deep Water lay down, too weak to go to the river himself and too weak to bury his family. He says he could hear the dogs and coyotes arguing over his grandfather's body where it lay by the river, and there was nothing he could do to stop them. He tried to fire arrows at them, dragging himself to the door of the lodge, but the river was too far away. And he hadn't the strength to pull his bow anyway.

"That was the worst, he said. Hearing the animals fighting over his grandfather's corpse. And lying there as the rest of his family began to smell of death. He drank the last of the water in the lodge and began chanting his death song. When he woke up, he was in the lodge of Big Bow. A Kiowa hunting party had found him and taken him there, knowing that Big Bow is a friend of the Wasps. The sores on his face began to dry up, but they left the scars you see now. The disease is like no other he has ever seen. It rots a person's face while he still lives.

"He stayed with Big Bow until he was well enough to travel. Then he went back to bury the bones of his family. He had to hunt up and down the river to find his grandfather's. He burned his family's lodges, even his own new one, and everything they owned. The horse he has is one Big Bow gave him. For months Deep Water has been traveling, looking for the source, the reason for the sickness."

"Did he find it?" Medicine Woman asked the question that everyone but Naduah wanted to ask.

"He traveled far to the north, north of the land of the Kiowa and into the territory of the Cheyenne. He learned that the sickness comes from the white man, from the places where he trades. The southern Cheyenne told him what they had heard from their brothers, the northern Cheyenne.

"North of the Cheyenne lived a tribe called the Mandan. They camped near the whites' trading posts. They are no more. Their tribe is gone. Their whole tribe." He stopped a moment as the impact of that hit them. "Deep Water says the Mandan went crazy with the sickness. That warriors would ram arrows down their throats, or dig their own graves and shoot themselves so that they fell into them.

"Deep Water does not know how the sickness came to the camp of our brother, or why his family caught it. He blames himself, I think. And he asks why he was spared. That is a hard thing to live with. I think there are scars on Deep Water that we cannot see, scars inside him."

"What did the council decide, Husband?"

Sunrise reached around to his waist and pulled his scalping knife from its scabbard on his belt. He held it up so that its metal blade glinted blue in the firelight. "There are many who favor trading with the white men. No one wants to go back to using flint and bone knives and stone ax heads. They say that Deep Water doesn't really know where the sickness comes from. That he has only heard from people who heard from people who heard from other people."

"What do you think?" Takes Down spoke softly, drawing Sunrise out as usual, getting him to state his own opinion, which he rarely did unless asked. That was why he would never be a chief, although chiefs consulted with him.

"I think Deep Water is right. We should avoid contact with whites as much as possible. But he is wrong too. We have traded with the white men and the Spaniards for many years. And this is the first time the sickness has come among us. We can trade with them. But very carefully. We should avoid the places where many of them live, and we should allow to visit us only traders that we know and have traded with in the past."

"Did you tell Pahayuca that?" Takes Down knew that Pahayuca valued her husband's opinion and would ask what he thought.

"Yes, he agrees. And so do most of the men on the council. Buffalo Piss would prefer to use only those things of the white men that we take from them. But he's always felt that way."

"Does this mean we will do anything differently than we have always done?"

"No. The most important thing now is to get through the winter. We have to have as much pemmican as possible. Pahayuca and I and some others will go hunting tomorrow for fresh meat. Use all the buffalo meat for pemmican. Do not save any of it."

For days the women had been coming in from their fall food-gathering expeditions. Their ponies were laden with pecans and mesquite beans, walnuts, acorns, fruits and berries and roots. In front of each family's lodges the women bent over piles of the nuts and dried meat, pounding them into powder to be made into pemmican. Takes Down and Naduah had a pile of jerky between them. The meat looked like strips of leather one to three feet long and one-quarter of an inch thick. Cut against the grain so they would have alternate layers of lean and fat, the strips dried in less than two days. They didn't even have to be watched, since they were too thin for flies to lay eggs in.

Inapa, the People called it. *Charque* in Spanish. Jerky. Jerked meat.

The word had been handed up the continent from Peru like the stone that gets passed from one team member to another in the hand game. *Inapa* had its uses as a ration, quick and easy to prepare on the trail. But pemmican, *tara-hyapa*, was better.

Using a log with the top sliced off as a cutting board, Takes Down chopped the strips of meat into small pieces, her wrist and hand flashing in a blur. She passed the pieces on to Naduah, who pounded them with a heavy wooden club. At that point, the meat was *tao*, powder, and could be saved to put into boiling water for broth. But they couldn't spare much for that this year.

The pounded dried meat would be mixed with the partially dried persimmons and melted fat. Then they would stuff it into large intestines, cleaned out and saved from the hunt. Takes Down would pour melted tallow over the top of the pemmican to make it airtight before she tied off the intestines. The pemmican would keep for years. What wouldn't fit into the intestines was stored in rawhide boxes, two or three feet long and about twenty inches wide. A good size for hanging on either side of a pack saddle.

"*Samarayune*, pound the meat thoroughly," said Takes Down as she chopped.

"I am," sighed Naduah. "Will we be camping with Old Owl's band soon?"

"Not for a while. His people haven't had a good hunt either. The men will try again before we camp together. So many people in one place makes hunting difficult. We'll see them later. And you'll see your brother. If he isn't off with a raiding party."

Naduah opened her mouth to protest that he was only seven years old. Then realized that her mother was teasing her gently as usual.

"Who will tell us stories this winter, Mother?" The thought bothered her. A winter without enough pemmican or Name Giver's stories was too dreadful to contemplate.

"There are many storytellers. Old Owl is a wonderful storyteller. And so is Medicine Woman."

"But none of them is as good as the blind one. And who will play Guess Who with us? Remember when the arrow maker put that white robe over his head and pretended to be a ghost? And we screamed and squealed and hid all over the lodge? My heart was thumping like Old Man's drum."

"Pay attention to your work, child." Talk of one who was dead made Takes Down anxious. And she couldn't help looking over her shoulder. Perhaps not all the blind one's bones had been buried. Perhaps one lay, gnawed and bare, outside a wolf's den. Perhaps the old man's soul still walked, sighing and moaning on the cold wind, looking for paradise, as in one of his stories. Who knew what terrible things the new sickness could do. Takes Down shivered as she took up a wooden club to help her daughter pound the dried meat.

❧ *26* ❧

In the cold hour before dawn, when the early December sky was the color of ashes streaked and smudged with soot, a buffalo blundered into the side of a lodge on the outskirts of Pahayuca's camp. The force of the collision and the animal's moans and bellows roused the family and the neighbors. As the bull staggered through the outer circle of tents, everyone turned out, clutching their sleeping robes around them. Fires flared to life, and several people brought torches with them. Naduah stood, her hand resting on Smoke's quivering back as the pronghorn cowered next to her, her huge eyes even wider with alarm.

The buffalo's hair had been singed off and his skin was shriveled like the warty bark of a hackberry tree. His knees were scraped raw, probably from falling, over and over again, as he raced blindly across the plain. His eyes were swollen shut, and his face was blistered and burned. He panted, steam blowing from his nostrils and his sides heaving.

The seared linings of his nose must have affected his sense of smell, which normally would have steered him well away from humans. But now the noise of camp, the shouts and the clamor, caused him to veer off toward the river, which lay close by at the base of a sheer, fifty-foot cliff. Before the men could catch him, he reached the edge, then he could be heard, still crying, as he fell, until he bounced on the rocks below. A few ran toward the narrow path used to fetch water, to try to recover the body, but Pahayuca's deep voice boomed after them.

"Come back." He pointed to the east where the sun would soon appear. It seemed to be rising early. There was a reddish glow that spread across the horizon. Naduah watched, fascinated, as it grew before her eyes. She had heard of grass fires, but she had never seen one. Medicine Woman stood next to her, her hand resting on her granddaughter's shoulder.

"We never should have camped here." She seemed to be talking to herself. "We're trapped."

Naduah looked up at her, startled. She tugged at her grandmother's thin hand, trying to pull her to action.

"If we hurry we can escape it. It's still a long way off."

"No, little one. We can't get around it. And we're backed up against that steep drop-off to the river. There's no ford here, even if we could get five hundred animals packed and down that narrow trail. When the wind picks up at dawn, the fire will move much faster." Medicine Woman never hid things from her granddaughter. And she never minimized a bad situation.

"Why can't we just leave everything? We aren't going to stand here and be burned alive, are we?"

"Quiet, child. Pahayuca and the men are discussing it." The knot of men that had formed broke up, and Pahayuca and Buffalo Piss were shouting orders. But still Medicine Woman and Takes Down stood quietly. Sunrise had gone on a hunting trip, as many of the men had, trying to find game for their families.

"At least the hunters are safe. They crossed the river farther down."

"How much time do you think we have?" Takes Down looked at her mother-in-law. Black Bird and Star Name had joined them, and their eyes asked the same question.

"Two or three hours at the most. Probably less."

Naduah fought down her panic. Why didn't they move? Why didn't they do something? This was only a temporary camp, a place to spend the night. It wouldn't take long to pack up. The horses were tethered nearby among some cottonwoods where they were grazing on the thick buffalo grass. The grass was dry and withered, but it had cured where it stood and it was still nourishing. It was also perfect fuel for a prairie fire.

Naduah wanted to scream at her mother and grandmother, to make them move, do something. She wanted to run blindly like the buffalo and throw herself off the cliff, into the cold, safe water fifty feet below. And onto the rocks, she reminded herself. At least she could run down the trail and get into the water and save herself. And leave all her family's belongings and the children and the sick and her pony.

Every muscle in her body tensed as she forced herself to wait until her grandmother had finished weighing all the aspects of the situation. When Medicine Woman finished, she came to the right decision, as she always did. She disappeared into the lodge and came out with the big buffalo rib they used as a shovel, and two sharp root-digging sticks. She handed the sticks to Takes Down and Naduah while Black Bird and Star Name ran to get digging tools of their own. Naduah took time to tie Smoke and Dog inside the lodge before running after the women.

Medicine Woman had broken into a trot, and women and girls joined her as she headed for the edge of camp. She shouted instructions as she ran. She sent women in a wide arc around the camp and set them to turning the ground over, clearing a swath in the grass. The boys had already headed for the pasture to bring in the best ponies. As they drove them into the center of the camp, those left behind, smelling the fire now, cried pitifully and pulled at their tethers.

"Upstream!" Naduah called to him as he went by with their family's horses. "Tie Wind and Rabbit Ears inside the lodge."

"They won't fit."

"Cut the door. Please, Upstream."

"All right." He had to yell to be heard over the din of horses and dogs, the men shouting orders and the women calling to their younger children.

A line of men and older boys formed at the top of the cliff, lowering buckets and kettles and buffalo pauches to men waiting at the river below. They filled the containers as they were lowered, tied them to the lines to be hauled back up. Then the water was passed from hand to hand and thrown onto the outer lodges, wetting them as much as possible.

Everyone strong enough to walk joined Medicine Woman's crew, forming a huge semicircle around the camp, stopping at the river bluff on each side. Desperately they pulled grass and threw it onto the prairie beyond. They dug at the tough roots with anything they could use as a shovel, some kneeling and stabbing at it with their knives. A few of the older men carefully lit fires to burn off the area being cleared, widening it and taking care of grass that had been missed.

Some of those with lodges at the perimeter of camp began pulling them down and dragging them into the open space near Pahayuca's tent. But there were too many lodges to dismantle them all, and the People would need many of them for shelter from the heat. As the sun rose Naduah could see her breath in the cold air, but sweat rolled into her eyes.

Her fingers were cut and sore and her fingernails broken off at the quick. Dirt had been forced under them until they bled and sent pain into her hands. Still she doggedly grabbed, pulled, and pitched, straining to dislodge the stubborn roots of the buffalo grass, roots that formed a solid, woven mass. She glanced over her shoulder now and then to check the progress of the fire. The flames were clearly visible, licking the sky and seeming to stain it with their own color as they marched closer.

The game that had eluded them for months began trickling into camp. Then the trickle became a flood. The faster animals, the deer and the pronghorns, arrived first, many of them racing through camp and over the edge of the cliff in their terror. Naduah was glad she had asked Upstream to tie Wind inside the lodge, or she probably would have broken free to join the stampede. As it was, the lodge was quivering as the four animals pulled and reared.

Jackass rabbits bounded after the deer, bouncing crazily, as though wound with steel springs. Their long legs were a churning blur when they hit the ground. A huge red wolf, his tongue flinging saliva as he ran, almost knocked Naduah down. More wolves passed her, and coyotes and badgers. The skunks began waddling by, their thick, silky pelts rippling with their rolling gait. The animals poured through camp, then turned and raced along the bluff in both directions.

Naduah was concentrating so intently on the grass she was pulling that she jumped and screamed when a seven-foot diamondback rattlesnake skimmed across her foot. Other snakes began streaming in like living rivulets of water: short vicious copperheads, rippling sidewinders, more of the beautiful diamondbacks, slender, irridescent racers and whip snakes. They slithered into every possible crevice in the folded gear and bedding.

Flakes of soot and wisps of smoke were blowing around Naduah's head when the lizards arrived. Brown and yellow and orange and blue and green. Scaled and horned, twilled and spotted and striped and checked. Rough and glossy, they skittered through the grass and over the stones until the ground seemed alive, moving and shifting. Long, plump, bright green collared lizards ran by, upright on their hind legs. Their mouths gaped and hissed in their big heads, and they clutched their short front legs to their chests like tiny dinosaurs.

The insects and the spiders were the last to arrive. Wasps and bees and beetles swarmed, their hard little bodies stinging as they hit Naduah's skin. There were hairy black tarantulas and huge bristling wolf spiders, each with eight eyes glowing as red as coals from hell. Many of them were as big as small birds. Daddy longlegs lurched by in lacy carpets, their legs a tangle of threadlike stilts. Worst of all were the scorpions, their evil, spiked tails curved and ready over their backs. Like a relentless army they advanced over the fallen, heaving bodies of animals unable to run any farther.

Black smoke rolled over them now, stinging Naduah's nose and eyes and setting everyone to coughing. Naduah felt as though her mouth were full of cottonwood fluff, and she could feel the heat intensifying. She gasped for air, sucking in each breath and wondering if there would be a next one. Still they worked on as the roar and crackle grew deafening in their ears, and the flames loomed over them like a thirty-foot wave about to break.

Fifty yards away, a fallen rabbit screamed as the fire engulfed and shriveled it. The flames stretched as far as the eye could see. They seemed to be consuming the entire world, eating it from the edges inward, coming closer and closer to the helpless village. Naduah knew they could never survive it. The thin, cleared area looked pitiful, like a thread stretched between them and the inferno.

The line of people moved back, their heavy winter moccasins crunching on the hard bodies of the spiders and insects and lizards that crawled around them. The last of the birds had flown overhead a while before. Naduah watched them go, wishing she could fly above the smoke and flames. Still she and the others hacked and chopped desperately, shielding their faces with their free arms, trying to protect themselves from the whirling soot and smoke and cinders.

The outer lodges were emptied, the well supporting or carrying the sick, mothers swinging their babies in their cradle boards. The circle of diggers finally had to give up. They dropped their sticks and ran from the intense heat. As they ran they grabbed as much as they could carry from the outer tents, taking their own or their neighbors' belongings with them. Medicine Woman was the last to give up, and she fell as she ran, her foot caught in an abandoned prairie-dog hole. When she pulled it out, it jutted at a strange angle from the ankle.

"Grandmother!" Naduah screamed and darted back to her, the fire towering over them both. Flames jostled at the edge of the cleared area, as though searching for the best place to jump it. Buffalo Piss appeared from the smoke, his young face smudged with soot. He and Naduah pulled Medicine Woman, already flaming like a living torch, away from the fire. Naduah fell across her grandmother with a buffalo robe, smothering the flames with her body. Other women crowded around, but they were too late. Medicine Woman was blind, her eyes seared by the heat, her face already raw and blistered.

She seemed dead, but as Naduah lay sobbing across her, she felt the old woman's heart beating. It reminded her of her first day in camp when Medicine Woman had put the child's hand on her chest and she had felt the delicate fluttering.

Buffalo Piss pulled her gently off as Pahayuca came running. He picked his sister up as though she weighed nothing, and Naduah and Takes Down followed him to see that she was safely laid in his lodge near the cliff face. He knew that Sunrise was away and that Takes Down and Black Bird would have all they could do to save themselves, much less look after Medicine Woman.

Small fires began flaring all around them as sparks landed on the lodges. They burned neat round holes whose edges burst into flames, like delicate petals opening. The roaring was that of an immense waterfall. Everyone who could grabbed a blanket or robe, shaking the snakes and lizards and spiders out of them. Naduah beat at fires until her arms felt like wooden clubs. Yet still the flowers bloomed, burning entire lodges and consuming more of the precious food supply. The heat was suffocating, and she gasped for breath. Several children lay unmoving, their mothers sobbing as they beat at the blaze.

Horses screamed, bucking and rearing in blind panic. Many of them pulled loose and veered off through the smoke and into the flames, or over the cliff's edge, trampling children in their flight. Past the cleared circle, in the grove of cottonwoods, the abandoned ponies shrieked as they were roasted alive. It seemed as though the fire was eating the air as well as the lodges and the food and the horses. The heat burned Naduah's nose and throat and cracked her parched lips. She couldn't cry anymore because her tear ducts had dried, and the linings of her eyes seemed to scrape against her eyeballs.

The world turned to blinding orange heat. Naduah staggered and fell, with blackness coming down on her like a heavy blanket. She waved her hand feebly, as though to push it away, then gave up. Before she passed out, she managed to pull a robe over her. That was all the preparation for death she could make.

Naduah awoke to a hissing of snakes, thousands of them. As she threw off the robe and sat up, she realized that two snakes had been sharing it with her, their bodies cool along hers. They slithered off in search of other shelter, their tongues flickering. Snow was falling, the flakes turning to tiny hissing points of steam as they hit the flames. She held her tongue out to catch the flakes, tantalizing with the hint of water.

Fire still burned in a circle around the devastated camp, but it was less ferocious. It had reached the bluff on either side of the cleared area and was dying from lack of fuel, sputtering angrily. As the snow fell more heavily, it beat the flames down.

From around Naduah came the moans and sobs of the survivors as they searched through the wreckage for whatever they could salvage. Their faces were blackened with soot. Pahayuca and the men of the council sat in the middle of camp. They huddled under their robes as they decided where to go from there. As far as the steel-gray horizon all Naduah could see was a smoking, blackened wasteland, broken only by a few ragged spikes of tree trunks and the charred lumps of dead animals, most of them too burned to eat. Snow was beginning to blow in thin sheets, piling up around the corpses and laying a cover over them.

Takes Down passed, swinging a dead rabbit by the ears and carrying a kettle of water in the other hand. She squatted next to Naduah and brushed the hair from her eyes. It was what she always did, showing her affection in her shy way.

"Are you hurt, Daughter?"

"I don't think so."

"Drink." Takes Down dropped the rabbit and scooped water from the kettle. Naduah drank from her hands. Then she reached in and splashed a little on her face.

"Medicine Woman is asking for you, Naduah. She says to bring her medicine bag when you come. I'll be gathering as many animals as I can to eat later."

"I'll go now, Mother."

Takes Down walked to their lodge, laid the rabbit down outside, and began carrying water to those who were hurt. Women were killing whatever animals they could find still hiding in camp, but there was little wood left to build cooking fires. As the ground cooled under the snow, some of them went beyond the village, searching among the larger animals for those with edible meat on them. The blackened carcasses of their own ponies and mules had the most. As the snow dampened the ground, the smell of wet charcoal pervaded everything.

Naduah shivered as she stood up. Less than an hour after she had thought she would never be cold again, she was shivering. Her robe and dress had black holes in them, and the wind seemed to blow through to her bones. She heard Wind's shrill neigh, and went to her lodge. It was crowded inside with two horses and the pronghorn and Dog, and all the animals were frightened. Crouched against the packs at the far wall was a large, buff-colored coyote, who stared at Smoke as though trying to mesmerize her. Now that the danger was over he was interested in his stomach. Smoke had backed the length of her tether and tugged at it desperately. Dog cowered in the bedding, whining softly.

When he saw Naduah, the coyote got up and stretched slowly and regally. He strolled across the tent, brushing against her as he left. She let him go, just as anyone else would. Coyotes were sacred. Not as sacred as wolves, perhaps, but brothers to the People anyway. No one would desecrate them by eating them.

Naduah stroked the trembling pronghorn, the thick brittle winter coat coming out in tufts under her hand. Smoke only weighed a hundred pounds, but perhaps a dog travois could be hitched to her. Wind would have to suffer the humiliation of serving as a pack animal too. Too many horses had perished to allow any of those left to go unused. She lifted her grandmother's medicine pouch down from its peg and collected rags and a bag of bear fat to take with her. Then she untied Smoke and Dog, and they trotted behind her as she ran toward Pahayuca's lodge.

Medicine Woman lay on a pile of robes, and only Something Good was with her, crooning softly as she glided around putting things into packs and sorting through the jumble in the tent. Outside, Blocks The Sun and Silver Rain were converting a travois into a stretcher. They lashed several crosspieces to the two long, scissor-shaped poles, then laid a thick pile of the softest robes on top. They covered the robes with an old hide to keep the snow off. Then they tied a curved willow lathe across the center to arch over Medicine Woman's body and hold her in place, no matter how rough the traveling might be.

Naduah mixed crumbled dried tree fungus with the warm bear grease. The fungus deadened pain and was used for burns and toothaches. Medicine Woman's hair had been singed off close to her head and gave off an acrid odor. She was naked under the fur robe. Naduah knelt beside her and gently rubbed the grease mixture over her face and neck and ears, covering the blisters and peeling skin that was blackened in place.

"Is the pain bad, Grandmother?" Medicine Woman's eyelids fluttered and opened, but the eyes were glazed and unseeing.

"Yes, little one. You must have my pouch."

"Yes, *Kaku.*"

"Good. You know what to use. The fungus seems to be helping."

"I had a good teacher." Naduah's tears fell onto the fur. She wanted to tell Medicine Woman that she would be all right. But she couldn't. Medicine Woman had never lied to her, even when the truth was painful. Naduah's grandmother reached out a thin, blue-veined hand and groped with it until she touched her granddaughter's cheek.

"Don't cry for me, little one. I've seen the world. Sight is only one way of seeing. There are others. I can still see in my memory. And you can describe things to me."

Naduah couldn't answer, and she busied herself with the tiny bags and bundles of leaves in the medicine pouch. She sat back on her heels, studying the contents and deciding what herbs to use. She could ask her grandmother, but she felt as though this should be her responsibility, that she shouldn't bother Medicine Woman and make her speak unnecessarily. The crushed leaves of the mimosa were good for pain and inflamed eyes. And there was the yarrow that she had discovered. She put water on the fire to boil the yarrow, and began grinding the mimosa leaves in the small stone mortar and pestle that was in the pouch.

222

"Little one."

"Yes, Something Good." In her preoccupation, Naduah had almost forgotten her friend was there.

"Hurry. Pahayuca and the council have decided where we will travel. Lance is riding through now with instructions. We have to leave soon. The snow is falling heavily."

Naduah raised her head and concentrated. Above the moans and cries of grief and the clatter of lodge poles falling, she could hear Lance's singsong chant.

The Wasps moved out in the teeth of the blizzard, with lines tied between each horse and walker to keep them all together. Pahayuca used the wind as a reference point, keeping it always on his right cheek as he headed slightly southeast, away from the precipitous river bluff, now invisible in the swirling clouds of white. The band followed the council's decision without question. They all knew that to stay where they were, snowed in miles from forage or game, would mean death for them all. Their only chance was to keep moving.

In good times the average family had at least five pack animals, five riding ponies, and two buffalo or war ponies. Now there weren't enough for everyone to ride, and many walked, taking turns on a friend's or relative's horse when they became exhausted. The children and the sick and hurt rode on travois like Medicine Woman's, spattered with the dark gray mud of mixed snow and soot. Behind them the abandoned wreckage was soon lost in the snow. The whitened lodge poles and tattered covers looked like the chewed bones of a mangled animal, left for the vultures to pick clean. Hanging from the highest pole still standing was a pouch with a piece of painted bark inside, a message for the missing hunters.

Naduah's fingers were red and stinging where they poked out of the wrapping of blanket strips. Her face was numb, and there was frost peeling from it. She could hardly feel her feet at all, except for the steady, throbbing pain. In front of her, Takes Down was an indistinct form, fading in and out of sight on Rabbit Ears. A dark form loomed through the white curtain and a figure trudged toward her, headed back the way they had come.

"Tahkobe Ano. Broken Cup." The woman stopped and looked up at Naduah. "Have you seen my daughter? Her name is Broken Cup. She must have wandered off." The wind whipped the words around the young woman's head before splintering them and sending them flying. She was shouting, but Naduah could barely hear her. Turning, the woman wandered off again.

"Stop, Gray Cloud. Broken Cup is dead. You know that. I saw

you bury her. Come back!" She screamed, knowing that the woman couldn't hear her and wouldn't turn back if she could hear. Knowing that she herself couldn't break from the line to go after her. The small figure vanished in the swirling snow as though swallowed in an ocean of foam. Grimly Naduah checked the stiffened hide rope that stretched from her pommel to her mother's. It would be easy to lose sight of the entire village in seconds.

The patched and blackened lodge was crowded. Star Name and Black Bird and Upstream had moved in to let a homeless family use their tent. Something Good had also loaned out her lodge, and she and little Weasel were staying with them. Weasel wailed as Medicine Woman rocked her futilely in her arms.

It was February, the Month The Babies Cry For Food, and spring was more than a month away. Winter had set in with a vengeance after the first blizzard, and they still camped alone. Game was too scarce to combine the bands in their usual winter encampment. The ponies were skeletal, their long, shabby coats rough and matted with dirt and burs. Their hipbones jutted from the hide stretched tightly over them, and their bellies were swollen and lumpy with sticks and bark. Like their owners', their eyes were listless from hunger.

For weeks the Wasps had grubbed for roots, chipping at the frozen ground. They'd eaten lizards and mice, snakes and rats and the bark from trees. The week before they'd feasted on a turtle that Star Name had found. Takes Down had thrown it on its back alive, onto the fire. They had all sat around watching it intently as it kicked its legs feebly, its head craning from side to side on its scrawny, wrinkled neck as the flames curled around the shell. When it had cooked, Takes Down raked it out and broke the bottom carapace open, releasing a thick, pungent steam. They gathered around to eat from the bowl of its shell, dipping through the broth and scooping the soft meat out with horn spoons. The children were allowed to eat first, but they handed their spoons over without taking much.

"Daughter, eat more. You've only had a mouthful, and you need strength."

"It's all right, Mother. I don't want any more." Naduah knew how many still had to be fed.

Now she could taste the oily meat in her memory and wished there had been more. Most of their meals were gruel made of mesquite meal laboriously ground from the beans, or a thin soup of pemmican mixed with water and a little parched corn from the precious supply. Naduah kept a close watch on the food dwindling in the rawhide boxes, most of which sat empty under the bed. She counted, over and over, the number of people to be fed and mentally measured out the daily amounts for each.

Sunrise went out on foot again and again, because the ponies weren't strong enough to carry a hunting party. He almost always came back empty-handed. He rarely spoke these days, despair gnawing at him as much as hunger. Something Good brought some food from Pahayuca's household, but there wasn't much there either. He fed everyone who came to his door hungry, and sent food to those who had none. And no matter how many times Naduah counted and measured, she always came up with the same answer. There wouldn't be enough.

She sat with her arms around Smoke, who nuzzled her hand. The doe was looking for the wisps of dry grass that Naduah searched the cold, wind-scoured plain to find. The pronghorn's thinness made her eyes seem even bigger and softer under their fringe of heavy black lashes. The lodge was empty except for the two of them and Dog and Medicine Woman, who slept. The women were out searching for food. Sunrise, in desperation, had gone with some of the men to raid the Texas settlements for horses so they could hunt again.

The bells on Smoke's collar jingled merrily in the chill stillness of the tent as she tried to push Naduah into playing with her. She butted her friend with the tiny buds of horns on the top of her head, and danced a little on her delicate, elfin hooves.

Naduah made one last calculation of the food supply, more to postpone what she had to do than through any hope of avoiding it. Tears spilled from her eyes, blurring her sight, and she gulped back sobs as she groped in the bag where she kept her skinning knife. With the knife in one hand and her other on Smoke's back, she led her out of the lodge and away from the village. Dog trotted a little ahead of them, and the doe frisked. She was looking forward to one of their runs out on the open plain. Naduah's family would have meat tonight, but she knew she wouldn't be able to eat any of it.

❧ 27 ❧

The border into Oklahoma Territory wasn't inviting especially in November. The Red River was lined with dry sand hills thirty feet tall and covered with a sparse growth of brittle weeds. A month earlier, Terrible Snows, his women, and their few ponies had waded over the sand hills and splashed through the shallow, muddy river. They had been wandering from band to band for almost a year, moving gradually farther and farther north.

With each move Terrible Snows thought vaguely to improve his fortunes, either by finding new medicine or by buying more from yet another medicine man. He wandered with the belief that things would be better somewhere else. But they never were. The fall hunts had been scant everywhere, but his hunting had been even worse.

North of the Red River they had caught up with Tabbe Nanica, Sun Name, and his band of Yamparika, Root Eaters. A Little Less and Mountain and Rachel put up the lodge on the muddy hem of the village as usual, their tent smaller and shabbier than the rest. The smell of rotting animal carcasses left outside the village and the dung from the horse pasture was stronger here. But at least the ponies were closer and Rachel didn't have to walk as far to tend them. And the children left her alone. By now they avoided her as one who was touched by spirits. No one questioned Terrible Snow's right to be there. The People were free to live with whatever band they chose, and to leave it when they wanted.

The plain rose and fell in graceful swells that the lodges rode like small ships. But the ground was cold and dry and brown, as though crusted over. And the icy winter northers howled across the wastes with nothing to stop them east of the Rocky Mountains, hundreds of miles away. Many of the lodges had brush windbreaks around them, but there was no brush left when Terrible Snows arrived.

Now Rachel and Terrible Snows and A Little Less were in Sun Name's lodge. It had finally happened. New Mexican traders, Comancheros, were in camp. And they were bargaining for the white slave. Rachel's eyes flicked from the two mestizos to the meal they were eating, her body's hunger vying with her mind's hope.

"*Cuánto cuesta la mujer, jefe?*" José Piedad Tafoya swallowed the last piece of buffalo steak speared on the point of his long knife and wiped his hands on his vest. The grease added to several years of dirt that had dyed his clothes the color of old coffee grounds. Across from him, Chino used his lank black hair as a napkin. The flames carved his face into that of a cadaver. His ferocious, slanted black eyes and hawk's nose made him look like a bird of prey. Chino was restless. He was too new at this, or not suited for it. He wasn't used to even asking for something, much less paying for it.

José watched Sun Name through narrowed eyes. How much could the chief ask for the woman? She wasn't worth much, that was plain. He wasn't even sure if he could get her back to Santa Fe alive. And Anglos didn't pay much for carcasses. They paid handsomely for stock on the hoof, though, even if it was as bad off as this one was. When ransoming captives, one dwelt on the sentimental value of the merchandise.

As though reading his mind, Rachel tried to run her fingers through her hair. She couldn't penetrate the tangle as far as her ears. In the smothering heat of the leader's lodge, she shivered inside her thin dress. She constantly stroked her face and smoothed her torn clothes, picking at imaginary lint. Her eyes would focus briefly, then empty. She seemed to dart into reality, look around, then run back to her cozy den of madness.

In the past year and a half, she had learned enough Comanche to get along. Commands mostly. But now the men were speaking in handtalk and pidgin Spanish. Somewhere in her battered mind, she knew something important was happening. In her lucid moments she stared at the men's faces intently, as though trying to read meaning in their expressions that she couldn't get from their words. Her lips moved in silent soliloquy pleading with them to help her.

Sun Name was not one to be rushed. Because José was young, he forgave him the breach of courtesy. Discussing business before establishing the proper atmosphere with small talk was like bathing with your clothes on: it just wasn't as effective. Sun Name would settle things in his own time. He took his pipe out, and A Little Less pulled Rachel roughly out into the night, harsh with the crystal edges of frost.

In broken Spanish and Comanche and graceful, flickering handtalk, the bartering progressed. It wound its slow way through the night, meandering and doubling back on itself like the slippery trail of a snail. Sun Name did most of the talking, since negotiations could hardly be trusted to Terrible Snows. The People didn't distinguish gender in their pronouns, so his pidgin Spanish translated something as follows.

"Terrible Snows loves the white-eyes woman very much. He won't want to sell him. You have to pay plenty blankets, coffee, guns, arrowheads, and horses. Maybe ten horses. Maybe twelve. Terrible snows be plenty brokenhearted if white-eyes woman leaves."

"*Jefe*, Terrible Snows loves only his stomach and his dice game." José knew it was going to be a hard winter, and Terrible Snows didn't look like he could even feed his slave. "She'll die soon. We'll take her off your hands." He thought of the tiny stock of goods, maybe twenty dollars worth, packed on their worn-out burros. Guns and horses indeed. "We'll pay you a sack of coffee, a sack of sugar, three blankets, and a keg of whiskey." The whiskey was José's ace, though it wasn't always successful with the Comanche. If he could pull this trade off, it would set him up, give him the profit he needed to expand his inventory.

"Ho-say." Sun Name laughed and slapped José on the back. "Often have we traded together. We will trade for many seasons to come. I love you as my brother. I love you because you make jokes all the time. But this is serious talk. The white-eyes slave works hard. Without him Terrible Snows' kind old mother will be sad. Maybe die from so much work to do alone. Everyone loves the white-eyes woman as his own. The men enjoy him often. We could not part with him for less than eight horses. Good ones. Not the broken-down ones you sell to the Kiowa. And the blankets and the sugar and the coffee and the guns. And do you have any of those red beads? The big ones? We don't want your stupid water, though."

"All right. One horse and the coffee and the sugar and the blankets." Chino would have to walk back to Santa Fe.

"As long as we're joking, did I tell you about the time Dog Foot got drunk on stupid water?"

The pipe was lost in Sun Name's huge brown hand as he passed it to José. The hand reminded José of a bear's paw, with its long, dirty nails and short, stubby fingers. The leader's eyes twinkled with the joy of driving a bargain. José took a deep drag on the pipe and settled back for a long story and a longer evening. A cold wind whistled outside and he had no better place to go. He had no place to go at all, in fact.

From here they would head back to Texas and the Valley of Tears. Then they would go south and west, threading their way through Palo Duro canyon to the Palo Duro River's headwaters. They would water at Trujillo and cross the Puerto de los Rivajeños, the gap in the cap rock called the Door of the Plains. From there they had only to journey up the Valley of the Taos to Santa Fe. With the shape their burros were in and the miserable weather, it would probably take them at least two weeks to make the trip.

Donaho's in Santa Fe would be the first stop. He had put the word out that he would pay for any white captives ransomed from the tribes. Maybe there would be enough money to buy a wagon as well as more trade goods. Then José would head out again, zigzagging through the wild, barren Llano Estacado, the Staked Plains, and across the prairie in search of the Comanche. Tonight he'd talk to Sun Name about arranging a regular meeting place. It would save time and trouble. At twenty-two, José had ideas that were new to the Comanchero trade.

Like most of the Comancheros, José Piedad Tafoya was part Pueblo Indian. His Indian mother had named him Piedad. Pity. Compassion. The irony of the name never occurred to José. It was just another part of him, like the coarse black hair and the piercing dark eyes in his gaunt face. Already his skin was toughened and beginning to crack from the hundreds of blast-furnace days he had spent scrabbling with the crude, heavy hoe, spreading the moisture evenly from the irrigation ditches into the stony ground before it evaporated.

He had decided early that the life of a New Mexico farmer wasn't for him. Even if he could grow something, the bureaucrats of the south, from their offices and mansions in Mexico City, would strangle him. All they knew, those men, were regulations and tariffs and monopolies. Why be a poor honest man in a world of rich, dishonest ones?

So here he was, bantering with Sun Name, civil chief of the Yamparika Comanches. Sun Name wasn't much older than José, but he had the dignity of command and the respect of thousands of people. Indians maybe, but it still counted for something. José could never hope to attain that kind of position. He would have to make do with money instead. And he intended to make a lot of it. It was the only thing that mattered to him. Ransoming this woman would be a good start.

If they could get Terrible Snows drunk they might be able to pass off that goose-rumped, knee-sprung paint they'd found on the Staked Plains. Terrible Snows looked like the type to take to whiskey, if he could be pried away from Sun Name long enough to make the introduction. He must be desperate for horses to ask for them in payment. Usually the Comanche used them for currency. But Terrible Snows didn't look prosperous. Not even by Comanche standards.

The next problem would be to get the woman back to Santa Fe alive and unraped. Donoho had some crazy religious reason for ransoming captives. It wasn't a profit-making enterprise for him. Gringos were funny. They'd pay good money for a woman who'd been used by the entire Comanche tribe, but take offense if the loveless traders got a little use from her too. There was no understanding gringos. The Indians were much easier to get along with.

From a distance the city of Santa Fe looked like a feature of the landscape, a geologic formation raised from the surrounding clay. José and his partner, his merchandise and burros moved down onto the open plain, a plaid mantle of corn and wheat fields and irrigation ditches laid out around the city.

Santa Fe from closer up looked like a gathering of beached Ohio flatboats. A prairie-dog town, traders called it. A town of low mud houses on streets that were little more than trampled footpaths between scattered farm settlements. It was the capital city of a Mexican province and the home of three thousand people. To the west soared a snowy mountain, waterfalls cascading down its sides. The water rushed to join the clear stream that flowed through Santa Fe, but the stream wasn't as clear when it slunk out the other side.

It was twilight when Rachel, exhausted, aching, and coated with dust, rode into the main plaza behind José and Chino. Her moccasins had shredded on the stones of the mountain trails, and she was wearing a pair of Mexican straw sandals. Grateful not to be walking, she perched on the haunches of the little burro. And he in turn was probably grateful to have her light, accommodating weight rather than the heavy, awkward packs. Most of the ugly sores on his back were beginning to heal.

The group ambled past the governor's palace. It was a sprawling, one-story, four-hundred-foot-long mud hut. The crude portico was held up by roughly hewn tree trunks, and the doors were so low the tall Missouri traders had to stoop to enter. There were few traders in town now though. Most of them had headed back toward Independence. Their huge caravans of covered wagons wouldn't be pulling in, along with the rains, until July or August. Around the plaza, the stores they rented for the summer and fall were shuttered and bare.

In the traders' absence, Santa Fe seemed almost asleep. The Indians and farmers, the merchants and housewives, their faces shrouded in seven-foot shawls, looked like sleepwalkers. It seemed as though time had slowed here. It was an easygoing city of rounded edges, flat, weed-grown roofs, and crumbling clay walls.

Rachel stared around her and clutched her only possession more tightly. José had given her a comb, a dirty, broken-toothed horn comb, that he'd found in the bottom of the pack. She had had to use a knife as much as a comb, but her hair was fairly untangled. José had watched her carefully as she used the knife. She wasn't right in the head, and he didn't want to lose her after going to so much trouble. Luckily, he had traded off the last of the mirrors, and Rachel couldn't see the pink scar tissue of her nose. She was spared the sight of dirt caked on her face, collecting in the wrinkles and accentuating them, and the spikes of chopped hair sticking out all over her head. Perhaps in her state of mind she wouldn't have recognized herself anyway.

From the military chapel across from the palace, a huge, brass bell began its solemn evening tolling. All movement ceased except for the clicking of rosary beads and the murmur of lips as everyone whispered their evening prayers. José and Chino weren't religious, but they stopped too, and bowed their heads. One can disregard law, but not custom. Jangling smaller bells interrupted the tolling, and the slow parade of strollers started up again.

José led the caravan around the fires that were being lit in the big square. Far into the night, men would stand around them, warming the seats of their baggy, white cotton pants and talking. In front of the palace a white-haired porter with long, drooping mustaches lit the torches that flared on poles jutting from the walls. The flames sent great gushes of greasy black smoke spiraling into the darkening sky. From a bar somewhere down a winding alley drifted the music of a guitar, rising and falling.

Nodding and speaking to everyone he met, José made a slow progress through the crooked streets. Through it all, Rachel sat patiently on her burro. Her mouth twitched in a flitting smile, tickled by hidden little thoughts, like insects crawling in one's clothes. It was dark when they finally drew up in front of a long, low fortress with walls three feet thick. The rafter beams stuck out under the roofline, looking almost like cannons in the dim light. The two windows were narrow and barred and set far back in the adobe. The big door was also recessed and made of heavy planks several feet wide and eight inches thick. When José pounded on it with his bone-handled quirt, it opened slowly, creaking on its wooden hinges.

"Who is it, La Paz?" A woman's voice, speaking English, echoed through the hall behind the servant as he stood blocking the door. Tears welled up in Rachel's eyes. When the door opened far enough to admit Mrs. Donaho's round face, Rachel could hardly speak. For a few moments she was totally sane again. Her words had to force their way through the tightness of her throat. They came out in a harsh, strangled whisper, the English sounding strange in her own ears.

"Please, for the love of God, help me."

The Donahos dispatched a message to Independence with a trader who was headed there. From there the message was to be sent on to Rachel's husband in Texas with whomever was going that way. And there would certainly be people going. Independence was a funnel, a spillway of humanity, sending settlers and trappers westward.

Santa Fe wasn't safe. Two plagues stalked its streets, typhoid and revolution. The first punched holes in its victims' intestines, invaded their arteries and rotted the marrow of their bones. It left them to die in their own vomited blood. The Pueblos were responsible for the revolution. Every hundred years or so they were pushed too far by the authorities and rose up against their masters, leaving corpses as fodder for the rooting hogs.

Violence lurked among the baskets of fruit and vegetables in the market and blew around the corners of the buildings. And so the Donahos only ventured out when necessary. They decided to risk the uncertainties of the Santa Fe trail rather than stay where they were. As soon as Rachel was well enough to travel, they hitched up their own small caravan, left their adobe fortress in the care of La Paz, and began the eight-hundred-mile trek to their small frame house in Independence.

It took the Donahos six weeks to make the journey. When Comanche stopped them and demanded the customary tribute, Rachel cowered, hysterical, among the barrels and boxes under the wagon's cover. Mrs. Donaho crouched next to her, her plump arms encircling her, and murmured while her husband handed over the goods he had brought along for just such a possibility. Mrs. Donaho chattered cheerfully for eight hundred miles, up mountains and down, across boiling rivers and baking deserts. She gossiped through torrential rains and mud that mired the wheels and collected into heavy and heavier weights on the soles of their shoes.

Starved for a woman's ear and understanding, she talked to Rachel while they leaned into the wind, their voluminous skirts billowing out behind them. She was still talking as their wagons wound through the mud and noise and turmoil of Independence, Missouri. She was the first to spot the sagging roof on their cabin.

"Looks like the porch could stand some repair, Mr. Donaho. Like as not some riffraff has been camping on it all summer and fall. There's probably someone keeping house in the necessary out back."

"I wouldn't be surprised. Housing's short here," Donaho answered.

"So are necessaries. This place smells worse every time we come back." Mrs. Donaho began setting her hair to rights, chasing stray gray wisps and herding them back into her bun. "Looks like we have company."

He was waiting for them, sitting on the corner of the low porch, his legs hanging over the edge. The message had been delivered to Rachel's family.

"Mr. Plummer, we're glad you're here." Mr. Donaho held out his hand. L. D. Nixon's face became even pinker than usual as he took the hand gingerly.

"My name is Nixon. Lawrence Nixon. I'm Rachel's brother-in-law. I live in Independence now."

"And where is Mr. Plummer?" called Mrs. Donaho from the wagon. "Did anyone deliver the message to him that we were coming?"

"Yes, ma'm. The Parkers are beholden to you for ransoming Rachel." L. D. cleared his throat and looked up at his sister-in-law, sitting in the wagon. She spoke so low they could barely hear her.

"Have they found little Jamie, L. D.?"

"No. There's been no word. Your father has been searching, though. We hoped you'd know something, Rachel. Your aunt Elizabeth was ransomed a year and a half ago."

"Where's Luther? Is he alive?"

"We're all glad to have you back." L. D. helped her down from the wagon and held her at arm's length, trying to keep the pain out of his face.

"Where is he?" Her hands fluttered like birds, but her face was still, except for a small tic in the corner of her right eye.

"He's alive. But he couldn't come."

"But I'm his wife, L. D."

She would have to be told, but he couldn't do it now. He avoided her eyes.

"Rachel, the past two years have been hard on him. Losing you and little James Pratt, and not knowing . . ."

"The past two years have been hard on him." Rachel started to laugh, tumbling into hysteria. L. D. shook her to make her stop. The light went out of her eyes and wasn't rekindled during the long trip home.

She crossed James and Martha Parker's doorsill in east Texas on February 19, 1838. She never saw her son or her husband again, although Luther and his new wife, Angelina, lived in the next county. She died in her parents' house at eighteen, exactly one year later.

❧ **28** ❦

As time went on, Comanche raids on the settlements intensified. While President Sam Houston sent envoys to bribe the Indians with presents and honey talk, Texans were tortured and scalped, mutilated and murdered. Others would come home from plowing or hunting and find the smell of smoke and death, a pall over their homes. They found the mangled bodies of their families or an empty cabin and a bloody trail.

Some of them, like John Wolf, went mad. John found his wife naked and dead and almost slashed to ribbons. His two teenaged daughters were still alive, but they didn't live long. They had been stripped and raped repeatedly, then nailed spread-eagled to the wall. Their breasts had been cut off before they were scalped. They died as their father was lowering them down.

John Wolf became a Comanche hunter. They called him Lone Wolf, and he roamed the frontier for years, ghosting in and out of Ranger camps. He made everyone nervous with his wild talk and his string of black scalps. But everyone fed him and in their hearts wished him well. Hollow-eyed and filthy, with gray hair and beard as matted as the tangled felt of a goat's fleece, he dangled his strings of scalps like fish on a small boy's line. Women's scalps. Children's. It didn't matter to John. Just as long as they were Comanche.

And it didn't matter to many of the Texans. They wanted the freedom to rid themselves of the Comanche forever. So they elected Mirabeau Buonoparte Lamar, the man who would give it to them. "Mark the boundary of the Republic with the sword," he said. He was a poet, and not a man who looked the part of a warrior. But then, he didn't have to lead the charges, just charge the expenses. He was willing to drive the country deeply into debt to rid Texas of the plague of Indians.

"Put honor before expense," said President Lamar, and the Texas legislature voted a million dollars to buy Comanche blood. Two thousand men volunteered to join the army, newly formed to fight Indians.

"He wants us to do what, Sergeant?" Noah Smithwick didn't mean to be insubordinate. He just wasn't sure he heard the order correctly.

"The colonel says to dismount and prepare to attack."

"Dismount?"

"Dismount, Smithwick. Dismount!" The sergeant rode along the line passing the word to the sixty volunteers. There was a jingling and a clanking, bridles, saddles, spurs, and weapons ringing the changes of war. Noah's stomach cramped with hunger. The food had almost run out, and they were all on short rations. They were sharing out the last of the mule that had frozen to death on bivouack.

Some of the men were suffering from frostbite after the snowstorm had caught them. They had huddled in the rye bottoms of the Lampassas for two days, sleeping together to pool their bodies' warmth. Now, from the sleeping Indian camp somewhere around the hill Noah could hear the faint sound of dogs barking, horses neighing, and roosters crowing. Stolen, no doubt, from a Texas farmstead. The comforting sounds taunted them as they shivered in the icy wind.

Above them, on a hill overlooking Old Owl's scattered camp, Colonel Moore sat with Chief Castro of the Lipan Apache. His scouts had done well. The camp was still asleep, its people staying in bed longer this winter to conserve their scanty food and fuel supplies. The village spread along the clear San Saba River. Thin lines of gray smoke, like pencil strokes against the lavender sky, rose from the smoldering cooking fires. It was a tranquil scene, but Moore didn't appreciate it.

Smug bastards. They haven't even posted lookouts. We'll teach them that they're not safe anywhere. Colonel Moore turned his horse and rode down to join his men, dislodging pink granite rocks and pebbles as he went. Leaving his mount closely tethered with the others, he waved his men in behind him. The column started through the cedar brake and around the base of the hill toward the sleeping village.

Noah Smithwick passed through the thick growth of cedars that scraped along his leather pants and jacket. He had a strip of torn blanket wrapped around his neck and more strips stuffed into his moccasins. There was an uneasy feeling in the pit of his stomach, somewhere between last night's dinner and this morning's hurried meal. He had fought Indians before, but never this deep in their own territory and never in a village. His friend, Rufus Perry, walked alongside him. Old Rufe was seventeen, and he usually followed Noah when they patrolled together with the Rangers.

"You always look so calm, Noah. I'm as jittery as a bird in a butter churn." Rufe spoke in a low voice that carried less than a whisper.

"Don't be fooled, Rufe. I took too large a helping of fear with breakfast, and it isn't sitting well with me."

"I'd feel better on a horse."

"I'd feel better back home in bed."

"I know what you mean. It's different, isn't it? It's so quiet down there. All of them asleep."

"And no telling how many there or, nor any trees to hide behind. No, sir. Line 'em up and let 'em yell, out where I can see and hear them. Rufe, I don't like this at all."

Then the sergeant turned and made a chopping motion, and their talking ceased. The company's single file became a rank as they lined up for the charge. Noah grinned over at Perry.

"Time to put all that fear to work." He tensed his chest and shoulder muscles and crouched, ready to sprint toward the lodges, plainly visible now through the brush and scattered trees. The men broke into a trot and then into a full run. As they ran they screamed whatever occurred to them. "For Texas" was the most popular. Followed by "Remember the Alamo," which had become an all-purpose phrase. But Noah had his own war cry. He bellowed it as he ran, the wind blowing his long red beard behind him. "Sheeeee-it!"

The Texans' war cries and their rifle fire woke Cub. His heart pounding, he sat up, disoriented from sleep. If this was an attack, where was the sound of galloping hooves? And that wasn't an Indian war cry. His father had his breechclout and moccasins on and his weapons in his hands before Cub could even find his clothes. Cub's hands trembled as he dressed. How humiliating it would be to die without his breechclout on. And it seemed to take forever to find his left moccasin.

"It's white eyes. Scatter. Head for the horses." Arrow Point left the lodge at a stooping run and cut his war pony's tether with one slash of his scalping knife. He mounted as the pony reared and started running. Cub hesitated. Should he stay with his mother? Should he stand and fight with his father? Should he take anything with him? Should he look for Old Owl? What he never asked himself was if he should try to join the white attackers.

Then a bullet ripped through the lodge wall and buried itself in his tumbled sleeping robes, in the spot still warm from his body. He bolted after his mother. The camp was in chaos, the lodges laced together with smoke and noise. Horses reared and whinnied, and the din of rifle fire was deafening. Cub could smell the powder and the blood and the horses' fear.

The People fled in all directions, their robes and blankets flapping like a covey of quail taking flight. Afoot or on horseback, the men followed the women and children, covering their retreat with arrows and lances and their old rifles and muskets. They withdrew slowly in a ragged, expanding circle, out of the camp and after their women.

As Cub ran, he looked back over his shoulder for a glimpse of the white men. They were the first he had seen in three years. One of the camp dogs darted between his legs, and Cub went hurtling over him. He sprawled on the ground, his head ringing and his elbows and knees raw. Cactus was imbedded in his chest. He scrambled to his feet and started running again.

He didn't see Noah Smithwick draw a bead on him, squinting through the dust and smoke. What Noah saw was a small, brown Comanche boy, his thick braids dark with grease and his upper body bare in the January cold. He held his rifle steady, but he couldn't shoot the child. Colonel Moore and President Lamar might be demanding brutal force with no regrets, but Noah had his limits.

He swiveled and aimed for the slender warrior just whirling his pony and heading after the boy. Noah swore when the ball only hit the man's arm and he kept riding. The boy had already dived into the underbrush and disappeared.

Colonel Moore and his men were left alone in the camp. Their victims and enemies had scattered like chaff in a high wind, and they could hear only the moans of the wounded as they tried to crawl to safety. One of the men walked through camp methodically shooting those who still lived, and several others began arguing about who would get the scalps. Smithwick could hear them laughing about it, and he winced when he heard the pistol go off. Most of the wounded were women and children.

"Are they any better than the Indians, Noah?" Rufe looked out from under his wild thatch of curly black hair.

"Maybe not as good. Not as smart, anyway." Noah turned slowly in a circle, taking in the whole situation. "Start easin' toward the horses, Rufe. They've foxed us."

The colonel planted himself in the center of the empty dance ground. With his hands on his hips, he looked around him like someone who's just caught his best friend cheating at cards. His face was purple and his hair blew in tatters around his head. What kind of cowards were these people, that they wouldn't stand and fight like men?

"Set fire to their tents," he bellowed against the moan of the wind. "They can warm themselves at a big fire. Burn everything." He swung his arm wide, enclosing the whole camp in its sweep. But before his men could obey, they heard shots from the hills around them. Chief Castro rode up with his mounted scouts behind him. His gaunt face held no more emotion than a snake's, but the fury at Moore's stupidity darkened his skin ever so slightly. More shots landed among them as the hunters became the hunted.

"Retreat to the horses. We'll regroup there." Moore started running before he had finished shouting. Castro yelled after him.

"Too many late, Colonel. Horses all gone. Comanche take him." Castro spat something else in his own language, then wheeled and led his sixteen men away at a gallop, leaving the white soldiers to their fate. Shielded only by a small cavalry patrol, the Texas volunteer army backed down the Colorado River. With their newer rifles they held off the swarming Comanche, many of them mounted on the soldiers' horses. All in all, Colonel Moore only lost one man, but Texas couldn't afford many victories like that one.

Looking like a discarded buffalo robe that someone had dropped in a heap, Cub huddled in the lee of the lodge. He was trying to overhear what the men of the war council were deciding. Their voices were muffled, and he could understand only what the loudest were saying. As he listened, he dreamed of the day when he would be a teenager and allowed inside to light the ceremonial pipe and tend the fire.

It was an honor for which he'd have to compete. He couldn't

count on having it just because he was Old Owl's grandnephew and Arrow Point's son. But it never occurred to him that he wouldn't earn the right. Just as it never occurred to him that he might not sit on the war council itself someday, or lead his men on raids.

Inside, Old Owl was chanting a prayer for the souls of those who had been killed in the white men's raid a few days ago. This was the first place they'd stopped to set up camp since then. They had slept only a few hours a night, traveling hard to get as far away from the white men's reach as possible. Their dead had ridden with them, strapped to travois, or lying across the ponies.

They had been frozen when it came time to bury them, finally, in this place. Those who had lain across a horse's back had to be buried in that position. The crevices around camp all had bodies in them and offerings of food and weapons at their edges. It was late at night, and the stars glittered like ice shards flung across ebony. Still Cub could hear the wails of the women mourning and the dogs howling in sympathy.

Cub wanted revenge. Revenge on those who had murdered his people. He strained to hear if the men would be riding to avenge the attack. If they did, he planned to sneak away and join them. Lots of boys did it, though he had never heard of a nine-year-old going on a raid before. Food was low this winter, and he worried about how much he should take from his family's stores. Perhaps he should just depend on his wits to find game.

He was startled from his thoughts by the clink and jingle of the bells and shell decorations on the men's leggings and shirts as they stood to leave the council lodge. Cub shrank farther back into the shadows and pulled his robe entirely over his head. The younger men filed out, led by Old Owl's nephew, Arrow Point, who had his arm bandaged over the hole left by Noah Smithwick's ball.

As soon as the dark swallowed them and their voices, Cub slipped inside the lodge. He squatted by the door as inconspicuously as possible. He knew better than to ask his father for information. Arrow Point firmly believed that a child's rearing should be left to grandfathers and uncles and great-uncles, as the case may be. Cub knew his father would go to bed assuming his foster son was asleep under the pile of robes. If Arrow Point knew that Cub often rolled out under the skirt of the lodge wall to go roaming with his friends at night, he never said anything about it.

When Cub wanted information he went to the man he called Grandfather. Old Owl let him do anything he wanted. Including listen in on conversations. Old Owl was talking now with his friend, the war leader Santa Ana, and some of the older men.

"Winter is no time for raiding," grumbled Santa Ana.

"Tell the white men so." Sanaco was offended that the whites would so inconsiderately ignore the winter truce that the tribes had always observed.

"They know nothing of war," rasped Many Battles. "They must be very stupid to leave their horses unguarded and raid on foot."

"It was a profitable attack. We captured seventy horses from them, one for each man in the band," said Sanaco. "We beat them soundly and sent them crying back to their lodges."

"And we lost a warrior and five women and two children. The horses were not worth it." Old Owl spoke softly. Then there was a silence.

"Can you talk Arrow Point out of leading a raid, Old Owl? We need the men to hunt." Age had tempered Santa Ana. He now weighed more carefully the consequences of raids. He was still among the first to go raiding, but only when the time was right.

"You know how young men are. I don't think I can change his mind. Arrow Point has a right to organize a war party. And there are many who will want to join it."

"They didn't even steal *our* horses." Sanaco still couldn't believe the Texans' stupidity. "And they milled around in the middle of the village like buffalo in a magic circle surround. We should have killed more of them."

"But we didn't. Even with them on foot, we couldn't kill more of them."

"Their guns are better than ours." Many Battles was indignant that Old Owl would hint that the warriors hadn't fought correctly. Santa Ana smiled inwardly. He had seen Old Owl work a conversation this way many times, leading people to his own conclusions.

"Yes. Their guns are better than ours," said Old Owl. "And they attacked in the winter, deep into our country. Where no white raiding party has ever come before." In the war council the talk had been about the necessity of avenging the deaths, and teaching the white man a lesson. Arrow Point and the younger men were confident to the point of arrogance. They were sure that the white men were ignorant, feeble enemies. Old Owl knew better. He went on. "Their guns are getting longer, and so is their trail. There are wooden lodges now where there were none a year ago. They do not respect the old ways, the ways we have always waged war."

"But we beat them. They're children when it comes to war."

Old Owl nodded in agreement. "Yes, we beat them. This time. But even children learn. Do you think their war leader will attack on foot the next time? And will he leave the horses unguarded?"

There was no need to answer. The men stared glumly into the fire. Finally Santa Ana spoke.

"Perhaps it's well that the men want to raid the white men's camps. But they should steal guns, as many of the new guns as they can." The others grunted in agreement, before they began talking of other things.

Cub slipped out and ran to his lodge. He passed by the weighted hide over the door and went to where his sleeping robes lay on the other side of the wall. Lying on his stomach, he wriggled under the hem and inside. He was happy with the thought that there would be a raid, and his own father would be leading it. And he would be a part of it.

Cub raged and paced around the confines of the lodge, kicking at robes and sending his mother's kettle clattering across the floor. He cursed his grandfather, who sat calmly by the door like a benign vulture roosting half asleep.

"How did you know I was planning to go with the war party?"

"I'd have been surprised if you didn't plan on it. But you're too young."

"That's what you always say."

"Have I ever told you an untruth?"

Cub sat disconsolately, his dreams of joining his father's raid destroyed. As though he could read Cub's mind, Old Owl had showed up in the lodge the night before and had not let Cub out of his sight. He even followed him outside when Cub went to relieve himself against his favorite cottonwood. He had not slept at all as he kept his vigil.

"I'm tired, Cub. Will you swear to me that you'll stay here? Your mother needs you."

"Why should I swear? Why should I stay here? If I'm too young to go with father, I'm too young to be of any use to mother." His lower lip dangled low enough to trip on, and he glowered to keep from crying.

"You are of use, and you know it. Besides, you'll slow the men down." Those were fighting words.

"I won't!" Cub jumped up as he shouted and started pacing again. Old Owl shook his head and smiled as he watched the boy.

"There's another reason, Cub. Can't you guess it?"

The boy pondered as he paced.

"I'm white. I'm not good enough because I'm white."

"Yes. You're white. But you're one of us. You know that. Look at me, Cub. Do you know that?"

"Yes. I know it."

"But yes, you can't go because you're white."

"I don't understand. If I'm one of the People, what difference does it make if I go?"

"Think." *Think, my beautiful child with hair like the sun and eyes like the sky. I can't give you all the answers. In the end you'll have only yourself to depend on.* Old Owl waited patiently while Cub thought.

"The white people will try to recapture me."

"Yes. Do you want them to? Is that why you want to go on the raid?"

"No! You know that isn't why I want to go. I want to take care of the ponies and help. I want to be a warrior. And count coup. Please can I go, Grandfather? I can still catch them. You taught me to track well."

"The first answer I gave you is still true. You are too young. Your father will be distracted worrying about you. You might cause a needless death. And if the whites see you, they will try to get you back. You'll be a special target for them."

"Arrow Point won't worry about me. He doesn't even care about me."

"That's what you think. You should hear him bragging about you to the other men."

"Does he really?"

"Yes, he does. Constantly. In fact, some of them are beginning to tease him about it. He asked me to make sure you stayed here, although I would have anyway."

"How did *he* know I would try to go with him?"

"Because he did the same thing, although he was older at the time than you are. And I did it before him. And I suppose you will too. But not yet. Not on this trip. Not against the Texans. Now will you swear you'll stay here? I want to take a nap." Old Owl gave a huge yawn, threatening to swallow his own face.

"Yes, Grandfather. I'll stay. This time."

In the fall of 1839, high on a bluff overlooking the Colorado River, Pahayuca and Buffalo Piss and their war party sat on their ponies. They knew they were clearly silhouetted against the pale pink, postdawn sky, but it didn't matter. There would be no raid. The four cabins they remembered being in this valley were no longer alone. A small city of tents and lean-tos, wagons and shacks had sprung up around them. Even at this early hour, the valley was swarming with surveyors and engineers laying out the streets of a town. The men of the war party could hear the crack of axes and falling timber, and the shouts of the wagoneers drifting faintly up from below. Sunrise rode up next to Pahayuca.

"What are they doing?"

"Stealing the land," Buffalo Piss answered. He had made the connection between the surveyors' mysterious activity and the hordes of white people that seemed to follow everywhere they dragged their strings and planted their dead trees. He had declared a special war on them.

"How can they do that? How can anyone steal land? It's our mother."

"With them land is a thing to possess. They divide it up the way we divide loot from a raid. And they think it belongs to them alone, each man with his piece of it. They even put fences around it to keep others out."

"They're mad," said Sunrise.

"Yes. But that only makes them more dangerous, like rabid wolves," said Buffalo Piss. "Come. There are too many of them for us to fight today."

The men backed their ponies away from the bluff's edge and rode off through the trees, leaving the whites to their antlike scurryings. Soon the four-cabin hamlet of Waterloo would be transformed into a city with wide streets and lots, and ground set aside for a university. President Lamar had chosen his favorite hunting spot for his new capital. And he renamed it Austin, after the founder of Texas. The site of Austin was an insult, an offense, a gauntlet thrown down to the People. Lamar had purposely placed it far from the thin fringe of the settlements, deep inside the wild, unknown country the People considered theirs to roam and hunt.

❧ 29 ❧

The hunt was plentiful in the autumn of 1839. Along the hills and in the valleys of the Penateka's hunting grounds the trees blazed red and yellow and gold against the deep gray of the sky and the glittering waters of the Lampassas River. Many bands made their winter camp together along the river. The lodges stretched for fifteen miles among the tall live oaks and hackberries, the cottonwoods and willows. Thousands of ponies grazed, herded by small boys riding bareback.

Naduah and Star Name, Bear Cub and Upstream roamed the length of the vast camp on their ponies. Their days were full of new people, new friends, dances and games and stories. The children of the Tekwapi, the No Meat band, taught the Wasps to play Guess Over the Hill. The game was usually organized by two older children. One would go out of sight on the other side of a rise while the other helped the players hide under blankets and robes. Then "it" came back and tried to guess who was hiding by feeling the blanket. And poking. And tickling. As usual, there was a great deal of tickling.

Cub and Upstream were usually gone, which was the way Star Name and Naduah preferred it. When they were in camp, they were in trouble. Or they set up their archery contests in the middle of everything and got in everyone's way. But it was a good time to be young and to be one of the People.

Naduah chose not to join the games this day. Instead she went with Medicine Woman to dig for roots and look for useful plants that might still be around this late in the year. They went on these expeditions often. At first she'd tried to lead Medicine Woman's horse on a line, but she'd been scolded for it.

"I can still ride, Granddaughter. My pony and I have traveled together for ten years. He won't wipe me off on a low limb. I can follow the sound of Wind's hooves."

As they rode, Naduah described the countryside in detail. She called out what was growing, and where, what the soil and terrain were like, and what the sky was doing. She named the plants she could, and dismounted to bring her grandmother samples of what she couldn't identify. Medicine Woman would stare ahead of her with her glazed eyes as she smelled the leaves, then felt them with her long, delicate fingers. She could almost always tell what it was and if it was useful. On this trip they were looking for bear root, a plant that belonged to the carrot family.

"How do you know which plants to use, Grandmother?"

"Other people told me, just as I'm telling you. And I used to watch what the animals ate, especially the bears. Bears know medicine. Why do you think they call this bear root?" She held up the gnarled root she was holding.

"I suppose because bears eat it."

"Yes. They eat it in the wintertime and it keeps them healthy. Sometimes, if a plant is new to me, I try it on myself. Some of them are very strong. I've made myself sick from time to time, but it's worth it. Don't you do it, though, until you're much older. Are the willow trees nearby?"

"Yes. We're coming to them."

Medicine Woman would dry the willow bark and pound it fine. "Mix it with water then," she'd told Naduah. "It'll start things moving in the most stubborn set of bowels. Be careful not to give too much, though. Pahayuca once broke up a war council after I'd given him some. Buffalo Piss said it sounded like a tribe of mad Cheyenne trapped inside my brother's gut. And when the explosion came . . .'' Medicine Woman laughed. "Pahayuca's a big man, and he hadn't relieved himself in a long time. They're still laughing at him about it. He'll burst before he'll take any more dried willow bark.''

"Naduah. Naaa-duah.'' Star Name came pounding over the low bluff bordering the river bottomlands and slid her pony down the slope in a shower of pebbles. She pulled up out of breath, Paint in a lather and steaming in the cold air.

"Takes Down said I'd find you here. Spirit Talker's band finally arrived. They're camping way down the river, at the end of the line.''

"So what?''

"There's a white man with them.''

"Did you see him?''

"No. But I heard he has red hair all over him, like a bear. Even on his chest and back. He's been with Spirit Talker's band for three moons.''

"Is he a captive?'' Naduah knew that was unlikely. White men were almost always killed. Slowly.

"No. He's a messenger from the Texans. They want to have honey talk and give everyone presents. Maybe I'll get a new mirror to replace the one I broke. Let's go see him.''

"Granddaughter, it would be better if you didn't see the white man.''

"It's all right, *Kaku*,'' broke in Star Name. "Cub saw him already. He counted coup on him and got away without the white man even recognizing that he was white.''

"Don't worry, Grandmother. I won't let him steal me. I'll pull my robe over my hair and stay far away.'' Naduah reached out and held her grandmother's fragile wrist briefly as they rode knee to knee.

"Just be careful, little one. Those eyes of yours flash like the white patch on your doe's rump. Your antelope was a nuisance, but I miss her.''

"So do I, *Kaku*. Maybe I'll find another one someday.''

The three of them headed toward the Wasps' campsite. As usual, Pahayuca had deliberately arrived early and picked the best place. On the other side of the river a waterfall slithered down the dark gray cliff face and splintered on the boulders in its path. It sent a fine spray into the creek that cascaded to the river. In summer it was a cool green glade. In winter it was a lacy sculpture of ice patterns. Naduah could see the sun glinting on it from her lodge door.

When they left Medicine Woman, the two girls rode slowly toward the place where Spirit Talker's people had set up their lodges.

"There's something else I wanted to tell you when we were alone."

"What?"

"There are two captive white girls with Spirit Talker's band. I wondered if you would want to talk to them." Star Name looked over at her sister and friend, and there was worry in her eyes.

"I don't know. I'll think about it while we ride."

"They haven't been adopted, those two girls. I don't know why. The older one is too old, but the young one isn't." Naduah knew that if she had been two or three years older she probably wouldn't have been adopted either. The People would have considered it too late to train her properly. The thought frightened her.

"Have you seen them, Star Name?"

"No. They just arrived. This is only what I heard. Naduah, they're slaves, those girls. They're not of the People like you are."

"What are you trying to tell me, Star Name? Does that mean they have to work harder?"

"It means they might not have been treated well. I wanted to warn you before you see them or talk to them. In case you decide to talk to them."

"I don't know if I can remember my old tongue. It's been so long."

"They speak our language. They've been with the band a year and a half. Some white men attacked Spirit Talker's camp last winter, like they did Old Owl's. The girls' owner hid them and threatened to kill them if they cried out. I hear that their father was with the white soldiers, and they had to lie silent. He walked through the gunfire and arrows and flames, just calling them. It must have been terrible for them. It must be sad to be a slave."

"Why are they treated so badly?"

"They're slaves, Naduah. Do white people have slaves?"

"Yes."

"And how are they treated?"

"It depends on their owners. Sometimes badly. Sometimes well. Sometimes they pay men just to whip them and make them work."

"It's the same with us. Not everyone is like Takes Down and Sunrise."

As they rode into the outskirts of Spirit Talker's camp, Naduah noticed slight differences from Pahayuca's or Old Owl's. When they had all camped together two winters ago she had been too new to notice, but now she did. It was hard to say why she felt a little out of place there. True, more of the women chose to raise the hides they were tanning on frames rather than stake them on the ground. And there seemed to be more shouting and less laughter than she was used to. But outwardly the camp seemed very much like her own.

She sniffed, tasting the air with her nose. What was it? Bread! Wheat-flour bread. And more coffee than she ever smelled in her own camp, although there was usually some brewing somewhere. Where did they get the flour? The white man must have brought it. For some reason she felt uneasy. This looked like a village of the People, but with differences so subtle they only teased her senses. Once she'd recognized the smell of baking bread, she noticed more women in cloth blouses, and more ribbons.

"Pull it up farther. Shade your face more." Star Name reached out and adjusted Naduah's buffalo robe, forming a deep hood around her face and head. They left their ponies tied to a tree and walked through the bustle.

"Where are the white girls?"

"I don't know."

"You seem to know everything else about them, Star Name."

"Deer."

"Oh." Takes Down's friend, Deer, would sometimes know a piece of gossip before it happened. And she often embroidered it with designs of her own.

Then the girls saw her. She was carrying water from the river. Even in the winter's cold she had no robe to throw over her shoulders. Her wrists, where they stuck out from the tattered sleeves, looked like sticks. Her face and head, arms and legs were covered with bruises and raw, running sores. Her hair had been burned from her head in patches. Her nose was charred to the bone, and there was no flesh left on the insides of her nostrils. Her face was puffy and purple with welts.

She limped and staggered under the weight of the heavy paunch. Then she turned her head and looked their way. At fourteen, Matilda Lockhart was an old woman, a walking nightmare. Naduah whirled, her stomach churning, and ran. She ran all the way to where Wind was tied, and her hands trembled as she fumbled with the knot. She galloped back to her own camp, crying the whole time. She never tried to see the white girls again. Nor would she go near Spirit Talker's camp.

Spirit Talker's council lodge was crowded. The leading civil and war chiefs from all six bands camped together were there. In the center, opposite the door, in the warm place of honor, sat Noah Smithwick. Noah had been in Texas a long time. Ten years before he had made his living as a blacksmith in Stephen Austin's original colony.

This gathering of Indians in the council lodge reminded him of the stag parties he and his friends used to hold in Austin. They called them "love feasts," and demanded that everyone perform. Three-Legged Willie would give minstrel shows, patting juba with his wooden peg and playing the banjo. Noah accompanied him on fiddle. *On second thought,* mused Noah, *maybe the scene is more like the ongoing monte game run by old Vincente Padilla.* In any case, Noah felt at home.

Noah's huge, bushy red beard flowed down his shirt front like a napkin, and he used it as such while he ate the greasy stewed meat. There was plenty of food. A regular fireman's line of women paraded back and forth to the lodge, bringing more steaming kettles of stew. Noah belched loudly, feeling a little queasy from too much meat and too much tobacco smoke and too many unwashed bodies in too close a space. He was used to all those smells, but not so closely packed together. He felt like he could slice the air with his knife, spear it, and eat it. He turned to the solemn Delaware who sat next to him.

"Jim, tell Spirit Talker that this is very good stew. Ask him if there's anything in it besides buffalo meat."

Jim Shaw was elegant. He was the only Indian Smithwick had ever seen whose leggings looked like they'd been tailored in London. He spoke English and Spanish and six Indian languages, and he trailed like a wolf. Made mean biscuits too, when pressed. He would never lack work on the frontier. He knew what Noah was getting at.

"It's okay. Comanche don't eat dog."

Santa Ana reached a beefy hand across Shaw and stroked Smithwick's beard, talking all the while. There was a roar of laughter.

"What did he say?"

"He says white eyes has very fine beard. Wishes he had a beard like that."

"Tell him thank you."

"Are you sure you want me to? He wishes he had a beard like that to hang on his shield. Wants to know if you have hair all over your body. Make a very powerful scalp. They like to take it all off in one piece. I saw one once like that. Ears and all."

"Don't tell him thank you. What's he saying now?" Noah had done most of the talking in Spanish in his three months with Spirit Talker. He had only sent for Jim Shaw to help him with the delicate maneuvering necessary for this council. For three months he had been in the Comanche camp alone, as Spirit Talker's guest. And he had enjoyed it. But now he found himself depending on Shaw's knowledge of Comanche and handtalk.

"Santa Ana wants to know if your women like your beard in bed.

Does it tickle them?" Noah thought about how long it had been since he'd had a white woman. Whoever had nicknamed the Penateka *tenyuwit*, Hospitable Ones, had known what he was talking about. Comanche were a lot more thoughtful and generous in some ways than Christian folk.

The women came slithering under his lodge wall late at night, no mean feat for a couple of them. Those prairie belles must have outweighed him by fifty pounds, and he was a big man. They left before light and he never knew who they were. But Spirit Talker always grinned broadly in the morning when he asked how Noah had slept. The toothless, bawdy old goat. If he hadn't sent them, he damned well knew they were there. Noah wondered what stories about him were circulating through camp. Well, at least women were safer subjects than beards as ornamental items.

He had learned that Comanche didn't consider brevity the soul of wit, and he launched into a lengthy listing of all the fine qualities of their women. He ended with the conclusion that they only had one fault. They giggled so much about his beard it was hard to make love to them. The hide walls almost shook with laughter as he told one story after another on himself.

Noah was at home with story-telling, and he'd refined his technique after watching the Comanche. When it came to story-telling they could hold their own with any barb-tailed Texas yarn-spinners. And the Texans were no slouches either. When a situation got so bad there was nothing left to do, they made jokes about it. They were a lot alike, the Texans and the Comanche. Tough, mean, stubborn, and always ready to laugh at themselves.

"Boys," he said, finishing his last anecdote, "I even tried tying my beard up, you know, the way you tie your ponies' tails before you fight. The little lady laughed so hard that my sturdy pine tree here," he waved grandly at his lap, "wilted like a dry daisy on a hot day." He held up his hand and forearm, then circled the hand and dropped it limply, palm up, onto his thigh. The hand rose slightly, quivered once, and fell back like a dead animal. His audience whistled and applauded, shouted and stamped their feet on the hard dirt floor. The wizened old buzzard next to Santa Ana laughed so hard he began to choke. Santa Ana pounded Old Owl on the back, almost knocking him over.

"Why don't you cut your beard off?" Santa Ana asked the question while he pounded on Old Owl.

"Cut my beard off!" Noah covered his beard with both hands, his eyes saucer-wide in horror. "Cut my beard off! Why, boys, you might as well ask me to cut off something almost as near and dear to me." Again he gestured toward his groin, framed by his crossed legs. "My beard is my strength and my medicine." Everyone grunted. They could understand that.

"Let me tell you a story about a great warrior who lived a long time ago. So long ago Spirit Talker wasn't even born yet. He wasn't even a glint in his father's eye, as we say in Texas. This warrior's name was Samson, and he had the most magnificent mane you ever saw." Noah had gotten warmed up now and had almost forgotten why he was there. Everyone else seemed to have forgotten too, as they listened raptly. And the night wore on.

When Noah finished his tale of Samson and Delilah, Spirit Talker reached for his ornate medicine pipe. A hush fell over the lodge. The friendly, frolicking hounds turned into hungry wolves. The orange flames flickered on their solemn, chiseled faces, carving their stern lines even deeper.

Noah looked around at them in the silence of the pipe-lighting ceremony. He thought of the hours he had spent with the men of Spirit Talker's band, and the times he had stood by their campfires and fiddled for them with three or four of their dogs asleep around his feet. The women and children and the men too had laughed and clapped and stamped and danced their own version of "Haste to the Wedding."

The real business was about to begin, and Noah had a moment's pause. He was alone here, at the mercy of men with whom he was at war. Never mind that Spirit Talker had told him the custom. That anyone who asked for hospitality from the People, even if that person was an enemy, was received as well as a friend or loved one. Spirit Talker had told him that when treaty talk was going on, both sides were guaranteed safety and good treatment. Noah knew that he had almost undoubtedly charged into the sleeping camp of some of these men and had tried to kill their people. He was little comforted by the fact that these men had also raided his own folks and done worse than kill them. *Oh, Lord. I hope we white eyes all look alike to them.*

Spirit Talker was the one who had proposed this council and had introduced the white envoy, so he gave the first speech. He drew deeply on the pipe before talking. His hair was graying, and he was the first balding Comanche Noah had ever seen. He looked like a chicken that had been half-heartedly plucked. His spare body was covered in leggings and high moccasins, with a breechclout so long it almost grazed the floor when he stood. His chest was hidden by a breastplate of bone cylinders laced to form a bib. It was so heavy it seemed to be pulling him forward by its weight. His voice was high and quavery. He talked for a long time, while Shaw murmured the translation. Finally he came to the point, his voice rising to a crescendo.

"We have set our lodges in these groves and swung our children from these boughs since time immemorial. When the game beats away from us we pull down our lodges and move away, leaving no trace to frighten it. And in a little while it comes back. But the white man comes and cuts down the trees, building houses and fences, and the buffalo get frightened. They leave and never come back, and the Indians are left to starve. Or if we follow the game, we trespass on the hunting grounds of the other tribes and war comes.

"The Indians were not made to work. If they build houses and try to live like white men, they will all die. If the white men would draw a line defining their claims and keep to their side of it, the red man would not molest them."

There it was. The crux of the matter. Summed up beautifully by an ignorant savage. Ignorant, hell. They wanted their land and the freedom to hunt on it without interference. A reasonable request. But it could never be. Lamar wouldn't agree to any kind of boundary barring Texans from taking as much land as they wanted. He planned to spread Texas all the way to the Pacific Ocean, and to hell with anyone who got in his way. Even if he did agree to a boundary, it would be worthless. Sam Houston had summed it up: "If you built a wall a thousand miles long and a hundred feet high between the Texans and the Indians, the Texans would find a way to get over it."

This treaty would be like all the rest. The Indians gave and the white men took. If he were a Comanche he doubted that he would even discuss the demands, much less give them the solemn and dignified consideration these men were giving them. One of the other chiefs rose to give a lengthy oration on the love the Comanche felt for the Texans, and, "By the way," he asked, "did the messenger bring more presents?"

The worst part of all this had been living in the village with Matilda Lockhart and her six-year-old sister. He had seen Matilda's eyes pleading with him to help her and knew the agony her family was suffering for them. He had tried to ransom her, but their owner wouldn't part with them. Noah dared not push too hard and ruin the chance of keeping Spirit Talker's cooperation. It was more important to bring all the leaders to the talks, and win the release of every captive, than to jeopardize the treaty over these two. But the picture of them gave him the determination to stand and repeat the Texans' demands one more time.

"The Texans want peace with their red brothers." *Well, that much was certainly true.* "It grieves them that there must be killing and bloodshed. They are sad when their children are taken from them and must live far from their families. It is impossible for them to feel love in their hearts for their brothers, the People, when their children are kept from them. Father Lamar asks that you meet with his war leader in San Antonio and that you bring all the white captives with you to return to those who gave birth to them and love them."

Then the shriveled old man who sat silently, like an emaciated and unhappy gargoyle, reached for the pipe. Until then Noah had thought he was there by mistake, someone's favorite grandfather, perhaps. A family retainer kept around out of kindness. Old Owl drew long on the pipe, his cheeks caving in until they looked like they would meet in the middle and be held there by the suction. Then he rose. His joints snapped loudly, and his breechclout hung between his bandy legs. After half an hour of rambling, he finally got to the point.

"For as long as we can remember we have taken captives in war. We do it because our own children are taken. It is the custom. The lodges of the People are often filled with the mourning cries of the women for a dead child. Our women do not have enough children. If our people are to grow strong and prosper, we need children. And you Texans have more than you need. So we steal them and raise them as our own and love them." Noah refrained from pointing out that no one loved Matilda Lockhart here. He wouldn't have dared interrupt. No one ever did. And what the old man said was true as far as it went.

"If we must part with our white children, it will cause us great pain. The grieving mothers and fathers, the uncles and aunts, sisters and brothers and cousins and grandparents must be compensated for their grief. And the slaves must be paid for, too. That is even your custom, I hear.

"What is the White Father, La-mar, going to pay us for our children and slaves? We will need horses and mules and blankets. And many knives and guns, lead and powder and flints, as well as coffee and sugar and mirrors and cloth for our women. My own wife is fond of those fancy Mexican shawls, and I am too old to ride down and steal her one. When my horse runs I grunt." He fingered his elbows, swollen with arthritis. "I would like a dozen of those shawls and a dozen more white vests like the one I wear now."

Solemnly, Old Owl detailed an impossibly long list of items that his people would want in payment. He ended with horn pocket combs, files, indigo and vermillion, brass wire, and silk handkerchiefs.

Noah didn't know Old Owl at all, much less well enough to know he was being taken. People who had been acquainted with Old Owl all their lives sometimes didn't know it. Old Owl had no intention of either going to the treaty talks or of giving up his grandnephew. But he knew better than to refuse directly and for a purely personal reason. So he fanned the spark of greed in the others, in the expectation that the negotiations would go up in flames. He demanded more horses than existed in Texas, at least in the hands of the settlers. He was deliberately creating obstructions.

Noah listened impassively to Old Owl and his mind raced ahead to his own response. He could promise them presents, but nothing in the way of payment. And not many presents either. He remembered Lamar's purple face at the very suggestion. He had pounded the desk in rhythm to his own words. "We won't be blackmailed by savages! We'll pay them nothing. We won't allow our women and children to be sold like cattle. Just get the Comanches here, Smithwick," Lamar had said, his voice low and dangerous. "Just get them here and we'll deal with them after that." Just get them there. Noah knew he had to proceed carefully.

But before he could reply, the second mistake at the council stood up. If Old Owl looked like someone's moss-grown grandfather, this one was a kid who should be out playing pranks with the rest of the boys. How could he take a pudgy scamp seriously? Smithwick had never met Buffalo Piss either. Buffalo Piss's style was direct. He wasted no time, and he aimed his words for the vital organs.

"We of the Wasps do not deal with the white men. They bring sickness of the body, and worse than that, they bring sickness of the soul. We have seen what their stupid water does to a man's reason. We have seen what their disease does to our children's faces. We have seen warriors sell their manhood for the sweet sugar of the white men.

"Last year Spirit Talker made treaty talk with the Texans. He has told us of it. He has told us that the People must not molest the settlers in any way. The People must not raid. The People must trade only with the government traders. The People must be punished by the Texans' laws. The People must fight the Texans' enemies. And what will the Texans do? Will they be punished under our law for the wrongs they do us? Will their traders treat us fairly? Will the Texans fight our enemies? Will they leave our land to us? No. They will not.

"The Wasps are not so foolish as to expect any different of them this time. Nothing but bad comes from their sweet words, their honey talk. We will have the things that Old Owl said we wanted. But we will take them."

Buffalo Piss sat down hard, and there was a low murmur in the lodge. Pahayuca remained silent, his broad face unhappy. Like Old

Owl, he knew his nephew's wife would be brokenhearted if her white daughter were taken from her. And he knew better than to go into a white man's town. He and his band had seen what smallpox could do, and he feared it. And he dreaded what Medicine Woman would do if he sold Naduah back again. There would never be a moment's peace. On the other hand, all those presents would go to the other chiefs and to the people of their bands. The chiefs' prestige would be enhanced. It was a difficult time for Pahayuca, but Buffalo Piss prevailed.

The first pale wash of dawn was diluting the black night sky when the council finally broke up. All of the bands there had agreed to follow Spirit Talker to San Antonio in the spring, except Old Owl and Santa Ana and the Wasps with Pahayuca and Buffalo Piss. Spirit Talker said that others who were not camped here would join him also. There would be more than six bands of the Penateka represented at the council talks. It would be the biggest group of Comanche civil and war leaders ever assembled to meet with the white men.

Smithwick was satisfied. Perhaps there would be peace after all.

❧ *30* ❧

In late March of 1840, four months after the council with Noah Smithwick, Pahayuca and Buffalo Piss again sat on the crest of a high hill overlooking a town. This time it was San Antonio. The Alamo was still in ruins at the edge of town. Nearby were the lodges of Spirit Talker, the twelve leaders who had come with him and their families. They knew that treaty councils, honey talk, could take a long time, and they would all be safe while the talks went on.

The chieftains' camp was almost deserted. Everyone had gathered in the center of town. The Comanche and the Texans milled around in the square outside the small limestone courthouse where the talks would be held. The bright March sun seemed to whitewash the gleaming stone and adobe walls with light. The town's plazas were paved in a shifting layer of gray dust, stirred by the sweeping hems of the Anglo women. The shorter, gaily colored skirts of the Mexican women fluttered in the breeze. A large crowd of people had come to see the wild Indians wandering so peacefully among them.

Texans threw coins in the air for the Comanche boys to shoot at

253

with their small bows and arrows. The chiefs' wives were dressed in their finest clothes, and the bells of their fringed ponchos jingled merrily. From time to time one of the women would reach out and grab a handful of a Texan's skirts, holding her captive while she fingered the cloth and discussed it with her friends.

Several miles away, along the river to the southwest, Pahayuca and Buffalo Piss could just make out the vast camp of the six bands represented at the talks. The tips of the lodge poles, with feathers and streamers fluttering from them, could be seen scattered among the trees. They looked like new foliage growing along with the pale green canopy of the pecans and the brilliant rose patches of the redbud trees. The surrounding hills were speckled with thousands of ponies grazing.

"Maybe we should have gone with Spirit Talker." Pahayuca's broad face was a study in misery. The other leaders would be flaunting their presents and new finery when this was all over.

"No, we did the right thing." Buffalo Piss stared across the gently rolling, green countryside. "I had a vision. I saw a buffalo pass by. A single buffalo walking very slowly toward the northwest. We must follow him."

"I've had bad feelings about these talks too. But what if we're wrong?"

"If we're wrong, we'll just start raiding. The whites will come to us to make peace, and you'll get the presents you want."

"I suppose so."

"It's always worked before. The bad Indians get the presents. The good Indians get their land taken from them. Look at the Wichita and the Cherokee up north. They tried to cooperate, and the Texans massacred them. They hadn't even pulled the bodies off the battlefield before the stick men were there, dividing the land."

Pahayuca grunted. They sat a while longer, then turned and rode down the slope toward their camp, thirty miles away.

Gonzales, the interpreter, was uneasy as he watched the twelve war and civil leaders follow Spirit Talker into the courthouse. The Comanche carried their weapons casually under their robes, sauntering in with an easy arrogance. But President Lamar's two commissioners were tense. The hostility vibrated from them like heat waves shimmering on the plains. It would have been much better if the Indians had brought no captives to the talks than to have returned only Matilda Lockhart, and in that condition. The Comanche didn't understand the effect her poor ruined face and body would have on the whites.

Even Gonzales, who had been a captive himself, didn't know how bad the situation was. He didn't know that Secretary of War Johnston had wanted to kill Spirit Talker and the other two chiefs when they had ridden in asking for the truce a month before. Johnston refrained only because there hadn't been enough Indians to make a difference. This wouldn't be a council. It would be a fiat, a listing of conditions that must be met before the chiefs were to go free. They would be held as hostages.

And the Penateka had come prepared with their own set of demands. They were under the delusion that they had come as equals. They were children, on both sides, playing with matches when they didn't know what fire could do. It would be a miracle if the whole situation didn't explode in that tiny room.

"Dios me bendiga." As Gonzales asked for God's blessing, he crossed himself surreptitiously. Then he followed Colonel Fisher across the rickety porch and through the heavy door. It closed with a thud after him. A dozen soldiers lined up along the wall outside, their shiny new carbines planted in front of them, muzzle-up on the splintered floor.

Inside the courthouse, with its small, barred windows, the air was becoming hard to breathe. If hatred had been edible, everyone would have been well fed. Gonzales was no fool. He stood by the door. Colonel Fisher waved away the amenities and pounced on the main point.

"Where are the other captives? We know you have more than one. We must have them all here before we can go on with the talks."

Old Spirit Talker rose from the circle of painted chiefs sitting impassively on the floor in the center of the bare room. He held one wrinkled hand in front of him, as though calming troubled waters, and delivered his people's position. He realized that these men weren't like his good friend Noah, and he too dispensed with the preliminaries.

"Our hearts are heavy that we are not able to return more of your people today. Bands that did not send leaders to this talk hold many of them. But I, personally, will try to convince them to turn their captives in. To do that, you must give me things to take with me to pay for them." Spirit Talker chanted the list that he had memorized, a list at least as long as Old Owl's had been. His plan was to ransom the captives one by one and receive a larger price for them that way than by delivering them all at once.

"We wish to live in peace with our brothers, the white men. We will make a road to our red brothers who do not have the love in their hearts that we do. We will tell them of your generosity and return your people to you. How do you like that answer?" Spirit Talker finished on a high quaver and sat regally with a flourish of his breechclout. Gonzales translated his words while the old leader listened. Spirit Talker would have made a good poker player, but not a great one. There was a hint of satisfaction on his face at a hand well played.

Colonel Fisher gave a loud command, and the door opened. Twelve soldiers filed in and positioned themselves along the wall, carbines aimed and at the ready. The chiefs stirred uneasily.

"Tell Spirit Talker that until the captives are returned, all of them, he and the other chiefs will be our prisoners," said Colonel Cooke, the second commissioner. Fear blanched Alirio Gonzales's rich, dark skin.

"*Señor Coronel*, I cannot. They will kill us all."

"Tell them, damn you!"

"I cannot, *mi coronel*."

"Tell them or I'll kill you myself." Cooke's patience snapped under the strain.

Gonzales's hand was on the latch as he blurted the message. He bolted from the room, slamming the door behind him. As he clattered across the porch, the sounds of gunfire, warwhoops, and shouts followed at his heels.

The door burst open again, and old Spirit Talker appeared in the opening. He stood for a second, his hand out as if to speak, then fell. He toppled full length and lay still, blood spurting from the back of his head and his brains oozing out onto the dry wooden floor.

The Anglos and Mexicans of San Antonio stood dazed, but the People reacted instantly. The circuit judge fell, a child's tiny arrow sticking out from the rusty black coat over his heart. Skinning knives appeared from under the long fringes of the women's ponchos. The Texan women ran screaming in all directions, their long skirts stirring up clouds of dust. Soldiers stationed around the area began firing into the Comanche families trying to escape the courtyard. But the shots hit more than just the enemy. Soon people were tripping over bodies in the dirt, and falling only to be trampled themselves.

The Indian boys and men tried to cover the retreat of their women and children, but they were trapped in the stone labyrinth of a white man's town. Texans who weren't armed ran to get their guns. The fight became a hunt through the streets and from house to house. Two teenage boys darted into a cookhouse and it was soon surrounded by a mob of shouting, jostling men. Someone came with a barrel of turpentine, which was sloshed onto the walls and roof. Another man casually lit it with his cigar. As the flames billowed and the heat became intense, the boys ran out, coughing and choking. The Texans were waiting on each side of the door with axes ready.

When the dust and the screams had settled, there were seven whites dead and ten badly wounded. Thirty-three Indians were killed, and twenty-seven women and children, many of them wounded, were herded into the city jail. One of the women, Spirit Talker's wife, was released later that day. She would be the messenger.

"Gonzales, tell her to tell her people that they can have their chiefs' families back when the white captives are returned." Colonel Fisher's face was stern but triumphant, like a father who has just chastised his children. He had these people where he wanted them now. The only thing they understood was force.

Gonzales closed his eyes wearily. The white captives. Always and only the white captives. The small Mexican knew that Fisher didn't care about his interpreter's people. There were Mexican women and children suffering too. Some of them were the families of men who had fought beside the Texans during the revolution. But of course they didn't count, any more than the negro captives did. Gonzales tired once more to reason with the two commissioners.

"*Señor Coronel*, I don't think that's a good idea . . ."

The lid was beginning to jitter on the colonel's simmering patience. His face reddened. He had the entire southern Comanche nation under his thumb and a stupid little greaser was arguing with him.

"We don't pay you for your opinions, Gonzales. Translate. Tell her they have twelve days to decide. If the captives aren't returned by then, the chiefs' families will be killed."

It was hopeless. It was the way of those in authority to assume they had all the answers without ever asking any questions. Gonzales had lived with the People for five years. He knew how they would react to the ultimatum. And no one asked him. He shrugged and translated the message.

Spirit Talker's wife listened stolidly. She would have beaten her husband at poker. Not a flicker of expression passed over her broad, seamed face. She took the bag of food they offered her, mounted the pony they gave her, and rode slowly off toward the wooded hills and the camp to the northwest.

"I would like my pay now, *mi coronel*," said Gonzales. And he added under his breath in Spanish, "Make it thirty pieces of silver."

"You'll get it in a few weeks. We have to make a written request for payment and send it to the legislature. These things take time, and there are important matters here to deal with." Cook shouted the last words at Gonzales's back. The interpreter had mounted his burro and was riding out of town toward his tiny farm.

Wailing, Spirit Talker's wife rode among the first lodges of the enormous camp. She had slashed her arms in grief and her horse's back was wet with blood. The People swarmed to meet her, taking up her cry when they heard the news. All night long the screaming went on, while the men sat rocking to and fro, sobbing and moaning under their robes. When morning came, three women lay dead. They had cut themselves fatally as they grieved. Then the slaughter of the horses began. It had been years since grief had taken such a toll, but never had the Penateka suffered a calamity like this.

They had lost almost all the men who led them. It took two days to kill all the mules and ponies that had belonged to the chiefs. Their shrieks mingled with the People's. Finally their carcasses lay everywhere and the odor of death soon joined the sound of death. The village looked like a sacked city.

Leaderless, the men galloped off to take vengeance on the town. In their hysteria, the women turned on the hapless captives who hadn't been adopted. They stripped them, children and adults, and staked them out on the stony ground. They tortured them all night, laughing as the victims screamed and pleaded for mercy.

Squatting around the captives, like crows picking at carrion, the women filleted the flesh from them, slicing and mutilating them. At last they burned them slowly alive, starting with their battered and crushed fingers and toes. With them, screaming under the cold moon, died Matilda Lockhart's six-year-old sister.

With them also died any hope of peace or trust between the Texans and the Penateka Comanche. In the months to come the two sides would glare at each other over a barrier of hatred much higher and more enduring than the limestone walls of San Antonio. For the People, raiding was not now merely a matter of sport or livelihood or even defense. It was for blood.

As he broke up the clods of dry, pebbly gray soil with his wooden hoe. Gonzales knew he shouldn't be out in his field. He knew there were parties of Comanche scattered throughout the hills around San Antonio. In their fury and frustration they were killing, aimlessly and wantonly, anyone foolish enough to go out unprotected. But two months had passed since the fight at the courthouse.

One white captive, a woman, had escaped the horror of the Comanche slaughter and had made her way to San Antonio. So the townspeople knew of the charred corpses that lay out on the rolling land near the river, but they were unable to go out to bury them. Nor could they bring themselves to exact a like retribution on the Indians within their grasp. Unwilling to kill the hostages, the army had allowed them to be divided out into the homes of San Antonio, for the women to train as servants. One by one the Comanche women and children had slipped away to join their bands.

It was spring, almost summer already. Gonzales knew if he didn't tend his crops, there would be none to harvest. And his whole family would starve. The government hadn't even paid him for his interpreting yet. At least his wife and children would have something to eat and sell in the fall if he planted now. If the Comanche left them alone long enough to harvest it.

Gonzales's wife and children were sheltering in town. The one-room *jacal*, a shack of twisted cedar poles, looked forlorn without them. The faded, torn curtain flopped listlessly in the glassless window. The wooden shutter, hanging on one hinge, banged gently in the breeze. Then Gonzales heard the other noise. He heard the hooves before he saw the lance points rise from the crest of the hill as though pushing up through the soil. They were followed by the heads of the warriors and then their ponies. Gonzales whirled, his hoe held up to fight.

He didn't return to his family that night. And in the morning an armed party of Mexicans went out to bring in what was left of his body.

He was the last casualty in the area. The Penateka disappeared from the hill country they had roamed for two hundred years. The people of San Antonio went back to their daily lives, grateful that the Council House Fight, as they chose to call the massacre, was finally over. They could at last bury the charred bodies that were weathering into the ground. They were relieved that the Comanche had admitted defeat and retreated to the north to live. The Texans were sure they would be bothered no more.

Pahayuca's camp was huge, swollen with refugees from the south. They had come straggling in for days, their hair shorn, their faces drawn. There was a hopelessness about them, a fear that they would never be able to replace the leaders they had lost. They gathered among the Wasps to ask the help of the one Penateka leader left who could take them into battle. While the haggard women set up their tents, the men went directly to Buffalo Piss's lodge.

Those who couldn't fit inside squatted around the door, smoking and waiting to hear the outcome of the council. The talks had been going on for three days, but there was little doubt after the first day about the final decision. Already the People were preparing for war. They didn't wait for Lance to ride through camp announcing it.

Word had filtered out from the secrecy of council. It spread invisibly, inaudibly. The shame and the sorrow would be washed away with white men's blood. And the mood of the camp began to shift from despair to a grim kind of elation. Drums throbbed ceaselessly, day and night. Hunting parties went out daily, and others returned laden with meat. The village was a forest of drying racks. Women gathered outside their lodges to mend and decorate their men's best clothing. They cleaned them by rubbing white clay into them, letting it dry, then brushing it off. Men repaired their equipment, and the pungent odor of glue permeated everything. The camp resounded with the chants of warriors, each calling his own spirits to aid him in the battle to come.

There was no way to hide the fate of the captives who had died, screaming for an eternity under the full moon that night outside San Antonio. Two white boys had been spared, their families refusing to part with them. They told Naduah and Star Name what had happened. Naduah went back to her lodge, stiff with dread. She was unable even to voice the fear that gripped her. But Medicine Woman noticed it almost immediately.

"What's the matter, little one?"

"The two *tosi tuinahpa*, the white boys, told me about the killing of the white captives."

"Surely you don't think you'll be killed?"

"How do I know? They hate Texans. They have reason to hate them. I'm a Texan."

"No, little one. You're not a Texan. You are a Nerm. One of the People. No one will harm you. No one hates you. You have a big family among the Wasps. And the Wasps are the most powerful among the Penateka. You are safe here."

But still she felt uneasy as she went about the camp on her daily errands. She rarely went anywhere now without Star Name or one of her family. She let her hair get dirty, and she rubbed grease into it to darken it. She kept her eyes lowered and avoided strangers. Finally, after two days, Star Name became tired of it.

"Naduah, stop acting so humble. It's not your fault you're white. No one cares but you."

"I feel like they're all staring at me."

"So what if they are? They stared at Something Good too, remember. And she didn't go around all hunched over, with her nose dragging the ground. She held her head high. You're one of the people. And the People are proud. They don't hang their heads like the Nermateka, the People Eaters. Put your head up."

Naduah raised her chin, her eyes still shifting from side to side.

"Look me in the eye and say, 'I am *Nerm*, one of the People.' Say it."

"I am *Nerm*, one of the People."

"Say it again, like you mean it."

"I am *Nerm*, one of the People."

"Louder."

"I am *Nerm*." Those around them turned to stare.

"Now act like one."

"All right, Star Name." They linked arms and strode through camp, the two of them dressed identically, as usual. They were coming back two hours later, their arms piled with brush, when Naduah saw the black pony threading his way through the confusion of war preparation.

"Nocona, Wanderer! Star Name, look!" Naduah dropped her bundle of wood and pointed. "He's back. Wanderer's back!" In her excitement, she left the wood lying and ran to meet him.

"My heart sings to see you again, my brother." Naduah looked up, staring at him, falling into the depths of his eyes. She had forgotten how big and luminous they were. He was twenty-one now, and the angles of his face were sharper, the planes more finely etched. There was nothing left of the boy he had been at times. Naduah was so happy to see him she wanted to laugh and skip. Instead, she walked beside Night, stroking his neck. He flicked his ears in greeting and whiffled softly to her.

"I'm glad to see you too." Wanderer stared at her in the way he always did. But she had learned not to flinch when his eyes roamed over her. He inspected everyone that way. At least everyone who counted with him, either for good or for bad. Naduah was glad she and Star Name had bathed at the river and washed each other's hair. She didn't feel like the urchin she had been two hours before. Star Name caught up and walked beside her sister.

"Will you stay long with us, Wanderer?" Star Name peered at him from around Naduah.

"I don't know. I heard about the treaty talks in San Antonio. And Buffalo Piss sent word for me to come. Spaniard and a few other men have come with me." Still he stared at Naduah, with the old, amused smile that wasn't a smile on his face. Finally she became embarrassed.

"You must have important things to do," she mumbled, dropping her eyes. "And I left my wood. I have to go back for it. Will you come to see Sunrise later?"

"Not for a while. There's much to talk about in council."

"Sunrise has been there for days. He only comes home to sleep." Naduah wanted to ask Wanderer if he had married, but she didn't dare. She had never discussed personal things with him. She'd go ask Deer. Deer would know. Naduah backed away and raised her hand slightly in salute. Then she and Star Name turned to go, walking slowly around the knots of busy people. Naduah forced herself not to look over her shoulder at him. She didn't want to see his back as he rode away, his thoughts only on war.

But Wanderer didn't ride away. He halted Night and watched Naduah, taking in the graceful, fluid way she moved. *She's been studying Something Good, and now that gait is part of her.* She was thirteen years old and three inches taller than Star Name, who was a year older. Naduah's skirt twitched as she walked, her thick, shiny, waist-length braids swinging in time to her stride. She might act like a child acting like an adult, but the woman inside her was beginning to show. Wanderer smiled a little as he squeezed his knees slightly and Night resumed his steady pace toward the council lodge. As he rode, speaking to those who called out greetings, his thoughts weren't totally on war.

Wanderer studied the young faces ringing the council fire. It must be small consolation for Buffalo Piss to know he had been right. Treating with the white eyes, trading with them, always ended the same way. The People came away from every such encounter diminished in power. Every useful or pretty thing the white eyes brought had some terrible, unseen price on it. *Never let a white man get closer than the point of your lance,* he thought. *And never stay around them longer than the time required to take their scalps.*

They were so young, these new war leaders. And at twenty-six, with his ragged, tousled hair and eyebrows plucked smooth, Buffalo Piss looked younger than any of them. His skin was baby sleek and his features soft and full. He usually wore a fierce scowl to mask the feminine beauty of his big black eyes, and he was never very successful at it. But Wanderer had seen him on the war trail. He was one of the best, one of the few whose judgement Wanderer trusted.

Since he had come into the lodge that morning, nodding briefly to Buffalo Piss, Wanderer had sat silently in the humble position by the door. He was a northerner. A Quohadi. This was not his fight. He sympathized, but he knew he could offer little support from his people, the Antelopes. They felt it was best to stay as far from the whites as possible, only penetrating their settlements to raid. They struck fast and disappeared into the wild wastes of the Staked Plains. They had never been comfortable among the tumbled hills and groves of the Ito is, Timber People, as the Penateka were sometimes called.

Still, it was a magnificent plan that Buffalo Piss was proposing, something that had never been tried before. And Buffalo Piss might be just the man to bring it off. It would be something to see, and to be a part of. The council had Wanderer's total attention now. He studied each man in turn, sizing him up, trying to predict how he would react in battle. He had never seen many of the warriors before. And that made him uneasy. Buffalo Piss would have been much better off with the old leaders behind him. But if they hadn't been killed, this council and this plan wouldn't have been necessary.

Suddenly, overnight, important positions as civil and war leaders had become vacant. Wanderer could imagine the days spent recounting coups, the time in council as each band decided who would replace its dead chiefs. The likeliest candidates had been considered and one asked to serve in each position.

There wasn't much official about it. Being asked and being followed weren't the same at all. The People would follow the man chosen only as long as he made good decisions, only until his medicine failed him once too often, or another became more successful on the raid trail or the hunt. Then the old leader found that his opinions were no longer asked and his advice no longer needed.

Most of these men had been eager for the chance to lead. But now, under some solemn masks, Wanderer detected the strain of responsibility. He could understand that. In fact, he distrusted those that showed no strain. They didn't know the importance of what they were doing. Overconfidence was more dangerous than cowardice.

Responsibility for an entire band was something to assume with time and training. But to have it thrust on one, to wake up one morning knowing that hundreds of people were depending on one for the decisions that meant their survival, that was not a thing to take lightly.

After four days, the council was finally ending, as the pipe passed to each man in turn. If the man smoked, it meant he would go with Buffalo Piss. If he declined, he would stay behind. Pahayuca let the pipe pass without smoking. Wanderer couldn't see the relief on Buffalo Piss's face, but he knew it must be there. It would be hard to maintain one's position of authority with Pahayuca around. Many of the men in the lodge might not know Wanderer, except by reputation, but they all knew Pahayuca.

It must have been tempting for him to go along. But as usual, his judgement won out. Those of the Penateka who stayed behind would need leadership too. And if Pahayuca stayed, Medicine Woman and Sunrise and his family would too. That was good.

As the pipe came closer, Wanderer had still not made up his mind. He glanced up and caught the fleeting look in Buffalo Piss's eyes. The look was so fast only he could have seen it. And it decided him. He took the pipe and drew long on it. As he held it cradled in his hands, he made the briefest speech of the council.

"I am not a Penateka. I am a Quohadi. But my heart is here with my friends and family. Their enemies are my enemies. Now the Texans have taken the lands of the Honey Eaters. Someday they may even try to do the same to us. Buffalo Piss plans to stop them. He wants to kill them or drive them from our country forever and show them the might of the People. I will go and help in any way I can."

Buffalo Piss was declaring war on the Republic of Texas. He would need all the help he could get.

❧ *31* ❧

Hundreds of shields and lance points glittered in the light of the full moon. As they moved through the night they were escorted by millions of fireflies that swarmed around them. The rough hills seemed alive and shifting with them, like schools of fish swirling in the water around a reef. There was a steady, eerie creaking of leather and the soft thud of thousands of hooves. There was the occasional slap of a quirt on a recalcitrant mule, and the nickers and the explosive whoof and mutter of horses blowing. There was the clatter of long poles being dragged across stones, and the dry crackle of brush against leather.

But there was no talking or laughing. No human sound. And no metal clinking. Buffalo Piss and his people, over a thousand of them, traveled mostly at night, pressing always south and east. It was an army, with women and children riding along for support. They had passed so close to the new capital of Austin that their scouts paused on the bluffs and looked down at the campfires flickering and the candles in the cabin windows.

They had avoided that settlement. There were still many soldiers there. Buffalo Piss was heading for the more populated areas, the gulf coast and the defenseless towns there that had never felt the People's wrath. He wasn't going to waste all his effort and man-power on the small, outlying cabins strung along the frontier.

Ben McCulloch pushed his battered, sweat-soaked leather hat back on his head. It held his thick, chestnut hair out of his eyes while he squatted to get a better look at the tracks. He had been a Ranger for five years, but he had never seen anything like this. The trail was half a mile wide, and the ground looked as though an army had come through dragging plows behind it.

"Buffalo this far south?" Ben winced. John Ford was a good

lawyer, a good doctor, surveyor, reporter, and politician. Someday he would be a good Ranger, but not yet. Ford caught the wince. "No. Of course they're not. Indians. Right?"

"Right." McCulloch studied the crushed blade of grass he had picked out of a hoofprint. "They're traveling at night, and they passed here about two days ago. If there are less than a thousand of them, I'll eat their horses."

"Maybe you'd best just offer to eat your hat, Ben. It's closer to hand and easier to salt," said Ford.

"If I saw that hat lying in a cow pasture, I'd step over it." William Wallace stood with his hands on his hips, surveying the trail. McCulloch and Ford were both six feet tall, but Wallace towered over them. Ford ignored him and went on peering at the blade of grass.

"How'd you know that? About them traveling at night and all?"

"They plowed through mesquite bushes instead of going around. And nothing goes through mesquite bushes if it can avoid them. Hell, armadillos go around them. And the grass is past the limp stage and getting dry. Feel it. Been in the print two days or so. Look at the insect trails crossing the print. They make those at night. So the prints have to be at least a day old."

"If you say so. But it beats me how you can know."

"You learn, John."

The lessons had been painful. And sometimes fatal. But the Rangers had learned a lot from John Coffee Hays in the past five years. And Jack Hays had learned from the Comanche. The Indians he hunted called him El Diablo, The Devil, but he hardly looked the part. He was five feet ten inches tall. He weighed one hundred and sixty pounds dripping wet and with his pockets full. He was dapper, with thick black hair and the long, dark lashes of a boy. He should have been a fop, a dandy, entertaining the ladies in their lace-curtained parlors on lazy Sunday afternoons. He should have been spending a remittance on slender cigars and elegant poker games.

He wasn't even a good shot. But he had a way of coolly calculating the odds and pulling off audacious maneuvers. Legends were already being told about him. One of his Apache scouts once said to a friend, "You, me, we ride into hell together. Captain Jack, he ride into hell alone."

Hays roamed the frontier, training men to follow him and to follow no one. He didn't create an army. He created hundreds of them, each composed of one man. His Rangers tracked the Indians ruthlessly, finding their camps by the languid wreaths of vultures and crows that hung over them. The Rangers were officially an arm of the Texas government, but neither Hays nor his captains wore insignia of rank. "Chicken fixings" was what they called gold braid, when they were being polite. Hays had trained Ben McCulloch as one of the first Rangers. And now Ben was one of the best.

Ben went on searching the ground, reading it for more information. "Comanche. Not that there was much doubt. Just wanted to make sure."

"And how do you know that?"

"Here's a track of the foot. Short and stubby. That's the way Comanche feet are, square as tobacco tins."

"You are a wonder."

"The wonder is that they got this far south with no one discovering them. I'd like to know who's leading them. He's brilliant." But already Ben's mind was churning over the next move. It would be suicidal to chase them and attack now. He had ten men with him. Even figuring the Comanche had their families with them, which they surely did, judging from the travois ruts, there must be at least five hundred braves. Ben knew his few men would be better deployed scattering through the countryside, rounding up recruits and warning people who might be in the Comanche's path.

My God. No wonder they've been so quiet lately. Every Comanche in the country must be with this mob. They've even brought their dogs. McCulloch would never have believed that the Comanche could have gotten this many people together for a raid. But for once, he was wrong. Entire bands of the People often had raided a thousand miles into Mexico before the whites came and provided easy pickings closer to home. Now they were on the march again, the largest force any chief of the People had ever led against the whites, an avenging army in a war of extermination. Ben could picture the devastation they would find as they followed the war party. War army. This was no party.

Well, best get on with it. He'd try to round up as many men as he could. And when he ran out of reinforcements, he'd attack with what he had. There was no choice, and he never considered not attacking. It was his job and his way of life. It was what the Republic of Texas paid him a dollar a day to do. When he was paid at all.

"Shit!"

Wallace and McCulloch and Ford and the three dozen men they'd gathered stood around the body. Those in the rear craned to see. The man had been shot and scalped, of course. They were used to seeing that. It was his feet they were staring at. The soles had been sliced off. From the torn and lacerated flesh it was clear that he had been forced to run a long way on the flayed surfaces. He'd probably been tied behind a horse.

"What kind of people would do a thing like that?"

"Comanche, John." There was a hint of exasperation in Wallace's voice. "If you'd studied Indians the way you study that Bible of yours, you'd not ask that question."

"You don't have to study them very hard," said McCulloch. "Just run across their handiwork now and then."

"We're going to be paying for the Council House stupidity a long time, aren't we, Ben?" Noah Smithwick came up to stand with them. Ben nodded and turned to him.

"You lived with them for three months, Noah. And you were at the council when the chiefs decided to meet with Lamar's gang. Who's left to lead this bunch?"

Smithwick mulled it over. "Well, there was Santa Ana and one dried-up old geezer, Old Owl, and a big, fat chief who probably couldn't find a horse to carry him. Pahayuca, I think his name is. The only other one was an onery, snot-nosed kid. I don't know if one of them is in charge here or someone else altogether. Spirit Talker said there were bands not represented at his council."

"Save one bullet in your pistols," Ben called over his shoulder as he mounted his weary horse. He didn't have to say for whom they should save them. A few men started digging a hole for the body. They'd done a lot of digging and no fighting. Ben still didn't know who was responsible for this sweep to the sea, but he was going to find out. He had put the word out to catch a live prisoner if possible, so he could question him. He checked off the list of those killed in San Antonio. Who was left? It was a mystery that nagged at him.

Each day the Rangers gathered more men and buried more dead. The Comanche leader, whoever he was, had formed his army into a huge, thin crescent, a scythe that mowed everything in its path as it moved relentlessly toward the coast. The people of Victoria were lucky to have gotten off with only fifteen killed. The Indians could easily have massacred the whole town, if they had been more adaptable. That might be the key. As brilliant as that chief was, he was stuck in the traditional way of doing things. He'd tried the old surround maneuver on the town. The medicine ring, riding in a circle around the victims, shouting and firing. It might work on a herd of buffalo, but stone walls didn't stampede.

At least he had made one mistake. And he was bound to make more. For one thing, his retinue was becoming unwieldy. They must have stolen a couple thousand horses and mules, five hundred from the Mexican traders in Victoria alone. Those, added to the ones they'd brought with them, meant a lot of forage. And a column that moved slowly.

They were headed for Linnville on the coast, and there was little to stop them from taking it. There were no fortifications or even strong buildings in which to make a stand. There were only the homes and warehouses for the port that fed San Antonio's appetite for gewgaws.

Buffalo Piss had led his army safely through the hill country and into the alien, swampy land of the coast. They had passed, hushed, through the gloomy tunnels of overarching live oaks hung with curtains of silvery-gray Spanish moss. The People had gathered the moss. The women would weave it into saddle pads, and the men would dry it as tinder for their pipes. They had all been scratching ever since as the tiny red bugs that nested in the moss crawled under their clothes and burrowed into their skin.

One of the dogs had been eaten by an alligator. Several people had come down with malaria and had to be sent back. But otherwise, they had traveled and raided unmolested. Not one man had been lost in battle.

As they neared the coast, the land flattened out and became veined with mangrove-lined rivers and tributaries. The live oaks dwindled in size and were punctuated with tall, spindly cabbage palms. The trees all leaned inland, twisted and sculpted by the prevailing winds from the gulf.

The low, flat land, the brushy scrub oak and palmettos, the sky and the distant town itself had a bleached, weathered look. The pale, gently curved shoreline lay along the blue water, the tiny waves licking at it lazily. Overhead the white August sun seemed to be trying to bleach everything to the same non-color. Even the people, Wanderer thought as he wiped the sweat from his forehead. He could feel the heat, like flames from a campfire, toasting his back. Only the waters of the gulf refused to fade. They sparkled a brilliant, blinding blue in contrast to the land and sky.

Wanderer sat next to Buffalo Piss on a knoll outside the Texans' wooden village. It was the highest point around. They could see the women lining up in the sand behind and below them, waving their arms, hooting and calling out to their men to bring them scalps and presents. Dressed in their finest, the warriors formed their battle wedge, their ponies restless in the steamy heat. The men looked toward Buffalo Piss and awaited his signal.

As he watched the young leader, Wanderer wondered when he had begun to change. Probably before they had left the main encampment, two weeks ago. The adulation would have been enough to turn anyone's head. For an entire day the war party had paraded, chanting its war song. They had ridden, double-file, through the huge camp. The women had lined their route, handing them pieces of clothing to carry as good luck, and promising them a warm bed when they returned. The celebration had lasted over a week. The People praised Buffalo Piss everywhere he went. He was their avenger, their weapon to regain lost glory. They believed he was invincible. And now he believed it himself.

To believe one's medicine was powerful enough to make one indestructible was normal. But to believe it would make a thousand people indestructible was putting a great burden on one's spirits. As the days and miles passed and the People stole and murdered, took captives and swept unchallenged toward the big water, Buffalo Piss had become less approachable. He was now more hostile to suggestions and criticisms from his captains.

Now Buffalo Piss raised his shield and dropped his other hand to the war whistle hanging on a thong against the elaborate bone bib that covered his chest. The whistle was made of an eagle's wing bone and had been painted and decorated with a long, beaded pendant fringed with downy breast feathers. He blew a shrill blast on it, like the cry of an eagle, and dipped his shield at the same time. With a howl, the warriors urged their ponies forward and the wedge formation opened into wings as they raced toward the town.

Wanderer and Buffalo Piss spurred their horses after the men, all of whom were headed toward the first building on the outskirts of the settlement. One white man stood outside the customhouse door, a breechloader in his hands. He got off one shot before he was overwhelmed, but he went down swinging. The warriors trampled him as they leaped from their horses and tried to crowd through the doorway all at once.

Cruelest One came back out first, pushing upstream against those who were still trying to get in. His friends, Skinny And Ugly and Hunting A Wife, followed him. They dragged a woman with them, hauling her kicking and screaming outside where there was more room to maneuver. The customs office itself was pandemonium. Men were tearing open every chest and emptying every drawer. When they found only paper, they threw it and the furniture in destructive abandon. Buffalo Piss had told them that the white men's goods entered Texas here, and he had promised them loot. All they found was paper.

Those who couldn't get inside waited for Skinny And Ugly to finish stripping the woman. Many of them had never had a white woman, and they figured the town would still be there when they finished with her. Besides, she was beautiful, by anyone's standards. She had hair like the sun, and although she was almost as buxom as one of the People, she had a waist like a wasp.

"Let's see what she looks like under all that cloth."

"Hurry up."

Skinny And Ugly ignored them and tugged at the stubborn blouse while Hunting A Wife tried to figure out the complex row of tiny hooks and eyes that fastened it up the back. Cruelest One pushed Skinny And Ugly aside and pulled out his knife.

"Don't kill her yet" said one of the men. "She'll get cold before we all have a chance with her." Cruelest One scowled around him. Pulling the cotton away from her body, he made a slit at the waist. He slashed the material up the front, between the soft swells of her breasts, and pulled at the edges, ripping the blouse apart. The woman no longer screamed or struggled. She had fainted, and hung limply between Hunting A Wife and Skinny And Ugly.

They began tearing at her skirts. Under her calico skirt she had several cotton petticoats, with flounces. The crowd moved in for a better view. Some of them jiggled their breechclouts, grinning in anticipation. Others began rubbing bear grease onto themselves so they would slide in easier. White women were delightfully tight, they'd heard, but dry. Of course, she wouldn't be dry after the first few men had used her, but it never hurt to be prepared.

More cloth. Cruelest One tore the white linen chemisette with his strong, bony fingers, then stood back, puzzled. He studied her as she hung there between his two friends. In the middle of August, on the steaming Texas gulf coast, Mrs. Watts was securely strapped into a whalebone corset. Cruelest One reached out and yanked at the buckles and straps, lacings and hooks and eyes. Frustrated, he tried to cut the corset off, but his blade bounced off the bone strips encased in the cloth.

Wanderer galloped up a little ahead of Buffalo Piss, and headed toward the other buildings. He was curious to see if this was indeed the source of the good things the white people had. Buffalo Piss was in a foul mood. He knew Night was faster than his own war pony, but he never got used to the idea. He pulled his horse so sharply to a halt that he reared, spraying the men with sand and gravel.

"Leave that woman!" He was almost shrieking in fury. "Drop her. Throw her away. We came here to fight, not fuck." Cruelest One turned and glowered at him, one hand still on the corset straps.

"I'll leave when I'm finished here." There was a quiet menace in his voice.

"Stay, then. But the rest of us will get the loot while you waste your time with that woman." He yanked his horse around and set off at a gallop toward the center of Linnville. The others ran to their mounts and followed him, shrieking and howling. Skinny And Ugly, Cruelest One, and Hunting A Wife threw Mrs. Watts and her armor over the back of her own horse, tied her there, and set out after them.

As Wanderer and the first wave of warriors swept into Linnville, the townspeople fled out the other side. They raced to the beach and pushed off in anything that would float. The raid had lost its most important advantage, surprise, because of Mrs. Watts and her corset. As the disappointed warriors ran up and down the shore, they screamed and fired their guns at the precariously loaded boats bobbing in the gentle swell. The people of Linnville shouted insults back.

Wanderer cantered past the wharves with their piles of bundles and sacks, kegs and hogsheads, barrels and neat stacks of fresh, resinous lumber. There was a strong odor of tarred rope and raw cotton and burlap, rising with the heat. Some of the men were already breaking into the kegs and barrels, scattering flour and grain, coffee and bolts of cloth. Wanderer pulled Night to a stop at one of the weathered buildings near the docks.

The sturdiest part of the building was its double door of solid, six-inch oak. It had a huge beam across it, fastened in place with a heavy lock and chain. Wanderer pushed at the door with one hand and saw that he would never get in that way. He walked all the way around to the back of the warehouse, and pulled his war ax from its loop on his surcingle. The boards at the back of the building were flimsy enough to shoulder his way in if he wanted to, but he had left his shirt off in the heat, and he didn't feel like pulling out splinters.

Soon he was joined by others, hacking and chopping and kicking with their moccasins until they had a hole big enough to ride a horse through. Sunlight streamed through the opening and played on the heaps of goods, piled to the ceiling. The first box Wanderer broke open held the new percussion breech-loading carbines. He whooped, forgetting everything as he stared at the bright polish of their barrels. He handed them out to the others, keeping three for himself. He began smashing box after box, searching for powder and lead and bullet molds, metal and knives. Finally, in the stack of boxes next to the rifles, he found something better, paper cartridges. They were of a new design, but he knew immediately what they were. Ten cartridges and twelve percussion caps nestled in each package. And there were a hundred packages in each pine box. He quietly piled them with the rifles and began tying them onto Night.

By this time the rest of the party had arrived, and the sounds of jubilation and destruction echoed up and down the hot, sandy streets. The warriors had torn apart the bales of cotton stacked by the docks and thrown it about until the streets looked as though snow had fallen in the August heat. Soon Linnville was littered with pieces of crates and scattered goods, sinuous trails of cloth and broken china.

Buffalo Piss sent a reluctant Skinny And Ugly back to where the woman and young boys waited with the pack animals. Theoretically Skinny And Ugly was supposed to get a fair share of the loot, but he could tell that the usual procedure might not apply here, and it was every man for himself. He kicked his pony viciously, racing to carry out his task and return as soon as possible.

Warriors began dancing through the streets, sporting their new finery. They wore top hats and morning coats, ribbons and ladies' bonnets and silk scarves. The air was filled with their shouts and laughter and the bawling of cattle as the raiders tried out their new guns. They rode around the milling herds shooting into them, like ducks in a barrel. Hugging one of the shiny, newfangled brass spittoons to his breast, Spaniard staggered up to Wanderer. He held it up, offering his friend a drink of what was inside. He had found a hogshead of whiskey. Wanderer sniffed at it and wrinkled his nose.

"You know what that does to you, Spaniard."

"Of course. That's why I'm drinking it. If it didn't do anything to me I might as well drink skunk piss." Spaniard howled at his own joke, slopping some of the whiskey over the curved rim of the spittoon.

"Look!" He nodded toward the beach, not trusting his arm to hold the precious whiskey while he pointed. A lone man with white hair was wading ashore, leaving his leaky dugout to founder and sink. Judge Hayes brandished his rusty Revolutionary War musket over his head and shrieked at the warriors running by him.

"You miserable swine. You destructive sons of bitches. You misbegotten spawn of the evil saint!" His voice rose to a shrill scream as the Comanche ignored him. "Maggots! Those are my cattle you're murdering." Spaniard was impressed.

"He must have very powerful spirits with him."

"Or he's crazy." Wanderer continued methodically sorting through the boxes he had pulled into the sunlight.

"In either case, he's very holy." Spaniard reeled off toward the beach for a closer look at the brave man. The others seemed to agree with his opinion of Judge Hayes. None of them dared touch him. They dodged around him as they continued to shoot at the people baking in the boats.

Finally the old man blinked, as though waking from a deep sleep, and looked around. He was standing alone on a bare beach swarming with murderous, drunken Comanche, and he was armed with a nonfunctioning gun. Judge Hayes started backing gingerly into the water toward the skiff that was being rowed in for him. When his friends pulled him over the side, his legs were trembling and he collapsed, quaking, in the stale, muddy water of the bilge.

"Hell, Hayes, while you was there you could have at least brought us back some of that there whiskey."

"Looks like it's going to be a long, dry day."

"What possessed you to take on the Comanche nation thataway?" Judge Hayes finally got his voice back. "I was angry," he said meekly.

"Angry? Judge, you was chewing iron and shitting nails!"

"You suppose Doc has anything in his kit for sunburn?"

"Maybe the ladies will part with some of their petticoats for sunshades."

"Outstanding idea."

Cursing and laughing, the men heaved the oars that pushed the sluggish skiff, its gunwhales almost awash, back out of range of the arrows and balls.

On shore, Wanderer could see that there would be no official division of the spoils. While the others celebrated, he packed the things he wanted onto his animals. He took coffee for himself and for Sunrise and Pahayuca. They had all developed a fondness for it. He had knives and metal barrel hoops for arrowheads, bolts of cloth, a large silver soup ladle, ribbon and braid for the women— Something Good, Blocks The Sun, Silver Rain, Takes Down The Lodge, and Black Bird. He packed a white enamel chamber pot with small items of clothing, sewing notions, hardware, and gifts for Star Name and Upstream. Then he loaded five more mules with presents for his family and friends among the Quohadi. Most of it was weapons and ammunition.

He carefully wrapped Naduah's present last, winding it in a length of soft wool blanket material. It was a Spanish bridle of tooled leather, heavily decorated with beaten silver disks and bells and tassels of silken cord. Then he went looking for Buffalo Piss.

He found him riding among the revelers, urging them to finish packing so they could leave before sundown. He wasn't having much luck. The men were dancing around roaring fires in the summer heat. The women had butchered the cattle and were boiling stew in the most popular item, the large white chamber pots. They set them directly on the fires, and they were blackening with soot. The fires were built of smashed packing crates and furniture from the looted houses.

Almost everyone was festooned with their new finery, and delirious with wealth and the white man's stupid water. Wanderer rode up next to Buffalo Piss, who was one of the few who refused to wear anything that belonged to the white eyes.

"It's time to leave."

"I know that." Buffalo Piss also knew that he had lost control, and he was blustering to cover it.

"Will we be traveling south and west under the white settlements? There'll be no one to stop us there."

"No. That will take too long. We'll head straight home, back the way we came." Buffalo Piss could sense Wanderer's disapproval. "No one will stop us," he shouted. "The Texans have fled. We're too mighty for them!"

"They may be waiting in ambush to catch us when we return."

"Let them try!" Buffalo Piss snarled like a cornered lynx, his child's face contorted with anger. "I'll be glad if they are. They're cowards. Nowhere have they stood and fought us. My lance is thirsty. I invite them to fight us. I want them to fight."

"The stupid water has made the warriors crazy. They might not follow you."

"They'll follow me. And if some don't, it doesn't matter. There will be enough to take care of the groveling Texans. We've beaten them. We've taught them not to think us weak. All we have to do now is go home, distribute our presents, and celebrate. We will talk of this victory for years."

So, thought Wanderer, as he watched men stagger by him, singing and vomiting and falling down. *The whiskey has conquered the conquerors.* He felt suddenly alone, and he missed his friend who had died. He had disdained whiskey too. At least the two of them would have had each other for company.

Liquor made strangers of the men Wanderer knew, and he didn't know many of them to begin with. As he rode through the littered town, dodging the unconscious bodies and roaring fires, he looked for anyone who might go back the long way with him. In an alleyway between two of the warehouses near the beach, he found Deep Water chewing on a half-raw steak. His pock marked face was morose. His body was bare of white man's clothing, and his extra mules were carrying only what he had brought with him, except for one of the new rifles. He was keeping his vow to touch only those things of the white men that he could use against them.

"Deep Water!"

The boy turned and glared at him.

"It's time to leave this place."

"Tell those fools," he spat. "They're *hibipa,* drunk."

"Might as well piss into a high wind as talk to them. Come with me. The great war leader plans to take a thousand people and three thousand animals loaded with loot straight back through enemy territory."

"You mean Penateka territory."

"It's not Penateka territory anymore, Deep Water. No matter what Buffalo Piss says. There are still Texans there. And they're probably waiting for us. I'm going back by way of Mexico. Do you want to come with me or not?"

274

"All right." Deep Water turned and called through the window of the nearest warehouse. "Upstream." Star Name's eleven-year-old brother climbed through the opening and stood grinning at Wanderer. He wore a pair of boy's heavy gray linen britches with the seat cut out of them. His round little buttocks gleamed through the ragged opening like the full moon through clouds. He had tied a green silk kerchief around his neck and wrapped his braids in strips of white lace.

"What are you doing here?"

Deep Water answered for him. "He sneaked away and followed the army. I've been hiding him so you wouldn't send him home."

"Saddle your pony, Upstream. We're leaving."

"But the others aren't ready to go yet."

"We're not going with them. We're going the long way, south through Mexico and up the old desert raid trail, then back over. You can help with the extra horses and mules."

"That trail will take forever. I have presents for Mother and Star Name and Sunrise. I want to get home."

"Upstream, get your pony. I'm not going to waste time arguing with you."

"No! I'm staying with Buffalo Piss. And don't try to force me to go with you." Upstream half-crouched, ready to flee.

"Do whatever you want. I know better than to try to force a strong brave like you." Wanderer smiled down at the boy. "Tell Pahayuca that we'll be there eventually. As long as we're in Mexico, we might as well steal some horses." He spotted a familiar figure tottering into the alley where they stood.

"Spaniard. Get your animals together. We're leaving."

"I'm not through celebrating." Spaniard had lost his spittoon somewhere and was drinking his whiskey from an old powder horn. His braids had come loose and his hair stuck out from his head as though he had been struck by lightning. A lava flow of dried vomit fanned down the front of his chest, and he reeked of it. Deep Water turned to Wanderer and spoke softly.

"We could use his help with the horses. I know a cure for whiskey. We just have to get him to the water."

Wanderer nodded. "I know that cure." They both leaped from their ponies and tackled the befuddled warrior. Together they dragged him around the building and through the sand of the beach, his heels digging twin furrows. They threw him into the water and pounced on top of him, dunking him and holding him under until he stopped struggling. Then they pulled him out and dropped him on the shore. On his hands and knees he threw up again, mostly liquor and sea water. He stood unsteadily and shook like a dog, spraying water from his woolly hair, and almost falling back down in the process.

The three of them rounded up their share of the stolen animals and rode off. Spaniard drooped in his saddle and moaned piteously. Wanderer turned to Deep Water, a grin dawning.

"It was a raid to talk about, wasn't it!"

Deep Water smiled back, his eyes lighting his ravaged face. "Yes, it was." No one noticed their going except Upstream. He waved, then turned and ran back to the celebration.

❧ 32 ❧

Ben McCulloch was satisfied. The chief had made the fatal error. Maybe it was overconfidence. Maybe it was an arrogant challenge, a gauntlet thrown down to the Texans. Ben doubted that it was stupidity. It didn't matter. The Comanche were taking the most direct route home, retracing their route north along the Colorado.

As soon as he saw which direction the Indians were headed, he knew where to ambush them. He sent riders fanning out in all directions. Their orders were to assemble every able-bodied man available in the thick trees and brush along Plum Creek outside of Austin. The Comanche army would have to pass through Big Prairie, an open plain near the creek. They would be exposed there.

"They'll never make it back with all that baggage." Ben looked at the bolts of cloth strewn along the trail. Already the Comanche's mules were tiring and being abandoned as the Rangers hounded them, sniping at the army's rear guard. McCulloch's men had been pursuing them for three days, and were losing their own horses. The men would jump off them as they fell to lie heaving and convulsing before their eyes rolled up and they died.

Bill Wallace kicked one of the dented enamel chamber pots, sending it clattering down the hillside before it came to rest against a cedar bush.

"Ben, they aren't splitting up and disappearing into the brush the way they usually do. Can't bear to part company with all those trinkets they stole. If their captain were smart, he'd dump all that frumpery and skedaddle."

"He's smart, but he's not crazy. Would you tell five hundred blood-drunk, whiskey-soaked Comanche bucks to throw away more loot than they've ever seen in their lives?"

"I see your point."

"A reverse Trojan horse."

"What'd you say, Ford?"

"A reverse Trojan horse," John Ford repeated. "Instead of taking the fatal gift to the city, they've carried it out."

"Well, Trojan or not, I wish we had some more horses. This campaign's been hell on them." Wallace went to collect his own.

The group of men following Ben McCulloch and his little patrol of Rangers was growing. Seventy had joined from among the irate citizens of Victoria alone. All along the Comanche army's wake, small parties of Rangers, militia, and volunteers were gathering, growing, and coalescing. And more men were converging from the hills around the small, clear, tree-shaded stream known as Plum Creek.

The Texans' bivouack among the hills looked more like a series of trash piles than a military encampment. There were makeshift tents of stiff black gutta-percha sheets and old blankets. There were lean-tos of poles and heaped brush. The area was littered with feathers and rabbit skins and bones from meals. There were rag patches for the muzzle-loaders, and bits of paper from the cartridges of those lucky enough to have cartridges. Most of the men had to make their own ammunition in the field. The smell of hot lead hung over the camp like a cloud.

Noah Smithwick walked over to a group of men sitting around their campfire.

"What are you boys up to?"

"Just gassin' and a-prophesyin', Cap'n. Speculatin' as to the outcome of the day's fun." John Ford sat with them and had slipped into the protective coloration of their dialect. "These boys are from over San Augustine way." Ford was sitting comfortably against his pack. He held his makeshift steel-can coffee roaster by a long metal rod over the flames. The smell of the roasting beans overpowered the odor of boiling lead. "Care to join us for some coffee, Noah? Should be ready in an hour or two, after I grind the beans."

"More than the coffee should be ready in an hour or two, John. The war party's getting close."

"Good. I always did love a party." Rufe Perry had dropped out of the Rangers to farm, but the present trouble brought him back. He was mending his moccasins with one of the "whangs," the buckskin thongs he carried in his shot pouch along with a roll of leather for patching. "You lived with the Comanche for a season, Noah. How do they keep their moccasins from falling apart?"

"They marry three or four women to mend them all the time."

"Sounds good to me," said Rufe. "Don't know as I'd like an Injun woman, though. I hear they smell."

"Smell!" Noah Smithwick rolled his eyes around under his bushy red brows. "Lordy, I can tell you they smell. They smell just like smoked ham, the most delicious thing you ever sank your teeth into."

"The ham or the squaws, Noah?"

"Well now, that all depends."

"On what?"

"On what you ate last." He ducked the oily cleaning rag that Ford balled up and threw at him.

"Mind if I check your guns, boys? McCulloch said to." Noah spoke almost apologetically.

"Yes, I mind," said Rufe Perry. "We've patrolled together for years, Noah. You know I can handle a gun." Old Rufe was eighteen and sensitive about his age, afraid others would think him green.

"I know you can, Rufe. But a lot of these new boys put the ball in before the powder."

"And a lot of them carry their guns around loaded and with the cock down on the cap. Or blow their fool heads off standing in front of the muzzle while they pull them through the bushes. That doesn't mean we're all idiots."

"Don't get excited, Rufe. I'm just making a general check."

"Well, check someone else. I'm responsible for my own weapon and I don't take kindly to anyone else handling it. Even you, Noah."

"All right. You other boys hand 'em to me one at a time." *Yes, sir, the Texans and the Comanche are a lot alike. Onery and proud.*

"Looks like we have company." The men turned to look in the direction Ford was pointing. A group of Tonkawa had arrived behind their chief. Placido stood bent over, his hands on his knees and gasping for breath. Sweat ran off his gaunt frame like rivulets down a stony cliff face. He and his fourteen warriors had run thirty miles. They would have cheerfully run another thirty for a chance to destroy the Comanche.

"Where do you suppose their horses are?"

"Same place as most of ours are. The Comanche have them." Noah stood to go on with his inspection among the other men. "Can you boys be ready in an hour?"

"We can be ready whenever you say, Cap'n. I do wish we had time for some coffee, though."

"Meet me at the big plum thicket in an hour, then." And Noah ambled off in that shuffling way of his. John Ford turned to Rufe Perry.

"You didn't have call to get so riled. Noah and Ben are right to check guns. For people who have to depend on them daily, I never did see so much carelessness. I've seen men track a Comanche horse-stealin' party and charge them trying to fire rusty guns. The Injuns take better care of their gear than a lot of these men."

"Mine's not rusty. When we charge, I'll be ready."

"I know you will, Rufe. I just pray everyone else is."

Ben McCulloch rode with his men, part of a long line that was scissoring in to meet one like it a half mile away. The plan was to catch the Indians in the middle. There was little talking. Each man was wrapped in his own thoughts. They were a cool-looking lot, grim and rough, but Ben could smell the fear in their sweat. He'd smelled it often enough before.

The wind that blew in their faces was heated, as though someone had left a blast furnace door open somewhere. Heat waves set objects on the broad, rolling prairie dancing to silent music. They distorted the distant line of riders until it seemed to undulate. Under his arms Ben's shirt felt clammy, and sweat tickled as it rolled down his neck and sides and ran from under his knees. His mouth was dry, and his lips stuck together when he closed them.

The cloud of dust at the south end of Big Prairie grew larger. McCulloch studied it. Placido and his Tonkawa scouts agreed that there were at least five hundred warriors. And they had their families with them. That was bad. The one thing that would make a Comanche stand and fight was the need to defend his women and children. Otherwise, a fight with them could be like blind men chasing birds. They melted away into the country and disappeared.

Dark figures emerged from the dust, and Ben strained to make them out. He shook his head, thinking for an instant that he had fallen asleep and was dreaming. Or hallucinating. Next to him, Bill Wallace laughed softly.

"If that doesn't beat all. That's what's been terrorizing Texas." Buffalo Piss rode in front of his men, standing on his pony's surging back and shouting his challenge. His braids had been lengthened with horsehair and streamed five feet behind him. In one hand he waved his war lance, and in the other he held aloft a dainty, black, lace-trimmed parasol. He might sneer at white men's clothing, but a sunshade was too good to pass up. As it was, he was the most conservatively dressed.

"Looks like a damned circus, with the clowns and the acrobats and the fancy riders all rolled into one."

"Better'n any circus I ever saw. Look at the one wearing a lady's drawers."

"I like the one with the stovepipe hat tied on with ribbons. And the one with the swallow-tailed coat on backwards." The men almost had to yell to be heard over the drumming and the war whoops.

"Why don't they charge instead of showing off that way?"

"That's the way they do things," Smithwick shouted. "They have to challenge us to individual combat first. More manly." Noah squinted to see better through the dust that was drifting over them by then.

"And they're distracting us until their main column passes," shouted McCulloch. "Break through the outer circle of warriors and go for the horse herd. Drive them toward that swamp to the northeast. Get the animals on the run and the whole outfit will fall apart.

"But Lord Almighty, look at them ride." John Ford was lost in admiration. "That one just climbed clear under his horse's belly and up the other side. And the horse running as fast as it can."

"Only a Comanche can ride like that," shouted McCulloch. And he added in a much softer voice, "They ride horses the way eagles ride the wind."

Upstream was herding the mules when the Texans charged, screaming like mad banshees. He heard the screaming and the shots and the pounding hooves as their momentum carried them through the outer ring of warriors and headlong into the women and children and pack animals beyond. Then he was choking in the added dust, trying to hold the animals in his section of the herd. Bucking and braying, their loads slipping and clattering, the mules started to swerve, looking for an opening. Their big eyes bulged with terror, and their stumps of teeth were bared.

The young herders yelled and waved their arms to steer them back, but a few broke through, then others. A figure loomed out of the dust cloud, and for a moment Upstream thought he was seeing the great evil thunderbird with huge wings flapping. It was Bill Wallace, towering over everyone and waving a buffalo robe to spook the animals. His face was contorted in a howl and his fox skin cap with the ears standing straight up, tail flying, made him look half man, half beast. And quite mad.

Upstream's pony panicked and was swept away with the herd. The boy pulled his legs onto his pony's back to keep from getting them crushed as mules crashed into him, their loads sliding off. Loot went flying as the animals bucked and leaped. Upstream was wedged in so tightly he couldn't see the ground. He could only cling to his pony, hoping there were no holes or crevices that would trip him. He had no idea what the terrain was like until the first mules started to go down far ahead of him. They had been driven into the quagmire that Ben McCulloch had pointed out.

The animals went down struggling and shrieking as those behind fell over them or tried to climb onto their backs. Women and children, their own horses caught in the stampede, screamed as they were trampled. There was no way Upstream could stop, and he steeled himself to jump. He could clearly see the hundreds of fallen animals ahead trying to rise, pawing and rearing up halfway from the heaving sea of backs. Their necks and heads lashed from side to side with the effort, then sank again.

When he felt the first falter in his pony's stride, Upstream leaped clear. His foot slid on the curve of the next mule's back and he put a hand on the animal's sweaty neck to steady himself. Without thinking, he jumped from back to back, bounding across the mass. He dodged flailing legs and hooves and one human arm, the hand grasping desperately at the air. Using both hands to haul himself forward, he clambered over the bulky packs and rolling bodies, as though climbing the steep side of a boulder-strewn mountain shifting in an earthquake.

He moved reflexively, his legs and feet finding footing and balancing with no conscious thought. His whole being, his years of play and training, orchestrated his muscles and sinews, eyes and nerves. He didn't hear the snap and crunch of bones, the clatter of metal, the cries or the shots around him. He saw only the next place where his feet would land. He heard only his own blood pounding in his temples, felt only the slide of skin and muscle and hair under his feet and hands.

As he cleared the last fallen animal, he leaped for solid ground, and hit it running. His goal was a thicket of plum, but he didn't make it. He felt a pair of wiry hands grip him, the bony fingers digging into his armpits, as he was swung onto a pony's back. He turned to struggle and saw Cruelest One's face. It was grim and hideously painted, but comforting and beautiful to Upstream.

Panting, the boy lay against the pony's neck and gripped with his knees to keep from falling off. As though his body had delayed the relay of messages from his eyes, horrors from his flight across the floundering mules flashed through his mind. He saw people pinned in the crush, their faces looking up at him in agony as he bounded over them. The adrenaline washed out of him, and he went limp and shaking.

Cruelest One plunged into the dense growth of bushes and trees bordering Big Prairie, beating his pony viciously with his quirt to force him through the thorny tangle. They cleared the thicket and slid down the steep side of an overgrown ravine, the sounds of the battle dimming behind them. Cruelest One had no family to protect, and he didn't waste time fighting. They pushed on for a mile or two, always using the ravine bottoms and stopping still from time to time while white men passed on the ridges overhead. Finally Cruelest One stopped and listened. Then he hooted, and was answered by another call in the distance. He spoke for the first time.

"Skinny And Ugly." They headed in the direction of the sound and found Skinny And Ugly and Hunting A Wife and their captive. Mrs. Watts was gagged as well as tied, and she was still naked except for her corset. Cruelest One was absolutely calm, which was when he was at his deadliest. He spoke in an almost conversational tone.

"Why do you still carry that piece of baggage with you?"

Skinny And Ugly squirmed and tried to look defiant. "She's beautiful, worth many horses. I'm going to keep her for a slave."

"She'll be burned to a cinder by the sun before you get her home." Already Mrs. Watts was a deep pink color and her skin was peeling in huge flakes. Her terrified blue eyes stared at them over the tight leather strip in her mouth.

"I'll cover her." Skinny And Ugly wavered. He was as close to being a follower as one of the People ever came, and a leader had arrived.

"We have a brave here who needs a horse," Cruelest One said. And Upstream sat a little straighter in front of him.

"She's mine."

"Then you have the right to dispose of her any way you want. Do you want to take her here before you do it? We'll wait five minutes." It was an enormous concession on Cruelest One's part.

Skinny And Ugly was angry and sheepish all at once.

"I can't get her unwrapped. I tried yesterday during the rest stops, but we haven't stopped long enough to really work on it."

"Then she's of no use to us, and we haven't time to waste. We need that horse." Cruelest One leaned down and untied the ropes holding her on the pony's back. With his moccasined foot he shoved her off onto the ground. The other two men dismounted and helped him tie her to a nearby tree. Upstream watched with amusement as Mrs. Watts squirmed and struggled, tears streaming down her face and soaking into the leather gag. The men paced off seventy-five feet and nocked an arrow each.

"We'll see who can hit the heart." Cruelest One fired first, and his aim was perfect. The other two arrows split his.

"That was easy," called Upstream. "You should've stood farther back."

The woman's chin had fallen onto her chest, and she hung lifelessly.

"Upstream, get on that horse. Hurry." There was the sound of hoofbeats in the distance, and the three men ran to their ponies. They all raced off, leaving Mrs. Watts hanging near the trail.

She had revived and was almost hysterical when Noah Smithwick and his men found her. The arrow was deeply embedded in the corset, but it had wounded her only slightly, stopped by the tough whalebone. She was lucky. As the Comanche split up and fled, they unburdened themselves of the spoils that had slowed them down. The corpses of their captives, black and white, women and children, were found littering the trails.

The men of Smithwick's patrol stopped talking. Their faces were hard as they rode, or stopped to dig another grave. The last one had been tiny, for a baby whose head had been smashed against a tree trunk. This had become a hunt for dangerous prey.

"Hold up. I gotta take a piss." Ezekial Smith had run out of powder and was carrying a captured lance. Its slender shaft was dwarfed in his huge hand as he walked off the cleared trail and into the bushes that grew over his head.

"What do you need privacy for, Zeke? Do it where you stand." The men were tired and irritable and nervous. But they were grateful for even the brief rest. They heard a scuffle and a rustling, and everyone took aim at the spot where Smith had disappeared.

"Hey, boys, look what I found." Smith was a hulking man. His belly hung over the waist of his pantaloons, and his chest strained the filthy cords that served as suspenders. But he grunted with the effort as he pulled the body of the Comanche woman behind him, his free hand twined in her braids as though hauling on a rope.

Deer lay panting where he dropped her, her eyes sullen behind the pain. Her knee had been blasted and her arm was broken, the bone jutting through purple skin.

Before anyone could stop him, Smith kicked her hard in the ribs with his iron-patched boots, breaking a few more bones. Then he drove the lance between her eyes, pinning her to the ground like an insect specimen. She twitched and spasmed, then lay still, her eyes open and staring at the sky. Noah spurred his horse and grabbed Smith's knife arm as he was about to take her hair. The two men glared at each other, and Noah began to worry about whether his men would support him. Finally Smith backed off. They could hear him muttering as he rode along behind.

Ezekial Smith wasn't bright, and he wasn't easy to get along with, but Noah knew that in this case, many of the men agreed with him. She was only an Injun, after all. And a scalp was a souvenir to brag about to the folks back home.

"McCulloch wants a live Comanche. He wants to ask him some questions. You boys remember that." And Smithwick tried to ignore the looks that passed among his men.

* * *

As night fell, most of the men walked their weary horses toward their isolated homesteads, some close by, some a day or two away. They melted silently into the trees and copses of the tangled river bottoms. Many of them had been trailing the Comanche army almost a week, and they were ready to quit. Only a few kept doggedly in pursuit, and most of those were Rangers.

Ben McCulloch watched the Texas volunteers lead their extra animals loaded with the abandoned Linnville loot. There was no use trying to recover it, and no one even suggested it. On the rolling lawn of Big Prairie, the Tonkawa were celebrating the victory around roaring fires. McCulloch had ridden back to talk to them. There was still something he had to know. He had a sullen Comanche woman with him, a prisoner who could give him the information he needed. He searched out Chief Placido as he was enjoying a late dinner.

"Chief, ask this woman who was in charge of the Comanche war party."

Placido relayed the question. "Potsana Quoip."

"What does that mean?"

"Potsana means buffalo."

"And Quoip?"

Placido's hands spoke eloquently. The woman made an obscene gesture in the vicinity of her groin, as though a man were urinating.

"She say him name Buffalo Pizzle."

"Buffalo Penis?"

"Maybe so. I know Potsana Quoip. Brave man."

"Is he still alive?"

"Woman doesn't know. Maybe dead. Maybe alive." Placido was obviously eager to get back to his meal, and McCulloch rode off, wondering what to do with his prisoner. Around him the bodies of the dead Comanche were strangely truncated, their hands and feet missing. The Tonkawa had cut them off and packed them to take to their women and children for feasting. Then they had borrowed a huge washtub, and were boiling up a stew of sections of their enemies' thighs. They were in high spirits because they had helped defeat the Comanche and they had been rewarded with horses. Silhouetted against the fires' light, they danced and sang among the corpses, mutilating them even more.

After leaving his prisoner with a man who said he needed a housekeeper, McCulloch sat on his exhausted horse, looking over the scene. Tomorrow he would gather his men and track the Comanche. But now he would get a full night's sleep for the first time in a week.

"John." McCulloch tried not to smile at Ford. "You can't write the word 'penis' in an official report to the Texas Secretary of War."

"But Ben, you said to write it up as it happened. And that's his name. Buffalo Penis. You told me so yourself."

"Nevertheless, President Lamar will throw a shoe. The Texas legislature may not have money to pay us, but they still think they're in charge."

"How about Buffalo Balls, or Donkey Dick? Or Bison Pisser?" Bill Wallace looked up from his poker game.

"Wallace, that's enough." But Wallace was full of suggestions.

"I know, Ben. Call him Comanche Cock or Buffalo Humps."

McCulloch ducked his head and pretended to study John Ford's report on the splintered ammunition crate that served him as a desk. Four small rocks anchored the corners of the paper to keep it from blowing away.

"Buffalo Hump will do," he finally said, when he could do it without laughing.

Wallace left his poker hand face down on the hide spread out as a table. He walked over to the crate and pulled the corncob plug from the gourd he always carried.

"I christen thee Buffalo Hump. May your tribe decrease." And with a flourish, he poured a drop of whiskey onto the report.

"Wallace, what are you doing? We'll have to send to Austin for more paper."

"They have plenty of paper in Austin," said Ford. "The only thing they have more of than paper is lawyers. What is it about government that attracts lawyers?"

"Well, he'd have had to write it over anyway," Wallace sat back down with a grunt and surveyed his neglected cards.

"It's a waste of good whiskey, Wall-eye. Hand it over."

"Good whiskey!" It was Ford's turn to snort. "Wallace wouldn't know good whiskey from privy squeezings."

Ben McCulloch raised the gourd. "Here's to Buffalo Hump." They all laughed as they passed it around.

꙳ *33* ꙳

Upstream slept as he rode, stretched on his belly along his pony's back. His arms dangled at the horse's neck, and his cheek lay against it. His small, full mouth was partly open. His eyelid twitched and his lip jumped from time to time, as though startled, even in his sleep. Cruelest One rode ahead of him, leading the boy's horse. The tiny warrior was not much taller than Upstream. But his body was so lean and muscled, it was as though all excess had been whittled off, leaving only the tough heartwood of him. In another hour he would waken Upstream and sleep while his own pony was led. Skinny And Ugly had the same arrangement with Hunting A Wife.

For five days the party had eaten only what little jerky Skinny And Ugly happened to have in a pouch tied to his surcingle when the Texans attacked. The meat was gone now, and their stomachs cramped with hunger. Cruelest One was chewing on a piece of leather in an attempt to fool his muttering insides. He wouldn't stop long enough to hunt. They would make the rest of the journey on water, and not enough of that. They rested for an hour three or four times a day, and rode all night. This was the usual method of traveling when they were pursued. They were used to it, but it was hard on Upstream.

Far behind them smoke rose beyond the line of flat-topped ridges. It came from the fires they had set to cover their tracks. A day's ride from Plum Creek they had stopped for a night's rest, and had almost been caught by a Ranger patrol. They hadn't laid down to sleep since.

That morning they had ridden through steep hills carpeted with a dark green nap of scrub oak. Now they were at the Clear Fork of the Brazos, on a grass-covered hill overlooking the river as it flowed lazily through deep-cut banks. Cruelest One was headed for one of Pahayuca's regular campsites. There would be signs left there for those who knew how to read them.

The campsite had been occupied recently, and it was easy to find. The ground around it had been thoroughly trampled, although new shoots were already pushing up to cover it again. Cruelest One and Hunting A Wife squatted at a pile of buffalo bones thrown into a heap. They looked haphazard, but Cruelest One was studying the scratches on them carefully.

"Two days north. They must be at Pease River."

"This is all Tenawa country. We don't belong here." Hunting A Wife had been brooding the entire journey.

"We have no choice. The white man is crowding us together like cattle in one of his corrals. Let's go." Cruelest One didn't waste any more time on reflection than he did on compassion. He had picked Upstream up reflexively, acting on his training for tribal survival. If he had known how grateful the boy was, he would have dismissed the whole thing with a snarl. He ignored Upstream as they rode the swells of the grassy hills to the north.

In small groups the survivors of the Plum Creek fight wandered into the Penateka camps strung along the upper Colorado and

Brazos Rivers. They had lost at least one fourth of the army that had ridden out so proudly. They had buried their dead in crevices along the trails. Most of those who were killed in battle had to be left at Plum Creek for the wild hogs to eat. Many of the men were without horses and had run behind their comrades, holding onto their ponies' tails to keep them going.

The men separated when they entered camp, dropping in silently, one by one. They painted their faces black and shaved their horses' tails to show their sorrow and shame. The sounds of mourning went on for weeks. Buffalo Piss left on a journey to Medicine Mounds to bargain with his spirits and try to find out what he had done wrong. Upstream arrived safely and ate enough to carry him through the winter. Then he slept through two sundowns like a brown little chipmunk hibernating.

He began following Cruelest One around camp, ignoring the threats and scowls and finally the clods of dirt thrown at him in exasperation. He would squat nearby like a devoted dog while the warrior smoked or talked to the other men. And he would rush forward to bring a coal for the pipe or ask if there were any messages Cruelest One wanted delivered. At last, in disgust, Cruelest One packed his few belongings onto his animals and left on one of his meandering journeys. Upstream moped around for a few days, and then consoled himself by recounting his adventures to his friends. He could usually be found with a group of them, acting out the sacking of Linnville and the disaster at Plum Creek.

Summer finally relented and the days were cool, the nights cold. The huge fall moon was dwindling and misshapen, as though one edge had been torn off. Overhead, the leaves of the tall cottonwoods and pecans glimmered a brilliant gold where the moon's light shone on them. Piles of brittle leaves, driven by the wind, rattled around the sides of Sunrise's lodge, like dogs scratching to get in.

Naduah and Star Name sat by the fire cracking pecans from the huge pile between them. Medicine Woman was sorting the latest batch of bark and roots and herbs, feeling and sniffing them to identify them. Then she tied them in bundles to hang for drying. Sprays of them were already filling the air with a spicy scent. Black Bird was sewing by the fire's light, and Takes Down The Lodge was giving Sunrise the usual account of the day's gossip. Dog was on Naduah's bed, snoring lightly. No one knew where Upstream was. More than likely he was with his friends, rustling the band's ponies for a ride through the moonlight that washed the prairie.

There was a jingling outside and a dry rustle as the hide flap was pulled back. Wanderer stepped into the light, followed by Spaniard and Deep Water. They all walked around the fire, murmuring their apologies to Medicine Woman for blocking her from the heat as they passed. Medicine Woman recognized the voices.

"Wanderer, you have wandered back to us." Her smile wrinkled around her sightless eyes.

"Yes, Grandmother. And I brought you presents." He pulled a sack from the leather saddle bag he carried and handed it to Takes Down. She beamed at him.

"Coffee. We had run out. It will warm our hearts as well as our bellies, Wanderer." She rattled the beans into an iron skillet and began roasting them. Naduah leaned forward to sniff the wonderful aroma, and to get a better view of Wanderer. No one said anything else as the three men sat down next to Sunrise on his pile of woolly buffalo hides. It was courtesy to let guests warm themselves and relax before distracting them with conversation.

Star Name stood, shaking the pieces of pecan hulls from her skirt, and searched for a container to put the nut meats in. When she sat back down, she was close to Deep Water. Naduah saw the smile her sister gave him. Only Star Name could manage to look shy and impish at the same time. And there was now the hint of wantoness in the imp. Deep Water stared at her, a spark of joy in his big, sad eyes. They were so beautiful they made one forget the scars on his face.

Star Name was almost fifteen and too big for a simple one-piece dress now. She wore the poncho and skirt of a woman. And she filled it well. She had a heart-shaped face with a full, wide mouth.

It was Star Name who had sneaked into Wanderer's lodge when he had camped with Pahayuca's band in July, three month earlier, before Buffalo Piss's raid. She had stolen a pair of his moccasins and brought them triumphantly to her sister. Naduah needed them to take measurements for a pair she wanted to make him in return for all his help with Wind. She thought she was finally a good enough seamstress. They'd giggled, she and Star Name, as she traced around the sole onto the tanned hide, using Takes Down's sharp drawing stick to indent the lines into the leather. Then Star Name had sneaked them back to the guest lodge.

Naduah looked over at the box where she kept her present in the soft case she had made. Suddenly she didn't want to give the moccasins to him. They were crude. Poorly sewn. He probably had many pairs, all of them better than the ones she'd made. She decided not to say anything about them. She didn't have to. Star Name broke the silence.

"Naduah has a surprise for you, Wanderer." Naduah glared at her. Not here. Not in front of all these people. What if he didn't like them?

"Not now, Star Name," she said. Naduah could feel the blush heating her face and hoped it would look like light from the fire. "The men have important things to talk about." And she stopped in confusion. She didn't want the men to talk about those things. They might make her leave. She saw Wanderer so seldom, and he might leave tomorrow. Or tonight. He always put her off balance, making her self-conscious and shy. But she wanted to watch him and listen to him all night. And all the next day.

"May I see it, Naduah?"

She rose slowly, reluctantly, conscious of the bare skin at her waist. She wished she had her robe with her, and wondered if she would stumble or do something clumsy as she went to the box.

"They're beautiful! How did you know what size to make them?"

"That's our secret," said Star Name, giggling at the memory of her raid on his lodge. Wanderer held one of the moccasins against his foot to measure it. He turned it over to inspect the bottom.

"I made the soles from an old lodge cover, the smoked part near the chimney, so they won't get stiff. And I greased them to make them waterproof."

"She shot one of the skunks and I shot the other," broke in Star Name again. "From a hundred paces." The thick, silky skunk tails hung down the backs of the moccasins. They were designed to trail in the dust and obscure the wearer's tracks. Wanderer smiled.

"My paces or yours?"

"Ours. But we're good shots, Naduah and I." Wanderer passed the moccasins around so the others could admire the beading on the pointed toes. And Naduah glowed with pleasure, her head down. She could almost feel the warmth of his smile on the top of it.

"I have something for you too. I'll show it to you later. It's something from the raid to the Big Water."

"Of course you know what happened after you left." Sunrise spoke for the first time, turning the talk to the most important issue.

"Yes. We've been staying with different bands on the trail from Mexico." There was no criticism of Buffalo Piss's decision to come north through hostile territory. That was something to be discussed only among the men, and in council.

"The white men raided again." Spaniard spoke up.

"Rain's camp," said Wanderer. His face shifted, became angry. "They burned everything. They roasted Rain's people's stores of meat in the flames of their burning lodges. They attacked at dawn again."

"Had Rain posted lookouts?" Sunrise asked a question that should have been obvious, but wasn't.

"No. Of course not. We've never had lookouts in our big camps."

It was unheard of. A camp of one hundred and fifty lodges being attacked. It bothered Wanderer. The white men were braver and more reckless than he had given them credit for.

"Wanderer." Medicine Woman's soft, quavery voice called from a dim corner. "You tell the story. It's confusing when everyone speaks at once."

"All right, Grandmother." There was silence, broken only by Dog's whimpering as she chased a rabbit in her dreams. Wanderer sat staring into the fire and collecting his thoughts. The light flickered on his face, and Naduah held her breath, lost in the beauty of him.

Wanderer concentrated on the story he was telling, living it again in his mind.

"We had been following the trail of Rain's band and planned to stay with them. But we found several of them hiding in that cave in the humped bluffs near the Talking Water River.

"Many of the people in the cave were wounded, and one woman was mad with grief. She had seen her baby trampled under the hooves of the white men's horses. The woman sneaked out of the cave, climbed to the bluff, and threw herself into the river. And no one could mourn, except in silence. They feared the white men's patrols who might be hunting them still.

"Most of the men were away hunting when the white eyes attacked. They rode through the camp howling like a pack of angry panthers and shooting into the lodges. Many people ran to the river and were killed trying to swim across. The white men had stolen Rain's horses, and they chased the warriors a great distance, hunting them through the brush like prairie hens. Then they went back to the village and burned everything, except the tent where they piled the wounded.

"When we found Rain's men, they were waiting for nightfall to steal their ponies back. We went with them, of course. Deep Water would travel a long way to kill a Texan, and here were some close at hand. It was easy to steal the horses.

"The white men are so careless. They've learned to attack on horseback. And they've learned to steal our ponies before they attack. But they haven't learned to leave, to sting and fly away. And they never will learn that we're the best horse thieves there are. We sniped at them all the way back to that new village they're building farther down the Talking Water River. Every night we yelled as we rode away with a few more horses, so the white men would know we'd visited.

"They finally got home, though some of them were walking and they had few extra pack animals left. And they had a big dance to celebrate their victory. Their women were there too. So we decided to steal the horses we'd missed." Wanderer rose to a low crouch and stalked stealthily around the lodge, acting out their raid into Austin itself.

"We crept among the square lodges like coyotes coming into the village at night to sniff around the meat racks. We went to the pasture, but they had dug a ditch around it. We filled in a section of it and led forty of their best horses across it while the white eyes danced and laughed nearby.

"The three of us tied our ponies far away and went back to watch them when they came out and found themselves afoot. I wish I could have understood what they were yelling." Wanderer laughed, and the boy returned to his face.

"I understood it."

"I didn't know you could speak white talk, Spaniard."

"I can't. I didn't have to speak it to understand what they were saying."

"I wonder why one of them threw his hat down and jumped on it," said Deep Water.

"Maybe it was a sacrifice to their gods, asking for help getting the horses back," suggested Spaniard.

"Or a war dance they do," Wanderer continued. "Rain's people will need those horses to hunt and replace what they lost. They're living in caves now, or staying with other bands."

As she listened, Naduah felt fear in the pit of her stomach. It frightened her to think that they might be attacked in their beds. Sunrise must have been thinking the same thing.

"We will discuss this with Pahayuca and suggest that sentries be posted."

"I only wish we had killed more of the white men." Deep Water's voice was low but intense.

"We'll kill plenty of them," said Wanderer. "The Texans will wish they had never come here. And when we drive them out, they'll be walking."

Just as she had expected, Naduah saw little of Wanderer for the next two days. He was shut up with Pahayuca in the council lodge. The smoke was so thick inside, it floated out the door. Naduah tried to peek surreptitiously inside as she and Star Name passed on their way to Something Good's and then the river.

Something Good's lodge looked as it always had, except that things of value were hung high on the walls, and little Weasel's toys and clothes were scattered about. Weasel herself sat naked in the middle of the floor, near the fire, her chubby legs spread in front of her. She had dragged away some of the hide rugs to clear a space, and was deeply engrossed in her play. She was chanting to herself and pulling a crude twig travois over the mountains and trails that she'd made. Her mother sat sewing, a thick, furry robe thrown over her shoulders.

"Is the Weasel planning our next move?" asked Naduah.

"I suppose so." Something Good smiled at her daughter. "Any day now she'll want to sit on the council and tell the men what to do. She's very headstrong. I don't know where it comes from." Naduah thought of Wanderer's dead brother's cheerful obstinance, and of how he could charm anyone into doing whatever he wanted. The child's mother went on. "Yesterday, while I was gathering wood, she tried to make rivers in here. And she brought in water to fill them. You should have seen the mess."

Star Name squatted beside Weasel and was murmuring to her while she whittled a crude pony from a forked stick. Together they fastened the travois to it with a piece of thong. While they played, Naduah stated her business.

"We've come to take Weasel to the river with us. It looks like she could use a bath too."

"Just don't keep her in too long. She'll get chilled."

"When the afternoon sun hits the shallow part of the river it isn't bad. And the weather's warm for this time of year." Naduah carried a bag with shampoo in it. It was a thick ooze made of bear grass boiled with the pale, parasitic love vine. It looked disgusting, but it did the job.

It took them a long time to leave the village with the Weasel. They had to stop at almost every lodge so the women could admire her and give her sweets. No matter who her father had been, it was impossible to snub Weasel. Her eyes seemed to take up most of her face, and tiny lights danced in them. Her laugh was irresistible.

The three of them finally cleared the camp and trotted down the path to the water. They wove through the cedars, jumping out from behind them to scare each other. The thick mat of dry needles was springy under their moccasins. But it was cooler in the shade of the trees, and they worried that Weasel might get cold.

"We'll race you, Weasel." The child ran, pumping her small legs and grimacing while the other two pretended to be unable to catch her. They broke from the trees onto the narrow beach. The warm sun felt wonderful. They spent half an hour scrubbing and washing, then lay back in the water.

"We should get out now," said Naduah. "The Weasel pup is beginning to shrivel."

"I know. But the air is colder than the water."

"One of us should get out and dry her." Naduah felt as though she could lie there forever. The water washing over her left her completely limp and relaxed.

"You can do it." Star Name felt the same way.

"She likes you better than me, Star Name. You play with her more."

"You can stand the cold better than I can."

"All right," sighed Naduah. She stood up, and for some reason looked up. And sat back down so fast she felt the gravel cut into her.

"What are you doing up there?" she yelled. "Go away!"

Star Name and Weasel looked up too, and Weasel laughed with delight. Wanderer was one of her favorite people.

"Come play with us, Wanderer," she called. She stood and cupped her small hands around her mouth. She was in shallower water, and her naked little body glistened, her stomach jutting out over her sturdy, bowed legs.

"Go away," Naduah yelled again, an edge to her voice. Wanderer sat on top of the bluff, his legs dangling over the side.

"I'll dry her off," he shouted. And he stood and disappeared as though sinking below the horizon.

"Go away!" But Naduah was too late. She and Star Name moved out into deeper water. The cold was beginning to affect them. They felt colder patches of water surging around them, and their fingers and toes were becoming numb. Wanderer appeared, running from the cedars, and Weasel splashed to meet him. She leaped into his arms like a wriggly puppy when he squatted, and soaked his shirt front. He rubbed her hard with the rag they had brought, until there was a pink glow to her skin. Then he dried her hair, tumbling it all over her head, and he dressed her. Holding her by the hand, he came to stand at the edge of the water.

"Do you want me to dry you two off too?" Naduah had never seen him look that devilish.

"No!" By now even Star Name was becoming angry. "Go away so we can come out. We're freezing."

Wanderer held out his hands to show they were empty.

"I have no weapons. I can't stop you from coming out."

"Wanderer, I'll get even with you for this." Grimly, Star Name stood and stalked toward him, her fists clenched at her sides. The late afternoon sun turned the beads of water into small jewels on her dark, sleek body. Naduah knew Star Name was lovely, and suddenly she felt pale and ugly and jealous.

"Please, Wanderer. Leave us alone." By now her teeth were chattering.

"All right." He laughed and turned, leading Weasel by the hand.

"We'll wait for you at the top of the bluff. I have the presents I promised you both, and I wanted to give them to you before I left."

"No!" Naduah stood without thinking, sending the gray water out in surges around her. "You can't leave." She pulled her long, heavy, wet hair across her chest and waded in after her sister. By this time Star Name was pulling her dress over her head, regally ignoring Wanderer, who had turned around again.

"You just told me to leave." He was looking at Naduah solemnly, but she knew he was laughing. She could see it in his eyes.

"You know what I mean. Turn around." She said it imperiously, circling her hand in front of her to explain it further.

Wanderer made a complete circle and ended up staring at her again. She held her hands up, trying to cover herself and at the same time grab the clothes he held out to her. She tried to ignore him the way Star Name did, and she concentrated on the dress. The soft suede clung to her wet skin and made it difficult to pull it on in a hurry. She kept her eyes lowered, avoiding his. She could almost feel his look. Her body was still smooth and without hair, but her breasts were beginning to swell and she was self-conscious about them. She scolded to hide her embarrassment, hopping around as she put on her moccasins.

"You're always leaving. All I ever say to you is good-bye. Why don't you stay with us?"

"I've been away from my band a long time. I have to go back."

Naduah felt the sting of tears. He was so hateful. Why did she feel as if a big hole was ripped from her life every time he left and a cold, bleak wind was whistling through the opening? He didn't care about her. She was only a child for him to tease. He probably had someone back on the desolate Staked Plains waiting for him, someone more beautiful even than Something Good.

She gave Wanderer her robe and he wrapped Weasel in it. He carried the child lightly in his arms, her head nestled in the hollow of his shoulder. With one hand poking out of the robe she played with the fringes decorating the yoke of his hunting shirt. Naduah shivered in the shade of the cedars. Her hair felt cold and clammy on her neck.

Night waited at the top of the bluff, and he whickered when he saw them. Naduah ran her hand down the arch of his neck while Wanderer set Weasel on the ground. Naduah's robe draped over her like a tent, and part of it trailed behind her in a royal train. Weasel let go of it long enough to tug at Wanderer's leggings, setting the tiny bells there to jingling. Barely coming to the tops of his thighs, she tilted her head way back to look up at him.

"What did you bring me from the raid to the Big Water?"

"A nice rattlesnake for a friend."

294

"But I don't want . . ." Weasel caught on. "You did not," she said, aggrieved.

Wanderer searched inside the pouches slung on Night's surcingle. He pulled out a length of deep blue velvet ribbon and handed it to her. Next he found a turnip-shaped top, carved of wood and painted bright red above the string's groove and navy blue below it. The groove itself was white. He had made her a string of twisted sinew for it. She knew immediately what it was, even though it was more sophisticated than the crudely carved ones her friends played with. She smiled up at him.

"Will you show me how to spin it with the string?" The ones she had seen were spun with a whip, thongs attached to a wooden handle.

"Maybe Star Name will show you. I have to talk to Naduah."

He gave Star Name her presents wrapped in calico. She unwrapped them carefully and smiled her thanks for the mirror and the box of vermillion. Naduah might pretend ignorance of what was between herself and Wanderer, but Star Name was aware of it. She could feel the tension vibrating like hummingbirds' wings around them. She helped Weasel tuck the robe up and free her hands to clutch her presents to her chest. Together they headed toward the village.

Wanderer passed the bundle of blanketing to Naduah. She opened it and held up the Mexican bridle, turning it so the silver ornaments glinted in the slanted sunlight. She felt as though there were a cord tightening around her throat and she could barely talk.

"It's beautiful." Wanderer had to lean closer to hear her.

"I thought of you when I saw it."

"Please don't go," she whispered.

"I have to. But I said I'd be back."

"How many years will it be this time?"

"Only two. Or maybe three."

"Forever."

"The year will be gone before you've had a chance to miss me."

"I need you to help me with Wind."

"You're doing a good job with Wind. You only need me to fight off the swarms of men that'll be around you soon. Will you wait for me?" She nodded, her eyes down. He put his hand lightly on her bright hair, and brushed a lock of it over her shoulder. He rested his fingers there for an instant. Then he turned. He swung effortlessly onto Night's back, and the pony pranced a little, eager to be free and traveling again.

"I have to hurry. Spaniard is waiting for me." He rode off without looking back.

Naduah sat on a boulder, her shoulder still tingling from the light touch of his fingers. She draped the delicate, intricately tooled bridle across her thighs, and put the blanketing across her back to keep out the wind. Then she crossed her arms on her knee, lowered her head onto them, and sobbed.

Outside the lodge, thunder grumbled threats of rain. Inside, Wanderer quietly watched his mother, Hawk Woman, direct his father's youngest wife as she cut out a pair of leggings. Finally, satisfied that they would be done right, she picked up a large tin bucket and started for the door.

"Where are you going?" he asked.

"There's white clay by the river," she said. "I'm going to dig some to clean your father's clothes."

"It'll rain soon. Do it later." He studied her eyes, unnaturally large and bright in her thin face.

"Then the clay will be too wet."

"It's too wet and heavy even now. Ask Visits Her Relatives or Spotted Pony to do it. That's why father married them."

"They're both busy. And they don't bother to find the purest clay." She disappeared through the doorway.

She was so stubborn, like a mule at times. With a soft sigh, Wanderer rose and followed her. He would go along with her as though he had nothing better to do. And he would casually help her carry the bucket, leaden with wet clay. Hawk Woman wouldn't even slow down, much less quit her endless labor. Iron Shirt, Wanderer's father, had married two other women to help her. But whenever she caught up with her own work, she went off to help a friend or relative.

Iron Shirt seemed oblivious to the fact that his first and favorite wife was ill, and had been weakening for over a year. Or perhaps he chose to ignore it, thinking that if he refused to recognize her illness it would leave. Iron Shirt was a shrewd judge of character, a master at manipulating men, yet he couldn't see that the mother of his only son was in pain and dying. Nor would he listen when Wanderer tried to tell him.

Hawk Woman never complained, never indicated that she was being consumed by some slow inner fire. She denied it when Wanderer questioned her. He dreaded returning to his father's band after each trip he took. He feared that she might have died while he was gone. And when he was home, he spent as much time as possible with her, knowing her days were limited. He reminisced with her about his childhood, told her of his adventures, joked with her as he had when he was young, and helped her as much as he could.

Now he towered over her as they walked through the village. She seemed to be shrinking with time, and he wondered how much of that could be explained by the fact that he had grown taller.

"Wanderer!" One of Iron Shirt's friends ran after them, dodging around an empty drying rack.

"Yes." Wanderer and his mother stopped in the middle of the street. All around them women and girls pulled strips of drying meat off the racks and covered equipment to protect it from the rain that was coming.

"My son has just returned from his vision quest. He wants you to help him paint his shield."

"Why doesn't he ask Iron Shirt or one of the medicine men? They're the ones who should do it." Painting sacred symbols on a young man's first shield was a very holy task, one usually reserved for the oldest and most respected warriors.

"He wants you. He says the wolf spoke to him, promised to help him. And no one has more powerful wolf medicine than you."

Wanderer stood a moment, thinking. Iron Shirt boasted about his son's powerful medicine and the fact that more and more men, even the older ones, were seeking his advice these days. But tension was growing between them. The young cub would someday challenge the leader of the pack, and they both knew it.

"I will help your son," said Wanderer. "I'll come to his lodge tonight. Tell him to cut cedar and sage for the fire."

"My heart is glad. I will have a pony and other presents for you." The man beamed at him, turned, and strode off to give his son the good news.

"The young men all admire you, my son. They tell stories about you when you're gone. They await your return each time you leave. A warrior with your reputation shouldn't be seen helping a woman with her chores."

Wanderer smiled down at his mother. "A warrior with my reputation can do anything he pleases."

❧ 34 ❧

Tears glittered in Cub's eyes. In his right hand he held a sharp rock. In his left he brandished a hefty chunk of firewood, a club to defend himself.

"No! I won't go. Grandfather, help me." But Old Owl sat hunched and sobbing in front of his lodge door. His robe was pulled entirely over his head in deep mourning. Cub had the desolate feeling that he was already dead and being grieved. The men of the band were gathering outside their lodges, muttering angrily. Women collected in their doorways, watching and crying.

David Faulkenberry sat back on his heels in the dust. He ran a hand through his thick, gray-streaked hair and squinted at the child in perplexity. Getting down on his level and reasoning with him obviously wasn't the answer. He stood, towering over the boy, who was big for his age. Cub took a better grip on his weapons and glared at him. He'd be a lot to handle, and taking him by force might set the braves off. The woman who thought she was John's mother was wailing in a lodge nearby. His aunt and his mother's friends were comforting her by howling even louder.

The women were getting on David's nerves. This was turning out to be harder than he had figured. Then a slender warrior shouldered his way through the men and stood behind Cub.

"Who's that?" David muttered from the corner of his mouth. Jim Shaw, the Delaware scout, answered, looking straight ahead and signing as he talked. He knew it was dangerous to hold conversations in a language the Comanche didn't understand. They were quick to expect treachery from Texans. He signed Faulkenberry's question and the answer Arrow Point gave.

"Bear Cub's father. He will tell the boy to go with us."

Arrow Point leaned down with tears in his own hard eyes, and spoke softly in his son's ear. Jim couldn't hear but could guess what he was saying. Arrow Point would tell Cub to go with the men and escape at the first opportunity. Shaw neglected to tell the white man that. There was no sense complicating things even more.

But even Arrow Point had a difficult time convincing Cub. The child spat out a flood of chopped, explosive Comanche. Shaw chuckled a little as he translated it.

"Bear Cub says he has a pony and friends and a family here. He likes the taste of raw liver and he likes to hunt. He will be a herder on the next raid. When he grows up, he will kill Texans. And he'll start with you if you don't leave him alone." Shaw grinned, his handsome face mocking. "Do you think his white family will want him?"

It was a good question, but there was no turning back now. It had taken David Faulkenberry six years to locate the boy, tracking down elusive reports from soldiers and hunters, trappers and traders. If it weren't for his robin's egg blue eyes Bear Cub would have looked like any other urchin in the village. His blond hair had been darkened with grease. This would not be a simple matter of exchanging the goods and horses David had brought and taking the boy with him.

"What do we do now?" David asked. He was glad he had brought Shaw along. The man deserved his reputation, even if he was arrogant.

"We wait. John Parker will be delivered to us."

"If they want to keep him so much, why are they letting me have him at all?" Shaw answered with a shrug. They weren't letting the white man have the child. They were only loaning him, or rather renting him, until the boy escaped. Old Owl was putting on quite an act, though. He was a foxy old man. Shaw was impressed.

But it wasn't an act. Under the stifling robe Old Owl was genuinely grieving, sobbing uncontrollably. He mourned the loss of his beloved grandnephew, and more. There was a sense of loss that he couldn't define. The lost honor at San Antonio and Plum Creek. The loss of his own youth. The loss of the past, and a feeling of impending doom. He could size people up well, and he knew that Cub wasn't likely to escape from this white man. From some other maybe, but not this one.

He saw the stubborness in Faulkenberry's face. Old Owl had stayed a leader of his band for thirty years because he could read faces. If he hadn't agreed to sell the boy, this one would have come back with soldiers. And there was no avoiding them. They would have hounded his people across the plains. They never gave up, the white man. Burn them out and they built again, in the same place. They didn't know when they were unsuited for a country. They stayed and changed the country to suit them.

They were like the warrior ants that held on, their pinchers grasping their enemies, even after their lumpy heads had been torn from their bodies. They were like ants in many ways, the white eyes. They were everywhere and into everything. One year there were none, and the next their nests were spreading. Soon they'd be moving into the People's lodges and making treaties giving them rights to the honey supply.

The white men were changing the very patterns of life. Old Owl knew, somewhere in his gut, that the People could no longer depend on their world to function as it had since before their ancestors could remember. White men disturbed the order of things, sent it off onto strange paths, until it might never find the main trail again.

There in the dark under the robe, Old Owl came to a fork in his own life's road. If the boy came back, he would rejoice, and do whatever he had to do to keep him. If he didn't, there was no longer any reason for Old Owl to avoid the white men. He knew he and all the People's warriors could no more turn them back than they could turn back a flood, or the wind.

He would start down their path and learn all he could about them. He didn't have many years left to him anyway, and as much as he disliked them, they interested him. As would any new species of animal that intruded into his world.

Maybe, in the end, he would find that Old Man Coyote had been playing a practical joke and would resolve it, as he usually did. But Old Owl doubted it. Old Owl was sure of only one thing. Bear Cub, Wee-lah, was one of the People. He would never be a white man again. It gave him a grim sort of satisfaction.

"God damn it to hell and the four quarters!" David felt the cactus spine drive into his foot like a hornet's sting. He swore again under his breath, determined that the boy wouldn't see him rattled. He had been stupid to take his boots off when he pulled his blankets over him for the night, but his feet hurt. They were swollen from weeks in the saddle hunting little John.

He stubbed his toe and swore again, but he didn't slow down. He could see the small shadow flitting ahead of him, running straight for the horses. Cub had already slashed the tether and was leaping for his spotted pony's back when David lunged and caught him by one foot. They both rolled, kicking and struggling, under the horse's fidgety hoofs. It took all David's strength to hold the boy. Jim Shaw came running to help.

"Now I know why they call the Comanche Snakes." David was breathing hard when they hauled Cub to his feet. David couldn't understand the abuse John showered on him, but he knew it must be imaginative. John was certainly that. David was at a loss to know how the boy had gotten the line off his wrists without disturbing the other end, tied to David's own. He was like a little snake, wriggling out of anything.

Faulkenberry and Shaw rode across the cold, flat Oklahoma plain toward Fort Gibson. A norther blew against the men's left sides, trying to shoulder them off the pale, narrow ruts of the trail. The sky was heavy and gray and immense. It hung so low it seemed as though it would smother them. As far as David could see, the prairie lay cold and brown and lifeless. Dead to the horizon.

Dead to the horizon and beyond. One rode for days, expecting some change. And it never came. It was a place that bred loneliness like slums bred cholera. *Let the Indians have it.* David rode sunk as deeply in his own thoughts as he was in the heavy buffalo coat one of the captains at the fort had loaned him. He had a piece of wool blanketing wrapped around his head and face, and strips wound around the palms of his hands. His red, chapped fingers were bare to grip the stiff reins. *It's the wind. It never quits. It's like a child whining and tugging at you day after day, year after year. No wonder the women go crazy here.* He'd be glad to get back to the hills and trees of east Texas.

Behind the two men, glaring from under his long, filthy, tangled hair like a rat cornered in a haystack, rode John Parker. He was trussed as tightly as a bale of cotton on a gulf coast wharf, and David and Jim kept carefully out of spitting range. If Comanche boys had the same sort of contests white boys did, Bear Cub must be a champion.

David almost grinned at the thought of Lucy Parker Usery's new husband being presented with Wee-lah Parker. Leaving him with them would be like dropping a hornet's nest into the middle of a Sunday school picnic. David thought perhaps he should take John to Elder James Parker first. If anyone could handle him, he could. It would be more charitable for Lucy, if not for the boy. James Parker didn't believe in sparing the rod and spoiling the child.

Little James Pratt Plummer had been ransomed too, and was waiting for them at the fort. He would go home with his cousin. Jamie was younger and easier to handle. Luther and his second wife could take him back. Elizabeth Kellog had been returned relatively unharmed just six months after her capture. And Rachel Plummer had died three years ago. Poor woman. David shook his head slightly at the memory of her.

Now only little Cynthia Ann was left of those stolen at Fort Parker over six years ago. Six years ago. Was it possible? She wasn't little Cynthia Ann anymore. He wondered briefly what she must be like now. And how much she must be suffering. Perhaps John could tell them something, if he could ever be persuaded to speak a Christian tongue. And in time he could be. Children were adaptable. He'd forget all that Comanche barbarism soon enough.

"So how did little John Parker get along with his Uncle James?" Abram Anglin lay back against the riverbank, drew his bony knees up to trap his body's warmth, and pulled his wool shirt tighter around him.

"You remember when that grizzly got into Old Man Lunn's cabin and rearranged the furniture and decorated the walls with the larder?"

"Yep."

"Well, just imagine how it would have looked if *two* bears had been in there, and you have the picture." David chuckled at the thought of it. "James figured to take the damages out of the boy's hide, but he must have grown several extra layers of it while he was with the Indians. He didn't even miss the little bit the willow switch took."

"He'll give those Pre-destrian, whattayacallit Baptists a run for their money. Think I'll drop in on Elder James next time I'm Anderson County way and see the show. By the way, Faulk, there's something I've been meaning to ask you. Why'd you go after them boys? They ain't yours."

"I don't know, Abram. Seems like I had to. To tie up the loose ends, if you know what I mean. It's like when you're driving a pack train and a load comes loose and pieces are flapping in the wind. You've just got to stop the whole train and see to it. I can understand James Parker's obsession with it. He won't rest until they're all accounted for. And the only one left is Cindy Ann."

"It's a big country to go looking for a little flappin' end." Anglin's dark eyes drooped and he wriggled to dislodge a root that was poking him in the back.

"Who are you telling, Abe? I rode over every spiny inch of it, seems like. But she's out there, and someone'll find her."

David's son Evan shivered as the wind curled an icy paw over the edge of the bank and touseled his hair, like a cat batting at a ball. High overhead, the same wind whimpered through the naked tops of the pecans, swaying black against the steel gray sky.

"Do you reckon Hunter'll be back soon with that canoe?" Evan muttered. "It's getting right cold.

David grunted noncommitally. The remains of their foundered raft lay awash nearby. They had made it to cross the river and round up their scattered horse herd while Hunter and Douthit went back to Fort Houston for a canoe.

Anglin dozed off, and the lullaby of his soft snores crooned David and Evan to sleep. It had been a long, hard day, and they were all tired.

In front of them, along the edge of the river, a seam of moccasin tracks stitched the water to the sand. The men weren't worried about them. The massacre at Parker's Fort seemed to have settled the score in this area as far as the Indians were concerned. The Caddo had blamed the whole thing on marauding Comanche, and there had been no retribution. The Caddo had been quiet and docile ever since.

The gunshots were so close they seemed to be going off inside David's head. His ears rang with them and his skull vibrated. He was running before he was fully awake.

"Come on, boys, it's time to go." He plunged into the river, an arrow driven deeply into his back. Abram felt a blow on his thigh under his powder horn. The horn had been shattered by a bullet and splinters from it were driven into his leg. He felt the sting of them just before his leg went numb. He threw his gun into the river and leaped after it, swimming with powerful strokes toward the opposite shore. David was ahead of him, but tiring. The water faded from red to pink behind him, curls of blood swirling gracefully in the eddies of his passing.

Anglin swam alongside, turned David on his back, and grabbed him around the neck. Stroking with his right arm, he pulled him toward the far bank. The lead raindrops of rifle fire sent up small geysers around them.

When they reached the far shore, Abram felt the sting and burn of arrows slicing through his arm and burrowing in his leg. He hauled David into the cover of the brush, and they lay, panting, and gathered strength to go on. The arrow had punctured David's lung from behind, and his breath came in whistling gasps.

"Abram, get away. Bring help. I'll hide here someplace." They both knew Faulkenberry wouldn't be alive by the time Anglin could run to Fort Houston and back, but neither of them mentioned it. Anglin broke off the arrow in his calf and quickly tied pieces of his shirt around that wound and the hole in his upper arm. He held one end of the bandage in his teeth while he knotted it. He lifted David and helped him further into the thick undergrowth before starting down the river toward Fort Houston.

While David and Abram escaped, Evan held the Caddo's attention on shore. He took cover behind the trees while the renegades ghosted through the brush, circling him like hawks gliding lazily in for the kill.

The relief party found David dead the next morning. He had pulled grass to make a soft bed near a clear pool of water, and he had laid himself down on it to die. They never found more of Evan than his tracks leading to the river. But the Caddo talked of him for years, until the story became one of their legends.

He had fought like a cornered bear, they said, killing two of the renegades and wounding a third. One of the Indians crushed the back of his skull with a hatchet, and four of them held him down while a fifth scalped him. Still he found the strength to throw them off, dive into the river, and swim to midstream before sinking.

David Faulkenberry had many friends around Fort Houston, and his funeral was a large one, though simple. Most of the Parker clan stood at the edge of the hole and watched the yellow pine box lowered. John Parker, scrubbed and brushed, dressed in painful shoes and a tight collar, stood with them. Cub's legs burned under the scratchy black wool pants that had belonged to an older cousin. His calves and upper thighs and buttocks were crisscrossed with red welts from a willow switch.

Behind Cub's stony gaze, fury raged. They had cut his hair short, tying him up to do it. Now he looked like a girl in mourning. And his uncle had beaten him. Never in his six years with the People had anyone struck him. He had never seen a child, other than a slave, more than lightly slapped to get his attention.

John's pony had been taken from him when he tried to escape again. And he wasn't allowed near the horses. They were kept hobbled with a steel contraption for which only Elder James had the key. Without a horse he was nothing, not a man and hardly a person. He had to ask permission for anything he wanted to do, and it was usually denied. He was forced to sit each day and listen to his uncle read from the big book. He read words Cub couldn't understand and refused to learn.

He got up each dreary morning to face the same set of hills and trees, the same smelly yard, beaten bare and filthy with the dung of the farm animals. He felt as though he were wading in the years' accumulation of filth and being slowly poisoned by it. He had to go to bed when the sun did. And there were no dances or all-night talks to eavesdrop on. Other white people danced, but Elder James Parker did not believe in it. That's what he said. He didn't believe in it. Not to believe in dancing was like not believing in sunlight.

Never would Cub ride at the head of that wonderful, laughing, jingling, clattering procession as the village moved. Never would he stage mock battles with his friends and hunt small game as they traveled. Never would he feel the wind blowing his hair as he raced for the horizon. Worst of all, the white eyes expected him to grub in the dirt like a Tuhkanay woman, a Wichita. They imperiled his soul by forcing him to desecrate Mother Earth. He could almost hear her cry out in pain as the hoe and iron plow blade bit into her, ripping her hair, the grass.

Fighting back his tears, John stood absolutely silent and as straight as a lodge pole beside his uncle. He looked at his mother, her head bowed, on the other side of the grave. Next to her stood the stranger who was his stepfather. Of them all, he cared only for his mother. Their first meeting had been uncomfortable for him. She had cried and thrown her arms around him while he stood stiff and unresponding. But his heart went out to her, even if he couldn't show it.

He would stay for a while, until his hair grew out. And he would try to get to know her. But as soon as he was old enough to make it all the way back to Old Owl's band on his own, he would leave. And he would go on his vision quest and receive his new name and become a warrior. And someday he would ride back here at the head of a war party and kill the man who stood next to him.

The Caddo had saved him the trouble of doing the same to the one who had ransomed him. As David Faulkenberry's casket was lowered and Cub's great-uncle, Daniel, stepped forward to read the burial service, there was another small revenge that Cub couldn't appreciate. It would have galled David to know that one of the Parker Baptists was mumbling prayers over him.

Cub knew that word of his ransom would find its way to his sister. Old Owl had promised to tell her and to warn her and her family to take care that she not be caught. So he stood, forcing himself to remain absolutely still. He pretended to be a wolf keeping vigil on a mountain crest, looking out over his prey. And like the wolf, he would wait patiently.

A stranger passing through stood among the mourners. He was watching silently and tasting Texas, getting a feel for it and its people. Samuel Hamilton Walker was on his way to Bastrop to join Jack Hays' rangers. After he'd spent five years fighting Seminoles in the mosquito soup of the Florida swamps, his home in Maryland had been too tame. He'd heard that the Republic of Texas was the place for excitement and opportunity, so he'd come.

As he looked around him, Sam smiled a little. *They do grow them big in Texas.* There must have been a huge seine across the Sabine and Red rivers, sifting out men under a certain size and sending them back east. Or maybe they seemed big because they talked big. Or they just looked bigger under all that leather and fringe and those outlandish hats. *Nothing like a pair of bear's ears on a cap to add inches to a man's heighth and pounds to his courage.*

Sam was a small man, and slender. He had a shy smile and wispy, curly brown hair. There was nothing remarkable about him, although women noticed him immediately. Maybe that was because he didn't speak much. And men who didn't speak much often were fascinating. Especially when their eyes were as eloquent as Sam's. Quietly, Sam turned and threaded his way politely through the groups of people. A man killed by Indians. This looked like the place for him, all right. He mounted his wiry, long-legged gray gelding and rode slowly away.

✤ 35 ✤

It was the spring of 1843. A year and a half had passed since Old Owl had come looking for Naduah when his band arrived to spend the winter with the Wasps. She had known what he had come for as soon as he entered the lodge. He had sat with her and her family around their evening fire and told them that Cub had been ransomed and had not returned. Tears had splashed over the red rims of his yellowed eyes. They had rolled unheeded along the craggy bluff of his nose, and in and out of the crevices in his face. Finally they hung, poised, on the sharp edge of his jawbone before falling off.

Spring had come, then summer. In the fall, after the big hunt, Naduah began looking forward to seeing Cub in the winter encampment again. Because she saw him so rarely, it was hard to think of him as truly gone, almost dead. She wanted to tell him many things. She wanted to see if she could still beat him at footraces, and to measure which of them was taller. She wanted to watch him swagger through the village with his friends, leaving trouble strewn behind him in his path.

She kept busy that winter, helping at home and watching Deep Water court Star Name. Sometimes it was questionable as to who was courting whom. Time had softened and blurred the smallpox scars some, and his large, sad dark eyes overshadowed them anyway. But Deep Water was still shy around Star Name. Which was probably one reason why she was determined to have him.

"He's not vain like those others. He doesn't worry about his looks or strut and gobble like a turkey cock."

"You don't have to defend him to me, Sister," said Naduah. "I like him. He'll be one of the finest warriors some day."

"He already is. He doesn't waste his time staring at himself in the mirror and begging hair from the women."

"Remember the winter when Skinny And Ugly was parading around with his braids dragging the ground?" Naduah mimicked him. She stalked regally, then turned slowly, holding her head carefully on her rigid neck. As she turned, she kicked at the pretend braids to position them behind her.

"Only they weren't his braids." Star Name was doubled over with laughter.

"And when he got up to dance, they fell into the fire." Naduah held her nose. "They smelled worse than the time Weasel tried to light a fire with chicken feathers."

"He must have taken hair from every pony's tail in the herd. And

when he bent over to try to pull the braids out of the flames, Cub set
fire to the back of his breechclout." Star Name had to sit down to
keep from falling.

"He's never danced better." And Naduah joined Star Name on
the ground.

"Then Pahayuca pushed him down and sat on him to smother the
blaze. Can you imagine being sat on by Pahayuca?" By now the two
of them were helpless with laughter. They rocked back and forth in
spasms of it, and Naduah pounded the ground in front of her with
her moccasin. Finally they lay out on their backs, using their robes to
keep them from the cold earth. Star Name rolled over on her side
and propped her head on her hand.

"Which of the boys do you like best?"

"None of them."

"The men, then. Which of them do you like?"

Naduah laced her fingers behind her head and pretended to study
the tree branches above her. "I haven't thought about it."

"Yes, you have. You're waiting for Wanderer."

"I am not!" Naduah jerked up to a sitting position.

"There's nothing wrong with that. He's worth waiting for."

"I'm not waiting for anybody. And he certainly isn't waiting for
me. He's probably married already."

"Did he say when he'd be back?"

"Two years, or three."

"Then he still has time. If he said he'd be here, he will," said Star
Name. "You can be sure of that."

"I can be sure he has no interest in me. A child. A nobody."

Star Name smiled at her as she got up and threw off her robe.
"Enough chatter. I'll race you to the river. Loser cooks dinner for
everyone."

As winter passed, the sky turned from gray to blue and a pale
green fuzz covered the brown of the plains. The scent of flowers
saturated the air. Naduah lay awake each night breathing the fragrance. As the earth and the People celebrated spring, as the days
became longer and warmer and the flowers turned the hills into an
ocean of brilliant color, Naduah became more miserable.

While her family slept peacefully, she tossed and turned, searching for the cause of her misery. But it lay, tiny and hard, buried deep
inside her. It was like the root of a plant that has died back, leaving
no trace of itself on the hard winter earth. If she could find it and
identify it the way Medicine Woman found hidden roots in winter,
maybe she could help herself.

As she worked each day amid the laughter and chatter that surrounded her, she pulled deeper and deeper into herself. To her, the women sounded like the magpies and jays and wrens that rioted in the treetops all day long. Star Name was preoccupied with thoughts of Deep Water and walked around humming. Her joy only intensified Naduah's vague longings.

She couldn't hide her feelings. There was very little hidden in the warm lodge. One morning as they were all stretching and yawning and getting ready to bathe at the river, Takes Down spoke casually. As she talked, she went on shaking out her clothes and moccasins to make sure no little creatures had moved into them during the night.

"Has your time come, Daughter? Are you bleeding?"

"No, *Pia*. It's only been ten days since I stopped." And she knew that Takes Down knew it. Naduah had begun her monthly bleeding a year before. Once the initial excitement was over, she resented it. The men wouldn't let her ride or train their horses while she bled. It was very bad medicine. She had to stay away from everyone, and fast for four days. She couldn't wash her face or she would wrinkle sooner. She couldn't comb her hair or she'd turn gray. Now she almost wished she were bleeding. At least she wouldn't have to talk to anyone. Medicine Woman spoke up.

"Do you feel sick, Granddaughter? Does something hurt you?"

"No." She started to cry, and cried harder because there was no reason to cry. "Just leave me alone." She tried to dart out of the lodge, but Takes Down's round body blocked the doorway. She caught her daughter in her arms and held her. Naduah tugged and pushed to get away, but couldn't.

"What's wrong, little one?" said Medicine Woman.

"I wish I were dead."

"Granddaughter, never wish that."

"I do."

"Remember what Sunrise told you. Get up each morning and listen. Look around you. Give thanks for the sunlight and for your own body and spirit. For your family and food and the joy of living."

"Those things don't make me happy. I'm tired of living."

"Then there is a lack in yourself. Look carefully around you. Study the beauty of the world. We don't need you here today. Go work with Sunrise's new pony. And when you come back this evening, tell me the three most beautiful things you saw or heard or smelled or touched. Share them with me. Describe them so I can see them with these sightless eyes. Will you do that for me?"

Naduah was suddenly ashamed. "Yes, Grandmother." She hugged her mother, her arms almost reaching around Takes Down now. Then she went to Medicine Woman's bed and, kneeling down, held her close.

* * *

Water dripped from Naduah and from Sunrise's new sorrel pinto as she rode him bare-backed out of the river and onto the slightly sloping bank. He stood straddle-legged on the coarse red sand, trembling and snorting while she stroked his neck and rubbed the area in front of his ears. She often broke in a pony by mounting him in the water, where he couldn't run or buck as much. But she used that method only in warm weather, because she was always thoroughly soaked when she finished.

Gradually the pony calmed as she crooned to him, leaning over to put her mouth close to his ear. He flicked it, shook his head and sidestepped, but she clung to him. Her lean, strong thighs sensed his moves before he made them. Her long blond hair was braided to keep it out of her eyes, and she wore only moccasins and an old dress.

The water felt good, a cool layer between her skin and the heat of the sun's rays. When she was sure the pony had quieted and wouldn't bolt, she reached up and untied her braids. She shook her head so the hair would fall free and begin to dry in the heat.

"*Hi tai*, hello, woman friend." She looked up, startled by the familiar voice. He hadn't changed much in the past year and a half. His features were a little more angular, chiseled closer to the bone by responsibility. His eyes seemed deeper and more luminous, with golden glints in them, like phosphorescence in the black waters of underground pools. He rode toward her, Night picking his way delicately over the tumbled, polished rocks at the edge of the narrow beach.

"Hello, Wanderer." Naduah stopped in confusion. She was suddenly aware that her skirt was hiked to the tops of her thighs, and that she had become a woman since last she had seen him. The wet, thin suede dress clung to her body. With his leg almost touching hers he sat on Night, studying her in that way of his. *Enough*, she thought. *I'm no longer a child for you to tease and embarrass.* She lifted her chin slightly and stared steadily back at him, waiting for him to finish his inspection of her. Because that was obviously what he was doing. But though she maintained her dignity, she couldn't bring herself to ask him if he approved of the changes the years had made in her.

In silence they turned and headed at a walk toward the village on the terrace bordering the deep, rapid river. The sorrel followed docilely alongside Night, and Wanderer and Naduah rode almost knee to knee. The Wasps' lodges stood among the white oak and overcups, the elms and hackberry trees along Sac-con-eber, the Little Wichita River. They could hear the laughter of children as they dove and splashed and threw sticks for their dogs to fetch.

"I remember when we used to do that," said Naduah, breaking the silence. "Star Name and the dead Arrow Maker's granddaughter and I."

"Knowing Star Name, I suppose she still plays like that."

Naduah grinned at him. "She never changes much. Not inside. But now she wants to marry, you know."

"No, I didn't know. My sources of information aren't that good. And we just arrived, Spaniard, Big Bow, and I."

"Big Bow?"

"The Kiowa. He's running from an irate husband again. They've gone ahead with the ponies and the packs. I came to find you. One of the children said you'd be here. Tell me the gossip. Who's the unfortunate warrior that Star Name has picked out?"

"What do you mean, unfortunate?" Naduah bristled a little, and Wanderer laughed, raising his arm as though to deflect a blow.

"I mean she's such a strong-willed—" he hesitated ever so slightly "—woman. She'll be a lot for a man to handle."

"I like her that way."

"I like her kind of woman too, but not many men do." He stared at her solemnly. "Whom does she want to marry?"

"Deep Water. He's a very brave warrior, but he doesn't have enough horses to buy her. She said she was tired of waiting for him to steal them, so she's gone off on a raid with him. I think she intends to steal ponies to buy herself for him." Wanderer laughed, and Naduah looked at him with delight. She had missed that laugh, rare as it was even when he was around. *Tell me the three most beautiful things you saw or heard or touched today. That's easy, Grandmother. Wanderer. Wanderer. Wanderer.*

"How is Medicine Woman?" Naduah jumped a little at his question. Could he read minds too? She wouldn't be surprised.

"She's well enough, although I think she's getting weaker and won't admit it. It's amazing how she gets around. People who don't know her often don't realize she's blind."

"And Pahayuca?"

"He doesn't change either, unless he's gained a few more pounds. On Pahayuca it's hard to tell. Wind had a foal, a colt. I'll show him to you. I bred her with one of Pahayuca's best stallions.

"And Old Owl had to sell Cub back to the white people. They took him away over a year ago and he hasn't returned. Some people say Cub turned white again, but Old Owl swears that won't happen."

"What do you think?"

"I agree with Old Owl."

"Has anyone tried to buy you back, Naduah?" It was a painful question, but Wanderer felt he had to ask it.

"No, but some traders were here last month and stared at me. They were probably just surprised to see me. I suppose I stand out here."

"If traders come, keep out of sight." The intensity in his voice startled her.

"Wanderer, it's been seven years. They've forgotten all about me back there."

"They hadn't forgotten Cub. And have you forgotten them?"

"Yes." She didn't even stop to think about it. "I'm one of the People. I would die if I were taken away, like a fish dies when it's thrown up on shore."

He didn't answer her, and they rode in silence for a few moments. Finally Naduah asked what was on her mind.

"Will you be staying long this time?"

"That depends."

"On what?"

"On how long it takes me to do what I came here to do."

"What did you come here to do?"

"Find a wife."

Naduah flinched. *Stupid! So you thought you were finally a woman. You're still a child to him. You always will be.* She tried to keep her voice light.

"Do you have someone in mind?"

"Yes."

"Wanderer!" Pahayuca and Buffalo Piss and several of the men galloped toward them through the village, waving their robes over their heads. War ponies reared at their tethers and neighed in fright and dogs scattered in front of them. Naduah spoke fast.

"I suppose I won't see you again until you leave and come to say good-bye as usual."

He only had time to grin at her before he was surrounded and herded good-naturedly toward the council lodge. She watched him go, then slid off the sorrel and led him toward her tent. As she walked through the camp, she noticed the slight change that had come over it. The unmarried women were suddenly interested in their appearance. Several of them were combing and rebraiding their hair. And mirrors and paint were brought outside where the light was better. There was more tittering and more bustling as others tried to show how industrious they were.

They're disgusting. Like dogs groveling for meat scraps. If Wanderer wants one of them, he deserves her. Naduah's hair had almost dried in the sere air of the plains, and she tossed her head to shake stray wisps of it out of her eyes. It fell in gentle ripples to her waist, like a field of pale wheat ruffled by a light breeze. As she strode along, the rounded curves of her body flowed smoothly under her thin dress.

311

But inside, she was empty of everything but despair. It was finally going to happen. She had been dreading it for years. As she went looking for Medicine Woman for consolation, she remembered her grandmother's words the first time Wanderer had left, seven long years ago. "He belongs to all of us." Now, even worse, he would belong to only one.

Naduah sat disconsolately in front of her lodge, watching the evening fire die down. She had pulled her knees up in front of her, laid her arms across them, and rested her chin on her forearms as she waited to cover the fire with ashes for the night. She was using the chore as an excuse not to go to the dance, not to see the women flirting with Wanderer. The full moon was so bright she could see colors in the pretty quartz pebbles that littered the ground. From another part of the village she could hear the rise and fall of drumming and singing, carried on a fitful breeze.

The music had been going on for hours. She stood and looked toward where the drumming was coming from. The lodges glowed softly, like huge, fat candles set out under the canopy of trees. Overhead, the moon winked at her through the clouds, as though trying to cheer her up.

A pony trotted from among the lodges and headed in her direction. It was Night. As usual, Wanderer leaped off before Night had stopped completely. Wanderer dropped to the ground as gracefully and as casually as a mountain cat. The light from the fire and the moon gleamed on the rippling muscles under his smooth, chestnut skin.

As he turned to throw the reins over Night's back, Naduah realized that he was naked. He wore moccasins and a breechclout, of course, but he was naked. The straight lines of the breechclout only emphasized and framed his long, lean body. It was the first time she had ever stared at a man that way. And it frightened her. But he fascinated her too. She couldn't take her eyes off the flowing curves of his legs, the power of his haunches, and the straight line of his back. He wasn't handsome. He was beautiful. He was like a wild animal perfectly built for the life he led. And he was as unconscious of his beauty as a wolf or a panther. She took a deep breath, clenched her fists at her sides, and spoke.

"Sunrise isn't here. He went to the dance."

"I know. I saw him. I came to find out why you aren't dancing."

"I told Takes Down The Lodge I would cover the fire for her."

"How many hours does it take you to cover the fire?" He was mocking her again. Why didn't he find his wife and go back to the Staked Plains and leave her in peace? Peace, she thought miserably. Was it possible to mourn someone who still lived?

"Come. You can ride with me." He waited while she covered the fire.

"I'll walk." As she started toward the sound of the drums, she heard Night trotting up behind her. A strong pair of hands gripped her, and almost as easily as when she had been a child, Wanderer lifted her up in front of him. His arms were like gentle vises around her and she knew there was no point in struggling. He thought of her as a child still, and there was no way she could prove him wrong. He would call her sister, and marry someone else, and go away and never come back.

She sat stiffly until they came to the ring of dancers just beginning to sway to the slow drumbeat. Overhead soared the black sky, brilliant with stars. The leaping light from the fire danced counterpoint to the slow drums. Naduah dismounted and joined the watchers, humming the low chant of the love dance along with the other singers.

The circle of women faced outward, rising from their heels to their toes in time with the music. Then they glided to the left, holding their arms out and choosing a partner from among the men. Wanderer didn't wait to be chosen. He put his hands on Naduah's shoulders. His touch sent chills down her spine and spawned a slight churning sensation somewhere below her stomach. It was the first time she had ever danced with him.

For an hour they swayed in the moonlight, circling, rising, and gliding to the hypnotic beat of the drums. The beat surrounded them and permeated them like the heartbeat of Mother Earth. Naduah danced with her hands on his hard shoulders and her eyes closed. Perhaps he was only being kind to her, to his little sister. But if she should die right then, this night would have made life worthwhile.

"I don't want to get married." Naduah sat stubbornly against the bedstead. Her arms were crossed over her chest, and her mouth was set in the stubborn Parker line.

"Naduah, he is a chief. He will give you many things. It's an honor for him to ask you." Sunrise had given up and Medicine Woman was trying to talk reason into her granddaughter's head.

Naduah didn't want Wanderer to marry anyone else. But the thought of marrying him herself terrified her. It had taken her years to reach the point where she was comfortable with him as a friend, an older brother. Now they expected her to rush into marriage with him. It was preposterous. Besides, she couldn't believe he really wanted her. She'd convinced herself otherwise.

"He'll take me away from you. He'll always be in council or on the war trail. He'll take six other wives and have no time for me."

313

"You'll be lucky if he has six wives," put in Takes Down. "There'll be less work for you to do."

"I won't marry him."

It was unheard of. Sunrise shook his head in puzzlement. She couldn't refuse. He had made an agreement with Wanderer seven years ago. But Sunrise had learned from past experience that Naduah was as impossible to intimidate as a boy. He tried one more time to persuade her.

"We'll visit you often."

"Will you move to the Staked Plains with me?"

"No. Our place is here with my mother and her brother."

"And so is mine. How can I leave you and *Pia* and *Kaku*? Who will help Takes Down with all the work around here? Who will gather herbs for Grandmother? Star Name and Something Good and little Weasel and all my friends are here. I don't know anyone among the Quohadi. I'll be lonely. I won't go."

Sunrise sighed and went out into the night. If Wanderer wanted her, he would have to persuade her himself.

Naduah awoke with a start when a hand clamped tightly over her mouth. She stared up at the shadowy face above her, straining to see in the dark lodge. He slowly lifted his hand, and she looked around. As her eyes adjusted to the dim light from the banked fire and the moon shining through the leather wall, she recognized Wanderer.

"There's no one here." His voice was low and soft in the darkness. She lay, tense and afraid. She had heard the women talk of this, of what men did when they sneaked into a lover's tent at night. But she couldn't imagine it. The thought of him entering her, invading her, was terrifying. Yet she dared not cry out. She'd never escape the gossip and the shame.

She wore nothing under the thin blanket, and she felt helpless and vulnerable. Wanderer laid his fingers lightly on her lips and pulled back the cover. She shivered at his touch, and her heart tried to beat its way out of her chest. He placed a hand over it, cupping the full, round breast, and circled the nipple gently. She felt dizzy as his hands moved down her body, stroking and caressing, sending ripples of pleasure coursing through her. As his fingers wound into the golden hair between her legs, she cringed and whimpered, thrashing her head from side to side in protest.

He had been sitting on the edge of the bed. Now he lay down beside her, his long body warm against her. He half covered her while his hand rested between her legs. They both lay still a few moments until she calmed a little. Then he spread her thighs slightly. She couldn't stop him. Her muscles had ceased to respond to her will.

She felt his fingers probing, and there was fire in the tips of them. Waves of heat flared through her groin, and she felt a silky wetness there. He dipped into the source of it and spread it upward through her soft, swollen ravine. His fingers trailed fire in their wake until he touched the tiny mound. Her back arched and she threw her arm across her mouth to keep from screaming. Every nerve in her body seemed to meet in that nub. Her whole being was centered there.

As he circled and stroked it gently with his fingers, the intensity built. She whimpered again, tossed by the waves of ecstacy washing over her. They left her arched and straining, for more and for an end to it. The crest came in pure, undistilled sensuality. When it ebbed, she lay there panting, drained and helpless. Her body still pulsed with a warm radiance that spread from her groin to her toes and her fingertips.

She turned to look at Wanderer, whose face lay so close to hers. He was grinning. He was grinning like a wicked boy who's just pulled off a wonderful joke. She smiled back at him and, reaching out, touched his cheek with her fingertips. Remembering one thing from her past, she pulled his face toward her and kissed him lightly on his curved, sensual mouth.

He pulled away and frowned a little, as though tasting the kiss. Then he kissed her back. He tickled her gently until she rolled over and wrapped her arms around him to make him stop. They lay entwined, their hearts beating in unison. Finally he spoke.

"Will you come with me?"

"On two conditions."

"What?"

"That you let me raid with you."

"If you want."

"And you do that again sometime."

"We'll do it often. And we aren't even finished this time."

As she pressed against him she felt him move, his cock hard and insistent. She buried her face in the hollow of his neck and shoulder.

"Wanderer, I'm afraid."

"Don't be. We'll go slowly. I'll only cause you pain once, then never again."

Two days later, not long after dawn, Naduah hid in her father's lodge with her family. They went about preparing and eating breakfast as though nothing out of the ordinary were happening. But Naduah could hear the stacatto "Li-li-li-li" of the women. The cry swelled as more of them joined in along Wanderer's route. He was coming with horses to buy Naduah from Sunrise, but there was no call for so much commotion. Men were shouting raucous, good-natured taunts, and the children were cheering. How many horses was he bringing? Sunrise probably knew, but he wasn't talking. His face was a maddening, noncommittal blank.

The noise outside grew into an uproar. Naduah felt her face and neck heat up. She was blushing, and she was grateful that she was expected to stay out of sight. Then she heard the thud of hooves. She tried to estimate how many ponies there were by the sound. The blush deepened. The three women, Naduah, Takes Down The Lodge, and Medicine Woman, looked at each other. Sunrise stared at the ground to hide a tiny, secret smile.

"A hundred horses," said Medicine Woman matter-of-factly. Her ears were the sharpest.

"There can't be. No one pays that many horses for a woman." Naduah would have estimated that many animals too, but she couldn't believe it.

"Wanderer does," said Takes Down.

Unable to resist, Naduah pulled back the edge of the heavy hide door and peeked through the narrow crack. Outside, it looked as though a river of ponies had overflowed and flooded the village. They jostled in the spaces between the lodges. There were stock-inged bays and toasted sorrels, blue roans, horses the color of rust, fox-colored ponies, steel grays, and gaudy paints.

Naduah maneuvered the crack in the doorway until Wanderer filled the space. She shifted her position slowly to follow him as he rode toward the lodge. Her stomach churned with excitement, but also from pride and embarrassment and longing. He was beautiful, dressed in his finest clothes. But in her mind's eye she saw him as he looked best. Naked.

While Spaniard brought up the stragglers, Wanderer piled the pony he led with presents and tied her apart from the others. The horse was the best of the herd, a young coyote dun with black legs and tail and a black stripe down her backbone. She was a gift for Naduah.

Then, without a word, Wanderer turned and rode away with Spaniard. Sunrise waited an appropriate time, and then a little longer, before going outside. He had a wicked sense of humor that was so subtle many people didn't know it existed. It would be like him to let the village think he was spurning Wanderer's incredible offer.

Finally, when Naduah thought she couldn't wait a second longer, he beckoned to her. Together they went out to collect the horses. They led them to the pasture where their own herd grazed, and turned them loose. Sunrise had accepted Wanderer as a son-in-law.

That evening, as the sun was setting, Wanderer came for his bride. They walked side by side to the guest tent where he was staying. She stretched her long legs to keep up with his. It seemed as though the pounding of her heart must be loud enough to be heard over the muted noises of the camp. Activity had stopped as people watched them pass, and Naduah knew she was blushing again. She was relieved when they stepped inside the lodge and the hide cover dropped closed after them, shutting out the eyes.

Before Wanderer led her to the bed of thick, soft buffalo robes, he gave her the silver mirror that he had carried with him for seven years. He stared at her intensely as she held it in her hands, turning it over to trace the raised design with her fingers. It was the same kind of inspection he had given it in the yard of a ravaged fort so long ago. He searched her face to see if the mirror brought back memories of the day his people had killed hers. She looked up at him and smiled her thanks, and the tension drained from him.

She came to him silently, and he put his arms around her. She stood, caressing the small of his back and his firm haunches. She rested her cheek against his chest as he held her. They swayed there slightly, eyes closed, lost in the feel of each other. Filled with the comfort and the joy of each other's presence.

FALL

"On the plains the senses expand and man begins to realize the magnificence of being."

Col. Richard Irving Dodge,
Hunting Grounds of the West

❧ 36 ❧

The plateau loomed in the distance like a vast, flat-topped fortress. It brooded dark and solid against the wide, blue, cloudless sky. It was a citadel two hundred miles long, one hundred and fifty miles across, and eight hundred feet high. Its bulwarks seemed to soar straight up from the undulating swells of the plains around them. Vertical outcroppings of red sandstone looked like flying buttresses braced against the cliffs. Along the plateau's rim, the gypsum cap rock gleamed like burnished silver in the flaring sun.

It was a desert, or so the white men believed. A trackless waste. Nothing grew there but grass. The only water was alkalai, poisoned by mineral salts. And there was damned little of it, bad as it was. The three forks of the Red River meandered through the plateau, their single source lost in a torturous maze of ravines and gullies and plummeting gorges. No one had ever mapped the plateau, and no white man had ever tracked the Red River to its original spring. It was considered deadly country and few dared go there.

In 1541, the Pueblo Indian, El Turco, led Francisco Vasquez de Coronado and three hundred of his soldiers on a chase across the top of it. El Turco would probably have led them to hell to get them away from his own helpless village. And there must have been some in the expedition who thought that was precisely where he was taking them. *A la cola del mundo*, to the tail end of the world, as they put it. But they followed him doggedly. They couldn't resist the promises of a land where King Tatarrax ate off golden plates and listened to the music of gold bells hanging in the trees. By the time the soldiers were well into the high plain, they would have been grateful just for the trees, without the bells.

Mile after mile the Spaniards and their six hundred Pueblo slaves toiled across the high plateau. It was as level as a griddle and almost as hot. There was nothing, no trees, no boulders, no ridges or mountains, to measure their progress. There were ravines, but they were gouged into the surface of the plain, and invisible until one's horse teetered on the edge. The air shimmered and trembled incessantly. A raven in the distance would stretch and distort until it looked like a man approaching, giving the land the look of a place inhabited by phantoms. Groves and pools shimmered and beckoned, then vanished.

The summer sun heated the men's heavy metal helmets and curaisses until they were too hot to touch, much less wear. The

321

soldiers baked inside them. Men born and bred in the harsh, hot hills of Salamanca and Extremadura began to sway in their saddles. If they took off their helmets, spots would heat up on the crowns of their heads, as though a magnifying glass were being held there. Dizziness swept them from their saddles. Many fell with a clatter, losing their lances and trumpet-shaped arquebuses in the grass.

Sometimes they were dragged, their feet caught in the solid brass stirrups they wore like shoes. Many of them suffered dysentery, made worse by the brackish water. The sun blazed through their eyelids when they closed them, and they had seen no shade for days. The grass, only inches high and burned a dull yellow color, closed in after their horses passed. Almost a thousand men, their mounts and pack animals left no more mark of their passing, to the untrained eye, than a ship leaves on the ocean. So they cut slender saplings from among the few stunted cottonwoods and willows along the dry creek beds. And they staked their route with the poles. Some of them stood, years later, stark and mysterious sentinels against the sky. In time the plateau became known as El Llano Estacado, the Staked Plains.

Naduah had watched it grow for three days as their small party meandered across the rolling prairie. Now it soared over them, filling the empty sky. A patchy growth of stunted red cedars clung to its vertical face. Naduah tilted her head far back as she craned to see the top of it.

"We'll never be able to climb up there."

Wanderer grinned at her over his shoulder.

"You know better than that. Do you think I brought you all this way just to look at it?"

"How will we reach the top, Wanderer?" yelled Star Name from behind them. "Pull ourselves up the sides by the cedars?"

"There's another way," said Wanderer. "Be patient."

Naduah searched for a path upward and could find none.

Wanderer led them around the base of the plateau, picking his way through the labyrinth of ravines. Finally they all stood at the edge of the deepest one. Two hundred feet below them they could see the roiling water of the south fork of the Red River as it roared and churned out of the plain. Wanderer pointed out their route.

"We'll go down to the river bottom, then follow along the cliff wall or splash through the shallows. We'll follow it upstream onto the plain. It's the easiest path."

The easiest path. Naduah thought she'd rather haul herself up the side using the cedars. Wanderer disappeared over the edge of the deep gorge that pinched the river at its narrow base. Naduah followed him. As Wind braced and slid down the winding trail,

Naduah felt the paws of her new mountain lion skin brush against her legs. The hide was draped across Wind's hindquarters like the brocaded quilts of the Spanish *caballeros*. When the People stole the Spaniards' ponies they took more than just livestock. They lifted the whole horse culture.

The lion skin had been expensive. They had almost bought it with their lives. Naduah thought about how they had killed the lion, she and Wanderer. It gave her something to think about beside the high, narrow path she was following. The trail was so steep it would be easy to pitch forward and plummet to the bottom. She could imagine bouncing on the rocks below. *The lion skin, and the look in Wanderer's eyes when he pulled my arrow from its heart, think about that.*

It had happened several days before, when the party stopped to rest after a long, hot ride that had started before dawn. It was late afternoon, and they were all lying propped against their saddles in the tall grass under a huge, spreading cottonwood. They had found a deep pool and bathed, then they watched, mesmerized, as the clear, shallow stream raced and chortled by them. The high boulder-strewn bluffs around them were covered with round, dark green cedars and scrub oaks. There were pale green feathery mesquites, plum and grape, raspberry and currant bushes, and various kinds of cactus.

Naduah lay on her back watching the tiny vultures circle and glide on the air currents at the cliff's edge high above them. She felt lazy and at peace. She wished, in a way, that this trip could go on forever, traveling at their leisure across the plains, laughing and gambling at night around the fire. Telling stories with her friends. And loving Wanderer under their sleeping robes until they were both spent, then lying wrapped around each other until dawn.

"Do you want to hunt a deer for dinner?" Wanderer had stood looking down at her.

"Of course." She had gotten up, stretched, and yawned. Then she put on her moccasins and fetched her bow and quiver from the packs. Together, on foot, they walked down the river to where the canyon opened out and there was a large meadow of waving grass. Naduah moved silently and lightly, aware of everything around her. Sunrise had taught her well. It had rained the day before and the air was cool and clean, the bushes washed free of dust. Here, where there was enough water, the buffalo grass reached as high as their waists.

Wanderer found a spot near the middle of the meadow and sat, pulling Naduah down with him. He stretched out on his stomach, and she did the same.

"I thought we were hunting deer," she whispered in his ear.

"We are. Hasn't anyone taught you to make a fawn's distress call?"

"No."

"You know that a doe will leave her fawn hidden and graze away from it, don't you?"

"Of course. The fawn doesn't leave a scent trace when it's very young, and the mother knows it's safer hidden by itself than with her."

"Right. So we make a noise like a fawn in trouble, and the doe will come to help it."

"How do you know there are deer nearby?"

"This is perfect country for them. And it's the right time of day. They'll be feeding. They're here." He cupped a thin reed in his hands and blew across it, making a frightened bleating noise, then another. Then they both lay still.

Naduah listened to the wind soughing across the grass and the insects singing and buzzing all around here. Lying there in the tall, cool grass with the sun warm on her back, she felt like a child again. Wanderer made the call three or four times, and she inched closer to him. Finally her leg brushed his, and they lay with their bodies touching. That was the most difficult part of being Wanderer's wife and lover as well as his friend. She constantly wanted to touch him, to feel his body, his hands, his mouth. She never tired of watching him, when he sat quiet and pensive at the fire, or when he moved gracefully around the camp. Now, as he lured the deer, she realized something about him.

"It's a game with you, isn't it?" She said it suddenly and very quietly.

"What's a game?" He glared at her, pretending to be irritated at the disturbance.

"All of it. This. Hunting. War, life, love." He stared at her as though he'd been caught at something.

"Why do you say that?"

"The look on your face. I used to think you were laughing at me. But I just realized you're laughing at everyone. At life."

"I laugh at it." He thought a while. "But I take it seriously too. Enjoying life is serious business. You have to work at it."

"Your friend and brother who died didn't work at it." She thought of his smile, his contagious laugh.

"No, he didn't. He was a rare one." Wanderer rolled over to weave his fingers into her hair. She had washed it in the river and it hung loose and heavy around her shoulders. He leaned over and buried his face in it, breathing the clean odor of its warm dampness.

"I like the way it curls on the ends, like pale oak shavings." She turned onto her back and twined her arms around his neck. She arched her body, straining to touch every part of him. He murmured in her ear.

"You're right as usual, my golden one, my palomino. Life is a game. If it wasn't a game before, you've made it one."

Looking over his shoulder, Naduah saw the mountain lion first.

"Roll!" She shoved him off to one side and twisted in the opposite direction. She felt claws rake her arm as the cat's spring carried him to the spot in the grass flattened by their bodies. Without thinking, Naduah snatched her bow, nocked an arrow, and fired, in one flowing motion. Wanderer shot at the same time, and both shafts were fatal.

"Some deer." She laughed, partly with relief and partly to keep from trembling. She wiped at the blood as it ran down her arm. Wanderer looked sheepish, and she laughed harder.

"Woman, you have me so bewitched, I forgot that call sometimes attracts more than deer. Did Medicine Woman give you all her love potions before she turned you over to me?" He grumbled a little as they began skinning the animal. "You'll be the death of me if I don't break your spell." He looked up at her mischievously as they knelt with the carcass between them. "Of course, it wouldn't have been as noble as dying in battle, but not a bad way to go. Not a bad way at all." He rested his free hand lightly on her shoulder as they walked back to camp.

Now he rode in front of her down the steep canyon trail as comfortably as if he and Night were out for a stroll at the edge of camp. She could see the long scar that curved under his shoulder blade. It was darker than the rest of his skin and freckled where the sun had burned the new scar tissue many years before. She smiled as she thought of the times she had traced it with her fingers, running them along the soft, velvety ridge as he lay on top of her. As though guessing her thoughts, he turned to look at her and shouted over the noise of the water.

"Let Wind do the steering." He was trying to hide the fact that he was concerned about her, but she knew he was.

"Wind's never traveled this trail either."

"Trust her." Then there was no more talking. No one could be heard as the river roared down from the plain and crowded through the narrow gorge. The sound of it echoed and swelled as it reverberated between the two-hundred-foot high walls.

Wind's hoofs dislodged pebbles that rattled and clattered on the stony trail before launching off the edge and sailing out into space.

Naduah's stomach contracted with fear, and she tried to look down at the ragged boulders and blood-colored rapids of the river. Wind lurched forward with each step. She carefully placed each hoof, then braked to avoid sliding with her own momentum.

Naduah leaned over and pressed her cheek to Wind's cheek. Wind shook her head in response. Wind's ancestors had been raised in the desert, bred to eat sparse grass and travel long distances between water holes. Wind was only fourteen hands tall, a descendant of pure Arab mixed with tough little North African barb. A Texan would have called her shaggy, mean, and ugly, but to Naduah she was perfect.

If anyone could travel this trail safely, she could. But what about skirting that mad river? A fish couldn't do it. She searched for a trail and found only fragments, tiny beaches eaten into by the swirling water. *It's impossible. Maybe he's remembering when the river was lower.* But even as she thought it, Naduah knew she was wrong. He knew what he was doing. He always did.

She watched the dark, smooth skin slide over his shoulder blades as he eased Night down the slope. His muscles didn't bulge and swell like Pahayuca's, but Wanderer was strong. Sometimes when they made love, he held her immobile, paralyzed in his grip, as he stared down at her. It frightened her and excited her to see the wild hunger in his eyes then.

He was strong and he was tall. So tall there were those who claimed he wasn't born one of the People at all. That he was a Mexican captured as an infant. She had heard the rumors. Now maybe she would learn the truth. She was riding to meet Iron Shirt, Wanderer's father.

Wanderer's people, the Quohadi, ruled the Staked Plains. They were the fiercest warriors in a nation of them. They looked down on the rest of the world from their aerie, swooping from it to raid deep into Mexico or to plunder the Texas settlements. Then they disappeared back into their vastness. They lived confident and secure in the knowledge that white men would never dare enter their territory.

There was only one group of people who invaded the Quohadi's land regularly. They were called *ciboleros*, buffalo hunters, and were from the New Mexican pueblos. The Pueblo, or Anazasi, were peaceful folk. Each year they ventured onto the plateau to hunt meat to feed their families and to sell.

It was dangerous work. Not many were suited to it. But those who were came every year. They brought their families with them, their

326

women and children, their dogs and oxen and their clumsy wooden carts. The hunt had been good this year, and the men and women of El Manco's party were packing the dried meat strips into their carts. El Manco steadied himself with his one hand on the cart's tall side and kneaded the meat into a compact mass under his bare feet.

El Manco, One Armed, was still the mayordomo, the leader of the hunts. As he chased the buffalo, he held the reins in his teeth. Using one hand, he drove his lance in with the force of two. Now he climbed out of his cart, wiped his feet on the clumps of grass, and walked away to start the band moving.

There was a stir in the vast, straggling camp around them. The oxen began to low in protest as the men rounded them up and hitched them to the carts. The heaps of buffalo skulls and bones buzzed with flies. The odor of putrifying meat was lying heavier on the camp with each hour. The women shoveled dirt over their cooking and smoking fires. They stepped back, shielding their faces from the wind-blown ashes, sparks, smoke, and dust.

There were over one hundred men, women, and children, fifty carts and five hundred oxen and burros, and seventy-five horses to collect and organize and form into marching order. It was two hours before the procession pulled out. It looked like a band of gypsies on the move. Whips cracked, men shouted, the women screamed for their children. The oxen complained bitterly, and dogs barked along the edges.

A caravan of *carretas* had no chance of proceeding with stealth. Even without the high-pitched squealing of their axles they could be easily tracked by the broken cottonwood axletrees that littered their trail. The two wheels were sliced from solid logs and stood chest-high to a man. They were only roughly circular, and the holes for the axles were never exactly in the center. Supporting them as they ka-chunked over the rocky ground was a lot to ask of a cottonwood pole, especially since buffalo fat was the sole lubricant available.

The T-shaped tongue held the oxen's heads at an unnatural angel. That, added to the weight of the carts, made it necessary to use four times the normal number of animals to pull a load. *Carretas* were a ridiculous form of transportation, but they hauled away the remains of ten to twelve thousand buffalo a year. Their catch was insignificant when compared to the millions of animals that blanketed the plains, but it supplied the pueblos and outlying ranches of New Mexico with food for the winter.

El Manco rode to a place at the head of the line and led his people eastward.

* * *

327

As he watched the band of Komantcia approach, El Manco noted that one of the women was blond. But that wasn't unusual. And except for her hair she was Komantcia in every way. The men behind El Manco were nervous. They were a fierce-looking lot, but it was mostly bluff. They knew they were no match for Komantcia on an equal basis.

Fortunately, this wasn't an equal basis. The band coming toward them had only nine members. And of those, only five were warriors. So El Manco waited calmly. He had learned long ago not to worry about things he couldn't control. And death was the major one of those. The manner of it was unimportant, though he would prefer not to die by torture.

The sixty Anazasi *ciboleros* crowded behind El Manco would have given most men pause. Even in the hot sun they wore leather pants and jackets. Round, flat straw hats protected their faces. Their lances rode upright, the butt ends wedged into leather cases and the shafts held in place by straps tied to their saddle pommels. A forest of slender lance points waved overhead, each decorated with a long tassel of brightly colored cloth that fluttered in the wind. The Pueblo's old flintlock muskets were also carried vertically on the other side of each saddle. Each had a tasseled stopper in the muzzle.

The muskets were more for show than defense on the Staked Plains. The constant wind blew away the sparks and priming and made the guns almost useless. The men's long, wiry black hair was pulled back into thick ques. Their swarthy faces were grim as they fingered the fourteen-inch blades in their belts. They looked like a band of land-locked pirates among their beached spars.

"Jésus, help Eulalia bring up the cart with the trade goods." El Manco beckoned with his right arm, and he heard the creak of the wheels grinding against their axle. The noise drowned out the fainter noises of creaking saddles and fluttering tassels. The Komantcia conferred at a distance, and the mayordomo waited patiently. He felt the small black buffalo gnats swarming around his face. They crawled down his shirt front and up his pants legs. He dared not mar the dignity of the occasion by slapping at them. And he cursed them under his breath. They left ugly, pus-filled welts that took days to go down. He hoped they were biting the Komantcia as badly.

If they were indeed Komantcia. They could be Kiowa, but more than likely they weren't. He hoped not. The Kiowa were the Komantcia's allies. But they didn't have the same shaky peace with the people of New Mexico that the Komantcia had had for over sixty years.

Suddenly the members of the small party spurred their ponies and raced toward the waiting *ciboleros*. The tallest warrior and the golden-haired woman rode in front, side by side. As El Manco moved out to meet them alone, he heard Hanibal behind him.

"*Madre de Dios! ¡Qué mujer*, what a woman! I wonder if the chief would consider selling her."

"In your whole life, Joven," said Jésus, "you wouldn't have enough horses to buy her."

Then the Komantcia bore down on El Manco as if to crush him under their hoofs, but he slowly held his right hand up. With the palm forward, he moved it deliberately back and forth, signaling them to halt. If they didn't they were hostile, but it would probably be too late for El Manco. The ponies lurched to a stop just out of reach of a lance and danced there nervously. El Manco still held his hand up, but now he moved it from right to left and back again. "I do not know you," his hand said. "Who are you?"

The tall, lean young warrior held his arm in front of him, the forearm parallel to his waist. He made a backward wriggling motion with it, around toward his side. El Manco gave a tiny sigh of relief. They were Snakes Who Came Back. Koh-mat, the Utes called them, Those Who Are Always Against Us. Komantcia. Comanche. Dangerous, but not as bad as Kiowa. They didn't look like they were the advance scout of a war party. They had too much baggage with them. They were young families on the move somewhere.

El Manco raised his right hand and shook the stump of his left arm. "Are you friends?" he asked, giving the sign as best he could with only one hand.

The warrior held both hands up high and locked his two forefingers. "Yes. We are friends." Then he rode forward to claim the gifts he considered his right.

Gifts. Tribute. Bribe. It was all the same. It was a custom begun by a shrewd Spanish viceroy in 1786, and now no one questioned it. When the order first went out to buy off the ferocious raiders from the east, the Komantcia had tried to return gift for gift, as was their own custom. But they were assured it wasn't necessary. As the years went by, they took arrogantly what they considered their due.

The cart had been turned around so Eulalia could see her husband. She sat with her short, plump legs dangling. As she watched the hand talk, she whispered the prayer said over each child at his naming ceremony.

> May you always live without sickness,
> May you have good corn and all good things.
> May you travel the sun trail to old age,
> And pass away in sleep without pain.

Would this be the time they murdered El Manco? They were so unpredictable. It was hard to tell. A black shawl shielded Eulalia's face from the sun and shrouded her fear. Behind her on the bed of the cart were piles of flat, round, golden loaves of bread. She had spent many hours grinding the corn for them in a series of ever finer stone *metates*. There was always grit in the cornmeal, of course. "Every man must eat a *metate* in his lifetime," the saying went. But the Komantcia loved the bread. It was a major trade item. Not that they would be traded today. They would be given in exchange for safe passage across the Llano.

She knew that the Komantcia considered them trespassers. But the Anazasi's Ancient Ones had been hunting buffalo here when the Snakes Who Came Back were still living in the mountains far to the north. Before they ever walked out onto the plains on their stubby, highlanders' legs, carrying their possessions on their bowed backs or making their dogs drag them. Before they ever stole their first horse and became a menace to everyone around them.

Now bread and sugar, flour and coffee were the price the Anazasi had to pay to use what had once been theirs. Just as they had to pay taxes for the land that was theirs. Eulalia wished there were more left for themselves after the tributes and the taxes and the tithes. The Spanish took, the Komantcia took. The priests took. Especially the priests. Looking at her kind face and that of her husband, it was difficult to see the rage that made the Anazasi rise up every hundred years or so and slaughter when too much had been taken from them.

Eulalia gathered up as many of the loaves of bread as she could carry and slid off the cart to offer them to her husband. He in turn solemnly handed them to the young chief and his retinue.

❧ *37* ❧

As they rode away from the caravan of Pueblo buffalo hunters, *Naduah* could hear the *carretas* moving forward again. The oxen bawled loudly, and the wail of the axles against fifty sets of cart wheels sounded like huge fingernails scratching against slate. Naduah nibbled contentedly on the corn cake, glad she was one of the People and not a *cibolero*, crawling across the landscape like a slug.

"This is delicious!" She waved the cornbread at Wanderer.

"It's even better warm, with honey."

Star Name and Deep Water cantered to catch up with them, and they rode together side by side. Spaniard's new woman and Big Bow's latest conquest stayed to themselves, gossiping and taking care of the pack animals. Lance, the Wasps' crier, had decided to come too. He was remote and preoccupied as usual, keeping to himself and chanting his songs through his nose all day. Naduah had asked him why he had come with them. He looked at her as though surprised by the question.

"To see the world, of course." She knew it was probably the only answer she would get.

Star Name looked over her shoulder at the crude, clumsy carts disappearing into a cloud of dust. Ahead of them, off to one side, stretched the broad, ravaged furrow left in the grass by the heavy wooden wheels and the hundreds of plodding animals that pulled them.

"There's no mistaking their trail, is there?" said Star Name.

"Not when there are this many," said Wanderer. "They don't always come in such a large party."

Naduah studied the vast sweep of absolutely flat land all around them. The short, curly, yellow grass stretched to the horizon like a newly mown meadow.

"How do you track a small party here?" she asked.

Wanderer reined Night around in a tight circle to face in the direction they had come. The others did the same. He and Deep Water waited silently for the women to figure it out.

"I see it," said Naduah. "Do you, Sister?"

"Yes. The grass is slightly darker where we passed."

"It'll stay that way for two days or more, depending on how dry it is." Wanderer turned and started moving again. "You'll learn to see the trails in the grass more clearly after you've lived here a while. One day they'll be so obvious you'll wonder how you ever could have missed them. You'll know when a deer has passed."

Naduah unfastened her gourd canteen from the loop on her saddle. She took a sip and handed it to Star Name. Star Name tilted it up to drink, then looked over at Wanderer.

"Should I save this?" She held the canteen up. "When will we find water?"

"Soon. Drink as much as you want."

"How will we find water?" asked Naduah.

"The same ways you have always found it."

"We just climb a high hill and look for darker colored trees along the riverbed," laughed Star Name. "That's where the pools will be in dry weather."

"Star Name, you have no respect for maturity and wisdom." Wanderer looked aggrieved. "Look for ponies."

"If they're strung out in a line and walking steadily without grazing, they're headed for water. Right?" Sunrise had taught Naduah and Star Name that.

"Right."

"Or look for mesquites," added Star Name. "Mustangs eat the beans and drop the seeds in their dung. And ponies rarely graze more than a few miles from water."

"Right also."

"It doesn't look like there's much water to find around here." Naduah was daunted by the immensity of the landscape. She was used to seeing plains that seemed to roll on forever, but never had she seen country as empty and monotonous as this. There was nothing to relieve the eye, nothing to soothe her mind or distract her from the barrenness. She longed for a big, cool cottonwood, with its rustling leaves that sounded like rainfall in the night.

"It doesn't look like there's any water here at all," said Star Name.

"There's water, but it tastes like piss," said Spaniard as he rode up to join them.

"He's right. Remind me to tell you about keeping the horses away from alkalai water. And what it will do to them if they drink it."

"Hey, you Kiowa stud," Spaniard waved to Big Bow. "Get up here. I don't trust you back there with my woman."

"Very wise, Spaniard," said Deep Water. "I wouldn't trust Star Name with him either." Star Name gave him an evil look.

"I wouldn't trust any woman with him," grumbled Spaniard. "I don't understand it. I'm much better looking than he is. What makes him so irresistible to women?"

"He has five hundred horses and half as many mules. And he has so many women, none of them has much work to do," said Wanderer.

"That's why he goes on the war trail so often," added Deep Water. "To get away from his women."

Wanderer and Naduah rode ahead while the others bantered.

"It's so empty, Wanderer. I feel lost and helpless here." Naduah looked around at the barren land lying inert under the weight of the wide sky.

"It's not empty. It's boundless. Free. Nothing blocks your vision. Nothing stands between you and the horizon. Or you and the heavens. You'll like it when you get used to it."

"I suppose so. You were telling me how to find water."

He picked up the trail of his thoughts.

"Watch for doves. They find water every day. They're usually not far from it. And the dirt daubers. If they have mud in their beaks, they're coming from water. And if they're going to it, they fly straight and low. Also, there's a type of grass that grows around

water. I'll show it to you. Even if there's no water visible, you may
be able to bring some to the surface by walking your pony back and
forth in the sand. And listen for frogs. They'll lead you to a hidden
spring sometimes."

"All those methods sound chancy."

"Life is chancy. Maybe chancier here than in the country you're
used to. But you'll learn."

You'll learn. Naduah despaired of ever learning all there was to
know. Just when she thought she'd done so, Wanderer or Sunrise or
Takes Down The Lodge would spring something new on her. And
she would feel like an ignorant child again. Wanderer went on
talking in his low teaching voice.

"Be very careful of the water, especially for your ponies. Always
drink from a spring when possible. The rivers are safest when the
water's low. When it's high it leaches the mineral salts from the
banks, and it's worse. Don't even let a horse graze near an alkalai
river. Floodwater leaves deposits on the grass that can make him
sick."

"How do I know if a pony's been poisoned by it?"

"His stomach and chest will swell. And he'll cough. If it's allowed
to go uncured, it'll destroy his lungs."

"How can it be cured?"

"If you catch it early enough, you can pour grease down his
throat." Wanderer swung a leg over and sat on Night's back as
though on a log, with both feet swinging free. "Enough lessons. I'll
race you to the next ravine. It's about three miles straight ahead."

"How do you know there's a ravine three miles ahead?" Naduah
was a little exasperated with him. How could anyone know where
they were on this featureless plain?

"You'll know in time too. There's a spring there where we can fill
our canteens and water paunches."

"A race with Night is no contest. Even for Wind."

"I'll ride backwards."

"You could ride standing on your head. It wouldn't make any
difference to Night."

"*Mea-dro*, let's go!" He swung the other leg over and sat facing her
as Night surged forward. He made hideous faces at her, and she
returned them. Unable to resist the challenge, she kicked Wind's
sides and raced after him.

For four leisurely days, the party traveled across the plain. They
headed north and west into the sun. They took their time, stopping
to chase buffalo or pronghorn, otherwise riding slowly so Naduah's
dog could keep up. Dog was growing old, and sometimes rode on a
travois, her nose on her paws, her liquid brown eyes staring serene-

ly off into space. But she still chased anything that ran, her legs trembling with fatigue when she returned to them.

The party spent the hottest part of each afternoon lying under small shelters of hides or brush, or in the wispy shade of stunted willows at the bottom of a ravine. One day, they found a clear spring gushing gallons of water from the bottom of a shallow, brush-choked canyon. As they lay around the spring lapping the cold water, Naduah sneaked up on Wanderer and poured a canteen full of it on his bare back. He leaped to his feet with a yelp, scooping up water in his cupped hands and spraying her face with it. Star Name came to her defense, and the war was on. They threw water until they were all soaked. All but Lance. He hunkered at the rim of the ravine and smiled down on them, like a fond parent on his mischievous children.

But as they rode on and on across the flat plain, Naduah began to feel restless. Or maybe she was nervous, although she refused to admit she was afraid. They must be close to Wanderer's band by now. He had collected piles of green brush at the last waterhole and tied them onto two of the extra mules. He was planning to make a signal fire. And when they finally entered Iron Shirt's camp, what would she do? How would she be received? A white-eyes woman. Wanderer had told her of his mother's death two years ago. His sister had married and moved to another band. Now there was only his father.

"Will we find Iron Shirt's band soon?"

"Yes."

"What's he like?"

"Who?"

"You know who, Wanderer. Don't play with me."

"There's no reason for you to worry, golden one."

"I just want to know what to expect. What kind of man is your father?"

Wanderer rode silently beside her. The silence seemed to stretch and distort time, like the dancing mirages that shimmered constantly on the horizon.

"He's a great warrior," he said finally.

"So I've heard. What else?"

"What else is there?"

"There are other things about a man besides his ability in war."

"I suppose. But that's the only thing that counts."

Naduah tried another tack.

"Is he kind?"

"Kind? I don't know. He has great power. His breath is magic. It makes arrows fall harmlessly around him, like the gnats you slap away. He has a shirt of metal that keeps bullets from touching him.

He has more coups than six average men put together. I never thought about whether or not he was kind."

It was hopeless. Wanderer could see everything clearly, except his own father. Or maybe he didn't want to tell her. It would be like him to make her meet Iron Shirt knowing nothing about him but what was common knowledge. The stories were told around the fires of even her own band, far to the south. She would have to meet Iron Shirt and form her own opinions of him.

Late in the afternoon, Wanderer called another halt.

"There will be a celebration tonight," he said. "If you want to dress for it, now is a good time."

Using their ponies as screens, they each searched through their packs for their best clothes. Naduah and Star Name drew their horses close so they could dress together. Their new ponchos and skirts had been community projects. Takes Down The Lodge, Black Bird, Medicine Woman, Something Good, and even Blocks The Sun had helped with them.

"We can't send you to the Quohadi looking like miserable Tonkawa," Medicine Woman said. She muttered it through the sinew thread she was softening in her mouth. She was splitting more of it by the feel of it under her deft fingers.

Naduah pulled the clothes from their special rawhide case and held them a moment, remembering the afternoons spent with the women as they helped make them. Then she shook them gently to straighten the long, thick fringes. The bells on them tinkled. She dressed carefully, nervously, tying the new leggings to the thong around her waist and fastening the skirt over that. She pulled the poncho over her head, the horizontal slit in it forming a high, straight neckline. Finally she put on her soft, heavily beaded moccasins, lacing them up to mid-calf and letting the fringed tops fold down into a cuff.

Star Name was humming to herself as she dressed. As usual, she didn't seem to have a care in the world. But then, her father-in-law wasn't Iron Shirt.

"Sit on the edge of the travois and I'll do your hair." Star Name had finished and stood with her brush in her hand. She liked to play with Naduah's waist-length golden mane, and brushed it for her often.

"All right. And I'll paint your face for you."

"Be sure you make the lines neat," said Star Name.

"What makes you think I won't?"

"You hands are shaking."

Naduah fumbled with her round silver mirror, the one Wanderer had given her the day he had brought one hundred horses to Sunrise.

She could hear her heart pounding in her chest, and rested her hand lightly there to still it. Then she walked over to help Wanderer finish braiding his hair and wrapping the braids with the otter fur that made him a swift runner.

"You're even slower than I am, Husband. You're not nervous, are you?"

"Of course not."

But never had she seen him take such care with his appearance. For the wolf's rings around his eyes he was using his best paint, pure graphite from the Chisos Mountains four hundred miles to the south, rather than charcoal. He painted the circles painstakingly, dipping his fingers into bear grease and then into the black powder. The eagle feathers that marked his most important coups were reinforced with thin wooden sticks and fastened to his scalplock. Under them hung a vertical row of five polished silver disks on a thong. He wore a necklace of claws taken from the bear he had killed when he was fifteen. They were strung on a strip of otter skin, with the otter's bushy tail hanging down his back.

What pleased her most was the fringed hunting shirt she had made him that summer. It was well made, and she knew it. And she also knew that no other man would look as good in it. That made her hours of work worthwhile.

Finally he was ready, and he looked at her almost shyly for just a moment, as though asking for her approval. She smiled it. He was magnificent.

It was late afternoon when the canyon yawned suddenly in front of them. From a mile away she would never have guessed it was there. Wanderer halted at the edge of it to build a fire and lay on the green branches that would make the column of black smoke that said "Attention." Behind them the plain lay as flat as the surface of a yellow pond. Six hundred feet below them was the bottom of Palo Duro canyon.

The canyon was a fairyland of twisting valleys, dark green cedars, and sand-blasted sculptures in shades of pink and red, beige and orange. Water and wind had eroded the sandstone into weird shapes and figures. Bluffs had been terraced until they looked like the flounces of a Spanish dancer's skirts. The canyon was huge, one hundred and twenty miles long and twenty miles wide in places.

To the west, the sun was setting. Enormous piles of cottony cumulus clouds seemed to rest on an invisible shelf in a bright turquoise sky. The clouds were turning pink and gold on their undersides. The stripes deepened to lavender while Naduah watched, and then to a rich rose color, like the heart of a cactus flower. The reddish-purple spread upward until the whole mountain of cloud seemed to glow with it.

Patches of cloud tore off and floated free in the blue ocean around them. Shafts of golden sunlight poured in rivers and waterfalls through holes in the clouds. Outlined against the darkening sky, Naduah watched it in silence. She wanted to sit there on Wind forever. To halt time and keep the sunset from fading. She wanted to postpone the ride down the canyon's face and into the strange camp.

Below, on the canyon floor, Naduah could make out miniature smoke-yellowed lodges spread among the trees. Hundreds of spirals of slate-blue smoke from the evening cooking fires curled upward and shredded in the eddies of wind frisking between the cliffs. Now and then she could hear the bark of a dog, or the bray of a disgruntled mule, the laughter of children and the voice of a mother calling her family to eat. The sounds drifted up lightly, as disembodied as the smoke. And with them Naduah's worries seemed to lighten and dissipate.

I am Nerm. One of the People. Those camped below might be Quohadi, the fiercest of the nation's bands, but they were the People. And she was one of them. Resolutely she followed Wanderer over the cliff's edge and down the narrow path. The rest of the group came after them, with Lance bringing up the rear.

The trail was long and tortuous and the day was fading. But the full harvest moon rose early over the rim of the canyon wall, and flooded it with pearly light. From the village they could hear the sounds of singing and drums, signaling their arrival. As they rode among the first bright lodges, they were engulfed by a swirl of happy people. Naduah could hear Iron Shirt shouting in the distance before she ever saw him.

"Where is she? Where's the woman who stole my son? The women of the Quohadi must not be good enough for him."

She sat quietly on Wind, waiting for her father-in-law. She held her chin high and stared levelly ahead. If Wanderer was magnificent, Naduah was a good match for him. At seventeen she was as tall as she would ever be, taller than any of the other women. Her long blond hair, bleached almost platinum, hung in thick braids that reached her waist. They lay along the curve of her large, firm breasts, then swung freely. White-gold tendrils escaped from the braids and blew around her face. She was tanned to a brown the color of rich, golden honey. Her features were even, but her mouth was wide and full over a strong, stubborn chin.

At her waist the curve of her ribs flashed a paler color of honey with cream. Her long legs gripped Wind's sides, and her hips rode lightly in the saddle. She had a body that demanded to be touched, to be stroked. But it was her eyes that always made people turn to look at her again. They were sapphire, with inner adamantine sparks.

"Where is she?" Iron Shirt called again. There was a shifting in the crowd, and an opening formed. Iron Shirt strode through it with the rolling gait somewhere between a yaw and a swagger that most of the older men had. He had spent most of his fifty years on horseback, and his legs had accommodated themselves to it. There were a few streaks of gray in his coal-black hair. A small, hard paunch was forming over his breechclout belt, as though he had swallowed an oak bole.

He was shorter than his only son, and broader across the chest and shoulders. But Wanderer was in his piercing black eyes, the straight nose, and the arched lips. He scowled ferociously as he paced around the pair of them, inspecting them from all angles. *I'm used to this*, thought Naduah. *Maybe this is where Wanderer learned the habit.* Wanderer's leg brushed hers, as though by accident, before he swung down from Night. Naduah dismounted also. Iron Shirt stood in front of her, his hands balled into fists and digging into his hips.

"You're the woman my son has been addled over for the past three years." It wasn't a question.

"I'm Naduah. And Wanderer isn't addled."

"Who killed the mountain lion?"

Naduah was startled. She'd forgotten the hide that still lay across Wind's hindquarters. She glanced at Wanderer to see if he would answer. He stood silent, watching her and his father with the old amused look on his face.

"We did. Wanderer and I."

The creases in the older man's face aligned themselves into a smile.

"You did? You and Wanderer?"

Naduah translated the smile as disbelief. "I wouldn't say I had if I hadn't."

The words sounded harsh to her own ears. Two minutes in camp and she was fighting with her father-in-law, a legendary chief. But Iron Shirt didn't seem to mind. He grabbed her in a crushing bear hug, giving her a warrior's embrace. With one arm around her shoulder, he beckoned everyone closer.

"This is my new daughter, Naduah," he bellowed. "My son has chosen well." He turned to grin at her. "He's chosen very well indeed. Are you sure you wouldn't prefer an older man?"

Nadua smiled back.

"I like the one I have."

"Did you make his shirt?"

"Yes." Naduah had the disorienting feeling that Iron Shirt was carrying on several trains of thought at the same time.

"Would you make one for me? None of my women can sew that well. But don't tell them I said so." He didn't wait for her to answer. As they all walked toward the dancing area, he grabbed Wanderer's upper arm and shook it, like a dog worrying a bone.

"No wonder you were restless and heading south at every excuse. I have a new wife too. She's younger than yours. Introduce me to the rest of your group."

Star Name caught up with Naduah as Iron Shirt was leading Wanderer off, already firing questions at him about the Penateka and the situation in the south.

"I hope you don't get too bruised," Star Name said in a low voice.

"What do you mean?"

"When they fight and you try to stop them."

"Grown men don't fight."

"You're right. Wanderer will probably just kill him."

"I doubt it. But now I know why he left our packs near the edge of camp, away from his father's lodges."

"Would you care to bet that Wanderer suggests a long hunting trip very soon?"

"No bet, Star Name. He probably will. And I'll be glad to go with him. I'm sorry our trip here has ended."

"I know what you mean. It was fun, wasn't it, Sister? But there'll be many more."

"Here, come the women," said Naduah. "They'll probably want to know whether the Wasps put plums or persimmons or pecans in their pemmican."

"Or whether we prefer the lazy stitch or the overlay stitch for beadwork. Or whether our women are sewing their blouses and skirts together in the new style."

"And they'll finger the seams on our clothes, and study our moccasins to see if they're made well enough."

"And of course they'll want to touch your yellow hair, Sister."

"I don't mind, as long as they don't try to take any away with them."

The drums started, and the singers began to chant for the dance. Naduah and Star Name joined the group of women coming toward them. They would go to Iron Shirt's set of lodges for a feast, then join the welcoming celebration and dance the sun up.

❧ *38* ❧

Naduah lay on her back, feeling the warmth of Wanderer's long,
lean body next to hers. The gold chain with the eagle coin on it
trailed across his sleek chest. The sun had yet to heat up the east side
of the lodge, but it was June and the day would be hot. The robe had
slid down toward their feet and she had awakened with a start. Even
after ten months living alone with Wanderer in the Quohadi band,
she still felt self-conscious. She still thought, when on the borderline
of sleep and consciousness, that her family was sharing the tent with
them and would see her exposed.

She gently pulled the furry robe up to their waists and lay listening to Wanderer's soft breathing. His head was turned toward her,
and his face was totally at peace. He looked young and vulnerable.
The beauty of him made her eyes fill. She blinked and stared at the
blurred outlines of the lodge cover above her. The shapes of the
hides were familiar patterns to her. As her tears dried, she studied
the seams of Takes Down's neat stitches. She sighed. It was evident
which seams Takes Down had done and which ones she herself had
sewn. She'd do better on the next one. Just for practice, she would
offer to help anyone making a lodge cover. In the meantime, Takes
Down's seams were a comfort to Naduah, as individual as a signa-
ture.

Naduah listened to the birds whistling and squabbling in the
cottonwoods and cedars outside. Now and then a blackbird would
crash into the treetops with a sound like the tearing and crumpling
of paper. From nearby came the morning song of the first riser. As
she listened to Lance chant his thanks for the new day, Naduah felt
as though it had officially begun.

She turned over, raised herself onto her elbows, and started to
climb carefully over Wanderer. He always slept on the outer edge of
the bed, ready to leap up and grab his lance or his cherished carbine.
It leaned now against the pole by his head. He kept it oiled and
polished, and wrapped in a leather case when traveling. The brass
trigger guard and bands around the barrel gleamed, and the wooden
stock was satiny with handling. Next to it lay the pouch with the
balls, and the powder flask. He had taken the triangular bayonet
that fit under the barrel and had ground it down into a large knife
blade. The People's style of warfare had little use for hand-to-hand
combat.

Naduah thought she could slide over Wanderer without waking

him. But as her full breasts brushed his chest, he reached sleepily for her. He hugged her voluptuous body to him, nuzzling her neck and nipples. She gently bit his shoulder, her long pale hair cascading around them both. Then she pushed herself back up onto her elbows.

"I'm going down to the river."

"Mmmmmm." He smiled without opening his eyes. Then he let her go, rolled over with a faint grunt, and went to sleep again. They had all been celebrating until just a few hours before. Buffalo Piss had arrived with a dozen people from the Penateka, and there had been the usual carrying-on. Tonight the men would probably sit long in council. Buffalo Piss obviously had something on his mind.

Naduah pulled her one-piece dress from the pole rack where it hung next to Wanderer's everyday breechclout and leggings. She drew it over her head and shook out the fringe. She brushed her hair quickly, slipped on her old moccasins, and stepped out into the cool, fragrant morning. Next to the doorway Wanderer's covered shield stood on its tripod, soaking up the power of the sun. And it seemed to her like a sentry guarding them from harm.

Wisps of ground fog still clung to the bushes low to the ground. The air was scented with cedar and flowers and smoke. Around her, the red walls of Palo Duro canyon rose in a protective embrace. Tall grass grew along the shallow river that meandered through the bottom of the canyon. The lodges were thinly sown among the trees along the river. She followed the well-worn path to the best bathing place. Dog came with her, wagging her tail and frisking clumsily, zigzagging from one side of the trail to the other.

Naduah was careful not to disturb Lance. He preferred to take his morning bath in solitude. He would stand silently with his arms upraised to the rising sun. Then he would solemnly wade into the water and splash it over himself.

The most astonishing thing about Lance was that he had found time from his religious preoccupations to marry. He hadn't had many horses to pay for Tarkau Huhtsu, Snow Bird, but her father had agreed anyway. Everyone could see that Lance would be a powerful medicine man some day. Already people came to him to ask him to name their children, or give them amulets for hunting or war, or paint holy designs on their shields. And Snow Bird suited him. She was as quiet and shy as he was.

Naduah lay serenely in the water, naked in the morning sunlight. Her hair floated out behind her, and she drowsed. Above her a fleet of fleecy white clouds sailed by, shifting and billowing. Graceful vultures soared lazily around the canyon's lip. A few late bats flitted among the trees, like hallucinations seen from the corner of the eye. Soon they would disappear to dangle, little velvet sacks, in crevices in the canyon wall.

As she soaked, Naduah reached down and scooped up handfuls of sand from the bottom. She rubbed it over her body and felt the grains wash away and drift to the bottom again. She and Star Name, Deep Water, and Wanderer had returned from a hunting trip the day before, and she could still smell the lingering odor of the crushed mescal beans she had spread on herself. The powder kept the mosquitoes and buffalo gnats off her, but she didn't like the fetid odor.

Then she heard the distant laughter of children coming to wash, and she knew it was time to leave. She waded out, swinging her arms in front of her through the water and watching the glittering silvery spray of water it made. She dressed and filled the water paunches she had brought. As she walked along the path through the bushes and grass and flowers, cooled by the shade of the cotton-woods, she thought of the chores she had to do that day. Make breakfast, gather wood, see to the horses, pack the dried meat they had brought in yesterday, smoke the hides she had tanned, and gather herbs. Then there was the painted robe she was making for Wanderer and the shirt for his father, and the moccasins that always needed mending.

And there was the visiting and the gossiping. And dyes to boil. It was becoming harder and harder to slip away with Star Name for long, leisurely rides along the river or practice with their bows and arrows. And Wanderer had promised to teach her to shoot his carbine. But ammunition was scarce. There was little for practice. Naduah didn't like the gun anyway. It was loud and it hurt her ears. It bruised her shoulder and exploding powder burned her face. But she stubbornly kept on trying.

Without thinking, she hummed Lance's morning chant. The daily repetition of it and its simple monotony made it impossible to drive from her head at times. She stopped guiltily and looked around when she realized what she was doing. A person's medicine songs were his own, and sacred. They could be given or sold, but never taken without asking.

Buffalo Piss and his men had come to the Staked Plains. He spoke to the leaders gathered in Iron Shirt's council lodge.

"The white men are everywhere. They swarm like buffalo gnats. And the old Peneteka leaders, Pahayuca and Old Owl, Santa Ana and Sanaco, they meet with them and agree to their demands. The young men's bravery is eaten away by the whiskey that the white traders bring with them.

"Last fall, right after Wanderer left, three Texans came to meet with us. They invited the leaders of the Penateka to make honey talk with more of the treacherous cowards. They wanted us to walk into their town and be slaughtered again like helpless deer." Buffalo Piss was almost chewing on the pipe stem in his rage.

"Arrow Point and I wanted to kill them then and there. Or tie them in the center of the village for the women to torture. They have no honor, these Texans. They lured us to treaty talks and turned on us. And then they expected us to come meekly again.

"All afternoon we discussed it. Not whether or not to go to the treaty talks, but whether or not to kill the envoys. We were there all afternoon. And Pahayuca kept silent. Finally he spoke. He was the last to do so.

" 'These men's honor and the honor of the Texans does not concern me,' he said. 'My honor and the honor of the Wasps does. The Texans are not the People. They do not understand our ways or our honor. I will not be disgraced by the blood of men who have come to me under a flag of truce. Their blood is not worth it. The blood of all Texans is not worth it. For after they are dead, I will still have to live with myself, and with my shame. They will not be harmed while they are here under my protection. Any man who wishes to harm them must fight me. *Suvate,* that is all.'

"What could we say? After Pahayuca and Old Owl agreed to meet with them, we let them go. The leaders made honey talk with Sam Hyu-stahn a month ago. They agreed to allow trading posts. They agreed to stop raiding. To stop raiding! Why didn't the Texans ask us to stop breathing? A man who doesn't raid is not a man. And as usual, the Texans refused to set boundaries on themselves. They won't guarantee us our land, or promise to punish those who wrong us.

"So we came here, those of us who can no longer live under the conditions in the south. The Quohadi will never surrender. They will never allow the white men to set up trading posts and destroy their young men with stupid water. And they will never stop raiding."

The pipe passed to Wanderer, and he thought as he drew a deep breath on it. Then he stood and adjusted his robe, to signal that he would speak next. He wrapped it around his chest and draped it over his left arm, leaving his shoulders uncovered. Solemnly he recounted the war records of Pahayuca and Santa Ana, Old Owl and Sanaco. He told of their coups and their bravery, their wisdom and loyalty. He told the history of the Penateka, their courage as warriors. Then he talked of the white men.

"The Penateka have always lived in the lands the whites want, the easy lands where there is much timber and game and water. A hundred years ago the Spanish tried to take their lands, and the Penateka fought them and won. Their warriors rode fearlessly through the Spanish towns in daylight and took whatever they wanted. But the Texans are different. They spawn like rabbits, like fish in the streams, like mosquitoes in the swamps. Their lodges are crowded with children. And still more come from the east. They bring sickness with them, and death, and the stupid water.

"And they bring guns. If we're going to drive them out, we have to have guns like theirs. And powder and ammunition. I will lead a party south to steal more of them. We will raid until every man of the Quohadi has a gun. We will raid until the white men are beaten and leave our lands forever."

Iron Shirt spoke next.

"My son speaks wisely when he says we must continue raiding. But I do not agree that guns are the answer. Our arrows are better than the white man's guns. They fire more quickly, and they do not require powder and bullets. If a bow breaks, we can make another one. If a gun breaks, it is useless to us. Bows do not misfire, or explode or hang fire or rust or jam. They do not wound or deafen the man firing them. While the white men stop to reload, we can shower them with arrows.

"We should steal the white man's weapons whenever we can. It's better for us to have them than him. But we must not depend on them to defend ourselves. We must not depend on weapons that come from a source outside ourselves. When we do that, we will be as foolish as those who depend on the white man's wih-skee for their courage."

For the rest of the afternoon the men discussed the raid that Wanderer proposed. Wanderer's face was expressionless throughout it. If he was angry with his father for contradicting him, he never showed it. The council lodge was not a place of anger. Anger was undignified, and maintaining the dignity of the council was much more important than personal slights and offenses.

When he returned to his lodge that night, however, Naduah could tell he was raging inside. She served the stew silently, waiting for him to speak. Finally he did, in a low, calm, dangerous voice.

"There will be a raid. I will lead a party, but there will probably be more than one group going. Buffalo Piss is going to Sun Name's band to recruit more men. Everyone is restless after a quiet winter. Many will want to go, to teach the Texans a lesson."

"May I go with you?"

"No, golden one. We will be raiding far south, deep into the timber country where the Penateka used to hunt. There are many white men there now, and they will try to take you. I do not want to risk losing you."

"I could darken my hair, dress as a man."

He stared at her in his intense way, tenderness showing through the rage.

"No, my love. Darken your hair, dress as a man. You're still too much of a woman to hide it. And your blue eyes shine like signal shields on a high hill in the bright sun."

Naduah signed. She knew why Sunrise had insisted that she learn to shoot and track and hunt. There were many weeks, months, sometimes years, when the men were gone on raids. And the women were left to fend for themselves and their families.

They moved inside, and he began checking his war gear. While he cleaned his carbine and rolled fresh sinew bowstrings, she took out the envelope-shaped rawhide wardrobe case. She untied the flap and pulled out his war shirt, leggings, moccasins, blanket, braid wrappers, and bear claw necklace. She shook the clothes and inspected them for wear or stains. Then she hung them over the pole rack to let the wrinkles fall out. Next she took his eagle feathers from the stiff tubular case that kept them from becoming torn or broken. She retied one of them onto its bone holder, and polished the silver disks.

The she began an inventory of all the items he would need as he traveled: carrying cases, extra moccasins, his medicine bag, fire-making equipment, jerky, his pipe bag with its tamper and tobacco, a buffalo robe, his quirt, powder horn, lead balls, his knife, club, sinew, and awl in their tiny cylindrical case, spare leather for patching, his whetstone and its case, his war-paint bag and seashells for mixing the powders. She added a bag of *puoip* root from her supply of medicines and a bag of skunk musk to blot out any scent trails that the Texans' hounds might follow. Wanderer took out a lead ingot and his bullet mold. He built up the fire until it was hot enough to melt the lead. While he worked, he talked.

"None of them understands. None of them. Iron Shirt lives in the past. 'Arrows are better than guns,' he says. Never do they ask where the guns come from. Where do the Texans get them? We have raided all over the country, and rarely do we find a place where the guns are made. Who makes them? Who improves them?

"I remember the first gun I ever saw, an old smoothbore, muzzle-loading musket that took forever to load. Each year the guns get better. For how long will our arrows be more efficient? What will the next improvement be?" He shook the carbine in the air to emphasize his point. And he looked at Naduah strangely, as though she had changed while he talked.

"Do you know where the guns come from, golden one?"

"No, I don't." And she busied herself with her work. She told him the truth. She didn't know. When she was a child guns had always been in her family's houses, but she never asked where they came from. They were always just there. She had lived in isolation on the frontier since before she was old enough to remember anything. She could no more imagine an armory than Wanderer could. She could barely remember her family's last cabin.

"Pahayuca and Old Owl are treating with the whites now."

"Yes, I heard that," she said.

"You and Cub are gone. They no longer have a reason not to."

"Surely that has nothing to do with it. The Penateka have been hounded by soldiers and Rangers until there's nothing else for them to do."

"There's always something else for them to do. They can do what the People have always done. Fight." In spite of his anger, Wanderer sounded sad. "No. Like my father, they're getting old. They've won their coups, made their reputations. They have no more need for the war trail. And they're denying the young men the opportunity to become leaders. They've been seduced by the trinkets that the white men bring. Because you can be sure that the Great Texas Father, Sam Hyu-stahn, isn't going to allow his traders to sell us guns or horses. Nothing we can really use.

"They'll bring us trinkets, things we've always gotten along without. Ribbons and flour and coffee. They'll be coffee chiefs— Pahayuca and Old Owl and Santa Ana. Coffee chiefs!" He spat the words out as though they were bitter in his mouth.

"Wanderer, stop!" Naduah sat in misery in the middle of the pile of soft furry sleeping robes. Her knees were drawn up and her face was buried in her arms. He sat next to her and put an arm around her shoulders. With his other hand he pulled back the thick, flaxen hair to see her face.

"I love Old Owl and Pahayuca too. I respect their courage and their wisdom. I haven't forgotten their records as warriors. But the future is no longer theirs. They have nothing piled on the sidelines to bet on it. Their fighting days are almost over. We are the ones who will pay for what they are doing. We and our children."

"I'll fight with you, Wanderer. I want to go on this raid."

"Not this time." Outside, from different parts of the village, the sound of drums intensified, like a pulse beating faster with the excitement of war. Men were seeking medicine to protect them as they fought.

Wanderer rose to go and Naduah didn't try to stop him. She knew he would probably be away all night. He would find a spot with spirits inhabiting it, and smoke and pray to enlist their aid. There were many places like that in Palo Duro canyon, places where the rocks had been twisted by time and kneaded by the elements into mystical shapes. Places where the wind whistled and moaned eerily out of dark side canyons, and shadows seemed to writhe in the full moon's light.

"Yee, yee, yee!" Naduah screamed and leaped with the other women, waving her arms in time to the scores of drums. In the center of the cleared space the men of the raiding party had been dancing for hours. Silhouetted against the roaring bonfire, they leaped and stamped. Individuals stopped to tell of their bravery and to beg the others to shoot them if they faltered in the battles to come. They staged mock skirmishes, firing their rifles in the air. Outside the dance area, Wanderer sat watching on Night. When his men gave a screech that resonated against Naduah's eardrums and left her head ringing, Wanderer rode forward at a gallop. He ignored the bullets they shot over his head, and stopped at the center of the circle.

There was a sudden silence, broken only by the snapping of logs on the fire, the occasional jingle of bells, or the dry crackle of a pebble-filled gourd rattle. Wanderer's face was painted black, as were the faces of his men. In one hand he held his carbine over his head, and in the other his bow and quiver. Night, as though he knew the effect required, turned slowly so all could see his rider clearly.

"Men and women of the Quohadi," Wanderer's powerful voice rang in the stillness. "We are going on the raid trail. We will win horses and scalps, guns and captives and slaves to make us even stronger. We will take what we want, and we will leave our enemies crying in the ruins of their lodges. We are strong. We are fearless. We are invincible." He gave the People's unearthly, yodeling war whoop and his men joined him. The drums took up the war chant, and the dance began again.

As it went on, into the early hours of the morning, the people of Iron Shirt's band worked themselves into a frenzy. Naduah was swept along by it, drunk with fatigue and excitement, delirious with the drumming and the swaying. She had lost her sense of self and become a part of something bigger and grander and more exciting. The rhythmic pounding seemed to radiate out from the marrow of her bones, vibrating every cell in her body. The flames of the huge fire leaped and danced too, as though nature were joining in the effort. The fire hypnotized her as it would a moth.

It was almost dawn when she staggered to her lodge, fell onto her bed, and pulled the warm robe over her. As she drifted off to sleep her arms and legs felt light and alien, as though they belonged to someone else, and her head was whirling. She never knew when Wanderer joined her an hour later. He had only a few hours to sleep before it all started over again.

Once more he got up, dressed in his war clothes, and led the parade of his men through the village. He carried his banner of red flannel streamers on a pole tipped with the eagle feathers of his coups. The older men lined the procession's path, cheering them on and urging the women to sleep with the warriors. The women and children followed behind, dressed in their best clothes and chanting war songs. When the second night's celebration was over, Wanderer hurried to catch Naduah as she walked toward home, her legs feeling light and wobbly from dancing.

She laughed when he picked her up in his powerful arms and swung her around. He swept into the lodge with her and threw her gently onto the tumbled robes. He fell lightly on top of her. Neither of them said a word. As she had felt her mind and will blending with his during the dance, so now did her body seem to become one with him. The touch of him was intoxicating. He was slick and satiny with sweat and the beaver oil that made him impervious to bullets.

She wrapped her arms and her long legs around him to pull him as close as possible. She wanted to meld their flesh together, to feel him push deep inside her, engorging her and making her complete. The lodge seemed to whirl slowly with her and Wanderer entwined at its very center, at the center of the universe.

They coupled almost violently, silently except for her low moans. They were totally absorbed in the feel of each other's flesh and skin and muscle and bone. They were driven by the unspoken knowledge that he would leave in a few hours, and that she might never see him alive again.

❧ *39* ❧

Sam Walker groped around him, feeling among the sticks and pebbles and spiny tufts of brown grass. He was searching for the tiny screw that held his new Colt Patterson together. His fingers bumped into a tubby little barrel cactus.

"Dammitall, Jack." He shook his hand. "If we had a fire I could at least see what I was doing with this infernal machine."

"Sam, you know why we don't make fires after dark." Jack Hays' voice was low and pleasant.

"Hell, Jack, there aren't any Indians within a hundred miles of here," said John Ford.

"Not after yesterday. They must be at least a hundred miles away and still running," added Noah Smithwick.

"That bunch is gone, but there may be others. We follow the usual procedure. Eat before sunset, then ride a couple more hours and camp."

"Camp! I don't call this camping," grumbled Rufus Perry. "No fire. No grub, 'ceptin' old jerky that tastes like someone's been wearing it on their feet for a month. No smokes, no laughing. Can't even have Noah fiddle for us."

"Thank you for that!" put in Ford. Rufe didn't usually mind Hays' rules, but after routing the huge Comanche war party the day before he felt they should celebrate a little.

"Well, it isn't the lack of light that's a problem anyway," mumbled Sam. "It's this damned gun. You lose this little screw here, the one that connects the standing breech with the lock frame, and the infernal thing falls apart." He finally found the screw and held it up, as though the others could see it in the pale starlight. The fourteen men of Hays' Ranger patrol still sat in a circle around an imaginary campfire. They were vaguely silhouetted against the lighter sky. Far off an owl hooted and cicadas made the night air vibrate with sound.

"You can't reload it while you're bouncing around on a running horse," Sam went on. "And it's too light to club anyone. Poorly balanced." He hefted it in his hand. "Man that made this obviously never hunted Comanches." The pistol's three pieces lay on his rumpled, grimy red bandana spread on the rough ground. Squinting and working mostly by feel, he began putting it back together.

"You ain't tellin' us anything we don't know, Sam," said Perry. "But hell, who'd've thought we'd be close enough to Comanches to club them? We hardly even get a chance to see them."

"Whooee." Ford let his breath out in a rush. "Didn't they run though!"

"I don't care what you say, Sam. *I'd* like to find the man that made these pistols and kiss the hem of his robe. He's a savior. That's what he is." Noah kissed his pistol instead and cradled it to his chest. "How many Indians do you suppose there were? I didn't take time to count."

"There were seventy," said John Ford.

"How do you know, John?" asked Walker.

"I did what Bill Wallace taught me to do," said Ford. "I counted their horses' legs and divided by four." Smithwick dove into him, a solid shadow in the dark, and they tusseled on the ground like children.

"You boys keep the noise down. Or you can ride with another patrol." Hays said it lightly. He rarely gave orders. He rarely had to.

"Wallace got a nickname down in Mexico," said Walker. "There wasn't a pair of shoes in the whole benighted country to fit him. So everyone started calling him Big Foot. Bill says he doesn't mind. He'd rather be called that than Lying Wallace or Thieving Wallace."

"Big Foot. I like that," said Rufe Perry. "Remember when Johnny there was as verdant as a meadow in spring and fell under the influence of Wallace? Bill had him plumb convinced that the proper way to cook a buffalo steak was to put it under his saddle and ride on it all day. Told him it not only cooked the meat, but tenderized it and cured a sore-backed horse all at the same time."

Ford stood, dusted himself off and helped Smithwick up.

"Best steak I ever had. You ought to try it."

"Naw. The best steak is cooked over a buffalo-chip fire," said Smithwick. "Spices it just right. You never need pepper when you cook with buffalo shit. Remember when Wallace took John on his first Indian hunt? Damn. I wish Big Foot were here instead of rotting in that Mexican jail."

Walker and Wallace had been two of the men who had joined the ill-fated expedition to invade Mexico in December of 1842. They'd all been captured in the small border town of Mier and marched southward by the triumphant Mexicans. Sam and two others had managed to escape, but the rest were still prisoners. It was a situation that galled the Texans a great deal.

Hays and Walker strolled over to check the horses' tethers. In the two and a half years Sam Walker had been in Texas he had become one of Hays' most trusted men. The two of them were very much alike. Small, quiet, modest and deadly.

The steep hills around the Pedernales River were covered with stunted, dark green cedars and oaks, but in the sheltered canyons laced with seeps and springs, the elms and oaks and basswood trees grew tall and thick. The Rangers were camped near one of the clear, cold springs that bubbled up, then joined the river in its wild, boulder-strewn gorge. The Pedernales cascaded down the tilted granite slabs of the river and into a crystal pool not very far from the ravine where the men were camped.

"Listen, Jack, I didn't mean to mutiny back there. It has its faults, but that little pistol saved the day, didn't it!"

"I don't know about the day, but it saved our hides and hairdos. But it's frustrating that it should be so close to what we need, yet still not quite right. Why don't you write Mr. Colt a letter and make some suggestions?"

"I'm not much on letter-writing, but I just might. A few changes would do it. A pistol in each hand, and each one of them firing five shots without reloading. It'll solve our Indian problems."

"Until they get their hands on them." Hays had been fighting Comanche for seven years. He had patterned his form of guerrilla warfare after theirs. He knew better than to consider the Comanche whipped because one band of them had fled in panic. "I've been trying to get Houston to buy the five-shooters in quantity since that stand-off at Enchanted Rock, three years ago."

"They saved your scalp that day too, didn't they?"

"They and the rock. I've never known any Indian who would climb Enchanted Rock for any reason."

"Did you notice any haunts while you were up there?"

"Well, Sam, I don't believe in spirits, but it even looks strange, you know. There it sits, four hundred feet high and all humped up out of nowhere. Looks like the back of some sleeping animal." Hays stared off to the west, as though he could see the huge rock hulking there. "And it makes a creaky noise at night. The top of it glitters in an eerie kind of way in the moonlight. I figure there's a reasonable explanation, but fortunately for me, Indians don't hold with reasonable explanations."

"Three years, and we're just now getting the weapons that can mean the difference between defensive and offensive fighting." Sam shook his head as he absentmindedly stripped the papery bark from a cedar. "Houston seems to think the Indian troubles are over. That he can shake hands with them and buy them off."

"In all fairness, Sam, there's no money in the Republic's treasury to pay for guns." Hays spent more of his time in Austin these days, dealing with government officials. He was trying vainly to obtain pay for his men and feed for their horses.

"Lamar left the treasury busted, didn't he. A big spender."

"A high roller, all right. Houston was ready to take the French up on their offer of a three-million-dollar loan. Did you know that? We'd be jingling sous in our pockets."

"I'm glad it fell through. It would have given the Frenchies a foot in the door. A few more years and we'd be fighting them as well as the Mexicans and the Indians."

Hays laughed in his shy way. "I hear it was quite a meeting, Sam Houston and the French count, with his chest paved with medals and his shoulders dripping with chicken shit. Did you hear about it?"

351

"No."

"Old Sam had his boots up on the desk as usual when the Frenchy came rattling in. All those medals sounded like a wagon full of spare machinery parts. Our illustrious president threw back that dirty old Indian blanket he always wears and pointed to his scars. He beat on his naked, hairy chest and roared—let's see if I can remember it straight. He said, 'An humble Republican soldier who wears his decorations here, salutes you.' "

"Sam may be a lot of things, but humble isn't one of them."

Still talking quietly, the two of them turned back toward camp. They sat down with the rest of the men again. The talk was about the fight of the day before.

"I'll tell you, boys," said Smithwick, "I've fought a lot of Comanches, but never did I see the like of yesterday. I've seen them retreat in disorder, but never have they left their dead and wounded lying around like that. They usually sweep a battlefield cleaner'n my dear old sainted mother's kitchen floor."

"The trick," says Hays, "is to keep them guessing. Indians always play their hand the same way. If you change the rules on them in the middle of the game and up the stakes while you're about it, they get confused. They cash in their chips, push away from the table, and run off to find another game." Hays took out his pistol and turned it over in his delicate hands. "Boys, Mr. Colt's invention has definitely changed the rules and upped the stakes."

Naduah heard the slow hoofbeats, and she stepped to the door to look out. It was dark outside, but from the light of the lodges around her she could see Wanderer tethering Night. He left a pile of freshly cut grass for him.

"Is there any water you can give him?" It was the only thing he said as he brushed past her and went inside. She brought out a stomach paunch and rolled the rim back to the level of the water so he could drink. When he finished, she took some of the grass and rubbed his lathered body. She did it as much to give Wanderer more time alone as to soothe Night.

"Poor Night," she murmured. "You're getting too old for these raids." He shook his head slowly up and down, as though in agreement.

He stood with his head drooping with fatigue and his tail hanging limply. It had been shaved in mourning, and it looked naked and ugly. The raid had not gone well. Naduah dreaded going back inside. She entered the lodge silently and sat opposite Wanderer, studying him through the flames of the fire.

"Are you hungry?"

"Yes."

She sliced a piece of meat from the pronghorn she and Star Name had killed that day and hung it from a stick. Wanderer stared fixedly at it as its juices bubbled and hissed on the hot coals. The silence seemed to stretch out forever, but Naduah waited patiently. No matter what had happened, she was happy to see him back alive and unhurt. She inspected him with her eyes, going over every part of him, looking for wounds. Finally he spoke.

"We left them." And he was silent again, gathering himself to admit his shame. "We left the wounded and the dead. For a hundred miles we ran, the wounded falling onto the trail behind us and no one stopping to help them. I picked up Tuhuget Naquahip, Sore-Backed Horse and brought him with me. But he was the only one I could save. There were too many of them. Almost half the war party is gone.

"We had left our spare horses tied at a distance and we were preparing to split up and raid when we found the tracks of a party of ranging soldiers. There were fourteen of them and seventy of us, so we laid an ambush. It would be a simple thing to kill them, take their scalps and guns and horses." Wanderer sat as motionless as a statue polished by the fire's light. Only his mouth moved.

"We attacked them, and they dismounted as they usually do. They fired their rifles at us while we circled them, but we kept out of range. When their rifles were empty, we charged, thinking they were helpless. But they remounted and raced to meet us, riding right through our arrows.

"Knee to knee they rode with us. They fired into our faces with their little pistols. Our bows were useless at that range, and our guns had to be reloaded. But theirs didn't. Again and again they shot, so close they burned us with their powder." He turned his head slightly so she could see the long black line that raked across his right cheek. "And their leader, never have I seen one like him. He was everywhere, screaming and shooting. He cannot be human."

"What did he look like?"

"A slender man, with black hair. He looks young, but it's hard to tell with white eyes. They all look alike."

"Was there hair on his face?"

"No. He was beardless."

"El Diablo," said Naduah. "Pahayuca told us about him. They say he's a devil and not human. He strikes from nowhere, then vanishes."

"I can believe what they say." Wanderer pulled the stake from the ground and cut off a piece of the half-cooked meat with his knife. "Whatever he is, his medicine is more powerful than any I've ever seen. My men panicked. They fled, howling. There was nothing I could do to stop them. The Texans chased us, their new guns still spitting death. They chased us for miles. We couldn't even stop for our wounded."

"You're the first to return."

"I pushed Night hard. He deserves a rest. But old as he is, he's still faster than any of them. I wanted to be the first to tell Iron Shirt. I'm going to see him now."

"Won't you rest first and finish eating?"

"No. I don't want anyone else to tell him of his son's shame. It's for me to do." He gave her his old sardonic grin, and she was relieved to see it. "At least I have the small satisfaction of knowing I was right. These guns are better than arrows. We have to get them." And he walked out into the darkness.

The council members sat silently in Iron Shirt's lodge. Outside, the wails of the mourning women added to the tension. Buffalo Piss and other men who had been with the war party had made their reports to the council. Wanderer was just finishing his.

"Many men believed the Texans were demons, that they had supernatural powers. They became too frightened to fight. Those of us who faced the Texans can understand how men could think that way. But I believe the Texans only have a new kind of gun. A small gun that can shoot as many bullets as I have fingers on my hand. We know they change the designs of their guns often. This is the latest. We must find out where they are made, or who has them for trade. Or we must steal them. But we must get them. No longer can we fire arrows while the white eyes are reloading. This new gun gives them the advantage over us."

Iron Shirt stood next and intoned a eulogy for the souls of those who died. Then he turned his wrath on his son.

"Our band lost thirty warriors, thirty of its finest young men. We have heard that the Texans have magic guns that don't need reloading. We have heard that they chased the warriors, still shooting at them with guns this big—" he held up his hands to show the size of the small Colt Paterson"—and didn't allow them time to help the wounded.

"This is hard to believe. Never in my fifty seasons has such shame fallen on my band. To die in battle, to run from the enemy when it is foolish to stay and fight, these things happen to us. But to leave comrades on the battlefield, to abandon them, that has never happened. I ask myself if this story of guns that fire without reloading is only a tale men tell to cover their own cowardice. I wonder if perhaps they only thought they saw such guns."

The council sat stunned. To accuse a man of lying and of coward-

ice was unheard of. Buffalo Piss started to leap to his feet, but
Wanderer beat him to it. His robe was pulled over his head and his
face was withdrawn to show his anger.

"Father Behind The Sun." He raised his face upward, toward the
bit of sky showing through the smokehole. "You have heard this of
which I am accused. Of cowardice. Of lying to hide my guilt. If this
accusation be true, let the next bolt of lightning and the next roar of
thunder take my life." He paused, as though to give his god a
chance to prove Iron Shirt right. Then, without looking at his father,
he turned and stalked from the lodge.

Silence followed his going. The men sat, letting the words fade
before they moved. Rarely did anyone call down the curse of *tabbe
bekat*, sun-killing. Without speaking, Iron Shirt shifted his robe. He
draped it togalike around his chest and threw the edge of it over his
left shoulder. It was the People's way of showing a change of
attitude. It was Iron Shirt's way of asking his son's forgiveness. But
Wanderer didn't see it. And his father was too proud to go after him.

Wanderer lay staring up at the top of the lodge for hours that
night. Naduah lay awake beside him.

"Stop it," she finally said.

"Stop what?"

"Brooding."

"Golden one, how can you understand the shame."

"I can understand very well. I'm a hated Texan, remember? I
understand shame."

"You're one of the People."

"And so are you. And a great chief and a brave leader. What
happened was not your fault, and you could have done nothing to
prevent it. You couldn't know about the new guns. But now you do,
and the mistake won't happen again. Stop wounding yourself over
and over."

"My father called me a liar and a coward in front of the entire
council."

"If he called you that he was calling Buffalo Piss and Sore-Backed
Horse and some warriors of his own band the same thing. All of you
agree about what you saw. No one really thinks ill of you. Iron Shirt
speaks before he thinks sometimes. You know that."

"Yes, I know that very well." Wanderer even laughed a little. "But
I won't stay here. We'll leave soon. Head out on our own."

"Alone?"

"Alone, or with anyone who wants to come with us. I think Deep
Water will come, and Lance and Spaniard, and Sore-Backed Horse.

Perhaps even Buffalo Piss will come. You should have seen his face in council this afternoon. Tomorrow I'll smoke with those who might want to join us."

"Where will we go?"

"South, to the southern edge of the Staked plains. There's room there."

"Wanderer."

"Yes."

"I have something to tell you."

"Then tell me, golden one. But I would prefer it be good news if possible."

"When spring comes, Night will be a father."

"And Wind will be the mother?"

"Yes. And when spring comes, you'll be a father too."

It took a moment for the words to penetrate Wanderer's gloom. When he realized what she was saying, he rolled over and put an arm protectively around her.

"A son?"

"I can't promise that. But one or the other."

He drew her close to him, and she felt his breath stirring her hair. She slept cradled in his arms that night.

❧ *40* ❧

A winding procession of ponies and mules and travois stretched behind Wanderer and Naduah, Star Name and Deep Water. Ten families and several single men had fallen in line behind Wanderer when he left his father's camp. Iron Shirt stayed stubbornly in his lodge, smoking with his friends and pretending he knew nothing of his son's departure. Naduah could hear him inside, talking loudly, when she rode by at the head of the caravan. She carried Wanderer's shield and lance, as befitted the first wife of a leader. And her lion skin, edged now with red cloth, hung draped across Wind's flanks.

Buffalo Piss had come with them, although he probably wouldn't stay. As much as he complained about the Penateka, he kept returning to them. Spaniard was part of the group, as well as Lance and Sore-Backed Horse, his shoulder still bandaged from the wound the Rangers had given him. Wanderer had saved his life. Sore-Backed Horse wouldn't forget it.

Many of the men from that raid had left with Wanderer. Naduah had been right. Iron Shirt's son wasn't the only one offended by his rash words. The band had barely cleared the camp when a small group came pounding after them. The boy in the lead stood on his horse and waved his arms.

"Wait for us!" It was Upstream, Star Name's brother, sixteen years old now. He and Cruelest One, Skinny and Ugly, and Hunting A Wife had passed through the village on a run when they heard Wanderer was leaving.

"We came to visit and hunt with you this fall," panted Upstream as he pulled alongside them. Cruelest One rode up, looking dour, and Upstream beamed at him. Cruelest One was coming anyway and asked me to join him."

"I only wanted you to help with the horses. I figured I could leave you with your sister once we got here."

"Herd the horses!" Upstream looked aggrieved. "I've gone on my vision quest. I'm a brave now."

"So I've heard. You've talked of nothing else the entire trip."

"My new name is Esa Habbe, Wolf Road."

"That's a good name, Brother," said Star Name.

"Esa Habbe, Wolf Road. Asa Habbe, Star Road." Naduah played with the words, sounding them out. The People called the Milky Way by both names.

"Takes Down and Mother and Something Good made me my own lodge. You women can set it up for me."

"And what will you do for us, Brother?" asked Star Name, cocking one brow at him.

"I'll bring you scalps."

"Wonderful." Star Name turned to Naduah. "Sister, how do you like your scalps, roasted or boiled?"

"And I'll hunt for you too, of course. Women!"

"Wolf Road, how are Takes Down The Lodge and Sunrise and Medicine Woman and Something Good?" asked Naduah.

"And Black Bird and little Weasel?" added Star Name.

"Has Pahayuca begun trading with the Texans?" asked Wanderer.

"One at a time." Upstream, now Wolf Road, patiently went over all the gossip of the Wasps that he knew. And he knew most of it. When they had wrung every last drop of fresh news from him, Naduah turned to Wanderer.

"You said we were going south."

"We are."

"My sense of direction isn't that bad. We're headed north and east."

He grinned at her. Being away from Iron Shirt's camp seemed to have restored his good humor.

"We'll head north a while, then south. I want to see what the country's like. I haven't been up north for a year." Wanderer was a lone wolf now, searching for his own territory.

They camped that night on the Salt Fork of the Red River. Broad swells of grassy prairie paralleled it for twelve miles. The clear stream was twenty feet across, with huge cottonwoods along the river banks. The women rushed to raise their lodges before the rain that had threatened all day. They could see it as they rode, a rusty gray curtain hanging from the black clouds on the horizon.

Naduah didn't take time to lash a platform to keep their gear out of the mud. She leaned the loaded travois against the lodge poles and covered them with old hides. She fell asleep that night listening to the rain patter against the taut leather wall above her head. The next day dawned clear and cool and freshly scrubbed.

As they rode at the head of the procession, Wanderer continued their discussion of the day before. They did that often, sometimes picking up the end of a conversation that had been dropped a month earlier.

"Your sense of direction isn't bad at all, golden one. But traveling on the Staked Plains can be confusing."

"I've noticed." They topped a high ridge dividing the waters of the north and middle forks of the Red River, at the eastern edge of the plateau. From that heighth they could see the valleys of both streams, although the rivers themselves were screened by the heavy growth of trees along them. The Staked Plains were behind them now, rippling and wrinkling and blending into the rolling, high plains to the north. Wanderer pointed to the valleys.

"Streams are usually parallel. If you're traveling upstream, follow the ridges, toward the headwaters. You'll have to branch out when you hit a tributary, but at least you'll be headed in the approximate direction you want to go. If you're traveling downstream, that method doesn't work. Do you know why?"

"Because going downstream you'll run into dead ends where the tributaries meet the main stream. You'll have to descend the ravine, cross, and climb up again. You could use that method if you were willing to ford a lot of tributaries, couldn't you?"

"You could. But there are easier ways to orient yourself."

"What are they?"

"The wind. It blows steadily here."

"Does it ever stop?"

Wanderer thought a moment.

"I don't remember it stopping. Except just before a really bad norther. Tonight I'll show you stars that can guide you." He didn't bother mentioning that she should notice every feature of the landscape and store the image away in her memory. He knew she already did that.

As they moved northward, toward the Canadian River, more people joined them. They came in small groups, preceded by their dust clouds. Most of them were displaced Penateka, forced from their homelands by the Texas settlements. But there were Quohadi too, and Kotsoteka, the Buffalo Eaters from the lands to the east. They were men who knew Wanderer and wanted to ride with him.

Naduah had long since stopped being surprised at how fast news spread among the People as they camped in isolated villages scattered throughout their vast territory. The newcomers fell casually into line with the others. The women were soon chatting like old friends, and the children chasing after each other. The men rode forward to pay their respects to the leader of the band. No one questioned their right to be there. The People were used to coming and going as they pleased.

Finally the group halted on the flat top of a high hill that towered two hundred feet over the beautiful valley spread below it. The valley sloped gradually upward on the other side, and formed a ridge with outcroppings of rock along its crest. A spring flowed from it and fell in a series of narrow waterfalls to join the creek below.

The rains had turned the hills a vivid green. Cactuses were vibrant flecks of color in the grass—pinks and yellows, white and deep purples and crimson. The yuccas, thriving in the wet autumn, still had stalks of red flowers rising from the centers of their fanned, swordlike leaves. A small white yucca moth fluttered past Naduah. She was probably on her way to lay her eggs and, in the process, pollinate the plants that depended on her for their survival.

Meadowlarks sang, their yellow breasts bright in the sunlight. The air was sweet with their flutelike warbling. From the deep grass a pale coyote emerged and loped aloofly in front of them, down the hill and into the trees along the creek. Wanderer ignored it all, concentrating his attention on the scene below him.

At the bottom of the ridge across the valley, men swarmed. A depression about eighty feet square and a few inches deep had been paved with hard-packed adobe mixed with animal blood and ash to harden it and make it water resistant. Walls two and a half feet thick were rising around it.

For acres in all directions the ground was a grid of wooden brick molds. Each mold was ten inches by eighteen inches and five inches deep. Some were empty and some full of the buff-colored adobe laid out to dry in the sun.

There was a shout below when someone sighted Wanderer and his band. The Mexican workers scurried for cover, dodging through the latticework of molds and around the piles of gravel and burned grass waiting to be mixed with the clay. Fifteen-foot beams were dropped with a clatter and rolled down the slope. Men who were tramping the gooey mortar with their bare feet left buff-colored tracks to the low walls, where their muddy soles disappeared over its edge.

Under her stony stare Naduah smiled a little to see them scatter like prairie chickens before her husband and his warriors. Only one man stood his ground. He rode slowly to meet them.

"It's Hook Nose," said Wanderer. "It would be better if you hid, golden one."

Naduah drew back among the women and pulled her robe over her head. She felt safer here, away from the settlements, but the man coming toward them was white. She was taking no chances.

William Bent held his arms up over his head and shook hands with himself. Wanderer locked his forefingers in the sign of peaceful greeting. Then he beckoned his group to follow him. Bent was small and dark, with heavy, slate-gray eyebrows like gathering storm clouds over a hawk's nose.

The Cheyenne called him Little White Man, and they considered him one of their own. He had married Owl Woman, the daughter of their chief, Gray Thunder. The Kiowa and Comanche knew him as Hook Nose, but all the Indians knew him. Already the women in Wanderer's group were gathering their spare buffalo robes and the men were considering which of their ponies and mules they'd be willing to trade. William and his brother, Charles, had operated trading posts for years. And the Indians trusted them as they trusted few white men.

The People camped for two days near the site of the new trading post. And when they left, their pack animals were loaded with calico, lead, powder, coffee, and trade cloth. Naduah and Star Name both had bright new vermillion paint in the parts of their hair. They had painted the insides of their ears with it, and Naduah had carefully stroked three vertical lines onto her chin. Wanderer was silent, disappointed that there had been none of the new repeating pistols for sale at the post. He had come north to find them, and was now planning his next move. He had no way of knowing that the maker of the wonderful pistols, Samuel Colt, was bankrupt and that no more were being manufactured.

Naduah heard the cries first. She kicked Wind toward them, crashing down the embankment they were following and into the brush-filled ravine along the shallow creek. A mule bolted up the other side, scattering the split willow lathes that were only half tied onto his back. Wolf Road and Cruelest One took off in hot pursuit.

"Naduah, come back!" Wanderer would be angry with her. She knew better than to rush into a blind spot like that. There was always the possibility of an ambush at a watering place. But her instincts had taken over. She could no more have resisted that cry than a mother doe could resist the bleat of its terrified fawn. The cries were those of a child.

She found him crouched against a boulder, babbling in terror and holding his leg. There was a dry whirring sound and the crackle of leaves as a dusty brown and black rattler, six feet long, twined off among the stems of the plum bushes.

"Wanderer, the fire horn." She didn't need to explain. He quickly gathered twigs and dry leaves and pulled the horn's strap over his head. He yanked out the hardwood stopper and the moist rotten wood that lined the inside. He shook the live coal onto the twigs and fed it sprigs of dry moss, blowing gently to fan it into a blaze. Then he held one of his arrow heads in the flames, feeding the fire until the metal glowed a deep, translucent orange-red.

While he was doing it, Naduah ran after the boy, who bolted when he saw the men. She and Star Name and Deep Water darted through the bushes like children chasing a rabbit. They knew they had to stop him as soon as possible. The more he ran, the faster the venom would reach his heart.

Deep Water tackled him and sent him sprawling. He pinioned the child's arms while Star Name threw herself across his thin, heaving midsection. Naduah knelt on his unhurt leg to hold it and grasped his other ankle firmly in her left hand. With her knife she made small incisions over the punctures. She sucked blood from the cuts and spat it until Wanderer arrived with her medicine bag and the heated arrowhead. The boy had been jibbering in Spanish, but when he saw the metal, pulsing with intense heat, he screamed.

Wanderer ignored him and knelt beside Naduah. He quickly bored the point of the arrow into the holes left by the snake's fangs. Rows of teeth marks fringed the fang punctures. Already the skin was discoloring and swelling. The heat seared the flesh, cauterizing it and drying up the poison. The boy fainted. Naduah sprinkled pulverized tobacco over the raw, ugly wound and bound a prickly pear pad over it.

She mounted Wind, and Wanderer gently lifted the child and sat him in front of her. She held him in the circle of her arms until he regained consciousness. When she felt him begin to stir, she murmured to him, trying to soothe him with the little Spanish she knew. Spanish was the language of trade, and most of the People knew some.

"*Está bien, niñito. No te haremos daño.* We won't hurt you."

"*Déjeme. Déjeme. No me maten,*" the child sobbed it over and over, begging them to leave him, not to kill him.

"He must belong to the Mexicans who're building the trader's lodge," said Wanderer.

"What will we do with him?"

"Keep him. You'll need help when the child is born. This one can work for you."

"Will you adopt him?"

"No. We will have a son of our own soon." Wanderer had no doubts about that. "Adopting this one will make life complicated when our son grows up."

The boy looked about ten years old. An unruly pile of wiry black hair obscured big round eyes that stared wildly around him. He wore faded brown cotton pants, many sizes too large and tied around his narrow waist with a frayed cord. His shirt had been patched and repatched with scraps of different colors. Each patch had been appliqued from the inside, the edges of the holes neatly turned under, until the shirt looked like an intricate piece of artwork. Someone cared about him.

Wanderer tied him onto one of the extra mules, and the band resumed its travels, still to the north and now westwardly.

"Where are we going?" asked Naduah.

"To the Cimarron River to collect salt. It's only a few days' ride. There's a plain covered with salt. It looks like snow that has melted and refrozen into ice. It glitters in the sun. As long as we're this far north we might as well get some."

"And then?"

"We'll go to Medicine Bluff."

"To the east of here?" Naduah had heard of it, but had never seen it.

"Yes. I want to pray to the spirits for a son."

"Medicine Woman once told me why you were named Wanderer. I never realized how right she was."

"Would you rather stay in one place?" He looked over at her. "Are you unhappy?"

"Of course not."

Unhappy? She spent her days in the company of Wanderer and

her closest friends. She watched the awesome, immense landscape change subtly daily and from day to day. She watched the sun shine in shifting patterns alternating with the shadows of the huge, billowing clouds overhead. She saw the wind approach from far off, riding on rippling waves through the grass. She felt it arrive, cool on her cheeks and hair.

Even Wind and Night were behaving like colts in spring. Night would kick out and whinny. He swerved to bump into Wind, who butted him back. Naduah laid her hand on her own stomach and felt the small bulge there. No. She wasn't unhappy.

Naduah stood with her feet spread, one on each side of the shallow hole in the birth lodge. She grasped the stake to brace herself, giving herself leverage to push. She contracted her muscles and helped the child toward the light. The pains were close together now. Tawia Petih, Wears Out Moccasins, squatted next to her, her large, square hands held between Naduah's legs to ease the baby into the fur-lined depression. Star Name wiped the sweat from her sister's brow with a rag dipped in cool water. The tent was fragrant with the sage burned to purify it.

Naduah missed Medicine Woman often, but never more than now. She tried to imagine her grandmother's low voice soothing her as the baby moved toward birth. And she regretted that there was no grandfather waiting outside to ask the sex of his grandchild. They had not seen Iron Shirt since they had left his village in the fall, six months ago. It was Wanderer who stood outside, pacing back and forth, as he had been all night, waiting for word. Deep Water and Sore-Backed Horse waited with him.

"Here comes the head." Wears Out Moccasins was a big, solid woman who had followed them when they set out on their own. "Every band needs a medicine woman," she had said. "And besides, my son, the great war leader, wants me to stay home and help his wife with the children. I like children, but I've raised my own. I want to travel, to raid. I've been an obedient daughter, wife, and mother for fifty-five years. Now I want to try something different."

Naduah doubted that Wears Out Moccasins had ever been obedient, but she let that pass. It did no good to argue with her. And she was a welcome addition to the band. She was a powerful shaman. Her name meant Wears Out Moccasins And Throws Them Away. And she didn't wear her moccasins out by being an obedient wife and mother. She went raiding often with the men. Her horse herd was as big as any man's among them. But she didn't have Medicine Woman's soft voice or gentle laugh. Her hands were large and rough. Her manner was rough too. She had a way of reducing people to the size of children when she was angry with them. Her son had probably been glad to see her go. Her daughter-in-law was undoubtedly happy about it.

"Here he comes," she said.

"Is he a boy?" Naduah craned to see.

"He's not far enough out to tell yet. But he will be. Wanderer asked me to make medicine to be sure." Perhaps the People had so much faith in Wears Out Moccasins' medicine because she did.

The baby cleared the torn tunnel and dropped into her hands. She lowered him slowly into the silky rabbit and ermine furs. Her hands were more than gentle enough as she bit the cord through and tied it.

"It's a boy, Sister!" said Star Name. Wears Out Moccasins lumbered to the doorway.

"*E-hait-sma*, your close friend," she called out. There was a whoop outside and the sound of feet running. Lance could already be heard chanting the news, and the drums had started, picking it up.

Wears Out Moccasins cradled the squalling child in her huge arms and laid a big hand along Naduah's wet cheek. It was a brief touch, not lingering long enough to be accused of affection. Star Name tucked the coiled, bloody umbilical cord into the small beaded bag to hang in a hackberry tree. Wears Out Moccasins carried the baby to the nearby stream to wash him. Naduah could hear his cries rise to a shriek when the cold water hit him. She walked stiffly to the pile of thick robes and sat wearily, learning propped against the willow-withe back support. Star Name handed her a rag dampened with warm water, and she washed off the drying blood and placental fluid.

When Wears Out Moccasins returned, she rubbed the baby with bear fat and started to give him to his mother. He screwed his tiny face up and began to wail again. Wears Out Moccasins held his nose tightly closed between her thick fingers. His face turned pink, then red, then purple as he tried to cry and breathe at the same time. When he gave up the crying and chose to breathe instead, she let his nose go. He immediately began to cry. She repeated the process once, then again, until Naduah feared she would kill the child. When Wears Out Moccasins let go of his nose the third time, the baby was silent. She handed him to his mother.

"Now he's cured of crying."

"I was afraid he wouldn't survive the lesson."

"It seems that way. That's why mothers can't be trusted to teach their own babies."

Naduah looked down at his fuzzy black head while he nuzzled her breast. Star Name burned more sage and cleaned up the lodge. She carried out the hide of bloody water that had been heated for the birth. Women began arriving to admire the baby. Wears Out Moccasins boiled roots and onions and roasted bread on flat stones next to the fire. Naduah couldn't eat meat during the time of childbirth, and she nibbled on dried plums as her son nursed. Then she rocked him to sleep, crooning to him as he lay nestled in her arms.

She'd seen many babies, but she'd never looked at one this way before. She was awed and elated by his perfection. She picked up one of his hands, inspecting the tiny fingers, each one tipped with a miniature nail. Then she cupped one delicate foot in her hand and wiggled the toes, as though to assure herself that everything was in working order. He would be a strong, healthy baby.

Three days later, Naduah left the birth lodge to wash herself and her son in the river. Then she walked to her own tent. A black spot had been painted on the door to announce the birth of a boy. Wanderer sat outside, smoking with Deep Water, Sore-Backed Horse and Spaniard. Wanderer only nodded to her. But Sore-Backed Horse reached out for the child. A father wasn't supposed to pay much attention to his son, but an uncle or grandfather could. And Sore-Backed Horse had elected himself uncle. He bounced the baby in his arms, careful to support the child's neck, in spite of his apparent nonchalance.

"What a handsome brave. Look at him. When are you going to produce a man like this?" He asked Deep Water. Sore-Backed Horse himself had fathered two girls. "In a year or two he'll be a herder for us."

"I think it'll take at least three or four years before he's ready, Sore-Backed Horse." Naduah retrieved the baby and carried him inside. As her eyes adjusted to the dimness in the lodge, she saw that the new cradle board had a miniature bow and arrows and lance hanging from it. There was also a stuffed bat dangling for good luck. She recognized the bat. It was of Wears Out Moccasins' making, and Naduah smiled. She could imagine Wears Out Moccasins stamping into the lodge, thrusting it gruffly into Wanderer's hand, then spinning heavily on her heels and thudding out again. And Wanderer must have spent the past three days making the tiny weapons. They were perfect in every detail.

It was evident he hadn't spent the time cleaning up. In the three days she had been gone, he and their new Mexican slave, Tso-me, Gathered Up, had made a shambles of the lodge. Torn moccasins and clothes lay in heaps. The sleeping robes were scattered. There

365

was a pile of gnawed bones next to the fire, and scraps of leather and thongs and shavings lying around. But it was good to see her things again.

Her beautiful silver mirror hung from a pole. Her clothes hung on a line. There was the saddle that Sunrise and Takes Down had made her, and her lion skin was folded and draped across it. She saw the Spanish bridle inlaid with silver, and the beaded moccasins that Star Name had given her.

With Star Name helping, she had spent days making the cradleboard, working around the bulging belly. She had hammered rows of brass tacks along the two narrow boards that formed the V-shaped frame. The soft leather wrappings were solidly beaded, laced up the front, and hung with long luxuriant fringe. Strings of blue and white pony beads dangled among the fringes. The beads were large and lumpy and brightly colored. They had made their way across the plains on the backs of traders' ponies, hence their name.

The light in the lodge dimmed slightly as Wanderer stood in the doorway. Naduah held his son up for him to see, but instead of just looking at him, Wanderer took him from her. While Naduah prepared a meal, he sat by the fire with him. He rocked the baby in his hard, muscular arms and crooned in a low, pleasant voice. The infant seemed to be inspecting his father too. He stared fixedly up at him before his eyelids drooped and he slept.

Just before the meal was ready, Gathered Up, came in. The boy's snakebite had healed quickly and he had taken almost as quickly to the People's life. He seemed to enjoy being in charge of Wanderer's herd. He had just come from the pasture, where he had watered them and checked their tethers. He leaned over Wanderer's shoulder and lifted the robe slightly to peer into the baby's face.

"He looks like his father," he said, his big dark eyes solemn. Gathered Up had learned the People's language over the winter, but he still spoke it with a slight Mexican accent. His ragged clothes had been replaced by breechclout and moccasins.

"Sit," said Naduah, waving at him with her ladle.

Wanderer found the bag of pulverized dry rot gathered from cottonwood trees. He powdered the baby's bottom with it, then wrapped him in a rabbit-fur robe. He carefully laid the child, still asleep, inside the stiff rawhide tube that had been laced up one side to form a conical cradle. It would keep him from harm as he lay between his parents at night.

There was no particular ceremony when the child was shown to his father for the first time. And the father rarely had much to do with his children's early training and care. But Wanderer had shown, without words, how he felt about his new son. He would never again perform a mother's tasks. But his doing it once told Naduah a great deal. She served him and Gathered Up the steaming stew and sat between them to eat. She wondered briefly if there was anyone as happy as she at that moment.

❧ *41* ❧

Wanderer and Naduah lay together in a field of fire. The meadow was ablaze with masses of bright orange daisies. The smell of them overwhelmed everything else. She was on her side, her head resting on his shoulder, with her arm thrown across his bare chest. His head was propped in the crook of his free elbow, and their bare legs were entwined. Leaning against a plum bush nearby was their month-old son's cradle board. His bright eyes peered out from the layers of wrapping, and he seemed to be studying everything. He was especially fascinated with the birds that fluttered and sang in the bushes around him. Dog lay next to him, her nose on her paws. She was guarding the child, as she always did.

Naduah closed her eyes and breathed deeply. The flowers' aroma was so sweet and heady it made her a little dizzy. She tried to separate the odors of the different kinds. The bright orange ones were easy. There were thousands of them, and their smell was strong. They were like daisies trying to be gardenias. And the furry red balls on the sensitive vines had a distinctive odor too, like roses. But the others, the primroses and bluebonnets, clammy weed and larkspurs growing waist high, all blended into one intoxicating medley of smells. Naduah gave up trying to identify them with her nose.

"Quanah. We'll call him Quanah," she murmured against Wanderer's warm skin.

"Quanah, Fragrant." He tested the name out loud. "If that's what you want to call him, that's what his name will be." It wasn't the usual way to name a male-child, but Wanderer didn't question her decision. He felt, deep inside himself, that she had medicine too. That someday she would be as powerful a healer as Medicine Woman, as respected a shaman as Wears Out Moccasins. If she wanted to name the child, he would forego the usual naming ceremony.

He breathed in the fragrance of her hair, the smell of grass and flowers and sunlight. He took his arm from beneath his head and caressed the long, golden tendrils of it, combing them smooth with his fingers. He ran his hand down her side and up to the curve of her hip. He caught the hem of her dress as it lay high on her leg and pulled it up farther, slipping his hand underneath it. He stroked her firm thigh, and pushed her gently over onto her back. He rolled on his side to lean over her.

"Your skin is as smooth and pleasant to the touch as a snake's belly when he's warmed himself on a rock in the sun."

He raised her dress almost to her waist and studied the curly golden nest between her legs. It always fascinated him. He played with the coils of delicate gold hair, twining it around his fingers. Then he ran his fingertips lightly over the down on her thighs. She lay quietly, totally lost in the sensation of his touch. His hands sent shivers over her body. "My wolf, my lone wolf," she murmured.

She reached out and pulled his face toward her. She pressed her mouth to his. Like the gold between her legs, kissing was alien to Wanderer, but he had developed a taste for it. He continued stroking her as they kissed. Her tongue explored his lips, his teeth, his mouth. She twisted and moaned under his hands, loosening his breechclout and caressing him in turn. He rolled lightly over her. Gathered Up and a gang of boys on ponies thundered past the thicket where they lay hidden, but Wanderer and Naduah no longer cared if they were seen or not.

When they finished, they lay wrapped in each other's arms, drowsy and content. Naduah was almost asleep when they heard a shrill whinny from the horse pasture.

"That was Night."

"I know." Naduah was on her feet and reaching for the cradle board. "It doesn't sound like his trouble call, though." She swung the board onto her back, adjusting the straps and shifting it into place while Wanderer collected his bow and quiver. He sprinted up the rise and down the gentle slope to the river bottom where the ponies were grazing. When Naduah and Quanah and Dog arrived, he was pulling the placental sac from a wet, gangly foal and wiping the fluid from his nostrils. Wind still lay on her side, and Night pawed and paced nearby. He came closer to sniff his son and began licking him dry.

"You took your time, didn't you?" Wanderer lifted one of the foal's long, loosely jointed legs. "It's a colt. And he's black like his father." While they watched, another sac, slick and shiny and purple, bulged from under Wind's tail.

"Twins!" Naduah kicked a twisted cedar log to scatter any scorpions that might be hiding in it. Then she sat down, braced Quanah's cradle board between her knees, and studied Wind through the forked frame. "I thought I'd counted more than four legs kicking inside her. And she's been huge."

The second foal, a female, struggled out of her sac while the first one swayed his large head on his thin neck, trying to avoid the bright sunlight. He was soaking wet, and even in the warm spring air he was shaking with cold. Wind and Night began licking the foals dry, massaging them with their tongues and imprinting them with their scent.

Wanderer and Naduah watched. In half an hour the colt should be standing. They wanted to make sure he and his sister were all right. The colt gathered his awkward legs under him and tried to surge to his feet. His front legs splayed out to the sides and his rear ones buckled. He lay a moment, collecting himself, then mustered his forces for another attempt.

"He'll be a replacement for Night." Wanderer studied the colt intently. "He'll have what it takes."

"Night can carry you for many years yet."

"It'll take that long to train this one."

"Do you think he'll be as good?" asked Naduah.

"I don't know."

The colt had finally mastered his own legs and had pricked his ears in triumph. He tottered toward his mother, bumping into her and almost falling down again. He began nuzzling along her side, searching for the food supply. Naduah picked up Quanah. Then she and Wanderer and Dog headed back toward the village.

It had rained a few days before, and the rolling hills were a rich, lush green dotted with darker copses of bushes and patches of timber. Wanderer's people were on the move again. The long procession wound over the hills like an enormous black snake gliding across a green carpet. As they rode, Naduah chewed a piece of jerky into mush. She scooped it out and reached down to feed it to Quanah, whose cradle board swung from her pommel. As his mouth clamped down on her fingers, she thought she felt the hard nub of a tooth under the surface of his gums.

In front of them a buffalo loomed from the dust cloud of the wallow where he had been rolling on his back, his legs thrashing the air. He looked like a ship emerging from a thick fog. Black mud dripped from his back, covering the raw skin laid bare in patches by shedding and scratching. The mud would harden into a protective shell, keeping away insects. A cloud of thwarted gnats swarmed around his face.

It was early August, the end of the breeding season, and the bulls were vicious. This one rolled his bulging eyes at them and bellowed before he wheeled and lumbered away. Wanderer didn't bother chasing him. He was old. His feet were set more forward and his hind quarters dropped lower than the average. His hind legs were bent more in the hock joints. He would be tough.

Besides, the men had hunted as they rode. Bags of buffalo tongues and tender steaks from the humps were piled on the pack animals. They would cook slabs of the ribs over the fires that night. They would eat the succulent tongues and the sweet marrow roasted inside the bones. Naduah's mouth watered at the thought of the feast they would have. They had taken more meat than they needed because they would be sharing it. They were riding toward a rendezvous with José Piedad Tafoya and his Comancheros.

"Your men seem to like playing El Gallo, Wanderer." José Tafoya lounged against his saddle and watched the competition. Except for a few added scars on his face and arms, he hadn't changed much since the days when he brought a few loaded mules onto the Staked Plains and trailed after the Comanche. Like many of his men José wore leather pantaloons slit down the sides and baggy, white cotton drawers underneath. The rowels on his spurs were huge and jingled when he moved.

"I'd like to try it myself," said Wanderer.

"You'd better hurry. We didn't bring that many chickens with us." On the level bottom of the narrow valley below them, the Comancheros were teaching the warriors the rules of the game. It didn't take long. There weren't many. They buried a rooster up to its neck in the sand, and galloping riders tried to pull it out as they went by. The game didn't last long, because the men of the People almost never missed. More often than not the triumphant player rode away with only the head in his hand, and the supply of roosters was limited. José stood, cupping his hands, and shouted to his lieutenant.

"Chino, teach them El Coleo." He sat back down. "This one is played on foot. My men will have a better chance against yours."

"How is it played?"

"With a bull. The meaner the better." He stood to shout again. "Bring El Bravo, not that one. That one is a pet. A kitten." Then, in Spanish and handtalk to Wanderer, "The object is to run after the bull and throw him. But you can only throw him by twisting his tail until he loses his balance. Of course, sometimes the bull runs after you. I lost three men that way last year. Bulls caught them in the stomach and ripped them open like those puffballs that grow in damp ground. Poof. What a mess. But I had a wonderful time consoling their widows."

"Ho-say," Wanderer was unusual. He preferred to talk business first and then get on with the stories. "I'm looking for the new pistols the Texans have. The ones that fire many times without reloading."

"I've seen them. A man loads them on Sunday and shoots all week. They're hard to find. I can perhaps bring them for you on the next trip. If you'll supply me with horses and cattle from Texas. There's a market for them in New Mexico, my friend. I can use as many as you can steal." The lean, brown trader gestured toward the west and the Mexican province. He pursed his lips, using them to point. It was easier than disengaging his hands from his serape, and it had become a habit with all the Mexicans and Pueblos.

"Have you seen the Penateka this trip?" asked Wanderer.

"Certainly. They're among our best customers." José belched and scratched his crotch. "They're trading for more whiskey these days. I have some hidden in the hills, if you'd like it. The usual arrangement. When we're all ready to go our separate ways, you pay for it and a couple of my men, on their fastest horses of course, will lead you to it. It's not that we don't trust you, my brother. It's just that we know how excited your people get when they drink whiskey. Sometimes they go a little *loco*."

"We don't want your stupid water." Wanderer relit his pipe. Deep Water and Sore-Backed Horse joined them.

"Ho-say," said Deep Water, sprawling next to him and reaching for the pipe. "What news from the south?"

"Texas is now part of the United States." Tafoya groped for words to explain territorial boundaries, political organizations, annexation. "The Great White Father in Washington has made a treaty with the Father in Austin. They are now one tribe. Anyone who makes war on the Texans makes war on the United States. And that includes Mexico. A big United States war leader has gone to the Rio Grande. Texas soldiers are gathering there for a raid into Mexico. They say even El Diablo Hays and his Rangers will go. And the army will need all the horses it can get for supply trains. You have left the Texans with few animals."

"While the Texans are in Mexico we'll steal their stock and sell it back to them," grunted Sore-Backed Horse.

371

"It's not that simple, Brother," said José. "The United States is more powerful than the Texans."

"Children are more powerful than the Texans," Deep Water spat contemptuously.

"The United States will send soldiers to defend the settlements."

"Let them," said Wanderer. "I've seen those blue-jacket troops to the north. They move through the countryside like a flock of jays. 'Boom!' They fire off a gun in the evening so everyone will know where they are. 'Boom!' They fire off another one in the morning so we'll know they're still there. And in case we mistake their cannons for thunder, they blow horns all day long. Do the blue-jacket soldiers have the new pistols instead of those old, useless guns?" Wanderer looked like he was ready to leave in search of them if they did.

"I don't know. But I have one of the shiny brass horns they blow. I'll be glad to trade it to you for two horses."

"Ho-say," said Sore-Backed Horse. "You'd trade your mother for two horses."

Wanderer smiled, anticipating a fight. He had learned not to bring up Ho-say's mother. The man had no sense of humor about her. But this time Tafoya let it pass. He continued with his news.

"Envoys from the Great White Father of the United States have met with Old Owl and Pahayuca and Santa Ana. Old Owl is away now, on a long trip to the lodge of the Great Father in Washington."

"Where is Wah-sin-tone, Ho-say?"

"*Allí está. Lejos.*" Tafoya nodded and pouted again, this time toward the east, as though Washington lay somewhere in the country of the Wichita. "Nocona, Wanderer, my brother. I hear you have a son, an infant. Now you don't need the yellow hair anymore. I'll give you a good price for her." José saw Wanderer stiffen, saw the rage gathering in his hard, black eyes. He was so protective and possessive of that woman. One would think she was a prize horse, the way he treated her. "*Amigo.*" He held up a thin hand in the sign of peace. "I was only teasing. I have nothing left to trade anyway. Your women have taken everything. They almost trampled Chino as they fought to get to the wagons. They'll leave me a poor and broken man. Such advantage they take of me."

"To trample Chino, one would have to trample also his machete," pointed out Deep Water.

"And no one takes advantage of you. Your soul is a lump of lead and you would gladly trade it for a good price."

"And you would buy it, Sore-Backed Horse. I wish my soul were lead. Lead brings a good price indeed." José turned to Wanderer. "Later I'll come to your lodge to see your son. I hear he's handsome, like his father."

"Be careful, Wanderer. He may try to seal little Quanah to sell to the Pawnee," said Sore-Backed Horse.

"He wouldn't dare," said Deep Water. "Wears Out Moccasins would come after him with her battleax."

"If Wears Out Moccasins is here, your son is safe, *amigo*. Once she thought I had cheated her, and almost broke every fragile bone in my body with a shovel that I had just given her."

The men rose, stretched, and walked toward camp. The warriors and the Mexicans had tired of baiting El Bravo and were drifting toward the cooking fires too. Spaniard held his gored arm gingerly as he walked. The smell of coffee was strong, and Wanderer's stomach rumbled. Piles of crisp hump ribs and tongues waited for them. Every man would eat at least five pounds of meat. Then they would lie around the fire and talk until dawn.

Around their own fires the women would be studying José's stiff sample cards of beads. Each card unfolded to show examples of the different colors and sizes. The women would take hours deciding what they wanted. Already they were wrapping themselves in the coarse, heavy buff and brown and blue-striped blankets he had brought. They would be happily comparing their new finery and kitchen trinkets. It would be a pleasant night.

For acres in all directions the sprawling camp was astir. The women of Wanderer's band were toppling their lodges, shouting and laughing and racing to see which groups would finish first. *And probably betting some of their new trade goods on the outcome*, thought Wanderer. The huge lodge covers lay all over the ground, along with piles of rawhide food boxes, bags, painted buffalo robes, bone and horn utensils, axes, kettles, the envelope-shaped wardrobe pouches, and hundreds of other things. The horses stood patiently amid the noise and confusion, flicking their ears at the horseflies. Their mistresses lashed the travois poles to their sides and piled baggage on their backs.

Children were lifted into place on other ponies, and the smallest, those one to two years old, were tied in place. Other children were stowed into domed willow cages on travois. The older boys ran hither and yon, dodging between their elders. Some of the warriors, painted and decked in feathers, charged through the flattened village, sometimes two or three abreast, racing their horses. The dogs lay panting in whatever shade they could find, yelping and running with their tails between their legs when someone stepped on them by mistake.

The Comancheros were packing up too. They lifted the huge burdens, using their knees as fulcrums, their arms and bodies as levers. With grunts and shouts and curses, they threw them over the mules' backs. Then, bracing their feet against the animals' sides, they tightened the wide straps of woven sea grass, pulling them until they gripped like ladies' corsets. They tied crupper lines from the pack saddles around under the tails to steady the loads and keep them from sliding forward. The cruppers cut cruelly into the animals' flesh, and many of them bled.

Tafoya now owned the ungainly carts that the little trader had dreamed of seven years before as he sat in Sun Name's lodge, bargaining for Rachel, the white-eyes woman. He remembered her with a certain amount of affection. She was largely responsible for his success, she and the price she had brought.

There were curses and shouts and singing, the crack of whips or the thunk of stout sticks against mules' flanks. There was the bawling of animals and the grating squeals of the carts' axles. And over it all Wanderer could hear the delicate jingling of the bell on the *madrina,* the bell mare.

"*Que lio, amigo mio.* What a wonderful riot. And the *madrina* stands quietly through it all. You should have a *madrina,* a bell mare, for your herds."

"Yes, and tell everyone where the ponies are so they'll have no trouble stealing them."

"Seriously, Wandering One. The mules love that bell mare. They'll follow her anywhere. Mules form the most outrageous attachments. They're like women that way. *Sinverguenzas.* Shameless. They bestow their affections on someone, even someone not of their station at all. And when they do, beware, *hombre.* Don't try to change them. They maintain their love as steadfast as the mountains. I have seen mules devoted to colts, to dogs. To buffalo calves. Even to a duck once."

Wanderer laughed.

"Truly. The whole herd followed that duck everywhere. They are like women, wonderful beasts. Stubborn, loyal, stupid. Just like women."

"Chino, beat that *maldito* mule." José pointed imperiously with his bone-handled quirt. "That one. Hit him hard." He turned back to Wanderer. "But like women, they become spoiled, lazy, if you don't beat them regularly.

374

"My men are ready to go." Tafoya reached out his right hand, and Wanderer clasped his wiry forearm just below the elbow. Tafoya did likewise, clapping him on the shoulder with his left hand, in the Comanchero manner. Then, standing on tiptoe, he grabbed Wanderer in an *abrazo*, hugging him first to one side, then to the other.

"When will we see you again, Ho-say?"

"Same time next year, *amigo*." He considered the bluffs around them thoughtfully. "And next year I'll build a little cave up there in the cliff. It'll be a storeroom, with barred windows and a little roof. That way I can keep my merchandise dry and safe from . . . let's say coyotes. And I can meet more bands here.

"Remember, *jefe*, what I said about the horses and mules and cattle. Steal a lot of cattle. I'll bring you guns if you'll bring me stock."

"Not just guns. Repeating guns."

"*Entendido, amigo.* Understood. ¡*Dios te lleve, y la virgen y todos los santos!* God carry you!" he shouted. As he rode away in the wake of his ragtag caravan, Tafoya waved his arm in a broad sweep, a motion vaguely representing a cross.

Wanderer rode to find Naduah. She and Gathered Up were just loading the last pack mule. The arched wooden frames of the pack saddle fitted so snugly over the rawhide pads that there was no need for a cinch. Gathered Up handed Naduah the goods and she lashed them tightly. They worked efficiently together. The process of moving had been shaved down to its barest essentials. They knew where each small item would best fit in the packs.

Lance was walking his pony slowly through the campsite, calling out the marching instructions. Wanderer had been so occupied with Tafoya and his traders that he hadn't had a chance to tell Naduah where they would be going. He rode next to her now as they led the procession away from Cache Creek. As usual, she carried his lance and shield.

"Lance says we're headed for the Pease River," she said.

"Yes. I think that's where we'll hunt this fall. It's between the land of the Quohadi and the Tenawa. And there are buffalo there."

"It's pretty country."

"Then you approve?"

"Yes, of course. Why wouldn't I approve?"

"You might like some other place better."

"No. I'm happy anywhere, as long as you're with me. And I think I've seen all the country between the Cimarron and Mexico."

"I suppose I am a wanderer." He smiled. "I have more than one reason, you know.

375

"What's the reason, besides the fact that you're looking for your own territory and you like to roam?"

"I worry that someday traders will find you and try to take you back. Or they'll tell soldiers. I want to make it as difficult as possible for them to get you."

"No one's going to get me. They've forgotten all about me. I have one request, though."

"What's that?"

"I want to winter with my family, with Pahayuca's band. I want to see Takes Down The Lodge and Medicine Woman and Sunrise again. And Something Good and Weasel. I want to show them our son."

"We'll camp with them this winter."

❧ 42 ❧

Wanderer stared at the pictures crudely sketched with charcoal on the folded piece of bark. He had found it in the largest cottonwood. It was wedged into a cut made by a hachet.

"Pahayuca's planning to camp on the Canadian. That's good. When we get bored this winter we can raid the wagons headed for Santa Fe."

"Here's a track." Naduah dismounted to look at it. The hoof marks were near the cottonwood, at the edge of the churned trail left by a village on the move. "They were here only two days ago, in the morning." She brushed at the sand that had dried on the blades of grass crushed by the horses' hooves. The brittle coat of sand grains meant that the grass had been wet with morning dew when the hoofprints were left. And there had been no rain or dew since two mornings before.

"Pahayuca's still riding that bay. The horse with big feet," said Naduah. "But he won't last much longer. He's starting to favor his left forefoot." Naduah stared at the tracks, tears stinging her eyes. The rounded impression in the soft sand brought back a flood of memories. The hoofprint was as familiar to her as the patterns of stitching in the top of her lodge.

When they rode into the abandoned campsite, they knew immediately that it was last used by the People, even though the

Kiowa also preferred open timber for their villages. The fire holes were fifteen inches across rather than twenty-four. And each round lodge site had four larger holes rather than three, where the main poles had been. Naduah could tell from a distance if an occupied camp was Kiowa or one of the People's by the pattern of the lodge poles. When the Kiowa women laid their smaller poles against the three larger ones, they formed a spiral where they jutted out from the smoke hole. The People's poles grouped between the four main ones.

Naduah spurred Wind and moved ahead of Wanderer.

"Woman, where are you going?" he shouted after her.

"I want to see them. Hurry!" He laughed and obediently squeezed Night lightly with his knees. The pony broke into a canter to catch up with her, and the rest of the band quickened their pace. Wanderer grimaced as he thought of the days of travel to come. In their haste Naduah and Star Name would be dismantling the lodges around him and Deep Water and Wolf Road as they slept each morning. There would be no peace until they found Pahayuca's people and their own family.

"Star Name, come on!" Naduah shouted and waved her arms. "They're only two days ahead of us." Star Name came at a gallop, and the two of them took off across the hills in a race with the wind, their ponies' manes and tails streaming behind them. Naduah stood on Wind's back.

"I'm giving you a handicap," she shouted to Star Name.

Wanderer shook his head as he watched them grow smaller in the distance. Naduah was a good mother most of the time. But it was fortunate that Wears Out Moccasins watched over Quanah. He was riding in front of Wears Out Moccasins now. But soon he would be old enough to ride tied onto a pony by himself.

The group of women and girls gathered near Takes Down's lodge was larger than usual. They claimed they were there to work, but not much work was being done. Sewing projects lay forgotten on hides scattered around the area. Awls were stuck into half-finished seams. Half-tanned skins lay with their scrapers on top of them. Most of the scrapers were metal now, as were the awls and the needles. And some of the women's clothes were being made of the blue and white striped ticking and red calicos that the traders brought. The blouses wrinkled and soiled quickly, but the women liked their bright colors.

Most of them were sitting in a circle around little Quanah. He was delirious with the attention. He would crawl, laughing, to someone and sit in the red dust, his bare bottom coated with it. When he held out his pudgy arms and smiled, no one could resist his sparkling slate-gray eyes. He was passed from hand to hand and told how handsome he was.

When he tired of that, eight-year-old Weasel helped him to stand. He threw himself, shrieking with glee, backwards onto the nearest ample lap. Weasel helped him up, and he did it again, until all the women were laughing with him. His laugh was contagious, and the warm sun was intoxicating. It was unusually mild for December.

Naduah and Black Bird, Star Name and Something Good watched Takes Down The Lodge. They were waiting for her to finish painting the outline of the design she was putting on Naduah's lodge cover. The cover was draped over a framework of poles so she could draw the picture as it would appear on the cover when it was raised. Using a peeled willow stick for a ruler and a narrow, flat piece of bone for a brush, she carefully traced in black paint the lines she had indented earlier with her pointed drawing stick.

Naduah stood by with a paunch of water to dampen the hide as her mother worked. Medicine Woman was heating more water to mix with the pulverized mineral colors. The hot water made them set better. She fed sticks into the fire by feel, holding her palm up to test its heat.

"Finished." Takes Down stood back to check her work. "Help me lower it." The others caught at the edge of the heavy cover and dragged it onto the ground, where they spread it out flat. While the black paint dried, the women mixed large quantities of yellow powder into a thin paste. They needed a great deal of it to fill in the huge sun design that Takes Down had outlined. To hold the paint they used whatever containers they could find—iron skillets, large turtle shells, horn cups, stomach paunches. The sun design was five feet across and had four sets of black lines radiating out from it in the wind's four directions. Around the circumference, between the straight lines, saw-toothed designs represented rays.

Each women used whatever type of brush she preferred. Black Bird always used a chewed willow stick, but Naduah liked the end of a hipbone. The honeycombed structure of the bone let the paint flow smoothly. Takes Down filled in the larger areas by blowing the paint through a hollow bone. Star Name and Something Good rubbed it into the damp hide with wads of buffalo hair. They scrubbed hard, working the paint into the surface of the leather.

Wears Out Moccasins and Medicine Woman were making the sizing that would fix the paint permanently in the damp hide. They had a huge pile of prickly pear leaves between them, which they crushed between flat rocks. The sticky juice that oozed out would give the design a gloss when it dried and make it impervious to water. Blocks The Sun, Pahayuca's first wife, was too large to bend over the cover, so she worked on her contribution near Medicine Woman and Wears Out Moccasins. She was stringing tiny dried deer hooves on a long thong. Naduah would hang them from the tallest lodge pole, where they would clatter cheerfully in the wind.

While they worked, the women talked. There was two years of gossip to catch up on, and they weren't wasting any time. As she listened to them, Naduah felt as though she had never left her mother's village. She felt as much a part of life there as she always had.

"A scout from Old Owl's band arrived today," said Takes Down. "They'll be here soon to camp with us."

"Then he's back from his journey to the home of the Great White Father in Wah-sin-tone?"

"Yes. They say he's telling the biggest lies anyone's ever heard. Santa Ana threatens to change his name to Easop, Liar. Very entertaining stories. We won't be bored this winter." Takes Down's hair had fine lines of gray, like pencil strokes, in it. But otherwise she looked much the same. "In the spring Old Owl and Santa Ana and Pahayuca have agreed to meet with the chiefs from Wah-sin-tone. There'll be more presents for us."

The idea of so much contact with the whites made Naduah uneasy, but she was silent.

"Will you stay the winter with us, Naduah?" asked Something Good.

"Of course."

"Don't say of course," called Medicine Woman. "We hear you Noconi never stay in one place more than a day or two."

"Noconi?" Star Name and Naduah said it together.

"Yes. Haven't you heard, Granddaughter? That's what Wanderer's band is called. The Wanderers."

"The Wanderers, Noconi. I like it," said Star Name. It fits."

"They're calling us the Noconi."

"I heard that," said Wanderer. On the other side of the hide curtain that divided the lodge, they could hear Gathered Up's deep breathing. Between his chores and his long hours riding and playing with the other boys, he had no trouble falling asleep at night.

"Golden one, I'm restless. And so are the other men. We're going to raid the wagons that travel along the Canadian. Maybe they're carrying the new guns."

"I'm going with you."

"What about little gray eyes? Will you abandon our son?"

"Abandon him!" Naduah put a hand out to rest on Quanah's back as he slept between them. His legs were drawn up under his chest and his bottom waved in the air under the robe. "Half the time I don't even know where he is. Weasel begs to take care of him, and plays with him most of the day. And Takes Down The Lodge can barely pull him away from Wears Out Moccasins. She and Medicine Woman go out gathering herbs and he rides along in front of one or the other of them. There are more than enough women to take care of him. Besides, Star Name is pregnant and she won't be able to go on raids for a while after this one."

"I didn't say Star Name could go too."

"Of course she can. She's my sister. And she's a better shot than Skinny And Ugly."

"Don't let anyone hear you say that."

"Isn't she? And aren't I?"

"Yes, you are." Wanderer sighed. "Why didn't I marry Red Foot? She never bothers Buffalo Piss to take her on raids. And she never beats him in footraces either."

Naduah hit him lightly with her deerskin pillow.

"You had a thorn in your foot."

"I like to think that's why you won. All right. Just stay behind the men as much as possible."

"Wanderer, stop worrying. No one will steal me from you."

"Not while I'm alive they won't."

The freighters were reorganizing after crossing the swampy ground near a tributary of the Canadian. The last wagon, its blue bed and bright red wheels stained a purplish brown from the mud, was plunging down the bank toward the ford. The grade was so steep the wagon seemed about to pitch forward and roll end over end into the water. Its brakes gave a high grating squeal as they ground against the locked wheels.

The men who had just crossed were shoving their wagon through the mire churned up by the ones ahead of it. They had dug through the red sand and into the blue clay below, covering everything in purple mud. Their shoulders were against the huge wheels, and they were cursing and grunting in unison, knee-deep in the thick slime. Other men were cutting brush and throwing it in the path, trying to give the wheels a firmer footing.

It was a small wagon train, as the Santa Fe trade went. It was the last one out before winter closed in, locking them in an icy fist. They were in a hurry to get their eleven big Pittsburgh wagons to Kansas City and safety. Each of the Pittsburghs was drawn by ten or twelve mules and carried as much as five thousand pounds of cargo.

The hardware and bolts of cloth they had carried west had been exchanged for furs and raw wood, silver and gold bullion from the new placer mines to the south of Santa Fe. The newer traders in the group also had *mulas*, the unsalable articles they'd been stuck with at the end of the trading season. And there were the supplies each man needed for the two-month trip: fifty pounds each of flour and bacon, ten of coffee and twenty of sugar, plus beans and salt and cracknel, the hard, flat biscuits that some men called crackers.

The remuda of spare mules trotted behind the wagons, trying to sneak mouthfuls of the wild rye and nibble mesquite beans. Already their unshod hooves were worn smooth and beginning to slide on the slippery, dry grass. There was a jangling of yokes and chains, the clatter of bells and the crack of whips as the drivers raced to be first in line. No one wanted to follow, floundering in the quagmires of the wheels and hooves ahead of them, or choking in the dust.

"All's set!" The cry was taken up by those ready to move out.

"Stretch out!" The caravan leader tried to maintain order, but it was a thankless job. Each man figured the captain had only been elected to do the dirty work and to order someone else around.

"Fall in! Hep." The air rang with shouts while the drivers urged their teams on. Guns started popping as the men in front shot at rattlesnakes along the trail. One of the wagons had a hide nailed horizontally to its side. The skin was tanned and stretched and a tarnished copper color. It was human. The men of the train had encountered Indians, either on this trip or on the leg out from Kansas.

From a high ridge along the Canadian, Wanderer and his party had watched the wagons approaching for miles. Their billowing white covers dipped with the rolling hills, like ships on an ocean. The warriors were ready for them. They had tied their ponies' tails up and wrapped their robes around their waists. Each of them was painted and had his lance and war ax, his shield, bow, and arrows ready. Those with rifles carried them lightly in the crooks of their arms.

There was no talking among them. Each knew what he was to do. They'd done it hundreds of times before. Wanderer held his war whistle between his teeth, ready to give the signal to attack. It was a perfect time. His war party of fifty men outnumbered the twenty-five white eyes. And the men below them were too preoccupied with their wagons and the mud to even notice them, as they waited,

screened by the dense brush along the ridge. He blew a shrill blast
on his bone whistle, the cry of a diving eagle.

The war party attacked in a tight wedge, whooping as they flew
down the slope. Naduah and Star Name, caught up in the excitement, rode behind them, screaming as they went. The traders saw
there was no time to draw the wagons into a defensive circle. They
frantically pulled down as many crates and barrels and bales as they
could. They took cover behind them, shouting the entire time. The
People's ululating war cry was designed to make each hair on the
back of an enemy's neck vibrate, to set his heart to hammering, and
to stampede his stock. The cry was generally successful. Pandemonium reigned among the wagons.

"Oh, shit, boys. I've broken my ramrod. Anybody got a spare?"

"My gun's choked!"

"God blast it to hell!" Len Williams turned his rifle upside down
and shook it. "I rammed the ball in without the powder." It wasn't
the first time he had faced Comanche, but it was always an unnerv-
ing experience.

There were widly conflicting orders as everyone tried to take
command. But it didn't matter. No one could be heard clearly over
the yells of the war party, the pounding hooves, the braying of the
animals, and the noise from the motley collection of guns.

Most of the warriors formed a huge ring that circled the line of
wagons, coming closer with each precise revolution. Finally, one
section of the circle passed within firing range. The warriors
dropped behind their ponies' sides, using them as shields while
they shot from under the animals' necks. Then the loop carried them
out of range, to the far side of the ring, where they reloaded as they
rode. Wanderer's men taunted the freighters. They rode backwards,
or stood, waving broad, obscene gestures. They shouted insults and
challenges.

Seventeen-year-old Wolf Road, Star Name's brother, couldn't contain himself. He broke from the ring and bolted straight for the
wagons, through the ragged yellow fringe of gunfire along the
barricade of boxes. His whoop came out more like the yelp of a
puppy when his tail is stepped on, but he never faltered in his
course. Sliding down on the opposite side of his pony, he rode along
the barricade and off again. He repeated the performance two more
times. On his last pass, he leaned to the exposed side of his horse.
Taking his knife from his belt, he sliced off the tail of one of the
mules as he went by. Howling in triumph, he waved the bloody
trophy over his head as he rejoined the whirling ring of riders.

While the others kept the freighters busy, Wanderer and Deep

Water and a smaller group rode to investigate the last wagon stranded in the mud and the other standing hub deep in the stream. Their drivers had abandoned them when they heard the first war cries. They dove under the wagons ahead as the first bullets and arrows whined around their feet.

Now Wanderer ransacked the wagon beds, searching for weapons. He found one old rifle and handed it to Naduah. She waited patiently, as though nothing special were going on. The others began loading goods onto the spare animals that Star Name and Naduah had brought. Then he surveyed the scene ahead of them.

It was obviously a stand-off. And if it went on much longer, more men would follow Wolf Road's daring feat and someone might be lost. Losing a man was far worse than returning without scalps. And the party had stolen a great deal of loot and taken the extra mules and horses of the traders' herd. It was time to go.

"Wanderer," Naduah called to him from the bed of the wagon she was helping to unload. "What about these?" She held a pale yellow bar of metal in each hand, ingots of gold.

"Leave them. They're too soft for bullets. Take the lead, though." When he saw that the two women and Deep Water had finished, he blew another shrill call on the whistle. The men of the war party began unwinding their magic surround ring. They followed Wolf Road, heading for the broken country to the south, and the Staked Plains.

With his telescope, Len Williams watched them go. Around him he could hear the men whooping and hollering their relief. Williams' partner looked over at him.

"What're ya starin' at Len? Ya figure them red bellies to be comin' back?"

"No, I think they're gone, Bill. But there was something strange about their herders. They were women, I think. And one of them looked to be white. In fact, I'd swear she was white."

"Who do ya reckon she was?"

"I don't know. But my neighbor back in Limestone County is still looking for his little niece. The one who was stolen, oh, back ten years or more. Parker her name is. Cynthia Ann Parker. Rumor has it she's been seen up in these parts."

"Shoo. The Comanche nation must be half white, what with the children they've stolen over the years."

"I suppose you're right." Williams turned to help repack the wagons. "Still, no harm in mentioning to James Parker the next time I see him."

* * *

It was mid-March in 1846. There were a few tiny buds, an eagle flying north, solitary gnats, shallow puddles of warmth in the air. Naduah was scraping a hide in front of her lodge. Dog, so old now she always rode on a travois when they traveled, was lying in the morning sun. She was following the rays as they shifted along the brush windbreak built around the lodge.

Quanah was playing one of his favorite games with her. On his bowed legs he would stagger over to Dog and throw himself affectionately across her back, pushing the air out of her with a grunt. With a martyred sigh, she rose, shook him off, and moved to another spot. She curled up as tightly as possible and looked at Naduah accusingly. Quanah laughed and tottered after her. The child was into everything these days, and Naduah was glad to see Weasel coming.

"Weasel, rescue Dog. One of these days she's going to lose her temper and bite him."

Weasel picked Quanah up. He was almost a year old, and big for his age. He was becoming an unwieldy burden for a nine-year-old.

"*Tameh-tsi*, dear little brother, would you like to hear the story of how the grasshopper got his beautiful coat?" Weasel sat in the sun next to Dog, who looked at her gratefully, and she put Quanah in her lap.

As Naduah scraped, she could hear Weasel's mother, Something Good telling the same story, in the same words, and with the same inflections. And Quanah would insist on climbing into his father's lap when he came home and repeating his own unintelligible version of it.

She was listening so intently to the story she didn't hear the footsteps. And she didn't notice the man until his shadow fell across the hide pegged out on the ground in front of her. From the corner of her eye she saw Weasel disappear around the back of the windbreak, dragging a protesting Quanah behind her. Dog stood, stiff-legged, the fur on her back flared into a bristling ride. She growled far back in her throat.

The first things Naduah saw were his boots. They were big and dusty, the leather cracked from being wet, then dried countless times in the hot Texas air. Her eyes ran up his rumpled, baggy pants, stained with use and hard traveling. His back was to the sun, and there was a nimbus of light around his head. She squinted to see his features, putting an arm up to shield her eyes. When he spoke, Dog began barking hysterically.

"Cynthia Ann. Listen. I'm a friend. Friend." Len Williams tapped his chest. "I've come to take you home."

His words were jumbled, unintelligible to her, yet vaguely, disturbingly familiar. She rocked back on her heels and pulled the skinning knife from her sheath. She remembered Cub, gone without a trace, swallowed up. Maybe it was the memory, maybe it was the sun, bright in her eyes, but tears welled up. The white eyes wouldn't take her like that. She'd kill him. Len Williams tried again.

"Cindy Ann, remember your name? Remember your mother? And your Uncle James? They want you home with them." It wasn't working. She'd gone savage. And with a husband and child. But it had to be Cynthia. She had those piercing blue Parker eyes. And there was a hint of her mother in the nose and the chin. She was a handsome woman. But she was hunched over a stinking hide like any other overworked squaw in the village. No better than a slave, she was. Her hair was in braids and her face was hideously painted. She'd been burned as black as any nigger in the sun. Williams studied her for marks, bruises, signs of mistreatment. Then he noticed the tears streaming down her cheeks.

"Are they beating you, Cynthia? Have they threatened to hurt you if you talk to me?" He crouched to see her face better and his rank, sweaty odor washed over her. She leaped up and darted off like a startled deer. Her dog sank her teeth into Williams's leg before racing off behind her. Williams shook his head and limped toward Pahayuca's lodge, where the men of the council waited for him. Negotiations resumed. At least he felt fairly sure now that she was the missing Parker girl. And even if she wasn't, she deserved to be saved from these horrible conditions.

"Chief, I'll give you twelve mules instead of ten, and all the goods I have left." That was about three hundred dollars' worth. Expensive. Williams had no doubt but that Pahayuca was holding out, trying to raise the price as high as possible. Once again, in halting Spanish, Pahayuca tried to explain the situation to the ill-mannered white man. He was stalling for time, waiting for Wanderer to return from his hunting trip.

"I cannot sell her. She belongs to her husband. And I tell you he won't trade her. Neither will her father or her mother."

Williams bit his lip. Her mother was back in Limestone County, not in a camp of heathens.

"But you're the chief. You can talk her husband into it. Or just let me take her and I'll leave the goods and animals here. Her husband will forget her soon enough when he sees the price she brought."

385

There was a commotion outside, shouting and hoof beats, and the rattle of arrows in their quivers as men dismounted. Wanderer strode into the lodge, followed by Spaniard, Deep Water, Sore-Backed Horse, and Sunrise. Gathered Up stayed with the ponies. He and his own horse were winded. He had galloped to meet the hunting party and to tell them of the white man's offer. Then he had pushed his mount to the limit to keep up with the others as they raced for the village.

Wanderer's anger seemed to fill the lodge as much as his height did. The five men sat and listened in silence while Pahayuca explained the situation. He spoke quickly, worried that Wanderer, in his rage, would commit some breach of courtesy. Never, in the twenty-five years he had known Wanderer, had he seen him so angry. Not even when he rode out to avenge the death of his friend and brother.

Wanderer took the pipe. He didn't bother using Spanish or hand-talk. It didn't matter to him if the white man understood him or not. He didn't have much to say.

"If this man and his mules and his trinkets are not gone by tonight, I will kill him. If he touches Naduah or my son, I will kill him."

"Let there be not talk of killing, *Ara,* the nephew I love as a son. This man has asked for hospitality under my roof. He will not be harmed," said Pahayuca.

"Then let him not leave your roof."

There was a sharp intake of breath around the council ring. Men didn't argue in council.

"There will be no killing of someone granted hospitality in this village. Would you destroy my honor, my son?" Pahayuca said it mildly. But Wanderer knew their horns were locked. He spoke to ease the tension. This stinking white man was not worth the loss of dignity involved in squabbling with Pahayuca.

"I will not kill him, Uncle. But there will be no talk of selling Naduah, the mother of my son." He stood, gathering his robe around him, and left the lodge. His friends followed.

The next day the Noconi, the Wanderers, were gone. The circles where their lodges had stood were bare and trampled. They had left word with no one, nor any sign indicating their destination. But they left their mark across the frontier as Wanderer and his men raided. And wherever he went, Wanderer searched for the repeating guns that obsessed him. He knew that without them, his people couldn't survive in their war against the white men.

* * *

The white men were having problems obtaining the pistols too. They were no longer being made. In November of 1846, Sam Walker went east to find some. *If only people weren't as starched as their collars and the sheeting on the bed, it would be good to be home again. Maybe they need the starch for their backbones.* They seemed weak and dull to him after the Texans. Passersby had stared at him as he stalked the streets of Washington in his leather clothes and tattered moccasins. He felt as though he had been wrenched from all he knew and was comfortable with, and set down in a foreign country. Even the language seemed alien. And the politicians. Heaven save him from them. He had only so much patience, and his supply was running out. The fate of the frontier depended on these Easterners and they had no idea of what it was like there.

Walker had returned to his home in Maryland, and the farmlands outside of Washington. He was there to see his family and collect his commission as a captain in the newly formed Regiment of United States Mounted Rifles. War had been declared on Mexico.

"While you're home, Sam," Zachary Taylor had said, "recruit troops for us and order some of those repeater pistols you and Hays have been raving about." The general had turned pensive for a moment, something he rarely did. He scratched the thin gray hair along his square face. "We'll need all the help we can get. The Mexicans have more troops stationed along the border than we have in the entire United States army."

"Yes, sir." Walker turned to leave, neglecting to salute as usual.

"And, Sam. Try to act like a soldier. Wear your uniform. You're in the United States Army now. Not that dirty band of rowdy ragamuffins. Those Rangers."

Sam grinned at him, and left without committing himself, or saluting.

He sat now in his stained and dusty buckskins and soft moccasins. He scratched the bottom of his left foot through the hole in the sole. His soft-visored blue dragoon's cap with its gold eagle and R on the shield, lay on the desk in front of him. But his tight, gilt-buttoned forage jacket with the shiny epaulets hung in his mother's house. It had never been worn.

Samuel Walker was in Samuel Colt's office in New York City. If it could be called an office. It was a shabby cubicle in a rundown section of the city. The walls were decorated with yellowed and torn posters advertsing snuff and patent medicines and political candidates. Outside the filthy little window Sam could hear the heavy wagons rumbling over the cobbled streets and the shrill cries of the street vendors.

If Washington was bad, with its unpaved streets and half-finished building, its acres of mud, New York City was much worse. Samuel Morse had only perfected his telegraph two years earlier, but already wires were tangling over the rooftops. A pall of coal smoke always hung over the city, and the air was thick with the stench of dung left by thousands of dray animals. The streets were choked with the huge wagons and the throngs of people.

Walker sat with his moccasins propped on the rungs of a straight-backed wooden kitchen chair. The only other furniture in the office were the chairs he and Sam Colt were sitting on and the scarred old desk. In his pocket Walker carried the letter that Colt had written him in desperation two months before.

> I have heard so much of Colonel Hayse and your exployets with the Arms of my invention that I have long desired to know you personally and get from you the true narrative of the vareous instances where my arms have proved of more than ordinary utility.
>
> Such is the prijudice of old officers in our Army against aney invasions upon old and well known impliments of Warfare that as yet I have not been able to introduce my arms in the servis to an extant that has proved proffitable.

The last sentence was a masterful understatement. Sam Colt wasn't making a profit. He was bankrupt. His armory was closed, and the few pistols in existence had been snapped up by men going to Texas. Sam Walker had written Colt of their success with his repeaters at the battle of the Pedernales, when they had routed seventy Comanche. And he had offered some suggestions for changes that would make the gun better.

Colt had searched everywhere for a model of the Paterson that Walker referred to. He needed it to demonstrate the changes that were suggested. But there was none to be had, not even for its inventor. Finally he had commissioned an armorer to make one. It lay between them now, next to Sam's dragoon cap. Walker picked up the small pistol and hefted it in his hand.

"It needs to be heavier, so we can use it as a club if need be. And it could stand to be a bigger caliber, forty-four at least. Can you put a trigger guard on it?"

"Certainly. No trouble." Colt leaned forward, all business. His popping brown eyes were almost fanatical when he talked about his invention. His bushy hair was as unruly as his spelling.

"And simplify the lock so the trigger's visible even when the gun's uncocked."

Colt nodded and hunched over to see better.

"Also, why not make it a six-shooter instead of five? And the breech mechanism should be simpler for loading on horseback."

"We can do it."

"Taylor wants a thousand of them. Immediately. For the troops in Mexico. When can you get them to us?"

"Well, Sam." Colt slouched back in his chair and ran his fingers through the tangle of his hair. "That's a problem."

"What is?"

"I don't have an armory anymore. No place to make them. But I can work something out. There's a man making Jaeger rifles, has an armory in Connecticut. Does real fine work. All the parts on his guns are standard, interchangeable, and he puts them together in stages. It's a brilliant concept. Wish I'd thought of it. In other words, his people make all the barrels, then all the triggers. Finishes them all at once, rather than working on one gun at a time."

"Sounds good. Do you think he'll let you retool for the pistols?"

"I can talk him into it. Whitney's his name. Eli Whitney. I'll write him today."

"I like the idea of interchangeable parts. We'll write it into the contract. And we'll need spare parts too. And tools. And ammunition. Cones, screws, molds, flasks, screwdrivers, nipple wrenches, levers, that sort of thing."

Colt slapped the desk top with the palm of his hand.

"Damn it, man, I'm in business again!" Then he sank back in his chair. "Maybe."

"What's the problem?"

"The army."

"But Zachary Taylor's the one who wants them."

"Zachary Taylor's word isn't worth a hill of horseshit to the politicians in charge here in the east."

"I'll see what I can do."

Walker went to President Polk with the order for the pistols, his persuasive tongue, and the tight uniform jacket he detested. It showed the sacrifices he was willing to make to see his men supplied with the repeaters. The order went through.

Then he headed for Baltimore and Fort McHenry to carry out the second part of his mission, recruiting troops for the Mexican conflict. While he was there, he sketched a picture of the battle of the Pedernales, with himself on a black horse and El Diablo Hays on a white one. He sent the drawing to Colt, who had a die made of it. The scene became part of the cylinder on each nine-inch long, four-and-a-half-pound six shooter, the Walker Colt.

Finally he returned to the frontier to lead his Texans into Mexico.

They were a savage-looking bunch, with huge shaggy beards and ragged clothes. The only thing uniform about them was the dust that coated them and the Colt revolvers at their waists. Sam was thirty years old when he died, impaled on a lance while leading a charge at Huamantla.

❧ 43 ❧

Time had taken its toll of the men in Old Owl's group of friends. He looked around at those who were left, and he thought of the ones who had died. Many Battles, Snake, Spirit Talker in the smoke and treachery of the Council House massacre. White Robe, his face rotted by the white man's pox. Even dignified White Horse had died under a buffalo's hooves when his pony stumbled in a prairie dog hole.

The talk flowed over Old Owl's head, and he was content to let it do so. As he smoked, he listened and thought. Since his return from Washington there was much to think about. He knew his people didn't believe him when he told them about the white men's towns. And he felt terribly lonely sometimes. Like a man who has seen a great vision of paradise and yet must remain chained to a dreary world. Sometimes he himself doubted what he had seen. And he wondered if he had really taken that wonderful trip, or if he had only dreamed it.

He wanted to go back, to see more of the wonders of the white men. He and the other chiefs who had gone with him from other bands and other tribes had watched a metal key tap out messages. Soon, the white men assured him, they would be talking over many days' journeys, in an instant. No wonder his people didn't believe him. How could anyone believe such a thing? And he had seen it with his own eyes.

There was a stir at the door, and a horse's broad rear end appeared, backing into the smoking lodge. The old men leaped up, yelling and pushing the animal out before it soiled the floor. The boys would never leave them in peace. Just when one group outgrew such jokes, another came of age. There was no end to it. Old Owl crowded around the horse, which was kicking nervously in the confusion, and looked outside. He didn't expect to see anyone, of course. Most of the village was asleep. And the boys never stayed long enough to be caught.

But the culprit was still there, laughing in the darkness. Old Owl squinted to see better. As his eyes adjusted, he made out the white outline of a chest that seemed to glow softly in the pale moonlight. The prankster wasn't a boy, but a man, and he was leaning on a shiny new Springfield rifle.

"Good evening, Grandfather."

"Wee-lah!" Old Owl began to weep, his lips trembling and tears rolling down his cheeks. He grabbed Cub around the waist and pressed his head to his grandson's chest. "Bear Cub, you've come back." Then he stood back and circled him, inspecting him.

The other men filed out, each of them embracing Cub and slapping him on the back. Many of them had to stand on tiptoe to hug him. At seventeen, John Parker was over six feet tall and broad in the shoulders. He had split hundreds of cords of wood in the past five years. And while he'd hated every splinter of it, cursing it for the women's work it was, it had been good for him. His muscles rippled under the golden down on his arms and chest and back. He reached out to poke Santa Ana's bulging belly.

"We're going to have a hard winter. Santa Ana has stored up a lot of fat."

Santa Ana grabbed a handful of the hair on Cub's chest.

"And you're growing an extra thick pelt, like your namesake, Bear Cub. It'll be a cold winter indeed."

"This looks like Sanaco's horse, Cub."

"It is," grumbled Sanaco.

"He was easy to steal," said Cub modestly.

Sanaco gathered up the tether line and led his pony away. The other men called good night and left too, turning off to their own lodges and sleep. Cub followed Old Owl inside, ducking to clear the low doorway. He remembered to turn to the left and circle the fire. He sat across from it and waited while his grandfather reached for his pipe case. Santa Ana had carefully put the pipe away before he left the lodge.

"Let me do it, Grandfather." Cub took the heavily fringed case, smiling at the almost forgotten tinkling its metal bells made. He pulled the three-foot-long cottonwood stem from its slender pocket sewn on the outside of the bag. He pushed it into the hole at the projecting base of the soapstone bowl. Then he shook out the smaller pouches in the bag and the turtle shell that Old Owl had used since he was Cub's age.

Cub reached into one of the pouches and greased his fingers with buffalo fat. Then he shook some dried willow bark into the turtle shell and crushed it with his fingers, mixing the buffalo fat into it to make it burn better. He added an equal part of Arikara twist tobacco from Mexico and a small amount of fragrant sage. The large tobacco leaves had already been cut into long strips and pounded to shreds. He sifted all the ingredients together until they were well blended. Alone, the willow had a bitter taste, and his grandfather would know if Cub were careless with his mixing.

He tamped the tobacco down and passed the pipe back to Old Owl. Then he lit it with an ember held between two green sticks. Old Owl sucked deeply, his cheeks caving in. A tendril of smoke curled around his large nose, then upward. The old man sighed and watched the smoke float toward the stars in the smoke hole.

"You have a new pipe, Grandfather."

"Yes. The old one finally cracked. This is a good one, though." Old Owl took it out of his mouth and looked at it, as though seeing it for the first time. "Something Good made it for me. The stem is one piece, not split and hollowed and glued back together. She put a grub into a hole drilled in one end of it. Then she blocked up the hole and held that end near the fire. The grub bored through the pith all the way to the other end to escape the heat. Very clever girl, Something Good." Old Owl passed the pipe back to Cub and surrendered to one of his huge, gaping yawns. He kneaded his fingers and wrists, swollen with arthritis.

"To think I have seen you before I die."

"You've talked of dying for years. You look the same as you did the day I was taken from you."

"That was the worst day of my life, my son. To know that you were going and that there was nothing I could do about it. I still hear your cries for help. I wept for months. I still weep. I'm weeping now." He sniffed loudly and searched in the litter around him for a rag. Old Owl wasn't much of a housekeeper, and he discouraged his wife and niece from coming into his smoking lodge.

"They put things away and I can never find them again," he grumbled. He didn't find the rag and finally just held one cavernous nostril closed and blew the other, discharging a wad of mucus onto the ground. He did the same for the other side, and kicked dirt over the puddle. "How did you get here? And where did you get the rifle? Are there any more? You didn't bring any coffee, did you?"

"One question at a time. I brought you many presents. I wish I could have seen my white uncle's face when he discovered his rifle and food and kitchenware and his three best horses gone." Cub hesitated slightly as he spoke, searching for the words he hadn't used in five years. "I pretended to cooperate with my uncle. He's a powerful holy man among his own people. But their religion is all wrong. Grandfather, if I told you what the white people made me do, you wouldn't believe me."

"Yes, I would, Cub. I have traveled too. All the way to the Great White Father's lodge in Wah-sin-tone. But continue. I'll tell you about it later."

"They cut my hair. That's one reason why I waited until late at night to find you, I'm ashamed to ride through the village with my hair as short as a woman's." He tossed the tumble of yellow curls contemptuously. "Last year I refused to let anyone cut it. I told my uncle I'd kill him if he touched it. And last year I was finally big enough to do it.

"They made me desecrate our Mother, the Earth. When I go to Medicine Mounds for my vision quest, I'll seek forgiveness. I'll do whatever I have to do to be one of the People again."

"You're still one of the People, but you'll have to prove yourself a warrior. Just like every other young man."

"I know. And I've lost so much time."

"That never stopped you before."

"I've tried to keep in practice, but it's been difficult. Your pipe, for instance. My uncle calls holy tobacco the devil's weed. He won't allow it in his lodge. And I didn't see a bow or arrow for five years.

"For five years I've felt as though I were breathing and smelling and seeing through a heavy layer of dust. Their life chokes me, smothers me. I won't ever go back. I'm big enough to fight them this time."

Cub brooded, his hair gleaming, tipped with points of flame in the fire's light. He had stripped down to his heavy, soft woolen home-spun pantaloons. And he had cut the seat out of them, so he'd be more comfortable riding. He had discarded his shoes, preferring to enter camp barefoot. His chest and shoulders and back were pale. The deep tan of his arms and neck stopped in a ring where his collar and rolled-up shirtsleeves had been.

"I didn't see my father's lodge when I came through the village."

"Arrow Point left. He's gone to live with the Quohadi. It seems so natural to have you back, I forget how long you've been gone. There's so much you don't know. Your sister married Wanderer. They have a son. I suppose he must be almost three years old now. The seasons rush by as you get older, Cub. And for me they're starting to stampede like a herd of buffalo."

"I heard about my sister's marriage from a man who tried to ransom her. He lives near my white uncle."

393

"Many of the young men have taken their families to live with Wanderer and his band. They're called Noconi. Your old friend, Upstream, is there. He's called Wolf Road now. The northern bands roam and raid and cause trouble for us all."

"Then you don't approve of them?"

"Approve? Who am I to approve or disapprove? They do what they have to do. I understand how they feel. But we of the Penateka often pay for their raids. Our bands are large, although not half as large as they once were. Our lands are shrinking, like leaves in the hot sun. Each season they shrivel and grow more barren of game. Other tribes are being crowded into our hunting grounds, and we war with them constantly.

"And we have become used to the white trader's goods. Our children cry for sugar and our women want the bright dyes and cloths. We can no longer avoid the white men. And they are too powerful to defeat. The young men don't know that, but I do. I have seen their cities and their numbers and their medicine." Old Owl's sight might be failing, but his vision of the future was terribly clear. It kept him awake at night.

"Wanderer's band is small," he continued. "They move constantly. They refuse all contact with the whites. No one can catch them. Most of the time even *we* don't know where they are. And to the white people we are all the same. They punish us for the raids of others, even though we try to follow the white man's road." Old Owl yawned again.

"You're tired, Grandfather. We can talk tomorrow. We have a lot of time to talk."

"All right, my son. Sleep here with me." Old Owl began rummaging through his belongings for extra buffalo robes. He threw them over his shoulder and onto the ground for Cub to make a bed of. "My other lodge is full of women and children. I sleep here most of the time for the peace. Where are the presents you brought?"

"I left them piled outside." Cub knew they'd be safe there.

"Did you bring any of the round yellow disks white men use to buy things?"

"No."

"Too bad. Don't tell anyone, but I'm saving them to pay for another trip to Wah-sin-tone."

Cub smothered the fire, and the two of them slid into their robes.

"Grandson, I'm glad you're back."

"Not as glad as I am to be back, Grandfather." Cub paused, listening to the sound of insects, the howl of a distant coyote, a war pony's whicker, and a cough from a lodge nearby. "It's good to be home. I've missed you very much." He hadn't finished speaking before he heard his grandfather's deep breathing and a few light snores. He knew the snores would build in volume until they almost vibrated the taut hide wall next to his head.

It didn't take Cub long to establish his reputation in the village again. He was bigger than everyone else. And although the men of the People made up in ferocity what they lacked in size, Cub was both big and ferocious. He had the graceful, catlike walk of a large, dangerous animal. He wore a neutral expression on his face, a look that didn't allow an opponent to guess what his reaction would be to attack or harrassment. He had been fooling the white eyes for years, and he was a master at bluffing. Without a word being said, he was given a place in the life of the band and plenty of room when he walked down its streets.

He wisely kept out of archery contests, but he could outshoot anyone with his rifle. He had had ammunition to practice with, while the men of Old Owl's band had none to spare. But most of the boys he had grown up with had gone on their vision quests and become braves. Some of them even counted coups and were warriors. He had already heard the story of Wolf Road's heroic ride during the raid on the wagon train the winter before. He knew he wouldn't feel like one of the People again until he had spoken with the spirits that would guide him through life.

He was restless while he waited for his great aunt, Old Owl's wife, Prairie Dog, to make him a pair of leggings, a breechclout and moccasins. There were none in the village big enough to fit him. And he couldn't go to meet his spirits wearing white men's clothing.

Cub lay awake one night, almost a week after he had backed Sanaco's horse into his grandfather's smoking lodge. On the other side of the tent Old Owl's snores had reached their maximum volume. But they weren't keeping Cub awake. His own thoughts were. He had to make his vision quest, and then count coup. To prove himself in battle. Until then his acceptance in the band was tenuous.

There was a slight movement outside the lodge, and the hem of the wall was lifted. Cub felt for the large knife he always kept at the side of the bed. Someone the size of a large boy rolled under the edge. With one smooth motion she slid under the covers, leaving the robe she was wearing outside them.

"Manita, Small Hand!" Cub was astonished. She had been staring at him for days, but he assumed she was laughing at him. He couldn't believe any woman would be interested in him with his ugly, hairy chest, his short, touseled blond hair, and the freckles spattered across his nose and cheeks. The girl laid her slender fingers against his mouth, silencing him. He put his lips to her ear.

"It's all right," he whispered. "I could fire off a gun in here and Old Owl wouldn't hear it." He nibbled at her lobe, while he was in the neighborhood. Then, without thinking, he ran his tongue around the inside of her ear. She giggled, stifling the sound against his chest, sending chills through his body. He ran his hand hesitantly over her round, firm buttocks and up her soft, naked body, feeling the goose bumps his tongue had raised.

Cub had never lain with a woman. His heart was pounding and when his tongue touched the roof of his mouth it was like licking a hot rock. He was grateful for the need to be quiet. He didn't trust himself to speak. He was more afraid of this small, pliant Mexican captive than the warriors he had faced down silently when he came here. He was used to fighting, ready for it and good at it. But this was different. Very different. He had missed more than target practice while he lived with the whites.

Small Hand rolled on top of him and pressed sensuously against him, rotating her hips slightly, but urgently. She rubbed her cheek into the mat of hair on his chest, and he ran his hands all over her, stroking every slope and valley of her lithe young body. He felt his cock stir and swell, throbbing with pent-up pleasure against her hip. *What would Uncle James and Elder Daniel say?* He thought it with malicious glee before he lost himself completely in her.

She turned onto her back and guided him, stroking his balls with her fingers and firmly taking his cock, erect and hard now, in her hand. She spread her slender legs and pressed the head of it to her, easing it into the tight, slippery, wet hole. He whimpered as he felt her close snugly around him, felt the intense heat of her penetrate him, spreading through his groin. He was frustrated when he hit against a taut shield inside. He propped himself on his elbows to keep from smothering her with his weight. He looked down at her small, round face, and stroked her thick, wavy black hair.

"Is this your first time, Small Hand?" he murmured.

"Yes. The women told me it would hurt. I'm ready for it."

"How old are you?"

"I'm not sure. I was very young when I was captured. A baby. I've been with the People almost thirteen years. I'm old enough to bear children, though."

"You're very beautiful."

"So are you, Bear Cub. I heard you'd be leaving soon on your vision quest. I wanted to come to you before you left. Several of the young women teased about doing this themselves. They have never seen a man like you. You fascinate them. But I told them I'd cut off their noses if they even looked at you." She smiled wickedly up at him, and he lowered his face to kiss her gently on the lips. Her mouth was full and soft and for a second, yielding. Then she returned the kiss fiercely. They made love the rest of the night, to the serenade of Old Owl's snores. When Cub finally fell asleep, exhausted and happy, just before dawn, Small Hand slipped out and was gone.

Cub awoke early that morning to a hand rocking his shoulder. His grandfather sat cross-legged next to him, shaking him. He held a neatly folded pair of leggings, a painted breechclout, and a pair of beaded moccasins in his lap.

"Are you going to sleep all day?"

Cub threw back the covers, and Old Owl wrinkled his mountainous nose.

"Whew. What were you doing here last night?"

Cub started to explain that it wasn't his fault, that he had been taken advantage of, but his grandfather held up a hand, palm outward and waved it from side to side. The stop signal in sign talk.

"Never mind. I can tell. We'll have to burn sage in here before I can let anyone in. The smell of love is on everything. Somebody will think I've been entertaining women here. Santa Ana will never stop teasing me about it." Old Owl left the clothes for his grandson and bustled around. He piled green sage boughs on the fire and prepared meat for breakfast while the crackling fireworks from the green branches died down. As he scolded he kept his back turned so Cub wouldn't see him smiling.

"You're about to start on your vision quest, the most important event in your life, and you're wasting your time with women."

"The vision quest may be the most important event in my life, Grandfather, but now I know which event is the most fun." Cub yawned mightily and staggered to the fire. His legs felt a little wobbly. He sat with a thud, scratching his chest and looking very self-satisfied.

"Smug pup. Foolishness! After we eat you can take a nap. Then we'll talk about your journey."

Cub sat straighter, alert suddenly.

"I'm not tired. I want to talk about it now, and start as soon as possible."

"All right. Tell me what you're to do, my son."

"I take only a few things with me—a buffalo robe, a pipe . . ."

"I have a pipe for you."

"Tobacco and a fire horn. I wear only a breechclout and moccasins. I stop four times on the journey to smoke and pray. I will stay on the south slope of Medicine Mounds so I can see the sun rise and set. I will eat nothing until I've had my vision."

Old Owl gave Cub a small leather bag.

"This is powdered willow bark. It's a very powerful purgative. It will clean you out and make you ready for your vision. And you'll ride Eagle Feather."

"Eagle Feather's your favorite pony."

"Take him. And take this too." The old man searched through the piles and bundles heaped around the side of the lodge. It was a lifetime's accumulation of things. He pulled out a battered rawhide tube and opened it reverently. The tube was more scarred than Cub remembered and it seemed smaller, but he recognized it instantly.

"No, Grandfather. I can't take your sacred wolf skin."

"It's time for you to have it. I promised it to you a long time ago. I don't need it anymore. And I'll give you one of my songs too. Listen carefully." Old Owl composed himself in front of the fire, facing east. He began to chant his favorite medicine song in a high, quavery, pinched voice. Cub listened intently, the wolf robe spread across his lap. He could almost feel the power seeping from it and into his legs. The hypnotic repetition of the song's words intensified the feeling. It was his grandfather's holiest chant.

That afternoon, when Cub had hung the few things he was taking with him onto the surcingle, Old Owl embraced him. Cub was always surprised at how much power was contained in his grandfather's lean, bent frame. There were tears in Old Owl's eyes, and he wiped them on one corner of his filthy white vest, worn thread-thin now, and colorless with age. The white hairs on his head shone silvery in the bright sunlight. He looked old and fragile as Cub turned to wave his rifle at him in salute. He was taking the gun for food and for protection on the journey. It would be a longer trip than usual. Not everyone traveled all the way to Medicine Mounds to seek their vision.

He had left the village and was on the trail to the river when a figure stepped from the bushes.

"Bear Cub." Small Hand said it in a low voice. "I wanted to give you something to take with you." She held up a buffalo robe, straining under its weight. It was a large robe, five feet by seven feet. It was made of two separate pieces sewn down the center. A narrow line of red paint hid the stitching. It had a seal-brown coat of thick wool mixed with hair almost two feet long. It was warmer than four blankets.

"May this keep you warm until you come back to me and I can do it instead."

Cub rolled the robe into a tight cylinder and strapped it across his pony's back.

"My heart is glad, Small Hand. When I lie under it at night, I'll think of your warmth. But my heart is gladdest for the gift you gave me last night." He leaned down from his pony to kiss her lightly on the mouth. Then he righted himself and rode off at a trot.

In March of the next year, 1849, an army expedition left Torrey's trading post at the site of an old Waco village. The expedition's orders were to map a route for the emmigrants headed for the California gold fields. Its commander, Indian Agent Robert Neighbors, enlisted the aid of the Penateka to guide them. It was a peaceful expedition, and it was unmolested because of Neighbor's influence among the Comanche.

In April the party bivouacked near one of the cold springs that gushed from a gravel bed to form a clear pool before joining a stream nearby. The high, rolling prairie along the Canadian was spectacular at any time of the year, but it was at its best in the springtime. A tall gallery of hardwoods towered over the camp. The air was crisp. Each star in the soaring sky looked as though it had been polished and set in place on black velvet.

The horses and mules grazed on the thick, sweet rye. They had each cropped a neat circle, its radius the thirty feet of the tether line allowed them. If "Major" Neighbors was in charge of the party, Captain Randolph Marcy of the United States Army saw to its marching order and bivouack routine. He left nothing to chance. Each animal was double hobbled as well as picketed. Sidelines fastened their hind and fore feet on the same side. As added protection, the small A-shaped tents were set up neatly around the exposed side of the pasture. The pasture itself was in the wide curve left by the stream's meanderings. Attack from the water side was unlikely.

Once Marcy had checked the mounted guards for the herd and the lookouts posted on the crest of a hill over camp, he was ready to relax. He unfolded his long camp chair with a clatter. It was an ingenious device of oak and canvas. He sank into it with a sigh, and rolled a cigarette.

"That contraption looks like it's alive and about to swallow you, Randolph," said Neighbors.

"Not at all. It's very comfortable. And after all, if you can't be comfortable on these little jaunts, what's the use of coming?"

"Seems to me if God had intended man to use a folding chair like that in the middle of the howling wilderness, he wouldn't have provided all these fine, soft rocks for us to sit on."

"This is the life, isn't it, Major?" And Marcy blew a smoke ring. On the other side of the fire, John Ford was having a harder time relaxing.

"How can a man concentrate with all that caterwauling going on?" He slammed the Bible closed so hard it blew out the candle by which he had been reading. Old Owl had been chanting his medicine songs for hours. Lying flat on his back, he sang to the huge, star-strewn sky. It was getting on Ford's nerves.

"Don't get testy, Rip," said Marcy.

"Actually, Rip, I prefer Old Owl's singing to your temperance lectures," added Neighbors.

"Trouble with you is you don't drink enough," put in Marcy.

"I don't drink at all, and you know it. Drink is the devil's crowbar, prying us off the straight and narrow." John Ford had recently joined the Temperance movement. It was one more thing to goad him about.

"Now you've done it, Marcy. Don't get him started."

"How'd you get your nickname, Rip?" Marcy changed the subject.

"In Mexico, during the war. Just a year ago, actually. I was adjutant. It was my dolorous duty to write the families of the men killed in action. Of course, I ended each letter with R.I.P., *Rescat In Pacem*. Hence the name."

"It's a good 'un." Neighbors twisted his bushy muttonchop whiskers around his fingers.

Ford looked out into the darkness of the warm April night, toward the source of the chanting.

"He stirs up recollections of boyhood, the chief does," Ford said. "The calling of hogs, the plaintive notes of a solitary bull frog, the bellowing of a small bull."

"Hark," Neighbors joined in, cupping his hand to his ear as though to hear better. "The awful melody of a sonorous gong. The mournful howl of a hungry wolf, fading into the gobble of a lovesick turkey."

"Hard to believe that dried-up old man is a ferocious, brutal Commanche chief," said Marcy.

"They're surprising people, the Comanches," said Neighbors. "I met with Old Owl and Santa Ana and Pahayuca. Even that scalawag Buffalo Hump was there, a couple of months ago."

Ford smiled to himself, thinking of Buffalo Hump's real name and of how he and Wallace and Ben McCulloch had rechristened him almost ten years before. Neighbors went on with his story.

"That's when I got them to agree to help us scout the trail and to leave the wagon trains alone. They were a very jovial set. We spent the evening eating and smoking and talking about war and horses and women. I found myself, in the end, upon a good understanding with them."

"Are you on a good enough understanding with Old Owl to ask him to shut up before I pin his ears to the wagon bed and force-feed him his own vocal cords?"

"Ford, since you've gotten religion you've lost your sense of humor," said Marcy mildly.

"It's teetotalling that has him out of sorts," said Neighbors. "Rip's always had religion. You obviously never heard his famous Sunday School lesson about the prophet Jeremiah."

Marcy shook his head in a cloud of cigarette smoke, and the Major continued.

"According to Ford, here, the man's name was just plain Jerry. Then one day his stubborn old mule bucked him off into the slimy black mud of a swamp. Well, he came a-staggering back into town all covered with black goo. And the folks dubbed him Jerry-mire. Called him that ever after."

"That's not true." Marcy laughed so hard he choked on his cigarette smoke. "Ford, you didn't teach that in Sunday school!"

John Ford looked solemn and placed his hand on his tattered bible. His pale blue eyes, high forehead, and arched Roman nose gave him a patrician look.

"Yes, I did."

Marcy laughed, and then turned when he felt a warm weight on his shoulder. Reflexively, Ford's hand went to his waist where his pistols were stuck into the waist of his pantaloons. Behind Marcy stood a hulking Comanche with a good-natured grin on his affable face.

"It's all right, Rip," muttered Neighbors. "It's just Sanaco."

The Comanche held his broad palm up in the sign of peace, and Marcy stood to face him. Sanaco executed a rather snappy salute, which Marcy returned, as much from reflex as anything else.

"Sanaco," the man said pointing to his broad chest and tapping his grimy fingernail on the crescent-shaped, silver gorget that dangled there.

"Marcy," answered the Colonel, clicking his brass coat button. Suddenly the Comanche lunged forward and enveloped him in a smelly hug, almost smothering him with the odor of bear grease and sweat and the dung he had rubbed in his hair for this special occasion. Sanaco had seen Marcy holding sway in his camp chair and had assumed he was a plenipotentary of some sort.

"*Amigo*," he said, pointing first to himself and then to Marcy. "Nermenuh, *amigos, tabbay-boh*, soldiers. The People are friends of the white soldiers."

"And we are friends of the People."

Sanaco beckoned to Marcy to step closer to the light. He tugged his arm gently with one hand, and with the other pulled a filthy, tattered piece of paper from somewhere within the fringes and folds of his hunting shirt. Ford was nervous, and by now his hand was resting firmly on his pistol. He had spent too many years tracking Comanche to trust them. Marcy squinted at the faded, smudged writing on the paper, being careful to keep out of line of Ford's fire, should it come.

"Major, would you bring me a light?"

Neighbors brought a burning branch from the fire and held it so Marcy could read. Sanaco peered over his shoulder, a worried expression on his face.

"Is it a testimonial?" asked Neighbors. "Many of the Penatekas carry them to gain safe passage through the territory."

"Looks like it." Marcy chuckled softly. Sanaco's worried expression deepened.

"Him no good?"

"Not as good as it could be, chief. Listen." He read aloud to his two friends. "The bearer of this says he is a Comanche chief named Sanaco; that he is the biggest Indian and the best friend the whites ever had, in fact, that he is a first-rate fellow; but I believe he is a damned rascal, so look out for him."

Marcy folded the paper and handed it back to Sanaco, who looked crestfallen. He crumpled the paper, then threw it into the fire. He turned to Marcy, and slowly and somberly he shook hands three times. Then, gazing at him with a steady, sincere expression, he locked right elbows with him and pressed both their arms to his side. He did the same with his left arm, repeating, "*Bueno, mucho bueno*," the whole time. He melted back into the night, leaving the three men laughing and shaking their heads.

Pahayuca was the last of the Penateka leaders to arrive. When he did they all were ready to meet with Marcy and Neighbors to discuss details. They would talk about the possible routes, the meals and the presents they would receive in payment for their services as guides. The Delaware scout Jim Shaw was there to translate.

The Penateka leaders filed solemnly around the fire, circling it from left to right in their traditional way. Each of them was dressed in his finest clothes, in honor of the occasion. Sanaco had spent two hours that afternoon in front of his mirror. He had plucked every hair from his face and body. When they were finally seated and the opening ceremonies observed Old Owl's friend Santa Ana stood to speak. With his robe draped togalike around him and his classic profile, he reminded John Ford of a Roman addressing the senate. His big, good-natured face echoed the sincerity of his words.

He began by telling the white men how the People had come to this land in the beginning. And of how good the land had been to them. He gave a detailed account of their life-style and roamings, their wars and triumphs over the past few hundred years. He assured them that his people could lead their white brothers over every rise and through every arroyo of the territory around them. After an hour, he finished with a flourish. Placing his hand over his heart, he pledged his undying love for the white men. "There is no need," he said, "to station soldiers on the People's land. There will be no war with the United States. I am not a Comanche, but an American."

Marcy took the pipe next, drew a puff on it, and rose to speak.

"We know of your love for us, and we return it. I myself am not really an American, but a full-blooded, true-blue, one hundred percent, dyed-in-the-wool Comanche."

"Dyed in the wool?" Shaw looked at Marcy, unable to translate.

"Don't worry about it, Jim. The soldiers are stationed here for your protection, Jefe. They are to make sure that bad white men don't take advantage of you." When Marcy finished, Old Owl spoke.

"You tell us that the troops are placed here for our protection. That I know is not so." He turned to Agent Neighbors. "When you set the line for us a year ago, you said we could go south of it to hunt if we wished. That I only had to ask the captain at the fort for permission. I wanted to go south to hunt with a party of eight old men and their women and children. I applied for permission, and the captain denied it.

"I told him that I had no warriors with me, only my friends, the old men. That we needed the meat for our families. But still he refused. I told him that I was an old man. And that I had hunted on these prairies before he was born, before any white men came. It made no difference. Now you want us to help you make a road for more white men. And how will we be treated when they come?" Old Owl had apparently been thinking about the project a great deal since he had agreed to it. *Damn that officer, anyway,* Neighbors thought. He rose to assure the chief.

"The road we will mark will lead people through your lands. They will not stay here. They are passing through to the other side to dig for the yellow metal that white men hold as sacred medicine." Old Owl should be able to understand that. The crafty old goat had asked for his pay in coins. He must be planning another trip east. And he knew he couldn't buy passage on a steamship with horses and mules.

"I promise you, Chief," Neighbors held up his hand to give weight to his words. "The people who will use this road will mean no harm to you. They will not be Texans. They will pass through and you will see them no more. They will be as the wind that blows through your villages on its way to the ends of the world."

Robert S. Neighbors was a good and honest man, a friend of the Indians. He believed that he told them the truth.

❧ 44 ❧

Cub sat next to his grandfather's bed. He had renamed himself Esa Nahubiya, Echo Of A Wolf's Howl when he returned from his vision quest, but Old Owl continued to call him Cub. Now the boy sat with his head in his hands, his fingers pressed against his temples to relieve the throbbing there. His head ached from days of crying and nights without sleep. He had sent the medicine man away the day before, when it was obvious to everyone that the medicine was doing no good. Cub had known it wouldn't when his grandfather had shown the first symptoms. He had recognized the sickness as cholera. That morning Old Owl had chanted his song welcoming death, and he now lay waiting for it to visit him.

Why did you escort the wagon trains, Grandfather? I tried to warn you, but you're a stubborn old man. Once Old Owl had decided to walk the white man's road, and when he had seen what lay along it to the east, he sought more contact with them. *You were looking for coffee, weren't you? And the baubles that the white men buy cheap and sell dear. Buy cheap and sell dear. How much coffee is a life worth?* Four thousand gold seekers had passed along Old Owl's road that summer, and Old Owl was a familiar figure along it. He was the welcoming committee and the escort.

404

On the other side of the fire Cub's great-aunt, Prairie Dog, had fallen asleep. She was nodding over the broth she was making in a futile gesture for her husband. Suddenly a wail rose from the lodge next door, a ululating cry that pricked Cub's skin. It was the voice of Wild Sage, Santa Ana's wife. Santa Ana must be dead of the cholera. Cub could no longer even feel grief for his grandfather's old companion. But the sound awoke Prairie Dog, and she stood wearily, moaning and sobbing. Pulling her robe over head, she went to comfort her friend.

"Cub." The boy leaned down, putting his ear to his grandfather's blue-tinged lips. "Santa Ana?" The old man panted with the effort of speaking.

"Yes, Grandfather. He's dead."

"My bag."

Cub knew he could only mean one bag. He took the large, fringed medicine pouch from its peg.

"Yours, my son." Old Owl's cheeks were sunken by dehydration and starvation until the bones of his skull were clearly outlined. The bluish skin stretched across the bones seemed transparent. His eyes were closed, the chalky lids threaded with delicate violet veins. His dry tongue was too swollen to fit in his mouth, and protruded slightly.

Cub took one of his skeletal hands and rubbed it gently, trying to give some warmth to the clammy skin. He had to search for the pulse in the emaciated wrist. He almost panicked, thinking Old Owl had died. Then he felt the heart's faint flutter.

There was a horrible odor in the lodge, intensified by the summer heat. Cub and Prairie Dog had cleaned him thoroughly after each siege of watery diarrhea and vomiting, but the smell permeated everything. Now Old Owl had nothing left to vomit. He jerked, seized with violent, painful cramps in his stringy muscles. As the dehydration drained him of life, he sank deeper into the torpor of shock.

"Water." Cub was ready and poured a trickle of it between the shriveled lips. Then he sprinkled some onto the palm of his hand and washed his grandfather's face and chest with it.

"Bag."

"I brought you the medicine bag."

"Bag."

Cub held up one bag after another while Old Owl forced his eyes to stay open. He shook his head slightly each time. Finally Cub had shown him all of them.

"Bag."

"Where?"

"Bed."

Cub got on his hands and knees and searched under the tumble of boxes against the wall, next to his own sleeping area. He found a heavy leather bag hidden there. It was undecorated, but it clinked as it bumped into the other boxes and bundles.

"Yours."

Cub untied the thongs wrapped around the neck of it and peered inside. The bag held a large pile of gold coins, the hoard that Old Owl had been saving for three years. They were the coins he had gotten from the young men when they came back from raids. He had convinced them that they were useless, and offered to dispose of them.

"Yours," he repeated. And with something that was almost a smile on his face, the old man relaxed. "Love you, Cub," he whispered. "Proud."

"I love you too, Grandfather."

Old Owl jerked once more and lay still, his face somehow peaceful, released from his body's agony. Cub placed his hand on the cold, bony chest, searching frantically for a heartbeat. He knew his grandfather must die, but he wasn't ready for it. He would never be ready for it. With both his hands flat on Old Owl's chest, Cub tilted his head back and howled. It was an animal sound, as devoid of human reason as the howl of his new namesake, the wolf.

Perhaps that was what the wolf was trying to tell him when its howl echoed through the hills and Cub saw his vision. Brother Wolf saw the future and tried to warn him. And Cub had ignored the warning. He should have prevented his grandfather from helping the whites. He should have stopped him the way Old Owl had once refused to let him go on a raid with his father, over ten years ago.

By now the noise in the village was deafening. The mourning for the two leaders crescendoed with Cub's howls. Finally Cub shook his head and looked around him, as though waking from a nightmare and finding reality much worse. He pulled the buffalo robe over Old Owl's face and went to help Prairie Dog, the woman he called Grandmother.

It was strangely quiet inside Santa Ana's lodge. Cub peered in, squinting as his eyes adjusted to the dim light. There, in an expanding pool of her own blood, lay Prairie Dog. She had opened her throat with her skinning knife. The slash gaped like a grinning second mouth. Wild Sage lay next to her. He felt for her heartbeat and found it. His hand came away bloody from the deep gashes on her bared, pendulous breasts. She had fainted from exhaustion, hysteria, and the loss of blood.

Cub pulled the blanket over Santa Ana's face. The skin hung in folds from his large frame. His shrunken cheeks were a mockery of the robust man he had been. Women began rushing into the tent, screaming and tearing at their hair and clothes. Cub left Wild Sage to them. He scooped his grandmother up easily and carried her back to his grandfather's lodge. She had grown frail, resembling her husband more each year. He picked his way through Old Owl's friends, huddled and sobbing under their robes. The crowd was growing as the villagers converged like wailing sleep walkers on the smoking lodge of their leader.

When he had laid his grandmother gently next to her husband, he carried out the few things that he had to have, and those his grandfather had given him. Then he went back inside and, sitting crosslegged in front of the bodies, he lit Old Owl's ceremonial pipe. He blew the smoke toward the hole in the top of the lodge, sending a prayer for the old couple's souls after it. No one entered the lodge. It was as though they all recognized the special relationship Cub had had with his great-uncle, and they felt he should be alone.

At last Cub took a burning branch from the fire and set the things in the lodge alight. While the flames slowly caught, he went outside and hacked a huge armful of brush to pile on them. He heaped more and more branches until the heat was too intense to approach, and sparks were showering from the smoke hole. He chanted a death song and prayer while the lodge burned.

As he watched the hide covering buckle and shrivel, consumed from within, he thought bitterly that he couldn't even give Old Owl and Prairie Dog a proper burial. He couldn't bathe them or paint their faces red, or seal their eyes with red clay. There would be no wake for the bodies, dressed in finery and laid out on blankets for all to pay respects. Nor could they be carried through the village on the backs of fine horses. He couldn't even cut his hair to show his grief. The white people had already shorn him.

Old Owl and Prairie Dog would have to be buried in a cleansing fire that would help prevent the disease from spreading. He had his hand in the bag of coins, ready to throw them into the blaze and let it melt them. But he stayed his hand. His grandfather had insisted he take them. He'd find a use for them.

When the lodge was a ring of charred ruins, Cub headed for the horse pasture. Already there was chaos in the village as terrified families tore down their lodges and fled. They fled in disorder, and in all directions. They scattered to seek sanctuary with friends and relatives in other bands. And they carried the disease with them.

Cub methodically shot all his grandfather's ponies, except Eagle

Feather and one packhorse. Old Owl had a herd of five hundred animals, and it took Cub all afternoon and all his carefully hoarded ammunition. The horses' screams and the sound of his rifle could be heard over the din from the camp. Then he returned to Old Owl's lodge to gather his grandparents' bones. They were still warm, and charred black. He squatted in the ashes and sifted through them for the bones. He shook them before putting them in a large leather bag he had saved for the purpose.

Cub packed the spare pony and mounted Eagle Feather. He rode slowly, one last time, through the camp. There were gaping spaces left by the families who had run away. Those who remained seemed insane with grief. It was a scene from Uncle James's hell.

For the first time in his life, Cub felt totally alone. Even when he had been imprisoned with his white relatives he had known that Old Owl was here and that he would one day see him again. Old Owl had been a fixed part of his life, like the North Star even when obscured by clouds. And now he was gone.

With tears coursing down his cheeks, Cub left the village. As he rode, another horse ghosted from the bushes to join him, its rider shrouded. When she pulled the robe back, Cub saw that it was Small Hand.

"Small Hand, go back."

"I'm going with you."

"I have no ponies to pay for you. And many men will offer your father a handsome price."

"I don't care about the other men. I'm going with you."

"I don't even know where I'm going."

"It doesn't matter." Small Hand rode in silence for a few minutes before she spoke again. "Will you go back to the whites?"

"No!" He realized how bitter his voice was, and softened it. "No, I can't go back there." How could he tell her? He remembered one of his uncle's neighbors bragging that he had the answer to the Indian problem. How could Cub explain to Small Hand the satisfied look on the man's face when he told of how he had innoculated a captured Comanche with smallpox and turned him loose to spread the disease. Cub had heard the story repeated in his Uncle James's house, among righteous, God-fearing Christians. And no one had condemned the man. No. Cub knew he couldn't go back there. He had seen what the white people's ways had done to Old Owl. Besides, he thought pragmatically, if he went back, the Texans would hang him for a horse thief.

"I'll probably look for my sister," he said at last.

"Naduah? With the Noconi?"

Cub nodded.

"Small Hand."

"Yes, Echo Of A Wolf's Howl?"

"I'm glad you came with me."

Small Hand smiled shyly at him. Her eyes brimmed with love as well as grief.

Cub and Small Hand roamed the Comancheria, tracking down rumors and sightings of the elusive Noconi. At first the two of them had stayed with the bands they encountered. But almost every village they entered resounded with the wails of mourning, as cholera cut its way through Texas. Families, the basic unit of the People's society, were broken and destroyed. Terror and despair were on every face they saw. Finally, sobbing, Small Hand refused to sleep in another camp.

From then on Cub rode into a village alone while Small Hand waited outside. As warriors gathered, their weapons ready, he held his hand up in the sign of peace.

"Hi, *haitsi*, hello, friends," he called. Then he went to find the leaders of the band while the children swarmed after him. They were enchanted by his hair, bleached almost white in the sun. He smoked with the council in each camp and asked about Wanderer and the yellow hair, his wife. Then he rode away again.

Often a party of men and boys from the village accompanied Cub and Small Hand a few miles on their journey. They gave them gifts of food, and watched as the two grew smaller in the distance, leading their single pack pony after them. They had no lodge, no spare clothes, no cooking gear or personal possessions other than what Small Hand had hastily thrown into her saddle bags before she followed Cub from Old Owl's village.

At night they sought shelter in caves, or under brush lean-tos in protected breaks and ravines. For their meals, Small Hand scooped out a depression in the ground and laid a buffalo hide in it. She poured water into the hide and heated it with rocks taken from the fire. When the water reached the boiling point, she cooked a stew of whatever they had killed that day. When darkness fell, they slept in each other's arms.

One night, Cub felt her shake him gently awake, calling him by her pet name.

"Sun hair, listen."

Cub pushed to the surface of consciousness and lay still. He breathed shallowly, listening.

"Do you hear it?"

"You know you have better hearing than I do, small one. What is it?"

"I don't know. It sounded like an animal in distress."

"Maybe a rabbit caught by an owl."

"No. There it is again. Can't you hear it?"

Cub listened intently. Finally he heard the faintest of sounds, eerie and broken, carried on the light night wind. He pushed the robe back and searched for his moccasins. He shook them automatically to make sure they were empty, then slipped them on. Small Hand did the same. In silence they saddled their ponies, leaving the camp and the pack animal. Using the pale light of the moon, they picked their way over the sweeping hills. The sound grew as they approached it.

"What is it, sun hair?"

"Fiddles."

Small Hand looked puzzled.

"A fiddle is a musical instrument that white people play and dance to. Like drums or flutes or rattles."

"I don't like it. It sounds like dead souls in agony."

But Cub's feet had begun jerking in time with the music, in spite of himself, and to his pony's confusion. They dismounted just below the crest of the last hill and crawled to the top. On their bellies, they looked down at the wagon train below them. The wagons were in a circle, the tongue of one under the rear wheels of the next and laced with heavy chains. In the center of the ring was a huge bonfire, and the gold-rushers had gathered to dance around it. Over to one side stood two fiddlers, one of them a large man with a flowing red beard.

Noah Smithwick wasn't heading for the gold fields, but he was guiding the train part of the way. His fiddle was held against his barrel chest, and his arm was flying. The broken strands of his horsehair bow flailed around his head. He had laid boards of raw lumber down and was standing on them so the pounding of his hobnailed boot could be heard. It provided a thumping base line.

Another man played a cigar-box banjo with Gem razors cut down for frets. What it lacked in size it made up for in volume. The rhythm section was an iron pot and ladle and two big tin spoons. The spoons were held back to back and beaten in a clattering, jumpy cadence against a thigh. Someone in the group was Irish.

There were no women, so the men formed up and danced with each other. Those who took the ladies' part tied rags around their waists or arms. And between each dance there was a rush for the whiskey barrel.

Noah broke into "Arkansas Traveler" and the other fiddler joined him. They both stopped between choruses to tell outrageous stories, and the men howled with laughter. No one could tell a joke better or with a straighter face than Noah Smithwick. Cub and Small Hand lay watching them for an hour, mesmerized by the beat that seeped through them, permeated them with a fleeting sense of peace.

The sound of the fiddles conjured up strange longings in Cub. He remembered sneaking from his uncle's house at night. He would walk five miles through the dark forest to where he knew a dance was being held. He couldn't participate. Word would certainly have gotten back to the Parker house and his uncle would have whipped him soundly. So he stood, alone in the dark, looking into the lighted windows, tapping his feet and wishing he could join in the fun.

For Cub the music was more than a reminder of his isolation among the white people. Even in their gaiety, the dissonant notes were lonely and primitive. They called up something from deep within him, something fierce and martial. They were the skirl and drone of the bagpipes they imitated, calling soldiers to die in the moors and mountains of a far-off land. There was joy and death and love and war in them. And for some reason that Cub himself couldn't know, they brought tears to his eyes.

Finally, he noticed Small Hand shivering in the cold night air. He signaled to her, and they backed off the crest of the ridge. He put an arm around her shoulders and cut a little jig as they walked. Then, catching her by surprise, he whirled her around. He gathered her in his arms and swung her in time to the music, until her feet lifted off the ground and spun freely. She laughed silently with him, and they walked, holding hands, to where their ponies were tethered.

The next morning, they went back to the site where the wagon train had been. It was deserted, but not empty. The grass was trampled by the animals and by the men's dancing. There was a litter of cans and paper sacks blowing across the prairie. There were broken axles and scraps of metal. There were bits of discarded clothing, socks that were more hole than yarn, the mule-chewed fragments of a straw hat. Small Hand dismounted and picked up an empty bottle in the shape of a cabin. Imprinted on it were the words "Log Cabin Whiskey" and the name of its manufacturer, E. G. Booz. She held it up for Cub to see.

"We can carry water in this."

Cub whirled around.

"Drop it!" he shouted.

He startled her and she let the bottle slip from her fingers. It shattered against a rock at her feet.

411

"I'm sorry, small one. But don't pick up anything here. Don't even touch anything."

"There might be something we can use."

"The white men carry disease. They leave it lying along the path with their trash. Look." He pointed east, back the way the wagon train and hundreds like it had come. Even after it had disappeared among the hills, the trail could still be followed. It was marked by a line of vultures that circled over it, growing smaller and smaller in the distant sky. The trail was littered with abandoned wagons, broken wheels, garbage, and the putrifying carcasses of dead mules and horses, oxen and buffalo and deer. Cub and Small Hand crossed the dusty furrow and continued their journey. Even Cub didn't know that the whites left more than rotting trash behind. They contaminated the pools of drinking water.

At last Cub and Small Hand found the Noconi, camped on a high bluff overlooking the Pease River. The village had a commanding view of the countryside around. It was a land of rolling, grass-covered hills covered with the usual dark green cedars and pale green mesquites. Against the horizon to the north, flat-topped bluffs marched along in silhouette, like elephants in a line. And dotting the hills as far as the eye could see was a herd of wild mustangs, thousands of them.

Each of the smaller herds, or *manadas*, was converging at a leisurely walk on the river that meandered among the hills.

Wanderer's band had grown until there were over a hundred lodges spread out under the pecan trees. The tops of the tents and the lodge poles could be seen for more than a mile along the ridge. There were no cries of mourning, and no sign of the white man's diseases. Wanderer and his warriors disdained councils with the whites. And they stayed far from trading posts and wagon routes, except to raid.

His war parties struck like lightning, flashing down from the hills then disappearing into the wild labyrinth of breaks and arroyos. They stole only weapons and stock, horses and cattle and mules to add to their own herds and to trade with José Tafoya. The size of the Noconi herds rivaled the vast band of mustangs moving and shifting below them. The trained ponies, the cattle, and the pack animals grazed on one side of camp, and the wild mustangs that they had caught were tethered on the other.

Small Hand and Cub rode into the village together, and Wanderer stood to greet them. His lodge was the largest one and it was set in the center of the camp. It had a huge, bright yellow sun painted on its side, and a string of deer hooves clacked in the breeze. Wanderer recognized Cub immediately. But he did so probably because of the young man's resemblance to Naduah, rather than remembering the child he had known briefly many years before.

"Hi, *Tah-mah*," he said, smiling. "I welcome the brother of my wife, and his woman."

Cub smiled back, a feeling of relief washing over him, as though he had found a warm sheltered hearth in a howling snowstorm.

"Greetings, Brother." When he slid down off his horse, Wanderer embraced him.

"You have a nephew around here somewhere, Echo Of A Wolf's Howl."

"So I've heard. People say he's handsome." Cub didn't ask how Wanderer knew his new name. Perhaps he would find out later, after dinner and over a pipe. "Where's my sister?"

"She's busy." Wanderer glanced toward a lodge set apart from the others. It was near a small, spring-fed stream and a large hackberry tree. "She's giving birth. Most of the men have gone hunting. But I stayed until the child is born." Wanderer waved behind him. "You can stay in the guest lodge, that one over there."

Silently Small Hand led the spare pony toward it and began unpacking their few belongings. Some of the neighbor women helped her. When they saw the sorry state of Small Hand's household, they sent their children scurrying for things to loan and give. Soon there were people coming from all directions with robes, clothing, food, ladles, containers, even a tiny child struggling along under a big brass kettle. Small Hand accepted all the presents shyly, but she kept a strict accounting in her head. Someday she would repay each one's kindness.

Wanderer sat down again in front of his own doorway and motioned for Cub to join him. He leaned against a saddle, with his long legs stretched comfortably in front of him. He reached for his pipe and flint.

"I'm glad you're here, Echo Of A Wolf's Howl. Naduah will be very happy. I don't think she ever stopped missing you. She speaks of you often. Tomorrow we'll visit the pony herd. You can choose the horses you want."

Cub started to protest, but Wanderer held up his hand.

"You don't have to keep them if you don't want to. But they'll give you a start at regaining what you've lost. Soon you'll have many horses of your own. I'm planning a raid to Mexico for more." He grinned wickedly. "There are so few good horses left in Texas. Will you come with us?"

413

Cub nodded.

"Good. Tell me the news from the Penateka."

"You already seem to know most of it."

"One never knows all of it. And each man has his own version. I want to hear yours. I trust yours."

"That makes my heart glad, my brother. Especially since you haven't seen me in such a long time. I may have changed. Become a white man."

"I know you haven't. I've heard many good things about you from the other bands. And besides, you're my wife's brother.

"I also heard that you were traveling with nothing. That you burned everything when your grandfather died. And that you killed his ponies. That was as it should be. These days, people are greedy. They only shave the tails of the dead one's ponies, and then they keep them. You did things properly, as they should be done.

"My heart is in the grave with your grandfather, my brother. He was a great warrior and a wise man."

Wanderer's eyes filled with tears, and they were both silent. Then they heard the thin wail of a newborn baby, testing its lungs. Wanderer ran toward the birth lodge, with Cub close behind him.

◥ 45 ◢

An early norther had pounced on the camp and howled around the lodge, looking for a way inside. The heavily weighted hide door bowed inward with the force of it. Naduah sat on a pile of furs, her back against the pole bedstead. She was basking in the warmth of the fire and the joy of having her friends and loved ones with her. She looked up at the seams of the lodge, firm and taut in the fifty-mile-an-hour gale. The lodge was crowded with men smoking and quietly talking, and with children waiting for the first corn kernel to pop. Wears Out Moccasins was tending the corn, stirring it gently in the bed of hot sand.

Naduah was nursing her second son. His steady, rhythmic sucking at her breast lulled her and filled her with contentment. She knew there were terrible things happening in the southern bands, but they seemed far removed this night. She had left the birth tent sooner than usual when she heard her brother had returned. As Cub held her new son in his arms, he answered her questions about

Pahayuca's band and her family. They were safe. Cub had warned them to isolate themselves, as they had when the pox broke out ten years before.

Naduah looked down at her son's fuzzy little head, nuzzling her. He was called Nakahtaba, Pecan. Wanderer had named him.

"You named Quanah," he had said. "I name this one. He stared down at the tiny, brown, wrinkled baby. "He looks like a pecan." And Pecan he would be until someone gave him a better name.

Quanah, almost five years old now, sat on Sore-Backed Horse's lap, braiding the long fringes on the warrior's leggings. He studied his blond-haired uncle surreptitiously, his slate-gray eyes peering from under a heavy fringe of straight, dark brown hair. Echo Of A Wolf's Howl wasn't unfriendly, but he had a formal, preoccupied air about him. He always looked as though he was thinking about something else. It was a defense that Cub had used to keep his white family at a distance, and it was part of him now. Quanah wasn't sure how to react to him, so he stayed with Sore-Backed Horse. He was certain to have his own way there. Sore-Backed Horse had been filling the important role of uncle ever since Quanah was born.

If only Medicine Woman and Takes Down The Lodge and Sunrise were here, thought Naduah. *And Black Bird and Something Good and Little Weasel. Not so little anymore*, she corrected herself. *She must be almost as old as Small Hand.* Cub had also reported that Weasel was even more beautiful than her mother. He had visited them to tell Something Good of her parents' death. He spoke of it to Naduah through clenched teeth, fighting to keep his face impassive. Naduah loved Cub, but even she felt uneasy around him. He no longer had the openness and sense of humor of one of the People.

Star Name and Deep Water and their three-and-a-half-year-old daughter, Wakare-ee, Turtle, were there, as well as Spaniard and his wife and their little girl. But the most unexpected guest to show up at the lodge door that evening was Cruelest One, looking like some evil spirit blown in on the storm. He came in after Star Name's brother, Wolf Road, and he scowled at Naduah as he handed her the present of popping corn, traded from the Wichita. He brushed past her before she could say anything.

Naduah wasn't as surprised to see him as she should have been. She caught him once in serious conversation with little Quanah. He didn't know she had seen him, and she would never tell him. She still didn't feel any warmth for Cruelest One. Few people did. But he was given a place in the family circle because he had saved Wolf Road's life in the battle of Plum Creek nine years ago. And because he quietly, without words, asked for a place.

Gathered Up, fifteen now, sat next to Wolf Road. Wolf Road and

Cub had been entertaining everyone with stories from their boy-hood. Naduah knew they had played pranks, but she had no idea how much trouble they had caused, or the tight spots they had gotten themselves into. *On the other hand*, she thought, *no one knows some of the tricks Star Name and I pulled either*. As he reminisced, Cub's eyes rekindled, and his old charm surfaced. Small Hand watched him closely, as though seeing a stranger she had never met before.

The first small, dark kernel of corn exploded with a tiny pop, and the three older children crowded around to watch. They had never seen it before.

"Stand back," said Wears Out Moccasins, waving them away. "Give me room." The corn was exploding steadily now, and even Wears Out Moccasins couldn't keep the children away. The adults leaned forward too. Popcorn was a rare treat. As it popped, Wears Out Moccasins swept the top kernels off onto a flat piece of bark. Now and then, one would arc up and out of the sand, and the children scrambled for it.

Wears Out Moccasins divided the corn first among the children, putting some in each of the containers they held out. One had a turtle shell, one had a small piece of buffalo hide, and Quanah used a bandana that his uncle Echo Of A Wolf's Howl had given him. Then the rest of the corn was passed to the adults. Wears Out Moccasins stepped over the legs sprawled in her way as she served it. For a few minutes there was only the sound of people blowing the grains of sand off their corn, and the crunching of the kernels. Then Naduah spoke, handing Pecan to Star Name.

"Quanah, girls, did I ever tell you the story of the time turtle actually tricked Old Man Coyote, the Trickster himself?"

"No." It was a chorus.

"Long ago, it is said, Old Man Coyote was coming along, and he met a little turtle roasting a nice meal of five prairie dogs. Does Old Man Coyote like to eat?" she asked the children.

"Yes," they shouted.

" 'Hello, my friend,' said the Trickster. 'May I share your delicious-looking prairie dogs?' 'No,' said Turtle, poking up the coals with his little stir stick. Turtle knew that if he wasn't careful Coyote would find a way to eat all the prairie dogs himself. He watched him closely, like this." Naduah squinted her eyes and with her fingers wrinkled the skin around her mouth. She sucked in her cheeks until she looked like a turtle. She glared at Quanah out of the corner of her eye.

" 'If you won't share your dinner with me,' said Coyote, 'why don't we race?' Turtle was suspicious. 'You know I can't run very fast. You'll beat me,' he said. But Coyote said, 'I'll tie a big stone to my leg to give you a better chance. Let's race over that hill and through the trees and along the river to the big boulder. Then we'll circle back here.' Turtle knew that Coyote had some trick in mind, but he agreed to run the race. It would give him a chance to think of a plan to save his meal.

"They both started running, and it looked like the little turtle was going to win. He huffed and he puffed as his stubby legs hauled his heavy shell over the rough ground. But as Turtle became tired, Old Man Coyote drew alongside. They ran even for a while, and then Trickster slowly pulled ahead. He disappeared over the crest of the hill. Turtle slowed to a stop and drew his legs into his shell to think. 'That Coyote will win,' he thought. 'He'll get back to the fire first and he'll eat all my prairie dogs.' Then Turtle had an idea. He turned and plodded back down the hill.

"When he came to his fire, he pulled the roasted prairie dogs out by their tails. As soon as they had cooled he gobbled them quickly up. He carefully put the tails back, so thy stuck out of the ashes. Then he threw the bones into the lake. He heard the Coyote coming, so he hid in the weeds.

"Old Man Coyote arrived all out of breath. But he patted his stomach when he saw the prairie dog tails sticking out of the ashes. 'I'll have a wonderful meal,' he said, 'while that stupid little Turtle crawls along, finishing the race.' He pulled at the tails, but whoop, they came out right in his hand. He saw that he had been tricked and he heard Turtle laughing in the weeds.

" 'I thought I would cheat you, Turtle,' he said, 'but you tricked me instead.' Coyote went to the lake and searched for the prairie dog bones. He fished them out and made a meager meal of them. Then he went dejectedly off, with little Turtle's laughter in his ears. *Suvate*, it is finished." They all applauded, pounding their moccasins on the hard-packed dirt and clapping and whistling.

"Girls," said Star Name. "It's late. Lie on the bed, where you'll be more comfortable if you fall asleep." The two children climbed onto Gathered Up's bed. They curled at its foot like a pair of puppies, leaving the rest of it for Wears Out Moccasins to sit. Quanah crawled back into Sore-Backed Horse's lap, determined to hear the rest of the evening's talk. But within minutes he was asleep, his head against Sore-Backed Horse's chest. Wanderer stretched his arms over his head, recrossed his long legs, and spoke to Cub.

"Tell us all the news from the south, Echo Of A Wolf's Howl. We have heard reports, but they've been scattered. And often the messengers are too distraught to believe."

"You can believe whatever they say and more. No one can describe how bad the situation is there. It has to be seen to be believed. I would guess that half the Penateka are dead from this latest disease." He paused a moment to let the impact of that settle. They all knew that Cub didn't exaggerate. Naduah spoke up.

"There have been outbreaks of the white men's diseases before. Remember, Star Name, the camp we found ten years ago? The People will survive this and become strong again."

"No, sister," said Cub. "The People survived the sickness ten years ago, but it left them weakened, their numbers less. And this is far worse. Entire bands are breaking up, scattering. The major leaders are dead. There's not a family that hasn't lost someone. And now everyone's afraid of everyone else. A child with diarrhea is abandoned. A grandmother who vomits is left to die. The People are losing touch with their old ways. Fear is driving them from the traditions that have made them strong."

"What can we do?" asked Star Name.

"What you are already doing. Wanderer is right. Stay away from the trading posts and wagon trains. Don't touch anything that belongs to the white people, or to refugees from the stricken camps."

"We can't turn away people seeking shelter and protection," said Deep Water.

"I know. But stay away from them. Ask them to camp on the edge of the band. And don't let your children go near them."

"The best defense," said Deep Water, "is to kill the source. The white eyes have found another way to attack us by turning evil spirits loose among us."

"If it's any comfort to you, Deep Water," said Small Hand, speaking quietly from the shadows where she was rocking Pecan, "they die of it too. In our travels we passed over their trails. And always there were wolf-pawed graves along them. The wolves had dug up one of the graves, and we saw the remains. It was a white baby."

"But they breed like rabbits," continued Deep Water. "As fast as one dies, one of their women drops two more. We must kill their women and their children and burn their lodges and crops."

Cub thought of the Parkers in Limestone County. There was hardly a family that didn't have a child for every year of the marriage. And here, Naduah was exceptional. She had borne two sons in the past five years. And the People didn't even realize the worst, that back east there were thousands outfitting for the wilderness. Old Owl had seen them. That was why he had given up the struggle. He knew the hopelessness of it. Cub didn't have the heart to tell those sitting around him of the teeming cities beyond the eastern mountains and the big river. He knew they wouldn't believe him anyway. Even his own sister wouldn't believe him.

"Deep Water is right," said Wanderer. "We must raid. Only now we don't raid for loot in Texas, or even horses. We'll take the horses and cattle and captives when we can. But we'll burn and slaughter whatever we can't carry with us."

"When will we leave, Wanderer?" Deep Water was always eager to raid.

"We can discuss that in council. We can ride to Mexico for loot, and raid the Texans on our way south. We'll operate differently than in the past. We won't set up base camps near the settlements. The Rangers are there again and it's too dangerous.

"We'll divide into smaller groups and leave the main trail. We can sneak down the river bottoms at night and hide during the day. Then just about sundown we'll strike and run, and rejoin the main group."

Wanderer had been thinking about the plan for a long time. He was testing it here, among his friends, before he brought it up in council. Cub sat, silent, mulling it over.

"What do you think, Echo Of A Wolf's Howl?"

"It's a good idea, Brother-in-law."

"Will you ride with us?"

"Of course."

The winter of 1849 and 1850 was a hard one. It closed in on them and locked them in their camp. All their spare time was taken with hunting to stay alive. It wasn't until the spring of 1850 that Wanderer's party headed south. There were over three hundred and fifty men in the group. Word had gone out to the Yamparika and Quohadi, to the Kotsoteka and even to the Kiowa. Men gathered for weeks. The drumming and dancing and councils were incessant, and the encampments stretched for ten miles along the Pease River. The cholera epidemic seemed to have run its deadly course, and the People were going to extract their revenge.

Naduah and Star Name and all those who stayed behind watched the war party leave camp. Quanah insisted on riding with them a short way on his tubby little pony. The child's legs were too short to curve around the horse's barrel, and they bounced up and down as he jogged along. Wanderer rode on Night, in front, with his lieutenants ranged on each side. He picked as aides those men whom he trusted the most and who had earned the most honors in battle. On one side rode Big Bow and on the other Cub. Although he had yet to prove himself in battle, most of the warriors tacitly recognized Cub's knowledge of both the white culture and of their own. They realized that his advice would be valuable.

Night's tail was tied up with thongs and decorated with eagle feathers. Streamers and feathers and bells were braided into his mane. His eyes were painted with the yellow circles he always wore. There were gray hairs peppering Night's muzzle, and his five-year-old son, Raven, followed him.

Wanderer carried his coup stick in his right hand. It was a slender branch with a few eagle feathers and fur streamers that made its owner impervious to arrows or bullets. On his left arm he carried his shield, and in his left hand his lance. His men rode to the steady thump of small hand drums. The bells on their legging and shirts jingled, and there was the rustle of leather against leather.

Each man's clothing was smoked to pale yellows or browns or dyed in subtle greens and blues. Some were rubbed with selenaceous clay until they were creamy white. Their long, fringed shirts were hung with bells and tassels of scalp hair or animal tails. They wore breast plates of bone cylinders strung in parallel rows into bibs. Some had huge silver necklaces. Their hair was combed and oiled and allowed to flow over their shoulders. Some had woven horsehair into their own to make it even longer. Their scalplocks were hung with feathers of polished silver disks that flashed in the sunlight.

They each carried their fourteen-foot lanches upright, and a forest of them waved overhead, their streamers dancing in the breeze. The rifles and carbines that Wanderer and his men had raided so relentlessly to obtain were carried in special buskskin cases, strapped to their ponies' sides and within easy reach.

Not many women, other than Small Hand and Wears Out Moccasins, went with them. Unlike former years, the war party would be even more mobile than usual. The trail, down the valley of the North Concho River across the Edwards Plateau to the Balcones Escarpment near the Rio Grande, was more dangerous than it had ever been. Not only were the Rangers hunting them, but there were local volunteer companies. And there were United States troops, ineffective as they were. Worst of all, there were more and more settlers, each armed and looking for blood.

Wanderer's plan worked well. Small bands of his men left terror and destruction behind them as they pillaged and burned their way south. They killed every Texan they found, mutilating the bodies so the souls wouldn't be accepted into paradise. By the time a party of men could be organized to chase them, they were long gone, dividing as they left the scene of the raid. Half would drive the stolen stock and the other half would act as a rear quard. They rode a hundred miles without stopping. And they usually left the Texans with no horses, or at best a few poor ones. The warriors, on the other hand, had mounts to spare. When one pony tired, a companion would lead another alongside and the man would leap onto it without breaking stride.

The war party had already stolen a large herd of ponies and cattle when they reached the mountains near Eagle Pass. From there the broad, well-marked raid trail unraveled as the parties that had used it for decades scattered into Mexico. Wanderer and his men set up a large base camp, well hidden in the mountains. Smaller groups would leave from there, devastating the isolated ranches and helpless farms of Chihuahua and Coahuila. Once into Mexico, they would raid with arrogance, hardly bothering to cover their tracks.

After the base camp was established, the raiders would bring their stock and captives back to it, then leave again for more. The few women made temporary lodges, buffalo hides thrown around cones of short poles. The men cut brush for shelters and piled it against the small lodge framework. Small Hand and the other women settled down to a life rather like the one they had left, except that there was less work to do. As the captives were brought in, they would take over what chores there were. When Wears Out Moccasins wasn't raiding, she was bustling around, mothering the men of the Noconi band. Most of them treated her with good humor, but more than once she and Cruelest One locked horns in the middle of the encampment.

"Leave my moccasins alone," he shouted at her.

"They're tattered. You look like an unkempt Osage," she roared back at him.

"I can mend them, you meddling buffalo cow."

"They look worse after you mend them than before you started."

And around they went. When she wasn't collecting piles of mending from the men, Wears Out Moccasins was talking to Small Hand, whom she'd taken under her vast wing. She had accumulated more horses and was enjoying herself immensely. Each day more men rode in from their scattered raids north of the Rio Grande. Finally all of them had arrived, and Wanderer called a council for that night to discuss their plans for their forays into Mexico.

"Small Hand," said Wears Out Moccasins. "Is your husband feeling all right?"

"I don't think he feels good."

"He looks pale to me. Where does he feel bad? Maybe I have something to help him."

"I don't know," Small Hand mumbled. She was afraid, because

for the first time since she had known her sun hair she sensed fear in him. She made an excuse, and left Wears Out Moccasins to find him.

Cub sat alone, on a high outcropping of rock overlooking a barren, brown valley, spiny with cactus and agave.

"Sun hair."

"Yes, small one."

"How do you feel?"

"Worse."

"Do you know what it is?"

"Yes."

Small Hand waited for him to continue.

"Cholera."

"Ka-ler-ah?"

"The white man's disease. The one that killed my grandfather."

"Maybe you're wrong."

"I'm not wrong. My dung is running from me like water."

"Maybe you ate tainted meat, my dear one." Small Hand came closer, her hand out to feel his forehead. "Is your skin hot?"

"Stay away, small one. Don't come near me. Go find Wanderer and ask him to come, quickly."

Small Hand turned and darted away, calling for Wanderer. When they returned, Cub was leaning against a rock, wretching helplessly. Wanderer waited for him to finish, and Small Hand gave him the water she had brought. He spit out the first mouthful, trying to wash away the taste of bile. Then he drank deeply from the gourd. He replaced the carved wooden plug.

"Don't drink from this canteen, small one."

"Yes, Husband."

"Cub," said Wanderer, using his old, pet name. "Are you sure?"

"I'm sure. Take everyone and leave camp. Ride as fast as you can and as far as you can. And take care of Small Hand for me."

"I'm not going, Husband."

"Yes, you are. Don't touch my belongings, Brother. I'll burn them before I become too weak. But you must leave now. Immediately. Take everyone. And don't return to this campsite. Tell my sister I love her." His last words were almost lost as nausea seized him again. He was too weak to stand, and spread his knees to vomit between them.

"Cub, I can't leave the brother of my wife, the uncle of my sons, my friend."

Cub reached for the gourd of water.

"Because you are all those things, you must leave. You can do no good here. I'm not a wounded warrior that you can throw on the back of your pony and save. If you stay, you'll die too. And your family will have no one to provide for it."

Wanderer stood for a moment, staring at him. He raised his hand in salute.

"I will pray for you, Brother." He turned to go. "Come, Small Hand."

"No."

"Take her, Wanderer," said Cub.

Small Hand drew her long, wicked skinning knife. She crouched, her eyes steady and deadly.

"You can't kill me, Small Hand. You know that I can take that knife from you," said Wanderer in a low, calm voice.

"You can't take it from me before I slit my throat. Will you be responsible for the death of your brother-in-law's wife?"

"No, Small Hand. Stay," he said sadly. "It's come to this. We abandon those we love. The white men have brought us to such a miserable state." Wanderer took his small medicine bag from its place hanging inside his breechclout. He tossed it gently onto the ground in front of Cub and Small Hand, who stood next to him. "It's all I can give you. It's protected me. Perhaps it will do the same for you. I'll leave ponies for you. And cattle to eat. Small Hand can kill and butcher them. We'll leave whatever we can that will be of use to you. If you recover, return to us, Cub."

"I will, Brother." Cub didn't try to thank Wanderer for the medicine bag. He knew it was the most valuable thing his brother-in-law owned. It was more than valuable. It was priceless. It had taken Wanderer a lifetime to gather the things inside it. He picked it up and held it on his lap.

He and Small Hand watched Wanderer disappear through the corridor of rocks leading to the camp. Small Hand took the canteen to the trickling spring nearby. She squatted patiently while the water ran slowly into the narrow opening of the gourd.

"When they're gone, I'll make you comfortable." She knelt in front of him and washed his face and chest, splashing the cool water over his hot, dry skin. "Drink more."

"I'm craving salt, small one."

"I'll make you a broth and put salt in it." From the distance they could hear the shouts from camp as the men packed to move. Wears Out Moccasins appeared at the narrow opening in the boulders.

"Small Hand, Echo Of A Wolf's Howl," she called. "I put pemmican and jerky and stew near your shelter. And I'm leaving medicine for you. Hurry and get well and rejoin us."

"We will, Mother," said Small Hand. Then Wears Out Moccasins

423

was gone. They could hear screams. The women and children who had been taken captive in Texas were being killed. They might be carriers of the disease. Then they heard the sound of hooves diminishing in the distance. And silence. It had taken only minutes for the word to spread and the campsite to be abandoned.

"Come, Husband." Small Hand put an arm around Cub's waist and helped him to his feet. "When you lie down and rest, you'll feel better. You'll get well. I promise you."

Cub was too weak to argue with her.

❧ *46* ❧

Naduah and Star Name rode toward camp. There were two carcasses slung across their pack mule's back. They had raced their ponies into the herd of pronghorns and had each lassoed one of the darting, dodging animals. Now, with a week's worth of meals taken care of, Naduah was thinking of something else.

"They've geen gone almost two months."

"Yes. I doubt they'll be back before the next full moon. They'll use it to raid by. I hope they have a leisurely trip back. Because when they return, I'm going to wear Deep Water out. He'll walk around with his breechclout in his hand for a week."

Naduah laughed.

"Gathered Up had a visitor last night."

"Gathered Up?" said Star Name. "I can't stop thinking of him as a small boy."

"Not after last night. They thought I was sleeping. I could hear them giggling next door." The women had made Gathered Up his own lodge.

"I miss Wanderer, Sister," said Naduah. "I worry."

"Don't waste your time worrying about Wanderer. Worry about if it's going to rain. You can depend on Wanderer. He always comes back."

"It always rains too," said Naduah.

"Yes. But one never knows when."

"And one never knows when Wanderer will be back either."

They both smiled.

"The river's too low to swim, but at least we can lie back in it and let it flow around us. I'm looking forward to that," said Naduah. "It's about the temperature of stew water, but it's better than nothing."

Star Name wiped sweat from her face and slung it off her hand. She was too hot to even make her usual suggestion to race back to camp.

The village was quiet with the men gone. The older men and boys and women defended it and carried on as best they could. But they were used to it. War parties were sometimes gone for years. Perhaps that was why it was so important for the older people to train the children. They were often the only ones around to do it.

The two women were startled from their lethargy when Gathered Up came galloping toward them. He waved frantically for them to turn back. Little Pecan rode in front of him and Quanah clung to his waist, bouncing along behind. Without asking questions, Naduah and Star Name wheeled their ponies and raced for the cover of a high, dense growth of plum and oak and prickly pear. Once behind it, they jumped down from their horses and tied them to trees. They strung their bows and each nocked an arrow. Gathered Up arrived in a lather. He handed down the baby and turned to help Quanah, but the child had already tumbled off. He ran to his mother, his tiny bow drawn too.

"White men, Mother, and they're asking about you. But I won't let them get you." Quanah planted his feet and raised his bow, taking steady aim in the direction of camp.

"It's all right, Quanah. No one told them where your mother is."

"What's happening, Gathered Up?" asked Naduah.

"Traders. Sore-backed Horse is talking to them. They asked about you. He told them you and your husband were visiting his father on the Staked Plains. That ought to discourage them."

"If Wanderer were here, he wouldn't have let them in the village."

"But Wanderer isn't here. Sore-Backed Horse said he'd get rid of them as soon as possible. Here." Gathered Up reached into a saddle bag and pulled out an intestine stuffed with pemmican. "I brought food so we can sleep away from the camp tonight."

"We have food too, Gathered Up," said Naduah, nodding toward the two pronghorn carcasses. "Let's go." She led the small group back the way she and Star Name had come.

"No bath in the river," sighed Star Name.

Naduah didn't like the idea of traders in the village. Not only because she feared they would try to ransom her, but because of the death the white men were spreading. She was as fascinated with the

425

mirrors and combs, the bright beads and cloth as any of the women, but Wanderer had planted a fear of them in her.

Come back soon, Wanderer.

Naduah and Star Name were digging a hole for Dog's body when Wolf Road entered the camp.

"The raiding party is back," said Naduah.

"They're back early," said Star Name. "Do you think something's wrong?" They hurried with their task.

They had found Dog dead when they'd returned that morning after the traders had left. The white men had looked inside Naduah's lodge and Dog attacked them. The neighbor children said she'd tried to tear one of the men's legs off. He had kicked her hard in the head.

Quanah and Turtle, Star Name's daughter, appeared around the side of the lodge. Turtle clutched a fistful of wilted flowers. Quanah carried wild grapes in his cupped palms. They carefully left the traditional offering on the small grave as the adults watched.

They knew Wolf Road would come next to their lodges, so the two women waited outside. Lance was already announcing that no one had been lost in battle and that there were hundreds of horses captured, when Wolf Road walked up to them.

"You're back earlier than we expected, Wolf Road. Is anything wrong?"

"Your brother, Naduah."

"What happened to him? Has he been hurt?"

"No. He has the white man's disease. Ka-ler-ah. He told us to leave him. We didn't want to. Small Hand stayed with him. We left food. Perhaps he'll be all right. Naduah," there was a pleading tone in Wolf Road's voice. "He was my friend. I loved him like a brother. I didn't want to leave him. My heart is there with him still. And with his woman."

"I know, Wolf Road. I don't blame you." *We must leave them!* She remembered telling Medicine Woman that. She remembered helping to pack while her friend Owl lay burning with fever. "There was nothing you could have done," she said aloud. "And maybe he'll recover. Cub said that some do." Absentmindedly, Naduah herded Quanah inside, her hand on his tousled head. Was Cub lost forever this time?

The raid had been a success, even though it was cut short. But the image of Cub, dying somewhere in the bleak mountains of Northern Mexico, haunted her. She tried not to think of it, although the need to cry stung the linings of her nose and burned her eyes. Wanderer was back, and he was bringing seven hundred horses. He had lost no men in battle. Perhaps he had lost no men at all. Perhaps Cub was still alive.

Somewhere out there, Wanderer was painting Night and himself, and dressing them both for his triumphal entry into the village. Naduah could feel her heart pounding. If she hadn't had two children to dress, she would have jumped onto Wind and ridden bareback to meet him. Her fingers shook as she helped Quanah dress. She knelt in front of him and tapped his ankle.

His feet were buried in the deep pile of the bear skin he stood on. He lifted one of them, and she put on one of the new leggings she had made him. They were painted red and the fringes were decorated with metal cones, each stuffed with a tassel of horsehair. As she pulled on his leggings, he balanced himself by putting a hand on her head. Then he drew on his hunting shirt. Its yoke was solidly sewn with rows of gleaming white elk's teeth. And she made him wear his good, beaded moccasins.

"They're too tight," he protested.

"That's because you don't wear them very often. They'll loosen up." *Just in time for him to outgrow them,* she thought. He squirmed while she brushed his hair and rebraided it. Then he adjusted his small squirrel-skin quiver across his back and picked up his miniature bow.

"I'm going to show my new clothes to Sore-Backed Horse and Wolf Road," he said, posing for her in the doorway.

"Stay out of the dust, gray eyes. And if you see Gathered Up, tell him to hurry and dress. Then come right back. We will ride to meet your father."

Without answering, he ran out into the late afternoon sunshine. Naduah stood, trying to decide what to wear. She took one dress from its case, then another, until the bed was covered with them. She picked up the one in the latest style, with the blouse and skirt sewn together at the waist, the seam hidden under fringe and beaded panels. She had just finished it and Wanderer hadn't seen it. She laid it back down. It would be better to wear something familiar, something she knew he liked.

She chose one of her older ones. The poncho was a creamy yellow, its yoke area painted a russet and outlined in thick fringe. Long tongue-shaped panels hung down the front and back. The front one was beaded with medallion shapes, and the back one had dark blue slashes painted on it, one mark for each of Wanderer's battle honors.

There were clusters of blue and white beads with long leather thongs threaded through them and hanging in fringes. Red and white beads were scattered around the edges of the line of deep fringe at the sleeve hems. And there were the usual clusters of tiny bells.

She pulled on her tight dress leggings and crisscrossed a lacing around each of them, tying it at the knee. She brushed the dust off the bottoms of her feet and stepped into her high, soft moccasins. They were smoked a pale yellow with green stripes up the front, and laced through holes along the sides. The moccasins ended in wide cuffs folded over and trimmed with long fringes.

Studying her face in the mirror, she painted herself. Dipping her forefinger into bear grease and then yellow paint powder, she ran it from her nose across her cheek to her ear. She drew another line under that one, and repeated the pattern on the other side. She wiped her finger and drew three red lines fanning out from her mouth, over her chin. When Quanah came back, she would paint his face too. But there was no use doing it early. He would surely smudge it.

She put on an otter fur choker with the bushy tail hanging down the back and a polished clam-shell disk in front. The disk looked just like the one Eagle had bet on the honey hunt fourteen years before. She slipped several Mexican silver bracelets over her strong slender hands, and brushed her hair. By the time she finished braiding it with otter fur strips, Pecan had awakened and was whimpering. She chewed some pemmican and fed it to him.

Then Naduah went outside to saddle and decorate their horses. Finally, when they were all ready, they rode, side by side to meet the war party. The rest of the village ranged behind them, drumming and shouting and chanting.

Wanderer watched them coming. The edge of the red-trimmed mountain lion skin fluttered on Wind's haunches. Naduah sat tall and straight, her thin suede dress moving along her full, agile body. Little Pecan rode next to her leg, his cradle board swinging from her saddle. Quanah sat on his fat, sway-backed little pony like a miniature warrior. He was scowling fiercely under his paint. He had grown in the two months Wanderer had been away. And so had Gathered Up. Wanderer realized he would have to prepare him for his vision quest soon.

As he watched Naduah approach he wished, for an instant, that he were the youngest, most insignificant herder in the war party. He wished he could sneak away, unnoticed, with his beloved. He wanted to take her to some isolated spot and love her the entire night. But he wasn't a herder. He was a war leader, returning with plunder and horses, and the news that he had abandoned his golden one's brother. He would have to tell her about it, and it would be hours before he could even be alone with her.

He was expected at the feasts and dances in honor of the raiders. There would be visitors for days, coming to congratulate him and carry away presents in return. He would give away most of his share of the spoils and, in doing so, prove his disdain for material things. He would show that he knew he could always steal more whenever he wanted them.

And he would be given presents too. Families would ask him to name their sons. Warriors would seek his advice. Boys would want to discuss the proper conduct for their vision quests. Or they would ask him to paint a holy symbol on their shields when they returned from their quests. He was expected to attend all councils and to maintain diplomatic relations with the other bands and allied tribes.

Wanderer would have it no other way. He thrived on the responsibility. But just this once, for a few moments, he wanted to escape from it. To give Naduah the delicate white scarf he had brought her. To tell her of her brother. Most of all, he wanted to feel her naked body next to his again. To love her until he was exhausted, and then to lie, shrunken, inside her until her warmth aroused him again.

She was almost even with him now, and he raised his shield and lance in salute. She and Quanah and Gathered Up did the same with their bows and arrows.

Most of the village was asleep when the men of the council finally left their smoking lodge. Wanderer had gone home by way of the river to bathe. Dressed only in breechclout and moccasins, he carried his sweat-stained shirt and dusty leggings in his hand as he walked through the quiet camp. As he passed each lodge, he listened. It was a habit of watchfulness that was hard to break. He felt responsible for each family, and he smiled at what he heard. The returned warriors were being well received by their wives.

His own family was asleep when he reached home, the familiar sun glowing softly on the lodge wall. Quanah and Pecan lay curled together among their sleeping robes on one side of the buffalo robe curtain. They had thrown the covers off themselves, and he pulled them back up. Then he stood looking down at them for a long time in the light of the embers. He watched their chests rise and fall rhythmically and their long lashes flutter as they dreamed. Quanah was already taller than the other boys his own age, and his legs were lengthening, giving him a coltish look.

Wanderer slipped his breechclout and moccasins off in the gloom. He threw his clothes over the line stretched between two lodge poles. He luxuriated in the feel of the furs scattered on the floor, wriggling his toes and digging his tired feet into them. He felt clean, and weary and, in some way, let down. He wished he could wash the sorrow away as easily as the sweat and dust. As they had ridden to and from Mexico, he too had seen the devastation left by the latest white man's epidemic. And Naduah's brother might already be dead of it.

He sat down cross-legged among the tumble of bedding. Naduah too lay uncovered in the warm night of early summer. Wanderer ran his hand very gently along her smooth body, feeling the familiar, rounded curves once more. She sighed and turned over sensuously so he could stroke her breasts. He started to speak, but she was ahead of him.

"Wolf Road told me about my brother, beloved." She took Wanderer's hand, kissed it, and held it against her cheek. "I know there was nothing you could do."

"It's as bad as he said in the south, golden one."

"I want to go back for his bones, and those of Small Hand, if she died with him."

"We'll go. We'll wait until the spring to give them a chance to return. Then we'll search for them." Wanderer started to lie down wearily, and felt something hard on his pillow. He picked it up.

"Gathered Up made it for you," said Naduah. "He worked hard on it while you were gone. He thinks you're brother to the wolf and cousin to the bear."

The object was a handsome quirt. A rawhide lash, two feet long, was doubled to form a loop and inserted into a hole drilled vertically in a polished bone handle. A bone plug was driven tightly into a horizontal side hole through the loop and then through the hole on the opposite side, holding the thong in place. The handle was beautifully carved with a picture of a wolf, and had a beaded wrist strap. Another smaller hole was drilled at the butt end of the handle, near the wrist strap, and a tassel of fluffy white breath feathers and a single crow feather hung from a braided horsehair thong.

"I did the beading for him, but he made the rest of it."

"It's well made."

"Tell him so. Quanah has a present for you too, although he's much more excited about presents he might get."

"I brought you a present also, golden one."

She rolled over and wrapped her arms around him, feeling the lean, sleek contours of his shoulders and haunches and legs.

430

"This is the best present you could bring me," she murmured. "Welcome home, my wandering one."

"You've been with me the whole way. The thought of you."

She held his serious, handsome face between her palms and looked down at him in the dim light from the coals and the stars shining through the smoke hole. Words couldn't express her love. She would have to be content with showing him.

Wanderer spent most of his time at the pasture, working intensively with Raven, Wind's colt sired by Night. The pony was already as well trained as the average buffalo horse, but Wanderer still wasn't satisfied. He was teaching Raven to signal with his ears, waving them if buffalo were near, pitching them forward if a man approached. Raven was a replica of Night physically, but there were differences in their personalities. The colt was eager to please, but Night had a more businesslike approach to his training. It was as though he knew it was to their mutual benefit to work well with Wanderer.

Quanah had come along with his father, but had become bored. He had wandered off to practice shooting for distance with his bow.

"Gray eyes." Quanah came at a run. "Mount and show me how well you ride."

The child backed up and took a running start. He clutched his elbows to his sides and pumped his legs as hard as he could. At the last moment he leaped, grabbing for the loop woven into Raven's long, black mane. At the same time he hooked his toes into the stirrup loop on the surcingle and launched himself onto the pony's back. He adjusted himself and looked down, waiting for some comment. But while he concentrated on his father, Wanderer gave a cluck and Raven started off at a gallop. He threw Quanah backward, almost dumping him onto the ground. Quanah held on, grabbing frantically at the pony's mane. He bounced and slid, first to one side then to the other, until he managed to position his knees, grip with them, and bring the horse to a halt. He looked accusingly at his father.

"That was mean."

"Be glad it happened here and not in front of your friends. They'd never let you forget it. They'd bring it up when you're all old men passing the pipe in your smoking lodge." Wanderer smiled at him. "What did you learn?"

"To pay attention to my horse."

The two of them headed for the river, where Raven drank and Wanderer and Quanah rubbed him down with handfuls of grass.

Quanah concentrated on grooming the pony's legs, because that was about as high as he could reach.

"When we finish here," he asked, "will you show me how to shoot? Sore-Backed Horse said he'd show me, but he said you were the best."

"While I tether Raven, bring some buffalo chips."

Quanah darted about among the bushes near the river until he had gathered an armload of the large, round, dried disks.

"Now set one of them on edge against the trunk of that cotton-wood, and come here."

The child did as he was told. He knew he must take advantage of every minute with his father.

"Let me see your bow, son." Wanderer held it up, measuring. It didn't quite reach the boy's waist.

"You're growing fast. You need a new one. Either I or Sore-Backed Horse will make one for you. Show me how you nock an arrow and draw the bow. Get used to holding your arrows in your left hand with the points down. Then you won't cut yourself when you reach for one in a hurry." Wanderer knelt for a better view. He put his arms around his son to show him the proper position. "When you nock the bow, grip the string, not the arrow. That's why we cut a narrow slit in the shaft so the arrow will fit tightly around the cord. You don't have to pinch it between your fingers.

"The arrow shaft should rest loosely between your first two fingers, with your thumb on the butt end of the arrow to steady it."

The child concentrated on drawing the bowstring. His tongue stuck out of one corner of his mouth, and his eyes squinted.

"Relax, gray eyes. Use both hands and arms together. The left pushes while the right pulls. Rest your left forefinger lightly on the other end of the shaft, where it crosses the bow. You must learn to feel if the shaft is in the center of the bowstring without looking at it.

"Draw the arrow quickly and smoothly, in one sweeping motion, like a sapling that snaps back when bent down and then released. Don't spend time aiming or you'll lose control. Shoot first for distance. Build power. The aim will come. Nock, raise, draw, and fire. Try it."

The first arrow went wide.

"You're pulling up at the last minute. Do it without thinking about it. Do it as easily as you wave at your friends. Or steal stew from the pot." Quanah tried again.

"I came close that time!"

"Close isn't good enough. Close won't fill the kettle." Wanderer picked up his own bow and quiver. He had an arrow in the air and

432

arching toward the target before Quanah could even get his nocked. The arrow struck the middle of the chip and shattered it. Quanah ran to replace it.

All afternoon they shot. By the end of it, Wanderer was rolling chips for Quanah to shoot at while in motion. As they practiced, Wanderer passed on a little of what he knew, as much as he thought the child could learn in a day.

"When your arrows are damp, aim higher. They don't go as far wet. And try to keep them dry to begin with. Dampness loosens the sinew wrapping on the feathers. I prefer the feathers to be tied down only at each end so they bow a little in the middle. I think they fly better, but Sore-Backed Horse disagrees. Try them each way and decide for yourself.

"The arrow is the important thing. Any bow will shoot. But never be satisfied with an arrow that isn't perfectly balanced. Or the wrong size. You can measure it by holding it against your arm. It should be the same as the distance from your elbow to your fingertips."

Finally the sun sank almost to the horizon and cool shadows crawled over the plains, chilling the sweat on their bodies.

"It's time to go home," said Wanderer. "Stand perfectly still and I'll pick you up." He untied Raven and rode off a hundred feet. He turned the pony and galloped toward the child, who stood stolidly in his path. Even when it looked as though he would be run down and crushed under the pounding hoofs, Quanah didn't flinch. He watched his father with his solemn eyes, the color of gathering storm clouds, and tensed to help with the pickup. Raven passed so close his wind would have fluttered Quanah's long breechclout if he had been there. But Wanderer had swooped down and swung him onto the pony's back.

Quanah wrapped his small arms around his father's waist, and they raced for the village. As usual, the Noconi were camped on the highest hill along that part of the Pease River. As they approached the first lodges, Quanah gripped his father's shoulders and raised himself into a crouch. He planted his feet firmly and slowly stood, bracing his knees against Wanderer's back.

"Mother! Mother! Look!"

Naduah watched them career through the camp, scattering children and dogs in front of them. Then she reached down and scooped up Pecan, who was tugging on a piece of rawhide. His favorite puppy was on the other end of it, and they had both been growling at each other and worrying the leather between them. Naduah held Pecan astraddle her hip as Raven braked suddenly in front of her, rocking back on his haunches. The puppy tucked his tail between his legs and skittered, yipping, around the tent. But like Quanah, Naduah didn't flinch, even though dust kicked up by the pony's hooves coated her moccasins and made her sneeze.

Almost before Raven stopped, Quanah launched himself at his mother. He screamed a childish, high-pitched war cry as he leaped, arms outstretched. Naduah laughed and sidestepped, bouncing Pecan on her hip as she feinted. Quanah landed in a crouch to cushion his fall and rolled headfirst into a somersault. He jumped to his feet talking, telling her about his afternoon.

Gathered Up arrived with an armload of grass for Raven and Night, who was already tethered outside the lodge. Star Name and Deep Water and their daughter, Turtle, walked from their tent. Wolf Road trailed hungrily behind. Quanah dominated the conversation as they went inside to eat.

When the meal was over and the men sat talking and smoking, Naduah and Star Name walked outside and stood in the fresh air. To the west, the last of the sunset's lavender stain was being washed over with deep violet streaked with gold at the horizon. Late summer insects had started their evening concert, and from the hills below them the two sisters could hear the barking of thousands of prairie dogs, just before they dove into their holes for the night. The cool, gentle wind caressed their faces. Somewhere outside the village, a young man was serenading his beloved with a flute made of cedar. Its pleasant, whistling notes in a plaintive minor key wound sinuously through the camp.

All around, the plain rose and fell in huge surges, like the swells of a boundless ocean, rolling to meet the soaring dome of the sky. The plains' immensity should have dwarfed the People as they traveled constantly across its vastness. But it only made them more self-confident, more certain that they could survive anything. Its wild beauty made them more stubborn in defense of their right to roam it at will. It was their home, and they loved it. All of it.

When the last light of the sun faded and the stars began to glitter, the two women went back inside the softly glowing lodge. In the time they had stood outside, neither of them had spoken a word.

❧ 47 ❧

Wanderer sat in Pahayuca's council lodge and looked around him. He had the disorienting feeling that he had gone back in time ten years, to 1840. This council reminded him of the one he had sat at then, after the Texans had killed most of the Penateka's leaders at the Council House massacre in San Antonio. Even Buffalo Piss was here, as recalcitrant and adamant as ever. Most of the faces at that council ten years ago had been new to Wanderer. And many of the faces he saw today were new also.

As Naduah and Wanderer and their war party had traveled south toward Mexico, they had found Pahayuca's band back in the country along the upper Colorado River where they had always hunted. Cholera had run its course, and the Wasp band seemed as large and as prosperous as ever. But Wanderer knew the appearance was a false one. He could sense the difference even before Pahayuca talked about it.

Pahayuca was talking now. He hadn't changed much. He was too fat for wrinkles and too imperturbable to show the horrors he had seen. Deep Water had commented on how large the band was, and Pahayuca was telling him why.

"Many of them are refugees from the white man's disease, the sickness they call ka-ler-ah. It hit us too. Many of the Wasps died of it. But not as many as the other bands. For months the survivors have been coming to us. They have set their lodges up at the outskirts of our camp until there are as many of us as in the old days.

"But it's not the same. These people have lost parts of their families. They have lost their leaders. They have lost their faith in the old medicine to save them. Vomiting, bowels that flow, or a fever sends them fleeing in panic, even from their own loved ones. And the white traders bring more and more wih-skee. Many of the warriors crave it now.

"But the Texan leaders are weak these days. Not like La-mar and the Ranger, El Diablo. Their big council in Aus-tin sends men to make honey talk and give us presents. They expect us to touch the writing stick and give away the People's land as though it were horses or buffalo robes. They insist that I and the other leaders speak for all the People. We have explained to them over and over that we cannot do this. But they are fools, the white men. They hear only what they want to her. And they do not keep their promises. So we continue to raid. And they give us more presents to stop the raiding."

When he had finished, Buffalo Piss took the pipe and spoke.

"The United States has made a treaty with the Texans. They say they are all one tribe now. But I don't think so. The United States sends *tabay-boh*, soldiers, that aren't like the *Tejanos* at all. *Tabay-boh* soldiers are walking soldiers. Or walking soldiers on horses. They have handsome clothes, bright red and blue and orange. But they don't know how to fight. And they don't know how to ride. They use old guns that are inaccurate, and have a short range. We keep just outside that range and taunt them. They do not hunt us the way the Texans do, and they don't attack our villages.

"I would rather fight the Cheyenne or the Apache or the Osage. Fighting *tabay-boh* soldiers is like fighting children." Buffalo Piss turned to Wanderer. "We are glad to see our brothers, the Noconi. What are your plans? If you're raiding into Mexico, many of our young men will want to join you."

"We're going to Mexico to raid and to look for the bones of Echo Of A Wolf's Howl, Arrow Point's son and my wife's brother. He fell ill there of ka-ler-ah. We do not know if he died. We are going to find out what happened to him. And we will raid the Texas settlements on the way down and back. Your men are welcome to ride with us. We'll raid as we did last year. We'll divide into smaller groups, strike the Texans, steal and kill all we can, and run."

When the Noconi war party left the Wasps' encampment, their number had swelled. Twenty-five more warriors had joined them, some of them with their women and children.

"Now Quanah will have a few playmates," said Naduah as they rode out at the head of the procession. "I wish we had brought Pecan along. Medicine Woman and Takes Down The Lodge wanted to see him."

"He's better off with Star Name and Wears Out Moccasins at home. If Wears Out Moccasins doesn't spoil him. Did you have enough time with your family, golden one?"

"I never have enough time with them. But it was good to see them. To know they're safe."

"You were worried about them, weren't you?"

"Yes. Even if there had been no white man's sickness. I would have worried about Medicine Woman."

"She looked the same to me," said Wanderer.

"She never changes. And she still insists on doing everything for herself. But she's so old."

Gathered Up and Quanah joined them. Quanah was kicking his old horse's sides in a futile attempt to make him gallop like a war pony.

"Gathered Up," said Naduah, "Did you sleep last night? You look tired."

"I'm all right. My throat is a little sore. Wanderer, when will we raid the *Tejanos?*"

"Soon. Why? Do you want to go?"

"Of course. I've had my vision. I'm a man now. It's time I started gathering horses."

"I'm going with Gathered Up," said Quanah loudly.

"Not yet, gray eyes," said Wanderer.

"I am too." Tears welled up in his cloudy eyes and threatened to rain on his cheeks. "I'll herd the ponies."

"Not yet."

Quanah glowered at his father. Wanderer looked at him mildly, the way a coyote will look at a camp dog that has become too familiar. The child lowered his face.

"Quanah," said Gathered Up, "will you take care of the horses I steal on the raid? I'll give you one of them if you do."

"All right." His face brightened. "Can I pick the one I want?"

"I'll pick first, little brother, then you."

They rode off again, Quanah discussing horses as though, in his six years of life, he had learned everything there was to know about them.

When Wanderer and his small raid party returned, Gathered Up rode near the head of it, in a place of honor. A fresh scalp of blond hair dangled from his lance. The Noconi and their allies danced far into the night, celebrating Gathered Up's first coup.

Wanderer and Naduah and the others threw presents at his feet as he danced in the center of the circle. Some pitched sticks onto the dancing area, each one representing the ponies they would give the new warrior. Anyone could grab the presents out of the circle and keep them for themselves. But not many did. It was considered demeaning.

Finally, after midnight, Naduah and her family lay down to sleep in their brush lean-tos. She awakened an hour or so later and lay listening.

"Naduah. Mother," Gathered Up whispered to her from his own shelter.

"Yes, Gathered Up," she called softly. She rose and put on her moccasins. She wrapped her robe around her in the cold night air and walked to his bed.

"I feel bad." There was pain in his big dark eyes. And his long, curly black hair was plastered to his forehead with sweat. His face seemed thinner.

Naduah put her hand to his cheek.

"Have you vomited? Have your bowels run?"

"No. It's my throat. I can hardly swallow." Even talking seemed excruciating for him.

"I noticed that you didn't eat tonight."

"I haven't eaten in two days. I can't swallow."

"I'll be back with my medicine."

She returned with her bag and built up a small fire for its light and warmth. She sat by it and searched through the tiny pouches inside until she found the one with the crushed bull-nettle berries. They were mildly narcotic, and she used them often for sore throats and toothaches.

"Swallow these, Gathered Up. And eat some more in the morning."

The boy tried to swallow and gagged.

"I can't."

Naduah mixed them with fat to make them go down easier and held them out to him.

"You must."

He tried again and got some of them down.

Naduah kicked aside the bigger stones. With a stick she scraped away the cactus and lay down, still wrapped in her robe.

"I'll stay here with you. Call me if you need me."

The first light of dawn was spreading across the east when Naduah felt a hand shaking her. She sat up to find Gathered Up ashen and in agony. His breath was coming in gasps, and while she watched, his face began to turn red, then purple with suffocation. She rummaged frantically through her bag and pulled out a hollow quill. She knelt by the boy's bed.

"Open your mouth."

"What is it, golden one?" Wanderer stood over her.

"He can't breathe. Something is choking him." Gathered Up flinched as Naduah jammed the quill down his throat, past whatever was blocking it. He closed his eyes in pain, but kept his face impassive.

"Is he choking on a piece of meat?"

"He hasn't eaten in almost two days."

Gathered Up lay back, his eyes still closed, and his thin chest heaving. He was pulling the cool air in short gasps through the tube and into his lungs.

"Wanderer, build the fire up and heat the broth from last night's stew. I don't want to leave him."

Wanderer obeyed. He never questioned her powers with medicine. A few minutes later he brought some broth, steaming in a big, curved horn ladle. Naduah sipped some and leaned over Gathered Up. She put her mouth to his and blew the broth through the tube and down his throat. Most of it ran off his chin or spattered on his cheeks, but some made it inside him. Patiently she repeated the process again and again until most of the broth was gone.

"What do you think it is, golden one?"

"I don't know. Open your mouth as wide as you can, Gathered Up." She peered in, turning his head to catch the morning's rays. "It's swollen in there. And the back of his throat is coated with a thick, white skin. It looks dry and hard, and the flesh around it is red and inflamed. Wanderer, I've never seen anything like this."

"Can you help him?"

"I don't know. Call Gets To Be An Old Man."

Gets To Be An Old Man had come with them when they left the Wasps' land. He was so old he was entirely bald except for a few long, snowy hairs that sprouted here and there on his wrinkled scalp. They looked like the beaten, bleached fibers of the agave before they're twisted into sisal rope. He had brought no weapons with him when he joined the raiding party. He obviously wasn't interested in stealing horses. Naduah asked him why he was coming along. He had pointed a quavering, skeletal finger at her, as though waving a chicken bone in her face. Then he swept the finger in a wide arc around him.

"I want to see the old hunting grounds before I die, Daughter." And every day he rode off to one side of the party. He rode by himself, on a swaybacked old gray that looked as bony and dejected as he did. Old Man mumbled to himself the entire trip, pointing out each hill and ravine, each river and bluff. He looked as though he were instructing a band of young men about to go on their first raid, describing each day's terrain for them.

Wanderer had described Gathered Up's illness, and Gets To Be An Old Man had left his drum and eagle feathers behind. He trotted up on his bandy legs, still talking to himself.

". . . Cheyenne are good for something." He pulled his medicine bag from the folds of his baggy breechclout.

"What did you say, Old Man?" As Naduah grew older, she had developed more respect for Old Man's skill as a healer. And she understood now why even Medicine Woman called him for the cases she couldn't handle.

"I said the Cheyenne are good for something." He continued mumbling as he worked, and Naduah leaned close to watch and listen.

"Back in the year of the Council House fight, in San Antonio, ten years ago it was. When we made treaty talk with the Cheyenne. You remember, Wanderer, when we gave them all those horses. A lot of horses. Remember all those horses we gave those no-good Cheyenne, Wanderer? Or were you born then?"

"I was born. I heard of it, Old Man."

"I met one of their medicine men there. A very powerful man. He taught me this." With a slender trade needle Old Man had been trying to thread small, spine-covered burs onto a piece of split sinew. Finally he thrust it at Naduah, his fingers too unsteady and his eyesight too blurred for the task.

"Here, Daughter. This is woman's work anyway. Ugly." Old Man returned to his monologue on the Cheyenne. "That Cheyenne was the ugliest human being I ever saw. But powerful. He saved the life of Hook Nose, that white trader up on the Canadian River. Hook Nose told us so himself, when the Wasps were there a few years ago. And Hook Nose is the only white man I ever met who didn't lie."

Naduah finished stringing the burs, and Old Man covered them with marrow fat from a buffalo. He held the sinew up between his thumb and forefinger and, with his spidery fingers, kneaded the fat gingerly around the burs.

"Sit up, boy." Naduah helped Gathered Up sit, and supported him, watching the procedure closely. With a thin, notched stick Old Man rammed the burs down Gathered Up's swollen throat. Naduah and Wanderer held the boy as he gagged and retched. Old Man peered into his mouth, still mumbling and chanting. He pulled the sinew back out, tugging gently, as though he had a fish on a line. When it cleared Gathered Up's lips, there was a hunk of blue-white membrane, as dry and hard as tree bark, attached to it.

"Better?"

"Yes." Gathered Up collapsed onto the bed, gulping air in painful swallows. "I can breathe," he rasped.

"Cheyenne know a thing or two. Not much, but one or two things." Old Man began collecting his medicine.

"May I have that?" Gathered Up signed the request and pointed to the hard, scaly lump caused by diphtheria. It was powerful. It had almost killed him. He picked it up gingerly and laid it aside. Later, when he felt better, he would put it into his medicine bag. He plucked at the medicine man's breechclout to get his attention. He spoke in hand talk, to save his throat.

"I stole some ponies on this raid. You can have any of them."

"I don't want them. What use are they to me? I have my old war pony, Lightning." He nodded to the wreck cropping grass with thick yellow teeth worn down to stubs. "This is my last trip anyway. Keep your horses, young man. You're young. You'll need ponies to buy a wife. Women aren't cheap. And they're getting more expensive every year. When I was young, you could buy a good wife, a hard-working wife, for one horse and a few blankets." Still grumbling, Old Man waddled off to the spring. He rolled from side to side on his bowed legs as he went to take his morning bath.

Naduah lightly touched Gathered Up's hand as she rearranged his covers. He smiled up at her, and closed his eyes in sleep. While he slept, Naduah built a travois to carry him.

The party traveled on, through the desolate country north of the Rio Grande. It was a world where colors hadn't been invented yet. The rock-covered hills were painted in neutral tones of brown, yellow, buff, and ochre. The deep ravines were choked with tangles of dust-covered brush perforated by huge spikes of ocotillo cactus and threaded with long yellow rattlers. It was hostile, merciless country, defended by a hundred miles of spiny agave, cactus, and mesquite that tore at their legs.

The second day, they found the previous year's campsite in the mountains. The war party moved on to camp elsewhere, so that the old site would be undisturbed. Wanderer and Wolf Road and Naduah began casting around among the fallen drying racks, fire pits, and piles of brittle cut brush. They were looking for some sign left by Cub. They found the bones of animals and of the captives they had murdered the year before. Most of the bones were picked clean, anonymous and scattered. They were white and dry, like an element of the earth itself.

"Wanderer!" Naduah shouted and waved. "They're alive!"

They all squatted around a wedge-shaped pile of stones. There was a stone for each day Cub wanted them to travel. The point of the wedge gave them the direction. Naduah picked up each stone, counting it, until she saw a tiny leather bag buried under them. She opened it carefully and shook out into her palm a lock of pale yellow hair, curled up on itself like fine golden wire cut from a spool. The hair was tied in the middle with a piece of sinew. With it was another sheaf of hair, this one black and curly.

Naduah held her palm up for Wanderer and Wolf Road to see. She grinned at them. Then she slid the hair back into the bag and slipped the bag into a larger one hanging next to the beaded awl case on her belt.

When the band broke up into smaller raiding parties, Naduah went with Wanderer and Wolf Road, Sore-Backed Horse, Spaniard, Quanah, and Gathered Up, who was still weak. Because of

Gathered Up, they were the last to leave camp. Naduah looked over her shoulder as they rode away. On top of a ridge looking out over the broad valley was a solitary figure. Gets To Be An Old Man sat on Lightning and surveyed the land below him. From his perch he could see seventy miles into Mexico.

Naduah was carrying Wanderer's lance, and she waved it at him. But either he didn't see her or he chose to ignore her. He was probably remembering the past, when a thousand warriors and their families took this trail to plunder the isolated Mexican ranches. Maybe he was remembering the honors and presents heaped on them by the fawning Spanish, and the fear the People struck wherever they rode.

Now there was a ragged, ugly white man's fort squatting on the trail behind them like a sleeping dog that trips you when you leave the lodge to relieve yourself at night. As he watched the small groups of men and women disperse out onto the vast brown bowl of the valley below, Old Man was grateful that he was old and that it was his time to die. He sat all day, watching the shifting shadow patterns the clouds created on the pale brown palette of the valley floor. He watched a tiny, solitary coyote lope through the mesquite and cactus scrub, and he looked up when a silent hawk sent his shadow gliding across the land. And he felt the wind, his lifelong companion.

He watched the sunset paint piles of cottony cumulus clouds with brilliant, translucent colors, more beautiful in the soaring sky than the stained glass windows of a cathedral. And when the colors began to fade, Gets To Be An Old Man turned Lightning and went in search of a place to lay his bones.

The lodge looked out of place in front of the sprawling adobe ranch. There was a shield with a cover made of wolf's hide standing on its tripod by the door. A fourteen-foot lance with a slender war blade leaned against the three-legged stand. A string of long, black scalps fluttered from the lodge pole.

A few small burros stood in the yard, the occasional twitching of their ears the only sign that they were alive. Chickens, searching for crumbs they might have missed that morning, scratched around the single, scarred wooden door in the long, dingy mud wall. There were horses in one corral and cattle in another. Pigs lay panting in the dust, pretending that it was mud.

A pack of dogs, their hackles raised and their tails tucked at the same time, set up a fearful clamor. The four dogs with Wanderer and Naduah barked back, advancing stiff-legged on them. Spaniard leaned down and swatted one of his, and they all quieted, growling softly instead.

The door of the ranch opened and a man stepped out, stooping to clear the low lintel. He wore the tough leather chaps of a *vaquero*. A faded, striped *serape* was draped over his shoulders. He carried a rifle, obviously cocked, and he wore his big straw hat low, shading his face. He raised the gun as they approached.

Maybe we made a mistake. Maybe this is the wrong place. Naduah tried to see the man's features, but the sun was behind him. She remembered the scalps, long and black, hanging from the lodge pole. How many guns were hidden behind the parapet along the flat roof? Wanderer's palm was up in the sign of peace, but Sore-Backed Horse's hand rested on the butt of his carbine, easing it out of the saddle holster by his leg. Suddenly the man started running toward them, leaping the pigs that lay in his way. He shouted back over his shoulder as he ran.

"Small Hand, it's Naduah and Wanderer and Wolf Road."

A small woman, dressed in a white blouse and full skirt of bright red cotton, darted barefoot after him. When Naduah dismounted, she was almost knocked down by Cub's rush and bear hug. He picked her up and swung her around, sending one of her moccasins flying. She gasped for breath as his arms squeezed the air out of her.

"Cub, you're going to force my liver up into my throat and pop my eyeballs out. Put me down."

He dropped her and turned to Wolf Road and Wanderer. While they all cried and thumped each other, Naduah pulled her dress back down over her knees and checked to see if anything was broken in the various bags hanging at her waist. She hugged Small Hand, who stood shyly by, and they all headed for the ranch house.

Naduah hadn't been inside a solid building for fifteen years. She felt uneasy as the thick, heavy walls closed in around her, as if she were being sealed off from the world. She walked quickly through the main room and into the open patio beyond. From there she could inspect Cub's kingdom. She sat on a stone bench beside the small, circular fountain in the center of the courtyard. A spring kept the cachement trough full of cold water. Naduah trailed her hand through it as she looked around her.

A continuous open corridor with rooms along it enclosed the patio on all four sides. Each room had a massive door, but none of them was closed. Some of the rooms were obviously for sleeping. There were piles of buffalo robes and even a mattress or two. The floors had wolf pelts and bear skins scattered as rugs.

One storeroom was piled almost to the ceiling with dried meat and huge oxen stomach paunches of tallow. Another room was filled wall to wall with corn. The cobs spilled into the corridor, flowing over the low barricade that had been built to keep out the pigs.

"*¿Patron, qué haces tú con esos indios bravos?*" A tiny Mexican woman, brown and wrinkled as a smoked sausage, shook her finger at Cub. He answered her in Spanish, and she scurried away.

"She wanted to know what I was doing with a bunch of wild Indians. I told her that my house was theirs, and that she was to tell the herders to kill you a steer. You're welcome to stay as long as you want."

"I'll stay longer if I can do it outside, Cub." Naduah couldn't stand the trapped feeling anymore.

"My husband prefers it outside too," said Small Hand. "But at least now he'll sleep inside when the weather's cold. Which isn't very often."

"But the lodge will always be there for guests like you. And also to show that I'm one of the People."

"Have any of the People ever raided you, Brother?"

"No, Wanderer. They see the lodge first. But I do get raided. You can come on one of my hunting trips if you like."

"What do you hunt?"

"Apache."

"I wondered whose scalps were hanging from the lodge pole," said Naduah.

As Wanderer's group set up their camp near the ranch house, the Mexicans, who called Cub *patron*, began drifting cautiously back from wherever they were hiding. They stood around curiously as the steer was slaughtered and roasted, and joined in the eating of it.

"Cub," said Naduah as they ate, "how did you get all of this? Did you kill the ones who were here?"

"No, Sister." He searched for a word for "buy" and couldn't find one. "I traded it for a bag of the yellow metal that my grandfather was saving. He gave it to me before he died."

"Why didn't you come back to live with us?"

It was a difficult question for Cub to answer.

"I couldn't, Sister. I've changed. The People have changed. We're better off here, Small Hand and I. I miss the life of the People. But I'm the chief here. All this is mine." The sweep of his big arm took in the hundred miles of the brown valley and the deep violet, snaggle-toothed mountains that divided it from the royal-blue sky overhead. "I can do as I please. I probably didn't have to give the Mexican—" Again he searched for the word. Government? Officials? Politicians?

"—council of chiefs anything for this. No one wanted it. It's been deserted for years. Small Hand and I have been working to repair it.

"The Mexicans are terrified of the People and of the Apache. They had all left. But now they're coming back to work for me." He knew that working for someone was something else the People couldn't understand. They would never comprehend a man, his head bowed and his hat in his hand, offering himself virtually as a slave in exchange for protection and subsistence. Nor would they understand how dependent the Mexicans were on their strange, taciturn *patron*, a man who wore an eagle feather dangling from the sweat-stained leather band of his battered straw hat. A man who more often than not chose to sleep in a tent in his own ranch yard. But strange as Cub was, the *vaqueros* recognized him as someone who would prevail over any adversity.

For over a century the farmers and ranchers of Northern Mexico had been terrorized by Comanche and Apache. Even now, leaving the ranch's patio was venturing into a war zone. It was a no-man's land where there was no such concept as quarter, and where a man could expect mutilation and torture if caught by the enemy. Clanking with belts of ammunition, pistols, rifles, and the huge, razor-honed machetes, as well as their rolled blankets, coiled lariats, and big gourd canteens, the cowboys left the safety of the ranch only in large groups.

El Patron often rode out alone. And sometimes he returned with a grisly black Apache scalp dangling from the muzzle of the rifle he carried, its butt end resting against his thigh. His men cheered when they saw one of those scalps, looking like hair from a horse's tail, fluttering and revolving in the wind.

As the months passed, Cub had come to respect the men who worked for him. Next to his hulking size, they looked like children. But they had courage nonetheless. It was a quiet, fatalistic bravery that had endured every horror and hardship, even as they themselves had. They had been victimized all their lives. Because they had to live isolated and scattered to scratch a living from the stubborn, dry soil of their homeland, defense was impossible for them. But in a group, they were as good an army as Cub could wish for.

The stern discipline of James Parker and the wise counsel of Old Owl had turned Cub into a good administrator. He made every decision concerning the ranch. And he arbitrated almost every detail of his employees' lives. He did it not because he wanted to, but because they expected it of him. They needed him. And although Cub himself didn't realize it, he needed them.

Wanderer and Naduah and their friends stayed a week and the

time passed quickly. At last they packed to leave for the north. Cub stood with his arm resting around Small Hand's shoulders, and they both waved good-bye. The small group took with them twenty head of Cub's cattle as a present.

Quanah appointed himself chief herder and rode among them on his patient old pinto pony. Yipping and snapping his quirt and spinning his lariat, he harrassed them steadily. He practiced his roping on their horns, which were wicked and curved and longer than his outstretched arms. The cattle tolerated him as they did the horseflies and buffalo gnats, the mosquitoes and the snakes.

In the week he had spent with his uncle, six-year-old Quanah had become cock of the roost. He charmed the women, who sneaked him snacks of sweetened cornbread cakes. He spent each twilight squatting with the *vaqueros* against the rough adobe walls of the ranch. Solemnly he tried their long, slender cornhusk cigarettes. And he listened attentively to the strange, soft language that passed back and forth over his head.

Perched on top of the twisted cedar and mesquite rails of the corral fence, he spent hours each day watching the men break their horses. He cheered them as they "tailed" bulls. They would race alongside the animal, grab its tail, throw a leg over it, and pull it to the ground. Quanah wandered back to the guest lodge at all hours of the night. And he was usually hoarse from screaming at the cockfights.

"Maybe we should have left him with his uncle," said Naduah as she watched little Quanah bobbing around among the cattle. "He says he wants to be a rancher."

"No," said Wanderer. "He would drive his uncle *loco*. I would rather have your brother as a friend. He would be too formidable an enemy." Once again Wanderer's medicine bag rode inside his breechclout. Cub had returned it to him.

"It's very powerful, Brother," he had said. "It saved my life. But from now on, I'll make my own medicine."

"Gathered Up," called Naduah, twisting around in her saddle to look at him. "How are you feeling?"

"Fine. My throat is well." He grinned at her, his even, white teeth flashing in his brown face.

"He ate more than two of us last night," grumbled Wanderer.

"If he ate more than you and Spaniard, then he ate more than four," Naduah answered.

Laughing, they rode toward Eagle Pass and the rendezvous with the rest of the war party.

❧ *48* ❧

Late in the fall of 1854, Buffalo Piss again rode into the Noconi camp. This time he was followed by ten families.

"What brings you back, Buffalo Piss?" asked Wanderer. "You migrate like the geese or the buffalo. First you move north, and then you go south. Now here you are in the north again."

"I'm through with the Penateka." Buffalo Piss dismounted and untied the cinch on his saddle. "Pahayuca is no longer one of the People. He's a white man with red skin." He stalked into the guest lodge and threw his saddle in a heap, with the saddle bags on top of it. While his patient wife, Red Foot, began unloading the packhorses and sorting things out, Buffalo Piss sprawled in the middle of the group of men sitting in the shelter of Wanderer's lodge. He pulled his robe angrily over his head and crossed his arms on his raised knees, as much to contain his anger as to shut out the chill of the November wind.

"Are you hungry, Buffalo Piss?" asked Naduah.

"Yes."

The rest of the men sat silent, waiting for him to tell them what was happening. He ate the stew Naduah brought him, then took out his own pipe and lit it. He cupped his hands to keep the wind from blowing it out, and took a few deep breaths, still scowling. The pipe seemed to calm him a little. He went straight to the point.

"They want to pen us in a corral like their cattle. Remember that *tabay-boh* soldier, Marcy? The one who made the trail five years ago and brought ka-ler-ah to us? Now he and his agent, Neighbors, want us to move onto a tiny piece of land and stay there so there will be no more war with the Texans. Sanaco told them they should pen the Texans up. They're the ones who are causing the trouble."

"We saw the men who steal the land, measuring with their sticks near the Brazos," said Sore-Backed Horse.

"Pahayuca isn't going, is he?"

"He's thinking about it. There aren't many powerful leaders left who oppose him. Pahayuca likes the presents he's been getting at the honey talks. And he's an old man now. He's seen more than sixty seasons. He's so fat, he pants when he has to walk to relieve himself. Soon he'll have to ride on a travois. Can you imagine him leading his warriors to battle on a travois?" Buffalo Piss tapped the ash out of his pipe and relit it. "He might go, Wanderer. Things are

447

bad. Game is scarce. The hunt this fall was scant. It's going to be a long, hard winter."

"I know. Night's been studying the cottonwood bark. He seems to know he'll be eating a lot of it."

"The white people's trails and wagon trains have disrupted the herds' migrations and scattered the game," continued Buffalo Piss. "They shoot the buffalo and leave it to rot. They kill anything that moves. And the noise of their guns scares away what they don't hit." The People still preferred to hunt their food with bows and arrows. They saved the ammunition and guns for two-legged quarry. "More Penateka will follow me here. They want to raid."

"We welcome them," said Wanderer.

Pahayuca was uncomfortable in the wooden building. The floor-boards felt strange, and they shifted under his moccasined feet. They creaked, as though he were treading on small animals. There wasn't a chair big enough for him, but he wouldn't have wanted to sit in one anyway. He stood before the desk that separated him from the fort's commanding officer. There was no pipe, no fire, no circle of men discussing things as they should be discussed. People rushed in and out, interrupting Pahayuca, a humiliating dis-courtesy. Colonel Neill signed papers as he talked and listened. Jim Shaw stood nearby to translate.

In the dust outside the colonel's door was a body waiting for burial. The weather had gone from cold to very hot in its usual way, and the body would have to be buried soon. Pahayuca had watched it all night as he sat outside his lodge, communing with his spirits and thinking. The sheeting tied over the corpse had glowed dimly in the moonlight, and its edges flapped in the wind like a ghost struggling with its bonds.

Pahayuca and four hundred and fifty of his people were camped at the fort. They had come in search of the food rations that had been promised them by the agent. The rations were always late at the reservation on the Clear Fork of the Brazos, but never this late. Now the body outside gave Pahayuca another cause for unease. The man had died of smallpox. Even now the *tabay-boh* soldiers were lining up at the dispensary for vaccinations.

"Chief, the food will be here. The rivers are swollen with the spring floods. The freighters are having a tough time getting through."

"Colonel, the children of my band are hungry. They cry for food. The stomachs of our women are empty. We men have to watch our loved ones become thinner each day. There are no buffalo on the reservation. We want to go outside to hunt them. Think how it would be if you had to watch your family starving."

"I can't let you go." *A little starving will do the man good. Won't hurt that mountainous wife of his either,* thought Neill. "It's for your own protection, Pahayuca. The United States government says that any Indians found off the reservation will be considered hostile and will be dealt with accordingly. I didn't make the law. I'm just following orders." Shaw always had a hard time explaining the concept of "orders" to Comanche. Neill shuffled his papers, hoping it would encourage the chief to leave. He was a busy man, and the body outside was beginning to decay. He could smell it through his open window. *Where the hell is that burial detail? A rotting corpse and a herd of sullen, dirty Indians squatting on my doorstep. Damnation!* He thought. *What a way to start a morning.*

It didn't occur to Pahayuca to plead. He had stated his case as eloquently as he could. And his request had been denied. It was humiliating enough to have to ask for permission to hunt. He wouldn't demean himself further by arguing. But he did have one other plea.

"Colonel."

Neill looked up, exasperated.

"My people have been exposed to the white man's pox. Will you 'order' your doctor to scratch us to keep away the sickness?" Pahayuca had grasped not only the idea of chain of command but of preventive medicine.

"No. There's hardly enough vaccine for the soldiers and the officers' families. We can't vaccinate four hundred Indians. Shaw, tell the chief to take his people back to the agency and wait there for the food supplies. There's nothing more I can do for him. Britt," he roared at the open door. "Where is that nigger?" The orderly's black face appeared, shiny with sweat. "Where are those damned Micks and their shovels? There's a stinking corpse out there to bury."

"Yes, sir." And the face disappeared.

Pahayuca turned and walked out into the warm, redolent March sunlight. He shouted to Blocks The Sun and Silver Rain and Something Good to prepare to leave. Then he beckoned to Weasel, who was surrounded by a small group of soldiers. The enlisted men weren't allowed wives. Whorehouses had sprung up around the fort; hog ranches or blind pigs, they were called.

A few men were lucky enough to have a bit of muslin on the sly, as they put it. A woman hidden away somewhere. The Cherokee women were especially prized for their beauty. But there wasn't a woman in a hundred miles as beautiful as nineteen-year-old Weasel.

449

And she knew it. White men swarmed around her wherever she went. It was one more burden for Pahayuca to bear.

Humiliated and enraged, Pahayuca lumbered to his lodge. He searched through his belongings for the waterproofed bag that held his letters of testimonial from various white leaders. Sitting cross-legged in front of the fire, he fed them one by one into the flames while his wives and daughters and granddaughters carried the household goods outside and dismantled the lodge around him.

Pahayuca and his band of Wasps headed away from the fort in the direction of the agency so the soldiers wouldn't follow them. But once they were out of sight of the buildings, and past the wood details and the water details and the parties out hunting game, Pahayuca turned west and north, toward the Pease River and the country of the Noconi.

The Wasps made it as far as the southernmost fork of the Pease before smallpox caught up with them. As the wails of mourning arose from the lodges and the families began to scatter, Weasel saddled her pony and struck out alone, looking for Naduah and Star Name. Their families were sick.

Naduah arrived too late. As she and Star Name and Wolf Road and Weasel rode up to the familiar lodge with Takes Down's big yellow sun on it, she saw Pahayuca outside, his arms upraised. He had chopped off his right braid and painted his face black. He was chanting his prayer for the souls of his sister, Medicine Woman, his nephew, Sunrise, and his nephew's wife, Takes Down The Lodge.

Crying and wailing, Star Name and Wolf Road ran to find their mother. Black Bird had been spared, but her face was pitted. She was keening in her lodge. In her grief she had cut off the top joints of the middle and fourth fingers of her left hand. Her hair lay in piles around her feet.

In a daze, Naduah stood in the doorway of her mother's lodge. They couldn't be dead. Not Medicine Woman and Takes Down and quiet Sunrise. Not all of them. Something Good tugged at Naduah's sleeve, trying to pull her away. Even though Naduah was four inches taller, Something Good still used the old pet name.

"Little one, it would be better if you stayed out and we burned the lodge with them in it." Something Good had seen much grief, but tears streamed down her cheeks anyway.

Naduah didn't seem to hear her. She stood frozen in the doorway, looking around at the familiar objects inside. The square mirror with its dangling feathers and bells still hung on a peg. Sunrise's otter skin quiver hung with his bow. And Medicine Woman's rabbit skin pouch lay opened next to her bed, the contents of it profanely scattered out on the floor for anyone to see. Aside from this, it seemed tranquil in the lodge. As though everyone were merely sleeping.

Sobbing, Naduah crossed the lodge and scooped the bundles of leaves and packets of powders and roots back into the bag. She tied it shut and hung it at her waist. The bodies lay under buffalo robes on the beds. She stood over her grandmother's form, forcing her hand down to the edge of the cover. She had to see. Otherwise she would spend her days not believing it had happened. She pulled the cover back and gagged as she stared at the devastation that had once been her grandmother's kind, gentle, humorous face.

She did the same for her mother and father. Then she left in search of Wolf Road and Star Name. Pahayuca still chanted outside, and she circled around him. She brought the other two back with her. Weasel and Something Good helped them drag the shrouded bodies outside, and tie them onto ponies. Then they each mounted their own horses. The small funeral procession wound through the remnants of the camp toward the ravines of the river's banks. Naduah and the others buried Medicine Woman, Takes Down The Lodge, and Sunrise, wedging them deep into crevices and piling stones on top of them to keep scavengers out.

When they died Something Good had thoughtfully and bravely positioned each body properly with the knees drawn up before rigor mortis made moving them impossible. They picked handfuls of the spring flowers that grew everywhere and placed them on the graves along with offerings of food. Naduah lay Sunrise's bow and quiver across the stones of his grave.

As the shock wore off, she began to remember what she had lost. Her grandmother's elfin laugh, Takes Down's quiet instructions, the evenings talking and telling stories around the fire with them. Sunrise's soft voice teaching her to ride and shoot. Sobs shuddered through her body. Crying and wailing in shrill ululations, she pulled out her skinning knife. Grabbing hunks of her thick blond hair, she began hacking at them. She slashed her arms and breasts and tore at the ragged ends of hair she had left. She screamed her grief to the sky above her.

Bent over, on her knees, she cried and moaned for hours, rocking back and forth. Finally she sank to the ground and slept there in the open. Something Good and Weasel draped robes over her and Star Name as they lay unconscious from exhaustion. Then they sat under their own robes to watch over them.

Naduah grieved for another day. Then she burned her parents'

451

lodge. Star Name and Wolf Road helped her kill Sunrise's ponies, holding their tether lines and slashing their throats. As the three of them and Black Bird rode among the remaining twenty or thirty lodges of the camp, Naduah saw a child sitting alone in front of her tent. She reined Wind to a halt.

"Where are your parents, Daughter?"

The girl looked up at her dully, as though she hadn't heard.

"Where is your family?" Naduah repeated.

"Dead."

"All of them?"

"All of them."

"And what is your name, child?"

"Kuyusi, Quail."

"Come with us, Quail." Naduah held out her hand. Quail used it to mount Wind, settling down behind her. As they rode away, Quail's family's dogs roused themselves and trotted along after the procession.

In November of 1855, Company A of the newly formed cavalry regiment halted at the ford of the Red River. On the other side lay Texas. They affectionately called themselves Jeff Davis's Own, in honor of the cavalry's creator, the United States Secretary of War. But with the peculiar logic of the military, this very first cavalry regiment was officially designated the Second Cavalry. The cavalry was only six months old, and already it was the elite of the United States forces. Davis threw over established procedure when he formed it. And he'd roared at congressmen and generals to do it.

"I know it'll cost three times as much as an infantry unit, God damn it to hell. But it'll be ten times as effective."

Jefferson Davis went to the heart of horse country, Louisville, Kentucky, to organize his new unit. He personally selected each officer, disregarding seniority when he did it. And each senior officer was in turn permitted to chose his noncommissioned officers. Davis offered commissions to the seasoned Indian fighters of the Texas Rangers, and he made Albert Sidney Johnson, Texas's former Secretary of War, its commander. In effect, the cavalry was formed to fight Comanche.

He recruited troops from Kentucky, Ohio, and Indiana, the states famous for their horses and their horsemen, but the Second Cavalry was predominantly southern, both in its makeup and in its outlook. He sent special teams to select and buy the finest blooded horses available. Each of the regiment's ten companies rode horses of the same color.

The horses belonging to the men of company A were grays. They went well with their riders' black, round-crowned Jeff Davis hats. Each man had pinned one side of his brim up with a brass ornament, and soft gray ostrich plumes nodded from the officers' hat bands.

"By columns of four into line!" The bugle sounded as Sergeant McKenna called the command. There was a rattle from the heavy dragoon sabers that each NCO carried for show. "Old Wristbreakers," they called them. Saddle leather creaked as the men formed four abreast to cross the river. They splashed into the shallow ford, the sun glinting on the silver sprays of water sent up by the hoofs and on the brass-mounted saddles. Each man carried a new breechloading Springfield carbine socketed in a boot next to his left knee. And each had a brace of thirty-six-caliber Colt Navy model revolvers at his waist.

For their entry into Texas, the ninety men of Company A wore their dress uniforms. Their tailored, dark blue jackets were waist length, with high collars and twelve shiny buttons down the front. The officers and NCOs had yellow stripes down the outside seams of their blue trousers. Everyone's brass and tall, black boots were highly polished. Company A glittered as it moved. Each man in it rode with the unconscious grace of someone at home in the saddle. A retinue of black slaves and servants, mounted on mules or riding in wagons, followed.

The tramp of hoofs subsided in a diminishing clatter as the men halted on the Texas side of the river. They awaited further orders, and the arrival of the twelve-pound mountain howitzer that followed them.

" 'Tention! By squadrons! Left wheel into line. March!"

With the column once more moving forward, Sergeant McKenna rode alongside the man who was second in command of the entire Second Cavalry. Colonel Robert E. Lee was a quiet, gracious man, easily approachable, which was why McKenna chose to speak to him directly.

"Sir."

"Yes, Sergeant?"

"I think we had best find shelter now and stay put fer the rest of the day."

"I see the black clouds to the north, Sergeant. But they're on the horizon, miles away."

"It'll be cold afore you can boil a pot of coffee."

"Sergeant, I wouldn't want to doubt your word, but it's unusually balmy for this time of year." Snatches of wind blew the grass in ripples, like cat's paws across the surface of water. "The wind does seem to be freshening, but frankly," Colonel Lee tugged at his high, tight collar, "I find it a relief. Surely the storm won't hit before we've bivouacked for the night."

"Begging your pardon, Sir. But I've lived in this here state since I was high as a grasshopper's thigh. That's a blue norther acomin'. And blue northers move faster'n a snake with a bee up his ass. They blow the world inside out and freeze the linin'."

Lee flinched imperceptibly. It was easy to pick out the Texans in the ranks.

"We'll ride a couple more hours and see what the weather looks like then, Sergeant."

"Yes, Sir."

In an hour the temperature had dropped twenty-five degrees and was still plummeting, and the wind had already hit the bottom of the thermometer. The men of Company A unbuckled their overcoats from behind their saddles, unrolled them, and put them on. The huge black clouds rolling overhead seemed to sink lower and lower under their own swollen weight. A coyote skulked off shivering, his fur blown up in ridges on his back.

Sand began blowing around them. Then, as the wind picked up to gale gusts, pea-sized bits of sharp gravel stung them. Sand and gravel mixed with a cold rain drove slantwise into their faces. Finally it seemed to be raining mud that trickled down the men's collars and ran in grating streams down their backs.

"Column right. Double time for that bluff," shouted McKenna. The huge rock rose from the plain, a dark green skirt of cedar around its base. The wind whipped Sergeant McKenna's words from his mouth, and he had to ride along the line repeating the instructions. The rain fell even harder and turned to needlelike sleet as the temperature continued to drop. The trail became a morass of gluey red mud that formed heavy balls on the horses' hooves. Then the animals began to slide on the ice that formed over the mud. At three o'clock in the afternoon it was as dark as night, with lightning playing continuously all around the horizon.

Lord, just let us make shelter and I'll never take your name in vain again. McKenna pulled his coat up higher on his neck and turtled down inside it.

By the time they came to the dubious protection of the bluff, he was numb with the cold and the wet, and chills shook him. He hurried around, seeing that the men picketed the horses and mules in as much shelter as possible, and that they storm lashed their own little A-shaped tents and the large conical Sibleys for the officers. The canvas duck bucked and snapped in their hands, and it took six

to a dozen men to tame each one. Then he crawled into one of the
Sibleys with the other noncoms and huddled with them for warmth.

"Christ on the cross, how long's this gonna last, McKenna?"

"A day anyways. Usually three. Never know exactly. Mebbe a
week."

Rain began seeping under the tent, but everyone was already too
wet to care. There was nothing they could do about it anyway. They
sat on the canvas skirts of the tent, helping to hold it down with
their weight. They told stories to pass the time, shouting to be heard
over the wailing wind and the detonating thunder. About midnight,
after the thunderstorm had passed, another scream soared over the
wind. McKenna got up.

"Good God Almighty. What was that?" someone asked from the
darkness in the tent.

"You goin' out there, McKenna?"

"Shore. Hit's stuffy in here. Thought I'd jest take a stroll and have
a smoke. Mebbe check the horse pickets and see what the hell's
makin' 'em scream like that. Anybody wanna come along?"

"I'll go with you, Mac."

"You're crazy. It's ten below out there," said a muffled voice from
among the anonymous shapes in the tent.

"Who farted?" asked another.

McKenna and Casey stepped out into the wind and staggered as
the full force of it hit them. It was snowing, adding to the foot
already fallen. They felt their way along in the dark, their path lit by
the fires in the tents. McKenna's foot hit the body of a mule, the last
on the picket line. He felt around it.

"Dead. Frozen. Solider'n my sister's biscuits."

"Here's another one," said Casey.

Then they saw the eyes. Two, huge, glowing yellow eyes.

"Sweet Mother of God! They're as big as mess plates."

"Jest consider the size of the animal wrapped around 'em."

With an unearthly shriek, the cat leaped at them. They both fired
at once, emptying their revolvers into it. The panther fell dead,
almost at their feet. Although it was too dark to see it, there was
foam around its muzzle.

"Ferget the horses," said McKenna, backing toward the tents.
McKenna's heart didn't stop pounding until his hand brushed the
stiff canvas of a Sibley. He pulled aside the flap and poked his head
in.

"You gentlemen got any tobaccy you'd like to trade for coffee?"

"Come in or stay out, Sergeant."

"Jesus, it's colder than a polar bear's toenails."

McKenna and Casey crowded in among the officers, made equal to them by adversity. Someone passed them a cigarette from among the glowing points of light in the tent. The two sergeants shared it.

"Coffee won't do us any good," said someone. "Some damned fool forgot the stove."

"What was the noise out there, Sergeant McKenna?"

"Panther. Big'un. Dead now, though."

Casey hefted his empty revolver.

"Thank God for Colt's repeaters," he said.

"Well, sir, you know how it is," spoke up a young lieutenant. "God made some men big and some men small. But Colonel Colt made them equal."

By the time Company A pulled into Camp Cooper, the glitter was gone. They were so covered with dust and dried mud that it was almost impossible to tell what color their uniforms or their horses really were. The sky was a leaden gray and a fine mist began to fall on the barren hills. The first part of the fort they saw was the cemetery. Sergeant McKenna rode out of line to read one of the markers aloud.

> O pray for the soldier, you kind-hearted stranger,
> He has roamed the prairie for many a year.
> He has kept the Comanches away from your cabins,
> And chased them far over the Texas frontier.

On the bare, scoured square between the rows of half-built wooden, canvas, and mud barracks, five men marched wearily around and around in punishment drill. Two of them dragged balls and chains. A sixth had fainted, and lay where he'd fallen. A crowd of soldiers and dogs had gathered outside the headquarters building, and there was no one to greet the new troops. Then one man separated himself, mounted his horse, and rode to meet them.

Lee sat straight as a ramrod on his big gray. He managed to look washed and starched in spite of everything. He and Colonel Neill saluted each other and introduced themselves.

"Sweet Jesus," said Neill. "Am I glad to see you. Troops that actually speak English. All I have are Irish potato-eaters and thick-skulled Germans."

"Glad to be of service, Colonel Neill. What's going on over there?" Lee nodded toward the cluster of men.

"Come over. You should see this. And so should your men. Why don't you have them file by? Stand back. Move." He elbowed

456

through the crowd. "Let the new troops, fresh from the east, see what kind of enemy they'll be facing out here. Not that you'll actually be facing them," he muttered to Lee. "You'll rarely even see them. I doubt that West Point prepared you for this."

The men parted to expose a naked body lying at their feet. Lee fought back the need to gag.

"They're beasts, the Comanches," Neill said casually. "There's not a drop of pity or humanity or gratitude in them." He nodded toward the corpse. "An enlisted man. Strayed from his wood detail and was captured. Probably by the same Comanches we fed all winter. We just found him thirty-five miles from here. The Indians had staked him out on his back and built a fire on his chest and stomach. They cooked their meal over it, seasoning it with his screams, I suppose."

Neill pulled a small derringer from his pocket.

"May I suggest, Colonel Lee, that each of you carry one of these to use on yourself, should the necessity arise. Your men can pitch their tents over there. They'll have to build their own barracks, just as mine had to. And they'd better hurry. You must have already had a taste of our winters, with that norther that went through. The real thing will be here soon.

"Lumber's a problem. Has to be hauled ten miles. We've cleared the area around here building this. And the sanitation situation is bad. The water's often undrinkable. The alkalai in it will give you the flux. At my last command, over one hundred men died each year of disease and dysentery. Each man has to pay for anti-scorbutics by having deductions taken from his already inadequate rations. Not many do it, so there's a lot of scurvy. The dispensary's a pesthole.

"Boredom creates discipline problems. One out of every ten men is on punishment detail at any given time. Rabble. That's what we have here. The lowest scum the east had to send.

"And the rations. By the time the freighters get here the bacon has enough maggots to walk in by itself. And the flour's crawling with weevils. Winters are bad, but the summers are worse. I heard you served in Mexico, Lee, but if you've never spent a summer in Texas, you can't imagine what it's like. Your eyeballs will sunburn. When I die and go to hell, I'll take it amiss if the good Lord doesn't subtract from my allotted time the years I've spent here.

"By the way, Colonel—"

"Yes," said Lee mildly.

"Welcome to Texas."

❧ *49* ❧

Wind was too old for hard riding. But she was still useful for gentling freshly caught wild mustangs. She was tied now to a young colt, black spattered with white patches and spots. The pinto had been forced to follow Wind for three days, since the afternoon Quanah had pointed him out to his father.

"That's the one I want."

"Are you sure?"

"Yes."

"He's not very handsome."

"I don't care. I like his look."

"He doesn't look friendly to me. Have you thought of a name for him, or will you wait until you know you can ride him?"

"I can ride him. His name is Polecat. He'll be a good horse, He's smart and he's fast and he's agile. I've been studying him."

Wanderer smiled to himself. His instructions had taken hold. Quanah had indeed picked a good pony. And he had had to study the horse from the length of his twenty-foot tether line. Polecat wouldn't let anyone closer than that, with the possible exception of Naduah. She had a way of gaining the confidence of even the wildest pony. And this was a wild one.

Wanderer had caught the pinto by creasing him, something many men tried but few could do. He had shot him through the muscular part of the neck, just above the vertebrae. The shot paralyzed him for two or three minutes, long enough to get several lines on him. If Wanderer's aim had been off a hair's breadth, the spine would have been fractured. Many mustangs ended up as evening stew that way.

When the time came to gentle the pony, Quanah came looking for his mother.

"Why don't you ask your father or Sore-Backed Horse or Wolf Road to help you?"

"Because all three of them said you were the best at breaking ponies."

So Naduah had put down her mending and come with him. Now Polecat regarded them malevolently from around behind Wind's tail. His forelock fell in long bangs, giving him the look of a determined boy. He was small. Wanderer could have rested his elbows on the pony's back. He was wiry and tough looking, with a big barrel, thin legs, and a mane and tail matted with burs. The bones in his narrow head jutted out prominently, and his large, pointed ears were pricked forward. His erratic markings made him look as though someone had dropped a bucket of whitewash on him. His thick, dusty winter coat was coming out in patches in the warm weather of late spring, making him seem bedraggled and motheaten.

"Quanah, do you want to lead him to the river and mount him in the water?"

"No, I'll ride him here." Since his visit with his uncle on his Mexican ranch five years before, Quanah had been determined to break his first real pony the way the *vaqueros* did.

"Then we should put a surcingle on him and a line around his withers and chest for you to brace your knees under. Let's see if you're as good with your lariat as you've been boasting. I'll make him buck, and you lasso his hind feet.

Actually, Quanah had been doing more than boasting. He had ambushed and lassoed Naduah and Gathered Up and Quail and Pecan at every possible opportunity. He would lurk in the branches of the trees over the trails and drop his noose over their heads when they walked by. He lassoed the dogs until they all gave him a wide berth. Even the foolish chickens avoided him.

He coiled his rope in the Mexican fashion and stalked up behind Polecat. The pony crowded against Wind and watched the boy from the corner of one big, bright eye. Quanah hummed casually to himself until Naduah made a move toward the pony. Polecat bucked reflexively, and Quanah flicked the rope over his rear hoofs. The line moved too fast for the eye to follow, and Quanah jerked it tight before Polecat realized what had happened.

He looked chagrinned, and lassoing his forelegs was harder. Finally they had him tethered between two trees, his front and rear legs spread, keeping him off balance. Naduah untied his headstall and led Wind away. Then she fastened another long line to his neck and snaked one end of it around a tree for leverage. She cinched the wide leather surcingle around him and tied a second cord around his chest. Quanah vaulted on, disdaining the stirrups. Polecat flinched and laid his ears back. The boy wedged his knees under the cord and gripped tightly with his knees.

"Ready?" asked Naduah.

"Ready." And Naduah untied the rear line. Polecat didn't move.

"He's tame already. What did you do to him, Mother? He isn't going to buck."

Naduah untied the front line and flicked it to slacken it around the hooves. But the hooves weren't there. Polecat reared back, then tipped forward until he looked like he was standing on his upper lip. He whirled in place like a drunken top. He folded in the middle and took off on a series of jolting hops. Still clinging to the line, Naduah was dragged after him. She ran to keep up, laughing at Quanah, who was bouncing around like a drop of water in a hot skillet.

Polecat danced gracefully on his rear hooves, then suddenly reversed ends. He rocked on his forelegs, sending his rear ones skyward. Quanah finally lost his hold and soared off in a wide arc. He bounced when he hit, and lay still, taking inventory of his bones and letting the pain subside before he moved. Polecat walked over to him and solicitously whiffled in his ear. Then he began searching for the roots that Quanah sometimes brought and left him.

When Naduah arrived, Quanah was rolling on the ground and laughing. Polecat was still tickling him, blowing on his stomach and ribs and nuzzling his waist. He was nobbling at the bag of lunch Quanah had tied there. Naduah stroked the pony's neck and offered him a thistle to distract him. While he gingerly ate it, his eyes closed in ecstasy, Quanah rolled away and stood. He limped back to them, picking the bigger cactus spines out of his forearm.

"I brought my medicine bag," said Naduah. "I thought you might need it. I'll put salve on that scrape." Quanah's knees were bloody and raw.

"Later. I'm going to ride him again."

While Polecat was digesting a second thistle, Quanah leaped onto his back again. The pony gave a few halfhearted skips that ended in a general frolic. Then he pranced at the end of the neck line that Naduah still held. He circled her at a trot.

"I'm going to untie the neck line," shouted Quanah. "He learns so fast, I'll have him following knee commands by the end of the afternoon." He leaned forward to loosen the knot. Polecat, with supple grace and economy of motion, flipped the child over his head. Quanah lay on his back on the ground, looking up in astonishment. Naduah had to sit before she fell down laughing.

"This will take longer than I thought," said Quanah grimly. Polecat stood with his head down docilely. He looked as though the fall had been a terrible mistake, for which he was heartily sorry.

"Gray eyes, you picked the smartest horse I've seen since Night. He doesn't even signal his intentions with his ears. He fooled me too."

The child stood and brushed himself off. He strode toward the pony again, trying not to limp.

"Wait, gray eyes. Let it rest a few minutes." Naduah studied Polecat.

"I have to get back on him. I have to show him who's leading this party."

"I don't think that'll work with this one. He just wants you to know you haven't beaten him. He wants to be friends, but on his own terms. Why don't you take him to the river and water him, rub him down. Pick the burs out of him and clean him up. Talk to him as a friend. Then tomorrow I'll bet he'll let you ride him."

"Do you think so?"

"Yes."

"All right. If you say so." Quanah picked up the lead rope, but didn't pull on it. He draped it casually over his shoulder. Polecat whinnied for Wind to follow them. He had grown fond of the old mare in the three days they had been tied together. Naduah turned to go back to her mending and her gossip with Star Name.

"Mother, come with us. I'll cook us some grasshopper legs."

"I don't understand how you boys can play all day on a meal of grasshopper legs. It seems like there'd be more meat on lizards."

"There is, but grasshopper legs taste better."

"Did you bring Little Bit to eat?"

Quanah looked at her in shock.

"I wouldn't eat Little Bit. He's the best wrestler in camp."

Naduah was aware of that. Quanah's area of the lodge was piled with items he had won betting on Little Bit. The boys often tied two grasshoppers together with a short piece of sinew and goaded them into either fighting or fleeing. The first insect jerked over onto his back lost. Quanah had won many matches with Little Bit, who was enormous, almost as big as his owner's fist. Quanah had named him Little Bit to lure other boys into betting on their own grasshoppers. But his reputation was so widespread in the band no one would fight him. Quanah was saving him for when they camped with outsiders.

Elaborating on the career he would have with Polecat, Quanah strode off beside Naduah. He had to run now and then to keep up with her long legs. The two ponies followed behind. Whenever Polecat thought he wasn't receiving enough attention, he butted the boy between the shoulderblades, nearly knocking him over.

Sergeant McKenna laid a gunnysack over his horse's back and carefully folded the saddle blanket over it, smoothing out the wrinkles. A galled horse meant punishment and, worse than that, scorn. But McKenna would have been careful anyway. Casey was trying to treat a sore on his mount with calomel. But when he blew the white powder into the wound, the high wind whipped it back in his face. He sneezed mightily.

"Mac, does the wind blow like this all the time?"

"Naw. It'll blow this way fer a week or two. Then it'll change its mind and blow like hell fer a while. You'll get to where you find a steady diet of alkalai dust right tasty. A man can get used to any-

461

thing, 'ceptin' skinnin'. I once't saw some Tonks skin a pris'ner alive. Pore feller died real soon after."

"Good Lord!"

"Your mount got maggots?"

"Yeah. I never saw anything like it. Those damned flies lay their eggs in every cut and sore they can find."

"They will do that. Oh, hell," muttered McKenna. "Here comes the bugler. Wish they'd lose that infernal horn. Those West Point officers can't take a crap without one, can they? I think Cap'n Oakes has a bugler standin' by to give a flurry and a fanfare when he farts."

"You know what Sam Houston says about West Point men. You might as well take a dunghill fowl's eggs and put them in eagles' nests and try to make eagles of them, as to try to make generals of boys who have no capacity by giving them military training."

"Well, to tell the truth, they ain't as bad as most. If they could jest be weaned away from their bugles, they'd do all right."

McKenna's woolen trousers were threadbare. They had been reinforced with buckskin at the inner thighs and the seat. His loose navy blue fatigue jacket was unbuttoned halfway and faded a deep mauve. There were dark stains under the arms, and the collar was frayed. He had washed that morning, but already there was dust in the week's worth of stubble on his face.

He threw his light California saddle over his steel gray's back, and tightened the cinch. He shook the large leather pad that had served him as a mattress and ground cloth and tossed that over the saddle. He fitted the hole in it over his pommel. It covered the saddle and the horse's back, protecting them both from rain.

Casey stuffed a day's rations of pemmican and hard biscuit, preserved potatoes, flour, tea, sugar, and lard into his saddlebag. Before he buckled his flat, wooden canteen over the saddlebag with his rolled blanket, Casey took a sip. He made a face.

"Warm already and it's only seven o'clock in the morning. Hope we find a river with some water in it today. I could use a bath."

"We all could." McKenna wrinkled his nose. "Now I know why they call 'em the ranks." He swung onto his horse. "Saddle up. Fall in."

There was a jingling of spurs and clanking of metal.

"Count fours. Prepare to mount. Mount!" Saddles groaned as the weight of twenty-four men hit them. "Fours right. Harch!"

The men of company A moved out on another day of patrol. With their bugler, they were noisy. And they were restricted to the area south of the Red River and north of the Mexican border. But they were effectively disrupting the freedom the People had always had to travel their raid trails.

At first the cavalry had cut trail often, coming across the marks of war parties and following them for hundreds of miles. Captain Oakes and his men had proved that the heavier, grain-fed horses could run down the lighter Indian ponies over three hundred miles of rough country, if the patrols relieved each other. They had fought and killed Comanche without loss to themselves. And they had driven the raiders back into the wilds of the Staked Plains, and the broken high plains north of the Red and Canadian rivers.

Now their quarry was harder to find. There were few raiding parties venturing south. The patrol moved over territory mapped by Colonel Robert Lee and his engineers. They followed the Delaware scouts who were tracking the Comanche. The monotony of their job was equaled only by the monotony of the landscape. As they rode, Casey, a Virginian, grumbled from behind his bandana. He wore it in a futile attempt to filter out the dust.

"God must have created Texas as a place to get rid of all his surplus thorns and varmits."

"This would be fine country if it jest had water," said McKenna.

"So would hell."

"Cheer up, Case. We're goin' to Utah soon."

"I heard that rumor. You suppose it's true?"

"Sounds like the sort of fool thing brass will do. No one over the rank of cap'n knows his ass from his ears."

"Well, hell, Mac, we haven't seen hide nor hair of a Comanche for over a month."

"Now why do you spose that is?"

"We've whipped them."

"Casey, I like you. But if you think that, you're as big a fool as the brass."

"Then where are they?"

"Up thar." McKenna waved vaguely toward the north and the Staked Plains. "Can't conduct a campaign on the Staked Plains, they say. 'No water.' Iff'n that's true, then the Comanches've found a way to live without it.

"Onliest way to do them mean varmints is to thrash 'em soundly. And the ones who're left'll sorta take to you and mind their manners. But no. We have to stand at the border with our hats in our hands and wait for 'em to come out to play. Comanches may be red-bellied savages, but they ain't stupid. Not by a long ways. They can figure out our limits, same way they can gauge a carbine range. And they'll stay jest outside that range.

"Hell, it don't matter," said McKenna with resignation. "We can fight Injuns jest as badly in Utah as we do here."

"But we've fought a lot of them. And we've chased them away. You have to admit that."

"Oh, I'm the first to admit it. 'Course, they've been chased away before, you know. Onliest trouble is, they always come back. You'd think someone would've learned that by now." Over the clatter of shod hooves and the clank of gear, Sergeant McKenna's baritone rose.

> *Roll your tail*
> *And roll her high;*
> *We'll all be angels*
> *By and by.*
>
> *I got a girl*
> *In Tennessee;*
> *I love her*
> *And she lets me.*

The men joined in on the chorus. From somewhere in the ranks an Irish tenor soared into another verse. The verses became more and more ribald as the morning wore on.

The Noconi too had retreated back into the wilds of the Staked Plains. They were camped near a creek running into the Red River near its source. Naduah and Star Name had set up their lodges under the largest cottonwood on the plateau. Nearby was the clear, sweet stream, twelve feet wide and two feet deep. There were large cottonwoods all along it, and meadows of thick, wild rye. The valley was bordered on each side by twenty-foot bluffs of sandy red loam. On the plain beyond the bluffs were round, conical hills, thrown up by the constant winds.

Down the river from the camp were hundreds of acres of small plum trees, six feet high. They were closely meshed and so loaded with fruit that their branches dragged the ground. Beds of wild roses grew among them, as well as currants and gooseberries. They were all interwoven with huge masses of prickly pear. They formed a solid mat on which fat snakes and lizards lay basking.

Quanah and the other eleven and twelve-year-olds were having an archery contest on the outskirts of camp, with Sore-Backed Horse acting as judge. The object of the contest was to see how many arrows each boy could shoot into the air before his first shaft fell to ground. The arrows looked like flocks of birds as they arched upward.

Most of the men who weren't away hunting or who weren't mending their gear were gambling. They gathered around buffalo hides marked into sections with a chalky stone. The dice were two smooth, four-inch-long sticks, flat on one side and curved on the other. A player held the sticks between his thumb and forefinger and either tossed or dropped them on a flat stone in the middle of the robe. His score depended on which chalked sections the sticks fell into.

A few of the Penateka men, followers of Buffalo Piss, were playing poker with a greasy deck of leather cards. Buffalo Piss played too, shaded by his tattered black parasol. "Brag" or "Poker" was a game the Penateka had learned from bored soldiers at Camp Cooper when they had spent the winter there. And they had taken to it immediately. Once the men of the People learned the game, the soldiers started to lose. No white man could bluff as well as they could.

In the shade of the trees the women worked or played at dice or practiced kick ball. Seven-year-old Pecan and his friends were chattering among the roots of the huge cottonwood. Dwarfed by its immensity, the girls set up small lodges while the boys hunted squirrels with their tiny bows and arrows. Naduah sat in front of her lodge while Star Name plucked at the fine, pale hairs on her sister's face.

"Ouch!"

"I'm sorry. I'm trying to be gentle."

"Mother, look!" Pecan came running, holding a bottle in front of him. It was caked with the red clay soil and stoppered with a wooden cork. She pulled the stopper and shook the bottle, working the folded paper inside toward the neck.

"Where did you find this?"

"It was buried near the cottonwood. What do the magic marks say?"

"I don't know." Naduah stared at the brown lines crawling like worms across the yellowed paper. She could remember nothing of the little schooling she had had twenty years before. Still, she studied it, knowing it meant something. The ink was faded, but the letters were written in a crisp, educated hand.

On the 16th day of June, 1852, an exploring expedition, composed of Captain R. B. Marcy, Captain G. B. McClellan, Lt. J. Updegraff and Doctor G. C. Shumard, with fifty-five men of Company D, Fifth Infantry, encamped here, having this day traced the north branch of the Red River to its sources.

"There are marks on the tree too, Mother. Come see them." He pulled her by the hand to the cottonwood. A section of the bark had been sliced off and "Exploring Expedition, June 16, 1852" had been carved into the raw wood.

"It must have been made by white men," said Star Name.

465

"It must have. But what white men would dare come here?" The paper and the marks on the tree made Naduah uneasy. The Noconi were camped where no white men came, save the few Comancheros, and they weren't really white.

The United States military was sometimes slow to react, but Captain Marcy's four-year-old report of his mapping expedition was finally being considered by those in command. Marcy had proven that patrols, entire military columns, and support trains could cross the Staked Plains and find good water and forage along the way.

Marcy was a thorough man. He had a keen eye, an excellent memory, and a level head. He didn't just explore the territory, he took along artists and cartographers. He described in detail the flora and the fauna, the soil and the geological formations. He outlined the best routes to take. He detailed each day's march, with mileages between watering places. Marcy's report was a manual for anyone wanting to cross the wilderness. It was only a matter of time before someone put it to use.

When Wanderer returned that evening, Naduah showed him the paper and the marks on the cottonwood. He stared at them a long time, until the light faded too much for him to see.

"White men."

"They have to be," she said.

"White men here. And leaving messages. They would only leave messages for other white men to find." Beside her, in the darkening twilight, Naduah could sense Wanderer's outrage. But she felt only despair. There was nowhere left. No place the white people wouldn't hound them. The enormity of it engulfed her. Here, on the Staked Plains. She almost expected white men to appear from the trees and begin shooting at them.

She looked back over her shoulder at the looming columns of the cottonwoods and the flickering shades of the bats. The dry crackling of an armadillo crashing through the underbrush made her start, her heart pounding. Naduah hated the white people. She wished fervently that there were some way to do away with them all, forever.

"The *tabay-boh* horse soldiers are leaving," said Wanderer. "Buffalo Piss's scouts from the south report that the forts are empty of them. There are only the clumsy walk soldiers. There'll be a full moon soon. I'm planning a raid to the Texas lodges and villages again. What do you want me to bring you?"

"Scalps." Naduah said it ferociously. "Bring me as many scalps as you can. And I want to go with you."

"It's too dangerous. Even with the riding soldiers gone, the south is full of white people now. I don't want to lose you, golden one. I'm taking Quanah along as a herder. And I'll bring you scalps. That's why I'm going."

≫ 50 ≪

Naduah packed quickly by the light of the smoldering fire in the center of the lodge. Outside, the pale pink light of the sun, still buried below the horizon, was just beginning to hint that there would be another dawn soon. Wanderer's raiding party had left a few hours before, and Naduah was preparing to follow.

By the time Wanderer discovered her, it would be too late to send her home. She might have traveled alone to meet him, but she knew he wouldn't send her back alone. It was one of the few irrational things about him. He might send someone back with her, but she was depending on her ability to get her own way. She did it often enough.

She took only extra moccasins, her sewing kit, a change of clothing, some pemmican and jerky, her bow and quiver, and a buffalo robe. The items she used on a daily basis anyway were already in the bags she wore at her belt. She had a flint and tinder, and her awl, in its tiny beaded leather cylinder with a tightly fitting cap that slid down on the thong straps and was tied in place. She carried the bag for her paints and mirror, tweezers and hairbrush that Takes Down had given her many years ago.

She stood in the center of the lodge, taking mental inventory of her medicine bag. It was well stocked. And she decided to carry a hatchet with her, as well as her old trader's blanket that Sunrise had given her twenty years before. It was faded and thin, but it was a link with her dead parents.

She wore her leggings and one of Wanderer's breechclouts. She had on one of Gathered Up's old hunting shirts that had been packed away for Quanah to wear when he grew into it. It was a little small for her and stretched taut across her full breasts. She made wings of her arms and pulled them sharply back several times at the shoulders, expanding the soft leather to fit her better. The heavy fringe around the hem fell almost to her knees.

She threaded the end of her outer belt through the slots on the broad, beaded sheath of her knife and tied the belt tightly at her waist. The side of the sheath that the blade touched was studded with brass tacks to reinforce it. Finally she tucked her hair behind her ears. She still wore it cropped in mourning for her parents.

"Are you going after Wanderer, Mother?" Quail rose on one elbow, yawning. She called Naduah Mother, but she could never bring herself to call Wanderer Father. Sometimes Naduah remembered how self-conscious she had been around Wanderer when she was Quail's age.

"Yes. Take care of Pecan. He stayed with a friend last night. Star Name will help you when you need it."

"Wanderer will be angry with you."

Naduah looked at the child affectionately.

"It won't be the first time." She knew Wanderer's anger was never real as far as she was concerned.

She slung her quiver and bow across her back and her saddle onto one shoulder. With her gear under her arm, she padded through the sleeping village, threading her way around the drying racks. As she passed Star Name's lodge, she stopped and scratched on the hide where she knew her sister's head would be. It was their old child-hood signal. Star Name staggered sleepily out, her buffalo robe wrapped around her.

"You're going after him."

"Yes. I'm tired of staying home."

"So am I." Star Name patted her swollen belly. "But I can't go raiding for a while."

"Please look after Pecan and Quail while I'm gone."

"I will," said Star Name, yawning. "I'm making a new pair of saddlebags. Bring me some scalps to decorate them." Star Name grinned, the imp dancing in her eyes. Naduah laughed.

The birds were awake, chattering and crashing in the trees high overhead. The dogs were sniffing around camp. Naduah could hear the first quavery notes of Lance's good-morning song. It was time to go. She hugged Star Name and went off down the path toward the pasture. As they trailed behind her, the fringes of her saddlebags made wavy lines in the dust.

Naduah rode casually into the war party's base camp as the men were eating their evening meal. It had been easy to find them, following the columns of smoke from their signal fires on the hill-tops and their cooking fires. Wanderer had gone back to the old way of raiding. He was confident that the settlements were helpless again. The Rangers were disbanded and the riding soldiers had left Texas. And so Wanderer's scouts would leave the temporary camp to find the Texans' horses and cattle. Then the party would divide up and raid, driving the stolen animals back to their base.

Temporary shelters were set up in an open grove of huge, deep green oaks that spread like a canopy over them. The country around them was broken and wild. There were mazes of buttes, tall, narrow ridges, and deep, twisting gorges filled with brush and trees. It was country that few white men would enter, yet it was within an easy day's ride of their isolated farms and small groups of cabins north and west of Austin.

Once again the Texans would watch in fear and dread as the full Comanche moon rose in September. When its brilliance washed the tops of the trees and bushes, lapped against the door jambs, and seeped through the cracks in the shuttered windows, no one slept easy. And the settlers cursed its light.

It was twilight and the moon hadn't risen yet as Naduah rode among the camp cooking fires, the temporary drying racks, and the shields set on tripods. She nodded and spoke to the men as she passed, finally finding Wears Out Moccasins cooking under an enormous, gnarled, silvery old oak. She had come along as usual to add to her already large herds.

"Wears Out Moccasins, where are Quanah and Wanderer?" asked Naduah.

Wears Out Moccasins looked up from the stew bubbling in its buffalo hide. She tilted her chins, like flounces at her neck, pointing in the direction from which Naduah had just come.

"Following you."

"Following me?"

"Yes. They've been following you for two days."

Naduah dismounted and tethered her pony, the coyote dun that Wanderer had given her thirteen years ago. The dun was cream-colored with black mane and tail, black stockings and a black stripe running along her back. With the point of her knife Naduah fished a hunk of buffalo meat from the hide suspended like a kettle from a tripod. She ignored the ashes from the hot rocks that had brought the stew to a boil, and tore off a piece with her teeth. Through the steam she saw Wanderer and Quanah approaching on Raven and Polecat. She moved away from the fire to meet them.

She stroked Raven's neck and Polecat sniffed around her, looking for the treat he expected her to have. When he didn't find one, he bit her lightly on the shoulder.

"Wears Out Moccasins says you've been following me."

"Yes," said Wanderer. "I was teaching gray eyes to trail." He slid down from Raven, who began cropping grass. His hand brushing Naduah's was his greeting.

"Mother, I saw the strangest animals. I've never seen anything like them before." Quanah was bursting to tell her. "No one will believe me, and when I took Father to see them, they were gone."

"Gray eyes," said Wanderer. "If you're not careful, you're going to get a new name. *Esop,* liar, storyteller."

"I did see them. Two of them. They were bigger than elk and the color of coyotes. And they each had two big humps on their backs, like buffalo. And long skinny legs and big flat feet. And they were eating mesquite. Not the beans, but the thorns. And cactus too."

"Little liar," called Sore-Backed Horse from the group of men settling down with their pipes around the fire. "Come tell us about your coyote-colored, two-humped buffalo elk again." The men laughed.

"I told you they don't believe me. But I saw them."

"Maybe you had a vision and didn't know it," said Naduah.

"I don't think so. I was pissing at the time. Can you have a vision while you're pissing, Father?"

"I suppose it's possible."

"Quanah," called Sore-Backed Horse again.

"Your uncle wants to see you, gray eyes."

"He only wants to tease me." But Quanah pressed his heel into Polecat's side and headed for the group.

"He tells some wonderful stories, but this is the best one I've heard," said Naduah as they walked toward Wanderer's brush shelter. "How long have you known I was behind you?"

"I expected you to follow us. You were so meek when I told you to stay. The scouts spotted you the day after we left."

"Are you angry with me?"

"Yes. I'll beat you later. When I'm not so hungry." He dropped his saddlebags and gear and went back to Wears Out Moccasins' stew. When he finished eating he joined Sore-Backed Horse and Spaniard, Deep Water, Cruelest One, and the others whom he had chosen to help lead the raid. Quanah solemnly lit the pipe and tended the fire. His hands shook in his eagerness to do it right.

Naduah laid her sleeping robes out under the trees where she could watch them as, wrapped in their blankets and robes, they sat around the council fire. Their voices rose and fell on the still night air while they passed the sacred pipe carefully from hand to hand. They were strong and capable and familiar. She felt safe and comfortable with them nearby.

Fireflies winked on and off around them. Crickets sang. The light from the flames danced on their faces. She could hear Wanderer as he discussed the reports from the scouts. He detailed the countryside, going over the best routes and the safest retreat trails. Then they began chanting their war song. The other men joined until most of them were singing. When they finished, Wanderer sang one of his medicine songs. As the last note died away, Naduah heard Raven nicker nearby, and a solitary wolf howl somewhere far off. Her eyes drooped, and she smiled as they closed. She was where she wanted to be.

She heard Wanderer's soft footfalls coming toward her. She heard the faint swish of his leggings being drawn off and his breechclout dropping to the ground. She unrolled the thick robe so that there

was room for him on it. It left her uncovered, and she shivered in the
coolness. Then he lay down beside her and pulled his own robe over
them both. She luxuriated in the warmth and the touch of him. He
gathered her into his arms and nuzzled her neck.

"Woman."

"Yes."

"Are you ready for your beating?"

Before she could answer, his mouth was hard against hers.

When Naduah woke up, the golden rays of sunlight were slanting
among the tree trunks and splintering as they passed through the
leaves. The light poured in shafts through the pillars of smoke rising
from Wears Out Moccasins' fire. A ring of cows stood around them,
staring down curiously. Long strings of green saliva swung from
their mouths and they rolled their big brown eyes at her. She sat up
and waved her arms at them. Startled, they wheeled suddenly and
lumbered off to join the herd that the men had stolen.

The men of the camp were already moving around, getting ready
for their raids. They had divided up into smaller groups and would
follow different trails. Naduah wondered what Wanderer would
bring when he returned.

Rufe Perry had finished roasting the coffee beans and emptied
them from the iron skillet into a square piece of buckskin. He was
careful not to drop any of them. They were precious. Putting the bag
of beans on a flat rock, he began beating them with another rock.

"Rufe, I can't think of anything smells better'n real coffee, less'n
it's corn mash fermentin' or my woman's bread bakin'. It's been over
a month since I've had anything but parched corn biled up." Palestine Hawkins reached into the pouch made by the overhang of his
shirt where it tucked into his belt. He pulled out a wad of unspun
linen tow, as pale as Hawkins' own tumbled, sun-bleached hair. He
separated a piece of the tow and tucked the wad back into his shirt.
There it became just another anonymous lump under the dirty,
coarsely spun summer hunting shirt. He began cleaning his rifle
with the tow.

"You're a regular mobile commissary, Pal. What all do you have
squirreled away next to your belly?"

Palestine laid aside his rifle and reached behind him. He untied
the strip of homespun he wore as a belt. He pulled his shirt out of
his baggy breeches and spilled the bundles inside it onto the
ground.

"Le's see. There's whangs fer fixin' these damned moccasins. My
tobaccy, and flint. Some jerky and some journey cake." He unwrapped the heavy waxed cloth around the crumbled corn cakes

and offered some to Rufe. "Made with real Sam Houston corn, that is."

"You were at San Jacinto, Pal?"

"Yep. Jest a lad of fifteen. I saw Sam take a gnawed corncob out of his pocket and wave it at that little chicken-stealin weasel, Santa Ana. Sam told him he had fought for two days with nothin' to eat but a few kernels of corn. Then he divided what was left among those of us standin' thar. Told us to plant it and cherish it, as a remembrance. Quite a showman, old Sam is."

Perry took a chunk of the bread and ate it.

"At least the bread gets plenty of salt, riding there. Especially on a hot day, I imagine."

"Man shouldn't ever be without the necessities of life close to hand, Rufe," said Hawkins. "Or close to stomach, as the case may be."

"You remind me of a friend of mine."

"You don't mean Noah Smithwick, do you?"

"You know him?"

"I know of him. Anytime the talk's about eatin', people usually think of Noah."

"Did you ever hear about the time Noah and Big Foot Wallace sneaked into a Waco village one night to reconnoiter?"

"Don't believe so. And if I did, tell it anyways. A yarn before dinner whets the appetite." Hawkins cut a plug from his tobacco with his curved Bowie knife. In an ornate, spidery hand the words "Genuine Arkansas Tooth Pick" were etched on the eighteen-inch blade. Hawkins tucked his larder back into his shirt and returned to his gun. From the river nearby they could hear Carlin and Dunn shouting and splashing as they bathed and washed clothes.

Perry shook his thick shock of black hair from his eyes and poured the ground beans into the pot for coffee. He leaned back against his saddle and stretched his long legs in front of him. Rufus Perry was no longer the fresh-faced boy he had once been. He was thirty-four now, and a long scar, the track of an arrow, puckered his right cheek. The first wiry gray strands were beginning to appear in his coal black hair.

"Well, Big-Foot and Noah and the boys were hiding in this Indian village and planning to attack at dawn. Since they had a couple hours to wait, old Noah curls up and commences to snore like a pack of wild hogs rooting after the same acorn. Big Foot wakes him up and chides him just a bit. 'Cap,' says Noah, 'don't ever pass up a chance to eat or sleep, because you never know when you'll get another.' "

"Sounds like Noah, all right."

"The Indian dogs got wind of their soiree and set up a howl. The race was on, with Noah and Big Foot the favorites, on account of they had such a stake in the winning of it. 'Cap,' sings out Noah, 'looky here. A roast of buffalo ribs hanging there. What say we stop and have a bite of breakfast?' Well, by now there were Indian howls among the dogs' melody, and Big Foot says, 'Noah, I have better things to do.'

"He picks up steam and his legs are churning like pistons when the boiler's about to burst. Noah, he cuts off a slab of that meat as he runs by and he throws it over his shoulder. The Indians are so close now Big Foot says he could smell their breath. Like old bear bait. And he plumb doesn't feel the ground, he's skimming over it so fast.

"They reach shelter among some trees along the river, two miles away. They lie there panting while the noises of the Indians and their dogs fade. All that running has given Big Foot an appetite, and he turns to Smithwick. 'Noah,' he says, 'I believe I could do my duty by those ribs now.' Noah looks at him kinda sheepish like. 'Too late, friend, I ate 'em.' And he holds up a few bones picked cleaner'n your rifle barrel. He'd devoured the entire slab while he ran."

They both chuckled. Perry turned toward the river, where the other two men were.

"They're making a lot of noise down there."

"It's been quiet. No raids in this area. They're jest havin' themselves some fun."

"I heard there's been some Indian sign spotted."

Perry was pouring coffee into his big tin mug when an arrow sang through the air and thunked into his shoulder. Perry grabbed his own rifle, then dropped it as his arm numbed. He pulled his Colt from his belt and, firing with his left hand, backed toward his horse.

Arrows whined around them like angry insects. Rufe heard his horse scream as one buried itself in its eye. Hawkins' mount pulled his picket loose in his panic and fled. Perry and Hawkins ran, zigzagging, toward a huge fallen log. They leaped over it. While Perry fumbled with his pistol, trying to load it with tingling fingers, Hawkins pulled the arrow from his friend's shoulder. The raiding party was in full cry now, like a pack of hounds that has treed a coon. Dunn and Carlin waded from the river and, ignoring their clothes, ran for their horses.

"The river, Pal." Perry followed his own advice. An arrow drove into his hip and halfway out the other side. Another raked his temple. Almost blinded by blood, he stumbled and fell on his hands and knees near Carlin's horse. An arrow struck Hawkins in the back, paralyzing him from the waist down. His Colt spun from his hand, out of reach. Perry tried to crawl to help him.

"Git out of here, Rufe. You can't do nothin'. Take him with you, Carlin, Dunn. For God's sake, take him!" screamed Hawkins. But the other men ignored him. As they urged their horses toward the river, Perry limped after them. He managed to grab Carlin's horse's tail as they all splashed into the deep, swiftly flowing current. Winding the tail around one hand, Perry held his pistol out of the water with the other. The horse pulled him across the channel and he dragged himself onto the low bank.

The first Comanche, taller than the others and a faster runner, reached Hawkins, who was pretending to be dead. Perry could see the grotesque black circles painted around the man's eyes as he tucked the fallen revolver into his belt and leaned down to take Hawkins' scalp. Palestine made a sweeping slash with his Bowie knife, and the raider doubled over and dropped. But eight others ran toward him.

Perry wiped the blood from his eyes and raised himself on his elbows. Supporting his pistol in one hand, he took careful aim. It would be a miracle if the shot found its mark at this distance, but he had to try. He only had one bullet left. He leveled the barrel at Palestine's head and saw the thanks in the man's eyes just before he fired. Then he fainted.

Perry didn't see the bullet kill his friend. He didn't feel Dunn take his pistol and his knife before he and Carlin left him. Nor did he see the Comanche carry their fallen leader back into the bushes. In less than a minute, the clearing where the camp had been was empty and still.

When Perry woke up, he staggered to a thicket and lay there panting. He held his shirt to his head to stop the flow of blood, and packed dirt and leaves into his other wounds. He stayed there all day until the sun had set and he could crawl to the river to drink. He curled up in a hole among the roots of an oak tree and slept.

The next morning he started for Austin, seventy-five miles away. Seven days later, starving and crusted with dirt, he crumpled on the doorstep of the first cabin on the outskirts of Austin.

Wanderer was unconscious on the travois that Sore-Backed Horse and Deep Water had made for the trip back to the base camp. Naduah stifled a cry when she lifted the blanket and peeled back the bloody leaves and grass that Deep Water had applied as a temporary compress. Intestines bulged from the clean, purplish gash in Wanderer's smooth, golden-brown stomach. Frantically she searched through her medicine bag. She pulled out a pouch of *puoip* root, her fingers trembling in her haste.

· She chewed the root as she singed the spines off a prickly pear

pad. *What would Grandmother do?* She tried to calm herself by thinking of Medicine Woman. Had her grandmother ever seen the man
she loved, the most important human being in the world, gutted like
a deer in front of her? Perhaps she had. Medicine Woman had never
talked about her dead husband. He had been gone a long time. But
Takes Down had once told Naduah that Medicine Woman had loved
him very much. *What did you do when he died, Grandmother?* And she
wondered what she would do. *Help me, Medicine Woman,* she
pleaded silently.

She cleaned out the debris and washed the wound in warm water.
Taking a deep breath, she leaned over Wanderer's still body. With
the palms of her hands she gently and firmly pressed the intestines
back into place. Then she spat the juice into the wound. Wanderer
grunted once, softly. She looked into his dark, luminous eyes. He
smiled at her before he closed them again, his face tranquil.

Naduah made a slit lengthwise in the pad and not quite all the
way through. She spread the cut cactus and held it over the wound.

"Wears Out Moccasins."

"Yes, Daughter." The woman loomed behind Naduah.

"Press the wound shut."

Kneeling with a loud grunt and cracking knees, Wears Out Moccasins positioned herself over Wanderer. With the flat of her hands,
she pushed the edges of the cut together. Naduah fitted the cactus
pad over it, pressing the cut surfaces against the flesh on both sides
and holding the edges closed.

"Keep it in place." Wears Out Moccasins put slight pressure on
the compress with her hands while Naduah tore her old blue blanket
into strips. She used the strips to tie the prickly pear in place. Then
she sat back on her heels, drained and limp.

"Will he live, Mother?" Quanah stood at her shoulder, his eyes
big with worry.

"I think so. If the wound doesn't become infected."

Wears Out Moccasins made her buffalo medicine for Wanderer.
She chanted most of the night and shook her rattle made from the
scrotum of a bull buffalo. She waved a buffalo tail around her head
as she turned and circled in her ponderous dance. Then she put the
tail in her mouth and blew on Wanderer. Finally she went to her
robes to sleep.

Naduah and Quanah sat next to the travois all night, huddled
together against the cold. Naduah's robe was around them both.
Sore-Backed Horse woke them at dawn.

"Naduah, we must leave. The scouts have seen white men. They
may be trailing us."

"He lost so much blood. Can't we wait another day?"

"Sore-Backed Horse is right, golden one." Wanderer spoke in a low voice. "We must leave now. Gray eyes."

"Yes, Father." Quanah wore only his breechclout in the cold morning air, and his skin was covered with a rash of goose bumps.

"Bring the horses and the cattle. Hurry."

The boy scurried away, without stopping to put his moccasins on.

"He's a fine son, Wanderer," said Sore-Backed Horse. "He'll steal many horses and be a comfort to you in your old age. He's also a wonderful storyteller. Elks with humps." Sore-Backed Horse chuckled as he went to gather his belongings.

As Quanah trimmed the twigs from a long willow switch to herd the cattle, he stood gratefully in a spot warmed by a cow's sleeping body. The warmth felt wonderful on his cold, bare feet. Quanah looked at all the horses and cattle his father's men had stolen, and he was proud. Holding the switch in one hand, the boy took a running start and leaped onto Polecat from behind. He used his hands on the pony's rump to propel himself into position. By now Polecat could almost herd cattle alone, but Quanah made a great show of rounding up the animals. Yipping and slashing his switch through the air until it sang, he drove them into camp.

The war party moved out an hour after dawn. Some of the men had chosen to stay and raid longer, so it was a smaller group that followed Wanderer's travois. As they topped a high ridge they stood without moving, looking down in astonishment. There below them, in a long, sinuous line that wound slowly across the dry valley floor, were fifty of Quanah's humped elk.

"Look at that!" hissed Quanah. "See, Uncle. You owe me a pony." Sore-Backed Horse had been foolish enough to bet that there were no such animals.

"You can have any pony but the one I'm riding."

Naduah led the pack pony around so the travois faced the valley and Wanderer could see. She absentmindedly pushed her cropped hair away from her face and tucked it behind her ears. It was what she always did when she was distracted.

"What are they?" she asked.

"I don't know, golden one. I've never seen anything like them."

The pack train below them was made up of two-humped Bactrian camels, imported, along with riding dromedaries, at a cost of $30,000. The animals were part of Jefferson Davis's other brainchild, a camel corps. They were his hope for solving the transportation problems of a war in the Great American Desert. The idea should have worked. The camels were perfect for the terrain and the climate. They ate thorns and mesquite that a mule wouldn't touch. Their feet were impervious to the hot stony soil. They thrived, and they multiplied. And some were already escaping, like the pair that Quanah had seen. But they didn't appeal to the soldiers the way a hundred prancing thoroughbreds in matching colors did.

From their perch on the ridge Naduah couldn't hear the swearing that went on up and down the line of gangly, lurching, loose-limbed camels. Most of the *tabay-boh* soldiers couldn't keep their seats on the humps. The ones who could became seasick from the constant rocking motion. And they all felt like fools. Most of them would end up walking back to their base camp, Little Egypt, as Camp Verde was being called.

The People watched the bizzare procession until it passed out of sight behind a flat-topped bluff. Then they continued their journey home.

"Do you think Ho-say has a market for those?" asked Naduah.

"I'll ask him," said Wanderer with a small laugh that obviously caused him pain. "The scouts have been finding signs of raiding parties. Now that the riding soldiers are gone, everyone is making up for the year their patrols kept us penned up." Wanderer was fretting that he should be wounded just when the raiding was good again. "All the horses and cattle will be stolen before I'm well."

"Don't worry, my wandering one," said Naduah. "The white people always get more. You'll have plenty of stock to trade with Ho-say this fall."

Wanderer was very weak, and he fell into a deep sleep. He slept for hours, oblivious to the bouncing and rocking of the travois. Hawkins' pistol was beside him, tucked into the blankets like a child's new toy. It had taken twelve years, but at last he had one of Colt's repeaters.

୬ *51* ଈ

In January of 1858 the governor of Texas appointed John "Rip" Ford as senior captain and supreme commander of the re-formed Rangers. Rip's orders were to follow any and all trails of hostile or suspected hostile Indians, to inflict the most summary punishment, and to brook no interference with his plan of operation from any source.

By late April Ford had gathered his force, one hundred battle-tested, saddle-hardened Texans and one hundred and eleven Anadarko and Tonkawa scouts. The scouts were led by their Indian

Agent's son, nineteen-year-old Sullivan Ross, who was home on vacation from college. There was no bugle on this expedition. No rattling sabers, no drills, no heavy wagons, no fires, and no fancy bivouacs. Rip Ford followed Jack Hays' example of making cold camps and traveling fast, light, and silently.

After Chief Placido had given his report, Ford turned to the tall, earnest young man riding beside him.

"What did the chief say, Sul?"

"He says the signs lead across the Red River and into Oklahoma Territory. Says the Rangers were never allowed up there. Wants to know if we're going to turn back."

"My orders are to fight Indians," said Ford "not learn geography. When Placido comes back, tell him his men are doing a fine job."

"There's nothing they like better than hunting Comanches. 'Specially if there are a hundred white men with revolvers and Springfields behind them once they've gotten them treed."

"They're good scouts."

"They are that. If only they'd stop eating each other."

"Surely they don't eat each other!" Ford had seen a great deal, but he could still be horrified at times.

"My father suspects they do. On the reservation. There are more women pregnant than there are births reported. Many more."

"They eat their babies?"

"Boiled as stew. So the rumors go. But we can't catch them at it. And maybe it isn't true. People will believe anything about them because they eat their enemies."

Ford remembered the aftermath of the battle of Plum Creek and the hands and feet bubbling among the potatoes and carrots and turnip greens in the huge laundry kettle. Enough of that subject.

"Looks like rain," said Ford.

"I hope not," said Ross. "When these damned buckskin trousers get wet they feel like the skin of a corpse drowned three days."

When the column reached the Red River it disintegrated as the Rangers rushed to drink and fill their canteens before their horses stirred up the bottom. Scouts had reported no Comanche for miles, so the men stripped and sat in the water. They scrubbed themselves with sand and bellowed bawdy songs. They were bronzed or carmine above the neck and below the elbows, and as white as peeled chestnuts everywhere else.

Ford sat smoking a cornhusk cigarette and waiting patiently on the bank. Placido squatted beside him. Across the back of his pony was a freshly killed deer for dinner. The scouts did most of the hunting because their bows and arrows were silent.

"Got smoke, Cap'n?" asked Placido.

Ford took another cigarette from his shirt pocket and handed it to the Tonkawa. Then he lit it with his own and watched Placido from the corner of his eye. He tried to imagine the dignified old man eating a human baby. And he thought of the stories he'd heard. Of the Tonkawa's favorite way of cooking their food, driving burning splinters into a living prisoner's flesh and eating the half-cooked meat around them.

Best not to think about it. No white man could ever really understand how Indians felt about things, or why they did them. "They're the uncertainest creatures in God's creation," as one of his men had put it. Whatever their dietary habits, the Tonks were brave allies. At times old Placido seemed almost fanatic in his efforts to track Comanche. And everywhere he went, he carried a single arrow, unlike any of his own. It was an arrow with three red lines painted around its shaft.

"Chief," said Ford, to break the silence, although Placido seemed content to sit without talking. "Why don't you ever hunt the turkeys that are all around?"

The Tonkawa gave it some thought, working the English out in his head.

"Hunt turkey no good. Deer, him see Injun, him say 'Mebbe so Injun, mebbe so stump.' Turkey, him say 'Injun, by God!' and him gone." Placido flapped his bony elbows and gave a gobble of alarm that set a flock in flight far away. "We eat here, Cap'n?"

"No, we'll cross first as usual. This time of year we might find the river six feet higher when we finish dinner."

Twenty-four hours later, they were deep into Comanche territory and heading north toward the Canadian River. The scouts were finding many signs of their enemies. They could barely contain their excitement. The Rangers kept their weapons ready.

Naduah and Wanderer sat in front of their lodge, basking like lizards in the warm May sunshine. The flowers and grass and leaves of spring covered more than the scars on the land. They covered scars on the heart too. In the beauty of spring life became worth living again, no matter what sorrows it had brought in the past.

As though in reaction to being crowded together during the long, cold winter of 1858, the Noconi had scattered their lodges widely on the grass-covered slopes of Antelope Hills. Outside the village, narrow paths, beaten bare by the tread of unshod hoofs and moccasined feet, meandered through a pastel carpet of flowers. The air was heavily scented with them. Now and then a dog or a small child would wander off a path, and only the waving grass and flowers would mark his progress. Bees kept up a steady drone, and Naduah counted eight hummingbirds. Other birds flitted in and out of the clumps of small oaks and mesquite scrub that dotted the campsite.

Streamers and feathers fluttered from the lodge poles. The big yellow sun painted on the side of Naduah's lodge seemed to pulse with a cheerful heat of its own. The string of deer hooves hanging above them clacked gaily. Nearby, thirteen-year-old Quail, Turtle, Star Name's twelve-year-old daughter, and a few of their friends were scraping a huge buffalo hide. Quail was a good worker. She was stocky and solemn, and her eyes really lit up only when Gathered Up was around. No one had seen Quanah or Pecan or their friends since they had all left at dawn.

The younger children raced and played, laughing, while their dogs chased after them. Long, slender, scissor-shaped travois leaned upright against the lodge walls. Gear was heaped onto raised platforms to keep it dry in case of rain. The muffled clatter of Lance's medicine rattle and the thump of his drum could be heard. He must be curing someone. Gathered Up was sitting in his doorway, laboriously carving and fitting the pieces of a new Spanish saddle with high pommel and cantle.

In front of a neighboring lodge, Wears Out Moccasins was holding court with the older ladies of the village. She sat under her cherished sunshade, a large yellow umbrella that glowed like a miniature sun. She had traded two horses to get it from Cruelest One. He hadn't wanted to give it up and had driven a hard bargain. The camp had echoed with their shouts. Naduah had been afraid Wears Out Moccasins would squash the tiny warrior in her excitement. But she had gotten the prize in the end. And she had lashed a tripod to hold it in place over her head.

A small flock of scruffy hens and a bedraggled rooster scratched and bustled around the women. The hens roosted in Wears Out Moccasins' lodge if there were no bushes or trees nearby. When the camp was moved, Wears Out Moccasins tucked the hens' eggs into the cavernous cleavage of her bosom to keep them warm.

Her rooster, the Old Buzzard she called him, had a special hatred for men and dogs. He trained the dogs young. H would launch himself at a puppy's face. Squawking and flapping, he aimed for the eyes and tender muzzle. All the dogs went out of their way to avoid him.

Quanah was fascinated with him. He watched the rooster often from safe distance as he methodically mounted and serviced each hen. The boy had once tried to approach him from behind a thick piece of rawhide. The rooster attacked and sank his talons deep into the leather. Quanah figured he could win a fortune if he could get the Old Buzzard away from Wears Out Moccasins and go into cockfighting with him. But there was no hurry. So far, the Old Buzzard was the only rooster in the village.

Near where Naduah and Wanderer sat, a tiny wren, oblivious to the commotion in camp, was taking a bath in a shallow puddle of dust. She flapped and fluttered, fluffing her feathers so the dust would penetrate them and discourage mites. Wanderer was cleaning the old Hall carbine he had taken from the warehouse on the gulf coast, eighteen years earlier.

He rarely used it anymore. He preferred the newer Springfield he had traded from Tafoya and his Comancheros. It was an official United States Army weapon. With his keen nose for graft, Ho-say had sniffed out the officers in New Mexico who were willing to trade guns for Texas cattle.

The old Hall wasn't much good. The joint between the chamber and the barrel was worn and weakened. When the gun was fired, powder gases exploded next to his ear with a painful noise. But Wanderer couldn't bear to throw a gun away. The old Colt Paterson five-shooter that he had taken from the white man six months before lay wrapped in front of him. It was his most prized possession, and he planned to clean it next.

His wound from the raid last fall had healed cleanly, leaving a shiny ridge across his hard stomach. Sore-Backed Horse had tattooed lines radiating out from it. Even before the wound had stopped itching, Wanderer was back on the raid trail. All across the frontier he and his men and others of the People left farmsteads burning and corpses bloating in the sun.

Now he worked lazily and slowly, as he sat quietly in the sun, buffing the brass trigger guard to a fine sheen and wiping each piece of the firing mechanism clean with a soft piece of oiled calico. Naduah knelt behind him, brushing his hair. He liked to have her do it. Every once in a while he would close his eyes. A look would come over his face, rather like a dog who is having the base of his tail scratched by someone with a superb set of fingernails. Wanderer was thirty-nine years old, but he looked ten years younger.

"Hold still." Naduah tugged at a tendril of his hair. He had washed it and it was still slightly damp. It reached past his waist and hung thick and loose, raven black and wavy from being in braids most of the time. As she brushed, Naduah could see the russet highlights gleaming in the sun and a few strands of silver.

Naduah was not quite three months pregnant. She had told Wanderer that morning. She knew he was proud of her. All in all, it had been a fine day. When she thought Wanderer was as relaxed as he ever would be, she brought up what was on her mind.

"There's a rumor that your father is coming. They say he wants to camp with us and see his grandsons."

"I heard that rumor."

"Will you see him?"

His answer was a stony silence.

"My wandering one, you haven't seen Iron Shirt in fifteen years."

"If it were fifty years I still wouldn't see him. He dishonored me as no man ever has."

"Maybe he wants to apologize."

"Iron Shirt? He wouldn't know how."

"His coming here is an apology of sorts. He's an old man now. You're his only son. No matter what he did, he deserves to see his grandsons before he dies."

"Naduah, you have a way of persuading me to do what you want me to do. But not this time. I will never speak to Iron Shirt again. He is not welcome in my lodge. The worst of my enemies would be given hospitality if he asked for it. But not my father. *Suvate,* it is finished."

Naduah said no more. She braided in silence. As she worked, she studied his profile, stark and chiseled. There was strength in the sharp angles of his cheekbones and nose, and gentleness in the full, sensual curves of his mouth and chin. But now his face was a beautiful mask, shutting her out from the thoughts behind it. Suddenly, the afternoon lost its delight.

Neither of them spoke to the other for the rest of the day. As it lengthened, the silence seemed to become more solid, like fragile spun silk that forms a cocoon. Naduah was afraid to speak, afraid her voice would damage the love she knew was hidden inside Wanderer's silence.

She was relieved when Pecan came home, full of news about his day. Perhaps his chatter would distract Wanderer from his anger. But Wanderer's answers were so curt and slow in coming that Pecan gave up talking to him.

"Pecan," asked Naduah. "Where's Quanah?"

"I don't know. Here comes Gathered Up. Ask him."

Gathered Up left his pony tethered outside his lodge and walked toward them.

"Gathered Up, have you seen Quanah?"

"No. Maybe he's staying out tonight with his friends. He was talking about hunting for the humped elk we saw. None of the boys will believe they exist. And Sore-Backed Horse pretends he never saw them. He makes Quanah furious. At any rate, he wants to shoot or capture one."

Naduah had to smile a little at the picture of Quanah trying to lasso a camel.

"Quail, come eat," Naduah called. And they all filed inside.

Quanah didn't return that night. But he wasn't hunting camels.

On Polecat, he rode alone toward the west, looking for Iron Shirt. He had heard many stories about his grandfather, and he was determined to meet him. When night fell, he found a small hunting camp of five lodges. They belonged to Quohadi from Iron Shirt's band, and they insisted that he eat with them. They invited him to sleep there and travel the three miles to the main encampment the next morning.

He had eaten breakfast and was tying the surcingle on Polecat when the Tonkawa swooped down on them from the south. The people of the camp fled in all directions, racing for their ponies. Quanah leaped onto Polecat and spurred him eastward, back toward his father's camp. He and his pony arrived in a lather, and Quanah hit the ground running.

"Father." His voice was changing and it cracked as he shouted. "They're attacking Grandfather."

"Iron Shirt?" Wanderer put aside the arrow he was making.

"Yes. Tonkawa, I think. And white men. Hundreds of them."

"Tell Lance to spread the word. Then come back here immediately. You'll lead us to them."

Quanah ran to find the crier, and Wanderer ducked inside.

"You're going to help him." It wasn't a question.

"Of course. They're not just attacking my father. They're attacking the People. They're Tonkawa and Texans."

Naduah silently handed him his war clothes. She collected his weapons and ammunition while he quickly dressed and painted his face black. Within minutes he and Quanah rode out at the head of one hundred and fifty warriors. Naduah and the other women began dismantling the village to flee.

The Noconi warriors paused at the top of the tallest hill overlooking Iron Shirt's camp. Wanderer sent a protesting Quanah back to help his mother and Quail. Then he sat and studied the situation. The valley below them seemed alive and shifting with humanity. Three hundred hastily painted warriors from Iron Shirt's band raced back and forth outside the camp. Each man was showing off his riding skill and howling insults at the attackers. They were stalling for time, covering the retreat of their women and children.

The hills were dark with families who had packed what they could and had scattered, driving their animals in front of them. Women's shouts could be heard fading in the distance as they called for their missing children.

When the overzealous Tonkawa had attacked the hunting camp that morning, they had ruined the Rangers' advantage of surprise. Ford cursed his scouts as he watched the two Comanche galloping away to warn the main band. Now his Tonkawa were as hysterical as their enemies. They screamed their hatred, waving their arms and shouting obscenities. And the Comanche warriors circled them, calling challenges.

The Texans, bearded and ragged and coated with dust, sat in the center of the Indians like the calm eye of a hurricane. They watched the swirling bodies warily as they checked their weapons and shifted their quids. When they were as ready as they ever would be, they waited for Ford to give the signal.

He took his time. The show had been going on for almost an hour when Wanderer arrived at the crest of the hill. Then Iron Shirt gave them the chance for which Ford had been waiting. While Wanderer watched from the hill, his father cantered in front of his men. His voice floated up in snatches to where the Noconi sat unnoticed. Iron Shirt was calling on his men to follow him, and to put an end to the white eyes and their cowardly vultures, the Tonkawa, once and for all.

"I am magic," he shouted. "I am invincible. My breath blows away bullets." He waved his lance and shield over his head, taunting the silent Texans. He wore his metal curaiss, the platelets lapped like shingles, over his hunting shirt. His huge buffalo headdress had feathers and red flannel strips fluttering from the tips of the horns. He paraded back and forth, oblivious to the shots fired at him.

"Pockmark," Placido called his best marksman. "His iron jacket doesn't cover his head. Shoot for that."

Jim Pockmark took aim, one steady form in the confusion around him. He fired. There was a muffled clank when Iron Shirt fell from his pony like a sack of sand. He lay without moving. The Quohadi were stunned into silence. It was impossible. And it was just the chance Ford had been waiting for. The medicine had been broken. The Quohadi were demoralized. Ford shot a brown arc of tobacco from between his teeth, and ordered the charge.

Then everything happened at once. Ford led the Texans and Tonkawa, whooping and firing, into a force almost twice their size. And with a high yodeling yell, Wanderer lunged down the hill, as though chasing his own voice. His men, ready to fight, followed close behind him. But Wanderer had something else in mind. Without slowing, and running down anything in his way, he headed for the spot where his father had fallen. In the middle of the melee Wanderer could see Iron Shirt's war pony, and he focused on him. The horse never moved from his master and friend's side.

It seemed to take forever to reach the body. Wanderer dodged and feinted reflexively. He kept a steady pressure on Raven's sides, guiding him in as straight a line as possible. Once into the press it was harder to keep his bearings, but he rode toward the oak tree near where Iron Shirt had fallen. He defended himself when necessary, but he did it almost absentmindedly. The noise and stench, the acrid smell of sweat and the sweet odor of blood, were familiar to him.

He was concentrating so intently on reaching his father's body that he didn't notice Deep Water and Sore-Backed Horse flanking him. They deflected blows aimed for him and protected him from behind with their shields and bodies.

He arrived as Placido was standing over the old man. He intended to take off the curaiss and cut out Iron Shirt's heart. Later, when there was time, he would eat it and devour his enemy's medicine along with it. He looked up as Wanderer leaped from his pony. They stared at each other over the corpse. It had been twenty years since Placido and his men had killed his friend piece by piece, but Wanderer would never forget his face. Nor had Placido forgotten Wanderer's. He knew this was the man who had killed his family and destroyed his village.

The battle had scattered as Ford used Hays' trick of charging again and again into the Comanche. He never let them form their magic surround ring, because even if it wasn't really magic, it was effective. Soon there was no battle, but a series of skirmishes as the Comanche fled. Deep Water and Sore-Backed Horse melted into the fray, carrying on running fights with the Rangers who chased them. It was as though the two chiefs were alone. They both stood facing each other.

"Your father?" Placido signed to Wanderer. He could tell from the resemblance that they were related.

"Yes."

"Your arrow?" He held up the shaft with the three red stripes.

"Yes."

"You killed my family."

"Yes. I have had my revenge."

"But I have not had mine."

"I'll fight you. You can have your chance for revenge."

"No. I don't want your life. I want more. I've heard of you, Wanderer, and of your golden-haired wife and your children. Your woman's yellow scalp will decorate my lance. Every time you go on a raid or a hunt, you will wonder what you will find when you return. One day you will come home to a circle of ashes where your lodge once stood. Your woman will be violated and mutilated and your children burned alive." Tears streamed down the old chief's lined face. "Just as mine were."

He turned his back to Wanderer, ignoring the Colt five-shooter

485

held loosely in his enemy's hand. He mounted his pony and rode slowly away. Wanderer watched him go. Then he stooped and quickly hoisted his father's body onto Raven's back. There was nothing more he could do here. Once again the repeaters had routed his people. Few of his men had them. They were no match for the white eyes. Perhaps there were only half as many Rangers, but their weapons made them five times as strong.

He rode fast and hard in the direction his family and band had fled. His only thoughts now were to protect them. Placido's threat filled his mind with terrible images. The Red River was no longer a barrier holding back the white soldiers and their allies. For the first time in his life, Wanderer began to understand, in a small way, how a hunted animal must feel.

❧ **52** ❧

Wanderer and Naduah, their family, and eighty or ninety of their friends sat astride their horses on the highest ride overlooking the Red River. The Noconi had fled the Rangers for two days without stopping, until Wanderer's scouts reported that they were no longer being followed. This was the first chance they had had to hold Iron Shirt's funeral.

On the hills that flowed away in all directions below them, the leaves of the trees shuddered and flashed like semaphores in the constant wind. The same wind snapped the hems of the blankets wrapped around the mourners. It set the long streamers tied to their ponies' manes and tails flapping and fluttering as Wanderer led the People in a death dirge. His song was a wild, melancholy chant in a minor key that went on for an hour. Occasionally a woman's voice rose in a shrill note of despair. Now that it was late, now that there would be no reconciliation with Iron Shirt in the present life, Wanderer regretted his stubbornness.

Naduah sat on her coyote dun with the black mane and tail and stockings. She wore rags in mourning, and she steadied the corpse of her father-in-law as it sat on Iron Shirt's war pony. That morning, Naduah and Star Name had drawn up the old chief's knees, breaking his legs to do it, and had bound them in place. Ignoring the fact that he was beginning to smell, they bathed him and painted his face red. Then they sealed his eyes with red clay from the river. They dressed him in the finest clothes they could find in the disorder of their two days' flight.

After everyone had had a chance to look at him, they wrapped him in blankets and tied them in place. Then they brought him here, where he could look out over the land he loved. He rode in a sitting position on his pony, with Naduah and Star Name on each side to support the body. Thirteen-year-old Quanah carried his grandfather's war lance and shield, his bow and quiver.

When Wanderer finished his song, he and Gathered Up, Sore-Backed Horse, and Deep Water lifted the blanket-shrouded corpse off the pony. They lowered it into a deep crevice near the face of the bluff. Wanderer climbed down into the cleft to carefully position his father's body so that Iron Shirt faced west.

Naduah led the chief's horse to the edge of the opening. Before he realized what was happening, she slit his throat. The air escaping from his lungs caused the blood to bubble. There was an ugly rasping sound as he gasped for breath and died. His blood ran in rivulets that were soaked up by the thirsty ground.

More men helped push the horse over the edge and wedge it in place next to Iron Shirt's body. Everyone came forward and picked up large rocks from those scattered around. They threw them into the crevice until they reached ground level. Quanah raised his arms and his face to the sky. He closed his solemn gray eyes and chanted a prayer for his grandfather's soul. But as he chanted, the tears welling up, he thought how lucky Iron Shirt was. He had died in battle. He was assured a place in paradise. Quanah sent another silent prayer to the Great Father behind the sun. He prayed that he would die fighting also. Naduah brought wild flowers to lay next to the weapons Quanah placed on the grave. Other women left offerings of food. Then they all mounted and rode back to camp.

It was July, and the plains were parched. Day after day the sun pulsed in the white-hot, cloudless sky. Dust devils spun madly across the hills, throwing out a wake of leaves and twigs and gravel as they passed. Sore-Backed Horse called them spirits of the dead. The camp dogs lay panting in the speckled shade of drooping mesquite bushes. The air smelled like dust and horse dung. The river was dry but for a few pools covered with scum. Naduah had to lay grass over the surface and suck water through it to strain out the flies and bugs that swarmed there. Tomorrow they would pack and move on in search of a better place with a spring.

The sides of the lodge were rolled up a foot or so, and the rolls propped in place with forked sticks. As evening fell, the mosquitoes tuned up for their nightly twilight concert. Naduah unrolled the lodge hem so she and her friends could sit inside where the smoke from their small fire would give them some relief from the insects. As she pulled out the last stick and the heavy roll of dusty leather fell flat, a large scorpion ran out from the folds and leaped onto her arm. She shook it off, and the hundreds of babies riding on their mother's back scattered.

Naduah stamped on as many as she could. Then she went inside to resume her conversation with Star Name and Wears Out Moccasins. Star Name's daughter, Turtle, was sewing her first pair of moccasins by the light of the fire. Quail was restless. She got up and went outside from time to time. Naduah knew she was standing out there staring longingly at Gathered Up's lodge.

Weasel was with them too. Her husband had finally left Pahayuca's band and had taken her with him. She was twenty-two now and still beautiful. But her face was drawn and sad. So many of her loved ones had died, and the others looked desperate these days. Weasel's mother, Something Good, had pulled deeply into herself and rarely spoke to anyone.

Pahayuca had returned to the reservation on the Clear Fork of the Brazos. Weasel said he had been persuaded by his friend, Agent Neighbors. But still there was no peace. The Texans blamed the Penateka for every raid that occurred. They said Neighbors was coddling his Indians, giving them sanctuary after their bloody depredations. And sometimes the white men raided, stealing the People's ponies. Or they stole from other white men and left Indian arrows and moccasin tracks.

The reservation was too small, but the Wasps were afraid to leave it to hunt. When they did they knew they might become the hunted, shot on sight by any Texan who took the notion. They were not allowed guns to hunt or defend themselves. And even if they had been, defense would have only brought retaliation.

"And our women," said Weasel, "they sell themselves to the white men for wih-skee and bits of cloth. What will become of us, Sisters? How can I bring a child into the world as it is?"

"You must bear many children, Daughter," said Wears Out Moccasins. "Our children are our only hope. Look at Naduah, swollen again. In three months she will bear a third child for her husband."

"If I were you, Naduah," said Star Name, "I'd ask Wanderer to marry another wife or two so you won't have as much work to do. He can afford three or four wives if he wants them." Deep Water was negotiating for a second wife, and Star Name was pleased.

Another pair of hands would free her to go raiding with Deep Water again.

"Maybe Wanderer doesn't love you, Naduah, or he would marry someone else to make your life easier," teased Weasel.

Naduah didn't bother answering that. She might doubt that the sun would rise, or that spring would follow winter, or that the buffalo would continue to roam in their millions, but she would never doubt that Wanderer loved her. It was harder being the only wife of a chief. There was a great deal of work to do. But it never occurred to either her or to Wanderer to change the pattern of their lives.

As she listened to the women talk, she wondered how Quanah would do in the months ahead. In Gathered Up's lodge, thirty feet away, he was preparing for his vision quest. The older men were advising him. The tobacco smoke was thick there. Wanderer was speaking, telling of a man's duties, his obligations toward his family, his band, his spirits, and himself.

"A man of the People does not grovel at the feet of his spirits the way other tribes do," said Wanderer. "He doesn't plead or say he is unworthy. Nor does he need stupid water or bull-nettle berries or *wokowi*, the catcus buttons, to help him see his vision. His dreams come to him unaided, through the strength of his own will. He purges his body to be clean and worthy. He opens his mind to receive the messages of the spirits. He rids himself of the distractions of the senses, of pain, and of hunger. He learns what it is to be absolutely free of the things of this world and to soar above them like an eagle. He reaches another plateau of being. He knows what it is to be one with creation."

"When you return, Nephew," said Sore Backed Horse, "you will be a man. You will never look at life the same way again."

"You can no longer act like a child," added Deep Water. "You must be brave, wise, level-headed, loyal in friendship. You must be generous with others."

"But most important," continued Wanderer, "you must depend on yourself. In the end, you are the only one you can ever be truly sure of. Listen to everyone's council, but abide by your own."

No one discussed the possibility that Quanah wouldn't have a vision. If the thought worried him, he didn't let it show. He sat solemnly, with his medicine bag lying across his lap. Naduah had made it for him from the complete hide of a skunk, with the tail still hanging from it. Skunks were very powerful animals. They feared nothing. This one had walked boldly into their lodge one night two years ago. It had bitten seven year-old Pecan's finger. The child burrowed under the covers while the skunk pawed at them, trying to get to him. Quanah killed him, hacking his head off cleanly with his knife.

"Tell us how animals can help us, Quanah," said his father.

Quanah recited what he had learned.

"The bear can cure wounds, it can bring me back to life. The eagle and the hawk have powerful war medicine. If I have wolf medicine I can walk barefoot in the snow the way they do. The coyote tells me the future."

The talk went on long into the night, after the rest of the people in the village had banked their fires and crawled under their robes for the night. As with his ponies, Wanderer was determined that his son would have the best training he could give him.

It was late in the evening when Quanah returned three weeks later. He was changed. He rode slowly into camp, his face older, his bearing even more dignified and confident than when he had left on his vision quest. He dismounted and tethered Polecat while his mother and father stood waiting for him beside the lodge door. There was no need to ask if he had seen his vision. It was still on his face. Nor would either of them ask him to tell them about it. It was his experience and his alone.

"What should we call you now, my son?" asked Wanderer.

"Quanah. I am to keep the name my mother gave me."

Naduah saw that now he had the distant stare of his father, as though he were looking into and beyond people rather than at them.

"Star Name and Quail, Wears Out Moccasins and Weasel and I have made a lodge for you, Quanah."

"My heart is glad, Mother. I'll bring them all presents when I go on my first raid as a brave."

"Come inside and eat and rest." Naduah thought he looked thinner than when he had left. Perhaps he had starved himself for more than the usual four days. He had been gone a long time.

"Father," he said as he dipped into the kettle of meat, "the yellowlegs, the horse soldiers are back. I saw one of their patrols. I watched them in their camp. I wanted to steal one of their horses, but there were too many guards." He said it casually, but Naduah's heart jumped. She could imagine Quanah sneaking up to spy on a patrol of yellowlegs. And if their sentries had seen him . . .

It was so hard to let him go, to admit that he was no longer a child. It had been bad enough watching him leave camp to play with his friends, knowing the wild things boys did. But now the play would be deadly. The danger was multiplied many times. She wished, briefly, that she could halt time, prevent the change that must come. She wanted to keep him the wide-eyed rambunctious, loving child he had always been. The son she had cared for when he was sick, had fed and helped and listened to for hours, was suddenly a stranger.

She dismissed the thought. It was an unworthy one. Of course he would be a warrior. To be anything else was unthinkable. She smiled at him. And he grinned back at her, the old devilish, cocky grin she remembered. As though he understood what she was feeling, he leaped at her. He bowled her over onto the sleeping robes and tickled her. They tussled and laughed as they had when he was a child.

"Careful, gray eyes," called Wanderer. "Your mother is in no condition for that."

"I hadn't noticed," said Quanah, patting Naduah's huge belly. "When is my sister due?"

"In the fall. In another two months," she said. "So you want a sister, do you?"

"I suppose so. I already have a brother. I need a sister to wait on me and to help you." Then he was serious again. "Father, when are we going on a raid? I have to count coup."

"First we hunt. A buffalo can be a more dangerous adversary than a man. Now tell us about the yellowlegs. How many were there? What kinds of weapons did they have? Were there wagons with them? Where were they camped? Later you can report to the council about them." Wanderer didn't say so, but he was helping Quanah rehearse his first speech to the band's council. He wanted to be sure the boy had all the information he would need and that he presented it well.

As Quanah spoke, telling in minute detail what he had seen, Wanderer knew he didn't have to worry.

The cavalry bugle seemed to trigger the cramp that knotted Naduah's abdomen. It was still dark, not quite dawn, and she strained to see as well as hear. As though somehow she could see through the lodge wall and the darkness beyond. Wanderer's side of the sleeping robes was warm and empty. She could hear him collecting his weapons in the dark. The powder horn clanked against the metal rifle barrel. Naduah stifled a cry as the contraction gripped her. Wanderer didn't need to know. He had enough to worry about.

"Quanah, come with me," he shouted. "Pecan, bring the horses. Quail, help Naduah. Save what you can. Meet at the ford, ten miles upstream." Then he ran out the door with Quanah at his heels.

491

Outside there were screams and yells as the men ran to defend their families and the women packed what they could and made ready to flee. Naduah could hear distant gunfire.

When the pain subsided, she pulled herself heavily to her feet and staggered to the door. Under a lightening sky she could see forms running in all directions. Warriors raced on foot and on horseback toward the edge of camp. They would hold off the soldiers as long as possible, but there was very little time.

She pulled her dress over her head, tugging it over her stomach. She gathered her medicine bag and a sack of pemmican. She threw some blankets onto the pile, and her bow and arrows on top of that. As she straightened up, she ignored the memory of the pain that still lingered below her stomach and the burning ache in the small of her back.

Three of their travois stood leaning against the lodge wall. The Noconi moved so often they sometimes didn't bother dismantling them. Quail and Naduah worked frantically, bumping into each other and tangling the lines in their haste. When Pecan arrived with the ponies, they lashed the travois to the packhorses.

"Pecan, where's Night?" shouted Naduah. She could hear the guns and the men's shouts coming closer. And it was becoming lighter all the time. Only a few minutes had passed, but it seemed as though she was trapped like an insect in the slow-flowing sap that creeps down the trunk of a pine tree.

"I brought the strongest horses," said Pecan. "The ones we can use."

"Go get Night."

"He's old."

"Get Night." Her voice rose, lapped at the edge of hysteria. She had to shout to be heard over the howling dogs and the children wailing for their mothers. The boy turned and sprinted back toward the pasture. Naduah ran inside and grabbed the round silver mirror from its peg. She threw the Spanish bridle over her arm. She had treasured it for fifteen years, and she would lose her life before she lost it. She stuffed them into the blankets covering the packs.

She felt the pain start again, and doubled over with it. She leaned against the travois poles, her bow and arrows clutched in her hand.

"Quail, the baby is coming. I'll have to ride the third travois. Herd the ponies." *No, please,* she whispered. *Not now.*

Fifty feet away, Star Name, shrouded in her blanket, was tying a few bags onto her pony's surcingle. A figure in a battered slouch hat ran crouching from the shadows behind her lodge.

"Star Name, run!"

Star Name whirled around, and McKenna fired. One of the lodges

had been set ablaze, and through the smoke and dust Naduah saw
Star Name fall. She had her own arrow nocked and drawn and into
McKenna before he could load and pull the trigger again. He fell
forward with a surprised look on his face. The weight of his body
drove the arrow the rest of the way into his chest and out his back.

Gathered Up rode by. Leaning down, he picked up Star Name
and laid her across Naduah's coyote dun. Quail supported the body
in front of her as she rode the dun. Then Gathered Up grabbed the
rifle. He held it up in a salute to Naduah.

"You are a warrior now," he shouted. "Wanderer sent me to help
you escape." Naduah lowered herself onto the woven slats and
tumbled robes of the travois. She tucked the bow and quiver under
one of the straps that bound it together. Gathered Up began lashing
the ponies viciously with his quirt.

They galloped through camp, the travois bouncing crazily on the
stones and scattered equipment. Thorny mesquite whipped her face
and arms, embroidering long red welts on her skin. As the poles
bucked and swayed, she gripped them with white knuckes scraped
and bloodied by the bushes. The fingers of her left hand were
bruised where they had been smashed against a tree trunk in passing.

Dizziness, nausea, and pain swept over her, but she fought to stay
conscious. If she blacked out she would fall from the travois and be
trampled. The camp was a chaos of stampeding ponies and running
people. Mules kicked and brayed, sending their half-tied loads flying.

The pony swerved to avoid a small child standing bewildered in
its path, and Naduah tensed to keep from rolling off. The sky was a
lead-gray color now. Forms of soldiers could be seen ghosting
through the clumps of bushes in the camp. Their silhouettes, broken
up by the branches and leaves, looked fragmented, like the camouflage patterns on moths' wings. As Quail and Gathered Up and
Naduah plunged into a steep ravine outside the village, the sounds
of firing faded. They were replaced by the roll of thunder.

An hour later, it began to rain as they reached the ford of the river.
The water was running fast and deep, and a hundred refugees
gathered at the shallow place to cross. They splashed helter-skelter
into the river. Dogs barked as they were washed downstream by the
current. Small children clung to their travois, choking and shaking
their heads when the spray reached them. On one travois each of
the three children held on tightly with one hand and clutched a tiny,
whimpering puppy with the other arm.

Women held up their husbands' lances if they had them. They
used them as signs around which their scattered families could

gather. Naduah searched for Pecan and Wanderer and Quanah, gritting her teeth against the pains which were coming close together by then.

"Quail," she called.

"Yes, Mother."

"Star Name?"

"She's dead." Quail sobbed, her head bowed. Her tears mixed with the rain falling on Star Name's limp body as it lay across the pony's withers. Naduah was too distraught for the news to register deeply. She would grieve later.

"Gathered Up," she said, "tie my sister's body onto the other pack pony. Quail, look for Wears Out Moccasins. My time is near."

When Gathered Up finished transferring the corpse, he rode ahead of them, clearing a path in the crush of people and animals at the water's edge.

Wanderer. Where are you, Wanderer? Naduah gasped as the icy water hit her. It was even colder than the rain that was coming down in large drops. Thunder crashed in reverberating explosions that seemed to rip the sky open. Once on the other bank, the three of them stopped to look for Wears Out Moccasins and the rest of Naduah's family.

Refugees crowded past them, jostling each other as they hurried up the crumbling embankment. Someone picked up a child who had fallen from a travois and been unwittingly left. Mothers zigzagged in and out among the ponies, searching for lost little ones. People retied loads and redistributed weight on their horses, trying to save them from exhaustion. Sometimes three or four children rode on one horse. They sat in a row, each with arms tightly wound around the waist of the one in front. Their faces seemed to be all eyes.

On the far side of the river, the fleetest of those on foot were beginning to arrive along with the riders. Wanderer rode among them.

"Naduah!" The cry was wrung from somewhere deep inside him as he drove Raven into the water at a gallop. It wasn't until he was by her side that she began to cry, great gulping sobs. He shook her gently.

"It's all right. I'm here."

"Please don't leave." She clung to his arm. She felt so helpless and bloated. Unable to move or run or defend herself.

"I'll stay with you."

She began to calm.

"I'm sorry, Wanderer. I was afraid."

"I was afraid too, golden one. I was terrified I would find you hurt." He saw the pain cross her face. "Is the baby coming?"

"Yes."

"Quail, find Wears Out Moccasins. She crossed near me." He brushed wet hair from Naduah's face, leaning over to shield her from the rain. She had never seen anything as beautiful as his big dark eyes. "Wears Out Moccasins wouldn't leave the village until she had counted coup on a *tabay-boh* soldier." He smiled, and it seemed to warm her in the cold rain.

"Wanderer," said Gathered Up. "Quanah is coming. And Pecan has just arrived on the other side. He has Night with him."

Wanderer mounted and paced along the riverbank, waiting for his sons.

"He's going too far downstream," he muttered to Gathered Up. "Pecan!" Wanderer shouted and waved, but thunder canceled his voice. The child's pony waded into the water, with Night following behind.

"Quicksand?" asked Gathered Up.

"Yes." Wanderer galloped back toward his youngest son. Pecan crossed safely, but Night slipped on a shifting ridge of sand and floundered. As the lead line came up taut, Pecan turned around and saw what had happened. He began tugging at the rope in panic, trying vainly to pull Night out. But as the pony struggled, he sank deeper. His eyes bulged as he strained to free his feet. He neighed when he saw Wanderer coming, testing the bottom with the butt of his lance. Wanderer took the line from Pecan.

"I'm sorry, Father." The child was sobbing. Wanderer ignored him, staring only at his beloved pony. It was a bad stretch of quicksand. The worst kind. Wanderer knew that the harder Night fought, the deeper he would sink. And Night was fighting hard.

There was a stir among the crowd waiting to ford. Someone had brought word that the soldiers were coming. People rushed to cross, pushing and shoving. Wanderer looked from Night to the travois where Naduah lay wrapped in robes. Wears Out Moccasins had found her and was signaling for him to hurry. He drew his revolver from its oiled leather case. Naduah saw him point it at Night's head. She closed her eyes, and flinched when the gun went off.

Then they were moving again, and Wanderer, Gathered Up, Quanah, and Pecan galloped to catch them. The rain became a torrent, blown like sheets of needles by the wind.

"We have to get her to cover. The baby is moving down. Its head will be out soon." Wears Out Moccasins had to shout to be heard over the thunder, the wind, and the rain.

"There is no shelter." Wanderer led them into a ravine where the wind was blocked. He and Quanah and Gathered Up held hides over Naduah while Quail and Wears Out Moccasins helped the baby into the world. No one had to tell Wanderer that his third child was a girl. Wears Out Moccasins wiped the tiny body off as best she could and wrapped the baby up and buried her among Naduah's robes. She and Quail hastily lashed a domed framework of thin cottonwood poles over the travois and tied a covering of hides over it. They would protect the mother and child a little from the rain.

Rain continued all day and all night. The next morning dawned and was hardly noticed. The sky was still dark with clouds and the rain was still falling. They traveled another day in it. That night it slowed, but no one dismounted to sleep. The water had flushed tarantulas from their holes. The ground seemed alive and shifting with them. Everyone slept that night on their ponies, or not at all.

After burying Star Name, they spent a week hiding in caves or sleeping out in the open, gradually collecting the scattered people of the Noconi band. Then they returned to their village to salvage what they could. The rain that had plagued them in their flight had also saved most of their lodges. They had been too wet to burn when the soldiers returned from chasing the survivors. If the cavalry had been Texans and not United States troops, they would have wrecked everything they couldn't burn. For the cavalry, hunting Indians was a job. For the Texans it was a vendetta. The cavalry had yet to learn that to destroy the People they would have to destroy their entire way of life.

Even so, the rain had flowed in streams through the lodges and soaked many things. Scavengers had eaten most of the food supply. The drying racks were fallen and empty. The horse herds were scattered. And the soldiers had ransacked the tents in their search for weapons and souvenirs.

There was a cold wind blowing as the People rode into the deserted village at twilight. A flock of crows seemed to be caught in the tangled web of tree limbs, black against the gray-white sky. They cawed hollowly at the intrusion. While the men and boys went to find lost ponies, the women picked through the sodden piles of their possessions.

Naduah was glad when they had all packed what they could save and left, the next morning. The place made her uneasy, as though it was inhabited by ghosts. Which it was. There had been bodies lying where they had fallen or been dragged by wolves. Naduah couldn't look at Star Name's lodge without crying.

As the long column of Noconi moved out, Wears Out Moccasins rode beside Naduah.

"You found the cradle board, Daughter."

"Yes. It was still in the lodge, and unharmed."

"Seeing your daughter hanging in her cradle board from your saddle is like salve on a sore wound, or a fire on a cold day. She looks so peaceful asleep. So new and full of promise for the future. Looking at her, I can believe everything will be all right. Have you named her yet?"

"No. Quanah calls her Grub because she wiggles so. But she has no real name."

"I have a name for her."

"We would be honored to have you name her."

"She should be called Toh-tsana Kohno, Hangs In Her Cradle."

"Toh-tsana Kohno will be her name. But I'll probably call her Topsana, my beautiful little Flower.

As they rode, Naduah wondered what the future would be like for her daughter. It had always been uncertain. Winter was coming and there was a shortage of meat. They would have to hunt long and hard to make up for what they had lost. They had lost their food supplies before. And they had survived. They always survived. Naduah nursed the thought like a tiny ember in a bleak world.

It had been a long time since she had had the dream where time stopped. The nightmare in which everyone stood motionless with their heads turned toward an opening in a wall made of logs. Something horrible, ominous, was out there. There was a jingle of metal, and the scene exploded. Naduah was running, falling, screaming, struggling futilely in huge hands that gripped her. Then she was awake. Fear gagged her, and the drumming of her heart echoed in her head.

She lay, afraid to move, listening to the silence. She heard the gentle breathing of her children and Quail. Outside, a light wind jingled the metal cones on the shield cover by the door. Stars glittered in the patch of icy sky seen through the smoke hole. She looked up, dizzy from fear and the exhaustion of another long march and hunger. The lodge tilted and whirled around her. She seemed to be hovering like a hawk and looking down at the stars, as though into a deep pool. The stars seemed to glint at the bottom of it like shiny pebbles.

Wanderer stirred beside her. And the feel of him righted the world. She measured his smooth, taut body with her own, stretching to touch as much of him as possible. She smelled the smokiness of his skin as she pulled the warm, soft robe closer around them. Wanderer's hand moved lightly up her stomach and ribs. It stopped, cupped around the breast over her heart. He felt her heart pounding like that of a small, captured animal.

"It is winter," he whispered against her neck. "They will not come. We are safe." His strong, graceful fingers moved back down her body. His thick black hair trailed across her shoulders as he moved over her.

WINTER

"We took away their country, their means of support, broke up their mode of living, their habits of life, introduced disease and decay among them; and it was for this and against this they made war. Could anyone expect less?"

General Philip Sheridan

"The only good Indians I ever saw were dead."

General Philip Sheridan

ꙮ 53 ꙮ

Over a year had passed since the attack on Naduah's village. It had been a hard year. The Noconi moved constantly, avoiding the cavalry patrols that roamed the southern part of their range. The hunt that fall had not been good. The buffalo were elusive. Even though it was mid December, Wanderer and his sons and the men of the band were away hunting for them. As usual, the women and children and old people were fending for themselves.

The band was camped along a creek, a tributary of the Prairie Dog Town River. The red cliffs broke the wind some. The prairie dogs in their vast village among the sandhills beyond the bluffs usually barked a warning if anyone approached. But they had withdrawn into their holes and closed the openings with weeds and earth. It was their signal that a storm was imminent.

"Mother, there's a dust storm coming," said Quail.

"I know." Naduah panted as she ran. "Head him off." The armadillo she was chasing swerved, trying desperately to elude her. His gray plating rippled as he scuttled along, dodging under mesquite bushes and through cactus clumps.

The sky was dark gray. The clouds hung low overhead like the undersides of granite boulders. Already Naduah could feel tiny shards of sand stinging her face and arms. Her short hair blew in tangles around her head. She was dirty from falling as she ran after the animal.

Finally she was close enough to grab his tail. She lifted his hind feet, careful to leave his forefeet touching the earth. He scrabbled in the rocky soil, digging furiously with his powerful claws. He scattered gravel and a pile of dessicated pellets of rabbit dung. If she had hoisted him completely off the ground he would have twisted back toward her hand and wrenched free of her grasp. And too exhausted to chase him farther, she would have lost him. *I'm old*, she thought. *I don't have the stamina I once did.* Quail took the armadillo from her.

"Hold him tightly," Naduah said. "Or he'll wriggle free."

"I know." The girl held his sides and carried him toward the lodge. He struggled in, his legs swimming futilely in the air, his head snapping from side to side. Naduah followed, her body bent, her head bowed, squinting to block the sand blowing on the cold December wind.

She could feel her heart pounding in her chest, and she put a hand over it, as though to calm it. She was dizzy and panting, and her

501

lungs burned from breathing the icy air. For a moment she felt as bleak as the landscape around her. The sand hills were covered with brittle, rusty-looking brush, and the ragged buttes looked like stained, broken teeth to the north. The river and the creek were covered with a thin film of ice.

Naduah knew she couldn't have chased the armadillo any farther. No longer could she run for miles. There had been a time when she felt she could run forever. She remembered the exhilaration of races with Wanderer. Her long legs had rolled easily in their joints then. And she could pace him as he loped along, loose-hipped and graceful as a pronghorn. No, she wasn't the lithe young woman she had been.

It was a relief to enter the lodge and escape the shoving wind. Quail had already broken the armadillo's shell and was separating out the meat. Armadillo meat was delicious. And even if it hadn't been, they would have eaten it anyway. Naduah was hoarding their supply of pemmican. They would need it for the time when winter was in earnest, in the Month The Babies Cry For Food.

Right now winter was only playing with them, like a cat that catches a mouse and lets it go so she can catch it again. First it would be cold, and then there would be a few days of warmth. But the Indian summer didn't fool Naduah. She knew exactly how much food her family needed to live comfortably through the winter. And they had too little this year.

Sand gusted and blew against the lodge with a dry, scratching sound, like tiny persistent claws. It was not a good time to break camp and move. But some of the villagers were leaving. They were following Wears Out Moccasins in search of the men. Naduah could hear the clatter and shouts of people packing and moving into line. The dogs were barking, eager to be traveling, and chasing small game with the boys.

Let them go, Naduah thought. *Tomorrow is soon enough to pack.* She tossed the armadillo meat into the kettle along with the last of the horse Gathered Up had slaughtered. She wrinkled her nose at the odor that floated up from the pot. Naduah didn't like horse flesh. Mule tasted better, more like beef. Horse meat was stringy. It smelled bad and had a peculiar, slightly sweet flavor.

As much as she missed Wanderer and the two boys, she was grateful she didn't have to feed more than three people with what was in the pot. At least Quail never complained. And Gathered Up didn't care what he ate. His only preference was that there be plenty. He was like a ravenous dog that gulped down choice bits of steak and camp offal with the same relish. But when there wasn't much to eat, Gathered Up quietly gave part of his portion to the younger children.

Hangs In Her Cradle was fifteen months old now. Her mother called her Flower, or sometimes Grub, as the mood struck her. The child was banging Naduah's big, curved horn cooking ladle against an iron skillet. It took both her hands to swing the ladle, but she did it with great enthusiasm. That was the way she did everything.

"Quail," called Naduah. "Feed Flower."

Quail coaxed the child onto her lap. She scooped cold corn mush onto her fingers and fed it to her. Then she chewed some pemmican and gave that to her.

"Where's Gathered Up?" she asked.

"He's riding to the head of the valley with Wears Out Moccasins. He'll be back soon."

Gathered Up was a rare one. He accepted his status as part-time warrior and part-time servant with grace and dignity. He stayed home more often since the cavalry attack. He knew Wanderer had to leave his family to lead hunts and raids, so he remained to protect Naduah and Quail and little Flower.

Although Gathered Up had never been adopted, Naduah thought of him as a son. With his even white teeth flashing in a quick, shy smile and his thick, black lashes lowering over his eyes, it was no wonder Quail thought of him as something other than a brother. Naduah knew the girl's sleeping robes were often empty at night, and that she was with Gathered Up.

Lost in her thoughts, oblivious to the familiar noise of the wind and the sand and the clamor of those who were leaving, Naduah chased a bit of armadillo meat around the big iron kettle. She had just speared it with the point of her knife and was lifting it to her mouth when she heard hoofbeats. She stopped, knife poised in midair, and listened. The pounding was coming from the southeast, the wrong direction. Quail ran to the door.

"Soldiers!" she screamed.

Naduah dropped the knife and scooped up her daughter. She ran for her pony tethered outside. She balanced the child on the dun's back while she mounted. Then she enclosed Flower in the blanket she wore draped around her shoulders. With Quail riding close behind her, she headed for the mouth of the creek. It was shallow there and free of quicksand. Naduah squinted to see through the blowing sand and the confusion around her.

The pace of the Noconi flight quickened as the first shots rang out. Women dropped what they were trying to save, or lashed their pack animals into a gallop. Loads fell or dragged along behind. The

Rangers raced headlong into camp, firing as they rode. Most of the women were shrouded in buffalo robes and blankets and bent over in the stinging wind. It was impossible to tell if they were warriors or not. And the Rangers had no time for niceties. Even if they were women, they were shooting back.

It would have made little difference to men like Ezekiel Smith anyway. He hunted Comanche and Mexicans with the same enthusiasm. He whooped with glee whenever an Indian slumped and fell. And he swerved to trample children and the wounded.

Naduah rode with her legs, guiding her coyote dun with heels and knees and thighs. With one arm she encircled her daughter and with the other she shielded her eyes. She could barely see through the stinging sand, but she could hear. And she knew they were being followed. She tensed at the sound of a breech bolt clicking, and she waited for the shot. When it came she wondered fleetingly how long the bullet would take to reach her, and what would it feel like when it hit.

Then she heard a war cry. She looked over her shoulder and saw that Gathered Up had fired. He was racing behind them, trying to hold the white men off. The mouth of the creek was ahead of them. Once across it they could scatter into the maze of bluffs and ravines on the other side. Then Naduah saw fifty men rise up over the crest of the lopsided hill just across the creek. The bandanas they had pulled over their faces to filter out the blowing dust and sand made them look even more sinister. They fired down on the women and children and old men trying to cross the creek. Sul Ross had planned well when he deployed his one hundred and twenty Rangers and Tonkawa scouts. He had sent some to cut off escape attempts.

"Head up the creek," shouted Gathered Up, waving his carbine in that direction. Quail cried out as she fell, a bullet in her side. Gathered Up galloped toward her. He hooked his arm through the loop in his pony's mane and hung low, using his mount as a shield. At the last moment he swung down and lifted her up behind him. She slumped there, her arms around his waist and her head against his back. Naduah turned to help them.

"Keep going," Gathered Up shouted. From the corner of her eye, Naduah saw two men raise their guns and fire. She saw Quail and Gathered Up jerk as one of the bullets passed through her and into him. She saw them fall. Then she fled. Her daughter wailed in fright and clung to Naduah's arm as she bent over her, trying to shield her from the bullets. Naduah had a horror of one passing through her as it had Quail and finding her child.

Gathered Up raised himself to a kneeling position and felt Quail's chest for a heartbeat. There was none. He stood and threw down his empty gun. He unslung his bow and shot one of his pursuers before he was hit again. Ignoring the blood oozing from wounds in his chest and shoulder and flowing down his arm, he walked to a tree. With his back against it, he began chanting his death song in a loud, clear voice.

> Where I walk
> I am feared.
> There is danger
> Where I walk.
> Where I walk
> There is death.
> And I shall walk
> No more.

He held his knife ready in his good hand and continued to sing while the white raiders swirled around him. They seemed to be listening, admiring his courage, waiting for him to finish. Then one of them raised his rifle and leveled it at Gathered Up's head. Gathered Up ignored him. He stared straight ahead, looking far beyond the men who surrounded him. The gun went off.

Gathered Up was dead before his body slid down the rough bark of the tree and hit the ground. But he had done what he intended to do. He had died in battle and assured himself a place in paradise. And he had drawn the enemy away from Naduah and her child. Only two men continued to chase her, racing up the narrowing valley into the blowing sand.

Naduah could hear them behind her, and she knew their larger horses were gaining on her pony. Soon she would be within range of their rifles. In desperation she lifted little Flower over her head, hoping that these white men wouldn't kill a child. Many of them didn't.

"God damn it!" swore Ross. "It's a squaw. You go after her, Tom." He shouted to be heard over the wind and Lieutenant Kalliher's hacking cough. Then as he wheeled and headed back toward the village. Kalliher spurred his horse and began closing on Naduah's lead.

They galloped all-out for miles. Naduah's pony leaped rocks and boulders and clumps of chapparal. Kalliher's horse sailed after her. He was a thoroughbred, a racer, the lieutenant's pride. And he was in his element. Tom Kalliher wasn't. He coughed and spat. His head ached and his eyes burned from the sand. His face was red and sore from the wind. He cursed steadily under his breath.

The valley began to close in on them, the bluffs coming together at the head of it. The creek originated there, from a spring that was surrounded by a morass of icy mud. Naduah veered toward the cliff face and searched for a way out. She urged her pony up the talus slope, but he fell back, his hoofs slipping on the loose gravel and sand. Like a trapped animal, she tried again and again, until her horse was blowing with exhaustion.

Then her head cleared and she calmed. He hadn't tried to shoot her. He was one of those foolish white men who didn't kill women. Not deliberately, anyway, not unprovoked. He thought too little of her. He didn't consider her dangerous, a warrior in her own right. One who had killed an enemy in battle. It was demeaning, but at least it meant her daughter's life might be spared. If only she had her bow and arrows with her instead of her child. If only little Flower were safe with her father.

But she wasn't safe. She was here, clinging silently now in terror. And Naduah was defenseless. She turned her pony around and sat waiting for her enemy to arrive. Her blanket formed a hood that she pulled far out over her face. She was trying to keep out the sand and to hide her blue eyes.

Kalliher spared her face little attention anyway, once he had her headed back toward the village. He was still coughing, and his prisoner and his horse were both giving him a great deal of trouble. Naduah dodged, trying to escape into the brush and out of the valley. Kalliher had to constantly head her off, and his horse didn't fancy acting as a cow pony. He had a fiery temperment, and he reared and balked. Kalliher cursed himself for neglecting to bring a rope. Not that he was sure he could have gotten it around the woman anyway. She was an excellent rider. If she hadn't been burdened with the child Kalliher knew he wouldn't have been able to catch her, much less herd her along.

By the time he reached the Comanche encampment, his Irish temper had been pushed to its limits. Finally he had cocked his rifle and leveled it at his prisoner's midsection, where her child rode in front of her. He glared at her, to show there would be no more tricks or he would shoot the baby. He wouldn't have. But he knew a Comanche would expect it of him. They killed troublesome captives all the time, and not always mercifully, with a bullet.

With his gun still trained on her, he drove her to where Sul Ross stood in the shelter of a lodge. With him was Chief Placido. The wind had died some, and the sand was settling. Only small flurries scurried along the ground, biting at their ankles. But it was becoming bitterly cold. The lather was freezing on the two horses. Kalliher dismounted and tried to calm his thoroughbred. While he tethered him, he warmed the air with oaths.

"God damn it to hell, Ross. I've winded a fine animal for a dirty old shit-eating squaw. Should've shot her and saved all this trouble," he grumbled. "Holy Mother of God, look at Prince tremble, would you. He'll probably die of pneumonia, lathered up in this weather. My balls are so frozen they play 'Jingle Bells' when they knock together." Kalliher hawked and launched a large glob of phlegm downwind.

" 'Jingle Bells?' " asked Ross.

"It's a new song back home, in Boston. Everyone's singing it." Kalliher sang a few bars while Ross threw a line around the coyote dun. He snubbed it tightly to an exposed lodge pole. The lodge's owner had been getting ready to pack it when the attack came, and the cover was half pulled off.

As Ross was tethering the pony, a gust of wind snatched the edge of the blanket away from Naduah's face. She lowered her eyes, but not quickly enough. Ross saw them.

"Why, Tom, this is a white woman."

"White hell. She's a dirty old squaw. We should feed her to the dogs. Or to the Tonkawas," he added.

"We take." Placido stepped forward. As soon as he saw her eyes, he knew who she was. His face was almost boyish, eager, under his wrinkled stoic's mask. He had been waiting a long time for this.

"Hold your horses, Chief. You'll eat rations like the rest of us," said Ross. "Indians don't have blue eyes, Tom. She's white, I tell you. Who do you suppose she is?" He walked closer for a better look. She glared back at him sullenly, but without shifting her eyes she was looking around her.

She was aware of everything in her peripheral vision, and she was gauging her chances of escape. The chances weren't good. The village was full of Ross's volunteers. They were throwing things out of boxes and bags, looking for souvenirs. Some were scalping bodies, mostly women's, that were lying scattered on the cold ground. Ezekiel Smith was ecstatic. He carved a long strip from the back of a corpse and danced, waving it like a streamer.

"Gonna make me a razor strop outta this here Injun, boys," he shouted.

Naduah knew that even if she could get away she and her daughter would be without weapons or tools in very cold weather. She had dropped her knife in her hurry to save Flower. And the child wasn't dressed for the cold.

"Tom," said Ross, "tell Sergeant Spangler to post lookouts around the camp. We'll stay here a couple days until the weather gets better. And maybe we can ambush the menfolk when they come home. Throw a surprise party for them."

507

As Kalliher was leaving, two men rode up. Naduah recognized the horse they were leading as Gathered Up's.

"Guess who we got here, Cap'n," yelled Kelly.

"The Mexican cook says it's old Chief Nocona hisself," added Garret. "Kelly and I split his scalp. Fer a trophy." They each waved a blood-soaked braid with skin and hair attached. One of them pushed Gathered Up's body onto the ground.

With a wail of grief, Naduah jumped down from the dun. She set Flower on the ground and ran to Gathered Up's still form. Wrapped in her blanket, she knelt over him and rocked, sobbing inconsolably. She held his hand, which was already stiffening like some small animal whose soul had escaped and carried its warmth with it.

Flower wailed in unison with her mother, and Kelly picked her up. He patted her clumsily, trying to soothe her, but she only screamed louder. *Women and children,* thought Ross. *Some victory.* The man stretched in front of them was the only warrior in the lot. *Well,* he thought wearily, *the only way to beat them is to bring the war home to them.* But to find, when the dust had cleared, that one had killed only women and children and old folks, that was hard on a man. Even Kelly and Garret were chagrined. They all stood helplessly watching Naduah grieve. It was so like the grief of one of their own women.

Kelly jiggled the baby, trying to distract her. Like most of the Texans, he wore rusty, homemade trousers that gapped at the waist between his galowses and bagged at the knees. His stretched-out woolen socks hung in folds at the ankles, covering the tops of his patched, rundown moccasins. His coat was colorless as well as shapeless.

It didn't occur to Kelly or the others to compare themselves to the dead man lying in front of them. Even scalped, Gathered Up was handsome. His tight, fringed leggings followed the contours of his muscular legs. His shirt was tailored to fit him perfectly. In some unexplainable way, Gathered Up was the victor among them. In death he still commanded respect.

Then the crying began to grate on the men's nerves. Just like white women, Comanche squaws didn't know when to quit. Garret tried girning at the child as Kelly bounced her in his arms. He contorted his face ridiculously to make her laugh, and her screams escalated to shrieks. It was the shrieking that finally penetrated Naduah's grief. If the child irritated the white men too much they might dash her life out against a tree.

When she stood and held her arms out for her daughter, the blanket fell away from her head. They could see that the dirty, tangled hair underneath was blond. As she took Flower from the white man, she stared directly at him. Her deep blue eyes were awash with hatred. For an instant Ross was nervous. If she had a knife hidden under her blanket, she wouldn't hesitate to use it. He was relieved when she bent over the baby, crooning to quiet her.

Maybe Kalliher's right, Ross thought. *Blond hair or not, she's a squaw. A Comanche just as sure as if she'd been born in a teepee with a witch doctor mumbling over her. A hard looker, she is.*

"Ya reckon she's the chief's missus?" Kelly almost stumbled on the last word. A white woman married to a Comanche was difficult for him to comprehend. He'd known white women who'd been used by Indians. Victims. Chattels. Slaves. But a woman willingly submitting was beyond him. He wondered if she'd enjoyed it.

Word spread that the dead man was the infamous Chief Nocona who had terrorized Texas for twenty-five years. Men came to collect souvenirs. They cut pieces from the hunting shirt that Naduah had made Gathered Up, and from his leggings. Two men had a tug-of-war with one of his moccasins. Naduah cradled Flower in her arms and watched them. Her face was expressionless, but Ross could detect the disdain behind it.

Placido watched everything silently too. The Mexican cook, a former captive, must have forgotten more of the Comanche language than he'd admit. This wasn't Wanderer, although the woman was certainly Wanderer's golden-haired wife. Perhaps the dead man was a member of the family, or a beloved slave. Perhaps the cook had understood the word Nocona, but had missed the rest of it.

No matter. Placido smiled to himself as he walked away to help with the destruction of the village. Wanderer was alive. He would have to return eventually, after the white men had left. The Tonkawa knew that the Texans could sit here until the world ended, but they would never trap Wanderer.

Placido had only two regrets. He wished he could see Wanderer's face when he rode into his ruined camp. And he wished that he could leave the blue-eyed woman's body, naked and rotting, staked spread-eagle in front of Wanderer's charred lodge as a greeting from his old friend Placido.

The light and the heat of the campfires that night were augmented by the burning lodges. A few were left standing temporarily to provide shelter from the cold, but most of the men preferred to sleep outside. They complained that the smell was too bad inside the tents. In truth, they were nervous, as though the ghosts of the lodges' owners would come back to take revenge. Also, there was the chance that the hunting party would return, and Ross's volunteers didn't want to be trapped inside if they did. They made their own shelters and sat around the campfires.

509

Naduah sat near a campfire with Ross and Kalliher and a few others. She drew as far away from them as she could, but she couldn't go far. The night air was well below freezing, and little Flower had only one moccasin. Naduah had tried to find another pair when the soldiers let her choose items from her own things to take with her. But the lodge had been ransacked, and Flower's extra pair of tiny, beaded moccasins was gone. Perhaps they had been taken as a present for someone's child.

While she was in the lodge she looked for her knife, or for any weapon, but they were all gone too. And she was guarded carefully as she searched. No one mistreated her, but there was always a man with a rifle nearby.

The beautiful Spanish bridle that Wanderer had given her twenty years before was missing, and so were her good dresses and the silver-backed mirror. All she could claim were her saddle, which a white man would find uncomfortable, a few plain clothes for herself and her daughter, some blankets, and her mountain-lion skin. She had salvaged her medicine bag too, the one that had belonged to Medicine Woman, and carefully put its scattered contents back inside. Then she had stood back as the Texans touched huge crackling torches of cedar boughs to her family's belongings, the winter's food supply, and her home.

Tears streamed down her face as the flames devoured her lodge, eating at the seams she had sewn so carefully. She felt her life shrinking, shriveling, being consumed along with the poles and the hide cover, while around her the Texans laughed and joked.

As she sat with them now, she grieved inwardly. She refused to speak to the interpreter or to look at anyone. She held Flower on her lap, wrapped in the blanket with her.

Under the blanket she clutched the one thing of value that the white men had missed. The gold of the eagle coin and chain was warm and smooth in her hand. She could feel the embossed design with the tips of her fingers. As she held it she remembered Something Good and the night word was brought of the death of Wanderer's brother. It was the same night Wanderer had asked her to take care of his war pony for him.

She thought of the times she had played with the coin as it lay against Wanderer's strong, naked chest. She used to twine the chain around her fingers when they had finished loving and lay quietly, side by side. He always left it with her when he went away. He left it as a part of him and a part of the past, a reminder of his brother who was dead and of Something Good.

Absentmindedly, Naduah rubbed her daughter's bare foot with her other hand, trying to warm it. Then she noticed that one of the men was turning a small moccasin over and over in his hands. She stared at him fixedly until he noticed her. He looked from her to the child's bare foot, and then to the shoe. He had obviously been intending to keep it. Finally he held it out to them. Naduah nodded, and Flower crawled down from her lap. She toddled to the man, took the moccasin, and returned to her mother. Naduah put it on for her, then tucked her back into the blanket.

Puzzled, Ross watched them. Who was she? She stubbornly refused to answer any questions. The rumor was going around that she was Cynthia Ann Parker, missing for over twenty-four years. It was possible. She could be about thirty-three years old. The sun had tanned her face to a deep brown, and there were fine wrinkles around her eyes. She was dirty, but then everyone was. Ross could still feel the grit in his ears and in his hair from the sandstorm. Her hair had been combed, but it was chopped off short and tucked behind her ears. It wasn't a becoming style for anyone.

Still, considering the hard life she must have led and the years that had gone by, she was a handsome woman. Her features were regular, and her mouth was wide and strong. There was a sensuous curve to her full lips. Her eyes were the most arresting thing about her, though. Ross couldn't stop looking at them. They were large and expressive and a brilliant blue. She must have been a great beauty when she was younger. In a way, she still was. There was a feeling of strength and dignity about her.

If she was the Parker girl, she was lucky. Her family had become very influential in east Texas. And they never stopped searching for her. Most likely she would be welcomed back among them. And that wasn't something one could say of many returned captive women. She'd be better off away from this dirty, dangerous, degrading existence. But Ross wondered, briefly, why he had the feeling he was condemning a beautiful, wild animal to living out its life in a cage.

It was almost a week before survivors of the attack found Wanderer and his men. The three women rode wailing into camp. Wears Out Moccasins was one of them. Wanderer grabbed her by the shoulders and shook her, which was no mean feat.

"Where's Naduah?"

"I don't know," Wears Out Moccasins cried.

"What happened to her?"

"I don't know."

"Who were they?"

"Texans."

"Anyone else?"

511

"Tonkawa. I saw Placido."

"You must have seen her. Where is she?" Wanderer was shouting, his eyes wild. Placido's threat rang in his head. It was the first time Quanah had ever seen his father lose control.

"I don't know. I don't know! They killed so many." Wears Out Moccasins was sobbing.

Without stopping to do more than collect his weapons, Wanderer leaped onto Raven and galloped east toward the campsite on the Pease River. Quanah followed on Polecat. They neither rested nor ate until they stood on the bluff overlooking the village. A light snow was falling like sifted flour. It softened the charred ruins of the lodges and drying racks. The camp was deserted, the women were afraid to return without their men. They had come creeping into the village only to pick through the piles of burned things, looking for anything worth salvaging. Then they had gone back into hiding.

Even on the bluff there were signs of the attack. A saddle lay where it had fallen. There were boxes and bags, spilled from packs. As Wanderer and his son rode down the trail toward the valley, the debris became thicker. Small bows and arrows, dresses, a single moccasin, ladles and kettles, finely beaded pouches, a smashed mirror, tools, feathers, scraps of leather and pieces of rope. There was a daguerreotype album, stolen on some raid. The soaked pages were beginning to disintegrate. There was a long, curved powder horn studded with brass tacks. Strings of trade beads lay like bright coral snakes in the brown grass.

Wanderer and Quanah found the first body on the outskirts of camp. The attackers had missed it when they had neatened up. The rest of the corpses, twenty-six of them, were stacked like cordwood. They had frozen into the positions in which they had fallen. Arms and legs protruded from the pile like untrimmed branches. It had been so cold that the wolves had only been able to gnaw on the bodies. They hadn't eaten much.

There was a horse starved at its tether. But its body heaved as though it were trying to stand. When Wanderer and Quanah approached it, a vulture exited through the pony's enlarged anal opening. More birds moved about inside. They had eaten their way through the anus and were feasting until the pony froze too solidly.

As Wanderer and Quanah rode through the ruins, blackened, half-burned lodge covers fluttered listlessly. A lone dog howled his misery. When they came to their own lodge, they stopped. In the center of the charred heap of their life's belongings lay an undamaged arrow. It had three red rings painted around its shaft. Wanderer stared at it as though it were a ghost. With his heart pounding, he searched for some sign of Naduah and his daughter.

Not finding any calmed him a little. If Placido had been able to make good his threat, he would have left their remains where his enemy would surely see them.

Wanderer and Quanah rode to the stack of bodies. They began the grim task of pulling corpses from the pile, looking for Naduah among them. She wasn't there, but the bodies of many of their friends' women were. As they worked they both wept.

"What should we do now?" asked Quanah when they had finished.

"Wait for the men. They'll be here soon. They'll want to bury their own."

"And what will you do after that?"

"Find her." The calm, distant look on Wanderer's face unnerved Quanah as much as his shouting had.

"Where will you look for her?"

"Where I found her twenty-four years ago. In the east."

Wanderer pulled his knife from its sheath. He sawed at his braids and dropped them at his feet. The braids were three feet long, and his pride. He strode off to mourn his loss alone. It would be a strange mourning, grief for one who was not dead.

❧ *54* ❧

Sul Ross's Mexican cook served Naduah rations along with the men. The bread had dried to the texture of an iron wedge. It was tasteless, like dust in her mouth. She chewed it slowly, her thoughts far away, searching through the vast, empty brown land for Wanderer. When she finished eating, the cook tried to talk to her again. She turned away from him, pulled up the bottom of her poncho, and began nursing Flower.

She sat, her arms wrapped around the child, soothed by the tiny mouth sucking and the small hands pressing warm against her breasts. She felt contained, protected from her enemies. She was a soft kernel inside a hard shell of hatred and disdain. She ceased to hear the cook's voice and he shrugged his shoulders, lifted his eyes to the night sky, and left. When her daughter finished nursing and lay against her chest, Naduah crooned softly to her. Her song was a lullaby and a song of mourning.

As he watched Naduah, Sul Ross wondered what she was thinking. It was disturbing to see a white woman behaving like a savage. Perhaps she had been brutalized too much to ever think like a civilized human being again. At any rate, once they reached the fort, she wouldn't be his problem anymore. He'd already dispatched a messenger to report to Camp Cooper and then to notify the Parkers that Cynthia Ann had been rescued. If she was indeed Cynthia Ann Parker, Ross doubted that her family would have a joyous reunion with her.

It was a relief for Ross to see the rough wooden buildings of Camp Cooper on the deserted Brazos reservation. To protect his wards from vengeful Texans, Agent Neighbors had led the Penateka into Oklahoma and Indian Territory. He took them "out of the heathen land of Texas" as he put it. So at Camp Cooper there were no Comanche left who might try to help this woman escape. But there was still an interpreter, who could be of use in getting information from her.

Sul Ross would be glad to turn over his charge. "Prisoner" would be a better word for her, actually. He couldn't bring himself to tie her up after all she had suffered, but he had to post a guard on her day and night as they traveled. Even when she was staring stonily straight ahead, which was most of the time, she seemed to be searching around her for an opening through which to slip.

Naduah kept her face rigid as they approached the white man's fort. A slight twitch of the muscles around her mouth was all that betrayed her terror. As they entered the trampled parade ground, she saw the women waiting for her. Pale women, like maggots in voluminous dresses and shawls. They would torture her, of course. That was what the more vindictive women did to captured enemies. Naduah had a clear vision of the manner of her dying, piece by agonizing piece. She gathered herself to meet it with the dignity and courage of a woman of the People.

Her escort was greeted by the fort's commander and his officers. They accompanied the Rangers to a large white canvas tent. Ross motioned for Naduah to dismount. She did, and held Flower closer to her. She watched the men carry her few belongings into the tent and pile them next to the cot that had been neatly made up.

Chattering like magpies, the women fluttered across the parade ground and caught up with them. Clutching Naduah's arms, they herded her toward one of the long, low, sagging buildings that housed the officers' families. The chicken coops, they called them. A huge black woman, someone's slave, waddled along behind. She shook her head and tsk-tsked in sympathy. Naduah jerked slightly at the sound, which was so like her own people's cry of alarm.

The women tightened their grip. They weren't about to let this exciting find get away. Naduah's rescue was the most interesting event to occur on the post since Molly, the lieutenant's wife, discovered Rabelais among her husband's books. She regaled the other wives with selected passages when the colonel's lady was away.

The house closed in around Naduah and she focused her attention on the large wooden tub full of steaming water in front of the hearth. The ceiling was so low she felt it would fall and crush her. The large, heavy furniture crowded the room like buffalo milling in a box canyon. The dark wooden walls would never let in light the way the hide covering of her lodge did. The only cheerful thing about the place was the fire burning brightly in the big stone fireplace.

The black woman took little Flower gently and stood by the door, rocking her in her huge arms. She sang to her in an undertone. In the gloom, the brilliant white of her teeth and bulging eyes seemed disembodied in her dark face. For the first time since the attack, the child smiled and laughed, poking her fingers into the mammy's mouth. The woman was shaped like Wears Out Moccasins, and she had a similar gruff, sure touch with children. Naduah was comforted. No matter what happened to her, perhaps the child would be spared.

Naduah allowed herself to be stripped and bathed in the tub by the fire. At least she would die clean. She assumed they were preparing her for the victory celebration. With everyone crowded around her, she didn't see one of the wives carry her clothes outside and hand them to an orderly to burn. The woman held Naduah's old, stained work dress and moccasins at arm's length, as though she had a dead mouse by the tail.

When Naduah was clean, she stood, stolid and uncooperative and shivering with cold, on the rough plank floor. The others bustled around her, holding up skirts and blouses, discussing what would fit her and what would look best. She was a project for them, a doll to dress out of charity. In this godforsaken outpost they thought she was someone even worse off than they were. She was someone to pity, someone to take their minds off their own dreary lives.

The owner of a butternut brown wool skirt fastened it at Naduah's waist, while another buttoned a blue and white calico blouse. They decided to dispense with drawers. No one wanted to attempt putting them on. As the lieutenant's young wife, Molly, was knotting a yellow linen neckcloth at Naduah's throat, she stared into her eyes and shook her head in sorrow.

"Poor, poor woman," she said. "You poor thing."

Naduah was a chief's wife. She was a respected healer among her people. Her advice was sought by all the women in her band. She carried her husband's sacred shield and his lance when they moved.

And she rode at the head of the column on his best war pony. She was loved by a man such as none of them would ever know. She was prepared to die in agony, tortured slowly by the women of her husband's enemies. But she wasn't prepared for kindness or pity. The simple compassion in the woman's pale green eyes affected Naduah as pain and cruelty couldn't. She began to cry.

Before anyone could react, she darted around the lieutenant's wife, past the astonished black woman, and out the door. She ran sobbing across the parade ground, tearing at the clothes that bound her and tangled around her ankles. Ice crystals formed in her wet hair, but the cold wind on her bared chest felt like a welcome bath in a running stream after the suffocating air of the cabin. No matter what happened, she was Wanderer's wife and she would dress as a woman of the People.

The black woman lumbered ponderously in pursuit, waving a blanket to cover her. The men loitering around the parade ground watched in amusement and hoped she would get all her clothes off before anyone caught her. Wailing, little Flower tottered after her mother. When the women arrived, Naduah was in the canvas tent. She stood on the wool skirt as it lay in a puddle at her feet. She had pulled on the best dress she had among her clothes and was searching for a pair of leggings.

The women crowded around the door giggling and wondering what to do next. Someone had scooped up the child and set her down inside the tent. She ran to her mother and clutched her legs, wrapping her arms around them at the knees. Naduah held her leggings in one hand and stared defiantly at her enemies. Her eyes were trapped and desperate.

"She's like a wild beast," said Molly.

"We'll leave her here with a guard and let her calm down. She's had a terrible experience." The colonel's wife had steel gray hair with eyes to match and a parade ground bearing. If she had been a man she would have been a general. As they walked back toward their quarters, she lectured.

"All those years with savages, she's probably mad. There's no telling what bestial brutality she's been subjected to. Or what vile acts she's witnessed." The woman had everyone's attention. The other wives were hoping she'd elaborate on the vile acts. "We'll do what we can to get her safely back to her family and into God's fold, but we can't allow her heathen ways to infect us. This wanton display is evidence of her total lack of morality. You girls stay away from her. Do you understand?"

"Yes, ma'm," they chorused.

It was almost the shortest day of the year, and darkness came early. With it came Molly. Her thick pile of red-gold hair shone in the light of the guard's small fire like a halo around her head. She smiled angelically at him as he warmed his chapped hands near the flames. He had been so long without a woman that he was torn between the urge to fall on his knees and worship her and the desire to throw her down and ravish her. He stared at her dumbly instead.

"I came to visit the poor woman you're guarding, Private."

"Colonel says no one's to go in there, 'ceptin' to take her meals." The private recovered his voice, but it broke briefly into a falsetto, making his face even pinker in the firelight.

"The colonel means no men, of course. I'm here on an errand of mercy. I'll only be a few minutes." Before he could collect his scattered wits for a reply, she had swept through the door and stopped just inside it. The tent was cold and dark and smelled like musty canvas. In the dimness, Molly could see the mother and daughter wrapped in layers of blankets and sitting huddled on the bed. She had a brief twinge of fear. Perhaps the woman was really wild. Perhaps she would attack. Molly spoke softly in Spanish, using what little she had learned at Fort Bascom, New Mexico.

"*¿Señora, tienes frío*, are you cold?"

There was no answer. The new conical Sibley stove in the center of the tent was empty. The woman had taken the wood out and tried to build a fire on the ground, but she had nothing to light it with. Molly walked slowly to the wood, watching Naduah carefully. She stooped and picked up the tinder and kindling. She lay it back in the stove. Then she went outside and brought in a brand from the guard's fire. She lit the wood, and made sure it stayed lit. She warmed her hands at it as the sheet iron heated up. She smiled at Naduah.

"*¿Tiene frío la bebé*, is the baby cold?"

Naduah nodded. Molly opened her arms, asking without words if she could hold the child. Naduah handed her over, tears welling in her eyes. Molly rocked her, pulling back the blanket to look at her face. The baby's huge brown eyes looked like those of a fawn startled by the wide world.

"*Qué hermosa eres*, how beautiful you are," Molly murmured to her. "*Cómo se llama la niñita*, what is the little one's name?"

"Topsanna, *flor*." It was the first word Naduah had spoken.

"*Flor*, Flower. Little Prairie Flower. A pretty little black-eyed Susan." Molly carried her to the bed and sat on it next to Naduah. She searched for more words.

"*¿Qué puedo hacer para tí*, what can I do for you?"

"Nocona." Naduah began to cry, unable to hold it back any longer.

"*¿Qué es, pobrecita,* what is it, my poor little one?" Molly put an arm around her shoulders, and Naduah leaned against her, sobbing.

"Nocona," was all she could say. The two women sat, their arms around each other and the child between them, while Naduah grieved. When she finally quieted, Molly searched around inside the front of her bodice until she found a dainty, lace-edged hand-kerchief. She wiped Naduah's eyes and held it for her to blow her nose. She saved one corner of it to use for her own tears.

"Now lie down, my dear, and sleep. It's been a terrible time for you." Molly didn't bother speaking Spanish. The words were no longer important. Only the act of speaking was. She pushed Naduah gently back onto the bed and laid Flower next to her. She covered them both with blankets, checked the stove, and tiptoed out.

She didn't see Naduah get off the wobbly cot and pull all the blankets onto the floor in front of the stove. She lay down among them and held Flower in her arms. She cried softly all night. Outside the perimeter of the fort, the wolves were howling as they coursed through the bare hills in large packs.

"Carry my words to Wanderer, Brother Wolf. Tell him where I am. Tell him I love him. Guide him to me. Please, my brother."

She had just fallen into a fitful, exhausted sleep when the bugle jolted her awake with reveille in the predawn darkness. She bolted up, her heart jumping in her chest. She tensed for another attack, then remembered where she was. She lay back down and closed her eyes as though that would shut everything out. She had an intense longing to hear Lance's morning song. To hear it would mean that the world had been set right again.

Camp Cooper's interpreter, Ben Kiggins, was playing cards in the shack that was officially called the enlisted men's barracks. The north wind whistled through the cracks between the logs where the mud had fallen out. The men stuffed rags into the holes, but they never managed to cover them all. Navy blue army blankets covering the windows of the north wall luffed slightly with each gust of wind.

The card players huddled in front of the stove. A battered black felt cavalry hat sat in the middle of the blanket they surrounded. The hat was full of IOUs, small bags of tobacco, a couple of small knives, and a few coins. No one ever had much actual money to bet. The men were so absorbed in their game they didn't bother to look up when the door opened.

"Ben," called the corporal who had just come in. Kiggins grunted.

"Kiggins, they want you in the squaw's tent. She's about to know somethin'."

"God damn it!" Kiggins threw down his limp, greasy cards. "The hell she is." He got up and stalked out, a straight lying face up on the blanket.

Naduah's tent strained at its tethers and billowed in the moaning wind. Inside, she sat on a small, rough pine box. Her elbows were on her knees and her jaw rested in the palms of her hands. She stared down at nothing, and tears fell silently into the dust. Her daughter napped in a nest of blankets near the stove. Naduah's uncle, Isaac Parker, sat gingerly on the edge of the cot. He leaned toward Naduah, resting his forearms on his thighs. His strong, gnarled fingers were intertwined between his knees. His gray hair was short and brushed in a wave away from his broad forehead. He looked up when Kiggins entered. His clear blue eyes were pale and kind and guileless. His mouth resembled Naduah's.

"I had almost given up," he said. "Nothing seemed to reach her. I was about to leave, and I said 'Poor Cynthia Ann.' The name touched something inside her. She patted herself and said 'Cincee Ann. Me Cincee Ann.' Praise the Lord! I know this is my long-lost niece. God has delivered her from bondage." It looked as though Brother Isaac was about to launch a sermon or, worse, a prayer, so Ben Kiggins hurried to stop him.

"What do you want me to ask her?"

"Ask her if she remembers her mother. Tell her that her mother passed on, but we can visit her grave. Tell her that her younger brother, Silas, and her sister, Orlena, want to see her. Tell her I'm her father's brother. My wife and I would be pleased to have her come live with us."

Kiggins held up a hand.

"Don't stampede this thing, Mr. Parker." He hunkered down to be eye level with Naduah. In Spanish and sign language and some Comanche, he passed on her uncle's message.

"Nocona," was all she would answer.

"Is that the chief who was her husband?" Isaac Parker didn't flinch when he said it. He had prepared himself for what he would find when he met his niece.

"Yeh. He was killed defending her. She took it pretty hard." Kiggins turned back to Naduah and reminded her that Nocona was dead. He asked if she wanted to go back for his body. Comanche were great ones for carrying bones around with them. Disgusting, grisly custom. Naduah signed rapidly, fighting back tears.

"She says he ain't dead. She wants to find him. Says her sons are with him."

"Tell her if she'll go with us, we'll do everything we can to help her find her family again. I promise her that."

Naduah didn't believe him. She stared at Kiggins, then at the tall, smooth-faced old man on the cot. Isaac Parker stared back at her with a compelling intensity. His blue eyes held hers. They spoke to her without words, pleaded with her. She shook herself to break their spell, and looked stubbornly back at the pebbles and dust and twigs of the tent floor. She liked him. His eyes had the power to bewitch her into liking him. It was a trick.

Parker's knuckles were white with tension as he clenched his interwoven fingers together. So close. He had almost reached her.

"Mr. Kiggins," he said in a low voice, "explain to my niece that I am her uncle. How do you say uncle in Comanche?"

"*Ara.*"

"*Ara.*" He repeated it, and Naduah looked up at the familiar word.

"Tell her she is the daughter of my dear, dead brother. We share common blood, she and I. Tell her she has a large family in East Texas. They all want to see their beloved daughter again. I understand that she loves her husband and sons and wants to see them. We will help her. Tell her we have waited long years to see her. Our hearts are full of joy. Explain it to her." Parker spoke to Kiggins, but he never took his eyes off Naduah.

It was a long speech. When Kiggins finished, she searched her uncle's face, reading it and interpreting it. She inspected the lines around his eyes and mouth. They were made of laughter, not anger. The steadiness of his gaze and the size of his pupils showed he told the truth. His eyes were alive and eloquent, not blank, like so many here. His mouth was relaxed and tranquil, not tense and petty. He had the eyes and mouth of a storyteller, like Kavoyo, Name Giver.

For the first time since that terrifying, wrenching afternoon of the sandstorm, she felt hope. It was as light and fragile and drab as the bruised wing of a moth, but it was hope. She said one short word in Spanish.

"*Voy*, I go."

Isaac Parker wasted no time leaving with his niece. It was one thing to go in search of a Comanche chief. It was quite another to have one come searching for him. On the advice of Tom Kalliher, he sold the coyote dun to the camp's quartermaster.

"That snip-nosed nag is fast," said Kalliher. "Believe me, if you keep her and your niece gets aboard her, the last you'll see of them will be shoe soles and assholes. Pardon the expression. If I were you, I'd remove temptation."

But when Isaac loaded his wagon with her possessions, Naduah refused to go without the horse. She folded her arms across her chest and used the single word of English she had learned.

"No."

"I thought Comanche squaws were obedient and downtrodden," grumbled Parker as he bought the pony back.

"You must never have had one shooting at you," said the quartermaster.

The wagon finally rumbled out with a small escort of troops headed east. The women of Camp Cooper stood in the wind, the dusty hems of their long black coats blowing around their ankles. Molly waved as she watched them go, and the colonel's wife noticed the worry on her face.

"She'll be all right," she said.

"I hope so."

"I know so."

"How do you know?"

"I checked the seat on her uncle's wagon."

"What could you tell from that?" Molly looked at the colonel's wife as though she had changed into a completely different person.

"The seat was worn toward the far edge. You can tell a man's character by where he sits in a wagon. A generous man always sits on the side so there's room for the people he picks up by the road. A stingy man sits in the middle. She'll be all right."

As the wagon cleared the last of the buildings, Naduah began scanning the hills for signs of Wanderer and a war party. Her ears strained to hear his signal. She listened closely to each bird call. She knew he would come for her, but she also knew how futile it would be for him to attack the fort.

She tried to analyze his chances of finding this small party. He wouldn't be able to trail her, although she had insisted on keeping the dun in hopes he could pick up the horse's hoof marks. The countryside around the camp was a lacework of tracks left by wood and water and game details. There were tracks of the men who hauled garbage away in wagons and dumped it in the surrounding ravines. There were patrols and freighters, sutlers and traders and visitors. There were the trampled areas where the men held their Sunday horse races, and the trails that led off to the "flats," the small collection of shacks that housed camp followers.

But though she knew how impossible the situation was, she couldn't stop looking. And she couldn't stop imagining him swooping down from one of the thick stands of cedar and oak on the hills. She saw the scene over and over as the mules plodded along.

While Naduah was traveling slowly east with her uncle, Wanderer sat with Deep Water and Sore-Backed Horse and the other men of the band's council. They were gathered around a fire at the mouth of a large limestone cavern, out of the worst of the north wind. Behind them, in the cave, they could hear Wears Out Moccasins complaining loudly to her friends. It sounded as though she were trying to organize a revenge raid on her own.

Families had gathered what few belongings they could salvage from their old camp and had fled here. Now they clustered together, the lucky ones under the shelter of this cave and another one nearby. The others built makeshift lodges of brush and hides and blankets. They shared what food they had, but there wasn't much. A few boxes of pemmican had escaped the flames and had been strangely untouched by scavengers. When the women opened them, they discovered why. The white men had urinated in them, soaking the food inside.

The men of the council discussed the losses. It was a desperate situation. The worst of winter was waiting for them, patiently, inexorably, like an owl perched over a mouse hole. Life would become harder, not easier, in the months to come.

"I say we head for the Staked Plains," said Deep Water. "We can find the band of Wanderer's father, or camp with other Noconi bands. They will help us and loan us the ponies we need to hunt."

"No one's ponies are in shape to hunt," said Wanderer.

"Then we should walk to the nearest settlements and steal some of theirs. They grow food for their horses to eat in winter."

"Go where you will," said Wanderer. "I will go my own way."

"To the east?" asked Sore-Backed Horse.

"Yes."

There was silence. This would be hard for Sore-Backed Horse to say. But perhaps it would be easier for him than the other men, who were younger than Wanderer or who knew him less well.

"Wanderer, look around you. These are your people. They left their bands, their families to follow you. They left because they admire you. They believe in your power, in your medicine. They are Noconi now. Wanderers. You have made them as respected as the Quohadi. Now they need you. You can't abandon them."

"There are other leaders."

"No. There are few leaders left. And there are no more like you. Not among the young men. If you leave, these people may give up and die. You have strong medicine. It will bring us through this. Without it there will be more grief among them."

"My medicine hasn't protected us. It didn't even protect my family." His voice was bitter. "If only I'd been there when the Texans raided."

"Will you come with us?"

Wanderer stared into the fire, his face immobile. But Sore-Backed Horse knew what was raging behind it.

"Wanderer, when the people have recovered, when the children no longer cry with the hunger that cramps their bellies, when the men are not ashamed because their families are starving, I will go with you to find her."

"You're asking me to decide between my woman and my people."

"Yes."

No one else said anything. It was as if the two men were alone. Finally Wanderer spoke in a low voice.

"I thought I already knew every reason to hate white people. But all the reasons put together aren't as fierce as this."

Behind Wanderer's impassive face, Sore-Backed Horse could see the anguish. It shone from his black eyes like signal fires on a hill at night. He would stay with them.

"My heart is with your heart, my brother," said Sore-Backed Horse. "We'll find her, no matter how long it takes."

❧ 55 ❧

The huge harvest moon was brilliant, drifting in and out behind luminous, pearl-gray clouds in a black velvet sky. The ruined fort was ghostly in the moonlight. There were gaps on the stockade, and trumpet creeper had taken over large sections of what was left. Most of one wall was gone. Only charred stumps stood where a campfire had blazed out of control. The cabins inside had been dismantled over the years, cannibalized to build other houses. Weeds stood chest-high in the yard beyond the collapsed and rotting gate.

Wanderer sat astride Raven for an hour, staring at Parker's Fort near the Navasota River. Quanah sat patiently next to him, but Sore-Backed Horse was restless.

"We must go, Brother. There is nothing more we can do here. These walls will never speak to us. They give us no clues of where she is. And the white people are as thick as mosquitoes around a stagnant pond."

"We'll go soon."

"Is this where you found Mother?" asked Quanah.

"Yes. On this slope. She was a child then. A blue-eyed, golden-haired child."

"How can we find her again?"

"I don't know. I was sure they would have brought her back here. To this place." He couldn't believe she wasn't here.

"There are hundreds of whites' lodges scattered over a hundred miles," said Sore-Backed Horse. "We can't ride up to one and ask for her. We can't scout every lodge. We can't gather the men and attack them. There are too many. And she may not be anywhere near here." Sore-Backed Horse hated the harsh sound of the words as he spoke them. But they had to be said. He would follow Wanderer anywhere. He would fight by his side against any foes. But he would not allow him to fool himself.

Sore-Backed Horse had known how this would end when they first found clumps of houses instead of isolated cabins. The rest of the large Noconi war party had divided then to raid. But Wanderer had continued stubbornly eastward. And his friend and his son had come with him. Finally they were threading their way through a precarious maze of trails and roads, fields and fences and ragged stumps. The lights from faraway windows flickered like beacons on the hills.

There were no traces of Caddo or Wichita, Tonkawa or Kichiwa or Karankawa. It was as if they had never existed. As if the whites had medicine to wipe out even memory. If Wanderer had not been staring at the fort, he might have wondered if it had all been a dream. The land seemed different. The forests had been cleared, and the grass replaced by neat rows of crops.

You were wrong, Father, he thought. Iron Shirt had once said, "We grow old and die, but the land never changes." The white eyes had changed the land. They had destroyed so much in twenty-five years. In twenty-five more years Wanderer would be sixty-seven, as old as Pahayuca was now. What changes would he see if he lived that long? Suddenly he saw the future. He saw himself as a stranger in his own land. The shudder that passed over him wasn't caused by the cold autumn wind. If he couldn't find his golden one, he would seek death in battle soon.

For the first time, Wanderer admitted that he might not find her. He knew Sore-Backed Horse was right. Never had he felt this weak, this helpless. He wanted to ride pell-mell through the countryside calling her. He wanted to burst into every squat, square wooden lodge and demand her return.

In sheer desperation, he threw his head back and gave a ringing wolf's howl. As the last echoes died mockingly away, he waited for an answer. He knew Naduah would recognize the call as his. If she were anywhere within hearing, she would answer. But all they heard was the hysterical barking of dogs from some dooryard shrouded in darkness.

"Now will you return, Wanderer?"

"Not yet."

"Then we will stay with you."

"No. It would be better if the two of you rejoined the others. It will be difficult for me to hide here. Harder for three of us."

"She may not be in Texas."

"She's here. I know she is. I can't give up yet, Sore-Backed Horse."

"I'll stay with you, Father."

"No."

"She's my mother. I love her too." Quanah never argued with his father. He knew better. But this once he had to try. Wanderer seemed to understand.

"No." He kept his voice low and gentle.

Quanah and Sore-Backed Horse turned and were soon out of sight in the darkness.

In the fall of 1861, while Wanderer was searching for Naduah around Parker's old fort, she was one hundred miles away. Her uncle, Isaac, had built his small frame house near Fort Bird twenty years before. Birdville became the first permanent settlement on the upper Trinity, but it never grew much. The village to the southeast, Fort Worth, had just been voted county seat.

Isaac and Bess Parker's house faced west, like a gambler who sits where he can see the door. West was wild, unpredictable country. The Comanche raided out of the west. Late every afternoon, when Naduah had finished her chores and the sun was sinking, she sat in a hard, straight-backed chair on the sagging wooden porch.

Her face was always remote, but at those times she was even farther away. Her eyes refused to focus on the frame of rambling rose around the porch or on the tall trees and small hills hunched up around the cabin. She looked instead for the far horizon she had ridden toward all her life. She was used to wide spaces and vast distances that beckoned her, offered her freedom and change each day. "The prairie stare," her uncle Isaac called it.

The only time her attention was engaged here was when she played with her daughter or worked at her chores. She chopped wood and hauled water without complaint. She was learning to spin and seemed to enjoy it. Often in the evening she carded wool, piling the soft rolls of it, neatly combed, into a basket by her chair.

Bess Parker watched Naduah as she sat motionless. They all watched her. Constantly. She had tried to escape nine times in the first two months she had been with them. They had had to sell her pony. The dun had almost carried her completely out of their reach the first time. They had only caught her because she was burdened with little Flower.

525

Grain and good living had made the dun impossible anyway. She would only let Naduah near her. The more she was pampered, the better she was treated, the surlier she became. Finally she bit Isaac Parker hard on the arm. Naduah said nothing as she was led away, but two tears coursed down her cheeks. They had had to give her a room with no windows and a door that could be bolted at night from the outside.

"What do you suppose she's thinking, Mr. Parker?" Bess kept her favorite chair near the front window where she could sew by its afternoon light and watch her niece at the same time. Her husband sat nearby.

"I don't know, Mother." Isaac laid aside the single sheet of newspaper he was reading. He rested his spectacles on top of it, and rubbed his eyes. It's so hard to talk to her."

"It'd be easier if she'd learn a Christian tongue. She's not stupid, but I never did see anyone so stubborn."

"Yes, she's a Parker all right."

"Only on the outside."

"She's unhappy, Mother. She wants to see her children. I promised her she would. I told her I'd help her."

"I know you did. It bothers you, don't it, that you can't keep that promise."

"I can't even explain to her why I can't keep it. I try to tell her about the war, about how the men are either gone or needed here in case the Yankees come. There's no one to go with her. And the Comanches and Kiowas are raiding again. They always know when our defenses are down. She just looks at me with those eyes, wounded and proud and sorrowful all at the same time. Sometimes I wonder if I did the right thing, bringing her here."

"And what else could you have done, Mr. Parker? Leave her with those savages? Of course you did the right thing. Heathens is what they are.

"I fear, Mr. Parker, that her soul will be damned if we can't reach her. Today I finally threw out that nasty old rabbit-skin bag she had. Law, you wouldn't believe what was in it. Horrible things. A mummified mouse. And a rabbit's foot. And pieces of dried animal innards. Claws and teeth. Smelly roots and leaves and things whose devilish purpose I would be afraid to even guess.

"My, but she was angry when she discovered it gone. First time I've seen her like that. She always has that blank face, you know. She talked more than she has since she arrived, and I was glad I couldn't understand a word of it. She broke my good pitcher. Threw it against the wall."

"We'll buy another one. I don't think she would harm you."

"Oh, I don't think so either, now that she's back to her silent self. And the pitcher don't matter. It's only worldly goods. But she scared me at the time. She's so helpful, so good with the child. And I've gotten used to the wild look in her eyes. She don't mean nothin' by it.

"I took the last of her Injun clothes and buried them too. Bad enough she has to sit out there wrapped in a blanket like a squaw. I don't care what the neighbors think, but I get tired of people coming by here to gawk, like she was a freak show, a circus. And she acts like she don't even see them."

"I don't think she does, Mother."

Big Bow noticed the change in Wanderer's eyes immediately. He asked Sore-Backed Horse about it as they rode along.

"No," Sore-Backed Horse answered. "The anger never leaves him. The laughter is gone. I haven't seen it in his eyes or heard it in his voice since his woman was taken almost two years ago."

"There are other women. I would be glad to share any of mine."

"There are no other women for him. He's had none since then. He refuses to even discuss it. The happiest I've seen him was when you told him about this raid."

"I thought an attack on Placido's camp would interest him. The Shawnee and the Caddo are right. It's time we joined forces and fought the whites and their allies. And since the Tonkawa moved to the reservation, they're easy to find."

The war party moved across the gently rolling plain. The grass waved around the ponies' knees. There was nothing but the grass as far as the eye could see. They were following the Washita River into Oklahoma Territory, where Placido had his village.

Wanderer called a halt to inspect a collapsed soddy. The house had been dug into a hillside that provided the back wall. The other three sides were made of large sod bricks laid in double rows. Grass and flowers grew thickly on the partially caved-in-roof. The house hadn't been abandoned long. The canvas door still hung askew from the broken cottonwood pole that served as a lintel. With charcoal, someone had written on the stained, gray canvas.

> 250 miles to post office.
> 100 miles to wood.
> 20 miles to water.
> 6 inches to hell.

Quanah ducked inside to look around. Banners of tattered, dusty burlap hung from the rafters. The cloth had been stretched there to keep some of the dirt from raining down. There was an old pallet mattress in the corner. Most of its grass stuffing had been scattered by rats and mice in search of nesting material. There was a broken three-legged stool and a rusty candle mold. The air was thick with the smell of dust and animal droppings and dead insects. Quanah was glad to get back outside and mount again.

Farther on they found three boards nailed together like a stack of army muskets. They discussed what it could mean, sure only that it was the work of white people. They couldn't know that it was a "straddle bug," the mark of some homesteader's claim.

Nor could they know that five months earlier President Lincoln had signed an act giving one hundred and sixty acres to anyone who could live on them for five years and improve them. Soon the plains would be dotted with those mysterious markers, and then with more and more of the sod houses.

Wanderer and his men couldn't know that the new "grasshopper" plow made it possible to slice through the solid mass of buffalo-grass roots, laying back long ribbons of rich black soil. They couldn't know that the sound it made, like the tearing of canvas, would replace the booming of the prairie chickens and the long, plaintive whistle of the solitary hawk. However, they did know one thing that the United States government and the settlers didn't. They knew that one hundred and sixty acres wasn't enough for a person to live off of in such dry country.

"Wanderer," called Big Bow, "these are fine rifles your men have."

"Yes." There was a bit of pride in his voice. "Tafoya got them for us. The war between the white men has helped his cattle business. The bluejackets are paying him well for Texas stock. And he pays us well too."

"Father, Buffalo Piss is coming with Penateka men." At seventeen Quanah was almost six feet tall, and a stockier version of his father. He had a fine, aquiline nose and high cheekbones in his dark, oval face. His eyes were gray, tinted with blue. They were hooded and usually brooding, like his great-uncle Daniel's had been. His mouth was full and wide like his mother's. His thick, dark brown hair was long and loose and brushed behind his ears.

Wanderer rode forward to meet Buffalo Piss and embrace him. Whatever their differences may have been in the past, Wanderer now thought of Buffalo Piss as a comrade. He was someone who understood what it had been like to live without the interference of white men. Without their treachery and disease. Together they rode toward the main encampment of the combined war parties.

More than three hundred warriors from the Shawnee, the Delaware, the Caddo, the Kiowa, and the People grazed their ponies together that night. Their sleeping robes and neat piles of weapons and saddlebags were collected into groups according to tribe. But they mingled at small fires to brag and taunt each other. Their leaders sat in the center of the litter of equipment and tethered war ponies.

It was an uneasy truce, especially where the Delaware were concerned. But the soldiers at the agency were Confederate, and the Delaware were allied with the Union forces. And they had intermarried with the Shawnee who had initiated this revenge raid. The others cared nothing for sides in the white man's war. They knew only that it drained the frontier of soldiers and fighting men and left it helpless.

The camp was quiet. Even the boys roamed noiselessly from herd to herd as they guarded their ponies. They conversed silently in hand talk, sniffing out the future competition from other bands or tribes. There was no loud singing or drumming. The gambling was muted, which made it even tenser than usual.

But even though it was quiet, it was the largest group of warriors that had gathered this near a fort since the cavalry had begun patrolling seven years before.

When the council ended at midnight, Wanderer walked away from the sleeping forms and past the men who still sat smoking in small groups. The light from their pipes looked like tiny twinkling stars. He moved carefully through the dark, avoiding the piles of fresh horse dung that signalled their presence with their odor. The smell brought back memories of hot afternoons in the horse pasture, training Wind and working with the child who was to become his woman. The ache inside him hurt as much as the belly wound she had healed. He rubbed his fingers over the long scar. It would be a night of memories.

He remembered her eyes, as beautiful as a clear summer sky. She had been such a serious child. It had been hard not to smile at her when she wrinkled her forehead in concentration as he taught her. Wanderer paced through the still night with his fists tightly clenched at his sides. He fought the urge to reach for her, to try to touch her.

He wanted to stroke her thick, honey-colored hair. He wanted to see her next to him, scent her in the air as she rode and walked and slept beside him. If only he could feel her warm, naked body just once more.

He sat cross-legged in the cold, damp sand by the river. The tiny rushing sound of the water always different, always the same, masked other noises and helped him focus inward. His people didn't write. They remembered what they needed to know. And Wanderer was better than most at remembering.

He started by remembering the very first day, the raid where he had picked her up and swung her behind him on Night. He remembered her small arms wrapped tightly around his waist. She had been just another child to him. He had taken her because he had promised Pahayuca he would try to find a girl for Sunrise and Takes Down The Lodge. He hadn't kicked her or the others as the war party danced that first night. But that was because he never did, not because she meant anything special to him.

When had she become more than a captured urchin? He reviewed each day of the march toward Pahayuca's camp. It had happened the morning she had stared levelly up at him as he bent to cut the thong across her throat. When she thought he was going to kill her. That was when she ceased being his captive and he became hers. He remembered watching her at play with the other children in Pahayuca's camp. He thought of how her long, blond hair flowed out behind her as she ran.

When the pain became too great he closed his eyes and let the tears fall unheeded down his cheeks, until he was calm again. Then he picked up his memories where he had dropped them. He sat there, perfectly still, all night. He was surrounded by images and voices, traveling through his past. Just before the first pale pink streamers of dawn began unfurling along the horizon, he made love to her for the last time. He did it slowly, gently, and with great tenderness. When he finished, he kissed her lightly good-bye and memorized her face as she lay tranquil in sleep beneath him.

He had finished his medicine song and a prayer when he heard slow hoofbeats on the bank overhead.

"Father?"

"I am here."

It was time to go. He stood and walked to where Quanah and Polecat waited for him. He leaped effortlessly up behind his son, and they rode back toward the campsite. As they approached, there were the muffled sounds of low talk, the occasional clink of metal on metal, the mutter of a pony or the stamp of a hoof. As the sky lightened, three hundred men could be seen dark against the sky. Wanderer would be meeting his two oldest enemies that day, Placido and death. He was ready for them both.

The war party divided in half as it swooped down on the sleeping agency. Half of it, intent on plunder, attacked the office building, the store, and the commissary. Wanderer led the others at a gallop toward the Tonkawa encampment five miles away. As they approached it, a woman filling dented tin pails at the river screamed a warning. But she was too late.

The warriors swept into the village, shooting at anyone who ran from the patched-together lodges of brush and canvas. The women and boys, old men and the few warriors that weren't out hunting fought back. But they were no match for the People's new lever-action, rim-fire Henry repeaters. Wanderer had obtained two dozen of the rifles from Tafoya and had armed his men with them. That was something even the United States Army hadn't done yet to any great extent. Few of the Winchester Henrys were made in 1861 and 1862, and many of them ended up in the People's hands. Wanderer didn't know who the white traitor was who sold the army rifles to Tafoya. Nor did he care.

He rode to the center of the village and dismounted amid the shrieking, fleeing Tonkawa. With his bow and quiver slung over his back and his revolver tucked under his belt, he shouted over the din.

"Placido!" Each time he shouted he fired the rifle, until it was hot to the touch and he had emptied the fifteen cartridges in the magazine. Some of those he shot had fled their beds naked. Now, as they tried to drag themselves through the dust to safety, they reminded Wanderer of large slugs inching across the ground. He didn't waste ammunition killing them. Someone would do it later with a knife. Nor did he take the time to scalp them. He had earned all the coups he needed in his life. Let some young man take them.

Then he saw Placido walking toward him through the smoke and clouds of dust. Wanderer dropped his empty rifle and took off one of his moccasins. He pushed a large stone down into its toe. He whirled the moccasin around his head and flung it as far as he could. Then he turned on Raven, who stood patiently nearby, waiting to carry him away. He yelled at the pony and waved his arms. Raven ran a few steps and stopped, waiting again. Placido had broken into a trot and was coming fast. Wanderer drew his Colt repeater and aimed it at Raven's head.

"I'll meet you in paradise, my brother," was all he had time to say. He fired, and the pony dropped, kicked his long legs once, then was still. Wanderer threw his Colt away. He was rooted there now. He could neither run nor ride away. With his knife ready, he turned to face Placido.

Placido also held his long hunting blade loosely in his thin hand. He was older than Wanderer by more than ten years, but he was taller. His reach was longer. And he was still in magnificent condition. The two men circled each other, the muscles of their tensed shoulders and arms flexing and bunching under their bronzed skin. Wanderer danced lightly backward as Placido feinted, sweeping his knife in a wide arc that left a red line above the scar on his stomach.

Wanderer knew he had to get in close or Placido's longer arms would win. He lunged forward and grabbed the old chief's wrist on its upward swing. The two locked together and stood swaying, straining to drive the knives home. They both knew they would have to finish quickly. All around them the battle raged. Wanderer feared that he would be killed before he could take his revenge. Worse yet, one of his own men or a Shawnee ally might kill Placido and deprive him of the chance.

Wanderer gave his wrist a quick twist, jerking it from Placido's grasp. He used the momentum to strike upward, slashing the older man's throat. As the warm blood washed over him, Wanderer had the fleeting feeling that he was fifteen again and had just killed his first grizzly. Then Placido slid from his embrace and sprawled on the ground. Wanderer panted as with his foot he rolled the body onto its back.

He sliced Placido's chest and abdominal cavities from the neck to the navel. He made diagonal cuts along his torso, arms, and legs so that Placido would arrive in paradise crippled and mutilated. Then he ripped away the breechclout and cut off the penis and testicles. He pried Placido's mouth open with the blade of his knife and stuffed the genitals into it. Placido would be able to take no pleasure in the afterlife.

He stood a moment with his eyes closed, his hands and arms, his head and chest covered with bright crimson. He was drained, not of strength but of emotion. He had waited years for this moment, and now it was over. Even mutilating the body gave him no satisfaction. Placido had already been dead, so the mutilation wouldn't be as crippling in the afterlife. There was nothing more he could do, and he felt cheated. There had been no time for Placido to suffer.

"Father!" Two shots rang out almost simultaneously, but Placido's sixteen-year-old wife fired before Quanah did. Wanderer felt her bullet slam against his head like the heel of a hand. It plowed through his scalp and chipped a piece of his skull. As he fell, Quanah and Sore-Backed Horse raced to rescue him. As they rode by him they picked him up and swung him on Polecat behind Quanah. Then they lashed their ponies and galloped for safety.

They and the other Noconi warriors rode west for three days with Wanderer tied to a spare mount. They were sure the soldiers would follow them. Even in the midst of the civil war the whites couldn't allow an attack on an official installation to go unpunished. Wanderer was unconscious much of the time, and Quanah bound his father's head as best he could while he slept. But when Wanderer awoke he tore at the bandages, opening the ugly, ragged wound and causing more blood to flow.

"You must let us help you." Quanah glared at him in exasperation.

"No. Don't touch it."

"Flies will lay their eggs in the wound. It'll become infected."

"I know." Then Wanderer passed out again.

By the time they reached the band's camp, the area around the wound was painful and swollen. It was foul smelling and cool to the touch. It was also alive with small white grubs eating their way into his brain. The men carried Wanderer into a lodge and laid him on the robes. Quanah and Sore-Backed Horse sat next to him. Most of the other people in the band gathered at the door, waiting outside.

"Where's Pecan?" Wanderer asked in a whisper.

"I don't know," said Quanah.

Wanderer tried to raise himself, but was too weak. He could only open his eyes briefly.

"You left your brother behind?"

"We were trying to save your patched hide," said Sore-Backed Horse. "Pecan must be with Cruelest One. He was taking care of the ponies. He'll be all right. And Brother," Sore-Backed Horse leaned forward with the good news. "We took over a hundred scalps. Placido's people will never recover from that raid."

Wanderer relaxed. His mouth curved slightly, but it was still a taut, white line holding in the pain. Quanah knew his father had decided to die, but he tried once more to save him.

"Let me call Wears Out Moccasins. She can help you."

"No. If your mother can't help me I want no help." His voice was a whisper, and Quanah bent over to hear him. "My son."

"Yes, Father."

"Fight them. Never become a red white man like the coffee chiefs. White men work. A man who works cannot dream. And it is only through dreams that we achieve wisdom."

Then his voice failed altogether. He sang his death song silently, only his lips moving. His heart gave a final flutter and stopped.

Daily, for three years, Naduah asked her uncle Isaac when they would go in search of Wanderer and her sons.

"Soon," he always replied. "When the war has ended." But it never ended. White people didn't stop raiding when the weather was bad or when it was convenient to form temporary treaties with their enemies. They fought on and on, year after dreary year.

"Cynthia Ann, it's getting dark and cold out there. You and the child come in now," Bess called from the door. Then she pulled her head back in and muttered to her husband, "That child oughter be in bed, sick as she is, and not sitting out exposed to the bad night airs."

"Being in bed won't help her now, Mother. Let them be," said Isaac Parker.

They're afraid, thought Naduah. *They're afraid of the night and the full moon. They're afraid of the People, of Wanderer*. Comanche raiders were striking deeper and deeper into the settlements. The roads were crowded with people fleeing east. Naduah's aunt and uncle had packed as much as they could fit into their old wagon. They'd tied the cow to the tailboard and cages of squawking chickens along the sides. They'd called the hounds, shuttered the windows, and driven here, to the house of Naduah's younger brother, Silas, and his wife, Amelia. Naduah was one hundred miles farther away from the country of the Noconi.

Every day she prayed for the raid that her family and neighbors dreaded. She begged the spirits, if there were any here, to send the warriors swooping down on this house, this kind prison with the white picket fence and the long, airy gallery covered with trumpet vine. She would protect the people in it, ask that their lives be spared. But she would ride away with Wanderer and the war party.

"Cynthia Ann Parker, come inside."

Naduah rose slowly and carried Flower to their rocker in the corner by the hearth. The child whimpered softly in pain, as though by now she knew that crying was futile. Her joints were red and swollen and tender to the touch. "The rheumatics," Bess called it. For three days Flower had vomited everything they fed her. She was weak and emaciated. As Naduah held her, she crooned a lullaby of the People.

> *I will wrap you in a blanket of wind.*
> *I will swing you in a cradle of dreams.*
> *I will sing you a lullaby of grass.*

The child was five years old. She spoke the white man's tongue. She used the People's language only when she was alone with her mother. They sat for hours in the evenings on the porch until the mosquitoes or the cold became too insistent. Then they retreated to the chair by the hearth.

Aunt Bess had tried to insist that Naduah speak English to Flower, but Naduah had only looked at her in that stubborn, silent way. And Bess let the subject drop. So every night, in a low voice, Naduah told her daughter stories about her people. Sometimes she had to stop, a cord of longing tight around her throat, throttling her words.

In winter she recited stories about Old Man Coyote. In summer she told about swimming in the river and the games the children played. Or she described riding across the plains on a pony that flew like the wind. And she told Flower about the father she couldn't remember. Naduah knew that the stories were all the same to the child. The trickster tales were as real to her as the stories of her mother's own childhood. Her father was a mythical hero, like Old Man Coyote.

Naduah brushed the long, dark hair from Flower's dry forehead. She felt the heat pulsing under her hand. Aunt Bess had called a white man's doctor for her. He had stared down her throat and up under her eyelids. Then he had gone away shaking his head. Naduah had seen the defeat in his eyes.

Naduah did what she could for Flower. But her bag of healing roots and herbs was gone. She was only allowed to gather the few plants that the whites knew about. And many of the ones that Medicine Woman had used didn't grow here anyway. Her power was gone too. As time passed Naduah felt it shrink within her, like the river as it dries in a drought. The spirits avoided this country, where the land was mangled by plows and the trees were cut and their stumps burned.

Finally Flower slept for the first time in two days. Naduah held her tighter and willed her to live. Through both their dresses she could feel the heat from the child's body. Her arm began to numb, but she dared not move for fear of jostling her and waking her with pain.

The Parkers seemed to understand. They blew out the candles that they didn't carry with them, and went quietly to their bedrooms. Mrs. Parker returned with a blanket and draped it gently over Naduah and Flower. Naduah looked up at her with tears brimming in her eyes.

"Such a dear little girl. She's all you have, isn't she?" murmured Mrs. Parker, stroking Naduah's hair, and laying a cool hand on Flower's fevered forehead. "You poor, lost soul." She went to bed, her long, full skirts swishing like dry leaves across the clapboard floor. Huge, shifting shadows followed her candle across the room. Then there was only the fire in the hearth with its warm, flickering light and its comforting crackle. Naduah nodded and finally fell asleep.

She awoke with a start and knew something was wrong. Flower was cool to the touch. Frantically Naduah felt for a heartbeat. She shook the child gently to waken her, but Flower's small soul had slipped away while her mother slept. She had set off on her long journey alone. Soon she would be stiff.

Naduah's wail filled the room and pounded at the heavy walls. It burst from the cabin and spiraled off through the darkness in search of the child's spirit. The loneliness and grief pent up for years found a voice. Her screams were so intense and loud it seemed as though they would tear her inside.

"Oh, good Lord!" Bess Parker stood in the door of her bedroom, her fists crammed into her mouth, her eyes wide with horror. Isaac Parker and his nephew Silas held long, tapering candles high so they could see.

"Stop it, Cynthia," shouted Isaac. "Oh, my God." He gave the candle to his wife and rushed to grab her arm, but she was too strong.

The knife grazed his hand, cutting through the skin. She had bared her own breasts. They were red with the blood from long gashes across them. Before Isaac could react, Naduah laid the first two fingers of her left hand on the table and hacked them off. Still there wasn't enough pain to blot out the torment in her heart. The blade was at her throat when Isaac grabbed it.

Silas and Amelia held her while Isaac twisted the butcher knife from her hand. She collapsed onto the floor, sobbing and raking her fingernails across the boards. Bess ran around the room collecting all the knives and cleavers, axes and anything that could be used as a weapon. She fled into her bedroom to hide them, then returned to kneel next to Naduah. Ignoring the blood, she threw her arms around her and sobbed with her, rocking her as though she were a child.

It took Naduah a week to cry herself dry. Then she sat out on the front porch in the sepia light of winter. All day and into the night she stared toward the west. With her tears went all hope of seeing Wanderer again. She refused the food that Bess and Amelia brought her. The only reason to eat was to live.

❧ 56 ❧

The wonderful aroma of coffee lay over everything. Army cooks had emptied huge sacks of green coffee beans into iron pans. They had roasted them, then ground them. Now the coffee was steeping in thirty twenty-gallon iron kettles near Medicine Lodge Creek. The coffee was almost ready, and almost thick enough to slice. Crowds were gathering to dip their tin cups or their cups of horn or deer hooves into it.

Even in October the south Kansas sun was hot. Under brush shelters the sweating, swearing cooks dispensed bread and beans and salt pork to hundreds of Indians who had no concept of waiting in line. Tin ladles clattered against tin plates as the beans were dished out. Beyond the tangle of massed army supply wagons and ambulances, cattle bellowed as they were killed and butchered for the evening meal. Flies buzzed in thick clouds around the area.

The army field kitchens operated day and night. They had to. They were expected to feed four thousand warriors and their families and the one thousand soldiers who had come as an escort for the peace commission from Washington. It was autumn 1867, and the largest number of representatives from the southern plains tribes ever assembled had come for honey talk. There were Kiowa, Kiowa-Apache, Southern Cheyenne, Arapaho, and the People.

Sam Houston had once said about the Indians, "Either feed them or kill them. And leaving out the humanity of the thing, it is cheaper to feed them." Congress agreed. The congressional committee set up to study the Indian question in 1866 had reported that it cost one million dollars to kill each Indian. And so they had arranged this meeting.

It was a spectacle for the ears as well as the eyes. There were shouts and war whoops, galloping hoofs, drumming and bugling and sergeants shouting orders. There were horse races and close-order drills, flannel and calico streamers and neat military flags. There were feathers and flashing sabers. The even white rows of A-shaped army tents, each with the black chimney of its Sibley stove precisely aligned, were surrounded by pale yellow conical lodges scattered over the grassy hills. Many of the lodges, especially those of the Cheyenne, were gaudily painted with hunting scenes and geometric designs.

Everywhere, there were animals. Ponies and mules, cavalry mounts, oxen and cattle grazed for miles in all directions. Excited dogs ran about in packs, and so did boys.

The Penateka had arrived the night before from their reservation in Oklahoma Territory to the south. The Yamparika and the Quohadi and the Noconi were there too. Wanderer's people were no longer called Noconi, however. In respect for their dead chief they had changed their name to Dert-sa-nau-yu-ca, Those Who Move Often. Or, as they were more simply referred to by some, Messy Campers.

Sore-Backed Horse had taken over as civil chief of the band that Wanderer had led. He had adopted Quanah and Pecan, and when Pecan died of cholera, Sore-Backed Horse had mourned him as a son. But much as Quanah loved his father's old friend, he often disagreed with him. He was disagreeing with him now.

"Uncle, how can you even consider signing the white man's paper? They always lie, those papers." Quanah was twenty-two and far along the trail to becoming a leader. Sore-Backed Horse's deci-

sion to join the peace chiefs was an affront to Wanderer's memory. It
was also a threat to Quanah's future as a warrior.

"We cannot fight change, my son. Even your father said that
everything changes in a man's lifetime. One cannot kill change like
one can kill a grizzly or a Ute."

"Nothing could change my father. He would never have given
away the country he loved."

"We're not giving away anything. One cannot give away the land.
Black marks on a paper mean nothing. The white people make
promises and we make promises. They never keep theirs. So why
should we keep ours? The blankets they promised us two years ago
were so flimsy they fell apart under our saddles. We never bothered
to go back for the rest of them. And most of the things they promise
never arrive. But they're giving out presents here. They have saddles and bridles and sugar and coffee and tobacco and paint, too
many things to name."

"But not weapons or ammunition," Quanah reminded him.

"No. We'll have to steal those or get them from Ho-say and his
men." Sore-Backed Horse doubled over, wracked by a spell of
coughing that wrenched his insides. He spit and saw that there were
flecks of blood in the sputum. He had noticed them for the first time
that morning. *What a silent enemy age is,* he thought, studying the red
spots, like chips of bright paint. *It has crept up on me like a spider stalks
her prey, and it has clouded my eyes with webs.* But in return, age had
burdened him with a clear inner sight. He knew how the future
would be. He could see what the white men could do. He wished he
were still blind with the optimism and arrogance of youth, like his
beloved friend's son. Life was so much simpler and full of promise
when one was young.

A tall, thin, slightly stooped figure approached the group of men
sitting with Quanah and Sore-Backed Horse. Philip McCusker was
an official interpreter for the treaty talks. He was liked and respected
by all the tribes. He was the second husband of Weasel, Something
Good's daughter. He had married her after her first man was killed
in a hunting accident. He understood the People as few white men
did.

He sat down beside Quanah and accepted the pipe that was
passed him. His thick, droopy mustache draped over the stem of it.
He drew a puff and passed it on. He inquired politely about each
man's family. He discussed the weather and praised the new Remington rolling block rifles that were beginning to appear on the
frontier. Then he spoke in an undertone to Quanah.

"May I speak with you alone?"

Quanah nodded and rose. Together they climbed a high, grass-covered rise overlooking the vast encampment.

"What is it, Ma-cus-ka?"

"I have word of your mother."

"Is she alive?" Quanah grabbed McCusker's arm as though to shake the information from him.

"No, my brother," said McCusker. "The words I must speak are sharp and painful like knives. I do not wish to drive them into my brother's heart. But I must." He paused.

"Did they kill her? Torture her?" Quanah looked ready to take on the entire white race single-handedly.

"No. They were kind to her. They treated her as one of them. But she refused to become white. She was always one of the People. She died of a broken heart."

"When?"

"Three, maybe four years ago. They gave her a fine burial with an elaborate ceremony. The women wept for her, and they left flowers on her grave."

"Do you know where she's buried?"

"I can find out. But you can't go there, Quanah. They are so afraid of the People there that they would kill you."

"And my sister?"

"She died of a fever. She was five years old. Everyone loved her."

Quanah felt bereft, totally alone. His mother had been dead for three or four years. What had he been doing when life left her? Had he been eating, sleeping, lying with a woman, gambling perhaps while she suffered? Why hadn't he felt her going? There should have been some message from her spirit, some disturbance in the daily order of things. Some farewell. What had her life been like among the strangers that were her family? There were so many questions he wanted to ask, yet he knew that McCusker probably couldn't answer many of them. He tried an easy one.

"What manner of people are my mother's white kin?"

McCusker pondered that question.

"They're good people. They're very respected among the whites. And very religious."

"The white man's religion," said Quanah contemptuously.

"Religion is religion. You have to admit the whites have very powerful medicine."

"Bad medicine. They use sickness and destruction of Mother Earth as their weapons."

"The Parkers are far from the People's land. They do not covet it. Nor do they bring sickness."

"Pau-kers?"

"Parker. That's the name your mother's people use for their whole family. They add Parker after their own names."

There was a strange light in Quanah's gray eyes, the dawn of an idea that had never occurred to him before. Suddenly he saw his mother's wonderful deep-blue eyes. They were eyes that he had loved as a child for the light in them, for the laughter and tenderness in them, not for their strange color. They were the eyes of a white person. The realization hit him. He wasn't alone. He had kin he had never met. Might never meet. White kin.

"My mother's family is my family. I too am a Par-ker."

"Yes, you are. Fair and square."

"Quanah Par-ker." Quanah liked the sound of it.

"Pleased to meet you, Mr. Parker." McCusker laughed and stuck out his bony hand. Quanah shook it hard.

"Ma-cus-ka."

"Yes."

"This changes nothing. The white eyes are still my enemies. I will make war on them until I die. They have killed my entire family. And they are destroying the band my father led. Soon Those Who Move Often will be as much a joke among the warriors as the Penateka are now."

Below them there was a stir among the thousands of men. Criers from the various tribes were riding through their camps, beating their small hand drums and calling the warriors to the opening of the treaty talks. Most of them had been preparing all morning. Each man was carefully painted and dressed in his best clothes. Their shirts and leggings were heavy with decorations. The ponies were covered with streamers and feathers, bells and paint. The milling and confusion began to take on order as the horsemen converged on the plain where they would make their entrance. The leaders of the tribes had already decided what that entrance would be like.

"Will you join them, Quanah?"

"No. I will watch from here."

"I must go, then. They need me to translate."

Quanah embraced McCusker. He gripped him by the shoulders and stared him straight in the eye. Both men were over six feet tall.

"My friend," Quanah said, "the news you brought was sad. But I am in your debt for bringing it."

"Your mother and father were much loved by my wife and her family."

"Tell Something Good and Weasel that my heart grieves with them over the death of Pahayuca. I heard here that he died, but not how."

"Cholera. It was bad this summer."

"Soon all the old ones will be gone. Their smoking lodges will be empty and their fires cold. Who will replace them?"

"The People's leaders will have to change, Quanah. You can no more stop the white men than you can stop the wind or turn back the rivers. And you will be one of those leaders. You must make the choice. Continue stubbornly in the old ways and you will be like the buffalo that stampedes blindly toward a sheer cliff. I must hurry. The white men will be looking for me."

The two men saluted each other, and McCusker ran down the hill, his arms out to keep his balance. Quanah stood watching the spectacle below him.

The cavalry was lining up four abreast, rank on rank of them. The four civilian commissioners and the three generals rode at the head of the long column. The Indians had formed a huge triangle, like an arrowhead with the point aimed at the soldiers. There was a long pause, the massed, armed horsemen splendid and dark and shifting against the yellow grass of the slope. Then suddenly the wedge was in motion. Each man spurred his horse forward as fast as he could fly.

When the warriors reached the edge of the huge, level plain, the point of the wedge swerved and began to circle. Riders peeled away from it in precise lines, until they formed five concentric circles, all moving at a headlong pace. The enormous rings moved toward the white men, shifting forward as the riders closest to the soldiers swung out in imperceptibly wider arcs and those farthest away closed in.

About fifty yards from the column of tense soldiers, the wheel stopped as suddenly as it had started. A wild, ululating war cry rose from several thousand throats. Black Kettle of the Cheyenne, Satanta of the Kiowa, Ten Bears of the Yamparika Comanche, and Sore-Backed Horse of the Dertsanauyuca rode slowly forward. Each of them accompanied a pair of commissioners back toward the wheel.

The warriors parted to make a neat aisle through the five circles. The chiefs led the commissioners through the rows of riders, silent except for the fluttering of feathers on their shields and lances and the jingling of bells on their shirts and leggings. In the center a young man waited with the ornate, three-foot long pipe with the bowl of smooth, polished red catlinite. He held it carefully in his outstretched palms. Groups of eagle feathers, strips of white ermine fur, and a panel of intricate beading dangled from the carved stem. After the smoking ceremony, the talks began.

Quanah stayed with the Quohadi who refused to participate in

the talks. Big Bow reported back at the end of each day as they sat
around their evening meal of roast mule. The lights from the campfires twinkled over the dark hills for miles in all directions. The night
was cool, like black satin on the skin. The noises of the vast encampment were muted and remote. The starry sky seemed close enough
to touch.

"How do the talks go? What demands are the white men making?" asked Quanah.

"The same as always. We must change the road we walk or we
will suffer and die. The white men want to help us."

"That much is the truth anyway. They want to help us suffer and
die," broke in Deep Water. Big Bow went on patiently.

"They say they'll set aside part of the best lands for our exclusive
home before the white settlers take it all away."

"Let them try," said Buffalo Piss angrily.

"They'll set aside land that won't support even a few families."
Sun Name of the Yamparika had grown rounder with the years, but
he was still powerfully built. He glowered at those around him. "I
told them I would rather stay out on the prairie and eat dung than be
penned up on a reservation."

"You won't have to eat dung, brother. There will always be
buffalo," said Quanah. "When those on the reservation live better
than we do out on the Staked Plains, then it will be time to come in."

"What did the leaders of the People say, Big Bow?" asked Buffalo
Piss.

"Ten Bears made the longest speech. He said, 'You want to put us
on a reservation, to build us houses and make us medicine lodges. I
do not want them. I was born upon the prairie, where the wind
blows free and there is nothing to break the light of the sun. I want
to die there and not within walls. When I was in Was-in-tone the
Great White Father told me that all the Comanche land was ours and
that no one should hinder us in living upon it. So why do you ask us
to leave the rivers and the sun and the wind to live in houses?

" 'If the Texans had kept out of my country, there might have
been peace. But that which you say we must live on is too small. The
Texans have taken away the best places, where the grass grew the
thickest and the timber was the best. Had we kept that, we might
have done the things you ask. But it is too late. The white man has
the country we loved. And we wish only to wander the prairie until
we die.'

"He said more, but that was the important part," finished Big
Bow. "I sneaked among the wagons when it got dark," he went on,
with his old mischievous smile. "They really are full of presents.
One entire wagon is piled with pots and pans and buckets. Another

has mirrors and boxes of vermillion and beads. My women will be ecstatic. Ah." A blissful, lascivious expression crossed Big Bows' handsome, unlined face, "How they will love me when I bring them so many wonderful things."

"Big Bow." Quanah was shocked. "You won't sign the paper!"

"Of course not. But I'll collect the presents. One Indian looks like another to them."

"What other presents were there?" asked Buffalo Piss. And the conversation went on through the night.

After the last day of the talks, outside their tents, the peace commissioners sat in canvas chairs and listened to the sounds of drumming and chanting, shouting and laughter that surrounded them. Philip McCusker sat with them, his long legs on each side of the chair, his elbows on his knees, and his chin propped on the palms of his hands. He stared into the fire as the men around him smoked and congratulated themselves on their work. McCusker ignored them and thought about his recent trip to Washington. Getting the chiefs to sign the treaty was simple compared to getting Congress to ratify it. And then follow through with the promises.

Washington City. The very words depressed McCusker. He had been relieved to return west. The city was still a shambles from the five years of fighting that had gone on in and around it. There were still temporary hospitals in the parks. The cobblestone streets were broken and pitted by the iron-bound wheels of the heavy guns and caissons. All the trees were gone, fed into the soldiers' campfires. The Potomac was thick with raw sewage and debris. It stank. The whole city stank.

In the midst of it all, men tried to go on running a bitterly divided country. McCusker couldn't blame Congress for not paying as much attention to the Indian question as they should. The problems of Reconstruction made it seem trivial. Three hundred and eighty-four people had been murdered last year by fellow Texans. Twenty-six had been killed by Indians.

Men in Washington cynically blamed the Indian troubles on vengeful whites and profiteers, crooked freighters and contractors and railroaders supplying the army. They pointed to the federal Indian administration, which was most certainly corrupt. And they accused the conquered confederate Texans of exaggerating reports of Indian raids. Chasing Indians gave the federal occupying troops something to do besides harrass the Texans.

It was an impossible situation. McCusker could clearly see what would happen when this commission returned to Washington. Congress would tie the treaty up in endless debate, or table it altogether.

The Indians would become impatient and disillusioned and hit the raid trail again. Some of those politicians meant well, but they had no notion of the complexity of the problem. And others gave the Indians no thought once they had gotten their land from them.

McCusker saw the war stretching out for years, and costing millions of dollars and thousands of lives. As long as there were young men like Quanah Parker around, there would be war. And it would be the ugliest kind of war, with women and children the victims. McCusker shook his head to clear it. He felt the need to get away from the white men and their talk of killing for sport and their discussion of tumbling Indian squaws. Their smug superiority sickened McCusker. He rose and mumbled his good-night. He collected his bedroll from his tent and ambled off in search of Quanah and the Quohadi.

He awoke the next morning to a bizarre cacophony. The men dozing around the glowing embers leaped up and grabbed for their weapons. McCusker began to laugh.

"What is it, Ma-cus-ka?" asked Quanah.

"Bugles. Good Lord, I forgot. One of those wagons had over three thousand surplus army bugles. The stupid sons of bitches must have just passed them out with the rest of the trinkets. Those Injuns must have started demanding their presents at cock's crow. No more rest for the wicked, boys. Up and at 'em. Any of that mule left? I'm hungry."

They took their time eating and packing their equipment. Then they moved off slowly through the main encampment, looking disdainfully at the chaos around the army wagons. Indians were scattering in all directions with their arms loaded.

"Look at Kicking Bird," said McCusker. The dignified Kiowa chief wore moccasins and a breechclout and a tall, black stovepipe hat resplendent with yards of red ribbons. Four ribbon streamers hung down his back almost to the ground.

"What will you do now, Quanah?" asked the interpreter.

"Can I trust you, Ma-cus-ka?"

"Yes, Brother. I interpret. I don't carry tales or spill secrets."

"We will raid the new cattle trails. The white men have started driving large herds north through Texas. We will steal their stock and trade it with Ho-say Tafoya near Quitaque."

"Well," said McCusker, "the meek might inherit the earth, but they'll never possess its cattle. So you're going back to Texas."

"Of course. It's my home. I'll stay on the Staked Plains with the Quohadi and raid from there."

"Then you won't consider surrendering and collecting annuities on the reservation? They'll pay you every year." McCusker knew the answer.

"We don't need their presents. We'll take what we want. Tell the white chiefs the Quohadi are warriors. We'll surrender when the yellowlegs come to the Staked Plains and beat us." Quanah lifted his lance in salute to McCusker as he rode away with the Quohadi. "Good-bye, Ma-cus-ka," he shouted. "Remember Quanah Parker. Maybe someday you'll hear my name in Texas." Quanah grinned.

McCusker waved back. *I'm sure I will, Mr. Parker.*

➤ 57 ↩

In the summer of 1870, a blond, blue-eyed young hunter, fresh from the east, was killing buffalo to supply the army with meat. He shipped fifty-seven of the hides home to his older brother in New York City to see if they could be sold. As the hides were being trundled in an open wagon down Broadway, they were spotted by two tanners. The men followed the wagon to its destination and offered the hunter's brother three dollars and fifty cents apiece for the skins.

After experimenting with them, they ordered two thousand more at the same price, seven thousand dollars worth in all. The new tanning process they had invented made hides collected at any time of the year usable. The brother took care of his affairs, packed up, and left for the Great Plains to help obtain the hides. The stampede was on. Thousands of men, eager to get rich quickly, followed him.

Christian Sharps obliged the buffalo hunters by producing a heavy rifle with an octagonal barrel that could stand great pressure. The gun's rear sight was calibrated to one thousand yards. The rifle could drop a full-grown buffalo at six hundred yards, and a good marksman could kill two hundred and fifty animals a day with it.

Dodge City became the center of the trade as loaded wagons converged there to meet the new railroad. The huge mountains of hides and the men who brought them in could be smelled a long way off. And the hunters usually weren't the type to be fastidious anyway. Signs saying "No Buffalo Hunters" began appearing in Dodge City whorehouses.

A little over a year later, in late October of 1871, Quanah and a party of young men rode south from the Canadian River toward Blanco Canyon at the edge of the Staked Plains. They were headed for the supply camp of Bad Hand, or Three-Fingered Kinzie, as Colonel Ranald Mackenzie was called.

Quanah and his war party had been harrying Bad Hand and his soldiers for weeks. The Quohadi would swoop down from the high ridges in a long flying V-formation and then scatter into the tall grass before the useless massed charges of the yellowlegs. Now Quanah was determined to find the supply camp his scouts had reported and relieve Bad Hand of the neccessity of providing forage for his horses and mules.

Quanah's pony snorted and skittered a few steps to the side. Quanah put a hand on his neck to quiet him. The horse was all black and groomed until he shone like obsidian. He was a descendant of Night through Raven, and old Polecat was intensely jealous of him.

All the ponies were nervous, and the men knew why. Circling above the ridge ahead of them were swirls of vultures. As the raiders topped the rise, the smell hit them. The plain below them was dotted with putrifying buffalo carcasses. But there was something strange about the kill. The buffalo had been skinned, but the meat had been left to rot.

"Who would waste so much meat?" At fifty-five, Cruelest One was by far the oldest in the group.

"White men," said Quanah. He pulled his bandana over his mouth and nose to keep out as much of the stench as possible.

"Shouldn't we go around?"

"No. There isn't time. I want to find Bad Hand's camp by night-fall. We'll attack by the light of the full moon."

Mackenzie and his officers were just finishing the evening meal when the attack came. They were relaxing with their cigars and pipes when they heard the hoofbeats. They leaped to their feet.

"Stampede?" called someone.

"No," said Mackenzie wearily. "Quanah Parker."

By that time they all knew who the young war leader was. The Texans were even taking a perverse pride in him. He was one of theirs, after all. And he was leading the damn Yankees on a hell of a chase all over the Panhandle.

"God damn it!" yelled someone. "Not again."

The men ran for cover and grabbed weapons as the first riders thundered screaming into camp. The ponies' hooves sent sparks flying from the scattered campfires.

Quanah led the raid. He was larger than the others, and to the soldiers stranded on foot, he looked even bigger. His face was painted as black as the horse he rode. His expression of fierce joy was grotesque in the fire's light. The bells on his hunting shirt and leggings jingled madly as he pounded his pony's sides to hold his lead over the others.

With his right hand he fired his father's Colt repeater. With his left, he flapped a blanket over his head to panic the stock and send it stampeding in front of him. His men followed closely. They all careened through the camp. They leaped the small tents of the enlisted men, sometimes coming down in the middle of one and thrashing as it tangled around the horse's legs. They overturned wagons and scattered equipment.

Then, as suddenly as they appeared, they were gone. Seventy of Mackenzie's horses and mules went with them. The soldiers heard the Quohadi shouting insults and taunts. They yipped to their new livestock as they rode away into the cold, starry night. Mackenzie bent down to right his overturned camp chair and fold it. *All the plains tribes are fine horse thieves,* he thought, *but you have to give the laurels to the Comanches.*

"Round up what horses they missed. We're going after them."

"But, sir, there's a storm a-brewing."

"We're going after them, Lieutenant."

Overhead, the stars winked out like snuffed candles as clouds scudded over them. The wind began to blow colder. *Damn,* thought Mackenzie, *another Texas norther. They always arrive at the worst time. But then,* he asked himself wryly, *when would be the best time?* At least the same wind was blowing on Quanah Parker and his horde of ruffians. Somehow Mackenzie doubted that it bothered them as much.

He would have been gratified the next day to see his nemesis, wary of army reprisals, leading his entire village in a retreat through the blizzard. Men, women, and children braced against the stinging, blinding needles of ice that blew in their faces. When the sleet changed to a heavy, wet snow, they floundered through drifts of it.

In the three years that followed, the People's numbers dwindled in the wild. Bad Hand and his soldiers continued to hound them, destroying their camps and food supplies, taking their women and children hostage. But in the end, it wasn't the army that exacted the worst toll of them.

"The white buffalo killers, those are the ones you should fight." Sun Name was an old man. He was still ready to go into battle, but he didn't mind letting the younger men travel from band to band. Quanah was collecting warriors for the battle that would drive the white eyes from their lands for all time. And Sun Name was telling him where to concentrate his efforts.

Quanah nodded. Across the council fire he saw Esa Tai, Coyote Dung, stand to speak. And he curbed his impatience. He had heard what Coyote Dung had to say many times. Coyote Dung was young, but already he was a powerful medicine man. He had witnesses who swore they saw bullets bounce off him and who saw him belch wagonloads of cartridges. Others had watched him ascend to the sky and confer with the Great Spirit. *He probably bored the Great Spirit too,* thought Quanah.

Coyote Dung was a man with a vendetta against the whites who had murdered his uncle. And he had a need for recognition that was unusual even for one of the People. But he was useful. Warriors were flocking to join the war party. Quanah and Coyote Dung had smoked with the leaders of the various bands and tribes who refused to live permanently on the reservations.

They were with Sun Name's Yamparika now. They discussed possible targets for the raid, and planned where and when to meet. When Quanah received the pipe, he wrapped his robe around him and spoke.

"I have heard the words of Sun Name, and they have found a place in my heart. As we rode here, we passed among dead buffalo lying as far as the eye could see. Where once herds moved and grazed and followed the seasons, there is now only death. The crows and the vultures are so gorged they cannot fly.

"The Medicine Lodge treaty of seven years ago promised our people that the white men would not hunt buffalo south of the Arkansas River. But now their guns are heard along the Canadian. They break the law and the soldiers don't stop them. They have built houses near the crumbling walls of the trader Hook Nose's old store. From there they send east wagons piled with robes. They are far from the forts. The patrols do not go there often. I say we attack them and stop their slaughter of the buffalo."

As the men discussed Quanah's plan, he elaborated on it in his head. By the time the council was over he had a clear vision of the form his hatred and vengeance would take. Through a steady, misty rain he walked to Sun Name's guest lodge, where he was staying. A figure huddled outside the door, shivering under a blanket. The mist had covered the blanket with tiny drops that sparkled in the firelight coming from inside. Perhaps it was one of the women who had prepared the lodge for him. But why was she waiting outside? Then the figure coughed, and Quanah realized it wasn't a woman.

"Sore-Backed Horse," he whispered harshly, startled to see the old man. "Why are you here? The young men are talking of killing you and the Penateka who have sided with the white men."

Sore-Backed Horse coughed again, unable to stop. He choked on the blood caught in his throat. With a hemorrhaging lung, he had ridden for days through the cold rain of spring to find Quanah.

"Come inside," said Quanah, taking him gently by the arm. He dropped the flap shut after them, closing them from view. He replaced the soaked blanket with a warm, dry robe. Sore-Backed

Horse's large, sad eyes were bright with fever. His gray-streaked hair was cut short in mourning like a woman's. The deep lines that went from his nostrils to the corners of his drooping mouth were carved by sorrow. Quanah saw the hunger on the old man's gaunt face, and offered him some of the stew left by Sun Name's first wife. Then he asked again, "Why are you here, Uncle?"

"To ask you to come to the agency so there will be no more bloodshed."

"And do you live well on the reservation?"

"No. You know we don't. The rations don't arrive on time or they're stolen. There's dust in the flour and maggots in the meat. I'm too old to hunt, and my family is dead. I must beg my food from the officers at Fort Sill."

"And you want us to live like that? Give up our old ways for that?"

"Quanah, they'll eventually kill you all if you don't surrender and come in."

"And be counted."

"Yes, and be counted."

That was as bad as anything else the white eyes did. Everyone knew it was bad luck to count the People.

"I loved your father as a brother and you as a son. I do not want to see you hunted and brought in in chains. They hang renegades. Strangle them so their souls are doomed." Sore-Backed Horse didn't mention that the whites had given him the terrible responsibility of choosing whom among the raiders would be executed. "I do not want to go looking for your bones, bleaching somewhere among those of the dead buffalo."

"Uncle, I know that to fight the white men is to be doomed as a people. But they give us no choice. I would rather starve here as a free man than to be forever a prisoner."

"And your wives and children? What of their future?"

"We are fighting for their future."

"Then I wish you well. If one of us kills a white man's ox to feed his starving family, the white men come to punish us, they make war over it. But they continue to kill the buffalo that we need for food. They don't eat what they kill, and they go unpunished. I am an old man. My hope has been all used up, wasted. But I must have some left, enough to pray that you are successful."

Quanah began packing his supplies of pemmican and jerky into saddle bags. He added piles of blankets.

"Here," he said. "Take these. They will last you a while anyway. I'll ride with you until dawn. It would not be safe for you to be here when the sun rises."

Sore-Backed Horse hesitated.

"Take them, Uncle," said Quanah gently. "You would have done the same for my father or myself."

Unable to speak, Sore-Backed Horse took the food and blankets and went with Quanah out into the night.

Billy Dixon was staggering with exhaustion when he entered Jim Hanrahan's saloon at the tiny settlement of Adobe Walls. Like the other three buildings, the place was made of double rows of posts set upright in the ground and then filled in with packed dirt. Even at that hour of the morning there were men drinking at the splintery bar made mostly of packing crates.

"I need a drink, Jim."

"You look it, Dixon."

"Dudley and Williams are dead. God, are they dead."

"What happened?" William Barclay Masterson was a fastidious dresser, a dapper young man. He looked out of place among the grimy faces in the saloon.

"Injuns. They propped their heads up." Billy Dixon downed the glass of whiskey in a long swallow and coughed.

"What do you mean?" asked Hanrahan, leaning over the counter.

"The Comanches propped Dudley and Williams' heads up so they could see what was happening to them."

"I don't think I want to hear this," someone mumbled.

"The Injuns cut off their tongues and ears and stuffed their balls in their mouths. Williams had a stake driven through his belly. They were both sliced into neat ribbons." With his knife Dixon demonstrated the pattern of the cuts in the air. Then he tapped his glass on the bar for a refill.

"Where were their bites?" asked Hanrahan as he poured. Most of the men carried home-made fifty-caliber cartridges emptied of powder and filled with cyanide. "Bites," they called them. A man would no more be without one than without his extra keg of water. When Indians attacked and there was no escape or defense, a hunter could always bite the bullet.

"I don't know where their bites were. Jesus! Another drink, huh, Jim?" Dixon turned to the men around him. "Anybody got a gun for sale? I lost mine in the river. The Indians were after me. Lost a wagonload of hides and all my supplies too."

"There must be something to all the rumors about Indians," said Masterson. "Think I'll see to my own weapons."

"Hey, Bat, how about selling me that extra round-barreled forty-four of yours." Dixon and Masterson were the two youngest men in the camp, and more than a cut above the average. They didn't associate much with the others, choosing each other's company instead.

The men at the camp spent an uneasy week. Buffalo hunters and their crews of skinners drifted in to take shelter. And they brought word of more killings. Antelope Jack and Blue Billy had been found in pieces.

On Saturday, June 27, 1874, twenty-six men had thrown their bedrolls down in the two stores and the saloon. The only woman in camp was Mrs. Olds, who helped her husband run the restaurant in one of the stores. The horses were locked in a corral made of heavy, sharpened pickets.

On a ridge overlooking Adobe Walls, Quanah and his pony were poised against the predawn sky. The dark gray clouds overhead looked like rippled slate formed on an ancient streambed, but they were beginning to break apart. The sky would be clear soon.

If his mother could have seen her son and his pony, she would have been startled. Painted for war, they looked like Wanderer and Night. Naduah would have had to come much closer to notice that Quanah's face was fuller than his father's. His eyes were deep gray rather than black. And the lids drooped over them, giving him a sleepy, sensual look that was accented by his broad cheekbones and wide, full mouth. From the front he looked like a warrior of the People. But in profile his nose sloped like his mother's rather than arching like his father's.

His upper body was bare. Beaver oil glistened on the muscles of his back and shoulders and chest. The elaborate tassels on the ends of his red breechclout reached below his knees when he stood. The wide edges of his leggings and the tops of his moccasins were crusted with intricate beading. Two tiny stuffed birds dangled from his pierced ears. His thick braids were wrapped in silky otter fur. An eagle feather hung from his scalplock.

Slowly, forms became visible behind him. There were men from the Quohadi, the Yamparika, and the Kotsoteka as well as Arapaho, Cheyenne, and Kiowa. The warriors from each band and tribe were led by their own chiefs. Coyote Dung rode off to one side. He was naked except for his rifle and lance. He had covered himself and his horse with ochre paint, and he wore sage in his hair. He said he needed no other covering. His medicine would protect him.

Quanah almost believed him. Coyote Dung had predicted that there would be fire in the sky as a sign that the Great Spirit would help them. And the fire had appeared, a glowing ball with a long streamer, like smoke, that moved imperceptibly across the black sky. It hung there still, advancing a little each night. Coggia's comet was unusually brilliant. The nebulous, hazy region around its nucleus had sharply defined layers visible to the naked eye. It was an awesome sight.

This raid couldn't fail. Even if Coyote Dung's medicine wasn't as powerful as he and his followers claimed, there were seven hundred picked warriors, the finest of four tribes. And Quanah had planned the raid well. There were only twenty-five to fifty men in the camp. Asleep.

He felt excitement stir deep inside him, below his stomach. Soon they would ride screaming through the flowers of the hillside and kill the hunters in their beds. They would teach the white eyes a lesson and drive them from the plains. None would dare venture back after this defeat. The black bugler, a deserter from the cavalry, held his horn ready to sound the charge.

The day was getting lighter. Quanah could now clearly see the four square, solid buildings nestled at the bottom of the high valley. They looked tiny there. Yet the Canadian River was far below even that, its sinuous course outlined in willows, cottonwoods, china berries, and hackberries below the bluff that defined the valley. Beyond the river was a magnificent view of layers of dark blue hills sweeping to a pale, blue-gray horizon. Birds began to sing in the tall grass. It would be a perfect day to fight.

From his position Quanah didn't see the spots of light shining from the small windows of Hanrahan's saloon. Nor could he see that the men inside weren't asleep. The crack of a ridge pole, strained to the breaking point under the tons of dry dirt that roofed the saloon, had awakened the men inside. For two hours they had labored to replace it. While the warriors prepared to attack, the white men were lined up at the bar having a drink at Hanrahan's expense.

Billy Dixon and Bat Masterson walked out into the clear, crisp morning air. They were relieving themselves, trying to spell their names in the dust, when Billy detected a slight movement at the top of the hill. Masterson saw him tense.

"What is it?" he asked.

"I don't know."

The two of them were backing toward the saloon, searching the crests of the hills around them, when the bugle sounded. As if a sorcerer had waved his wand, the ridges sprouted Indians. Each man was painted in wild patterns of ochre, red, and black, or white and yellow. The ponies were also decorated with streamers and feathers and paint. The warriors flowed down the flower-covered hillside, their war cries blending into one loud yodeling call that filled the valley. They looked as though they were pouring out of the rising sun itself. And they were bathed in its golden light.

Dixon and Masterson sprinted for the saloon door. They pounded on it as the bullets began kicking dust over their shoes. The door opened a crack, and they tumbled inside. Billy braced the barrel of his Sharps forty-four on a window ledge and began methodically picking off the riders before they even came close enough to use their own weapons. Other hunters, not dressed yet, were loading their rifles from belts of ammunition slung over their scratchy long wool underwear.

"Whooee!" Dixon couldn't contain his exuberance. He turned to grin at his friend. "Isn't this something? There must be a thousand of them. I'm glad I got to see it. Wish I had my Big Fifty, though."

"Dixon, you're a crazed lunatic." Masterson crouched against the wooden wall. He fed cartridges into his Remington with trembling fingers.

In a fury Quanah assaulted the door of the saloon, backing his pony into it in an attempt to batter it down. As the white men knocked mud from the chinks in the logs and began shooting through the openings, the crossfire became murderous. Quanah retreated to a safer distance and joined the riders circling the buildings. He hung from the far side of his pony and fired from under the horse's neck. But a truly safe distance was far beyond the range of Quanah's rifle.

The booming of the buffalo guns began drowning out the popping of the attackers' smaller weapons. The hunters themselves could recognize the sound of each one's Big Fifty by the way its owner chose to load it. The fourteen-pound Sharps could land a heavy, homemade cartridge, overloaded with one hundred and ten grains of powder, farther and more accurately than any gun made. And while most of the men in the camp knew little besides drinking and gambling, swearing and whoring, and perhaps horse stealing, they did know how to shoot.

As the hours went by and the day heated up, it became obvious that Coyote Dung's holy war wasn't going well. Many men had fallen, and their bodies had to be rescued for later burial. Quanah's pony was shot from under him, and as he took cover behind a rotting buffalo carcass, he was hit in the back by a ricocheting bullet. It wasn't a serious wound, but it paralyzed his shoulder and arm for hours. And it seemed to mean that one of his own men had tried to kill him.

The war party withdrew to a ridge high above the camp to find out who had fired on him. They didn't worry about the hunters escaping. There wasn't an animal left alive in the corral. When every man swore he hadn't fired the shot, the leaders were faced with the conclusion that the white men could fire unseen from behind.

A low muttering began against Coyote Dung, who still sat aloof on his pony. Then, as though the gods were playing with them, a stray bullet hit Coyote Dung's horse and dropped him where he stood. After that, no one had the nerve to attack the camp directly. For the rest of that day and into the next they laid siege to it from the cover of wagons and piles of hides, bushes and the corral fence.

Finally, disillusioned warriors began drifting away, defeated by the hunters' marksmanship and the range of their guns. Coyote Dung had found another horse and stood at bay on the ridge. He glared at the angry leaders who surrounded him. Quanah watched stonily as one of them, brandishing his quirt, advanced on the medicine man.

"It's not my fault the attack failed," shouted Coyote Dung. "A Cheyenne killed a skunk before the fight. He destroyed my medicine." He backed his horse away from the threatening men.

That may not be the only skunk who dies. Quanah turned his pony. He would return to the Staked Plains. There was no more he could do here.

In the buildings below them, the hunters began to relax. The acrid stench of gunpowder was clearing and someone had brought water from the well. The saloon still stunk of unwashed bodies, made even more pungent by fear, but the men were used to that.

"Bat, hand me your Sharps," said Dixon.

"What are you going to do? They've withdrawn."

"I can see some of them on that ridge over yonder."

"You're loco, Dixon. You can't hit them. They're a mile away."

"You wanna bet?"

"Hell, yes." Masterson held out his natty black bowler, and men dropped money into it.

Dixon squinted into his sight and took careful aim.

Quanah saw the tiny puff of smoke from the saloon window and saw the man with the quirt fall before hearing the rifle's faint boom. That ended the fight. Warriors scattered, totally defeated by a gun that could hit a man at a distance of a mile.

Night was falling. It was bitter cold. The wind moaned around the columns and misshapen lumps of rock in the narrow corridor off Palo Duro canyon. Quanah pulled his buffalo robe more tightly around him and hunkered as close to the shelter of the cliff face as he could. He sat alone on the ledge, halfway up the high canyon wall. One hundred lodges huddled below him along the frozen river.

The dark poles splaying out from the blackened hides around the smoke holes were all that set the tents apart from the snow that covered everything. The pony herd foraged for bark among the bare cottonwoods in the grove. The horses' mouths were cut and bleeding from gnawing on the frozen wood. The ground there was gray with the litter of stripped twigs, but Quanah was too far away to see the spots of blood that dripped from the animals' muzzles.

Across the canyon, on another ledge, Quanah saw a slight movement, one of his own sentries. His men were on watch. Nevertheless, he felt alone and desolate. He had listened to the advice of the council, but he had to make the decision. That was why he had come up here. It was as though being above everything could give him a clearer view of the future as well as the past and present.

He looked down at the still, silent village. He knew there were people there, gathered inside around their fires and the kettles that were almost empty. The kettle of his own wives and children was almost empty too. They were rationing out the remains of their own dead ponies. Each morning the boys dug paths through the snow to the herds and retrieved those that had died. They had to saw limbs from the frozen bodies. At least up here Quanah couldn't hear the babies crying with hunger.

It was March 1875. It had been the coldest winter anyone could remember. That afternoon a foraging party had brought in the body of Spaniard. They had found him, dressed in only a breechclout and moccasins, standing with one arm thrown across the back of his favorite war horse. Both he and the pony were frozen solid. The snow had shaken like powder from his frizzy gray hair as they lowered him from the pack pony. Now, in his mind, Quanah addressed him.

Greetings, my father's old friend. You left the reservation and the whiskey and came here to die with us. You chose to surrender to winter, to the plains, rather than to the white men.

Quanah allowed himself the indulgence of briefly considering suicide. But he knew he couldn't do it, as easy as it would be. His family needed him. His band needed him. And he felt helpless in the face of their desperate need.

Bad Hand and his soldiers had harried the Quohadi all fall and winter. Mackenzie's own men froze and starved and thirsted and cursed him, but at least they had no women and children to protect. They were free to patrol constantly and keep the bands unsettled and fleeing before them even in the worst weather.

Quanah and his men had tied the weaker ones in the band to their ponies to keep them from falling into a stupor of cold and exhaustion and sliding off. As they traveled through howling northers Quanah lashed his men with his quirt or his bow when they lay down in the snow and refused to go on. During the day the snow melted, then refroze into a glittering hard curst of ice. Quanah rubbed soot around the children's eyes to protect them from snow blindness, but it didn't help much. Exposed parts of their faces became puffy and blistered. Their eyes swelled shut. Lips became parched and cracked, and skin peeled off in sheets. When the temperature dropped to twenty below, fingers and toes froze and fell off.

As the drifts reached four feet deep, even the men could no longer break trails by walking upright. They had to crawl, putting their hands and knees in the holes left by those in front of them. After twenty or thirty men had crawled over a section of the trail, it was packed down enough for the horses and mules to pass. The cattle had died early in the winter. They had inhaled sleet and suffocated.

Somehow Quanah kept his people just ahead of Bad Hand's relentless pursuit. The other bands hadn't been as lucky or as resourceful. And they had all been betrayed by José Tafoya. The wizened little Comanchero hadn't done it willingly. When Bad Hand caught him, he had feigned ignorance of the People's whereabouts. But Mackenzie dispensed with the niceties of civilized behavior. He had ordered Tafoya strung high on a propped-up wagon tongue and strangled until his memory improved. José's wits had sharpened enough to remember the trails and hiding places of the Quohadi.

And Mackenzie had learned not to try to drive captured ponies back to the forts. When he had attacked the largest band of Quohadi left, he had ordered the ponies shot. Thousands of them. And he had burned the camp, lodges, food, robes, everything. Quanah had wept when he came across the destruction.

Had Coyote Dung cursed them all when he prophesied a winter such as they had never seen? His prediction for the summer certainly had come true. After the debacle at Adobe Walls, Coyote Dung had said that the rains would cease. And they had.

Quanah remembered how it had been. Even in the freezing cold of his perch he remembered. For two months the band had traveled across the dry, baked plains, with the ground cracking, the surface shriveling in the intense heat. Day after torturous day, the sun pulsed in a white sky and the horizon vibrated constantly. Waterholes and rivers and creeks dried up. The People dug in the dry beds for moisture. They filled their mouths with damp sand and tried to suck water from it.

They had sliced their horses' ears and drunk the blood. Finally some had gashed their own forearms to moisten their lips. Gaunt, hollow-eyed warriors doled the water out to the children. Quanah assigned a guard to the water paunches. His men threatened adults with death if they touched the supply being saved for the young ones. Many of their ponies died. Those that were left had backs raw and bloody from the constant traveling. Flocks of magpies swooped around the herd, diving and tearing at the horses' exposed flesh until they screamed and rolled in a frenzy to escape.

It had seemed as though nature itself was trying to defeat the People that last summer. As though the whites had managed to turn Mother Earth against them. When the sky blackened to the east in August, they faced it, waiting for the first cool wind that meant rain.

But the blackness on the horizon wasn't storm clouds. It was swarms of locusts. They covered the land in a living, seething mass. They ate every green plant that had managed to escape the drought, then they ate the nap from the blankets. The members of Quanah's band roasted them for food. Quanah remembered their brittle shells crunching as he bit into them.

It had seemed then, when his skin was hot to the touch and the heat penetrated his bone marrow, that he would never again be cool. He would never feel cold water rushing over him, never run barefoot in the snow or tilt his head to catch snowflakes on his tongue. Now he shivered in the wind.

But worst of all had been the fall hunt. Or what should have been the hunt. There were no buffalo left to kill. The hunting parties rode for hundreds of miles across the plains, searching for signs. But all they found were carcasses and bones. The herds of millions of animals that had blackened the prairie were gone.

There were those who believed the buffalo would return, that they had only migrated as they had in years past. But Quanah knew better. And even he had to force himself to accept the fact that they were really gone. If the buffalo could disappear, then anything was possible, any horror, any tragedy.

More than Bad Hand, more than the terrible drought and locusts of the summer and the cold of winter, hunger drove band after band to surrender and seek refuge on the reservation.

"I would rather stay out on the prairie and eat dung," Sun Name had said. The white men had made sure that there was no longer even that. Sun Name had been the last, but he had finally led his people eastward. Quanah had watched him go, his head bowed onto his chest.

Now Quanah knew they were alone on the Staked Plains, he and his small band of four hundred men, women, and children. They were the last of the People to taste freedom, as bitter as it was. A messenger had come from the reservation several days before. The word from Bad Hand was, "Surrender or watch your women and children die." And Quanah knew that Kinzie could do it. The messenger had told Quanah that because he had never signed a peace treaty with the white men he had broken no promises; he had fought to defend his homeland. Bad Hand respected Quanah as a courageous foe and would not allow him to be punished as a criminal.

Even after he had made his decision, Quanah stayed awhile longer on the ledge. He felt the wind and the cold with all his senses, tasting it and smelling it and hearing it too. He looked down on the magnificent white kingdom of Palo Duro canyon for the last time. Then he stood and stretched his cramped muscles. He walked slowly down the twisting trail to the canyon floor. As he walked, he watched the lodges glow in the deepening twilight.

A month later, at the head of his ragged, starving band, he rode down from the Staked Plains. He held his head high, his rifle cradled in his arms. His favorite wife, We-keah carried his shield and lance. Scouts must have seen them coming, because Bad Hand himself rode to meet them. Quanah advanced until he was knee to knee with the colonel. He stared him straight in the eye as he handed over his rifle. He said only one word.

"*Suvate*, it is finished."

Author's note

Quanah Parker's starving band was the last to enter the reservation at Fort Sill, Oklahoma Territory. They brought the total number of those who had surrendered to 1,597. Only one in every twelve of the People had survived the previous twenty-five years of warfare and disease.

The Comanche's surrender and removal to Indian Territory opened their land to the Texans. The frontier advanced farther in the next eight years than it had in the previous forty when the People had ferociously opposed it. Soon the plains were swarming with farmers and ranchers. The countryside became overgrazed. Miles of waving grasslands were reduced to barren stretches of mesquite scrub. Plows exposed the rich soil to the constant wind, which blew away tons of it over the years. Rivers, diverted to irrigate crops, became muddy trickles.

Bad Hand McKenzie kept his promise to Quanah. Because the young chief had signed no peace treaties, and so had never gone back on his word, he was not punished or imprisoned. He was not among the rebel leaders caged in an unfinished stone icehouse and fed meat that was thrown over the roofless walls. Nor was he sent to Florida in long, lonely exile, as many were.

But life was hard for the People on the reservation. The promised rations continued to be in short supply or of poor quality. Much of the food was unfit to eat. There were stones in the sacks of bacon and coal in the barrels of pork. Even with the best of intentions, transportation of the goods was a serious problem. Freight had to be hauled three hundred miles, often through deep mud and across swollen streams. Oxen caught Texas cattle fever and died, stranding entire wagon trains.

General Miles reported that "the pitiful annual allowances given them by the government were usually exhausted in six months." And the handouts were degrading, given grudgingly and accepted with resentment. Soldiers hunted the already scarce game on the reservation. It was an illegal practice that the fort's commander allowed to continue.

Even the benevolent administration of the Quaker agents was cruel. At least the People could understand and respect the soldiers who had governed them. But the men of God stripped the warriors of their very reason for living, war. They no longer had any way to attain status within their tribe. Whiskey, the "stupid water" that the People had always scorned, became their solace.

The People and their Kiowa allies had to set up their lodges on the west side of Cache Creek, where the water was polluted after passing through the fort. While the officers and their wives gathered in the evenings for small talk and lawn croquet, the Indians suffered malaria in the mosquito-infested swamp where they camped. Quanah himself came down with the fever in 1875.

When he recovered, he asked permission to seek his white relatives and to see where his mother had lived out the last few years of her life. Dressed in the buckskins of the People, speaking almost no English, and armed only with a letter of introduction from the Indian agent, he set out through Texas to find the Parkers. The agent's letter said, "This young man is the son of Cynthia Ann Parker, and he is going to visit his mother's people. Please show him the road and help him as you can."

One can only imagine his thoughts as he traveled through what had once been the country of his people, or the reception he received from the Texans, his former enemies. It is said that some treated him well, proud to have met the famous chief, and that others were hostile. But his mother's family made him welcome. His great-uncle Isaac taught him something of the white man's ways while he stayed with him. Some stories say that Quanah also traveled to Mexico to visit his mother's brother, John Parker.

When Quanah returned to the reservation, he began to lead his people along the peace trail. But adjustment for the Comanche was difficult. The houses that the government built for the Indians meant that the old villages were broken up and families lived isolated from each other. The houses were not of much use anyway, except for storage. The Comanche said there were too many snakes in them. However, they did like to go inside and whoop, enjoying the echoes in the empty rooms. One Comanche child asked his mother to set up his bed in the fireplace so he could look up the chimney at the stars.

In 1878 the People begged the agent for passes to hunt the buffalo. With good intentions, the agent complied. The entire tribe, 1500 people, prepared for the event. They celebrated as in the old days, remembering the stories and the dances and the medicine they had used not many years before. They all set out joyously for the plains to the west. A small military escort went with them to see that no one was tempted to steal the Texans' horses.

Scouts were sent out, and the rest of the band watched for their signal fires. But none appeared. The hunters rode for days. All they encountered were the bare skulls and the bleached bones of the buffalo. Weeks passed. The leaves blew from the trees and the wind grew colder. But the old men swore that the buffalo would return as they always had. They made more medicine. Finally, unable to stand the hunger, many of the People returned to the reservation and the meager rations that awaited them there.

Others stubbornly refused to leave their old hunting grounds, and the military didn't have the heart to point out that their passes had expired. As it grew colder, the agent sent wagons of food to them. His emissaries found them huddled and starving in their lodges in a snowstorm. They were finally persuaded to return to the agency. In a long, shivering, silent column, they left the graveyard that had once been their home.

Quanah must have realized that herding, not farming, would suit his people best. As one warrior expressed it, farming put yet another burden on their overworked wives. Quanah became a cattleman and an influential leader of his people. He was progressive where economics were concerned and arranged for the leasing of Comanche lands to the Texas ranchers. Prosperous cattlemen like Charles Goodnight and Burk Burnett became his close friends.

They and other Texas ranchers had lumber hauled from Wichita Falls and built Quanah a handsome two-story, twenty-two room house at the foot of the Wichita mountains. Quanah had huge stars painted on the roof and identical apartments set up for each of his five wives. One of his wives commented that Quanah's greatness lay not in the fact that he was a diplomat and a chief among his people and the whites, but that he managed to maintain peace and order in a house with five women.

In 1884, the government appointed him chief of the Comanches. In 1886, while in Fort Worth, he advertised in the newspaper for a picture of his mother. Sul Ross, the man who had led the attack on Naduah's village in 1864, obtained a copy of the daguerreotype that had been made a few days after that raid, and he sent it to her son. In it she was shown nursing her daughter and staring sadly at the camera. Quanah had a large painting made from the picture and hung it in his house.

Little by little, white settlers crowded the Indians' territory. Pressure mounted for the tribes to sell their land. In 1889, President Harrison authorized the opening of the unoccupied Indian lands, and the "Boomers" moved onto it by the thousands. Then, a few years later, the Indians each received 160 acres, and 100,000 people lined up for the "run" to claim what was left.

Quanah met Teddy Roosevelt in Oklahoma City and arranged a wolf hunt for him. In 1905, he was invited to appear in Roosevelt's inaugural parade. He was chosen president of the local school district and deputy sheriff of Lawton, Oklahoma. In 1897, however, Quanah lost his judgeship on the reservation's Court of Indian Offenses because of his many wives. When an official explained that polygamy was illegal and that Quanah would have to choose his favorite wife and tell the others to go, he looked at the man solemnly. "You tell 'em," he said. The subject was dropped.

Although Quanah became a celebrity and worked closely with the whites, he was always a Comanche. He may have worn an occasional derby and boots and tailored suits, but he kept his hair in braids. Many of his children converted to Christianity, but Quanah never did. He used peyote extensively and upheld the Indians' right to take advantage of the cactus's dream-producing qualities. He is recognized as the founder of the peyote cult among the plains Indians and the beginner of the American Indian Church.

In 1910, he wrote to the Parkers of east Texas, requesting that his mother's bones be sent to him. The Texans refused, until his letter was read to them from the pulpit one Sunday. It said in part,

My mother, she fed me, carry me in her arms, pat me to sleep. I play, she happy. I cry, she sad. She love her boy. They took my mother away, took Texas away. Not let her boy see her. Now she dead. Her boy want to bury her, sit by her mound. My people, her people, we now all one people.

The bones were sent to Oklahoma, and Quanah cut his braids in mourning over them. He died a short time afterward, on February 11, 1911. He was buried in full Comanche dress. When he died, there were even fewer Comanche in Oklahoma than when he had surrendered thirty-five years earlier. White man's diseases were still taking their toll.

For many years after Quanah Parker led his band onto the reservation, long furrows could be seen in the surface of the prairie. The grooves undulated with the swells of the plains and stretched to the horizon. Even though overgrown with grass, they continued to mark the trails made by thousands of hooves, moccasined feet, and travois passing back and forth, following the seasons and the buffalo. The furrows were the paths of a people who were happiest when they were moving.

Perhaps if the wind is just right, and one listens carefully, the laughter and talk, the shouts and the songs of the People can still be heard there. Perhaps they still wander those trails free, as they always were, in spirit.

Suvate.

About the Author

Lucia St. Clair Robson has been a Peace Corps volunteer in Venezuela, a teacher in New York and Japan, and a public librarian. She now lives in Maryland, outside Annapolis, and devotes full time to writing fiction. While researching RIDE THE WIND, her first novel, Miss Robson made two trips to Texas and Oklahoma. She has spent days just sitting on the Staked Plains to get the feel of the land the Comanche roamed.